and

Swingboats on the Sand

Grace Thompson was born in Barry, South Wales. After her children grew up, she qualified as a nursery nurse and worked with children in care and in schools. Then, following six years in Berkshire watching her grandchildren grow up, she moved back to South Wales, and now spends her afternoons walking the cliffs and beaches of Mumbles and Gower with her Welsh collie.

Wait Till Summer

and

Swingboats on the Sand

Grace Thompson

PAN BOOKS

Wait Till Summer first published 2000 by Severn House Publishers Ltd
Swingboats on the Sand first published 2001 by Severn House Publishers Ltd

This omnibus edition published 2002 by Pan Books
an imprint of Pan Macmillan Ltd
Pan Macmillan, 20 New Wharf Road, London N1 9RR
Basingstoke and Oxford
Associated companies throughout the world
www.panmacmillan.com

ISBN 1 405 00439 8

1 3 5 7 9 8 6 4 2

A CIP catalogue record for this book is available from
the British Library.

Printed and bound in Great Britain by
Mackays of Chatham plc, Chatham, Kent

Wait Till Summer

One

Eirlys Price stood in the crowded school hall looking at the anxious-faced children and wondering how they could possibly find homes for them before nightfall. This first arrival of evacuees from London had been expected, but even so, the bedraggled and clearly unhappy group had been a shock. So many and most of them so young; how could tearing them away from their families be the best solution?

Eirlys was twenty-two and she worked as a clerk in the council offices. Today she had been given the task of helping Mrs Francis to find homes for the evacuees billeted on the town. She didn't mind the duty but would have preferred to have done it with an assistant of her own rather than the tedious Mrs Benjamin Francis.

She tried to stay uninvolved as she had been told, but the plight of the children got to her and she felt her heart squeeze with pity for the youngsters taken from everything and everyone they knew and brought to a strange town with only a luggage label pinned to them to declare their identity.

The school in St David's Well had been closed for the day to allow for the dispersal of the children to be arranged but the pupils hadn't stayed home. They had turned up to watch curiously as the newcomers were walked in a long crocodile from the station along the streets where other, older people stood on doorsteps to gawp at the children, offer sympathy and pat a few heads as they passed.

The forty-five evacuees were given a snack meal which had been organised by the WVS formed sixteen months before, in May 1938. Now, in September 1939, with war declared and the country in a state of turmoil, the new Women's Voluntary Service, local people who could arrange help and comfort wherever needed, was coming into its own.

Eirlys could see that there weren't sufficient chairs, with many taken by the adults who had come to collect them or simply to watch, so she encouraged the children, who were worn out with the travelling and the anxiety, to sit on the floor. Several went instantly to sleep, hugging their gas masks and their small bags of personal possessions in baby hands. She moved some into more comfortable positions, and stepped among them reassuring them, smiling, admiring a small toy here, a smart hat there, hoping that Mrs Francis wouldn't take too long before sending them on the final stage of their journey.

One little girl began to wail, "I 'ates it 'ere and I wanna go 'ome."

"Wait till summer," Eirlys soothed. "You'll love living beside the sea when summer comes round again."

She began to describe the various activities the child might enjoy but had no response. Tears glistened in the child's eyes and she repeated, "I 'ates it 'ere," to every attempt at comfort.

The murmur of conversations and the clatter of plates as the dishes were cleared and washed in the school kitchen was a constant hum that had a drowsing effect and didn't disturb those who were sleeping. The women who had been told to provide homes for the children for the duration of the emergency stood up and approached the bedraggled group.

As the women approached, all searching for the most respectable looking and hoping to avoid the poorest, some of the younger ones began to cry. Eirlys picked up the unhappy little girl she had spoken to earlier, who smelled unpleasantly of urine and unwashed hair, and cuddled her.

She saw three boys scuttle away from the table to stand in a corner, and guessed they were brothers and didn't want to be parted. She stepped closer to read their names. Stanley Love aged ten, Harold Love aged eight and a glum-faced Percival Love, just six. Sympathy for Stanley, who had clearly taken responsibility for his brothers, made her stand protectively near them as the process of rehoming began.

Mrs Francis, who was clearly in charge, stood on a chair and in a loud voice addressed the room. "Welcome to St David's Well, children," she began in an accent that made Stanley and his brothers stifle a laugh.

"Blimey, brovers, she talks like the wireless!" Stanley spluttered.

Mrs Francis didn't speak for long; she simply explained that the women would walk around and choose the child they wanted to take home with them. "And don't forget to say thank you," she reminded the children firmly. "Here in St David's Well we consider manners very important."

Slowly the children dispersed as the women of the town chose and collected their visitors. They gave their name, and the name of the child they had selected, to Mrs Francis and her assistants and walked off, hand in hand, to introduce the newcomer to his or her new family. Some smiled, some began to look uneasy as the numbers dwindled and the selection was reduced to the untidiest and in some cases the dirtiest children. Stanley and his brothers stood unnoticed in the corner, half hidden by a group of curious onlookers.

Eirlys moved around the sad group and reassured one or two who were afraid of being left to fend for themselves if they weren't chosen, embarrassed at some of the comments uttered by the women who were loudly discussing the merits and suitability of each child.

"See, brovers," she heard Stanley whisper, "no one 'ere wants us, so we might as well go back 'ome." They would need an extra vigilant eye, Eirlys thought grimly.

The door of the school hall opened and Eirlys saw her father enter. She waved and he came to stand near her.

"How's it going?" he asked. "Have you chosen our girl yet?"

"No, Dadda. I thought we'd wait till the end and take the one no one wants."

"I'm amazed that we persuaded your mam to take on an evacuee, aren't you?"

"It took a long time and I don't think she would have agreed at all, if I hadn't told her that in my job at the council offices I had to show willing," Eirlys confessed.

"Very proud of you, Mam is for sure," Morgan smiled. "You working in an office when all your friends could only manage shops. Always boasting she is, about how clever you are."

"What are you doing here?" Eirlys asked him. "Aren't you working at ten tonight? You should be asleep."

"I was curious to see the child we're giving a home to. Your mam is busy making piles of food, convinced this lot won't have eaten all day, so I came down for a bit of a walk, like."

The number of children dwindled. Voices became more disapproving as the children were loudly discussed. Seeing the three brothers standing apparently unnoticed, Eirlys wondered vaguely how her mother, Annie, would react if she and her father arrived home with three boys instead of the girl she had agreed to take.

She glanced at her father, nudged him and gestured towards the brothers who were trying not to move in the hope of being forgotten. He stared at the boys with an interested look in his eyes. No! They daren't!

They looked up as Mrs Francis closed her book with a slap and seemed prepared to leave. They heard her say peremptorily, "These last two girls will have to go to the vicarage. The dear vicar and his housekeeper will have to manage until other arrangements can be made. I simply can't wait any longer."

The two frightened little girls were led off. "What's a vicarage?" one of them asked the other. Then, as she picked up her handbag and moved away from the table she had been occupying, Mrs Francis stopped, suddenly noticing the huddle of children in a corner.

"You over there, come here where I can see you."

"What, us, missis?" Stanley Love didn't move.

"Yes, you," she said impatiently. "Why have you been hiding in the corner?"

"Hidin', missis? We ain't hiding. You can see us plain as plain."

"Just when I thought we were finished," Mrs Francis muttered to her assistants. "Now, who have we left?" There were still a few women edging out of the hall, thankful they hadn't been needed and anxious to get home before someone changed their minds and brought a child back.

"Mrs Casey," she called in a shrill voice. "What about one of these boys for you?"

"I can't, Mrs Francis. Two bedrooms I got and me with two daughters an' all; it isn't possible."

Two others were asked and had reasons to refuse one of the brothers.

"Just as well," Stanley shouted. "We ain't bein' separated. Me mum said we got to stay together."

"That won't be possible, young man. You'll go where there's a place for you. Now." She turned to a small, thin woman standing patiently near the door. "Mrs Evans, my dear?"

"I couldn't have three." She shook her head determinedly.

"No one is asking you to take three; just one, all right?"

"No it ain't all right!" Stanley's head-shaking was equally determined. "The three musketeers we are, all for one an' one for all. We read that at school," he said proudly.

The hall was practically deserted. Mrs Francis looked impatiently at her watch and sighed. "I have a meeting of the Air Raid Precaution group in an hour."

"Air raids? What air raids?" Stanley demanded. "I thought you wasn't goin' to 'ave any?"

"Tiresome boy," Mrs Francis said loudly. She took a deep breath in preparation for a lecture on how fortunate they were.

"Just stay with me," Stanley whispered to his brothers, "and when we get the chance, we'll 'oppit and clear off back to London. Our ma wouldn't want us standing 'ere like two pennorth of Gawd 'elp us, waiting for someone to like us, now would she?"

Eirlys looked at her father, head tilted in question. They were very close and often read the other's mind. She knew now that he was wavering, discarding common sense in favour of helping these unfortunate children. "Dadda? Could we persuade Mam, d'you think?"

"No, love, we couldn't!" He looked shocked but at the same time his blue eyes – so like her own – shone with excitement. He looked again at the boys standing so defiant and brave. "God 'elp, Eirlys. Persuading your mam to take one girl was a miracle. We'd never talk her into taking on three boys."

"Dad, we have to do something. They'll have to sleep in the school if we don't take them, and imagine how awful that would be. Frightened, away from their mother and everything familiar, unwanted by anyone, abandoned—"

"Go on then, and pity help us when your mother is told. Go on, tell that bossy Francis woman they're coming home with us. It's up to you to talk your mam round, mind."

Stanley continued to whisper to Percival and Harold, ignoring what was being said, when he became aware of someone standing beside them.

"Now what?" Harold asked rudely.

Eirlys smiled and said, "It seems you are all coming home with me."

* * *

Annie Price was predictably furious when the five of them walked in.

"Who are these boys?" she demanded, placing her hands on her ample hips and glaring at Morgan. "I hope you don't expect me to look after three boys. A girl was what I agreed."

"Don't worry, missis, we'll go back 'ome in the morning," Stanley said jauntily. "We don't want to stay 'ere anyway!"

Annie looked at the tired children and her heart softened, as Morgan and Eirlys had thought it would.

"They can stay until we find a place for them, can't they Mam?"

"Our Eirlys was responsible for organising all this, mind. She can't walk away from children, can she? It's her job," Morgan added. "And I'll do what I can to help."

As Annie served a rich stew with mashed potatoes to each of the boys, she said, "How can we manage? You work shifts at the factory, I work every morning in the baker's shop and Eirlys works from nine to five plus all the hours of overtime this damned war is causing."

"We'll manage between us, Mam," Eirlys said. "I don't think Stanley will mind doing his share, will you?"

Stanley didn't reply; he was too busy filling his mouth with the delicious stew. Eirlys was relieved to see her parents share a smile.

As her father left for work that evening, the boys were finishing their meal. Stanley and Harold had consumed second helpings but little Percival ate very little. He sat with his head bowed, chewing with little pleasure on a small amount of food, looking unhappy. When Eirlys tried to coax him, he said solemnly and in a low voice, "These 'taters is boverin' me."

"Percival can't eat no lumps," Stanley explained, scraping the offending potatoes from Percival's plate on to his own.

"I only like chips," the dejected little boy explained. "Chips from the chip shop."

It was late before the children had been bathed and fed and settled for the night and Eirlys knew she would not be able to keep the date she had with Johnny Castle. She had promised to take some magazines and books for his mother, who was unwell, but she knew Johnny would understand once she explained about the plight of the evacuees no one else had wanted. Johnny was kind and never anything but good-natured. He would sympathise with the boys as soon as she explained.

Annie was still angry and Eirlys tried to take the blame from her father. "It wasn't Dadda's idea, Mam, it was mine," she insisted. "How could I walk away and leave them to be pushed into a home where they weren't wanted and separated from each other? If you'd seen those children you'd have taken more than the one you'd agreed, I know you would."

"It isn't their fault, I know that. But your father should have thought it through."

"Mam, it was me, not Dadda."

"I don't suppose he needed much persuading. You two always think alike. You look alike and you think in just the same way, soft you are the pair of you, and I have to deal with the result of it. Remember the rabbits you brought home when someone had moved and left them unattended? And the stray cat you insisted on feeding?" She sounded angry, she usually did, but there was a smile around her dark eyes as she added, "What am I going to be landed with next then, eh?"

"No more waifs and strays, Mam, I promise."

Annie didn't seem to hear. She went on, "Always wanted a big family he did, your father. Never got over his disappointment at not having brothers or sisters for you."

It was a sensitive subject for both of them. Unfading regret for Annie, and unreasonable guilt for Eirlys, who knew that it had been during her birth that her mother had been damaged with the result that she could have no more children.

Eirlys looked at the pile of clothes she had taken from the three boys and wondered where she would find more. The clothes they had brought were not suitable for school unless the Love brothers were able to cope with the teasing they would surely get from the locals. They were crumpled and very worn. There was a small weekly allowance intended to help feed them, but it was not enough to completely clothe them.

When her father Morgan came in from the factory the following morning she was awake and still trying to decide what to do about clothing.

"You'd better start on that washing, hadn't you?" he said as he reached for the kettle to make a pot of tea. "First thing I'll do is fetch the washing bath in and get the boiler lit."

"Yes; I have to be at work at nine so it'll be an early start. Like now this minute," she said.

Together they sorted through the worn clothes, picking out the least worst for the three boys to wear the following day. Today they would have to wear the clothes in which they had travelled. It wasn't ideal but it was the best she could do. None of the clothes were particularly clean and, looking at the threadbare material and frayed ends, at the holes where buttons had once been, Eirlys wondered if any item was worth the effort of mending.

"Your mam's hopeless with a needle, but you could go and ask Hannah Wilcox if she can turn a couple of my things into clothes for them. Good at that, she is."

"She's had to be, with her husband gone and her parents unwilling to help. She keeps those girls of hers beautifully turned out she does, and all by her own efforts. I'm sure she'll make a few things for these three, but we'll have to pay her, mind, she can't afford to do it for nothing."

"It's half seven, she'll be awake. Go and see her now, while the boys are still sleeping. I'll listen for them waking. I won't be going to bed yet. I thought I'd stay up and help your mother with breakfast."

Eirlys hugged her father affectionately. "Thanks, Dadda. I knew you wouldn't mind me taking them on."

"Go on with you. I'll chuck 'em though the window if they don't behave, mind. Oh, and call at the bake house and ask for a loaf of bread, will you? The shop won't open till nine and the lads ate all we had last night. On second thoughts, better get two."

Hannah Wilcox and Eirlys were friends even though their age and their circumstances were different. Hannah was twenty-nine, and had been married to a man who, she had soon realised, was a heavy drinker. While alcohol was in control he had been violent towards her. After a fourth stay in hospital, to her parents' embarrassment and shame she had sued for divorce – something unheard of in most families – and they steadfastly refused to accept it. They were both members of a local chapel where punishment was considered to be ennobling, and the rules of life were rigid. No mitigating circumstances were ever considered.

Hannah knew the religion was one that suited her parents' needs. They hated her but couldn't admit it, so the breakdown of her marriage was something of which they could disapprove and for which they could punish her.

Their hatred of her and the need to punish her was because her brother Rupert, whom they had adored, had died of pneumonia after she had passed the flu on to him, and they blamed her for being alive when he was dead. Her refusal to stay with her husband was a gift to them in their unhappiness. They constantly pressurised her to take him back, insisting that he was her husband until death. That solution was something Hannah had thought about often, after a severe beating had left her in pain and she could see no way out of her situation.

It had been Eirlys Price and her parents who had helped her and supported her through the traumatic early months of the divorce procedure. Every move she made had been discouraged both by her parents and their friends, and the solicitor together with his staff also lacked sympathy, believing that a wife had to stay with a husband through everything.

Members of her parents' chapel called on her and talked until she thought her head would burst with the frustration of stating her case to uncaring ears, and listening to their lectures on her wickedness. She was "selfish", "thinking only of herself", "a wicked daughter", she was told repeatedly. She should "spare a thought for the shame her parents were suffering", she was reminded. It was only Eirlys and her parents, Morgan and Annie Price, who saved her sanity.

After the separation and the plans for the divorce had shamed them in front of their Chapel "friends", Hannah's parents, intent on a reconciliation, had twice allowed her husband back into the house and tricked their daughter into being there alone, and twice he had made Hannah pregnant, each time also landing her in hospital with cuts, bruises and broken bones.

Even when her parents visited her in hospital, they still refused to consider Hannah a free woman and insisted that she was married and should take her husband back. They quoted the marriage vows at her whenever she tried to reason with them, chanting them to drown out her reasoning. When they had reluctantly allowed her to return to their house, after she had been forced to give up the flat above the china shop, they had made sure she lived as unobtrusively as possible, confining her and the children to the two small rooms she had been allotted, not even allowing her to take the babies into the garden to play. Her shame was never to be forgotten. The world had to see they did not condone their daughter's behaviour.

When Hannah opened the door to Eirlys on the morning after the evacuees had arrived, she greeted Eirlys with a warning finger on her lips and they tiptoed into the living room where a fire burned low and a gas light flickered and popped in the draught.

"Eirlys, this is a nice surprise." Hannah smiled as she poked some life into the fire and turned the gas light up a notch. "Anything important?"

"I went to collect our evacuee and came back with three," Eirlys laughed. "Dadda was fine about it but our Mam wasn't pleased." The smile slipped a little as she thought about her mother's reaction, wondering if her mother would be persuaded to allow them to stay.

"She'll be as kind as your dad, don't worry," Hanna assured her. "Her bark is always worse than her bite." She waited for her friend to say something more but recognising the hesitancy, guessing there was a favour to be asked, said, "Can I help? Mam and Dad can't take one, not with us being here – at least that's a point in my favour," she laughed. "But if I can do something to help you?"

"The fact is, they don't have many clothes and the ones they do have are very worn. I wondered if you could make them some trousers and shirts out of some of Dad's old ones? It will be expensive to buy new for all three of them. We'll pay of course."

"Bring around what you've got and I'll look in my odds-and-ends cupboard and I'm sure we'll sort out something. Good practise maybe. There was a piece on the paper last week about us having to manage without new clothes if the war lasts more than a year or so."

"But it won't, will it? This time next year we'll be laughing at all the scaremongering, won't we?"

"The last war went on for four years," Hannah said doubtfully.

"Yes, but we've learned something since then, haven't we?"

Hannah didn't think so but she said nothing. Talk of war was frightening and rumours varied from a brief skirmish, over by

Christmas, to years of deprivation and horror. Hannah didn't want to think about it. Like many other women she preferred pretending the battles would happen far away and to people she didn't know.

"How is Johnny?" she asked, hoping to change the subject. "What does he think of Stanley, Harold and Percival Love?"

"Oh, I didn't see him last night. Sorting out the evacuees took most of the evening. Luckily we were meeting at his mam's house so I wasn't letting him down. Besides, he knew the evacuees were coming; he'd have guessed what happened and understood."

"What is he doing now the beach is closing for the winter? Has he got a job yet?"

Because Johnny Castle's family ran Piper's Café and their stalls on St David's Well Bay during the summer months, when the town was filled with day-trippers and holiday-makers attracted to the small town and its lovely sandy beaches, they all had to seek other employment during the winter.

"He's decorating old Mrs Piper's house at the moment, and hating it. Johnny loves working on the sands, and likes to be out of doors, working with people. He dreads the end of the beach season. He never minds painting the stalls and swingboats and the like, smartening them up for the season, that's a part of the work on the beach, but painting Granny Molly Piper's house is not a favourite pastime."

"Poor Johnny. Mrs 'Granny Moll' Piper isn't even his real gran, is she?" Hannah smiled.

"No, but she acts as though he is. He and Taff have to do as she says the same as their cousins."

The friends said goodbye, with the decision made to use the newly washed clothes as a guide to making new outfits for the boys in time for the following week when they would all be starting at the local school.

Eirlys was thinking about Johnny Castle as she closed the gate behind her. She knew something of the protest about the name of the cafés and stalls owned by Molly Piper.

It was the Castle family who ran the businesses belonging to Moll Piper, which had been started by her grandparents, Joseph and Harriet Piper, with a small wooden café close to the sands. Moll Piper's daughter Marged and her husband Huw Castle had worked on the sands since they were children and Huw's brother Bleddyn had worked beside them. As soon as they were old enough, their own children had become involved, the cousins working happily as a team. Although most members of the workforce were called Castle, the name of Piper was still used and would be, Moll told them, until the last Piper was dead.

As she and her unmarried daughter, Marged's sister Audrey, were the last two, Huw and Bleddyn constantly tried to persuade her to change her mind and rename the business – but to no avail. Bleddyn and Huw felt it was an injustice, as they had managed the business since Moll's husband had died and Moll had practically nothing to do with the day-to-day organisation. Huw's wife Marged avoided discussing it; agreeing with her husband, agreeing with Moll, using lots of words but saying nothing.

It was past eight o'clock that morning as Eirlys walked thoughtfully back to her parents' house in Conroy Street. She hastily prepared breakfast for them all, offering toast and eggs to the subdued boys. Then, leaving her father to look after them until her mother returned from work at one o'clock, when he would at last be able to get some sleep, she made her way to the council offices and the continuing work of arranging schools and checking on the accommodation for the children.

Every placement had to be investigated, the schools prepared for the extra pupils, meetings arranged for the families to sort out any difficulties before they developed into problems. There were endless reports and forms to deal with, people to send out with questionnaires regarding the evacuees and their welfare. She ate a snack lunch at her desk, stopping only briefly to look out at the bustling town. As all the shops and offices closed between one and two o'clock, the shoppers gradually disappeared and only a few people walked the pavements.

She saw Johnny riding past on his bicycle and guessed he had been sent to buy more paint to finish his decorating for Granny Moll Piper. She didn't wave. He wouldn't expect to see her there at her window high above the street.

He was whistling and wobbling his way through a group of workmen standing examining a delivery of buckets and stirrup pumps that had been unloaded on to the road. How everything was changing. Even though not a single bomb had been dropped, the town was being turned inside out in preparation for war.

She shivered as she thought of the dangers to come in the pretty little town, and the young men who were leaving in droves to fight an invisible enemy far away across the sea.

She thought of Ken Ward from whom she had parted recently. He had wanted so badly to join the army and fight, but asthma had meant he received Grade Four at his medical, too low for any kind of enemy action. His family had moved to London and Ken had accepted a job with a small theatre group there and had asked her to go with him, but she had refused to leave St David's Well. She had often wondered if the decision had been the right one and each time decided it had been.

She wouldn't have stood on the railway platform without regret and watched him leave if she had really loved him. An unwillingness to leave her parents and a job she enjoyed wouldn't have entered her mind. She missed him, though; they had been friends for several years.

At five thirty, when she began to tidy her desk and prepare to leave, she was handed another pile of papers and asked to try to get them filed before she went home. With a sigh, she agreed. She was anxious about the evacuees, and wondered how they had fared during their first day, but the work at the council offices had to be kept up to date. With so many men already gone to join the forces she couldn't refuse to work longer hours.

She stretched her arms, yawned widely, walked around her desk a few times to refresh herself. A cup of tea, then back to the paperwork. She gathered the papers and began to sort them out. Judging by the size of the pile, it looked like being two more hours before she could go home.

As she walked up the back path towards the kitchen door later that evening, she almost fell over a bike. With the blackout already in force the nights were dark with only the occasionally ground-facing light of a bicycle passing, or the partially covered car lights that only made the night seem darker.

"Who left their bike where I could fall over it?" she demanded as she closed the door and switched on the kitchen light to examine her shin.

"Me, and I'm sorry," Johnny Castle grinned.

Her spirits lifted at the sight of him, her tiredness was forgotten. He was small, as most of the Castle family were, only five feet seven, dark and strong and bursting with an energy that seemed to have laughter as its main ingredient. Johnny, more than the others, seemed to be filled with the joy of life. No one, Eirlys thought as she leaned forward for a brief kiss, no one could be miserable with Johnny Castle near.

"Sorry about last night, Johnny. I'll take the magazines to your mam later. Did you hear about the three boys? Stanley Love, aged ten, Harold aged eight and little Percival who is six."

"Yes, the news has spread, so I thought I'd call to see how you're managing. Granny Moll said she has some bedding if you need it, and some boys' clothes left from my cousins. Heaven alone knows why she kept them but perhaps we'll be glad she did, eh?"

"Thanks. I'll go and see what she's found at the weekend."

"Who looked after them while your mam was at the shop?"

"Our Dadda. He's so good about taking them in." She turned and smiled at Morgan, who was reading the paper. "He should have been sleeping after working the night shift, but until we get them into school and properly settled we have to muddle through."

"I took them to the park," Morgan told them, "then Mam made them some chips. Harold said they weren't bad, but little Percival told her they weren't as good as the chip shop," he laughed.

"He's going to be hard to please, that one," Johnny smiled. They crept upstairs and looked at the three sleeping children. Stanley and Harold looked peaceful, but there was a scowl on Percival's face that made them smile.

"He's a cheerful-looking chap, I don't think!" Johnny said as they went down again.

"He's only six and I don't think he can possibly understand what's happening to them."

"I'll bring them a stick of seaside rock tomorrow, and at the weekend perhaps we can introduce them to the joys of the beach, eh? The swingboats and the helter-skelter and the stalls have all gone but Auntie Audrey is still opening the rock and sweet shop this month."

"Do you know, Johnny," Eirlys said in wonder, "Mrs Francis told us they might never have seen the sea. Isn't that amazing?"

When Eirlys's mother came into the kitchen and saw the pile of old clothes on the kitchen table, sorted for Hannah to use as patterns for newer ones, she put her hands on her hips, a well-known gesture meaning she was not pleased.

"When am I going to get this table cleared so I can set it for supper?" she demanded.

Seeing them together it was clear that Eirlys had inherited little from her mother. Annie was not tall, but she was plump, with dark eyes, and her long straight hair was always falling out of the bun with which she tried to control it. Eirlys was so like her father with their fair curly hair and blue eyes, and the wonderful milk-and-roses complexion to match. Johnny thought Eirlys would be ever young and Morgan would look as youthful when he was fifty as he did today. They were both slimly built and with an elegance in the way they walked, and a neatness that was always apparent, whatever task they undertook.

After greeting Johnny, Annie turned to her husband and daughter. "What were you thinking of, girl?" she demanded. "I was told we had to have *one*." She waved a solitary finger in front of Eirlys's face. "One girl. Now you and your father tell me we have three and you expect me to have them permanently? And boys at that. I never could cope with boys!"

"I'm off," Johnny laughed. "Remember the Queensbury Rules, mind, Mrs Price!" He could hear the shrill voice complaining as he jumped on his bike and wobbled his way down the path and on to the road. Thank goodness Eirlys followed her father in temperament as well as looks, and not her quick-tempered mother.

Johnny Castle lived in Brook Lane with his father Bleddyn, his mother Irene and his brother Taff. Apart from his rather sickly mother, Irene, who refused, they all worked on the sands during the summer months, sharing responsibility for the various entertainments as well as Piper's Café on the cliff above the beach and Piper's fish-and-chip shop and café in the town. Bleddyn's brother Huw and his family were the owners of the businesses together with Granny Moll, whose parents had begun it all, but Bleddyn had helped since he and Huw were children and he was very much involved, although, to his occasional irritation, Granny Moll, Huw's mother-in-law and owner of the business, always had the final word on any decision.

Running the fish-and-chip shop in town was Bleddyn's main duty, and as Johnny parked his bicycle in the shed and went into the house, he was closely followed by his father, who had just closed the café for the night.

"Been somewhere nice?" Bleddyn asked. "Pictures?"

"No, Eirlys couldn't come. She's been helping find homes for the evacuees who arrived yesterday and guess what?"

"Don't tell me we've got to have one?" He frowned. "Your mother couldn't cope, could you Irene?"

"No, not us, but Eirlys only came home with three boys!"

"What did Mrs Price have to say to that?" Bleddyn laughed. "I bet she let everyone know she wasn't pleased. Annie Price doesn't whisper at the best of times and they probably heard her reaction in Grange Road!"

"Mr Price seemed all right about it. He's a good-natured man, isn't he?"

"Yes," Bleddyn agreed. "I get on well with Morgan Price. He's all right, isn't he, Irene?" He looked across the room, trying to encourage his wife to take part in the conversation.

"What are they like, these kids from London, then?" Irene asked, ignoring his comment about Morgan Price.

"Most of them were tidy enough but a few of them looked real poor. Eirlys said theirs were clean and well nourished but they need clothes and a few possessions to make them feel at home. I was wondering, Mam, would you mind if I took my old train set over? And perhaps a few of our games and books?"

"Good idea, love. I'll sort through and see what I can find."

"I'm working for Granny Moll tomorrow so could you take them over?" Johnny asked.

"No I can't." His mother's voice was sharp. "You go tomorrow evening – you'll be seeing Eirlys, won't you?"

"Go on, Mam, they're so unhappy, a few toys would brighten their day."

"No. You go when you can. A few more hours won't hurt them."

Johnny frowned. Since he and Eirlys had begun going out together Eirlys's mother had invited his mother over several times but Irene had always refused. He shrugged. Perhaps the two women didn't get on, although it was disappointing for his mam to refuse an evening out. She was always complaining of being bored, and blaming his dad for never taking her out.

His brother Taff came in and they all sat down for supper. Twice a week Bleddyn brought fish and chips home; on other evenings they had something on toast, or a bowl of soup. It was Bleddyn's conviction that they should eat a meal together and talk about their day so they kept in touch with each other and didn't allow the family to drift apart. Lately, though, Irene had frequently set out the meal and wandered off to bed without joining them.

"Nice bit of hake for you tonight, Irene," Bleddyn said, hoping to persuade her to stay. "Saved it special, I did."

"I had a slice of cake earlier and I don't feel hungry. I think I'll go on up."

With Johnny and Taff arguing over possession of the fillet of hake, they didn't see the hurt disappointment on their father's face.

"Why don't you go and meet the evacuees, Mam?" Johnny asked as Irene went through the door. "Fancy that daft Eirlys taking home three boys! What her mam said when they all walked in I daren't think. She had plenty to say about it tonight. I hopped out as soon as she started on." Then he turned to share a smile with his mother and realised he was talking to himself. He began to tell his brother and Bleddyn instead.

Bleddyn knew Irene would be feigning sleep when he went up. She had no time for him lately, couldn't even spend a few minutes to share the family supper, something they had once both enjoyed and considered important.

He forced a cheerful tone as he began telling Taff and Johnny about some of the customers he had served, encouraging their laughter to cocoon him from his worries. He and Irene were more like strangers these days.

When he went upstairs after dropping the plates into a bowl of water to soak, Irene wasn't in bed. But when she saw him enter the room she hurriedly covered her semi-naked body with a dressing gown.

"It's all right, Irene, it's only me and you haven't got anything I haven't seen before," he joked.

"Don't be coarse," she said.

"What? Since when have you lost your sense of humour? That remark wouldn't have upset you a few months ago. What's happened? Do you find me so repulsive?"

"Of course not, Bleddyn. I'm tired, that's all."

"You aren't ill, are you? You don't seem to be with us these days."

"I'm all right, I'm just tired and it's late, so let's go to sleep, shall we?"

Bleddyn heard her breathing fast as though angry or upset. He didn't move when it slowed and became even as she dropped off to sleep. He slept fitfully, worrying about the way Irene was distancing herself from them all. He was awake when the hooter sounded to tell the factory workers it was time for the morning shift.

He was the first to rise that morning, knowing that Irene would probably stay in bed until he and their sons had left for work. With her present attitude he did more of the house chores than usual, hoping that his willingness would help her get over whatever was troubling her.

Irene had never been robust, or even truly happy. There were periods when she drifted through the days, half sleeping, reading magazines and novels, and then went out when she should have been cooking their meals. But between these spells, she had managed the house and cared for him and the boys reasonably well, until the mood came on her and she began hiding away from him again, into this shell she built around her; a situation that usually eased once more after a few weeks. He never learned the reason for the strange periodic indifference and aloofness. When he tried to talk to her she ignored him until he went away or changed the subject to one she was willing to discuss.

This time was more worrying. She had never been so indifferent to them for so long. Bleddyn had always been afraid that a more serious mental state would develop, which was why he was careful to help her and reassure her whenever these moods, euphemistically referred to as "nerves", occurred.

Johnny called on Eirlys the following evening when he had finished work painting the outside of Granny Moll's house in Sidney Street. He had gone home first to change out of his working clothes and gather up the toys he had chosen to give to Stanley and Harold and Percival.

Eirlys was just in from work too and she whooped with delight when he staggered in carrying a large cardboard box filled with his abandoned treasures.

Stanley, with assistance from Harold, set up the clockwork train set while a solemn Percival looked on.

Eirlys asked them what they had done that day but they were either too shy or too wrapped up in their new toys to answer her. "It's as though we're invisible," Eirlys whispered to Johnny with a laugh.

"What say we take them to the pictures tonight?" Johnny whispered back and was rewarded with the three boys' full attention.

"What have you done today?" Johnny then asked but Stanley shook his head.

"Nothing. That woman with the posh voice sent someone to collect us and we went to the school hall and listened to the headmaster chatting on about how we have to behave. What do they think we are, strange animals from a zoo?"

"What happened after the meeting?" Johnny asked, stifling a grin.

"Nothing. We just sat here and waited for you to come home. Your ma" – he addressed Eirlys – "said she was too busy and your pa was out."

"We'll make up for it at the weekend," Eirlys promised, disappointed that her mother couldn't spare an hour or two for the lonely and confused children.

"Too soft you are," Johnny smiled when she commented on this later. "I was telling our Mam about you coming home with three when you were supposed to have one."

"What did she say?" Eirlys grinned, expecting a humorous comment.

Johnny's smile faded. He couldn't tell her his mother had shown no reaction at all. "I told her you were daft. But, really, Eirlys, you're such a sweetheart."

He kissed her, startling her with his intensity. Until then his kisses had been nothing more than a peck, a greeting such as her father and mother gave. She felt the pleasure of it warming her and the embarrassment of it colouring her cheeks. Perhaps they were becoming more than friends. Shyly she looked at him and he kissed her again.

Eirlys was an only child without cousins or aunts and uncles. If envy could be said to be part of her character, she was envious of

Johnny's large family. A growing fondness for Johnny was tinged with a longing to become a part of the Castle family's closeness. A lively throng of relatives all involved with each other's lives, caring and sharing, had long been yearned for. Johnny's kiss had given flight to that dream.

A few days after the evacuees had arrived she went to call on Johnny, but found his father, Bleddyn, there with Taff. She was invited in but immediately sensed a tension, as though an argument had taken place. Both men were standing. Bleddyn walked around the room as she entered and words hung in the air, waiting to be said.

At home in the place she visited often, she offered to make tea and went out into the small kitchen to do so. She hummed to herself, aware that things were being said that Bleddyn did not want her to hear. Rattling the china unnecessarily to make sure they knew she was re-entering the room, she was surprised to see Taff's girlfriend Evelyn there.

"Hello Evelyn, I'll get another cup, shall I?"

"Thanks," Evelyn said, in a low voice. Something was seriously wrong, Eirlys could see that and she wondered whether she should pour the tea and make an excuse to leave. This was clearly not her concern.

When she had filled the cups she reached for the jacket she had abandoned with her handbag and said, "Best I go. You're obviously in the middle of a discussion. Tell Johnny I'll be home all evening if he wants to call."

"No, don't go," Evelyn said. "You can be the first to congratulate us."

She looked at Taff, who forced a smile and went to stand beside her before saying, "Evelyn and I are getting married."

Throwing down her coat again, Eirlys hugged them both and wished them every happiness. "This is sudden, isn't it? I didn't know you were even engaged!"

"We are now, from today, and the wedding will be very soon."

"Wonderful," Eirlys said. But she was curious to know the reason for the rush. Surely Evelyn wasn't— Her eyes dropped from Evelyn's face to the region of her waist and quickly back again.

"No, I'm not expecting," Evelyn said. "We've just decided, that's all."

Making her excuses to get away from the strange atmosphere which should have been joyous but was not, Eirlys hurried home. She was at her back gate when she heard Evelyn calling and she waited for her, wondering what to say. More congratulations? Or should she wait for Evelyn to speak first?

"I'm sorry you walked into that scene," Evelyn said.

"I thought it best to leave." Eirlys hesitated. "I had the impression that I interrupted something. I'm the one to be sorry."

"I don't want this talked about, mind," Evelyn told her, "but I want you to know what happened."

"Only if you want to tell me. Will you come in? We can go to my bedroom."

"No. It isn't a long story. Taff and I were kissing and, well, it was getting a bit out of control, and well, my mam walked in and thought we'd been – you know. She and our Dad insist that after debasing me – what a way to talk about love, eh? – after 'debasing' me in that way, we had to get married before it went too far and I was 'ruined'.

"Taff's mother seemed relieved somehow, glad to be getting one of her sons married and off her hands. She was in one of her strange moods, you know, as though she was there in body but not in her head. I wouldn't be surprised if she's forgotten all about it before tomorrow."

Eirlys could see that Evelyn was upset. It was a sad way to begin planning a wedding. "I am sorry, Evelyn, but you do love Taff, don't you? You and he have been together for years. It isn't such a dreadful thing, is it?"

"I love Taff, yes, of course I do, I think I always have, but I don't know whether he loves me and now I'll never know, will I?"

There didn't seem to be anything to say to comfort her and Eirlys watched as she walked away, head down, dejected. It was not a good way to begin a marriage. She hoped Taff would be kind and loving and convince her that he would have proposed anyway. Evelyn needed to be reassured of his love or her life would be incomplete.

Excited by the story in spite of her concern for her friend, her thoughts flew to the kiss she and Johnny had shared and she wondered if, one day, she and Evelyn would be sisters-in-law and be able to share all their confidences.

To her surprise and pleasure, Evelyn was waiting for her at lunchtime the following day and they went to a café for a snack, for which Evelyn insisted on paying.

"I need to talk to someone or I'll burst," she explained. "You know that Taff and Johnny and their father all work for Granny Molly Piper over on the beach and in the cafés, don't you?"

"Yes, of course. They all help during the holiday season." Eirlys nodded. "It's a family concern."

"That's the problem. Granny Moll came to see me this morning to welcome me to the family as though she was Taff's grandmother, which she isn't. She's related to Bleddyn's brother Huw, she's his mother-in-law in fact, but although she acts as though she's the head of the whole family, she's no relation to Bleddyn. But as Bleddyn and his brother Huw have worked for Pipers all their lives she has taken it upon herself to become matriarch. And her control includes Bleddyn and Irene, Johnny and Taff."

The family-hungry Eirlys could see no problem with this.

"What's wrong with being accepted into the whole family? They work together, don't they? I think it's wonderful that Mrs Piper welcomed you."

"Mrs Piper, or Granny Moll as she likes to be called, welcomes me as an extra pair of hands during the summer months. I'll be expected to give up my job and work on the sands or in the café."

"They all give up their winter jobs and work on the beach. They've done so for years. You wouldn't like that?"

"No, I'd hate it and I've no intention of giving up a job I enjoy because Granny Moll Piper tells me I should."

"Is that what you were discussing with Taff and Johnny's father?"

"They all do what Granny Moll says. I don't understand it. Taff's and Johnny's father, and his brother Huw, started on the sands when they were still at school and Huw married Granny Moll's daughter. Fine. But that doesn't give her the right to tell Bleddyn and Irene and their sons what to do, does it?"

"Bleddyn and Taff and Johnny work on the sands because they love it. Johnny's mother hates it so she doesn't, so why do you worry about it? Surely you can choose? I wouldn't give up my job if I were in your position. I enjoy it too much. But I'd love to help when I could. And if I found it more enjoyable than what I do now, I might be pleased to be involved and be a part of a big family like the Pipers. Why don't you talk it over and tell them how you feel?"

"You don't know Granny Moll! It's a family business and new members are expected to automatically give up their job and help."

"I'd love it," Eirlys breathed happily, seeing the dream and not the reality.

"Then you'd better tell Granny Moll and she'll make sure Johnny proposes to you!"

Eirlys was startled at how much that thought excited her.

She went inside and told her parents that Johnny's brother, Taff, was marrying Evelyn.

"Not before time if what I've heard is true. Carrying on they were and in her mam's house too."

"Kissing they were, Mam," Eirlys protested. "Her parents have made too much of it and now they're shaming her."

"If that's what's called kissing in this day and age, then you'd better watch out or you'll be in a worse position than her, my girl," her mother warned.

"Mam!" Eirlys ran upstairs in embarrassment.

"I don't want no hasty marriage for you," her mother called up the stairs. Eirlys covered her ears. She didn't want to hear any more. Loving someone was being reduced to something sordid, and the love she felt for Johnny was nothing like that. It was calm, and tenderly affectionate. Then she relived his kisses and thought of what Evelyn had said about the way she and Taff had been kissing and she was overcome with the reminder that perhaps love was more exciting than she had yet experienced.

Two

Eirlys and Evelyn did not know each other well, but once the engagement of Evelyn and Johnny's brother Taff was announced they began to meet more frequently. Neither had a sister or a brother and Evelyn needed someone with whom to discuss the arrangements for her special day. She didn't want to approach Beth or Lilly, Taff's cousins. The Castles would take charge of things soon enough.

Eirlys and she went together to look at wedding dresses, "Although," Evelyn explained, "my mother will want to be with me when I make the final choice."

They talked about the Castle family at first, Evelyn having some doubts about belonging to such a possessive group, Eirlys, in her euphoric mood of burgeoning love, convinced it would be heaven. "I love Taff," Evelyn said, "but I'm uneasy about taking on the Castle family with Granny Molly Piper at its head. She's kind at first but you soon realise how manipulative she is, persuading you something is your idea when she wants you to do something."

"Come on, she isn't that bad, surely?"

"Did you know Taff wanted to train as a carpenter? But Granny Moll insisted he was needed on the sands and his father agreed with her."

"Taff loves it though, like Johnny does."

"Yes," Evelyn said cynically, "it's childhood for ever, Moll running their lives."

"He'll stay in the family firm though, won't he?"

"Unless something crops up to give him the strength to leave," she said thoughtfully.

"And Johnny?"

"Oh, Johnny has never wanted anything else . . . You know, Granny Molly Piper has all but taken over the arrangements for the wedding," Evelyn complained as they watched the assistant removing a dress from its layers of tissue paper.

Eirlys sympathised but, surrounded by the magical displays of wedding gowns and all the extras, she imagined that if it were her marrying Johnny Castle, she'd be thrilled to be made so welcome.

As time went on and dress after dress was slipped carefully over and then off Evelyn's head, the two girls laughed and oohed and aahed and frowned and considered their way through the gown department of the largest shops in the town, and eventually selected two from which Evelyn would finally make her choice.

Saturday afternoon was the only time when they were were free to meet and shop, as both worked office hours five and a half days a week; Eirlys at the council offices and Evelyn in a factory making cables for army vehicles. When they finally settled for two, Evelyn whispered, "The truth is, Eirlys, I'm not really thrilled with either. D'you think Hannah Wilcox would be able to make one for me?"

"I don't think there's time, unless you delay the wedding for a few weeks."

"Come with me to see Taff. Johnny will probably be there and we can scrounge a cup of tea and a sandwich."

"Do you mind if I call for the boys first?" Eirlys asked. "I try to give Mam and Dadda a break from them when I can."

After collecting Stanley, Harold and Percival they went to Bleddyn and Irene's house but it was empty.

"Of course, they'll be at the chip shop, won't they?" Eirlys said.

"I thought today was his father's Saturday off." Evelyn frowned. "Never mind, we'll go for a walk instead."

"A walk to the chip shop?" Stanley said hopefully.

"I 'ates walking," Percival complained.

Bleddyn Castle had gone to see his brother to discuss the wedding of his son to Evelyn. As usual the house was full, with Huw and his wife Marged entertaining Marged's mother, Granny Moll, her sister Audrey and Audrey's fiancé of many years, Wilf Thomas.

"Where are the kids?" Bleddyn asked as he flopped into a chair near the fire.

"Our four are all out, thank goodness," Huw sighed.

"Our three now Ronnie's married," Marged corrected. "Our Lilly's got a date but we don't know who with."

"Secret meetings with a bloke she won't talk about," Huw grumbled. "Twenty-six she is, mind, and going out with someone she won't even put a name to."

"Our Beth is at a dance with Freddy," Marged went on, glaring at Huw to remind him they didn't want to discuss Lilly and her secret boyfriend, "and young Eynon is at the pictures."

"Beth at a dance? I didn't think Beth liked dancing."

"She doesn't, but that Freddy Clements does, so she goes with him and sits while he dances with other girls." Huw shrugged. "Daft, but there you are. They've been friends for so long they don't seem like a couple about to get engaged, do they?"

"Where are your lot, Bleddyn?" Granny Moll Piper asked. "We haven't seen your Irene for ages."

"I don't see much of her myself," Bleddyn admitted. "Irene isn't very well. You know how tired and depressed she gets sometimes. As for Taff and Johnny, they're probably out courting and it's Taff I came to talk to you about. He and Evelyn are going to get married as you know."

"D'you think that's wise, with the war and everything? There's the conscription that will soon take the eighteen-year-olds away, and the future isn't that cheerful," Moll warned. "I think they should wait."

Bleddyn shook his head. "All the more reason to get settled. It'll give the boys some comfort, knowing there's someone at home waiting for them."

"Just so long as it's what Taff really wants," Marged said pointedly.

"When are they planning to tie the knot?" Huw asked. "If it's soon, then it's best we get some food hidden away before the food rationing threatened for next year, eh, Marged? We'll want to give them a good spread."

"Don't be so hasty, Huw," Marged laughed. "They've only got engaged now this minute! Give it a bit of time."

"Fact is," Bleddyn said slowly, "they plan to marry very soon and we wondered, me and Irene, whether you'd make the cake and do the food, Marged."

"When exactly?" Moll asked, suspicion quirking an eyebrow.

"Three weeks' time and no, before you ask, she hasn't got a bun in the oven!"

"We weren't—" Marged protested.

"Yes we were," Huw grinned. "At least I was! So, Bleddyn, boy, what's the rush then?"

"Her mother and father want it sooner than later because they think they're getting a bit too passionate on the way they say goodnight," Bleddyn grinned.

Within an hour the plans had been discussed and finalised. The wedding would take place on Saturday October seventh at St Cenyth's church. The wedding breakfast for family and close friends would be held in Piper's Café over on the beach, specially opened for the occasion, and the bride would wear white as she walked down the aisle of the church, as befitted an innocent young girl and to stop tongues wagging.

Bleddyn wondered when Evelyn's family would be brought into the discussions but didn't ask. He knew it was best left to the women, although, he thought sadly, it was doubtful whether Irene would contribute much.

Bleddyn's brother Huw and his wife Marged had four children: Ronnie, now married to Olive; Lilly, with her mysterious lover; Beth, about to become engaged to Freddy Clements who worked in the local gent's outfitters and Eynon, who at sixteen was the "baby" of the family and hated it.

When seventeen-year-old Beth came in from the dance, her dark eyes were glowing and her smooth black hair cut in a bob with a straight fringe was a shining cap around her smiling face. Everything about her revealed a woman in love.

She was delighted to hear that her cousin Taff was to marry. Having just left the arms of the man she loved, her reaction was more enthusiastic than the others. She decided to go and see Evelyn the following evening after finishing work in the greengrocer where she was working throughout the winter. Like the rest of the family she worked on the beach during the summer season and found other work for the colder months.

"Pity they didn't wait a while longer, though," she said. "Me and Freddy are getting engaged on my eighteenth birthday and we could have had a double wedding next year."

Huw and Bleddyn went out into the small garden and stood looking around at the dark night. "Everything's all right, is it, Bleddyn?" Huw asked. "There's no pressure from Evelyn's parents that Taff doesn't want, is there?"

"No, nothing like that. He says he wants to marry Evelyn, but they didn't intend to marry in a rush like this. Engaged for a couple of years first is the usual carry-on, isn't it? To give themselves time to gather the things they need, fill their 'bottom drawer' and get to really know each other."

"What happened to change that?"

"Evelyn's mother got home earlier than planned and found them in a passionate embrace and insists that if she hadn't, her Evelyn would be in the pudding club."

The brothers smiled in the darkness, remembering their own courting days and the haste with which Huw married Marged before tongues wagged.

"Runs in the family, eh?" Bleddyn laughed. "You and Marged facing the wrath of Moll, and me and Irene not far behind, so your Lilly and our Taff were as good as twins, eh?"

"Irene bad again then, is she?" Huw asked after a while. "What's the trouble this time?"

"The usual depression. I've tried to work out what starts her off but there's no accounting for it. She walks around the streets and the beaches and I never know where she is or where she's been. Stays out for hours she does. When she is at home she's morose and won't talk. I don't understand it, but I do what I can to help keep the house running for the boys' sake. We just wait till she crawls out of the pit that she creates for herself, and gets back to normal. Then I just hope, every morning, that the black mood hasn't returned."

"Can't the doctor do anything?"

"Tells her to pull herself together and insists that she's fit and well and maybe doing it to avoid the work she hates."

"Rubbish. She never has done anything she doesn't want to." Huw coughed, embarrassed that his irritation with his sister-in-law was allowed to show. "Sorry, Bleddyn, I shouldn't comment when I don't know the full story."

"You know as much as I do, and that's practically nothing at all. It's as though she shuts herself off from her life with me and the boys, for weeks and sometimes months, then she comes back. But where she goes in her mind during those times, I don't know."

"Where does she go bodily, that's what I'd want to know. She can't just walk around. There has to be a place where she goes. Nobody sees her wandering about, do they?"

"Sometimes, yes. She's seen in the fields sometimes. But she's never been seen in a café or the pictures or anywhere like that."

"Strange," Huw frowned. "Now if she'd only help us on the beach in the summer months, keep herself busy, like, it might take her mind off herself and maybe it would help her."

"You know how many times I've asked her to come on the sands."

"I know, but if you told her how much we need her help . . . ?"

Bleddyn shuffled his feet, a sign that he was getting tense and didn't want to discuss it further, and Huw dealt with the blackout curtain as he opened the door to return to the others. Irene was Bleddyn's wife and he couldn't interfere, although he believed that the basis of Irene's "illness" was idleness rather than medical.

Eirlys knew that her mother was being kept busy with her part-time work and looking after the boys as well as dealing with the housewifely chores. Annie hadn't wanted the extra work involved in caring for Stanley, Harold and Percival, and she still threatened occasionally that they would have to go somewhere else to live. Eirlys spent as much time with them as she could. On the following day, a Sunday, it rained, but she was determined that they should see the sea.

In borrowed clothes, and wellingtons that were either tight or too loose, they made their way through the dreary streets towards the beach. Stanley asked a stream of questions, Harold was rude about everything and Percival walked head down, his rare comments making it clear that nothing interested him except getting back to his mother.

As they reached the promenade at St David's Well Bay, a light rain still fell, but across the water the sun showed its face and provided a rainbow – specially for them, she insisted, as she showed it off. With the low, dark clouds, the brightness across the sea on the distant shore and the magical appearance of the rainbow, Eirlys thought that considering the time of year, their first sight of the sea could have been a lot worse. Even Percival seemed impressed.

Then the rain stopped and everything sparkled like new, the sun giving the horizon a band of gold. Gradually they emerged from their outerwear and walked along the almost deserted, off-season beach while she tried to explain to the young Londoners what it would look like in the summer, when the entertainments were going full tilt and the beach was crammed with noisy families having fun.

She had walked a few yards before she realised that she only had two. Looking back, she saw Harold staring over the sea wall, where she had stopped for their first sight of the sea, amazement opening his mouth wide.

"Come on, Harold, you look like a dead fish standing there," she teased.

"I never thought it would be so big. What's that on the other side?"

"That's Somerset. Wait till we get home and I'll show you on the map," she promised.

With wellingtons coming into their own, they were able to run in and out of the water, pretending to run in fear from the white edged waves, laughing, sharing the joy of it with each other by occasional glances. Even the solemn Percival managed a glimmer of a smile.

A few entrepreneurial stall-holders had arrived and opened for the few hours of daylight left and soon the sands were full of people. It was as though summer had returned. Only the Pipers' helter-skelter and roundabouts and swingboats were missing. They had been stored away at the end of August.

The three boys watched in amazement at the sight of children running about, laughing, chased by assorted dogs, at dads formally dressed in suits trying to walk on the soft sand without getting any in their shoes, or sitting to make sandcastles. The women were neatly dressed and some carried baskets from which they took a few biscuits and a bottle of lemonade.

Eirlys smiled at a little girl carrying two cones which dripped, were licked and which finally fell into the sand. The child's mouth opened in a silent cry, easily recognised as such from a distance.

Crying could soon become commonplace, Eirlys thought sadly, as more and more fathers and brothers and sons were taken away to fight against Hitler.

They were returning to the promenade when she saw a figure she knew coming towards them waving and calling.

"Johnny!" she shouted, thankful for the release from her morbid thoughts.

"I called for you and your Dad said you'd be here," he said. "Have you shown them Piper's Café yet?"

She shared a hug and an affectionate kiss with him, then bent down to Percival's level and pointed to where, high above the beach, Piper's Café stood precariously on the cliff path, jutting out over the beach. It could be reached from the path and also from the beach, when the tide was low, by means of metal steps.

"I've got the key, what say we take a look?" Johnny suggested, waving the bunch of keys in front of her face.

Walking up the open-work metal steps that echoed each footstep, clanking in an alarming way, was an excuse for laughter and a few yells of fright which resulted in Johnny carrying Percival, who travelled upward with his eyes tightly closed.

The café was larger than it appeared from below and consisted of a dining area and a kitchen which was fitted with a frying range and an enormous sink as well as a cooker on which sat two large kettles.

"This is my family's business," Johnny explained as the boys prowled around examining everything. "We feed the hundreds of summer visitors that come to St David's Well Bay for their holidays every year."

"Got anything to eat then?" Stanley asked.

Johnny regretfully shook his head. "We closed at the end of August and we won't be open again until next summer."

"Not much of a caff then," Harold complained. "Some places are open, why not you?"

"Partly because we need to get jobs and wanted to take our pick, but mostly because of the blackout. We didn't fancy working here with the windows blacked out, or packing up in the dark, so rather than closing early, we finished altogether."

"What did you bring us here for if we can't get nothin' to eat?" Harold asked rudely.

"I ain't 'ungry," Percival said. He was a poor eater and even in the short time he had been staying with Eirlys's family had become anxious at the thought of mealtimes and the persuasions to eat.

"Sit at the table," Johnny instructed, pointing to the table close to a barred and partially boarded-up window. Little Percival sat disconsolately with elbows on the table, his hands supporting his chin, the epitome of misery. Then Johnny produced three sticks of seaside rock and his face changed. Now *this* looked more like food.

Leaving the boys chomping happily and discussing the sea and the sand, Johnny put an arm around Eirlys and asked, "They're great kids and I admire the way you're helping them settle in, but are we going to find a few hours for ourselves? Or will I have to wait till Hitler's been beaten and they go back home?" he teased.

"Sorry Johnny, but I thought I'd spend the weekend with them, get them out from under Mam's feet and show them around the neighbourhood."

"Of course, love."

The word "love" hung in the air. He had never called her that before, or greeted her with a real kiss when they met. She realised he was speaking, and pulled herself together and asked him to repeat it.

"It might be an idea to introduce them to some of the boys they'll meet at school so they won't feel so strange when they start there on Monday."

"You don't mind?"

"I can spare you for a while. I realise how important it is to help them." He turned his head and looked at the three brothers whispering, sharing opinions and most likely making fun of some of the things they had learnt.

Eirlys tilted her head to one side, smiling as she watched them. "It makes you realise how lucky we are to be here and not in one of the cities where they are theatened with bombs, and have to send their children away to live with strangers. I don't suppose we'll get off scot-free, though."

"No. For one thing, the call-up hasn't missed out St David's Well. Even the smallest village has been touched by that. I'll have to go next year unless they allow that the work on the beach justifies an exemption on the grounds that it's war work. That's not likely, is it? Taff will probably be going before me, so Evelyn won't be enjoying life as a married woman for very long. Living on her own she'll be, in the rooms they've rented in Curtis Street."

"Got a drink of pop to wash that sticky stuff down?" the cheeky Harold called hopefully.

Once again Eirlys was glad that he had broken the sober reminders that St David's Well was at war, and she replied cheerfully, "All right; as Johnny supplied the sticks of seaside rock, I'll treat you to a drink of pop in Piper's fish-and-chip shop."

"That's ours too," Johnny explained to the boys as they left the café perched high above the sands and walked back towards town. "My father runs it, but it belongs to the Piper family, same as the café. He takes a boat out for pleasure trips in the summer. You'll enjoy that next summer," he promised. "Right out across the bay he goes."

"Why isn't it called Castle's, then?" Harold asked.

"That's a long story, for another time, Harold."

"Rich, are yer?" Stanley wanted to know.

"Not rich enough to be idle; we have to work long hours for what we get. We earn our money by working in the café and the chip shop and, in the summer, we have swingboats and helter-skelters, stalls and hoopla and the like, right there on the sand."

"I do want to go home," Stanley explained, "I do want to see our Ma, but I'd like to be here in the summer and have a go on the helter-skelter and land on the sand. It sounds like fun."

"Softer on your arse than concrete," Harold said, looking wide-eyed at Eirlys, who chose to ignore the swear word.

"Swingboats make me sick," Percival said, with a brief demonstration.

Plans for the wedding of Taff Castle and Evelyn Power were set in motion, most of the arrangements being made by Evelyn's parents and swiftly changed by Granny Moll. Irene seemed happy about her son's wedding plans but did little to help. It was Bleddyn and Taff who liaised with the bride's family and dealt with ordering cars and other tasks allotted them by Evelyn's parents. The catering was firmly in the hands of Granny Moll Piper.

"D'you know what Granny Moll did?" Evelyn confided in Eirlys when they met one day to go and see how the wedding dress, being made by Hannah after all, was progressing. "Only went straight to the paper she did, and told them it would be the wedding of the year and for them to be sure to have photographers there. This was before Taff and I had decided on the church! And Mam wanted the reception in the church hall but no, that wasn't good enough for Granny Molly Piper. It had to be a wedding in Piper's Café. My wedding, mind!" She frowned. "I wish it was all over, and I think Taff does as well."

"You still want to marry him?" Eirlys asked anxiously.

"Of course I do, but not with this circus arranged by Granny Molly Piper!"

* * *

Marged and Huw made arrangements to cater for thirty people, which was all Piper's Café could comfortably hold, for the official wedding breakfast. The rest would wait for the real party at Sidney Street in the evening.

"Pity it isn't a summer wedding, we could have spread out across the clifftop and had a wonderful buffet meal-cum-picnic," Marged said, smiling as she envisaged the scene.

"Oh no," Mrs Power said in alarm. Whatever would the woman think of next? "That wouldn't do at all. It has to be a proper sit-down, three-course meal."

"And it will be," Marged assured her. "If there's one thing we Pipers do well, it's providing food in the right quantities and with the appropriate choices. Piper's Café was started by my great-grandparents and has maintained a reputation for excellence ever since," she reminded them firmly.

Eirlys wanted to be involved, she wanted to be considered a member of the family, but there didn't appear to be anything needed that she could do. She could hardly offer. She wasn't sure she would even be invited. Weddings were for family and close friends and she hadn't known Johnny very long. They had met at the beach a few days after she and Ken Ward had parted. That day she had been glad of the lively crowds to conceal her loneliness and the fear that she had made a mistake by not going to London with Ken. The beach atmosphere and Johnny's gentle teasing had soothed her and convinced her that her heart and her future was here, in the warm, friendly seaside town of St David's Well.

Watching Johnny flirting with the customers as he helped them on and off the swingboats, and comforting a child who wailed that he didn't want to go home, with the promise that it would all be there for him next year, she had felt her unhappiness fade away.

Later, when they had met by accident in the town, and talked and made a date for a visit to the pictures, she had become more convinced that her decision had been the right one. But they hadn't known each other long enough for her to expect an invitation to his brother's wedding.

When she received an invitation to the wedding a few days later, she was so excited she ran out and accepted it within minutes of the postman delivering it. She brushed aside the thought that it might have been Evelyn's idea rather than Johnny's. She would be attending a Castle wedding with Johnny. It was all going to happen; she and Johnny would be accepted as a courting couple before the year was out.

On the night before the wedding, Johnny and Taff went out for a drink. They had invited a few friends to join them but Taff didn't want the traditional pre-wedding booze-up. Taff was not an enthusiastic drinker and he didn't want to face his bride with a hangover.

His cousin Ronnie was there – as Taff's best man he had arranged it. The choice of Ronnie for best man rather than his brother Johnny had been Moll's. "It's a chance to show everyone what a united family we are," she had said.

To begin with it was a friendly chat around the table they had chosen near the bar-room fire, but, as the evening progressed, they were joined by more and more as news of the occasion spread. Other tables were joined to their own and the talk and singing grew more and more bawdy. The room became full and very warm and noisy and the party was no longer Taff's as the crowd increased to include people he hardly knew. Slipping away unnoticed, Taff went out into the street to cool off, wishing he'd never agreed to a stag night and wondering how soon he could leave.

Johnny saw him go through the double passageway with its heavy curtains hung to prevent the light spilling out during the hours of darkness, and followed him.

"You are happy about tomorrow, aren't you, Taff?"

"I wish it was over, that's all. I want to be married to Evelyn but I don't want to go through all this fuss. Why couldn't we have just gone and got married and forgotten all this nonsense?"

"Because the family would kill you, that's why," Johnny said mildly.

"Evelyn and I wanted a quiet affair."

"What, miss the chance of a party? An opportunity for Auntie Marged and Uncle Huw to show off their expertise at catering for a wedding? And Granny Moll to get a piece in the paper? You wouldn't deprive them of that, would you?"

"I suppose not."

Taff didn't want to discuss it. His wedding was not turning out to be the day he had imagined. Some of Evelyn's resentment had wriggled into his mind and had grown into discontent.

"What about you, Johnny?" he asked, to switch the conversation from himself. "Are you and Eirlys thinking of tying the knot? She seems very keen on you."

"Me and Eirlys? No fear! I'm too young. I want to have a bit of fun first; I'm only twenty-one."

"I just wondered, you know, whether Eirlys is hoping for something more permanent. The way she looks at you, you know, admiring glances and the like."

"Never. Just friends we are."

"You've invited her to the wedding and she'll be coming as your guest, sitting next to you for all to see and comment on. Serious stuff that. Is it wise, brother mine?"

"You don't think that she'll think – that I think—? No. We're just friends, that's all, she won't see anything more in an invitation shared by three dozen others to come to your wedding and the other three dozen who'll join us for the party later on."

"And you haven't kissed her or – anything else?"

"We've kissed, yes, but there's no 'anything else', you cheeky sod, and there won't be. I want to stay free for a few years yet. No, Taff, Eirlys is great, but she isn't my one love for life, like your Evelyn is yours."

It was almost ten o'clock and everyone had reached the maudlin stage when Johnny suddenly sobered up fast. "Damn Hitler!" he said to everyone's surprise. "I forgot to fix the blackout on Piper's Café!"

Amid shouts of "The wedding's off!" and "Lucky escape!" Johnny left the pub and hurried to see Eirlys. Inexplicably he had a sudden desire to see her, to find out perhaps whether what he felt for her was the beginnings of love. Talk about weddings often had this effect, he'd read that in a magazine somewhere. He'd better be careful!

In the boys' bedroom, Eirlys was reading *Swallows and Amazons* to them as a bedtime story. It was very late, but she had promised them and didn't want to let them down by refusing them even the smallest thing.

So far, apart from Stanley, they weren't impressed and Harold had explained, reasonably politely, that he and Percival preferred comics. She promised to order one for them to be delivered each week. "Something to look forward to," she explained. "In the mean time, we'll go on with this, right?"

The promise of the weekly comic persuaded them and they settled down to listen. On Stanley's pillow were the three letters they had so far received from their mother, Teresa Love. Scrappy notes written in pencil, the writing large and ill formed. The boys treasured them, reading them again and again. Eirlys knew she would be asked to read them aloud once more as soon as she closed the book.

When they were asleep, the precious letters tucked under Stanley's pillow, Eirlys stood for a while looking down at them and imagining herself in a few years' time, her and Johnny happily married and with children of their own.

Working on the beach in her spare time and being a part of the Castles' large family was a wonderful prospect. The recent kisses which had been more than the traditional peck, the hugging when they met and hearing him call her "love" had changed her expectations in the most exciting way, and she was convinced that they would stay together for always.

Tomorrow she would be going to his brother's wedding, that was a big step forward in their relationship. It was Johnny's way of telling everyone they were together. Everyone would see them as a couple after that.

She went to her wardrobe and stared at the suit she had bought specially for the occasion, a light blue-grey two-piece with tan accessories. She was having her naturally curly hair specially set in the morning. She wanted to impress his family, and the suit and the hair-do and the Californian Poppy perfume would be just perfect.

There was a knock at the door and her mother opened it to Johnny.

"Eirlys, can you and your dad spare an hour or two to help? We've just realised the café will need blackout curtains as the wedding isn't till four and it's bound to go on a bit. There'll be no time in the morning."

"Where will you get material at this time of night?"

"Granny Moll bought it ages ago in case something like this happened. It's in the café ready to be fitted."

"Dad's working but I can help if you like?" Eirlys offered.

Johnny turned to Annie as Eirlys reached for her coat. "I'll see her safe home, Mrs Price, don't worry."

They went on bicycles, Johnny borrowing Morgan's, packing the saddlebag with a few simple tools and necessary oddments. The roads were quiet, but with their poor lights they were extra careful when vehicles overtook them. Since the blackout began, there had been a large number of accidents.

The blackout "curtains" were in fact paper, forty inches wide and costing ninepence a yard. With a generous supply of drawing pins it took them two hours to complete the job.

Walking up the path to put the bicycles in the shed at one o'clock in the morning, Johnny put an arm around her and kissed her lightly on the cheek. "Thank you, Eirlys. I'd never have managed it on my own."

She turned her face as she smiled at him, hoping that the next kiss would touch her lips, but he hugged her then released her and increased his pace, hurrying off through the silent streets and leaving her with a feeling of dejection.

Hannah had made the wedding dress, after long discussions, using the skirt of one pattern and the bodice of another, embroidering it with pearls to a design of her own. She had worked long into the nights to get it finished in time as much of it was hand sewn. Her own two girls, Josie who was three and nine months and Marie aged two and a half were to be flower girls in white dresses matching, in a much-simplified style, the bridal gown.

On the day of the wedding, Johnny was up early, waiting on his brother and determined that the day would go smoothly in spite of his mother's inability to help.

He was the first to arrive at the church after making sure Taff was ready to leave. He stood back as the ushers welcomed the families and directed them to their seats. When Taff came, he would wait with him until their cousin Ronnie, who was best man, arrived to stand with him.

He guessed from the excitement engendered by the crowd that the bridesmaids had arrived and he couldn't resist going out to look at them. He knew their mother, Hannah, would be with them. He saw Hannah first. Dressed in a simple two-piece in a soft blue he thought she looked lovely. Her face was always rosy, as though she had just stepped away from attending to the fire. Her eyes, dark like his own, and large enough to lose himself in, glanced his way and she smiled shyly, turning his heart in a surprising way.

He went across to help the little girls in their long skirts, holding tightly clutched posies of flowers, out of the car, while Eirlys looked on, smiling happily at the pretty scene. Then Evelyn's mother came running up and elbowed Johnny out of the way, but he stared at the shy but proud mother and her two small girls for a long time before going with Eirlys into the church.

Ronnie was late. He was cleaning Taff's old shoes because Taff had insisted the new ones were too tight. He was battling with Taff's stiff collar, searching for a collar stud that refused to slip into place and repeatedly fell on the floor. He was assuring the over-anxious groom that the borrowed suit was an excellent fit. And that the ring was safely in his pocket.

Johnny returned to sit beside his brother, anxiously glancing from time to time towards the door, until his cousin Ronnie Castle running in late, arrived in the role of best man and took his place, leaving him free to join Eirlys.

Eirlys was smart in her new outfit but she felt uneasy, convinced that Johnny didn't like it. He had barely looked at her and they had exchanged very few words. She must be embarrassing him in her ill-chosen clothes. She felt the heat of humiliation and longed to run away.

He seemed indifferent to her presence, sitting well away from her and looking around at all the guests, smiling, waving, and ignoring her. She must look a sight, she thought and shrank down in her seat wishing the whole affair was over.

Johnny was uneasy. He knew he should have complimented her on her appearance; she did look rather lovely. But uneasy about how she would behave, not wanting to give the gossips any further fuel, he treated her like a casual aquaintance, and felt mean and unkind. He really would have to make up his mind or slip out of her life completely. Somehow he didn't want to do that.

"Where are the boys?" he asked, more for something to say to break the iciness of their situation than because he wanted to know.

Eirlys gestured with her head to the back corner of the church where three solemn boys sat in silence beside her parents Annie and Morgan, over-awed by the spectacle of so many smartly-dressed people and the whispering silence of the church. Johnny chuckled. "I never thought them capable of sitting so still. Or looking so well scrubbed!"

"I made them bathe at the very last minute. They've developed a knack of finding mud and water or anything else that's smelly or dirty. Thanks to Hannah's help, we managed to dress them in something that fitted them for a change. None of their own clothes would have been suitable."

"Have you known her long?" Johnny asked.

"Hannah? We got to know her when she was having trouble with her husband. Her parents refused to support her even though he used to beat her," she whispered. "Mam and Dadda helped her a lot and we've kept in touch with her."

"She's very kind, isn't she, Hannah?" Johnny said after a brief pause. "I wonder that she had enough time to help so willingly. Dad says she cleans for some shops every morning while the children are at school or being looked after by her friends, and again in the evening after the children are asleep. It must be exhausting to do all that, then settle down to work at her sewing machine for hours."

"Shush, the bride is coming!"

Every head turned to catch a first glimpse of Evelyn as she entered the church on her father's arm. She looked very beautiful, the dress was stunning, and there were many gasps of admiration as the organ music swelled and she came to stand beside her groom, who looked justifiably proud. In the silence that followed, as the congregation waited for the vicar to speak, Harold was heard to say, "Is that what we've been waiting for? Can we go back with you, now, Uncle Morgan?"

"Hush up, boy, you're in church!" Morgan whispered back.

Eirlys frowned. "They did promise to behave," she said ruefully.

There was a brief moment of amusement when Taff was called by his real name of Arthur Brian Castle, and the vicar interrupted the service to remind them of the seriousness of the occasion.

Eirlys glanced at the three boys from time to time and saw her father stride out of the door before the service was half-way through. She gestured to her mother with a philosophical shrug of her shoulders. Morgan Price wasn't one to sit dressed up in church for long. Always neatly dressed, even in his work clothes,

Morgan preferred casual wear and had always hated wearing a suit and stiff collar.

He'd clearly been there on sufferance, tugging at his viciously starched collar and fidgeting worse than the boys. But when the boys stood to go with him he had shaken his head and they settled disconsolately to wait till Annie took them home.

The photography session seemed to go on for ever. Unable to decide whether to go or stay, Eirlys took the three boys for a walk around the beach where most of the photographs were taken, and answered questions about the people they had met.

There was no professional photographer engaged; Huw and Bleddyn took turns at snapping the various groups. Granny Moll insisted on taking one of the whole family, which consisted of her daughter Marged and Huw, their children and daughter-in-law and also Bleddyn, Johnny, Taff and his new bride. Irene wasn't to be found. With her usual authority, Moll waved for Eirlys to join them and, feeling rather self-conscious, aware it had not been Johnny's idea, she did.

This was what Evelyn had been trying to explain, she realised. Granny Moll was making it clear that this was a Piper wedding even though the couple getting married were Castles. But she smiled anyway. Today she was Johnny's guest at a family affair. That was a good sign. His strange mood during the ceremony had faded. It had clearly been nothing more than worries about Ronnie being late.

Arranging everyone so nobody blocked anyone else took some time and there were laughs about the evenness of their height. Apart from Bleddyn who towered above the rest, all the Castle family were average height or below. Eventually some sat on chairs, some formed a line behind the rest by standing on more chairs, so a formal arrangement was achieved.

Huw shouted insults at his brother, telling everyone jocularly that Bleddyn must have been a by-blow or had been changed at birth because he was taller and heavier than the rest.

"Or better fed!" Moll added.

Johnny was slightly uneasy at the happy expression on Eirlys's face and as soon as the camera gave its loud click, he hurried away.

The party was held in the home of Granny Moll in Sidney Street as her house was the largest. Irene didn't seem to mind that her son's wedding party was held in someone else's house rather than her own. "It's less work for me," she said honestly, "and if everyone else wanted it, why should I complain?" She disappeared a short while after the crowd arrived and apart from Bleddyn, who searched for her to drink a toast to the young couple as they set off for their honeymoon in Weston-Super-Mare, and Johnny, who wanted her to talk to Eirlys while he looked for Hannah, no one missed her.

Stanley, Harold and Percival had sat in a row at the wedding breakfast and were plied with food. Percival hid his under the chair but the others enjoyed the fancy food, the like of which they had never before seen.

When Bleddyn came and talked to them, he asked them about their home.

"It ain't nothing like this," Stanley said. "We got two rooms for the four of us and the lavvy's in the yard."

"What about your father? Doesn't he make five?"

"Nah. He 'opped it years ago," Harold told him flippantly. "Good riddance too, Mum says, don't she Stanley?"

"I want to go home," Percival muttered.

"Go on with yer, it's all right with Auntie Annie and Uncle Morgan. And Johnny's going to show us how to make a treehouse next Saturday."

In a convoy of cars they had moved to Granny Moll's house and continued the party there, with the numbers increasing as friends and neighbours came to join in. Marged's sister Audrey had left the wedding breakfast early with her friend Wilf Thomas, and they had already prepared trays of glasses and set out food ready for the second half of the celebration.

Taff and Evelyn didn't stay long. They had arranged to take a train at seven.

Seeing the couple off by taxi to the station meant everyone was out on the pavement. Up and down Sidney Street, doors opened and neighbours crowded out on to doorsteps, adding to the cheers and good wishes. Bleddyn looked for his wife but Irene was not among the crowd of well-wishers. Her son was going on honeymoon and she wasn't there to see him off. Irritation flared and died. She was ill, he told himself, and couldn't be blamed. He just hoped that Taff hadn't noticed or would understand if he had.

Finding Eirlys with Annie and the three boys sitting in a corner, while Johnny began to play records on the gramophone, Moll sat near them. "I just hope Taff will be able to make that young girl understand that she's now part of the Piper family," she said. "She can't refuse to help on the beach next summer, not with the boys having to register for the armed forces. The family will have to stick together more than ever now. Piper's will need every pair of hands."

So filled with the happiness of the day, Eirlys was on the point of offering to help on her days off, but she stopped herself in time. How embarrassing to be so forward. She would have to wait to be invited. She wondered if Moll was leading up to do just that, when Marged and Huw and their son Ronnie heard what had been said and came nearer.

"Oh, Granny Moll," sighed Ronnie. "Give the girl a chance. Married five minutes and here you are, complaining about how she'll be next summer. Besides, we don't want to think about the war, not today."

"Why not? It won't go away because we pretend it isn't happening. The boys will have to go, but the business carries on as usual. Evelyn must realise that."

"Olive doesn't help, Granny Moll, we manage without her; perhaps Evelyn feels the same."

"I know she likes what she does," Eirlys dared to say. "She's an inspector on a factory bench, isn't she?"

"I know full well what she does, and I also know that checking up on someone else's work isn't more important than working on the sands."

For a moment Eirlys felt sympathy for Evelyn. Marrying Taff meant belonging to the family. And the head of the family, Granny Moll, was unlikely to allow her to forget it. Yet she was so anxious to impress, to make Moll look at her as a useful member of the family if she and Johnny became close, she swallowed her brief compassion, smiled at Mrs Moll Piper and said sweetly, "I agree, Mrs Piper. Piper's is more than a business, isn't it? It'll be helping to win the war by keeping up morale. I've read about how important entertainment was in the last war in keeping up morale. I'm sure Evelyn will see it too, as soon as she calms down from the excitement of her wedding day."

"Yes, I must give her time, mustn't I?" She looked thoughtfully at Eirlys's bright face and smiled. "You understand about Piper's, don't you Eirlys?"

"Oh yes, I understand fully the importance of Piper's," she replied as enthusiasm and the need to please blotted out common sense. She could give up her job and – She looked for Johnny, wanting, needing to tell him that she would accept what belonging to the Pipers really meant, and that she would willingly give up her job at the council offices to become a part of it. Then she felt colour suffuse her cheeks. What was she thinking of? Apart from a few kisses, Johnny hadn't given the slightest hint that he thought about her in that way. Acting as though he had already proposed? She must be crazy! She had let today's celebration, the romantic occasion, go to her head. But the dream warmed her for the rest of the day. At least she had Granny Moll on her side and that was a start.

Johnny found Hannah raising the fronts of the skirts of Josie and Marie's dresses a little, with the aid of a couple of kilt pins attached to ribbon bows, to allow the little girls to run around more freely.

"Is there anything they need?" he asked. "They've been so good today. If there's anything they want they only have to ask." He was bending from the waist and looking at the girls as he spoke. A shyness prevented him looking at their mother, a shyness which confused him.

"Go and smack that boy over there," Josie said haughtily. "He's been calling me names."

Without looking, Johnny guessed that Harold was the culprit.

Hannah laughed, a pleasant musical sound, and Johnny was caught by the humour and joined in. "I think we'll forgive him today, as he's new, shall we?" he said.

He walked Eirlys home with a sensation of doing a duty instead of it being a pleasure.

Eirlys lay on her bed for a long time without sleeping, wondering what had gone wrong. She went over all the conversations of the day. It was only during the one with Granny Molly Piper that she had presumed too much. Perhaps Granny Moll had repeated it and passed that presumption on to Johnny. Dismay filled her and she knew embarrassment would spoil her next meeting with Johnny.

On the morning after the wedding, Johnny's first thought was of

Hannah and her merry laugh. He lay there in the bedroom he had shared with Taff all his life, and wondered why.

Eirlys waited for Johnny to call the following morning, a Sunday. She had promised the boys a walk through the fields to search for a likely place to build a treehouse and she had hoped that Johnny would go with them. When eleven o'clock came and he hadn't appeared she dressed the three musketeers, as they liked to be called, and set off.

Their route led them through the allotments where her father had once grown a few vegetables, though since the call to grow more food, urged on by leaflets issued by the Ministry of Food, more enthusiastic gardeners had clearly taken it over. Its neat, evenly dug surface was broken only where sprouts and a few leeks survived, all that remained of her father's half-hearted efforts.

On through the lanes until they came to the field where more vegetation had been cleared. The field belonged to Mr Gregory, the owner of a small holding of a few acres, who was increasing the crops he grew. As well as vegetables and a few flowers, he had ducks on the pond and chickens in the large hen-coops and wire runs. He was a well known figure, as he ran donkeys on the beach during the summer with his son, Peter, who was now away from home in the army.

Eirlys was strolling along enjoying the pleasant walk when she was startled by a yell of fright from Harold.

"What the 'ell's that!" he shouted, and after the initial shock, Eirlys saw to her amusement that the boys had been frightened by the sight of a cow walking along the lane, followed by the rest of the herd, returning from the fields to the milking parlour for milking.

"Surely you know what a cow looks like," she teased.

"No one told us they was that big!" Harold said in awe.

Eirlys explained their usefulness in providing milk, butter and cheese and, after studying the creature with disapproval on his face, Percival announced that he wouldn't touch another drop of milk till he was home where it came in bottles.

The oak tree at the furthest end of a sloping field was the site Eirlys had chosen but she knew that without Johnny or her father helping, she would be unable to do what she had promised.

There was a stone building in one corner of the field and as they approached, the boys running about and shouting in delight at the wide spaces where they were allowed to roam, she saw someone leaving the place and, for a moment, thought it was her father. But it couldn't have been him. Why would he be out here when he should be at home?

Curiously she began to head for the place to investigate but once the boys realised which tree would be "theirs" there was no holding them back. As though they had been climbing trees all their lives they clambered up into the ancient branches and for a while played happily as the tree became a house, then a mountain, then a ship.

When they had decided on the position of their house, Eirlys led them back to the corner where the stone barn stood. She was just about to enter when a voice called and she turned to see her father waving to her.

"Didn't I see you coming out of this old stone barn?" she asked. He shook his head.

"No fear, love. Mud, rubbish and rats is all you'll find in there." He waved an arm to encompass the whole field and went on, "There used to be a rubbish dump in this field. Crawling with rats it is. Best you keep right away."

"I will," she said with a shudder.

"What's this about a treehouse then?" he asked the boys. He listened to their plans and instructions and told them that he had found just the thing. "But a lot closer to home than this," he said, frowning at his daughter. "We need to be able to get hold of you quick if the air raid siren goes, don't we?"

"Sorry, Dad, I didn't think. I remember there was one here years ago and thought we might use the same spot."

By evening Morgan had the base of the treehouse made. When darkness came the work continued as he used his skill of splicing thick rope to make the all-important ladder. The boys went to bed contented, but Eirlys was disappointed that Johnny hadn't called. Everything had been so wonderful until the day of the wedding, so what had happened overnight to change it?

Johnny didn't go out that day. Several people had referred to Eirlys as his girlfriend and his denials were treated as a joke. Then Granny Moll cornered him and told him how pleased she was that Eirlys realised the importance of Piper's and would be more than willing to take her place if she married into the family.

"But Granny Moll, I'm not marrying her. Friends we are."

The knowledgable look that appeared on Moll's face as she said slowly, "We'll see," terrified him.

How easily things could get out of hand. Taff had been right, it had been a mistake to invite Eirlys to the wedding. He needed to be very careful if he wanted to go on seeing her, and he did. There was no one he enjoyed being with more. But he wasn't ready to commit himself to a permanent partnership with her. Her kisses pleased him but had so far failed to engender that special excitement he knew they should.

Just how much of his reticence was due to the sight of Hannah as she tended her little girls he wasn't sure. But that was silly. Hannah was far too old for him, getting on for thirty. Yet in his imagination, when he felt his lips touch her soft, generous mouth it was a joy and a happiness, and he longed to make the dream a reality.

He decided that if he stayed away from Eirlys for a while, then casually invited her and the boys to go out for a walk, and avoided even the most casual of kisses, then things might return to how they had been. It was nice having a pretty girl on your arm. He enjoyed her company, but didn't want things to develop an impetus of their own and take him along a way he didn't want to go.

Three

Later that month, Morgan joined the local Air Raid Precaution group. Working shifts at the factory he was able to spend some time on most days helping to organise the rotas and deal with finding a place in which to meet and get the unit under way.

Because he had once owned his own business, the others presumed it was something he would do well, and it was. He wrote letters, persuaded the council to allow them to use a room in the school for their meetings, he acquired equipment and gathered information and set it out in leaflet form to distribute among the members of the organisation.

On being congratulated, he sighed and wished he had found it as easy to cope with running his own business. He had lacked the enthusiasm for the complicated store his father had left him; it had been too big and he felt he had failed because its success had been so essential for Annie and Eirlys. If he had been able to treat it as a hobby rather than a necessary full-time commitment, he might have managed better. It had been its importance that had made him fail, he was sure of that.

Annie didn't mind his involvement in the air raid precaution group although she did doubt its usefulness. The war showed no sign of ever coming to St David's Well; it was centred on France and how could that make their little seaside town vulnerable? She understood that the war effort needed everyone to do their bit, though, and she decided that looking after three evacuees between them was not enough.

"Perhaps I'll join too," she said to Morgan one day. "I can't do any evening work with the boys to look after, but I could help with the training classes, once I have been trained myself."

Morgan discouraged her. "Plenty of people at the moment," he told her. "It's later, when the novelty wears off and the enthusiasm wavers, that people will probably stop bothering. That's when we'll need new recruits."

Annie shrugged. She wasn't very keen to give up more of her time;

there was plenty to do now she had evacuees as well as the part-time work in the bakery.

She didn't enjoy working in the shop. It was hard to forget that they had once owned a business and employed four people besides having help in the house. Reminded of it, she showed her irritability with Morgan and asked why he didn't do more to help her instead of spending so much time with the ARP.

"You let the allotment go and you never do the decorating that the house needs. I work all the hours the day holds and you just disappear and meet your friends."

"More than that, Annie," Morgan protested.

"It isn't even needed at the moment," she went on. "I think you men just use the meetings as an excuse to get out of the house and idle away a few hours."

Aware that she was steamed up and ready to argue, Morgan said nothing, just waited for her to continue.

"Years I've had to work at the bakery. Years of people talking to me as though I were their inferior. Ever since you lost the business your father left you. Comfortable we'd be now if you'd looked after it properly."

"I wasn't made to run a business. I tried to tell Dad, you know I tried to persuade him to sell. But he was convinced that given the chance I'd do all right."

"Wrong he was then, wasn't he?"

Morgan's father, Reginald Price, had owned a successful business fulfilling the various requirements of farmers and smallholders. Fencing, barbed wire, chicken wire and the like. Creosote and special paints. Sheep dip, harness soap and polishes, cart-grease, buckets. Everything he was asked for he somehow found room to stock.

Morgan had allowed the business to run down and down until it was sold as a property only, a property on which he had borrowed until there was nothing left. He had taken a year to pay off the remaining debts. He didn't think Annie would ever forgive him.

He waited until Annie had finished listing her complaints, then told her he was going to work. It was early, but sitting chatting to the men was kinder on his ego than listening to her telling him how he had failed everyone, including his poor dead father.

On Sunday morning, leaving the three musketeers helping Annie to make a cake, Eirlys went to take a closer look at the barn where she thought she had seen her father. There was no real reason, it was simply an excuse for a walk, a destination to head for. On an autumn day when the sun shone weakly with a pretence of warmth, it was a pleasure to be out of doors.

Around the entrance, deeply rutted mud revealed the regular visit of cows and she almost turned back but she forced herself to ignore the mess creeping up the sides of her shoes and delicately made her way across to where she could look inside, although by this time with little hope of seeing anything of interest.

The door was partially open and she squeezed inside and stood a while waiting for her eyes to become accustomed to the poor light. There was nothing there but old, abandoned farm machinery. A broken-down tractor that looked as though it had been cannibalised to repair others stood drunkenly against the far wall and other, less easily recognisable pieces of metal were strewn carelessly around amid empty sacks, coils of baling twine, oddments of barbed wire rusted and decorated with dead leaves and rotting hay.

Everything was covered in mud and there was an air of abandonment that suggested that little had changed over past years. She must have been mistaken. Her father couldn't have been coming out of here.

She smiled as she thought that the man must have been a tramp who had just been given some new clothes. Shirt, Fair Isle pullover, grey trousers and a sports jacket were almost a uniform for the working man on his day off these days.

She stared around looking for clues to suggest the barn's use as an occasional night shelter but found none. She had been wrong about the tramp. No one could live here. The man she saw had obviously been just passing by and had chosen not to talk to them – or, she thought with a grimace of distaste, he had been using the place as a urinal!

She noticed an area just inside the door that had been spread with paving stones and was clean of mud. On the wall above her head there was a nail on which hung a key. She smiled to herself. It must be a long time since anyone had bothered to lock this place against thieves.

Standing outside, thankful for the mild clean air away from the dankness within, she still didn't feel like going home. The air was fresh, the sky an unbelievable blue and although there wasn't any wind, leaves fell from branches as a reminder that summer was gone. She ran and tried to catch a falling leaf. Catching one as it left the tree and before it touched the ground meant a day of good luck in the year to come. Like a child, she ran about idiotically until she had caught three.

Thinking of Johnny Castle, she whispered to herself, "One for a proposal, one for our engagement, and one for our wedding day."

Through a hedge she spotted a caravan parked near the corner of the next field. Not a healthy place to choose if Dadda had been right about rubbish and rats. She climbed over the gate and walked around to examine it. The curtains were clean, as were the windows. Beside the steps a pair of wellingtons stood, thick with mud. These gave her the feeling that the place was occupied, even though the curtains were drawn and no smoke climbed out through the chimney. Afraid of being seen and accused of nosiness, she crept quietly away.

She didn't see the curtains move and a pair of eyes watch her until she regained the hedge and disappeared.

There was a stream at the bottom of the field in which the barn stood, and she made her way down and stood for a while looking at the water glistening as it made its way towards the distant sea. A movement to her right caught her eye and she turned to see Johnny's mother walking, head down, along the other side of the field. She was not wearing a coat and, even though the sun was bright, there was an autumnal nip in the air. The green cardigan and thin brown dress Irene Castle was wearing did not seem suitable for a country walk.

Eirlys was about to call out and go to meet her but held back. Johnny's mother was known to be ill and she didn't feel confident enough to engage her in conversation. She spoke strangely at times and Eirlys felt guilty, but not sufficiently so to walk across and say hello. Besides, the woman probably wanted to be on her own and wouldn't appreciate her intruding into her thoughts. She would tell Johnny and make the excuse that she was too far away.

She was pleased to have an excuse to call on Johnny. Home was suddenly a more enticing idea. Turning uphill away from the stream she cleaned her shoes as well as she could with the aid of a stick and handfuls of grass, and headed for Brook Lane.

Invited in, Eirlys removed her muddy shoes and explained that she had been for a walk and had seen Irene, Johnny's mother, inadequately dressed for the crisp autumn weather.

"Mam often gets upset and goes off for a walk on her own," Johnny said, signalling for her to lower her voice. "Dad worries about her but can't stop her. She'll be back when she's calmed down."

"But she was wearing a thin brown dress and no coat," Eirlys whispered. "Frozen solid she'll be when the sun goes in, in nothing but a skimpy green cardigan."

"She'll be back long before then."

Bleddyn had heard Eirlys arrive and he appeared from the kitchen bearing a tray filled with steaming cups. Gratefully she took one and settled near the roaring fire to drink it. Johnny didn't seem at ease and he hadn't sat down, just wandered around the room restlessly. It was as though he was expecting her to leave. He took the tea offered by his father and eventually sat down, not near her but at the table some distance away. Perhaps her visit had been ill timed and there was something he had planned to do.

"It's all right if you're going out, Johnny. I just called to tell you that I saw your mam, you don't have to change your plans for me, mind," she said cheerfully.

"Oh, I wasn't planning much. In fact, if you're free this afternoon we could go for a walk. I want to see Taff and Evelyn but you could come with me."

"Thanks, I'd like that. I'd like to see their rooms. Done them out nice, have they?"

Johnny shrugged. "They look fine to me."

As she was leaving, Irene came in and to Eirlys's surprise the woman was wearing a thick brown coat with a fur collar. Johnny looked at his mother then turned to Eirlys with a frown.

"I thought you said— Hello, Mam, had a nice walk?"

"Lovely, Johnny. And I'm starved. I hope your father has kept an eye on the meat and roast potatoes."

"Yes, I have," Bleddyn said, emerging from the kitchen. "And the vegetables are simmering nicely."

Eirlys looked at Irene and saw not a sick woman, but a woman with a face glowing with health, her dark eyes shining as though she had just been happily surprised. Surely she hadn't been mistaken again in the area where she thought she had seen her father? Had the sad woman she had watched walking along with her head dropping low, and without a coat, not been Irene Castle? The place must be haunted by ghosts of the living!

"I thought you said she wasn't wearing a coat?" Johnny demanded in a whisper.

"But, I saw her, and she had a green cardigan and a thin brown dress on," Eirlys said, confused.

At that moment Irene took off her coat and hung it on a peg. Eirlys stared when she saw that Irene was wearing the clothes she had described. Stumbling her way out of the door, unable to think what, if anything, to say, she shouted back, "Call for me later, Johnny."

"No, meet me at fifteen Curtis Street at three," Johnny replied. "Where have you been, Mam?" he asked his mother as she washed her hands and began to make the gravy.

"Oh, just looking at the shops. I want to choose something for Evelyn's birthday next month. D'you think she'd like a new purse?"

"Not across the fields?"

"Fields? At this time of year?" she smiled.

Johnny looked at his mother's shoes. They were clean and well polished. Eirlys must have been mistaken, or had made up the story about his mother. He wondered why.

He arrived at the rooms occupied by his brother Taff and his sister-in-law Evelyn long before Eirlys was expected. He told them Eirlys's story about seeing their mother.

"Johnny, that's an old trick, making an excuse to call on the boy you fancy. I remember finding a button and knocking on your door to ask if it belonged to Taff," Evelyn laughed. "She likes you and—"

"She couldn't find a button?" Taff finished with a grin.

"Mam said she hadn't been near the fields. She walked around the shops looking for a birthday present for you, Evelyn."

"Eirlys said she saw your mother in the fields?" Evelyn said.

"That's what she said. Why would she make up a story like that?"

"Evelyn's right, she likes you and wanted an excuse to call," Taff said.

"Trouble is, Taff, I don't think I like Eirlys as much as she likes me," Johnny said seriously.

"Then keep out of her way, make arrangements so you're never free when she calls; she'll soon realise you don't feel the same," Taff advised.

Evelyn looked thoughtful, staring into space with a frown crinkling her eyes.

"I have a feeling that she'll be a bit clingy," Johnny went on. "I like her, but how do I tell her it's no more than friendship, without hurting her feelings?"

"Perhaps Evelyn could have a word," Taff suggested.

Evelyn shrugged and agreed.

Eirlys arrived just before three and Evelyn invited her in. The rooms, which consisted of a bedroom, living room, a kitchen into which a small table and two chairs had been squeezed, and – rather grand – a shared bathroom, were examined and admired. Then, while the brothers sat in the small, neat living room, Evelyn took Eirlys into the kitchen to prepare tea.

Evelyn had made a cake, a few sandwiches and fruit and custard. As they were setting it out on the table, she said quietly, "You don't want to crowd Johnny too much, you know, or you'll frighten him away."

"What d'you mean?" Eirlys asked.

"Don't always be available when he wants to go out, make him see that you have a life of your own without depending on him for the social side."

"But I do sort of depend on him," Eirlys explained. "I like doing things with Johnny and I want him to know that."

"Men respect you more if you have other interests. It gives you something fresh to talk about when you're together."

"I work from nine till five thirty. I don't have a lot of time for hobbies. If I did, I'd want to share them with Johnny."

Evelyn placed the sandwiches on the centre of the freshly-ironed blue-edged white tablecloth and said firmly, "Don't drift through the days waiting for marriage, Eirlys, get out and do things while you have the chance."

"My job—" she began to explain.

"Come on, Eirlys, like so many young girls you dreamily sit in a safe job waiting for a safe marriage."

Stung by the harsh truth, hurt by hearing it from Evelyn, whom she had begun to consider to be a friend, Eirlys was relieved when Johnny stood up and offered to walk her home.

She said little on the short stroll to Conroy Street, said goodnight at the gate without giving Johnny the opportunity for a kiss. Going inside, she announced, "Dadda, I want to learn to drive, so I am joining the ARP."

"What? Never, my girl. I don't want you to even think of it. I don't know what's got into you and your mam to want to deal with the things we might have to face. So it's no! Right?"

Surprised at her father's vehemence, Eirlys insisted rudely, and on the verge of tears, that it was none of his business and she would go to the headquarters the following lunchtime and sign up.

Seeing the distress on her daughter's face, Annie Price urged her husband to be quiet.

"No, I won't hush up. I don't want our daughter having to face fires and injured people and risking death by driving around while bombs are falling." Morgan was adamant.

"What bombs?" Eirlys demanded. "If there was a chance of us being bombed we wouldn't have been chosen as a safe place for evacuees, would we? I am going to join and I am going to learn to drive."

Trying a different tack, Annie asked, "What if Johnny wants you to go to the pictures or somewhere? It will take a lot of your time, love."

"Johnny will have to go on his own. We all have to do something to help the war effort and if he doesn't understand that, well, it's too bad!"

"They've had a row," Annie mouthed to Morgan, who nodded and wisely said nothing more. But he was worried. He didn't want Eirlys knowing his movements. Spending a few evenings with the Air Raid Precaution group gave him some welcome freedom and his daughter or, worse still, Annie belonging to the same organisation would interfere with that.

"Perhaps we can persuade her to run the Girl Guides pack instead," he said to Annie.

"That doesn't have the same ring as fighting Hitler, now does it!" she retorted. "Let her go if she wants to. What harm could it do?"

Morgan didn't reply. He coped with his marriage and with Annie's disappointment by escaping sometimes. He needed time away from the home. The instigation of the ARP had been a lifesaver.

Eirlys began to think about the things her father had promised to make for the boys, among them a treehouse. She decided to go back to the area near the barn where she had seen the sturdy oak tree that would be perfect for a hideaway house for them.

As she approached the field she saw two dogs and recognised them as belonging to Evelyn's parents. She looked around and, seeing Evelyn some distance away, called out and began to make her way towards her. This was nice; someone with whom to discuss her ideas.

She called out again as she saw Evelyn stop, then turn away from her and hurry off. Surely she had seen her or heard her shout? Why hadn't she at least waved? On her way home she knocked at the house in Curtis Street but there was no reply.

Stanley, Harold and Percival had settled down in school surprisingly well. Stanley amused the others in his class with his spurious adulthood, understanding things of which they were unaware. His different background and upbringing added a freshness to the class that even the teacher – after a few misunderstandings – began to encourage.

Stanley's love of books led him to the library too, and he was reading *A Christmas Carol* to his brothers, reading ahead then changing the wording to make it easier for his brothers to understand. There weren't many books in the Price household but Morgan's copies of *The Three Musketeers* and *Twenty Years After* found their way into Stanley's bedroom, where he was allowed to read for an inch of a candle after the others were asleep. Eirlys knew he also sneaked a torch under his pillow and used that to read a while longer when the candle had burned down to its mark.

Stanley looked through the daily paper too and it was he who read out the tragic news of the *Royal Oak* being sunk at her base, Scapa Flow. That disaster was a shock to everyone and was on the lips of customers in every shop and bus passengers as they travelled to and from work. For many, it was the realisation that the enemy could strike them in their homes too. Sobered by the ship being struck with the loss of so many men when it was supposed to be safe, with that incident people were made more aware of being at war than by anything that had happened previously.

They were at the library one Saturday morning, when Eirlys had a rare few hours off, and they met Evelyn there. Smiling a welcome and walking over to talk to her, Eirlys was struck by the angry look on her friend's face.

"Evelyn? What's happened? Is anything wrong?"

"You should know that, Eirlys Price! I don't know how you can look Johnny in the face and smile your sweet innocent smile, knowing what you do. Shamed you should be."

Puzzled, Eirlys watched Evelyn walk out of the library, pausing only to turn and give one more devastatingly furious glare. She had no idea what had happened. Since they had last met she had been at work. She hadn't seen Johnny for several days. What on earth was wrong? First the incident near the barn when Evelyn had run away without speaking, and now this.

She had defied her father and gone along one lunchtime to make enquiries about joining the ARP. She had arranged to attend a lecture explaining the various ways she could help. Her enquiry about driving lessons was noted and she had thought at the time it might justify a visit to Johnny to ask for a few lessons from him in Piper's van. Now, after Evelyn's strange anger, she wondered how she would be received, and also whether a visit might result in an explanation. It was this thought that made up her mind. She would call on Johnny Castle and demand to be told what was wrong.

She knocked on Bleddyn and Irene's door that evening but there was no reply. A walk around to the back lane showed the house to be in darkness, but whether that was due to the blackout or because it was empty she had no way of telling. Disconsolately she walked back home.

"Johnny called," her mother told her as she went in through the back door. "Said he was going to meet Taff and Evelyn and would you like to go with him."

Remembering the attitude of Evelyn to her and Johnny's friendship, she decided she would be better staying away. Evelyn's home was not the place to go for explanations. She needed more neutral ground than Evelyn and Taff's home. Settling near the roaring fire she looked idly through some magazines, not taking much in, just using them as an excuse to allow her thoughts to wander.

There were several articles about handiwork. Mostly knitting but other crafts as well. One attracted her attention. It showed attractive rugs made from strips of material and the idea looked simple.

"Mam, have we any old coats I could cut up to make a rug for my room?"

"Rug-making? You? You'll never finish it. There's me having to complete the gloves you started last winter, and the angora jumper is still on its needles from months ago."

"This is different, it uses a sewing machine."

"You want me to let you loose on my precious sewing machine? You've got a hope, my girl!"

"Mam, you only use it to mend sheets and the like and you never let me use it."

"No, and ask yourself why. You muddle it up and it takes hours to sort it out. Bad-tempered you are when you get a needle in your hand. You lack the patience to learn and I lack the patience to teach."

"I thought I'd ask Hannah to show me how; I can't learn from you. We end up arguing every time."

The method was simple, and used as a base a piece of sacking. It entailed winding lengths of cloth or thick wool around a length of thick wire which had been bent into the shape of a large hairpin. By machining a line up through the centre, then removing the wire, a double row of loops was left. Then the wire was covered again and sewn as close to the first as possible. This was repeated until the piece of sacking was covered in loops of coloured wool or material.

Eirlys found Hannah working at her machine and when she explained about the rug-making Hannah was intrigued enough to experiment with the instructions. Two days later, Eirlys took delivery of a second-hand treadle sewing machine and a corner of her bedroom was transformed into a workshop.

Over several days, friends supplied material. The colours were mostly drab, with the occasional camel coat the only cheerful addition to the dark navy, browns and black. Sacking was easy to obtain; flour sacks from the bakery where Annie worked and any amount of potato sacks collected from the greengrocer where Johnny's cousin Beth worked. To Annie's surprise, Eirlys's interest began to grow. Instead of simply covering the sacking with strips of material, she developed ideas for designs, usually after a discussion with the talented Hannah, who helped work out some simple patterns on the sacking for Eirlys to follow. The whole family, including Stanley, Harold and even Percival were intrigued. They helped with the cutting of strips and Percival asked her to make one to take home to his mother.

"What about one for this treehouse then? When we get it," Harold demanded in his abrupt manner.

"No, but I will make you one for beside your bed," Eirlys promised.

The new hobby helped to take her mind off the mystery of Evelyn's sudden dislike and Johnny's absence. Johnny did call one evening. She was alone, her parents having taken the three boys to the pictures, and she jumped up, guessing it was he. Then she stopped and, in the darkness of the front bedroom, looked through the blackout curtain and watched as he picked up his bicycle and walked away.

Johnny was restless. Twice he had called on Eirlys and twice she had been out. Now he began to wonder just what Evelyn had said to her. He didn't want to display feelings stronger than he felt, but he did miss her. Wherever he went, whatever he did, it was more fun with Eirlys. Most of his friends were either courting seriously or flirting with several girls. He was the only one without female company and he was beginning to feel regret for worrying about Eirlys taking their friendship too seriously. He had obviously been mistaken and now he was on his own, a situation he found displeasing.

One evening, unable to wait any longer, he met her from work, standing outside the council offices and watching the door through which the staff left. She was the last to leave, emerging in deep conversation with a colleague. She smiled when he called to her and ran to greet him.

"Johnny, this is a surprise. Don't say you've come to walk me home?"

"Well, yes. I was in town and I thought as it was almost half five, I'd wait. D'you fancy a walk later?"

"I'd love it, but I've promised to go to a friend's house to collect some old coats."

"Old coats?" he laughed. "Don't tell me you're going into the second hand business?"

She was reluctant to tell him about the rug-making. He might misconstrue and think she was making it for her bottom drawer in preparation for their marriage – which it was; but that was a private thought, not for anyone else to know, especially not Evelyn!

"I could help you carry them?" he offered.

"Thanks, but perhaps we could meet tomorrow instead?"

This was agreed and a curious Johnny left her at her gate and walked slowly home.

An hour later Eirlys and the three boys set off, Stanley pulling a bogie cart borrowed from a neighbour, in which Percival was given a ride. They called at three houses where friends had promised Eirlys some unwanted coats and another where huge parcels of wool were handed to her, remnants of a sewing circle long since disbanded.

Although it was dark, a sliver of a moon gave a little light and near Curtis Street Eirlys saw Irene, Johnny's mother. She knew she wouldn't tell him; he wouldn't believe her. Besides, the woman was wearing a coat and there was nothing strange about her walking along the street properly dressed against the cold evening.

Irene stopped near a shop on the corner and as Eirlys passed they exchanged polite "good evenings" as though both were uneasy about the meeting.

"Nice bit of stuff in that coat," Harold said loudly. "Bit of old tom cat would trim the edges of our rug a treat, eh?"

A cowardly Eirlys pretended not to have heard.

Percival couldn't manage to sit on the top on the way back but Eirlys carried him pickaback while his brothers struggled with the assorted load. Annie grumbled about the chaos of collecting so much material, but was pacified when she realised how excited her daughter was with her new interest.

Morgan made shelves and Annie found a pine box which held the wool. A washing bath that had sprouted a leak and had never been thrown away was used to hold the cut-up strips of material. Eirlys was grateful for her parents' support, especially when they went on helping with the boring job of unpicking the coats and cutting the material into strips. Twice Johnny called but each time she was too busy to go out.

She was grateful to Evelyn for saying what she had, even though she had been very hurt by her strange antipathy since. She had never discovered what had changed Evelyn from a friend into someone so critical and unkind. Yet she might not have started on this fascinating hobby without her harsh words.

The first rug was a bit lumpy and uneven, but it found a place of honour beside the bed Stanley shared with Harold, with another promised for Percival's corner. Hannah came once to see how the work was progressing and declared herself impressed.

"You could earn yourself some money with these," she suggested. "Hand-made rugs are prized and you could use shades to suit the customer's colour scheme."

Eirlys laughed disparagingly but the idea didn't quite go away. The main difficulty was finding material in sufficient quantities and in suitable colours.

In despair, Johnny began working on the treehouse. Rain had prevented it being completed during the first weekend, but with a dry cold snap coinciding with a day off for both Morgan and himself, he arranged with Eirlys's father to carry the ready-made platform to the tree Morgan had chosen, and begin to fix it securely into place.

Working all morning and returning in the afternoon to stain the wooden structure an unobtrusive brown, they walked back to the house tired but satisfied.

"Tomorrow we'll have a grand opening," Morgan announced to the three boys who were eating their evening meal.

Eirlys smiled and blew her father a kiss. "Thanks, Dad."

"All except Percival," Annie said sternly, "unless he eats that egg on toast."

"I'm havin' a bit of bover with me crusts," Percival complained solemnly. Stanley reached out and helped himself to the crusts pushed to the side of his youngest brother's plate then Percival began to cry. "I wanted that bit! There was some egg on that bit!"

Annie ignored him and removed the plates to where Eirlys was washing up in the kitchen. Percival ate very little. The appetites of his brothers had increased and their improved weight had shown it clearly, but Percival's hadn't. He chewed for ages on a mouthful, lips open, dismay clouding his eyes, insisting that he only liked "proper" chips, by which he meant those from a chip shop.

"And sweets and chocolate," Annie said with a frown. "You never have any 'bover' with chocolate, do you?"

"Everyone can eat chocolate," he replied disparagingly.

"Cup of tea, Johnny?" Annie asked, hiding a smile. Percival really was a character. "There's egg on toast for you too, if you're hungry."

While her father and Johnny washed their hands, Eirlys and Annie cooked fresh meals and the two men settled down companionably to eat.

"Do you fancy going to see the treehouse?" Johnny asked Eirlys, but she shook her head.

"Tomorrow I'll come with you for the grand opening. Tonight I have something to finish."

"Tell him what you're doing for goodness' sake, Eirlys; he'll think you're making illegal whisky or something!" Annie said in exasperation.

So Johnny was taken up to her bedroom where cloth strips and hanks of wool covered the floor and a half-made rug hung over the single bed.

The most recently completed one was wrapped in brown paper and she unfolded it to show him. She had improved her technique and also her choice of colours, no longer taking randomly from the box of strips but choosing with greater care. The result was a simple pattern with each shape filled with a blend of hues making the overall rug an attractive and well-made item. This one had a diagonally striped pattern, with assorted blues filling some and assorted greens others, with a border of rust and browns.

"It's really smart. Is it for anyone special, or for your bedroom?" Johnny asked.

"This one is for Hannah to thank her for helping when I started. D'you think she'll like it?"

"She'll love it for the kind thought as well as for the quality."

They went together to give it to Hannah, who, as usual, was sewing, busily finishing off a child's dress she was making for a client. Johnny sat and watched as Eirlys and Hannah examined the rug and admired its colours. He watched Hannah and marvelled again at the aura of peace and calm surrounding her, when life for her must be so hard.

Disturbed by his attraction for Hannah, he kissed Eirlys with more enthusiasm than was wise. Remembering Evelyn's warnings, he said goodnight without suggesting anything about the following day. Although, he thought as he walked back to Brook Lane, the arrangement to meet and show Stanley, Harold and Percival their playhouse in the oak tree had already been planned.

He couldn't sleep for a long time, even though the work on the treehouse had pulled at a few rarely used muscles and he had been pleasantly tired when he and Morgan had finished it. It was thoughts of Hannah, not Eirlys, that drove away sleep. There was something very appealing about Hannah; a tranquillity overcame him in her presence. He told himself he was being foolish to even think about her in that way. She was too old for him, and Eirlys was a good friend in the way that would eventually lead to love. Why was he agonising about Eirlys? He knew deep down that when he had reached the stage when marriage was what he wanted, she was the one for him. But he couldn't put Hannah out of his mind.

When Annie Price went to the newsagent to pay the weekly paper bill, she thought she would give the three boys a treat and buy them some sweets. They didn't receive pocket money, except the occasional two-shilling postal order their mother sent for them to share. She chose smarties and handed the money to Mrs Downs, the manager of the shop.

"There's a face for sweets young Percival's got," Hetty Downs smiled. "He eats them as fast as his brother buys them, hardly waiting till he gets out of the shop. I tease him that I put them in a bag for fear of him biting my fingers off."

"Percival? Our Percival you mean? I don't think so. He doesn't get money for sweets that often. Poor his mother is and she can't send money very often. There's no father, see," she explained confidentially. "Morgan and I buy for them occasionally and I know Eirlys does, but they don't have money to spend of their own."

"Someone is being generous then," Mrs Downs insisted. "Come in here two or three times a week for sweets, they do."

"No wonder he'll never eat his dinners!" Annie frowned. "But who is giving them money?"

Annie asked the boys whether they had received any money from their mother without telling her and the answer was a firm "No."

"Then who is giving you the money to buy sweets several times a week?" she demanded.

Harold and Percival looked at the oldest brother, utterly confident that he could explain.

"All right, I'll tell you," he said. "We was in the park and I found a ten-shilling note. I went to the post office and got it changed into shillings and I've been spending it on sweets because that's what Percival likes to eat. Never no dinners, just chocolate and cakes and stuff like that."

"Chocolate an' cakes," affirmed Percival with a knowledgeable nod or two.

Annie looked thoughtful. Ten shillings was a lot of money and they should have handed it in to the police station, although she could understand the temptation to keep it. But how long would ten shillings last if what Mrs Downs had told her was true? Three or six bars of chocolate each time would soon see the end of a ten-shilling note. She wondered uneasily whether the boys were stealing. She couldn't accuse them, but decided that in future she would keep an extra careful check on the amount of money in her purse.

Stanley was thoughtful too. His decision was to use different shops for his purchases. Going to the same place where Mrs Price bought her newspapers had been a stupid mistake. That Mrs Downs would know them too well. He made a mental list of the sweet shops and cake shops he could use, determined that Percival wouldn't be deprived of his sweets and cakes, whatever he had to do to keep him supplied.

Johnny called on Eirlys on Friday evening and found her clearing the dishes from their meal. He felt ill at ease, still unsure what his sister-in-law had said to Eirlys to discourage her from thinking of him too seriously.

"Evelyn and Taff are going into Cardiff tomorrow. Fancy coming?" he asked her. "They want to do some shopping and we could eat out and perhaps go to the theatre for a change."

Eirlys's heart began to thump unpleasantly. This was a chance to persuade Evelyn to tell her what was going on in her mind.

"Please?" he added as the silence lengthened.

She turned and smiled at him in a way that made his heart behave oddly. "I'd love to, Johnny. What time are we leaving?"

"About two. Taff fancies going to Roath Park to feed the ducks, would you believe? I think he's trying to build a few memories before he goes into the army."

"Don't talk about it," Eirlys shivered.

"I'll be off soon, sure to be. I only hope Dad can cope all right without us. Mam isn't much company for him these days."

"I did see her without a coat that day, you know. I didn't imagine it."

"What could she be doing?" Johnny said, as though believing her, although he still wasn't convinced that Eirlys hadn't mistaken another woman for his mother.

Sensing his doubts, she added, "I described her clothes before she took her coat off, didn't I?"

"Mam is behaving oddly," he admitted. "I think Dad is afraid she'll get worse and he won't be able to cope."

"Has she always gone off like this?"

"I think she might have done, but Dad has always protected us from knowing."

"It isn't – it isn't other men?"

"I think Dad would know if she went off with other men," he said disparagingly. "No, it's nerves. A lot of women suffer with nerves and it shows itself in different ways." He was quoting his father's explanation. "Thank goodness it isn't drink or fighting," he added, quoting Bleddyn again.

Eirlys felt uneasy as she waited for Evelyn and Taff to join them. Why had she agreed to this day out? She began searching her mind for an excuse to go back home.

When they arrived at the station, it was swiftly obvious that Evelyn didn't want to show Taff or Johnny how she felt because she greeted her with every impression of pleasure. It was only when they were on their own that she allowed her dislike to show.

When Johnny and Taff went to check on the times of the return trains, Eirlys turned to Evelyn and demanded angrily, "What is the matter with you? What am I supposed to have done?"

"You know very well what's happened." Evelyn began to walk away and Eirlys pulled on her arm roughly to make her face her.

"If you won't tell me, then will you at least stop creating this atmosphere and ruining my day out? I work long hours and an afternoon out with Johnny is a rare treat. I don't think you should spoil it. If you can't bear my company, please go home now, for Johnny's sake if not mine!"

"You Prices think you can do anything and get away with it!"

"Get away with what?" Eirlys said in exasperation.

"You two look serious," Johnny said as he and Taff returned unnoticed by the two girls.

"Yes," Eirlys said lugubriously, to cover their argument, "I've brought the wrong colour lipstick." It raised a smile and the atmosphere cleared.

The four of them did manage to enjoy their day out. The uneasiness remained hidden from the two brothers and Evelyn made no reference to the affectionate way Johnny and Eirlys behaved, to Eirlys's relief. When she stepped on to the train to travel home, and sat close to Johnny, arm in his, head on his shoulder, she was light-hearted and convinced that her reticence toward Johnny over the past days had cleared the air and allowed Johnny to decide whether or not they should continue to see each other. Surely nothing would spoil their courtship now? Evelyn had said nothing more. She was happier than she had been for a long time.

Johnny was contented too. The four of them had enjoyed their day and there hadn't been a moment of dissension. Plans were suggested and carried out amicably. Laughter had been plentiful and he didn't think there was a cloud in his particular sky.

He left Eirlys after a loving kiss and walked home, passing the house of Hannah's parents, where Hannah lived with her two little girls. Suddenly it was as though a cloud had burst and brought rain and storm and misery.

Eirlys was too excited to go straight into the house. She stopped at the door, the key in her hand. She could hear the radio playing dance music and the buzz of conversation, rising and falling, punctuated occasionally by thumps as her mother banged to emphasise a point. They were arguing again, her father's voice low, reasonable, her mother's more shrill and obviously angry. She was glowing with the joy of Johnny's kiss, dreamily reliving it and allowing her thoughts to travel with it to other, as yet unlearned delights. Walking in to a quarrel would be a cruel awakening.

She had hoped that after all these years the quarrelling would have ceased. Dadda losing the business left to him by his father had been a devastating blow. But it was years ago and life had moved on. Mam had been forced to find work and she, Eirlys, had given up hope of further education. Her father had worked cheerfully enough in the factory now making munitions and she had found a good position in the council offices, thanks to their determination. Paying for her to learn shorthand and typing had been a struggle and she was grateful to her parents for depriving themselves of other things to do so.

She looked up, forgetting for a moment the blackout which enclosed the house and gave no clue to what was happening within. The boys would be in bed and fast asleep by this time. The euphoric mood expanded to remind her of how grateful she was for the way her parents had accepted Stanley, Harold and little Percival. Fortunately they had been very little trouble, apart from Percival's refusal to eat proper meals, handing much of what he disliked to his brothers below the level of the table, in the hope of not being seen. Like Annie, she sometimes wondered how he managed to survive on the little he ate.

A number of the evacuees in the town had already gone back home. There were others who had been giving problems to the families who had taken them in. Their three musketeers had settled well and for that she knew her parents could take most of the praise.

Moving away from the house and its warring occupants, she walked back on to the pavement and stood for a while on the corner of Conroy Street allowing the quiet of the night to settle her before she went inside. She still savoured the happiness of the day out with Johnny and the resumption of their friendship, and was not yet ready for it to end.

There was no moon, yet she gradually made out shapes and began to recognise buildings and even the lamp post into which several people had walked when the blackout had begun. A sound across the street disturbed her and a cat skidaddled across the road before disappearing into a hedge.

A light shone brightly out of the side of a house opposite. She put a hand to her mouth in alarm, imagining a lone German plane with a beady-eyed pilot, circling around waiting for such an opportunity, then laughed at her stupidity. On tiptoe she crossed the road to investigate and saw, coming backwards out of a side window, a figure. A thief? Had she disturbed a thief? If so, what should she do?

Fear of confronting a dangerous and angry burglar ran through her mind but she hurried towards him, still making hardly a sound. He was smaller than she expected, only a boy. Grabbing him around the shoulders as he touched the ground, she turned him and gasped in horror.

"Stanley!"

Four

Stanley stood at the kitchen table red-faced and defiant, while Morgan and Annie threw question after question at him. He refused to answer, except to say, "Got plenty they have. They won't even know they've gone!"

"That's not the point," Annie said in exasperation. "It isn't yours. And breaking into someone's house and taking things belonging to them is a criminal act."

Threats of calling the police didn't move him. Jaw tight, eyes defiant, he stared into space and told them he didn't care. Threats of every kind of punishment had no visible effect. Sending him away from his brothers did.

"If we call the police they will probably take you away from us and who will look after Harold and Percival if you aren't here to look after them?" Eirlys asked softly.

Stanley's head rose and he looked at her with questioning eyes.

"Don't let them take me away," he said, and Eirlys saw not a defiant thief but a very frightened young boy. She opened her arms and he clung to her while sobs racked his body.

Annie turned away, affected more than she would have imagined by the little boy's fear. She had tried to remain aloof from the evacuees, knowing their sojourn would be brief, but they were only children and had been taken away from everything familiar without fully understanding why. "I'll make you some cocoa," she said, glad of the excuse to leave them and hide her own distress.

Stanley eventually told them that the money they had found in his pockets had been in a rent book on a shelf and there were several shilling pieces he had taken from a pile stacked near the gas meter ready to feed it when needed.

"We'll sort it out," Eirlys murmured. "No one will take you anywhere. Dadda will find a way of getting the things back to their owner, won't you, Dadda?"

Morgan looked at the things taken from Stanley's pocket and wondered. Beside the one pound seven and sixpence, there was a small ashtray, a cut-glass posy jar and a wooden musical box, plus a bag containing some biscuits. "Were you going to sell them, Stanley?" he asked. "Why? Is there something you want that we don't give you? And why the biscuits? I mean, why take food?"

"The biscuits were for the birds in the park," he explained. "Percival likes to feed the birds."

"And the rest?"

"They was for our mum. She ain't got nothin' like this. They got so much nice stuff they have it packed away in the back of a cupboard where no one can see 'em. Waste, that's what that is!"

"You still can't take things that don't belong to you," Eirlys admonished.

Tired out with the shock of discovery and the questioning, Stanley yawned and Annie reappeared and told them she was putting him back to bed.

"Now what?" Morgan asked, rubbing his face with his hands in a kind of despair. "If they were mine I'd give them a wallop they wouldn't forget, but how can I deal with someone else's kids over something like this? Out of my depth here I am, Eirlys."

Eirlys was thinking and after a while she suggested a solution. "If we hide the stuff somewhere far away from this house, then tell the police we'd found it, they might find the owners and return it all."

"Where do you suggest?" her father asked.

"Well, there's a barn on the field leading down to the stream. Cows gather there so there wouldn't be any footprints to find. If we covered some of them with mud . . . ?"

"Why that smelly old place?"

"Because it's a place people are unlikely to go."

"It might work," Morgan agreed.

"I'll take them on Saturday. Johnny will help."

The plans to hide the stolen items were delayed, however. Eirlys's boss, Mr Johnston, called her into his office on Monday morning and told her he needed her to work on the following Saturday. They were expecting a visit of important dignitaries who would arrive on Friday evening and would attend a special meeting that would go on through lunch on Saturday. It was Eirlys's responsibility to arrange hotel accommodation, organise drivers to ferry them about over the weekend, as they wished to travel around the area, and also to prepare luncheon for sixteen people at the office on Saturday. It was something she had never been asked to do before and was at once daunted by the importance of it. Mr Johnston hinted at promotion and she knew she couldn't refuse.

She felt guilty at letting Stanley down; they had hoped to have the whole unpleasant situation dealt with before Sunday. Yet she felt excitement too. She enjoyed her work and had ambitions to make progress, even though marriage to Johnny was her strongest desire. Or was it? Johnny, yes, but giving up her job was beginning to be a less attractive prospect. She realised then how difficult it could be to have Granny Moll insisting on making Piper's the number one priority.

She felt guilty at this new attitude to work as she remembered her declaration to Granny Moll of the importance of the family business. She might not have that commitment after all. Allowing her imagination to soar, she thought that she could even become manager of a whole section one day. Although those positions were usually held by men, with the outbreak of war and men being conscripted, she knew she had a better chance than ever before. That thought brought on more feelings of guilt. Perhaps being selfish was an essential part of success?

In the office that morning she spent a lot of time on the telephone making bookings, then writing confirmations, besides running across the town to speak to people who had no telephone. She was exhausted when half past five came.

The catering was in the hands of a firm who supplied cafés and hotels and, although costly, they were reliable and that, she had decided at the outset, was her number one priority for this special weekend.

The culmination of a frantic week was a smooth-running weekend in which she acted as minutes secretary taking notes at the Saturday meeting. The main subjects under discussion were the delivery and erection of air raid shelters and other needs, beside ordering some of the many leaflets being distributed giving information and advice to the local people. It was the ARP and the WVS who figured large as these things were discussed, and Eirlys went home at three o'clock to tell her father all she had learned.

Although she was very tired she went to the barn with Johnny as promised, late in the afternoon, as darkness was falling. To add to the gloom it was raining when they set off, Johnny carrying Stanley's stolen treasures: heavy relentless rain that seemed set to continue for hours, with gusts of wind to add to the torment. They felt the cold immediately, carrying boxes in their arms and being unable to swing them to keep warm. Wearing wellingtons and heavy raincoats they walked with heads bent against the driven rain and were relieved to see that a dozen Hereford cows were standing near the entrance to the barn.

"Good. They'll mess up our footprints within minutes," Eirlys said and they went into the barn, their boots squelching in the deeply churned mud and sometimes becoming lodged so that Johnny needed to pull her free. They messed up the objects a little then left them and made their way back to the slightly less soggy grass.

As they were about to turn for home, Eirlys hesitated. "I wonder if that was the first time Stanley had broken into houses and stolen things?" she mused. "It might be worth a look in the treehouse in case he's hidden other stuff there."

Johnny agreed and after wiping the worst of the smelly mud and manure from their boots they headed for the oak tree not far from Mr Gregory's smallholding.

The walk through the dark countryside was neither pleasant nor romantic. They talked a little, mostly about Stanley who, at ten, had taken responsibility for his brothers and even tried to help his mother with beautiful gifts.

"He's such a mixture of adult and child," Eirlys said. "He's lost the chance of a normal happy childhood, hasn't he, having to grow up so fast?"

"Perhaps, but people aren't all the same. Living in a flat in London, he wouldn't have had the same values or expectations as the children around here. He probably thinks we're deprived."

He waited to help her climb the gate into Sally Gough's field where Mr Gregory sometimes kept his donkeys. Taking her arm as she clambered down, he didn't let go when they were both safely over. "It's very dark," he explained. "A torch is useless and I don't want you to fall over this hummocky grass."

"I can't see a thing," she laughed, holding him tightly. He guided her to where the branches of the oak tree were just visible in the dark night.

"I'll go up," Johnny offered and, feeling rather than seeing, he took the rope-ladder from its hiding place, shinnied up and went inside and carefully used his torch. "Eirlys! Come and look at this lot!"

With difficulty, holding the rope and occasionally a branch, she managed to reach the four-by-three-foot building set in a wide fork of the old tree. The floor was made from wooden planking and the sides had three narrow windows and a doorway through which to enter. As she crawled in there was very little light from Johnny's torch and it took a while for her eyes to accustom themselves to the darkness and the thin beam. Johnny was standing bending over on the far side and between them was a piece of old carpet. Moving it he revealed an assortment of household objects: a teapot and silver-and-glass sugar bowl and matching jug, a few plates and a picture of some children playing on the sands. There also were two books, one of which was about Orlando the Marmalade Cat and had a small stick as a bookmark showing the reader was half-way through.

"Stanley is probably reading it to Harold and Percival," Eirlys whispered. "He tries to make a life for the boys that's separate from us. He knows this life is a temporary one and constantly reminds his young brothers that their home is not with us, not to forget the life they left behind when there were only the three of them and their mother."

A cardboard box was underneath the rest and while Johnny shone a torch, Eirlys opened it. Wrapped carefully in layer after layer of newspaper was a delicate porcelain cup and saucer. In lustre, with a wide top and an ornate handle, it was a very pretty object.

"The boy has an eye, I'll give him that," Johnny whispered. "He doesn't steal rubbish."

"Why hasn't it been missed?"

"Because they're someone's treasures, stacked away for safety and probably only used on very special occasions. My mam has stuff like that, hasn't yours?"

"Oh yes," Eirlys agreed wryly. "In fact, I recognise the teapot!"

The rain continued to fall around them like a curtain and although there was no warmth and hardly room to move, they settled themselves as comfortably as they could to discuss what they should do.

"Funny that your father chose this tree," Johnny mused. "I wonder why?"

"He said the other was too far from the house in case of air raids."

"Yet this one isn't any closer, is it?"

"Rats," she said.

"What?"

"The area near the old barn is infested with rats, or so he said. Although perhaps this tree was an easier one in which to build."

"Fond of the boys, isn't he? Wants to do what he can to make them feel wanted. Everyone needs to be wanted."

His voice was low and intimate, their bodies were touching in the most exciting way and he seemed hesitant to move.

Eirlys began to feel tense, wondering whether Johnny felt as aware of her closeness as she did of his. Then a mundane remark made her realise she had been alone in her thinking.

"We ought to take this and put it with the rest of the stuff, in the barn," Johnny said.

"Except the teapot," she laughed. "Little devil. He told us he wanted to take all his loot back for his mother."

"Strange that he stole from you."

"He thought anything hidden away had no value." She chuckled. "He'd have had a job getting all this into the little case he brought with him!"

Eirlys wondered when Johnny would suggest leaving their uncomfortable perch. She didn't want to. In spite of the discomfort of soggy clothes and mud-covered hands and boots that felt as though they were encased in lead, she could have stayed close to him all night without complaint.

Struggling in the confined place, Johnny put an arm around Eirlys's shoulders and she was glad of the warmth of him. She snuggled closer and they stared unseeing out of the entrance, their wet cheeks touching, listening to the gentle hissing of the rain through the leaves above them. It was a cosy sound and if only they had been dry it would have been heaven. Now and then a gust of wind stronger than the others seemed to move the weaker branches of the sturdy tree and they clung closer.

The kiss when it came was sweet and gentle and Eirlys thought she had never felt greater happiness than this reunion with Johnny in the peculiar hideaway in the oak tree surrounded by the spoils of a child's robbery.

They were both reluctant to leave but knew that if they were to transport the items from the tree and put them in the barn, they had to get it done soon, in case another lone walker took shelter and discovered the items already left there.

Carefully rewrapping thc teapot, the cup and saucer and the rest, they carried them down and set off to retrace their steps to the barn where the patient cows stood exactly where they had left them.

"I hope they shiggle about a bit after we've gone," Johnny said. "We don't want our footmarks to be seen."

"Hardly a problem; we're going to tell the police we found them while sheltering, aren't we?"

Johnny went back with her and they explained to her parents about the extra items. Harold and Percival were listening while Stanley read to them out of the most recent Beano comic, which had been first issued a few months before. Harold laughed at Stanley's ad libs and his interpretation of the drawings but Percival was stony-faced, as usual refusing to be amused.

When Johnny and Eirlys explained to Annie and Morgan about removing the treasures to the barn, their explanations reached Stanley's ears and he handed the comic to his brothers. "Now, I've started you off, and you got to see how much you can work out for yerselves."

On being confronted with the teapot he looked, shame-faced, at Annie and explained, "I took it ages ago, when we first came, and I thought we was going 'ome the next day. I've been tryin' to get it back without you knowin'." He was shouting and Eirlys knew he was close to tears.

As Annie turned to place the teapot on a shelf, he suddenly grabbed a mac from the back of the kitchen door and ran from the house.

It was Johnny who ran after him, talked him into calming down and brought him back to the house. Johnny said nothing but secretly admired the boy for doing what he could to take care of his family in a situation for which nothing could have prepared him. Stanley was only a child himself, although to hear him talk you'd imagine he was an old man, he thought with a chuckle.

The police called and listened to Eirlys's explanations about finding the stolen goods when she and Johnny were sheltering from the rain.

"Sheltering from the rain? Wasn't it raining when you set off, then?" the constable teased. "I don't know, what it is to be young, eh, Mr Price?"

Eirlys's father grinned and winked at Johnny. "I reckon that's why half of us get married, because there's nowhere to go for a bit of a kiss and cuddle, don't you, constable?"

Eirlys blushed and Johnny looked uncomfortable.

A few enquries were made around the area and most of the items were returned to puzzled owners. They hadn't been missed.

"Nor would they be, not till Christmas, and then we'd have been searching the house trying to remember where we'd put them," one old lady laughed as she claimed two pretty blue lustre fruit bowls.

"I wonder who owns the caravan in the field next to the barn?" Eirlys asked anxiously. "Someone there might have seen Stanley there and will tell the police."

"Oh, it's a mess of a place, used now and then by a couple from Brecon when they want to do a bit of walking," Morgan explained. "Certainly never in winter. I met them once. Better than a tent, I suppose, but only just."

The excitement and fears faded. Nothing more was heard about the robberies and the Price family were convinced that the Love boys, especially Stanley, had learned a powerful lesson.

Eirlys eventually went to a training session organised by the ARP but she was disappointed. The request regarding her driving lessons had been noted, but, it was explained, "We have to use the skills you can bring to us and yours, Miss Price, is the important skill of typing, making rotas, that sort of thing." She guessed her father was responsible. When Mr Johnston gave her a ten-shilling increase in her wages and told her she would be kept extra busy, she happily accepted and told the ARP officer that she no longer had the time to help.

Her next task at work was changing the offices around so a room could be cleared to hold the fire-watchers, who would be on duty every night once the air bombardments, which were already expected, had begun.

Moving furniture, placating staff who had to accept smaller accommodation or even share with a colleague wasn't easy but the job was completed in a week. To be given a job to do and told to use her own initiative to do it was frightening at first, but immensely satisfying. She was hardly at home in the days following the "discovery" of the stolen items. It was cold and misty and she wondered how Stanley and Harold and Percival were amusing themselves.

Morgan had made them a sled in readiness for the snow that would come after Christmas and possibly before. He had also promised them a bogie cart using a set of pram wheels and some planks of planed wood when the better weather returned.

Annie still complained about the amount of work they caused, rarely missing a chance to remind Morgan of the big house they had lost and the servant they had employed to enable her to work for various charities. Morgan seemed unaffected by her tirades and having Stanley, Harold and Percival clearly added joy to his life. He told Eirlys several times that he dreaded the day when they would go home.

Annie didn't spend a lot of time talking to the evacuees. It had been Eirlys's choice to take them in and it was her responsibility to look after them, she reminded her daughter when her help was requested at an inconvenient moment. But the distress on Stanley's face when he had been threatened with separation from his brothers had upset her.

"What do you think of my taking the boys up to London for the day to see their mother?" she suggested one evening when the boys were settled in bed. "They have to stay with us, but if they think they can visit now and then, it might be easier for them."

"Or they might refuse to come back, or Mrs Love won't let them! And where would that get them? Blown up and out of it. Is that what you want? Hitler might not have sent any bombs yet, but he will. And the IRA have planted a few, haven't they? Some of them have been sent down, but there'll be more. Take them back to London for a visit? Damn stupid idea, Annie!" Morgan spoke with unusual anger. "If those boys go back home they'll never come back and settle."

"You'd miss them, wouldn't you, Dadda?" Eirlys said.

"Well, yes, I definitely would."

"What if I use it as a promise, then, for good behaviour?" Annie said. "A bit cruel maybe, but I will take them, one day soon. There hasn't been any bombing yet, or I wouldn't suggest it. We should be safe enough. I don't want to have my head blown off any more than theirs."

Next morning she put the idea to the three boys. "Would you like me to take you back to your mam, just for a visit? You could all write her a letter asking her to find somewhere for me to stay. Then you can come back knowing she's all right. Or if you prefer, she could come and stay with us for a night or two. How would that be, eh?"

"I want to go home to see Mum," Percival said. "I eat when it's chips from the chip shop, don't I, our Stanley?"

"Not yet," Annie warned, "but soon. Only as long as you behave yourselves, mind. Any stealing, either sweets or anything else and you won't go, do you understand me, Stanley Love?"

"Yes, Annie Price," he replied cheekily.

The postman was becoming increasingly important in the town of St David's Well as elsewhere. Families waited for news of their sons and husbands and the Love brothers were no different. Teresa Love was not a great letter writer, but she managed to scribble a short message for her sons every other week. Eirlys made sure they wrote to her, Percival laboriously writing a brief message as a PS on the end of Stanley's letter, with Stanley's patient help.

One morning the postman brought two letters for the boys, the usual scribble and a reply to Annie's suggestion that she take the boys to visit her.

This excited the boys and they whooped and cheered as they danced around the small kitchen until everyone was laughing. Plans were discussed, but Annie made sure they understood that no date had been fixed.

By the same post Eirlys heard from Ken Ward, who, she learned had been turned down by the army but had found a job with the NAAFI, met someone called Max Moon and hoped to join a concert party travelling around entertaining the forces. Ken had a pleasant voice, she remembered, and also played the mandolin well.

She wrote straight back, friendly, affectionate, giving him impersonal news about the people he had known. She ended by wishing him luck.

She had no regrets about telling Ken goodbye, but hoped they would always be friends, wherever they ended up. His letter did unsettle her though. Everyone was doing something to support the war effort; there must be something she could do!

Annie was late leaving the bakery. She had been serving Hannah and had spent a while talking to her after locking the shop for lunchtime closing. She dashed into the house, handed Morgan his packed lunch, which she had bought in the shop, and saw him hurry off to work for the two o'clock shift. When he had left for work she settled to the sewing basket which was overflowing with the boys' clothes, needing darning, replacement buttons and other repairs.

"I would never believe how boys rip and dirty their clothes," she complained to Eirlys who was home for lunch that day. "I've heard people tell me how lucky we were to have a girl when you were born, and I didn't know what they meant until now." She held up a pullover that had once been a carefully knitted Fair Isle design but which was now a tangle of pulled woollen threads with no recognisable pattern at all. "Climbing trees on the way home from school they were. This was given to me by Mrs Daniels last week. Almost new it was. I daren't let her see it now!"

"I was given a pile of wool yesterday, to knit things for the Christmas Bazaar in aid of soldiers' comforts. There might be something suitable to repair it," Eirlys said without much hope.

"I doubt it! We've been told to keep all our rags for some savings scheme or other – well, they can have this for a start-off," Annie said, throwing the offending article in the corner of the couch.

"Why didn't Dadda want me to go with him to the ARP meetings, d'you think?" Eirlys asked.

"Tell the truth, I think he and his cronies like a bit of an evening out without the women, and you'd cramp his style. They go for a drink after and he wouldn't take you, would he?"

"I'd still like to help, Mam, once things at work have calmed down a bit. Everyone is doing something."

"Heavens, girl, you do plenty! All those extra hours of work and no overtime pay? What's that if it isn't helping the war effort?"

"Will you have a word?"

"I'll try, but I don't think he'll be persuaded. You know what men are like, wanting to get together 'off the leash' as they call it. Talk a lot of old nonsense and act the fool like a bunch of schoolboys they do. They're all the same."

Morgan didn't go to the factory at two o'clock the next day. He drove a van on an errand for a friend, missing a shift, hoping Annie wouldn't query the difference in his pay packet. When the van spluttered to a stop seven miles from St David's Well he gave a groan. Now what could he do? He turned to the woman sitting beside him and after a brief conference and an affectionate kiss she left him and caught a bus back home.

Fortunately there was a phone box not far away and he telephoned his daughter at her office in greatly exaggerated panic.

"Don't tell your mam, she'll kill me for missing a shift," he said. "Can you find your Johnny and ask him to help? Keep his tongue in check he will, for sure."

Eirlys gave him Moll's number as very few people had a telephone and Piper's didn't run to the expense of providing Bleddyn with one.

Eventually, after a second even more frantic call from Morgan, Eirlys used her lunch hour to go and find Johnny. He took the firm's van and went to Morgan's rescue, and, on seeing the ladies' scarf fallen down between the seats, promised to say nothing about the incident.

He told Eirlys though. "Seems he was giving a lift to a lady waiting for a bus that had failed to arrive and he knows how suspicious your mam would be," he laughed. "Left her scarf she did or I'd never have known."

"You're sure it was innocent?" Eirlys asked. "It's odd him losing a whole shift to do a favour for someone and then giving a lift to a mysterious woman."

"Some people seem to court trouble and it's often good-natured people like your father," Johnny told her.

Thinking of Ken and his recent letter, Eirlys was reminded about how important it had been for her to stay at home where she could keep the peace between her parents.

Johnny went home and under promise of secrecy, told Bleddyn and a disinterested Irene something of Morgan's problem.

"What was he doing?" Bleddyn asked.

"Collecting some leaflets from Cardiff on how to deal with incendiary bombs was what he told me," Johnny replied, "I didn't see any, mind!"

Irene walked away from the table and put on her coat with the fur collar.

"You aren't going out again?" Bleddyn complained. "Only now this minute you've come in!"

"If I don't get some fresh air I can't sleep," Irene replied.

"Shall I come with you?"

"No, I'll be all right."

Irene kept well away from the field in which the barn stood. The police had hinted that they would be watching it in case the thief returned with more of his stolen goods. Instead, she went along the lane towards the next village, turned in through a farm gate and walked around the field, feeling her way in the darkness, wary of unseen branches, guessing how far she had come before crossing to come up against the caravan. Three knocks and the door was open and she slipped inside.

"Hello love, it's perishing cold. Isn't there anywhere else we can meet?"

"I've got the fire ready to light."

"Well done, love. Well done." Slipping off the wellingtons she kept hidden in the barn, she stepped inside.

Eirlys was walking out of the office a few days later when a tall, thin young man approached her.

"Miss Price?" he asked hesitantly. "Eirlys Price?"

"That's me," she replied pleasantly, amused at the height and the thinness of him and the sparseness of the red hair on his head. "You are . . . ?"

"My name is Max. Max Moon and I've been sent to ask for your help. I am starting to arrange for children's entertainment in the locality next summer and although it's looking a long way ahead, we want to get a few programmes in place."

The name rang bells but she couldn't place it. Frowning, she said, "I'm sorry, there must be a mistake. I don't know anything about children's entertainment. I think you want to talk to the Pipers who work on the beach. They'll know all about what's available."

Max Moon took a pad from a pocket and ran a pencil down a list of names. "Would that be Mrs Molly Piper and her family?" he asked.

"If you wait while I go and tell Mam I'll be late, I can take you there," she offered. "I know them quite well."

He thanked her and, bending slightly to talk to her and referring to his neatly written list, explained a little more of his plans.

"With the war creating shortages of fuel, we are already starting to think about encouraging people to stay at home instead of going away for a holiday," he explained.

"Going away for a holiday? Who does that? I've never been further than Cardiff!" she laughed.

"Well, you live in a town where people come for a break, so you know what I'm talking about and you can imagine the saving in travel costs if they all stayed home."

"I know a few families here who would go hungry too! We depend on holiday-makers and day-trippers," she said. "What d'you think will happen to this town if we discouraged visitors?"

"It has been worked out that the local people would make up for the lack of visitors and there would be very little difference in the income of the town. Everyone would cater for their own local people, that's all."

"Rubbish! We cater for our own people already."

"We need to keep the railways and roads free for the troops," he patiently explained.

Unconvinced, Eirlys led her new acquaintance, who insisted she called him Max, to have a brief word with her mother before they set off for Johnny's house in Brook Lane.

"What did you want from me?" Eirlys asked curiously, as they reached the door of Johnny's house. "The only time I've been involved with children is when I helped Mrs Francis with the evacuees."

The door opened then and she left Max to explain the reason for his visit to Bleddyn.

Bleddyn invited them in but shook his head when asked for help. "Trouble is, we're very busy in the season. Working from early morning to eleven at night sometimes, with the sands then the chip shop. I don't think I'll have time to help with extra entertainments. Now Eirlys knows a lot of people at the council offices and I'm sure she'll put you in touch with a few willing and able people with a few hours to spare, eh, Eirlys?"

Max turned once again to Eirlys. "Seems I'll need your help after all," he smiled.

Johnny was out so Eirlys didn't stay. "I think you'd better come back to the house with me and see if I can think of a few likely names for you," she said to Max.

Talking about entertainers brought Ken Ward to her mind and the name Max Moon found its slot in Eirlys's memory.

"You're a friend of Ken!" she said in delight. "He wrote to me about you!"

After exchanging news and giving Max messages to pass on to Ken, they continued the walk back to Conroy Street like old friends.

Johnny was visiting Hannah. He had a box of apples which he planned to offer to Hannah for the girls. Carrying the box of fruit he manoeuvred his way around a new, shuttered porch, lifted a heavy curtain hanging outside the door and knocked.

She opened it, and seeing him, said, "Johnny? How nice. D'you have some sewing for me? How can I help?"

"Not work this time, Hannah. I've brought a few apples for the girls. Some are cookers and some are eaters," he explained. "I know they like to take an apple to school. Given to me they were, a friend at the wholesaler had a lot left and as Piper's is such a good customer, what with the potatoes for the chip shop all the year and the beach café in the summer, he asked if I could find them a good home."

"Thank you." Hannah smiled her delight. "Will you come in?"

The door to the front room stood open and he could see into the over-crowded room. A sewing machine stood against the window with material spilling out of it across the couch beside it. Hannah was making curtains. He wondered how many of the night hours she spent earning a living for herself and her daughters.

He stepped backwards and pushed the front door shut behind him, but to his surprise Hannah moved around him, reopened it and propped it open. It was a chilly night, dank with unshed rain, mist wreathing the trees and hedges. Curious, he asked her why she didn't close it and keep the warmth in.

"One of Mam's latest rules," she said, clearly embarrassed. "That's why she had the porch and the double curtains fitted, to keep the light from showing. The door isn't to be closed when I have a man caller. A lot of fuss, eh?"

"Why? Do you have many callers?" Johnny asked, disbelievingly amused.

"Oh, the man delivering groceries. The man come to read the meter, a husband collecting some sewing for his wife, a friend bringing apples." She tried to smile but there was deep sadness in her lustrous eyes.

He put the box on the table and asked, "Are we all suspect, then?"

"No, not the men, it's me my mother doesn't trust. Wicked and wanton I am, didn't you know? I divorced my husband and that is something my parents will never forgive."

Impulsively Johnny gave her a quick hug and said, "Never think you're without a friend, Hannah. If there's ever anything I can do you only have to ask."

After he left, Hannah stood watching the movement of the curtain until it was still, separating her from him. She heard his footsteps crossing the road and daydreamed, imagining how sweet life could be.

Johnny stood across the road and heard the door close and the house became anonymous, just one of a row, but with such sadness locked inside he imagined it stood out from the rest. He felt moved by Hannah's plight and wondered what he could do to ease her misery.

There were no lights either from the street lamps or from shop windows. Usually during the dark months, the window displays would light the way down the main road, enticing passers-by to stop and look and then come back to buy. Now, with the lighting restrictions so diligently kept, there wasn't a glimmer.

Another month and the windows would be showing Christmas delights. This brought his mind back to Hannah and her children. What sort of Christmas would they have, with a disapproving mother and nowhere to have fun? He wondered whether he could persuade his mam to invite her to share their day. They usually joined Uncle Huw and Auntie Marged and his cousins on Christmas afternoon; there would be plenty of company and plenty of food. An escape from the sad little overcrowded room.

Irene reached home at the same time as he did and when Bleddyn opened the door to them he stared at his wife but said nothing.

"Was Hannah pleased with the apples?" he asked his son.

"Yes, but Dad, she has such an awful time of it, no husband and a miserable mother."

"Don't interfere, Johnny. She's better off than some. Being alone isn't the only way of being miserable." The words were harsh, the words pointed.

Johnny watched his mother take a glass of water and make her way up to bed without a word for his father, and understood what was being said. But it was Hannah for whom he felt concern. Mam and Dad had to sort out their own problems, he daren't interfere in that quarter. Hannah was different. She needed a friend to stand up for her and persuade her that there was more than one way of dealing with a problem, and it wasn't necessary to deal with it alone.

Eirlys came into his mind as he was making a hot drink for himself and his father, and he wondered why he found Hannah filling his thoughts more than she. Hannah was too old and she was a divorcee with children. Why couldn't he accept that and put her from his mind? Tomorrow he would call on Eirlys and ask about the boys.

"Eirlys called while you were out," Bleddyn said, breaking into his thoughts. "There was a tall, skinny bloke with her, wanting help to set up some extra entertainments next summer. Max Moon he called himself – what sort of a name is that? Know him, do you?"

Johnny shook his head. "What did he want with Eirlys?"

"She thought we could help, but I explained we were always too busy during the season. This Max Moon chap said there'll be more people staying home next summer. That's what he thinks!"

Johnny glanced at his watch. It was a bit too late to call on Eirlys now, and besides, he admitted to himself, he wanted to sit and think about Hannah.

At the Prices' house in Conroy Street, there was something of a party atmosphere. Max had produced an accordian and he played a few chords. This brought the three musketeers out of bed and running down the stairs.

"We 'aving a party, Auntie Annie?" Harold asked, eyes shining. "Always having parties when we was 'ome, wasn't we, Stanley?"

To everyone's delight, Max sat and played several popular tunes, party songs in which the boys lustily joined. Even little Percival seemed touched by memories of other days and mouthed a few words of "Knees Up Mother Brown", which brought tears of laughter to Annie's eyes.

It was eleven o'clock before the boys settled back into bed. As Max prepared to leave he made a suggestion.

"I've been thinking," he said. "Wouldn't it be fun to give the evacuees and some of the local children a Christmas party? We could hire the hall and, if we could persuade the council to pay for it, we could ask various families to help with the food and give them a good time."

"What about entertainers?" Annie asked. "Are you volunteering to play the piano for pass the parcel and things like that?"

"Better than that. I *am* an entertainer, it's my job. Ken and I are getting together a concert party and we hope to travel around giving concerts as soon as everything is sorted. For the children I'll do a puppet show and if we can arrange a small gift each, I'll be Father Christmas, with the aid of a few cushions. Or, if you prefer, I'll be Maxie the Clown."

Eirlys stared at him. "You do that as a job? Entertain children?"

"And adults." He smiled. "I was turned down for the army as I have a weak chest, but I have arranged to reapply and I think they'll take me for ENSA, the organisation for entertaining the forces. I'm going to London in a week or so to be interviewed. Ken too."

"Max knows Ken Ward," Eirlys explained to her parents.

Max stayed another hour and talked about his work with children in which he was helped by Ken. It was as though they had found a long-lost friend.

Eirlys was filled with excitement at the thought of being involved in arranging the party for the children. Several families had already returned to London, as no bombs had yet fallen, but there were still a large number of them staying in the town.

Mr Johnston agreed to fund the hire of the hall as it was good publicity for the forthcoming arrangements for local holiday entertainment. It was no surprise that he put Eirlys in charge of arrangements and allowed her to take two members of staff to assist her.

"I think I'll take the boys to see their mother next week," Annie announced one day in late November. "If you'll go and buy some fresh eggs from Mr Gregory, Eirlys, I'll take a dozen or so with me. I don't expect they get fresh eggs up there. Not still warm from the hens like we do, eh?"

Eirlys was apprehensive about the proposed visit. Not because of the danger, should German bombers begin to attack, but because she was afraid that once they were back on home territory the boys would refuse to return.

"Don't worry," Morgan said when she expressed her fear. "I doubt their mother would want to risk their lives when they can be safe down here. Stands to reason." He was trying to reassure himself, Eirlys and Annie both knew that.

"There haven't been any air raids and people are starting to think there never will be," Annie said doubtfully. "They might stay with their mother."

"There's always Plan B," Morgan smiled. "I'm getting bikes for them for Christmas. Old ones, mind, but I'll paint them up all smart and Johnny has promised to help me replace the old brakes with new ones and check everything is sound. With fancy new handlebar grips and a shiny new bell each, they'll look a treat. If we accidentally let them see the bikes, well, that'll bring them back for sure."

Johnny and Eirlys were ill at ease when they met and even when they went to the pictures there was no hand-holding, no real togetherness when the film was romantic or scary or funny. Neither could explain what was wrong. Johnny suspected it was thoughts of Hannah getting in the way of his growing attraction for Eirlys. Eirlys wondered whether Evelyn had passed on her unexplained animosity. They were both relieved when the boys went with them and they didn't have to pretend that everything was all right.

When she mentioned going to see Annie and the boys off at the station, she was pleased when Johnny offered to take them in Piper's van. He carried their luggage on to the platform and paid for the platform tickets they needed.

The boys were very excited and insisted on Annie repeating their travel plans again and again. She told them they would change in Cardiff, then they were being met at Paddington by Teresa Love, the boys' mother.

The journey was an exciting one for Annie as well as the boys. She had never travelled so far away from home before. They had a picnic on the train, which they shared with a young soldier who was returning to camp after a week's leave. He amused the boys, showing them card tricks and a few simple sleight-of-hand mysteries to confuse their friends. She was grateful to him. He wasn't much more than a child himself, she thought sadly.

He talked bravely about what lay ahead of him, and the new friends he had made to replace the ones left behind. Annie felt sorry for him. He looked so young and was obviously unprepared for the dangers he would certainly face in the next months. He lived only a few miles from Conroy Street and she promised to call on his parents one day and tell them that she had travelled with their son.

Mrs Love, the boys' mother, was a surprise. She looked hardly any older than Eirlys and was dressed so smartly that she stood out like an exotic bird among the navy-blue, black and khaki surrounding them. She was dressed in a rather smart white coat and a hat with a cheerful feather, stockings that looked like pure silk and high-heeled red shoes to match the feather. Annie was still looking around her trying to recognise a woman in her thirties who looked poor and downtrodden and when she saw the boys running towards this smart young girl she tried to call them back. "Wait for me, come here, I don't want to lose you!" When they stopped and hugged the girl she decided it must be a sister they hadn't told her about.

A hand covered in a good-quality calf-leather glove was offered for her to take and the girl said jauntily, "How-di-do! I'm Teresa, the boys' mother. Mrs Price, I'm pleased to meet yer."

"You aren't what I expected and that's a fact," Annie smiled. She turned to the trio and added, "Why didn't you tell me you had such a beautiful young mother?"

With Stanley and Harold either side of her and Percival clinging to her skirt, they made their way off the platform and down to the Underground trains. Annie had never been so nervous in her life but hid her panic well. She picked Percival up and held him as a shield when the train came rushing out of the tunnel and pulled up like an impatient and bad-tempered animal at the platform.

"I feel as startled by this as you lot did when you first saw one of the farmer's cows," she laughed, as they pushed their way into the already crowded carriage.

Mrs Love lived in a single room and had managed to make bedspace for her three sons by pushing chairs together to make a bed for herself and putting the boys to sleep widthways along her double bed.

Although Teresa Love was smartly dressed in good-quality clothes, Annie thought the room was not very clean. The bed was covered in satin sheets that slithered as the boys sat on them, and there were several pillows, but it looked, to Annie's fussy eyes, very impractical and it all needed a thorough washing. But then, she excused, it must be difficult keeping such an inconvenient and cluttered space clean. And with dust floating in from the road outside, from where there came the continuous noise of traffic.

"Well, now I know where to find you, I'll make my way to my hotel," Annie said when she had been plied with tea and biscuits. "I'll come to collect you for the four o'clock train tomorrow, shall I?"

"Oh, don't go yet," Teresa said.

"But I thought you would want to talk to each other, catch up with family news and all that."

"Look, stay and have a bite to eat; we could go to the chip shop. Our Percival loves chip, don't yer Percival?" She looked around and frowned. "It'll have to be chips in paper. I don't think I can find enough plates for us all. They get broken, don't they? I'll put the kettle on and Stanley will show you where the chip shop is. Go on, Stanley, while I find the forks. Although, we don't need forks do we? Fingers is fine, eh, Percival?"

Annie bought the fish and chips, Stanley insisting that his Mam only liked the best bit of hake. When they had finished the food, Teresa put on her coat. "There's no need to take me, I can find the way if you'll give directions," Annie protested.

"Well, I wondered if you'd hang on a bit longer, Annie dear. I have to go out and I'd be much happier if you stayed with the boys."

It was three thirty a.m. when Teresa returned, smelling of drink and hardly aware of her being there. Dozing lightly on the chair, with Teresa opposite her, the night passed.

The next day Teresa didn't feel well, so it was Annie who found a shop selling bread and made them some sandwiches for their breakfast, and Stanley who led the way and took them to see the sights. He showed them the Thames and boasted about the bridges, found a place for them to eat, then took them to Buckingham Palace, guiding them through the intricacies of the Underground train system like an expert, while the tickets were paid for from Annie's dwindling purse.

"There's just time to feed the sparrers," Stanley announced and he dodged through the traffic and took them into the park, from where they made their way, via the Underground, back to Paddington station.

"There isn't time to go and say goodbye to your mother," Annie said, having repeatedly tried and failed to persuade them to return to the bedsit and Teresa.

"It's all right, Mrs Price. She'll be sleepin' it off," Harold said. "Won't she, our Stanley?"

Annie had a lot to think about on the journey home, with Percival snuggled against her and with the other two fast asleep on the opposite seat. Morgan met her in Cardiff and during the last leg of their journey she whispered some of her observations to him, trying not to let the boys hear her disapproval.

"Mum is only twenty-six and she says she wants a bit of fun," Stanley said in a spuriously adult tone. "Had me when she was only a kid."

"Sixteen," Harold supplied sleepily. "Lovely, ain't she, our mum?"

"Absolutely beautiful," Annie agreed, hugging them. "You're such lucky boys to have a lovely young mam like Teresa."

"Ain't we just," Stanley said sleepily. "Now, how long do we have to wait for them bikes, Uncle Morgan?"

Five

Plans for the Christmas concert for the evacuees went ahead with few problems. The entertainments committee refused at first to pay for more than the use of the hall but changed their minds when Max pleaded for some compassion for the poor children taken from home and everything familiar, on account of Hitler. Then they agreed to pay for the hall plus his expenses and something towards buying a gift for each child. Everything else needed for the concert, including stage and curtains, had to be found by Max and his supporters, who at that moment seemed to include no one except Eirlys.

For Eirlys, the organisation of the concert seemed to be an extension of her work at the council offices and she began to enjoy the challenge more and more. Marriage to Johnny was still enticing, but she beginning to like the idea of giving up her job less and less.

Johnny, Taff and a still suspicious Evelyn were persuaded to help, a carpenter was found to knock up a rostrum or two and Max was encouraged sufficiently to arrange auditions for a number of local people prepared to take part. Ken Ward wrote to tell Eirlys that although he was unable to help beforehand, he would definitely be there in time to support Max on the day of the concert.

Eirlys found it all very exciting and involved herself enthusiastically. It was easy to forget everything else. She would hurry home from work and start at once carrying out the instructions Max had left for her.

Johnny called twice and found she was out. He made his way to the hall, lent free for auditions and rehearsals, where she would be running around sorting out lists of names and skills, a pile of jugglers' equipment in one corner, ventriloquists' dolls and puppets in another.

Annie had to remind her that Johnny was feeling neglected. Ashamed that her enthusiasm had left him out, and to make sure he felt really involved, Eirlys put him down for various tasks, mainly searching for the hundred and one things they needed to get the hall ready. She also included him in the team of scene painters, using paint scrounged from a local shop and many garden sheds.

Hannah too offered her help and, after being given the material, made a pair of curtains for the makeshift staging Max had managed to acquire.

"It's all good practice for ENSA," Max told Eirlys. "I expect to be faced with worse than this if I have to entertain forces in strange places. There won't be doors to knock on and kind neighbours to ask, if I'm up where the fighting is taking place. Scavenging and making do will be a way of life for me if this war continues to run."

"You sound as though you want it to," Eirlys commented.

"No," he protested. "Like every other thinking person, I'd be relieved if it ended now, this minute. Many are going to be killed before it's over – how can you think I want that?"

"Sorry, Max. I didn't really mean it."

"I hope you didn't. I want you to think better of me than that, Eirlys." He looked at her and when she met his gaze, he smiled and she saw an interest in his bright blue eyes that made her turn away. She didn't want to see that look on anyone except Johnny Castle. But it was flattering just the same.

Between work, meeting Johnny, helping Max and amusing the evacuees, Eirlys still managed to work on her rugs most evenings. With the wireless for company, she worked until past eleven o'clock and had soon used up all the material she had gathered. If she were to continue, she had to find more unwanted coats and skirts. She was toying with the idea of making more attractive rugs using good quality wool, better colours as well as texture, but, it would have to be cheap if she were going to make a profit.

She saw an advertisement for Readicut rug-making kits which included a pattern set out in squares to represent each tuft, the canvas marked into sections to make the pattern easy to follow. The wool needed to complete the design was also included. Impulsively she sent for one. Heaven knew when she would find time to work on it with so many calls on her time, but an idea was growing in her mind about one day running a business of her own. Her father hadn't managed it but there was no reason why his failure should discourage her from trying.

That brought her thoughts back to Johnny. She didn't want any ambition to come between them: whatever the future held, she hoped Johnny would be a part of it. She smiled inwardly. Evelyn could hardly accuse her of sitting waiting for marriage; she had filled her life with so many things since that rather unkind remark. Life was full and it made her feel more confident. She was important and needed by her boss Mr Johnston, by the three musketeers, and hopefully by Johnny too. When things had settled down and she had more free time she would concentrate on a business of her own, earn lots of money and make Johnny proud of her.

Money was on her father's mind that night. He had missed a couple of shifts that week and he knew Annie would demand her usual housekeeping. He had nothing in his pocket, not a penny. When Eirlys had gone to bed, he asked Annie for the loan of ten shillings.

"Where do you think I can find a spare ten shillings?" she asked. "If you didn't get to work too late to start your shift you wouldn't be broke all the time. I have to work and I manage to get there on time, so why can't you?"

"I hate the job, that's why," he muttered.

"Pity you let the business fail then, isn't it!" she snapped.

"But I can't go a week without any cash at all," he pleaded.

Annie went on in her usual way, reminding him about how he had failed her and Eirlys by not looking after the successful business his father had left him.

Upstairs, Eirlys covered her ears with her hands. When the argument went on and Annie's voice grew louder she ran downstairs and begged them to be quiet before they woke the boys.

Annie eventually gave Morgan a half-a-crown coin – two shillings and sixpence. He stared at it in the palm of his hand until she went upstairs, then he took another one from her purse.

He needed money. How was he going to get some without working extra shifts in that damned factory?

Johnny worked well beside Max most evenings when he wasn't needed to help out at Bleddyn's fish-and-chip shop. They soon had their stage sets worked out and, with Max drawing the scenes in outline, and Johnny and several others filling them in with paint, they had all the scene changes they needed, and stored them in a garage behind one of the shops. Lighting was the province of Johnny's cousin, Ronnie, helped by Morgan.

With a week to go and only final reheasals of the acts to worry about, Max felt content.

"Will the invitations be for the evacuees only?" Johnny asked him one evening when they had closed the door of the local hall on another evening's work.

"I think we'll have room for a few more. In fact, I was intending to go to the school to ask the teachers if there are any children who would benefit from a night out."

"There's Hannah, who made the curtains," Johnny suggested. "She has two girls, Josie, four, and little Marie who's three. There's no father and I don't think they get many treats."

"I think that's an excellent choice. Thank you for telling me, Johnny. Will you invite the girls when you next see them?"

Johnny excused himself from walking Eirlys back to Conroy Street and called on Hannah on the way home.

As usual, the sewing machine was in use, with pretty pink-and-white material under the foot, the needle poised for Hannah to continue.

"Don't you ever rest?" he asked as she propped the door open and invited him in.

"I'm lucky to have this much work," she smiled. "This dress is one of five I've promised for the end of the week. They're for children who are to sing at Max's concert. Aren't they pretty?" She held one up for him to admire.

Josie and Marie were still up, looking at a book, sitting beside the fire in their nightdresses.

"I'm good at reading stories," he offered and Josie handed him the book. Trying to ignore the open door, he settled beside them and began to read, accompanied by the sound of the treadle machine as Hannah continued with her work. He gradually ignored the words in the book and instead invented a story using the characters in the pictures. Josie frowned and looked at the page as though searching for the part of the story he had found, but soon they were both sitting enthralled as he wove tales about beautiful princesses and magical animals and tables that only needed a tap to produce the most wonderful food.

Reluctantly, he stood to go when Hannah said it was time for bed. He waited while Hannah attended to the nightly routine and settled the girls in their bed in the next room.

"It's about the concert I've called," he explained when she returned and settled once more into her seat. "Max would like you to take Josie and Marie."

"Oh, they'd love it. But isn't it for the evacuees?"

"More a practice run for Max," he grinned. "There are some spare places. A dozen or so of the London children have gone home and we don't want the entertainers to perform to a half-empty room, do we?"

"Thank you," she smiled.

"Don't thank me, thank Maxie Moon."

"I think the invitation comes from you, and I appreciate it," she insisted.

Johnny ran home with her voice ringing in his head and a happy feeling around his heart.

When Eirlys had completed a small woollen pink and blue rug of which she felt reasonably proud, she went to see Hannah and gave it to her for putting beside the girls' bed. "It's a practice piece to see how well the wool works," she explained. "I made a smaller hairpin shape of wire, of course. The tufts are smaller and the pattern easier to plan."

"But I can't accept this!" Hannah held up the neatly patterned rug, which was pink squares on a mid-blue background. "You've already given me one."

"Why ever not? If it wasn't for you I'd never have tried."

"Nonsense. You and Johnny are more than generous to my girls."

"Johnny?"

"He called yesterday and told me that Josie and Marie are going to the concert. There are a few spare seats, he said, but I know he arranged it as a treat for them."

"Oh, the concert. Yes, he knew you'd be pleased," Eirlys said, although it was the first she had heard about the idea.

"He loves children, doesn't he? He plays so well with my two, and he reads to them like a professional actor. I can see he'll make a wonderful father one day."

A twist of jealousy went through Eirlys and she didn't stay for the proffered cup of tea. Johnny seemed to be seeing rather a lot of Hannah, and, she decided, it was her own fault. She had begun to take him for granted.

She stood for a moment outside the door to allow her eyes to become accustomed to the darknesss, and to allow her painful thoughts to settle.

Morgan was walking past when she moved away from Hannah's door. He recognised his daughter's voice as she and Hannah called their goodnights, and darted into an alleyway between two houses, before crossing a garden into the next road. One good thing about this blackout, it meant you could take short-cuts over gardens without being seen.

He stopped when he came to the house of Bleddyn and Irene and melted into the shadows.

Eirlys set off home, but for some reason she was edgy. It was only half past nine, and on that Friday evening there was a slight remnant of a moon and the night was crisp and clear. Yet there was an eeriness about the streets lit only by moonlight, and with no lights to mark the pavements. Deep shadows in doorways, beside trees and in the entrances to lanes and alleyways gave a sensation of emptiness that was unnerving. Her footsteps echoed in the silence and it sounded as though someone was following her. She hurried, anxious to get inside and warm herself at the fire. She wished she had asked Johnny to go with her. Voices and laughter would have driven away her foolish imaginings.

Her anxieties were not all that foolish, she reminded herself. The blackout had caused numerous accidents and she didn't want to be a victim of a fall from unmarked kerbstones or a knock from a bicycle gliding almost soundlessly past, or trip over an unseen cat, as someone had done the previous week, resulting in a broken leg.

She remembered that it was one of the nights for the ARP meetings and decided, impulsively, to go and wait for her father. The place where they met, a small stockroom in the school, wasn't far and it was better than allowing her fears to build up and make her afraid of the familiar streets. If she allowed that to happen she would be a virtual prisoner, as many already were, afraid to go out once darkness fell.

Like every other building in the town, the room in the school building was in darkness. Blackout restrictions were strongly upheld and no chink of light was allowed to be seen. She felt her way through the school gates and walked warily across the yard. In the wan moonlight she could make out the walls of the building and made her way to the main door. She pushed but it was locked.

She called but there was no reply. Perhaps they used another entrance.

She made her way back along the wall and screamed when a voice close to her said, "What are you doing here, miss?"

Even in the weird light she recognised the unmistakable outline of the warden with his blinkered torch and his helmet.

"It's me, Eirlys Price. I was hoping to catch my father and walk home with him," she explained.

"No one here, miss. There isn't anything here on Fridays."

"I thought the ARP—"

"Not Fridays," he said firmly, and she began to smile. Mam was right, he used the ARP as an excuse to meet his friends. He was probably in the pub!

"I'll walk you to the end of the road, miss. Conroy Street won't be far then."

She thanked him and was grateful for the chatter that drove away the emptiness of the dark night.

In Brook Lane, Irene stepped out of the empty house. Bleddyn was working at Piper's fish-and-chip shop, and Taff no longer lived at home since he and Evelyn were now married. Johnny hadn't been home since morning.

A shadow separated as Morgan stepped away from the fence and reformed as she melted into his arms.

Teresa Love, the boys' mother, wrote more frequently for a while after their visit. She wrote separate letters to Annie too, and in these she usually asked for money. Once it was the gas bill. Being unable to settle it would mean she had no heating and no way of cooking food.

As Annie had seen no sign of anything to suggest she ever cooked, she wasn't too concerned. Percival's famous chip shop was only a few houses away, she thought wryly. She had sent five shillings on an earlier occasion and two shillings on another, but this time Teresa had asked for ten shillings to pay the rent, stating that unless the money was found she would be out on the street in less than a week.

Annie put the letter away in her drawer, wondering whether Teresa was telling the truth. She had told Annie she worked in a shop where the wage was likely to be low, but from what she had surmised during her short visit, Teresa depended on men friends to feed her and the expenses of that tiny, drab room could hardly be crippling. She didn't dress like a struggling mother either. And those fancy sheets told her plenty!

She said nothing to the boys but discussed it with Morgan and Eirlys when the boys were in bed.

"I don't think she can be that desperate," Annie said. "She hasn't got the boys to feed and there's only the rent and heat for that one little room."

"You've seen it, we haven't," Morgan said. "You know better than us if she's telling the truth."

"I don't think for a moment that she can't find the rent. So I think I'll write back and tell her I haven't any money to spare. What with us feeding her sons an' all, she's got a real cheek, hasn't she, to ask for money as well? Besides," she couldn't help adding, "we aren't rich. You hardly earn enough to keep us in plenty, do you?"

Morgan looked away. Annie never missed an opportunity to remind him.

Eirlys looked thoughtful. "What if it is true? What if she's got herself into debt and she really is threatened with eviction? How would we feel if we were told she had been thrown out on to the streets because she hasn't enough to pay the rent?"

Upstairs, clinging to the banisters and leaning as low as he could to catch every word, Stanley's heart was racing. He was shivering from his chilly eavesdropping as he got back into bed, but it was nothing to the chill in his heart. His sleep was disturbed by frightening dreams, seeing his mother lying ill and neglected on a pavement, while Annie walked past her uncaring, and the snow slowly covered her lovely face. He had to do something. He was eleven now, and head of the family. There was no one else to help her. It was up to him. The promise to Auntie Annie didn't count any more, not with Ma in need of help. He needed money and he needed it fast, and there was only one way to get it.

Harold and Percival picked up on his concerns and when he explained about the lack of rent money, they began to feel afraid.

"If she sleeps on the pavement, will she end up stiff like that dead cat we found once?" Percival asked in a trembling voice.

"Don't be daft, our Percival! I look after you, don't I? Ma sleep on the pavement? Course not! Got friends up there, ain't she? One of them'll 'elp until I can get her some cash. An' I will, I promise yer.

Not a word to Auntie Annie or Uncle Morgan, though. They mightn't understand."

Morgan and Irene spent many moments together in the various places they had discovered during the past months. As the increasingly cold weather made spending time out of doors less and less appealing, they began to use the caravan for most of their illicit meetings.

Irene still used her depression, from which she genuinely suffered, as an excuse for her wanderings. Since very early in their married life Bleddyn had been aware that his wife suffered from "nerves" and twice she had threatened to take her own life. Because of this he didn't interfere when she spent days living apart from them in a world of her own. He looked after the house as well as he could and made sure their sons didn't suffer neglect. He had no way of knowing that several of these periods of "depression" coincided with a brief love affair, although that special glow in her eyes when she came home straight from a lover should have told him.

For Irene the affairs had never before been important, just a way of adding a little spice to her boring days. This one, with Morgan Price, was different. She wanted him to leave Annie and take her away from St David's Well so they could start a new life together. So far she had failed to persuade him. He treated her suggestions as part of a game they played, a "let's pretend" game of which they were very fond.

If only something would happen to change the game into reality, to make him understand that a fresh start was possible.

Then her prayers were answered.

They met one day when Morgan came off the morning shift and walked deep into the bleak countryside to meet her at "their" caravan. Morgan lit a fire in the tiny grate and they lay on the bed and pretended.

"This is a beautifully furnished room, isn't it darling? So spacious and with such wonderful views of the garden."

"I love the smooth bedspread, such a rich green satin, and the eiderdown is so warm."

They played the foolish game for a while, pretending they couldn't smell the damp rising from the cushions or hear the wind on the windows, or the tin-kettle sound of rain on the roof.

"Why don't we make it all come true, Morgan?" Irene whispered. "We've only one life and why should we spend it in misery? Annie expects too much of you; Eirlys is grown up, earning a good wage and doesn't need you to stay. I'm stuck in that house all alone, while Bleddyn is so tied up in routine I know what he's doing every moment of every day. I feel I'll go mad with the boredom of it all."

"We'd be so happy, wouldn't we, Irene darling. Just you and me with no one else to think about."

"Just us, and maybe later our children."

"If only we could. We'd be so happy."

"Then why not do it? Take ourselves off and start a new life?"

"We'd need money. I'd have to make sure we had enough to see us through until I found a job. A job I enjoyed, not that damned factory."

"I'd work too, Morgan. I'd work if it meant being with you, even though I wouldn't help Bleddyn and that Molly Piper. She expected me to work on the sands every summer once we married. Who did she think I was, to expect me to do what I was told by the likes of her! Bleddyn, Huw, Marged and Moll, they all tried to persuade me it was my duty to help the family business. I soon put them right on that. But I'd get a job if you were with me, Morgan, love."

"First we need some money, a lot of money," Morgan said, but to him it was still fantasy, still the unattainable vision of sitting in a beautifully furnished room in a beautiful house in dream country. Irene was extending the game they often played; she didn't really mean they would abandon their families and walk off together into the sunset. He wouldn't know where to start.

Irene put a hand against her stomach and imagined the tiny speck of a thing that was hers and Morgan's child, and smiled contentedly. "One day soon everything will be perfect, Morgan, love."

"Just perfect," he agreed.

Johnny found himself searching for excuses to call on Hannah. With the decorating in Granny Moll's house completed, he now worked as general dogsbody in a shop selling linoleum, hardware, kitchenware and tools. Boring jobs: tidying up, cutting customer's requirements and delivering goods in the firm's van.

There were no leftovers in this business to offer her. No more apples. The invitation to take the girls to the concert seemed to be the last excuse. Then he thought, Why do I need an excuse? Eirlys is busy at the hall, I could just stop by and ask if I can read to the children, take a few sweets. A friend would do that, surely?

Hannah answered the door to him and invited him in, making sure as always to prop open the front door with its protecting porch and heavy curtains.

"No one can see in," he whispered, "so what's the point of letting the icy cold wind into the room?"

"I find it easier not to argue," she whispered back.

"Who is it?" A voice from the back of the house asked.

"Johnny, Johnny Castle," he shouted back.

"Don't be long then. It's blowing a gale through this kitchen."

"Sorry. I only brought some sweets for Josie and Marie, and I thought I might read to them again."

"Sorry Johnny, but they're in bed. Only on Fridays are they allowed a late bedtime as a sort of treat."

"Oh, well, I really came to see you, to ask if there's anything you need. I might be able to get a bit of firewood from where I work, if you need it. You know, boxes the goods are delivered in that are only thrown to the rubbish or burned in the yard."

"Thank you; I'm often a bit short of sticks to start the fire."

"Is there anything else? I mean, if you have a problem you only have to ask and I'll sort it."

He stood close to her, feeling the warmth of her filling his body in a way he had never experienced before. "I didn't really call to ask about firewood," he whispered, staring at her, willing her to feel the same as he did, wanting to gather her in his arms, make everything right for her, smoothing the tiredness from her gentle face.

"Johnny, I like you a great deal and I love the way you are with the children, but don't make the mistake of thinking there could be anything more." She touched his face and then stepped away, backwards towards the door, and stood there waiting for him to leave.

"I think I'm falling in love with you, Hannah."

"How old are you, twenty-one? I'm almost thirty. I'm divorced – disgraced according to some. I have two children. You need someone younger so you can start at the beginning and write your own story."

"Why do I feel this way if it's wrong?"

"It isn't wrong. It's never wrong to love someone, but I'm not the right one to accept that honour. Thank you for being such a wonderful friend to the three of us. We will stay friends, won't we? I haven't driven you away by my frankness?"

"You haven't driven me away," he said as he left.

He walked swiftly from her door and headed away from the town and out into the dark anonymity of the lanes. He felt a little foolish but that passed and he thought seriously about how he felt. The moon was almost done and he could hardly see where he was going. Once or twice he stopped to get his bearings and eventually found himself at the edge of the field in which the barn stood, just visible, a bulky black shadow looming out of the darkness.

He smelled smoke and wandered, feeling his way with care across the hummocky grass and the unevenness caused by cattle, hard now in the grip of frost. He was led by curiosity. He hadn't seen any gypsies, but it must be them, back for their winter stay, choosing a different field by choice or necessity. He moved closer, expecting every moment that one of their dogs would bark. The caravan was close and he went to stand in its shadow, then realised that the smoke was coming from its chimney. Not the gypsies then.

He heard someone approaching, walking fast, confidently, a thin torchbeam pointing at the ground, and he stood back not wanting to be seen. He didn't want to talk to anyone, he needed to memorise every word Hannah had said to him; relive it, gather comfort by altering, in his mind, the tone of her replies.

Irene Castle was waiting for Morgan. The evening was raw, with frost already glistening on branches as she had made her way to and from the woodpile and fed the fire she had lit in the caravan. Once it was burning satisfactorily she went outside. She didn't bother to put on her coat but walked a little way to see if she could hear Morgan coming.

She got as far as the lane and turned back, hugging herself to contain her shivers, anticipating the warm fire waiting for her. She didn't see her son hiding in the shadows but he saw and recognised her.

"Mam? What on earth are you doing out here, and without a coat?"

"Johnny!" The name came out as a scream as she came upon him. "Have you been following me?" she asked as she quickly recovered.

She continued to shout loudly, her voice high and shrill. Morgan had to be warned if he was in the vicinity.

"I came out for a walk and my feet just led me here. But what are you doing and where's your coat?" He took off his overcoat and wrapped it around her shoulders.

Her shoulders drooped and she said, "I don't know why I'm here. I just had to get out of the house. Your father's working at the chip shop and won't be back till eleven, Taff has moved out and you're never there. What am I supposed to do with my time?" She still shouted and he tried to soothe her, leading her carefully away from the caravan across the field and on to the level surface of the lane.

"Come home, Mam, and we'll sort something out. Evelyn and Taff will come and stay with you sometimes and I don't have to be out every night, do I? Once this concert is over, Eirlys and I will enjoy a night in with you, listening to the wireless, playing cards."

He went on talking to her, telling her about the concert preparations and relating stories about the three evacuees. She walked beside him, saying nothing and from the hedge Morgan watched them disappear into the dark November night. He had made an excuse to change his shift from eight hours to four, something, the foreman warned him, that very soon wouldn't be allowed. He had finished at six instead of ten for nothing.

Stanley found it a simple business to push open the door of the greengrocer where Johnny's cousin Beth Castle worked. The door was old and the lock poorly fitted. One good shove and the weakened wood offered no resistance.

He had heard people talk about float and understood it meant that some money was left in the till ready to start the following day. He didn't think it would be much, but a pound was all he needed to keep his mother safe for a week or two. He found fifteen shillings and pocketed it happily before going to try somewhere else.

He even managed to close the door after him. The damaged wood was pushed into place and he heard the lock click as he pulled on the door knob. "Knackered," he muttered succinctly.

Morgan was walking back from the caravan after sitting there for a while wrapped in Irene's discarded coat and staring into the fire. So long as they weren't suspected, they could start using the place again in a week or so. Until it was safe, he wondered whether the school caretaker was still careless about locking the door to his room. He had the keys because of his occasional attendance at the ARP meetings. There was an electric fire they could use as long as they were careful to shield its glare, and a comfortable chair.

He was in no real hurry to get home; Annie wouldn't expect him until after ten and he had told her he might be late, using the excuse that he might join others on ARP business looking for possible sites to station fire-watchers in the event of air raids. He wandered disconsolately through the lanes and back streets of the town.

He was filled with self-pity. He was broke, doing a job he hated, Annie did nothing but remind him of his failures and his daughter was too busy to speak to him.

A shadow separated itself from the dark and he leaned into a hedge and watched as a body emerged from a ground floor window. He ran on tiptoe to intercept the thief, for that was what he must be, leaving a property in such a suspicious manner. A pretty stupid one at that, climbing out where he was in full view from the street.

He was grinning at the story he'd be able to tell as he grabbed the surprisingly small figure and whisked him around to see his face.

"Stanley! What the hell are you thinking of, boy? Why aren't you in bed?" he demanded stupidly. Then, "You've been thieving again! Do you want to be sent to prison, boy? Is that what you want?"

Stanley tried to run but Morgan held him firmly. "What have you been doing, boy?" he hissed. "I thought you'd promised us—"

"I had to get money so our mum won't get pushed out and have to sleep on the pavement, that's what – and don't expect me to say sorry, 'cos I ain't!"

"You won't find much money in a shop. They take the money home or put it into the night safe."

"The float. I took the float." Stanley was still defiant.

"Pubs, now they're the places where you'd find money," Morgan said with bleak humour.

"Pubs is where wardens hang about. And they lock and bar them places," the expert told him. "Shops is easier."

"You've done this before!"

"Course I 'ave. Mum's often broke and I look after her and my brothers."

"Pubs might lock up downstairs," Morgan said thoughtfully as though to himself. "But they don't worry about upstairs windows, do they? And pubs aren't the only place worth a visit. We could go to the pictures for the late showing and on the way back—"

"You mean you'd help me get Mum's rent?"

"Let's say we'll help each other, is it?"

"Blimey!"

Since preparations for war had begun in 1938, several stores of food for feeding the army had been set up in the vicinity, and Morgan knew just how to get inside the Nissen hut built close to the perimeter fence. Stanley, long and slim, was just the right person for the job.

The following day Morgan's shift changed to afternoons and he offered to put the boys to bed so Annie and Eirlys could go to the pictures. When Harold and Percival were asleep, he and Stanley left the house.

Prising up the slightly damaged window was easy. Sammy Richards had unwittingly told him which was the faulty one. Sammy had helped supply the glass for the windows and had noticed the poor fit of several of them. Made of metal, they had warped and no longer fastened properly.

"Don't forget, boy," Morgan said, repeating his instructions. "If there's any sign of trouble, you run for it and leave the explanations to me, right? Get out of it fast and make sure you're not seen till you get safely home."

In less than half an hour, Stanley had handed out half a dozen six-pound tins of corned beef and some tins of ham. Tinned fruit was found in a far corner and after helping the boy out through the window and fixing it as well as they could, they carried the loot in sacks across their shoulders and hid it in an elderly neighbour's yard until it could be retrieved later.

"Not a bad night's work, Stanley my boy," Morgan said and promised the boy four half-crowns. "Maybe more once I've got rid of it. We'll have no trouble selling this little lot."

He was dozing when Annie and Eirlys returned. The wireless was playing dance music, the fire blazed cheerfully.

"Enjoyed a quiet evening then?" Annie said.

"Fell asleep I did," he said, getting up to make the night-time cups of cocoa.

Ken Ward arrived on the day of the concert and found accommodation in the same boarding house as Max. He and Max were experienced at producing shows in small halls and the minor problems that developed as curtain-up approached were quickly dealt with. The hall was very overcrowded. Intended to seat forty, Max counted at least fifty-two before the doors were closed for the performance to begin, and he saw them open several more times before the introductory music began.

The excited chatter from the audience was counterbalanced by the hushed nervousness behind the curtains, where Ken confidently organised the adults and children into the order in which they would appear. With a chord on Sammy the carpenter's accordion, it began.

Five little girls in the dresses made by Hannah sang a few favourites and the audience was encouraged to join in with the choruss. A clown appeared next: Maxie Moon juggling and falling about in the casual way perfected by clowns over hundreds of years. Then a comedy duo with their humour aimed firmly at children so everyone had fun; the children laughing at the entertainment and the adults enjoying the children's laughter.

As the interval approached, three men came on dressed as rats and sang:

"Nobody loves a rat, boo hoo,
Nobody loves a rat.
They'll cuddle the cat and admire the bat,
But nobody loves a rat.
Three cheers for the rat!"

"Boo!" went the audience.

"Three cheers for the cat!"

"Hooray!" the kids shouted.

"It's true what we say,
Do what we may,
Nobody loves a rat. Boo hoo!"

At that moment there was a commotion at the entrance and the air raid warden came running down the aisle, blowing his whistle and shouting, "Put that light out!"

The rats squeaked and began to chase the man around the hall, through the seats and out of the door.

"Three cheers for the rat!"

"Hooray," the laughing audience shouted.

Stanley was not in the audience. He had made his excuses to his brothers, promising them a Cadbury's chocolate bar if they didn't give him away, and made his way to the corner of Sidney Street where Morgan was waiting for him.

After repeating his instructions to run for it if there was any sign of trouble, Morgan led him to a small window at the back of the newsagent run by Mrs Hetty Downs and her daughter Shirley. Both women were out as, having given a contribution to the concert fund, they had decided they were entitled to see it and had gone to the hall determined to bluff their way inside with several others.

As the "rats" were giving an encore, Morgan was entering through the door opened by the lithe Stanley after he had slipped in through the window.

It wasn't difficult to find the day's takings and it was a sizeable sum. With cigarettes and sweets as well as newspapers being sold, they guessed the leather bag used at weekends to put the money in the bank would be full.

Morgan cut the bag open, intending to put it under some rubbish in the allotments as they went home, and Stanley excitedly watched, imagining his mum's face when she saw the money he was going to present to her one day soon.

The sound, when it came, was slight and for a moment neither of them reacted. Then they realised that someone was pushing against the front door of the shop.

"They've come home early!" Morgan gasped. "They didn't get in after all."

He didn't have to tell Stanley to run. The boy pushed the door shut, locked it and pocketed the key before he wriggled out through the window with Morgan close on his heels. The original plan was for Morgan to use the door and Stanley to lock it after him and escape by the window. Stanley didn't stop to think, he ran.

Morgan listened and the sound seemed to have stopped. Someone sheltering, that was all. Where was the boy? Dammit. Now he'd have to leave the door open and their theft would be discovered straight away, when the police did their usual check of shop doors. No breathing space until the morning as he had hoped.

It was then he realised that the door was locked. He was trapped unless he could break the door down. Panic began to rise and he looked around him, wondering if there was another way out. Perhaps the shop door? But he couldn't get out of the store room.

He looked at the window and wondered if he could get through. Pushing it closed after him would mean no one would notice before Mrs Downs and her daughter Shirley opened up in the morning. He wasn't all that big; it was worth a try, especially when he thought of the alternative.

He stretched up and began to climb on to a cupboard. But overcome by curiosity he looked inside. It was full of cigarettes packs of 200 Player's Weights, Park Drive, Kensitas with "four for your friends", Woodbines, Du Maurier, Player's Navy Cut and Wills' Capstan. And, utterly irresistible, pink, elegant packets of Passing Cloud. He grabbed three cartons, stuffed one into his inside pocket and held the others under his arms and tried to slide out of the window.

He managed to get half-way out by throwing the cartons on to the yard below the window but when he greedily went back for more cigarettes he fell. His foot went under him and all his weight pressed on it. He tried to stand but the pain was frightening. There was no escape. He would be here when Mrs Downs opened up in the morning. His deepest fear was having to explain to Annie.

Stanley, meanwhile, hurried back to his seat and at once joined in with the rest, singing loudly, "It's a long way to Tipperary."

Morgan was writhing on the floor behind the shop, holding his ankle, cursing his stupidity, and Stanley laughed louder than the rest, making sure people remembered he had been there, blissfully ignorant of what had happened.

In the aisle the audience stood to dance to "Knees Up Mother Brown" and sat again while Max the clown played and sang a silly song about a lazy hen, standing up at one point to reveal an egg on the piano stool, to the delight of the children.

The applause was rowdy and it took a while to empty the hall. Max and Eirlys and Johnny and the others stood exhausted and declared themselves satisfied. Outside, Stanley looked for Morgan.

When they reached home, having been met by Annie, there was no sign of him.

Stanley said he had left his new cap at the hall and before Annie could tell him not to, he was out, running down the dark streets to the newsagent. If Morgan hadn't got out, he'd be trapped. Mrs Downs and her daughter Shirley were on their way home for certain now.

Racing past the hall he was relieved to see that groups of chattering people still stood around, reluctant for the evening to end. Jumping over fences and skirting through gardens to save time he reached the shop, clambered up and called through the window.

"I can't get out, boy, my ankle's busted I think."

"I'll go for help."

"NO!" Morgan shouted. "Get me out of here, and fast!"

Taking the key from his pocket, thankful he hadn't thrown it away as they had intended, Stanley unlocked the back door and, with Morgan grimacing at every move, managed to help him out of the building and into a nearby lane.

"Now you can go for help," Morgan groaned. "Fetch young Johnny Castle, he's sure to be with our Eirlys."

His chest was tight with all the running he had done, but Stanley ran back and to his relief found Johnny talking to Eirlys and Max as they dismantled the stage.

"It's Mr Price," he whispered to Johnny, his chest heaving with the effort. "He's hurt himself and he doesn't want Mrs Price to know."

"I won't be long," Johnny excused himself. "I have to take Stanley back home. I'll be back for you, Eirlys." It must be a woman, Johnny thought, half with disgust and half with admiration. How did he get away with it with Annie? How dare he even try!

"Don't worry," Max called after him. "I'll make sure Eirlys is safe."

"'E's got a nerve, muscling in on your girl," Stanley puffed as he led Johnny back through gardens and across the corner of the allotments.

"Where are we? Where are you taking me?" Johnny asked.

"Short-cut this is. Blimey, mate. Don't you know your own back yard?"

They found Morgan with his coat covering his spoils, from which he refused to be parted. "I can't suffer all this for nothing," he argued when Johnny tried to persuade him to leave them behind. "What, leave them for someone else to pinch?"

"Not ruddy likely, eh, Uncle Morgan," Stanley encouraged.

The sharp-eyed Stanley had noticed an abandoned pram not far from the allotment gate and he and Johnny went to fetch it. On this contraption, with two wobbly wheels and no handlebar, Morgan made his undignified way home.

"I'll make you a good bogie cart with this at the weekend, young Stanley."

"Big enough for the three of us I 'ope, Uncle Morgan."

"Stop it you two!" Johnny was angry, just realising the seriousness of his involvement. He had been so caught up in the haste, he hadn't been thinking clearly. "I can't help you with a robbery! You casually make plans as I rescue you after you've committed burglary and chat as though nothing has happened? I haven't decided yet whether or not to inform the police! I can't just ignore it!"

"You can't inform on your girl's dad, now can yer?" Stanley said reasonably. "She wouldn't never forgive yer."

"At least promise you won't ever do anything like this again." Johnny was confused, he didn't know what he was supposed to be thinking. This was a completely new experience.

"I can promise that, hand on me heart," Stanley said seriously as they stopped to catch their breath. "I only did it to get the rent paid for our mum. I'll never touch another thing that ain't mine. Never. Not even a pencil from the boy sitting next to me at school and that's a God's promise."

Johnny accepted the boy's word but he was embarrassingly aware that no such promise came from the wounded warrior in the broken pram.

Six

Johnny felt like a thief himself as he walked through the streets pushing the injured Morgan on the old pram. The man was obviously in pain although he tried to hide it. He was concerned about Morgan but anxious about the cigarettes young Stanley had hidden in spite of his entreaties to hand them over to the police.

"I hope you haven't put them where the police will find them, Stanley," Morgan said as though Johnny wasn't listening.

"Give them up," Johnny pleaded. "It'll go better for you if you do."

"Give over," Morgan said with a weak laugh. "If they find them I'll be stuck in prison and I'll have to face Annie at her worst." He winced as the pram lurched over a kerb. "And you want me to do all this for nothing?"

"I don't want my ma sleeping in no gutter," Stanley said. "I did it for my ma and I ain't doin' it for nothin' either!"

Johnny gave up. He was bemused by the bizarre situation and felt as though he had been caught up and driven along with them without a mind of his own.

Eirlys and her mother were waiting at the door when the peculiar procession appeared out of the darkness accompanied by Morgan's moans to generate sympathy. Once they were inside, a glance at Morgan's swollen leg made it clear that a doctor was needed and the rest of the night was spent dealing with hospital admissions, waiting for news and all the other alarms and confusions and irritations that go with an accident.

Johnny stayed with Eirlys, wondering how much of the night's adventure he should tell her. It was two o'clock the following morning before he told her the full story. They were in the hospital waiting for news, having asked a neighbour to sit with the boys. He felt uneasy and ashamed at the casual way he had accepted the situation and helped Morgan and Stanley to hide stolen goods and outwit the police. Dammit, he'd even carried some of the spoils!

He tried at first to avoid her learning the truth and at first said, "He fell in the lane."

She only had to look at his stricken face to know that wasn't true. "Come on, Johnny, you don't just fall and do that much damage."

"He climbed a wall or something, chasing a burglar he told us."

"Burglar," she muttered. "A woman more like."

"What? Your father doesn't chase other women does he?" He widened his eyes, feigning ignorance.

"Forget I said that. Dadda needs flattery sometimes. Mam reminds him constantly of his failures. He needs someone to tell him he's wonderful. There's nothing more to it than that – and don't try to change the subject!"

"I wasn't. I just don't know any more than he told me. Why is it so hard to believe?"

She hesitated to reply as they heard someone approaching. They smiled encouragingly at a young soldier, bandaged and using crutches, who was being helped and gently teased by a pretty young woman.

"It doesn't make sense, that's why," Eirlys said when they had passed. "For one thing, how did Stanley know exactly where to find him?" She sighed. "Please, Johnny. Before Mam comes back I need to know the truth. I need to if I'm to protect him."

"You always protect your dad, don't you? Why do you think he needs your help?"

"I love him, but I know he's foolish sometimes. Remember when we had to rescue him when that van broke down? Mam thought he was at work. He hates working. He never had to work hard when his parents were alive. They indulged him and did everything for him. When they died he couldn't cope. The business failed, then he lost job after job. I've always been afraid that one day Mam will have had enough and tell him to go."

"You're very loyal," Johnny said. The vision of the soldier had remained with him – the soldier and his loving girl. He imagined himself in uniform, coming home on leave like the soldier. How fortunate he was to have a girl waiting for him, helping him, loving him. He knew he needed someone if he were to go away and that was very likely. He looked at her and knew she would be loyal and loving and very good to come home to.

"Loyalty can be misplaced," Eirlys then said. "I didn't go to London when Ken Ward asked me and my decision was partly because of loyalty to my parents."

"Do you have any regrets?" he asked, his dark eyes staring into her slightly troubled blue ones. Her response was important to him. He felt a flood of relief when she shook her head.

"No, Johnny. No regrets. I couldn't have loved him or I wouldn't have been able to refuse, would I?"

"I'm glad you stayed," he said, drawing her into his arms, holding her close.

She broke away and stared at him as though deciding whether it was right, before moving close to kiss him again.

The hospital seemed deserted at that late hour. Just occasionally a nurse would walk briskly through the tiled corridor, stiffly starched clothes swishing, shoes squeaking on the highly polished floor.

"Does this mean you feel the same way as me, that we're more than friends?" Johnny whispered.

"I feel more for you than I've felt for anyone."

"If I asked you to move to London, would you come?"

"Whatever you want to do, Johnny, I'll support you." She smiled as she added softly, "I think we'd have to come home to separate my warring parents quite often, though, don't you?"

"I love you, Eirlys. I know this isn't the best time to say it. I'll be leaving next year to join the army, unless I manage a deferment which is doubtful. We'll be getting to know each other through letters, mind, not meetings like this. If you don't want to stay with me, I'll understand."

"Johnny, it's never the wrong time to fall in love. We'll deal with whatever happens, together."

He felt relief as he held her tightly and succumbed to the pleasures of a deep and emotional kiss. A huge decision had been made. No more dreaming about the quiet and gentle Hannah, who was eight years older and had two lovely daughters. He was committed to Eirlys, he was the luckiest of men and they would be very happy.

"Mam will be back any minute." She stood up and brushed her hair back and glanced in the mirror, knowing that whatever she did she wouldn't be able to remove the shining excitement in her eyes, a tell-tale sign of love. Then she returned to the subject of her father.

"Johnny, please, quick – before Mam comes in, tell me what really happened." When he told her, coldly and briefly, she stared at him – but not with love in her eyes; that look had been wiped away by horror.

"Dadda was breaking into a shop?" She stared at him, a half-smile on her face, waiting to be told it was a joke.

"He used young Stanley to get in through a window, then when they thought someone was coming in through the front door, he told Stanley to run, which he did, but your father tried to get out through the window Stanley had used and, well, he slipped and couldn't get away."

"What was he stealing – money?"

Johnny hesitated and she insisted on knowing the full story, so he said, "Cartons of cigarettes, and some money."

She was silent while horror and disbelief filled her thoughts, then she said, "Mam mustn't know."

"Young Stanley hid the cigarettes. I don't know what happened to the cash."

"We'll have to find it all and send it back."

"That's too risky. There's more chance of being caught than when they stole it."

"Dadda a thief? I can't believe it, Johnny. He's always been lazy, he hates his job, but stealing? Entering someone's house and robbing them? Why did he need money so desperately? Is he in trouble, d'you think?"

She was white with shock, trembling so much that her arms shook uncontrollably. Johnny felt a strong sympathy extending the love he had declared, and he took her in his arms and held her, talking soothingly to her as the tremors slowly left her.

A nurse appeared with a pale-faced Annie and they were told that her father was all right but would stay in hospital until the ankle had been set.

"I'll stay with him, you two go home and get some sleep," Annie said.

Johnny hardly heard what was being said until Eirlys told her mother that Johnny would walk her home.

Walking through the silent streets his thoughts were confused again. In a corner of his mind was a picture of Hannah, but a part of him wanted to hold Eirlys again, repeat that exciting kiss that had been full of promise. It was a powerful sensation, the arm-aching need to hold her again, to experience once more that almost overwhelming love and protection. She made him strong, with a newly born ability to deal with someone else's problems, take them on to his own shoulders.

Words of love teetered on his lips but this time he held them back, afraid to say them while the image of Hannah was still there in his heart in case they sounded as insincere as he felt. Hannah had been right to discourage him, common sense told him that. She was eight years older and at times it seemed she was a generation away from him in experience. But did common sense matter when love had spread its web?

Going back into the house, Eirlys revived the fire while he made tea. He watched as Eirlys poured, such a homely everyday act, yet with his newly declared love, a sensual one. He wondered if she knew how confused he felt? She had been strange lately, avoiding him, seeing rather a lot of Max Moon too. Perhaps that was why he had declared himself, afraid that if he didn't, then he might lose the chance. Perhaps if Max had spoken first, Eirlys might have already turned away from him. He couldn't really love Eirlys, he was simply playing safe, afraid of ending up alone, stuck in his father's house with no life of his own. His thoughts were like a tangled ball of string, not making any sense.

"Are you going to tell your mam?" he asked as they sipped their tea. When she shook her head he added, "She might find out from the boys. Kids of that age aren't reliable about keeping secrets, are they?"

"Why did Dadda involve Stanley? That's what I find hardest to accept. He's only just eleven. It was a wicked thing to do."

"I think Stanley wanted money to send back to his mother."

"He should have told us, not try and steal it. We'd have done something if only we'd known about his worries."

Johnny stood up, reached for his coat and was preparing to leave when a weary Annie returned from the hospital.

"Keeping him in, they are," Annie told them. "They have to set the ankle and put him in plaster." She frowned as she took off her coat and hat. "I still don't understand what he was doing in that lane. Thought he saw a burglar and climbed a wall for a better look, he said, and he fell awkwardly with his weight on the ankle."

"That's what he told me," Johnny told her.

"The police seemed to think he was right about the burglars," Annie went on with a yawn. "They had a call to tell them that Mrs Downs has reported a break-in at the newsagent."

"So he was telling the truth, then," Eirlys said, glancing at Johnny to support her lie.

"Seems that he was, but I still don't know why he was there in the first place."

"Dadda often goes for a walk, Mam. Nothing strange about that."

"Working in a factory like he does makes him a bit stale," Johnny added. "He says he needs fresh air and some exercise."

"Did they find what had been stolen?" Eirlys dared to ask.

"They wouldn't say. Now, I'm off to bed. Thank you, Johnny, for staying with Eirlys. What an end to the night of the concert, eh?"

"Great, wasn't it, Mrs Price?" Johnny enthused. He looked at Eirlys. "Max Moon did a marvellous job, didn't he?"

"I hadn't realised how talented he was," Eirlys said. "When I first met him he looked so – so—"

"Ordinary?" Johnny offered.

"What's ordinary? Everyone is capable of surprising us!"

Annie was surprised at the vehement way her daughter responded to Johnny's comment. Hastily, Eirlys smiled and added a few complimentary remarks about Max, with which her mother concurred.

Jealousy surged and for a moment Johnny forgot Hannah and feared to lose Eirlys to the man who had suddenly entered their lives and taken such a large role in Eirlys's.

"Pity he has to go. We'll miss him," he said.

"Oh, he won't be going back just yet," Eirlys said airily. "He's staying on to discuss next summer's plans with the council."

Johnny kissed her as he left, almost fiercely, reinstating his claim.

Stanley was frightened, wondering what the outcome of the robbery would be. Every time he saw a policeman he edged away as though his guilt were written on his face. He didn't talk to Percival, who was too young to understand, about the seriousness of not paying rent, but he and Harold discussed the problem whenever they were alone.

"If Mum doesn't get the money, she won't have a home and neither will we when we go back," Stanley explained. "She'll be thrown out into the streets."

"You mean we could go back and she wouldn't be there?" Harold began to cry and Stanley punched him affectionately on the shoulder.

"Come on, I ain't going let that 'appen, am I? Look after you, don't I?"

"What are you going to do, Stanley?" Harold looked hopefully up through tears.

"I'm going to ask Auntie Annie to take us to see Mam again, then I can hand her the rent money and everything'll be all right."

They asked her that evening as she was leaving to visit Morgan in hospital.

Annie refused. "I can't afford to take you all to London again so soon. But," she added quickly as faces fell, "I will take you after Christmas, how's that?"

"I'm bovered about Christmas," Percival said solemnly, in his low, defeated voice. "If we don't go back 'ome and leave a note, how's Father Christmas going to know where we are?"

"I've sorted that," Eirlys said at once. "There's a special address and I got it from the Christmas Fairy at the council offices. If you all write a note I'll see they get sent off."

When Johnny called to enquire after her father, Eirlys was advising and helping the three boys to perfect their letters, Harold optimistically asking him to kill Hitler so they could all go home.

Annie came in a little while after him and they all admired and more or less approved of the boys' efforts.

"I got to see Mam," Stanley said. "Can't you just take me, Auntie Annie?"

"Sorry, Stanley, but you'll have to make do with letters for a while. I can't afford it. Besides, I can't take the time off work," she explained. "In fact I'm working longer hours than usual with all the Christmas orders to see to."

"What if I pay for the tickets; will you come then?"

Annie laughed. "How can you pay for the tickets? Giving you too much pocket money, are we?"

Eirlys stood up, dropped the letters, talked about her hectic day's work, offered to cook, trying to distract her mother from continuing the conversation. Johnny stood up too and asked if he could have a cup of tea. Annie laughed, ignored the distractions and asked again, "How much d'you think it costs to go to London, Stanley? Tuppence ha'penny?"

Stanley drew from his pocket several pound notes and ten shilling notes and a handful of silver coins.

"Where did you get that?" Annie demanded. Johnny reached out and put an arm around a shocked Eirlys.

"It was what me an' Uncle Morgan got when we went into the shop, when he hurt his leg," he said, as though surprised they had to ask.

Eirlys's mind closed down. She was aware of the shouting that went on as Annie demanded a full explanation, but couldn't remember a word that was said. She clung to Johnny, who tried to calm Annie down, begging her to think before she did anything, as her actions would have long-lasting effects.

Eventually Annie's storm of anger was reduced to tears and Eirlys went into the kitchen to make the inevitable tea.

"I can't face him. You mustn't go and see him either," Annie said to her daughter. "All these years of marriage and I don't know him. How could he do such a thing? And involve a little boy too. I'll never forgive him. Never."

"She will," Johnny comforted Eirlys. "People who are married usually do."

"Mam's had so much to forgive him for, now this," she sobbed. "Can you see why I stayed when Ken asked me to marry him and move to London?"

"Things will be rough for a while but I bet in a few months they'll have put all this behind them. Look at my mam and dad. Mam's been ill with her funny moods for years and Dad doesn't give up on her, does he?"

"Better or worse, richer or poorer?" Eirlys said sadly. "I sometimes think it's a lot to ask of someone, don't you? Think of Hannah. I don't think she was wrong to leave her husband, do you?"

"Hannah is a brave woman," Johnny said. "I admire her a lot."

The decision to give back the money was not easy to put into action. Morgan came out of hospital to a storm of abuse. He didn't get the chance to ask why he'd had no visitors during his last few days in hospital; Annie gave the explanation the minute he set foot in the door.

In the first tirade she told him the money had to go back. When she had calmed down from the first onslaught, he asked mildly, "How?"

No one could think of a way.

Morgan was soon out and about, with a plaster on his leg that he wore like a medal for bravery except at home. His friends wrote silly messages on it and asked for the story of his chase to catch the burglar time and again. He was a hero outside the home, a villain inside. Neither Eirlys nor Annie spoke to him. It was only the "three musketeers" who gave him any comfort.

He was careful not to mention it when Annie or Eirlys were around but he learned from Stanley where the cigarettes were hidden. Together they moved them to a safer place, in the shed of a stranger's garden. The man who lived there was elderly and rarely left the house. There was little likelihood of the goods being found during the days it would take for Morgan to find buyers.

Morgan was not unhappy. Besides the cigarettes and the money, there were the tins of food to sell. It was more fun than working. Pity Annie had to find out.

Eirlys saw a lot of Max Moon and Ken Ward in the short time they were staying in St David's Well. They arranged concerts around Cardiff, entertaining in the army barracks and also giving impromptu sing-alongs in a few factories. They also did some fundraising to buy comforts for the forces. They didn't organise the events themselves but were paid a small fee for taking part; a few of the concerts took place in theatres, but most were small affairs in village halls.

They called one evening to take Eirlys and Johnny out. Johnny felt like an outsider as Ken and Eirlys shared so many memories, but with his own calling into the armed forces imminent, he listened with interest as they talked about the NAAFI, the Navy Army Air Force Institute, which would supply food and shopping facilities to the men at the front line.

Both Ken and Max were unable to serve for medical reasons but both had decided to serve in the capacity of entertainers and would soon be using their talents to help the men in France to take a break from the stresses of battle. Johnny admired them and congratulated them on their bravery, but at the same time wished them gone. He didn't want Eirlys to admire them too much.

Their newly revealed feelings for each other and the events at the newsagent had brought Eirlys and himself closer together. Most evenings she worked on her rug-making for an hour or two, then went with him to spend the evening with Bleddyn and Irene – who seemed to spend more time at home these days. They listened to the wireless and to records, played cards and talked. Johnny explained that his mother seemed to be coming out of her latest depression, but Eirlys cynically wondered if it was simply the weather that made it less attractive to wander the streets without a coat and alone. Irene certainly appeared to be more cheerful, smiling to herself as though harbouring a secret.

One evening, Johnny invited her to go with him to see his Auntie Marged and Uncle Huw. "I think Granny Moll has found you some coats you might be able to use," he told her. She had sold all the rugs she had made and the shortage of material was slowing her production, so she was delighted.

Bleddyn encouraged them to go, assuring them that Irene would be perfectly all right on her own for a few hours.

"Don't talk around me as though I'm the family dog." Irene said mildly. Bleddyn laughed affectionately, pleased at her light-hearted mood.

Bleddyn had said nothing to his wife, for fear of worrying her back into the dark depression that plagued her, but had told his brother Huw that he was relieved to see Johnny spending time with Eirlys. "Better than him getting too fond of Hannah Wilcox," he explained. "There's trouble brewing there if that affair gets out of hand. She's been married before and with children too; it would be a burden for him to take on. Plus there's disapproving parents and an irate husband on the prowl. I feel sorry for the girl, she doesn't deserve such a rotten hand, but I want better for our Johnny than that."

It was due to that conversation that Bleddyn and Huw's mother-in-law, Moll, heard about Eirlys's hobby and had gathered a few unwanted coats. Eirlys was welcomed warmly when she went with Johnny to collect them and she felt an excitement, a feeling that perhaps it was going to happen, and she would one day be a part of this large, close family. With her father disgraced, her mother not speaking to him except to shout accusations, a place within this family had an even greater attraction.

When two more rugs had been completed, using coats given by Granny Moll, Eirlys sold them and posted the money to Teresa in London, unaware that Morgan had defied Annie and, as soon as he could walk on crutches as far as the post office, had bought postal orders for Stanley to do the same.

Teresa stared at the postal orders, which had arrived by the same post. Now she would be able to move to a better place.

Packing didn't take long. She put her tidiest clothes in a suitcase borrowed for the occasion, threw away all that needed washing, packed a few boxes with the odd pieces of china she possessed and was ready to leave when her friend came to take her to a larger flat in a street near Paddington Station.

Moving into the new place was even quicker. She simply threw open her suitcase and, using it as a drawer, she spread skirts and dresses across the table and left the rest of her clothes inside it. She draped her satin cover over the rather lumpy bed. The ancient cooker didn't work but the gas fire did. She'd manage just fine.

She checked to make sure she had the address of Annie and Morgan Price and promised herself she would write back and thank them for the money the very next day. She threw the piece of paper casually on to the bed; it fell to the floor and was picked up and discarded with rubbish and yesterday's newspapers, left by a previous tenant. When she couldn't find the address she put it out of her mind. When she had time she would easily get the address from the WVS who had organised the evacuation. Or she could even go to the town of St David's Well. After all, it wasn't like London. Tiddly little place like that, she'd find them easily.

Putting on her new high-heeled shoes and her last pair of silk stockings, she went to join her friends for a celebration drink.

The boys still wrote regularly to their mother, Eirlys and her mother made certain of that. They knew how important it was for the family to keep in touch so there wouldn't be any strangeness when they were eventually reunited. They didn't hear for a while, but Teresa had never been the most reliable correspondent and Eirlys made them keep writing.

There had been two bombing incidents in London in the month of November although these were not from German aircraft, but caused by the IRA. Nevertheless it was still worrying for Stanley, who listened to the news avidly, and he watched for the post every day, anxious to be reassured that his mother was safe.

"Perhaps she didn't get the money," he whispered to the still-ostracised Morgan.

"Can't you take me to London to see her if Auntie Annie won't?"

When Morgan refused, and Eirlys had explained that with Christmas in a few weeks she couldn't take time off work to go with him, Stanley called a family conference. In bed one night after the lights were out, he woke Harold and Percival and told them he was going on his own.

"I'll set off for school at the usual time, but I'll head for the train."

"I want to come," Percival said. "I'm bovered about bombs, but I want to see Mum."

"You can't come and that's that. I'm going to persuade her to come here and see us," Stanley promised. "I've got enough money to pay for my fare and she's bound to have lots of money now we've paid her rent. Didn't she tell us in her last letter that she was working in a big dress shop and selling posh clothes to the nobs? No doubt about it, she'll be coming back with me for a little holiday."

He found his way to London, assuring the guard that he was being met at Paddington by his mother. The Underground created no difficulties; he had been using the trains since he was five, ducking under the barriers and out-running the porter on occasions. As a precaution, he had written down what Annie had told him through careful questioning, in case things had changed. He stepped off on to the platform where they had alighted on their earlier visit. He found the flat, his heart racing as he knocked on the familiar door.

Back home, Morgan had hobbled to the school to hand in Stanley's lunch, which in his anxiety he had forgotten. Learning that Stanley hadn't arrived at school, he questioned the other two until they told him where Stanley had gone.

He went to the police and explained the problem. A boy of eleven on his own in London was a serious situation. The phone calls exchanged between St David's Well and the Paddington police failed to result in Stanley being met off the train, but at the moment Stanley learned, to his disbelief, that his mother no longer lived at the same address, he turned to be met by a smiling and friendly policeman, who promised to make enquiries for him and let him know where his mother had gone.

"Don't you worry, son, we'll find her. Now, I bet you're starving after all that travelling. Clever boy you are, ain't you, to have come all this way and found the right door? She'll be right proud of you."

Settled in an office with a tray of sandwiches and tea to restore him, Stanley answered the constable's questions. "If you could describe her, that would be a help," he was asked.

"She's beautiful," Stanley muttered, as he fumbled in his pocket. He handed the constable a crumpled photograph.

"Got a picture, have you? Marvellous. My, what a pretty mum you've got."

They were unable to find Teresa, but the police promised to search for her and let him know where she was living. "Only an oversight. She's a bit forgetful, what with the upheaval of the move an' everything. She'll be in touch before we even start looking, you can bet your life, young Stanley," the policeman said cheerily. "There might even be a letter when you get back home."

Stanley was tired and dejected, aching with disappointment at failing to find his mother. He felt in his heart that they would never see her again. He sat on the train with the guard keeping a special eye on him, and even sharing the man's sandwiches, thinking of the best story to tell Harold and Percival. In his pocket were two bars of chocolate to give them, but he and the guard finished them off before they reached Swindon.

Hannah called on Eirlys to ask about Stanley, whose story was the talk of the small town. Johnny was there and when Eirlys saw a shared look of intimacy between them, she was startled by her jealousy and somewhat ashamed of it too. As if Johnny and Hannah could be anything more than friends, she chided herself. She couldn't ignore it, though, and she moved closer to slip her hand into Johnny's, a proprietorial gesture which he seemed to resent. She must make sure not to be too demonstrative when they were together, some men found it embarrassing, she reminded herself.

Annie and Morgan were still not speaking and it was Johnny and Eirlys who met Stanley at the station. He emerged from the carriage accompanied by the guard, who had kept an eye on him throughout the long journey.

Stanley was full of his adventure, telling it with many dramatic moments to entertain his brothers. He told them a completely fictional account of seeing the policeman running up as the passengers emerged from the train and how he had darted around to avoid being spotted, "Just in case he was after me." He went on to describe how he had gone into the café at Paddington station and had sat eating crisps and drinking pop, looking around him at the other passengers, many in uniform. "I've never seen such a crowd, not since we got on the train to come here."

"What else did you do?" Harold encouraged.

"Did you buy chips from our chip shop?" Percival wanted to know.

"Nah. I bought Mum a leather handbag from a barrer boy," Stanley said proudly. "I brought it back so we can give it to her when she comes to see us. Lucky I had the money from the shop, eh? It was a real bargain, the man told me."

Eirlys and Johnny exchanged a look of horror. Johnny gestured with a tilt of his head for her to go into the kitchen where they could talk.

"If Stanley carries on boasting about the money he's spent, word could reach the ears of the police and we'll all be in trouble. Knowing who broke into the shop and not reporting it is an offence in its own right; besides your father being arrested, we'll all be found guilty."

Johnny looked serious and Eirlys said, "What can we do? I can't tell the police my father is a burglar. I'm sure he'll never do anything like that again."

What makes you so sure?"

"It was a dare, a bit of fun, a childish prank, showing off to Stanley, that's all."

"A one and only time?" Johnny looked so serious that Eirlys clung to him, prepared for worse news.

"You said he went out every Friday and told your mother he was going to the ARP meeting, and there isn't one held on Fridays. Where does he go?"

"You don't think . . . That's too frightening to believe."

"I'll look back through the local paper and see if there is a pattern of break-ins on Fridays, shall I? If there isn't, we'll be able to put our minds at ease."

"Johnny, I don't know what I'd have done without you being

here," she said. "Talk about a nightmare. I still can't see an end to it."

"At least he won't try any fancy footwork with that great lump of plaster on his leg," he chuckled, and succeeded in making her smile.

The voice of Stanley droned on, repeating his stories over and again until Percival fell asleep and Harold and even Stanley were yawning fit to split their faces. Annie herded them up to bed while Morgan sat listening to the late news. Bumps and shouts came from upstairs as the boys tried to prove they weren't tired at all, but could stay up all night, and in the privacy of the kitchen Eirlys and Johhny stood wrapped in each other's arms and kissed.

Morgan hadn't managed to walk far on his crutches. Living in an aura of misery, hearing nothing but criticism that he knew he deserved, he didn't think he could be more miserable. He wanted to see Irene. But how? He couldn't call at the house in Brook Lane and the caravan was too great a distance to walk to leave a note in the hope she would call there. Anyway, he was too noticeable to do either. Everywhere he went people stopped to speak to him. A face exposed on the local front page was disaster to someone having a secret affair, he thought miserably. Having a great lump of plaster on his leg didn't make him invisible either.

Then the problem was solved by Irene herself.

He was sitting morosely reading the *Daily Chronicle* and debating with himself whether or not to go out to walk to the park and freeze, when there was a knock at the door.

"Hang on, I'm coming," he called and struggled through the kitchen to the back door. "Irene!" he gasped. "What a sight for sore eyes! Come in. Annie won't be back for hours yet. Am I glad to see you. Bored half to death I am."

Irene slipped off her coat and they fell into each other's arms. They clung to each other and whispered endearments, then Irene explained the reason for her visit.

"I know you can't get to the caravan for a while," she said. "But our house is empty for most of the day; why can't we meet there?"

"Damned risky." Morgan frowned.

"The chance of us being seen is slight. Come though the back lane.

You can always say you called with a message from your Eirlys for our Johnny."

"What if we're caught in the house? Annie would never forgive me for that."

"So what? You'll always have me," she said.

The expression on her face as she made the remark gave him a jolt. Was that what she really wanted? For him to leave Annie and Eirlys and live with her? Did she think he had enough money for a fresh start?

As though aware of his thinking, she said, "Isn't that what we both want, now your Eirlys is grown up and no longer in need of you?"

"Of course, love," he said, pressing his face against hers to hide the consternation in his eyes. This was no longer play-acting, this was real. "Wouldn't that be wrong, though, with our Eirlys and your Johnny becoming so close?"

"How can that affect us? We aren't related, even if they marry, silly boy."

"No, but it does seem wrong somehow. They'd be upset to say the least and would certainly separate because of ill feeling."

"You don't want to finish with me just in case your daughter marries my son, do you?" she murmured, wrapping herself around him in a loving embrace.

"Come into the front room and you can convince me it will be all right," he murmured, guiding her, hopping about with her arm for support until they both fell on to the big, generously cushioned couch.

Bleddyn was busy with the fish-and-chip shop and restaurant for much of the day, opening at twelve until two thirty for lunches, and again at five until ten thirty most evenings. With Johnny working at the linoleum and hardware shop from nine until six p.m., the house in Brook Lane was empty for several hours during the day. It was such a relief to be able to talk to someone who didn't accuse him of stupidity and worse, Morgan decided the opportunity, when the chip shop was open for business, was far too good to waste.

It quickly became a regular event. Morgan walked through the lanes at the back of the houses and rarely saw a soul. It was so easy. He would take a bottle of beer, he and Irene would spend a happy few hours together and Morgan would stomp home on his plastered leg, discarding the empty flagon at a convenient place and carrying library books or a magazine.

It was a pattern that pleased them both. "A damned sight warmer than that caravan, too," Irene agreed.

For Morgan, the evenings at home were spent in an angry silence. Annie was still refusing to talk to him, and Eirlys either out with Johnny or working on her rugs. He fielded Annie's scornful looks with wide smiles and if she wondered why he was so happy, she never thought deeper than to presume it was bravado, or pretence.

Johnny didn't call on Hannah again, but when he passed the house he always looked up at the window, hoping to see her smiling at him. He dreamed of her beckoning him in, propping open the door and sitting with him to talk for a while. Her pale, gentle face often came between himself and Eirlys although he told himself it did not.

When they did meet it was not in such romantic circumstances. Hannah cleaned offices most mornings, leaving the children with a friend until it was almost time for school by which time she was always back home. On a cold crisp morning in December, Johnny was standing out on the lane behind the hardware shop loading goods on to the van for delivery. Hannah came running towards him and she looked upset.

"Hannah? What's wrong?" he asked as he intercepted her. "Can I help?"

"Marie is not well and my friend left her with my parents because I was late, and they'll be furious. Of all the mornings to be held up it had to be this one!"

"Wait a minute," he said, holding her still. "I can take you home in the van; I can always find an excuse to change my route. But why will your parents be angry because they have to look after Marie for a few minutes?"

Pink from her exertions, Hannah explained between deep breaths. "They allow us to live there but refuse to help me in any way with the children. 'You made your bed', and all that."

"But that's inhuman! I can't imagine any woman not wanting to help her grandchildren." He hurriedly pushed the last of the packages into the van, locked it and opened the passenger door for her.

"You'd better let me out on the corner or you bringing me home will be another excuse for criticism," Hannah said sadly.

"Why do you put up with it? Why can't you get a place far away from them? Is it because of the rent you'd have to pay?"

"I pay rent now. Only five shillings, but I have to earn that and enough to pay towards the gas before I start paying for food and coal – Sorry, Johnny, I shouldn't be talking to you like this. It's my problem, I made this situation and I have to deal with it."

"And take their punishment for the rest of your life? Why are they so uncooperative?" he asked as he slipped into neutral and applied the handbrake at the corner of her road.

"They want to keep on the right side of God I suppose. Their church strongly disapproves of any wrongdoing."

He watched her run down the road and enter the house, and wished he could have gone inside with her and protected her from the unreasonable anger of her parents. But he didn't have the right. He had to forget ideas of protecting her. If he could.

When he met Eirlys later that day he was confused, twisted up inside, not knowing what was wrong with him. Here was Eirlys, a beautiful, capable, uncomplicated young woman who was obviously in love with him. And there was Hannah, who had told him to go away and forget her, who had escaped from a deeply unhappy marriage and was struggling to bring up two girls. Two daughters who would be reluctant to see their mother bring another man into their lives. They would find it hard to share the mother who, because of the circumstances, was such an enormous part of their lives.

There were posters going up on every billboard. He didn't need to read them, he knew them by heart: they were asking people to join up, urging mothers and wives to let their men go. Women were required for the land army and munitions. It was clear that before very many weeks had passed, he would be going away to fight. A wife at home, someone to build a place for when he came back, someone loving him, caring about him. It was suddenly becoming more and more important to him.

The confusion of his thoughts, first about Hannah and Eirlys, then about being called to fight, led him to think far into the future. Marriage was for life and when he was being sensible, he knew that he would be fortunate to have Eirlys as his bride. She would manage his home, care for his children and never cause him any worries. Eirlys was the sensible choice and, with Ken Ward writing to her, keeping in touch, and with Max Moon still hanging about, this was no time to be undecided. He had told Eirlys he loved her and he had to stay with that decision. It was the best and most sensible thing to do.

He went out that evening telling himself how fortunate he was, and how others would envy him his future wife. He called for Eirlys that evening and suggested a walk. On the headland, high above the empty, silent sands, he asked her to marry him and she said yes. Her happiness showed in her shining eyes and her glowing face and in the passion of her kisses. For Johnny, however, there was a feeling of anti-climax that didn't leave him, even when they went to tell Annie and Morgan, and his father and his vague and indifferent mother.

It was Eirlys who went to tell Hannah. She took a few patterns for rugs she planned to make, and after handing them to Hannah for her approval or comments, she burst out with it.

"Oh, Hannah, I'm so happy. Johnny and I are going to announce our engagement in the spring and we'll probably marry before next year is out."

Hannah congratulated her and said all the right things. It wasn't until Eirlys had gone happily on her way that she collapsed into tears for herself and her stupid dreams.

Seven

The best Christmas present of all for the three musketeers was a letter from their mother. They painstakingly made highly decorated Christmas cards for her and Eirlys posted them off, ignoring the fact they had already sent others. The need to keep in touch, convey their love for her, was something with which she could sympathise. The approach of Christmas made absences far worse.

The boys followed her to the pillar box, watched as the envelopes slipped through the slot and listened while she told them of the journey by van and then train and by bicycle until they were popped through their mother's front door all those miles away.

"I'm going to be a postman when I'm grown up," Harold said. "Everyone's pleased to see you, aren't they?"

"I'll be pleased to see my mum," Percival muttered. Eirlys hugged him and promised him that it wouldn't be much longer.

The policeman had found Teresa Love and explained about her son travelling all the way to London to see her. He didn't quite understand about the money Stanley carried but when he said that he thought the boy had brought her money to pay her rent, Teresa cried.

She had paid a month's rent on her new place, but had been arrested soon after for prostitution, charged and fined, so she had no more money until she could get back the job she had lost in the gown shop, or go on the street and earn more. If only she had written to tell them her address before she lost theirs.

Standing on corners was not her way – she usually met clients in pubs – but she hadn't been lucky and one or two of the regular girls had aggressively warned her off the area. She was wondering how she would survive Christmas, and berated herself for not being there when her son had come to the rescue. She bought a newspaper and under its shelter stole a packet of greetings cards. She had nothing else to give them.

She had runs in her stockings and she stopped them with nail varnish. Then, after repairing her make-up, straightening the seams in her silk stockings and pulling down her skirt so the holes didn't show, she smiled and went out into the street.

Ken and Max had left St David's Well to audition in London at the Drury Lane theatre, for ENSA. They had realised that song-and-dance men who played an instrument moderately well were very thick on the ground so before they attended they wrote and perfected a comedy act. Max was tall and very thin and with a wig to hide his meagre red hair he made a passable "female" performer. His voice was deep and he sang well and they were accepted on a trial basis for a short tour in France. Ken wrote to tell Eirlys, adding that they hoped to spend at least part of the Christmas holiday at St David's Well.

There was an urgency about Christmas in St David's Well in 1939 that was difficult to explain. Since the warnings about possible food rationing had begun and before they had become a reality, people had built up stores against the shortages to come. Now, only three months into the war, they opened their hoarded tins of ham and salmon, and used the dried fruit and sugar to make one last splendid cake. Tins of fruit and Nestle's cream were taken from their hiding places too and were included on the menu over the holiday period.

It was bravado. People told themselves there was no need to hoard, that if they were bold and confident, by next Christmas everything would be back to normal. All the fears would have become a memory. Warnings about future shortages and statements about the reduction in the manufacture of everyday objects were treated with scorn. The war was on the continent, not at home, and anyway, it would soon be won.

The shops were emptied of food and gifts and even household items ran out as people bought a new mat or a fresh pair of curtains or some new china for Christmas. Even the wallpaper shops had a hectic few weeks as women cajoled their husbands and sons into redecorating a room or two – for Christmas. As savings clubs paid out, the money was spent. Economy was a word to make you smile. This wasn't the time to consider tomorrow, or next week or next year.

Temporary stalls appeared on street corners, moved on by the police only to open up again a few yards away. Many sold holly and mistletoe and Christmas trees of all sizes. There were also those selling paper trimmings for living rooms, and cards and calendars which the vendors waved enthusiastically, shouting that the calendars were special souvenir issues on which to mark the end of Hitler and his war.

Butchers' windows were filled with geese and chickens and a few turkeys for those who could afford them. Rabbits were displayed less noticeably for those who could not.

Bernard Gregory delivered his annual supply of birds to the butchers who had ordered them, stripped of their feathers and ready to put on display. He had worked through the night, two nights in a row, taking a nap occasionally to keep himself going so the job would be finished on time.

He wished his son Peter were there to help, but Peter had volunteered for the forces long before war had been declared and Bernard didn't even know where he was. Scotland maybe? Holland? Or even France? He hadn't heard for eighteen days and didn't even know if he still had a son, he thought sorrowfully, as he handed the last of his turkeys to Keys the butcher.

He accepted payment and went home and slept for twelve hours. Christmas was not worth thinking about, or planning for. This year it would be just another day. Feeding the donkeys and the remaining livestock, cooking a bit of bacon and a couple of eggs and listening to the wireless or reading the copy of *The Hobbit* that Peter had given him last time he came home.

In the house at Brook Lane, Bleddyn cooked Christmas dinner assisted by Johnny, Taff and Evelyn. Irene was there but vague, as though unaware of the importance of the day. She opened presents, smiled and put them aside, handed Taff, Evelyn and Johnny their presents – which had been chosen, bought and packed by Bleddyn – and picked at her dinner, all with hardly a word spoken.

The rest of the family wore paper hats, laughed and cracked jokes and pretended to be having a good time, but the ghostlike presence of Irene made it all a farce, Bleddyn thought, temper simmering as Irene made no effort to make the day a good one for them all. As soon as was polite, Evelyn and Taff left to spend the rest of the day with Huw,

Marged, and their family in Sidney Street, where the atmosphere was sure to be more cheerful.

Johnny went to call for Eirlys and her family, who were also invited to spend the rest of the day in Sidney Street with his Auntie Marged, Uncle Huw and the rest.

"I'll follow on later," Bleddyn said, and, when the young people had left, he tried to get a reaction from Irene by showing an anger he didn't really feel. Anger was spent long ago, and even concern had faded to become nothing more than mild contempt.

"Couldn't you make a bit of an effort for Johnny and Taff and Evelyn?" he demanded, raising his voice in frustration. "What will Evelyn think of you, acting like this on Christmas Day?"

"I don't like Evelyn. She doesn't look after Taff as she should; working all day in some factory, how can she?" Irene spoke softly, looking towards a cushion, as if talking to someone he couldn't see.

"You're a fine one to talk. When did you ever look after Taff? Or Johnny, or me?"

"I'll make a cup of tea," she said and went into the kitchen. When the sound of clattering cups stopped, Bleddyn went to investigate. Irene had made a pot of tea, poured herself a cup and gone back to bed.

Irene sat against the pillows, rocking slightly. Her life would be so different once Morgan and she told the world about their love. He wouldn't bully her or expect her to do things she hated. Her eyes were sharp and intelligent as she went over in her mind the plan to make Bleddyn accept her leaving. Non-communication was so easy. All she had to do was walk off as they were talking to her and sit in her room. They would be relieved to see her go.

Persuading Morgan to leave Annie might be more difficult. She shivered slightly as she thought about how she would deal with rejection if Morgan refused to leave his wife. That was something she wouldn't be able to face. She'd rather be dead than cope with the humiliation of being spurned by Morgan.

It wouldn't happen. Not now. He would never leave her now.

Bleddyn sat staring into the fire for a while, then decided that he was wasting his time here with a woman who refused to speak to him. Ill or not, Irene was driving him away and from where he was looking, it was deliberate. He left the remainder of the dishes, reached for his overcoat and trilby and went to join the other members of his family.

In his brother's house the atmosphere was completely different. Dinner had been cleared away and dishes of sweets and displays of party crackers decorated the table. Besides Huw and Marged, their four children were there. Ronnie with his wife Olive; young Eynon; Bethan with her soon-to-be fiancé, Freddy Clements. And Lilly, who was putting on a coat and preparing to go out.

"Where are you off to, Lilly?" Bleddyn asked as she fastened a scarf over her long dark hair. "Meeting some friends?"

"Don't ask," Marged moaned. "Not a word will she say. Got some secret boyfriend but he must have a face like a codfish, because she won't let us see him or even tell us who he is."

"I'm going to follow you one of these days," Huw said jokingly. "I want to know who my daughter is seeing that she can't bring home to meet the family. Ugly is he?" Then, "You aren't ashamed of *us*, are you?"

"You do that, our Dad, and I'll walk out of this house and never come back."

"Promises, promises," Huw sighed, winking at Bleddyn.

Johnny hadn't gone straight to Sidney Street. He had some chocolate money in his pocket for Josie and Marie and he went to see Hannah.

He felt slightly embarrassed, knowing his excuse was a feeble one, but took out the gold foil-covered sweets and handed them to the little girls. Avoiding looking at their mother, he began to squeak, pretending the sound came from somewhere else. He fooled about searching for the cause of the squeaking, making the girls laugh, then produced a couple of sugar mice, each in its own sugar bed.

If he was surprised when they didn't go at once to show their grandparents in the next room, he didn't comment. Instead, he said, "I'm off to visit my Auntie Marged and Uncle Huw and all my cousins. Then we'll all be going for a walk to get some exercise before tea. How would you like to come with me, you two and your mam?"

"Thank you, Johnny," Hannah replied softly as Josie and Marie turned to look at her questioningly, "but I don't think this is a time for strangers to turn up uninvited."

"Extra friends calling is what Christmas is all about. You *are* invited; *I'm* inviting you," he laughed.

Hannah shook her head. "Your Christmas is with Eirlys, with her family meeting yours. And that's how it should be."

The children complained a little but she promised them they would go with Johnny and Eirlys another day, when it was warmer.

She didn't emphasize the fact he and Eirlys were a couple, but it hung in the air, making him inexplicably angry – not with Hannah for quite reasonably refusing what she saw as an unofficial invitation, but with Eirlys, even though she would surely not have complained.

He forced himself out of the mood of melancholy that was settling over him and called for Eirlys. They arrived soon after Bleddyn, with Annie, Morgan and the three evacuees, who were carrying their new game of Ludo, hoping to find someone to play with them, and boasting about the bikes Morgan had bought for them.

There were already four empty flagons on the kitchen table and the gramophone was playing music to which Huw and Marged were trying to dance, and, in the impossibly overcrowded room, causing much laughter. There were gifts to exchange and Eirlys was delighted to receive several items for her "bottom drawer".

"I suppose you have got one?" Moll asked. "Most girls start one as they approach twenty."

"Oh yes," Eirlys assured her. "There's quite a lot of linen that Mam has given me which I've embroidered. Some china too. It's surprising how much you need to start off, isn't it?"

"I'll look in my cupboards and see what I can find," Moll promised.

Johnny smiled his thanks but there was little joy in it for him. Shouldn't he be more excited about collecting things for their future home? Or was it more the responsibility for women to make sure they had the necessities? He decided he would talk about it with a few friends and with his brother Taff.

Every seat that could be squeezed into the room had been taken, with neighbours calling, finding it impossible to leave, and adding to the numbers. When they had pushed a few children out of the way and found seats in the very crowded room, Morgan announced that he needed a walk and everyone had to move again.

"For heaven's sake, Morgan, sit down and stop disturbing people," Annie sighed.

"It's as hot as Old Nick's kitchen in here," he grumbled, loosening his tie and collar.

"Always like this, he is, never can sit still," Annie said as she glared at him.

"Likes to be out and about, doesn't he, Mrs Price?" Evelyn smiled, glancing at Eirlys as she spoke as though the exchange should mean something to her. Eirlys frowned then looked away.

With crutches supporting him, Morgan made his way to Brook Lane, swinging himself along at a fair old pace with the ease of practice. The streets were deserted. Everyone was either sleeping off their dinner or listening to the entertainment offered by the BBC. No one wanted to move; even the children had given up parading with their new toys and were indoors where it was warm and the food was plentiful.

He went along the back of Brook Lane and through the garden and Irene opened the door as soon as he touched the knocker.

Morgan wasn't the only one to need a walk. Eating more than usual and sitting in the overheated room put several of the others in danger of falling asleep. As the day was dry, if a little chilly, Eirlys and Johnny decided to take the three musketeers and walk down to see Mr Gregory's donkeys in Sally Gough's field.

Mr Gregory seemed pleased to see them. He found a bottle of pop for the boys and made tea for Eirlys and Johnny. Eirlys asked about his son and was told that he was on secret service for the government, and he knew nothing more than that.

"I'll see Peter when I see him." Mr Gregory shrugged sadly, then he forced a smile and put aside his concern. It was Christmas Day and no one wanted to listen to his worries about Peter out of touch in a foreign country, with the war beginning to threaten them all.

As they approached Sidney Street again they heard music.

"That doesn't sound like the wireless," Johnny frowned. As he opened the door he saw that the party had got its second wind and several others had arrived. Among them, as promised, were Ken Ward and Max Moon, on a brief visit to Ken's grandparents. Ken had brought a set of tubular bells made for him by the local blacksmith out of tubes of varying length, and Max had brought a piano accordian on which he began to play songs for the children to sing.

"Hang on," Johnny said, waving a hand to stop him. "There are two little girls who would love to join the party. Eirlys, why don't you and Beth go and fetch Hannah and Josie and Marie? They won't have had a party this year."

The others readily agreed and after Eirlys had greeted Ken affectionately and promised to talk later and exchange news not covered in their letters, Johnny saw her off on her errand.

The party seemed to slow into a neutral mood as he waited impatiently for them to return. The music was soft and sentimental and the food was prepared but not served. Crackers were temptingly on display but were held back until Josie and Marie could share the fun.

Johnny had difficulty hiding the delight on his face when Hannah came in, rosy-faced from the cold evening, with her two cosily dressed, very excited daughters. Moll found them a place near Ken and Max while Hannah sat between Granny Moll and Marged, both of whom made her feel very welcome.

Ken gave his seat to Johnny and went to talk to Eirlys, greeting her with an affectionate kiss.

"I've heard all about your war efforts and your promotion at work. You're doing a great job from what I've been told," Ken said, staring at her, admiring her, his eyes glowing and revealing his pleasure at seeing her again.

She left him as he and Max were asked to play and sing, and she hugged Johnny and told him he was the most thoughtful of men to have invited Hannah and her girls. When she looked up to see others agreeing, she saw that Evelyn was glaring at her in her usual belligerent manner. Eirlys hugged Johnny tighter and decided to avoid looking at her for the rest of the evening.

For a while it had seemed that Evelyn's dislike of her had faded. They had been out together, the two of them with Johnny and his brother Taff, and the atmosphere had been tolerably pleasant. Not as relaxed as when they had first became friends, but there had been signs of a thaw in Evelyn's previous frostiness. Eirlys wondered what she had done this time to upset the girl, and decided that Evelyn was one of the unfortunate people who had inexplicable moods. She fervently hoped Taff hadn't married someone like his mother!

It was as they both went out to wash a few dishes that Eirlys asked Evelyn why she was so unfriendly. "You seem to dislike me, but I don't know why. Have I said something or done something to hurt you? I certainly haven't intended to. I want us to be friends when we are sisters-in-law."

"I don't dislike you. I just don't think you are the right person for Johnny."

"But who Johnny marries isn't anything to do with you." Eirlys frowned. "Why are you so concerned?"

"Look to your own family. See what standards they set and you should understand only too well why I'm concerned!" Evelyn threw down the tea towel and left the room.

A chill swept through Eirlys's body. Did Evelyn know about her father and the robbery? Had she learned the truth about how Dadda had broken his ankle? Johnny knew so it wouldn't be too much of a surprise to know he had told Taff. Yet, she thought, the dislike goes back further than the robbery at the newsagent. Could there have been others?

Puzzled, more than a little frightened, but unwilling to follow Evelyn and question her further, Eirlys went on dealing with the dishes. When she picked up a tray of sandwiches Marged had made and went back to rejoin the party, Johnny was dancing with Hannah, with Marie in his arms. They were all laughing and she felt a pang of alarm. He looked so happy.

Hardly surprising, she chided herself, it was Christmas and everyone else looked just as merry. Drink, the occasion and having the family crammed in together plus a few friends could hardly have resulted in sad faces. Nevertheless, she was relieved when he put the little girl down and came to dance with her.

She looked at Evelyn, sitting close to her husband Taff. Was she simply trying to place doubt in her mind? Surely she didn't consider Hannah a better choice for Johnny to marry? That would be too ridiculous.

To try and ease her mind she asked Johnny if he had checked on whether many of the burglaries had taken place on Fridays, when her father pretended to go to the ARP meetings.

"There wasn't a regular pattern," he said, reassuring her. "Besides, your father has been seen once or twice drinking with some friends, and on many Friday evenings he works, because of the shifts the factory uses. Forget it," he said, squeezing her hand as he led her to what Marged laughingly called the dance floor.

The dancing was a comfort to her. There wasn't much room and it was little more than being in Johnny's arms and luxuriating in the sensuous delight of having him near. Soon everyone slowed down and sat where they could find a seat, until the music stopped and people succumbed to the lethargy of too much heat and too much food.

She was reluctant to let Johnny go, needing his nearness, but he left her and went into the kitchen to get cold drinks for Hannah's girls, leaving her standing, conscious of Evelyn's stony stare.

Ken came over and when Johnny rejoined them said, "Congratulations to you both. Eirlys is a special person and you're a lucky man, Johnny Castle." He thumped Johnny on the back, winked at Eirlys and went to take a drink to Max, who was teaching Johnny's cousin Beth to play "Silent Night, Holy Night" on the tubular bells.

Hannah had never beeen so happy. In the stuffy, overheated room, the fire was kept as large as possible, with chestnuts piled and slit ready for roasting. A washing bench had been brought in to provide extra seats and the youngest lolled against its legs with cushions to add to their comfort. Faces were red and damp with sweat, but no one wanted to move, although, Hannah thought with fascination, no one could if they wanted to! This family gathering was something she had never experienced before and she knew she would remember it all her life.

While they recovered from the effort of dancing, a few party games and tricks entertained them all, everyone contributing, even serious little Percival who sang "Daisy Daisy", da-di-da-ing when he couldn't remember the words.

Max put down the accordion and began to play carols on the tubular bells and they sounded magical. Ken sang once or twice and the others listened in silence, wallowing in the atmosphere of peace and contentment, the war a million miles from their thoughts.

Most of the children were asleep before he finished and the silence that followed was more telling than applause. It had been a perfect end to the day.

"Will you be all right going home with your mam and dad?" Johnny asked Eirlys as they all began to move and gather coats and hats. "I'd better make sure Hannah and the children get home safely – in fact, I think I'll have to carry little Marie, don't you?" He pointed to where Marie was sleeping, rosy-faced, in the arms of Granny Moll.

"Would you like me to come with you?" Eirlys asked.

"No, I'll be able to go straight home if I'm on my own." The truth was, he admitted to himself, he didn't want her to. He had spent very little time with her that day; even walking to Mr Gregory's had been more a walk for the evacuees than a romantic stroll with the girl he was planning to marry. What was the matter with him? He should be glad of the opportunity to extend the day and walk her home at the end of it.

"Thanks for a lovely day, Johnny," she said, offering her face for a kiss. In his strange mood, he thought the "thank you" was too casually said: polite, a necessity, but without any real feeling.

Walking back through the silent streets with their breath showing in balloons of steam on the cold air, he felt a greater happiness than he'd felt all day. First the mood Mam had been in had ruined the atmosphere at dinnertime, then, in some way he couldn't fathom, Eirlys hadn't behaved as he had expected either. Now, with the sleepy Marie in his arms, and Hannah beside him trailing a weary Josie, he felt as though this was what he had been waiting for all day.

At the door they went in quietly without turning up the gas light which she had left burning low. "For fear of waking Mam," Hannah explained. So, as she guided the children toward the bedroom behind their living room, Johnny took the opportunity offered, and held her in his arms and kissed her. He hurried away before anything could be said, and ran home feeling like a schoolboy after a first date.

Ken and Max left soon after Christmas. Eirlys was sorry to see them go. She didn't wish them luck as she normally would; with the job they were going to do it was too much like tempting fate. They had added a great deal to the celebrations and she knew that Christmas 1939 was one she would never forget.

A few days after the festivities had ended, Morgan called at Irene's house in Brook Lane after seeing Johnny in the hardware store and Bleddyn opening up the fish-and-chip shop ready for the lunchtime session.

She opened the door to him and fell into his arms with the usual enthusiasm, but then she stepped back and said softly, "Morgan, there's something I have to tell you."

"That sounds serious. You aren't going to tell me goodbye, are you? Irene, love, I couldn't bear that."

"No, it's more the opposite."

"We meet or we don't meet," he laughed. "How can there be another opposite?"

"I think I might be expecting. We're going to have a baby, Morgan love. A baby. Isn't that wonderful?"

"What?" The shock distorted his face as the horror of what she was telling him hit him. He stared at her, then shook her gently, forced a laugh. "Don't make jokes like that, love. Don't try and scare me."

"Don't say things like that! How can you be scared? It's wonderful."

"Irene, you can't be."

"It's true. I've been telling myself it's a mistake, but I've checked and checked and there's no other explanation."

"Will Bleddyn believe it's his?" She didn't reply and when he forced himself to look at her, let her see the dismay written on his face, she had tears in her eyes.

"No, Morgan, this is ours, yours and mine, and I think it's wonderful. I thought you'd be as happy as I am."

"But if we could persuade him, just for the present, while we made plans?"

Tears drizzled down her cheeks and she shook her head. "I can't convince him of that. We've lived like strangers for more than a year."

"I don't know what to do." He sat on a chair and hid his face in his hands.

"Leave Annie. There's nothing else we can do. We have to leave Bleddyn and Annie and the children and go away and start again. Preferably where no one knows us."

"I can't do that. Sorry, Irene, but I can't leave Annie and Eirlys. What would they do? How would they manage?"

"Let them try. We need you more than they do, me and our baby. They're always telling you how useless you are, well, let them see how they manage without you. They don't deserve you, Morgan, love, you know they don't."

They sat discussing it for a long time, each becoming more and more depressed as an alternative solution evaded them. Irene was insistent that Morgan leave Annie and look after her, and Morgan was equally sure that he wouldn't.

After the first subdued exchanges, the comforting words, the declarations of everlasting love, they became more heated and within ten minutes they were quarrelling. Irene was crying, her voice reaching higher and higher until she was almost screaming. Morgan stomped out, for once uncaring about whether or not he was seen.

Irene shouted after him, "If you don't tell Annie, then I will!"

He sat in the park where the grasses and trees were white with frost. A wonderland of wintery beauty, of which he was unaware.

He'd been in trouble before but nothing like this. He couldn't expect Annie to forgive him this. He couldn't tell them. He couldn't face losing Annie and Eirlys. His daughter wouldn't take his side over this. Pacifist she might be but she wouldn't support him now. The decision to stop seeing Irene was easily made but he knew that the solution to the wider situation was not. How could he just walk away and pretend the past few months hadn't happened? She was going to have his child. Whatever he decided, Irene wasn't going to allow him to walk away and face it alone. Scared as he was, he knew he couldn't ask her to do that. The best decision was to wait, do nothing at all in case it was a ghastly mistake. Then, when – or if – it became a certainty, he would have to tell Annie.

Eirlys had called at a wool shop which was closing down and ordered a large quantity of knitting wool at a bargain price. Some was for knitting but much of it, best quality but boring colours, she planned to use for her rug-making. As background to her designs, grey, navy, dark green and maroon were ideal. She was passing the end of Brook Lane when she thought she saw her father. Unlikely, she thought, as he was at work during the afternoons this week. She went to call out to him, but hesitated. Surely it couldn't be him, and wouldn't she look a fool if she chased after a complete stranger? He couldn't have been the only man with a leg in plaster.

A woman was watching her from her front garden: hair in curlers, wearing a cross-over apron, wellingtons on her feet, she was carrying logs she had collected from the pile at the side of the house.

"Looking for someone, are you?" the woman called.

"No, it's all right. I thought I knew that man, but I'm probably mistaken."

"Oh, him. He's always around here, going in through the back gate and thinking no one will see. Furtive he looks to me. That tells you something, eh?" The woman nodded knowingly.

Eirlys was embarrassed, understanding the insinuations. "Then it couldn't have been my father. He has no business around here."

"You can hardly make a mistake with that great lump of plaster on his leg, can you? Your father you say?"

"No, no. It wasn't him. Too tall," she said, inventing any reason to convince the woman she was wrong. She was probably making it all up, Eirlys decided; she looked the sort to enjoy spreading gossip. True or untrue, it probably didn't make any difference.

She hurried away, working hard to convince herself she had been wrong. Then she sighed with relief; if it had been her father he must have been calling on Johnny. Probably returning the scarf Johnny left a few days ago.

Morgan went to work on the bus and got off at the factory. They were pretty lenient about his timekeeping since his accident. He only had to tell them he had a hospital appointment and they didn't ask for proof.

He worked the last hours of his shift and left the factory with the rest. Going straight home he was relieved when Annie was there. After the shock of Irene's announcement he needed the ordinariness of home.

Throughout the late evening, after he had eaten the snack she had prepared for him, he was solicitous, making tea for them and bringing in the tin of biscuits, offering the last of the chocolate ones to her, raking out the fire before being asked, and even going out and, in the thin beam of a torch, bringing in firewood for the next morning in case there wasn't enough already dry. All the time Irene's words echoed around in his head. "Our baby, Morgan. Our baby."

How could he tell Annie he had been carrying on with another woman? She didn't deserve it, she hadn't done anything wrong. In fact, compared with wives of friends, he had been very fortunate, apart from not having a second child. He felt a leap of guilt. That would be another devastating blow for her, another woman bearing the child she couldn't have. His child.

Irene was right about one thing, if they decided to stay together they would have to leave St David's Well. The humiliation and embarrassment would be more than he could cope with. He looked at his wife, hard-working and strong, fierce-looking at times, gentle at others, with a full, generous figure, still very attractive. She was working away at the sock she was knitting, concentrating on turning the heel, counting stitches, frowning slightly. Such an ordinary task, such an ordinary scene, but one to which he might have to say goodbye.

A letter came for him the next morning and, seeing the scrawled writing, he took it from a curious Eirlys and stuffed it into his pocket. It wasn't until Annie had gone to the baker's shop and Eirlys had left for the office that he looked at it, staring at it for a long time before daring to open it. He had never seen Irene's writing, but knew in his heart that she had written it.

Surely it was good news. It had to be. She had been mistaken, she had miscounted the days, it was a false alarm. Several of his friends had told him about those.

In trepidation he tore off the top of the envelope and unfolded the single page. The writing, large and untidy, swam before his eyes.

"If you don't help me I will kill myself," it said.

Irene sat in the doctor's surgery. She was smiling slightly, her eyes glowing with an inner happiness. This was a wonderful thing to have happened. Now she and Morgan would be together. She could leave the boring Bleddyn with his fastidious routines and organised life. She could relax and enjoy herself with the easy-going Morgan. When she considered how they would live she promised herself that she would find work and help pay the bills. That was something she would never do for Bleddyn. He insisted that the only way to help was to work on the sands in the family business and the family made it clear they disapproved of her because she had always refused. She would show them how wrong they had been about her all these years. She wasn't sick or helpless, just bored.

The doctor reached for his pad when he saw her. "More tablets, Mrs Castle?" he asked.

"Not this time, Doctor. I think it's something far more interesting." She bowed her head shyly and said, "I think I am going to have another child."

To her consternation the doctor didn't gasp and tell her it was wonderful and exciting, or jump up and shake her hand and congratulate her. Instead he asked, "How old are you now, Mrs Castle?"

"Old enough not to expect such a wonderful gift."

"I make it forty-four. A little old for babies."

After asking a lot of questions, he examined her, then sat down again behind his desk. "Sorry to disappoint you, but there's no sign of a pregnancy. I think you might be starting the menopause. The change," he added when she looked puzzled. "A little early I agree, but we're all made differently, and there have been other patients of mine who have had a similar experience."

Irene was stunned. All the excitement, the hope of a fresh new life, the thrill of being a mother again, the attention, the pride, it was all gone in those few casually spoken words.

The doctor could see she was upset and added comfortingly, "Mrs Castle, you must realise that nature is kind not to allow us to have babies when we lack the energy to look after them properly. Of course, it might not be the change; what you are experiencing could be due to some other cause, and we will investigate further. Either way, you can relax and know you won't have to face motherhood again. What a relief that must be."

He wrote on his pad, giving her a prescription for her usual pills, and stood as a signal that her time was up. She said nothing, and seemed unable to rouse herself and leave his office. With a hand under her arm he coaxed her out of her chair. "You can sit in the waiting room for a while if you feel tired. Having surprising news sometimes has that effect. It will wear off soon and you will be relieved. Much the best result after your worries, Mrs Castle."

He emphasised that there being no baby was good news, but Irene hardly heard. She had taken in nothing since being told she was experiencing the change of life. She sat in the waiting room and stared at the dull walls. She was old, past child-bearing age, past the age when she could look ahead with hope. She was old, old, old. Her dreams were no longer possible. Her best years were behind her.

Mrs Grainer sat in a chair waiting her turn to see the doctor and she spoke to Irene, but received no response.

Morgan didn't start work that day until two p.m., and he went in search of Irene. He had hardly slept the previous night, worrying about what had happened. Since their talk, every knock at the door threw him into a panic, convinced she had come to tell Annie about their affair. Somehow he had to persuade her to wait, do nothing until they were sure. When she had spoken to him, she had not seen a doctor and it was on this that he based his prayers.

She wasn't at the house on Brook Lane and, finding Bleddyn there on his day off, he made some excuse about wanting Irene to help with the tea-making at the fire-watching station. Bleddyn didn't think it was worth the trouble of asking her. "She won't be keen to help, but I don't know where she is anyway." He was shaking a large mat out in the garden and seemed a bit impatient at being interrupted. "She walks around on her own for hours and I never know where she's been. Ill she is, you know that, don't you? I've given up trying to find out how she fills her time."

"Must be awful for her," Morgan said sympathetically.

"Awful for all of us," Bleddyn replied shortly. "You might try the shops, although shopping is something she rarely does, leaves it to me she does. Like everything else."

Morgan's leg was aching but he stomped along the main street looking for her in the shops without much hope of finding her. At one o'clock he gave up and went home to join Annie and Eirlys for eggs on toast before going to the factory.

Bleddyn didn't see Irene before leaving for the evening shift at the chip shop. He had spent his time off from the lunchtime session doing work that Irene could reasonably be expected to do and he was tired and irritable.

As the time came for him to leave the house, he was also concerned. He didn't like her going out after dark, although as he worked most evenings he could never be sure she was in as she promised to be. He left a note telling her that there was stew in the saucepan for her to heat, called at the hardware shop and told Johnny to make sure she ate it, and went to open up. Something was worrying him and he couldn't understand what it was.

Irene often stayed out until he was at the shop, and he didn't normally worry, but not having seen her all day and being told by Mrs Grainer that she had been to see the doctor set alarm bells ringing. At nine o'clock, unable to wait any longer, he left the assistant in charge and ran home. The house was empty.

He searched through the rooms looking for something – he knew not what – to give him a clue. Then he realised what had been worrying him. Her coat with the fur collar, her only winter coat, was on the back of the door. She was out in the harshness of the January night insufficiently dressed.

He ran to Annie and Morgan's hoping to find Johnny there. Gathering up several of the neighbours, Bleddyn and Johnny began to plan their route to search the streets. "She's done this before," Bleddyn told them as they each collected a blanket and some torches.

Eirlys looked at Johnny and said accusingly, "You didn't believe me when I told you I saw her in the fields without a coat."

"Sorry; I knew you weren't imagining it. I saw her myself a while later and brought her home wrapped in my overcoat. I should have told you, but I try to pretend it isn't true sometimes. She's ill and I can't cope with it."

"You should have told me, Johnny."

"Forget that now, let's just find her."

"I'll go to your house and wait, in case she turns up," she offered.

Morgan came in from work at ten, and was sent around to the ARP centre to ask the wardens to look out for Irene. Everything possible had been done, apart from telling the police, and Bleddyn didn't want to do that until they had tried to find her themselves. "The less fuss for her to deal with the better," he explained. He didn't admit to his fear that another result of police involvement might be her being taken away for treatment in the mental hospital, his greatest dread.

Irene had been given a lift to the outskirts of the town and had walked through the fields towards the caravan. She had left her coat at home and was shivering, dressed only in a black dress and a black cardigan.

She had stood perfectly still against the hedge when Bleddyn and Morgan passed her, stabbing the darkness with their torches and calling her name. The icy cold air had made her shake uncontrollably, but she had smiled as their voices faded away from her.

She sat in the caravan for a while, wrapped in the blankets smelling of mildew, seeking warmth and comfort from the memories it revived. With one of the blankets around her she walked over the now hard and brittle grass to the road and, throwing the blanket away, stopped a van and begged a lift.

The young couple inside were on a visit to the girl's parents and they chatted amiably but without getting much response from Irene. Thanking them for the lift, she got out of the van and went to a lorry park where there was a café, which she had visited several times in the past. It was closed.

A group of lorry drivers were huddled in a corner sharing hot drinks from their flasks and she drank gratefully from one and accepted a lift into the next town. She moved from one town to another and finally, at two a.m., she was standing near the entrance to the docks of a town some thirty miles away from St David's Well.

She knew that the access to the dock area would be heavily guarded, but dressed in dark clothes and being small she thought she might succeed in getting past the soldiers who stood, shuffling their feet, changing position, clearly bored and impatient for their shift to end.

Her chance came when the guard changed and at the same time challenged a workman going to deal with a consignment of food just arriving at the dockside. She slipped easily under the wire and slid out on the other side. She felt a chuckle swell and fill her throat. It was a daring game she was playing, outwitting the soldiers who were armed with guns.

Slowly she made her way to the very edge of the dock. It took her almost an hour but instead of becoming tired, she felt more awake with every minute that passed. She was clever, level-headed, resourceful, talented, all the attributes Bleddyn accused her of lacking. She would succeed without anyone even trying to stop her.

The search continued in St David's Well, hampered by the intense darkness. Once they thought they had found Irene, and the call that went around the countryside and the subsequent relief was felt by everyone.

It turned out to be a female tramp who, when woken, issued a stream of abuse that startled Johnny and Taff, then reduced them to laughter as they imagined their quiet mother knowing such words.

Irene sat near a bollard for a while thinking about the cheerful decorations still covering shop windows and showing at the windows of houses. Tawdry they were, she thought. A pathetic attempt to make Christmas a special time when it was nothing more than an excuse to drink and eat more than you needed. She tried to remember Chistmases when the boys were small, but then, as now, she had backed away from any fun. She blamed Bleddyn. The Castle family tried too hard and made it artificial. Yes, Bleddyn was to blame. And now Morgan was letting her down too. No baby, but he didn't know that. He had refused to help her. There was no one anywhere who cared for her.

There was little light but she could see the water, moving sluggishly, greasy and looking very cold. The surface was several feet below where she was sitting. If she went in there, she would not be able to get back out. She vaguely wondered whether the soldiers would be punished for allowing her to reach the dockside. She was curious but not concerned.

At two o'clock, as Irene was crawling through the wire towards the dockside, Huw called his brother and insisted on informing the police. "Damn it all, Bleddyn, we might be talking about her life here!" he said in exasperation.

Bleddyn agreed and then, as was often the case, their reaction made him wish he had spoken to them earlier.

At once teams were sent out and a series of signals arranged to report if Irene was found or any clues or ideas needed to be shared. The streets of the town and the fields surrounding became unusually busy and activity increased as the night wore on.

"She might have been wandering and now the cold might have made her try and find a place to sleep. We have to find her before her body temperature falls too low," one of the officers told them. Ignoring the fields, they concentrated their searches on the streets near her home. Frustrated by the lack of light, thin torch beams pricked the darkness in alleyways and lanes and on waste ground again and again. People who now worked in close proximity called to each other as the intensive search gathered momentum.

Bleddyn and Huw searched together and they knocked on the door of anyone who might know Irene to ask for news, but no one had seen her. Morgan sneaked off to see if she had gone to their caravan, but the air of neglect and the stale smell that greeted him made him doubt whether the place had been used that day. In the darkness and his melancholy mood he didn't notice the absence of one of the blankets. He told the police about the caravan and explained that it was a place where Irene liked to spend time. He told them he had searched it and thought it had not been recently opened.

Irene became aware of how cold she was. Her whole body was stiff, there was no feeling in her feet and her hands just wouldn't move. She rubbed her arms with her hands once or twice, to try to bring life back. She soon gave up and accepted the lethargic sensation of non-feeling like a friend. A deep sadness overwhelmed her and she slipped gently into the water, momentarily imagining that it was warmer than the air.

Eight

In the mortuary chapel, Bleddyn sat and stared at the body of his wife and wondered what had caused her to be so unhappy that she couldn't face another day.

"I failed her," he said, "but I don't know what else I could have done."

Johnny and Taff were with him, and Taff's wife Evelyn was waiting outside the room.

Taff said, "She was ill, Dad, you can't blame yourself for this."

"But I do. I should have cared for her more. I worked long hours, specially in the summer, and she was left on her own day after day."

"I can't remember a time when she was not ill," Taff said. "We were always making excuses for her. How can this be your fault?"

Johnny asked, "Did you know how ill she was?"

"I learned recently that she was a difficult and confused child and was suicidal when she was a very young woman, besides the attempts I knew about."

"I mean, when you married her, did you know about the depression? Her strange moods? The family must have known. Did they tell you?"

Bleddyn shook his head. "No, I had no idea. They kept it from me."

"If you had known, would you still have married her?" Taff asked.

Bleddyn stared into space but did not reply.

Johnny wasn't a man to show his emotions easily, certainly not within his family, but he had a strong impulse to hug his father.

Unaware that Irene's body had been found, Morgan walked up and down the living room. It was four in the morning and he hadn't slept. The air was painfully cold and most of the searchers had given up at three a.m. planning to begin again at dawn. Even the places they had looked for her would have to be examined again, as, with the limited light from weakening torches, no one could be sure she hadn't been there, tucked up small, hiding from them in her confusion.

Where was Irene? He dreaded her being found. This time she would have a reason to explain her black mood: his refusal to accept her child and go away with her. He had avoided her since her announcement. She was bound to tell Bleddyn, and Annie was certain to find out. Or, worse still, she would come here and tell Annie to her face about their affair. He had to save Annie from that humiliation. He had to tell Annie himself. At least then she would be able to prepare her response, salvage a little dignity. He owed her that.

He imagined Annie opening the door to Irene, inviting her in, smiling and welcoming, then listening as Irene told her about her affair with Annie's husband, told her she was carrying his child. That would be cruel, and, coward as he undoubtedly was, he had to save Annie from that.

His thoughts drifted and returned to the shock of the note Irene had sent him. He had to see beyond the words. It had been a warning that Irene would tell Annie and Eirlys if he didn't agree to take her away. She wouldn't kill herself as the note threatened, that was just a touch of drama, to frighten him into agreeing to go away with her.

He had kept the fire burning and the room was stifling. He opened the back door and to his surprise it was snowing. He imagined Irene lying somewhere, slowly, silently being covered by the beautiful but insidious and deadly flakes. Shivering more from the image than the temperature, he closed the door and leaned against it trying to blot out the fearful pictures his mind was creating. He had to find her, but where could he look? He searched his mind for clues but thought only of the caravan, their secret love nest. How pathetic that sounded now.

He went into the living room and lifted some ashes to liven the fire. It burned brightly in the frosty air. He still shivered. Would he ever feel warm again? Sticks snapped and blazed but he didn't add coal; he needed the flames to take away the darkness in his heart. But he knew the brightness was a sham, just as his pretence of loving Irene had been. The fire burned itself out, became a heap of grey ash, and looked dead.

At five thirty a.m. he could wait no longer. He made a tray of tea and went up. He shook Annie, pulling her reluctantly from a deep sleep. "Annie, love. There's something I have to tell you."

He would never forget the way his words altered her sleep-rosy face. The way her eyes – reluctant to open – suddenly widened in disbelief. Her scream of anguish woke Eirlys who came running, presuming her mother had had a nightmare.

"Nightmare? No, Eirlys, not a nightmare, this is real. Your father—"

Morgan stopped her by putting a hand across her mouth. "Think, woman. We don't want our daughter to hear all this."

He released his hand and Annie stared at him in silence.

"Go back to your room, Eirlys, love. Your mam and I have something serious and very private to discuss."

Puzzled and not a little worried, Eirlys did what she was told, getting back into bed and covering her ears with a pillow. It was yet another row and she didn't want to hear, to try to take sides.

Ashen-faced, Annie stared at her husband. "I want to hear the full story," she said, her voice distorted by grief.

"Irene Castle and I have been meeting secretly for months."

"Where?" Annie demanded.

"Sometimes at her house in Brook Lane, and we had a caravan where we used to spend some time."

"Go on."

"Now she says she's going to have a baby and she wants me to leave you and I can't. I don't expect you to understand this, but I love you, Annie, and I haven't the slightest excuse for the stupid way I've behaved."

"A baby? Irene was going to have a baby? Your baby? But she's past forty. I was told it was too late for us when I was much younger than that."

Both were momentarily distracted from the present, thinking back to the large family they had both wanted. Irene's baby was the greatest agony of all. Neither of them knew what to say.

Then Annie pushed the tray angrily from the chair beside her bed and stared at it as it clattered to the floor. Morgan bent to pick up the shattered china but stopped. Picking up broken cups, clearing up the mess was too ordinary. They stared at each other in confusion. Both were stunned. This was something for which neither of them was prepared. If only he hadn't had to tell her about the baby.

Annie's mind flittered over all her friends and their families, aware than none of them had ever been involved in anything as sordid as this.

"I'll go and see Johnny and ask if there's any news," he said, backing out of the room.

"No you don't! I'll go!" Annie announced, bouncing out from under the covers. "I want to see this Irene when they find her; I want to tell her she can have you as from now this minute. I never want to set eyes on you again. Ever!" Turning to her husband she stared at him as though he were repulsive and said harshly, "Get out! I want you and your things out of this house before I get back."

"Don't try to see her, Annie. You'll be better off hanging on to your dignity and saying nothing."

"Give me the pleasure of telling her to her face what I think of her and her nonsense about depression! Depression indeed. Just an excuse to hang around waiting to meet her fancy man. Or men! It's unlikely you're the only one, so don't kid yourself you're so special! Or that you're the father," she added bitterly.

"I told her I wouldn't leave you, that's why she went off like she did," Morgan said.

"Well, you were wrong! As always, I have to make the decisions in this house. You *are* leaving and you're never coming back." She held back a sob as she added, "You and that tart and her child – who might or might not be yours – gone from this house you'll be before I get back. Right?"

Morgan followed her downstairs, where Annie reached for a long mackintosh and wellington boots. "Annie, love, you can't go out like that!" he protested. "You have to get dressed."

"Why? The mood I'm in, how I dress isn't important. Scragging that woman's neck is!"

"You're in the position of strength here, you haven't done anything wrong. Dress and put your make-up on, look smart and in control. That's the way to best someone."

Annie sagged as though all the strength had flowed out of her. "You're right. For once in your miserable life! I'll have a cup of tea, calm myself down, then I'll dress and go and face her. She's bound to be home by now. Stupid woman. Forty-five if she's a day and having half the town chasing after her as though she was a runaway child!"

There was a knock at the door as she was filling the kettle and she opened it to Johnny. At once she felt a twisting pain. How could she face him, knowing her husband had been having an affair with his mother? She stepped back and invited him inside.

"Mam's dead," he whispered.

She gestured for him to go into the living room where fire glowed meanly amid grey wood ash. Behind her she heard Morgan gasp. She turned and he pleaded with his eyes for her not to stay what was on her lips. He pulled her aside and whispered, "Wait, Annie, please. Not for me, for others. If we don't want to ruin everything for Eirlys and Johnny, we have to keep this from her. Don't say anything yet. Think of how this would wreck her and Johnny's life if she finds out. Let him tell us what happened, shall we?"

Somehow the plea worked and Annie remained silent and continued to make the tea with hands that shook uncontrollably.

They went into the living room where Johnny was sitting upright and uncomfortable on a hard chair. His voice shook as he told them how his mother's body had been taken from the dock after being found in the water by soldiers. She had been seen as the dawn light exposed her body, caught in some lengths of wood, her dress tangled and holding her from the depths.

Morgan heard him out then ran upstairs and locked himself in the bathroom. Imagining the scene as Irene had been pulled from her watery grave, he was crying like a child. He kept pulling the chain of the lavatory to drown the sound of his despair. He needn't have told Annie; that was the cruellest part. She need not have been made to suffer the pain of his betrayal. He could have avoided her ever finding out. If he had only waited another hour, he would have been safe. What an irony to have ruined his life and Annie's, for the sake of an hour's silence. To think he had woken her at that unearthly hour instead of waiting till morning.

Johnny waited while Annie woke Eirlys so she could be told. Morgan left the house then, and went across the picturesque fields, white with the brightness of the rising sun, to sit in the cold caravan, wrapped in misery, shame and the remaining mildewed blanket.

Eirlys went at once to see Bleddyn when Johnny told her the news.

She expected to help, but Bleddyn told her firmly, "I've managed more or less on my own all these years, I don't think I'll suddenly become useless."

"I just thought, with the funeral, and all the running around you'll have to do, I might help Evelyn prepare the food or something."

"It's all in hand." Bleddyn spoke abruptly and Eirlys shrugged and looked at Johnny as though to say, Well, I tried.

For days the snow stayed on the ground and frost had the streets in such a grip that people had difficulty getting around. The pavements were cleared and immediately covered again with treacherous ice and a covering of snow, and several people fell and broke bones.

Morgan stayed indoors and grieved for Irene and for his ruined marriage. Annie went about her usual routine: the bakery each morning, household tasks and shopping during the afternoon. She and Morgan didn't exchange a word. The pain of his betrayal ruined every moment of every day for Annie, remorse and bitterness affecting his.

Eirlys knew something was wrong but had no idea what it could be. She did tell her mother once that with Johnny's mother dead they should be thankful they had each other and manage to agree at least until the funeral. Annie shouted at Eirlys in such anger that she burst into tears without, for once, Annie's comfort there for her.

The post mortem revealed no pregnancy. No rumours had reached Bleddyn's ears about Irene having a secret lover. He believed that her insistence that there was both had been pure fantasy. Irene had lived in a fantasy world, cut off from reality; the imagined baby and lover were just symptoms of her sickness.

The newspaper reports were kind. They said that she suffered from depression and had become confused, and added that her devoted family were in shock.

Having read the reports, Morgan was convinced he was safe from discovery, and on the day before the funeral he dared to visit Bleddyn. In a bag, hidden under a few apples, he had a large tin of corned beef.

"Don't ask where it came from because I don't know and I daren't ask," he said, lifting the heavy tin from the bag. "I thought it might be useful for you to make sandwiches when the mourners come back. Hide the tin, mind. It has Ministry of Food stamped on the side!"

"I want to get rid of her clothes as soon as possible," Bleddyn said accepting the tin and putting it on the table.

"Hide it, man, unless you want us both arrested!"

"It'll upset Johnny and Taff to see her clothes hanging there, and they wouldn't like to help me to clear them out." He seemed not to have heard Morgan's warning. "I don't suppose you'd help, would you? Perhaps your Eirlys would like some of the stuff for her rug-making. I hear she's sold a few. Clever girl she is, mind. A clever girl. Johnny's a lucky man."

Morgan felt sick. If Bleddyn only knew what he was asking him to do. Yet he couldn't refuse. He looked at Bleddyn's face, strong and without a sign of suspicion. If only he hadn't told Annie, the secret of their meetings would never have come to light. Confession good for the soul? That's a laugh!

Bleddyn handed him a clean sack and beckoned for him to follow. He began to sweat as he walked up the stairs and couldn't believe how casually Bleddyn was talking. It was more like a discussion on the possessions of a stranger than his wife, and the mother of his sons.

"You seem very calm," he said, as Bleddyn led him upstairs and into the room where, so recently, he and Irene had spent passionate moments.

"Outwardly perhaps. I show control and strength for the sake of Johnny and Taff. Inside it's different. I think anger is my greatest emotion at the moment. How could she have cared so little for the boys and me that she could kill herself?"

"Best you believe it was an accident," Morgan advised. "That would be easier to cope with, and she was wandering around the docks in pitch blackness, wasn't she? How are we to know she didn't slip?"

"Because she left a note, telling me she was sick of her boring life and sick of me."

Morgan's heart leapt painfully. "Did she say anything else?" He looked at the powerfully built Bleddyn. Had he found out about him and Irene? Had he led Morgan up to this room so he could thump the life out of him? But the man seemed in control.

"She said she had a lover, but I don't believe that."

"Trying to hurt you, was she?"

"Succeeded too, for a while, until I realised she was living a fantasy. She also said she was carrying this man's child. She was going on forty-five, for God's sake! Anyway, the post mortem found no sign of it. The doctor told me she was very upset at being told it was probably the change of life and not a baby. She had a fear of getting old." He pulled open a drawer and began throwing clothes angrily onto the bed, his control slipping for a moment. "Fantasy, that was how she lived, by pretending that some wonderful life was just around the corner. A life that didn't include me," he finished quietly, and for the first time Morgan saw a hint of sadness and grief in the big man's dark eyes.

The funeral was sombre and made worse by the messy snow that still lingered. Morgan attended and stood beside the family, shaking with fear lest something about his involvement should come to light. He began to work out an escape route, but with this damned plaster he couldn't even run away. What was he doing here? Annie had insisted, telling him he owed the woman this final show of regret and reminding him he must look at the coffin and take at least some of the blame.

He had the face of a grieving man, but the grief was for himself and his ruined marriage.

Annie wondered how she would manage on her own. With Eirlys and Johnny getting married soon and her insistence – so far ignored – that Morgan should leave, she would be on her own for the first time in her life. It was tempting to forgive him sufficiently to allow him to stay, but her pride was strong. She dug her nails into her hands, trying to make the tears come. If only she could have a damned good cry and release the awful agony, she might start to feel stronger. Thank goodness she had Stanley, Harold and Percival. It was partly for their sake she hadn't thrown Morgan out on that first day. They needed him and didn't deserve to be deprived of an important person in their lives because of her pride and unhappiness.

Stanley and Harold and Percival had integrated well at school and with the neighbourhood's children. Most of the other evacuees had left and they were separated from their school friends only by their spurious maturity and their accents, although Percival was already beginning to copy his friends, coming out with pronunciation different from his brothers' accent, and Welsh word patterns.

Sledging and snowball fights were not new experiences for them but walks in the woods and fields were, and they came home at night cold, soaked right through to their skins and starving. Their appetites were enormous apart from Percival, who still had trouble with anything that needed chewing.

The snow returned, and, much to the boys' delight, Morgan had to dig his way around to the coal house and cut a path to the street. As it was a weekend they were introduced to the delights of sledging.

Dragging the home-made sled through the field, with Percival sitting on it like a disapproving master pulled by servants, dressed in so many layers he could barely move, their progress was a noisy, colourful sight. Led by Eirlys and Morgan, with Stanley and Harold pulling their small brother, they were not the only ones heading for the steep field beyond those owned by Mr Gregory. They were soon at the head of an ever-growing procession with others appearing from different directions. Some had sleds and gathering around them hoping for a ride or two were several of their friends.

Once the snow had been flattened and the ice had done its bit, the rides became faster and faster, the shouts louder and the faces redder. Scarves and even coats were discarded as they toiled up the slope dragging the sleds ready for another ride down the steeply sloping field, to come to a juddering stop on the hard furrows of the ploughed field below.

There were moans of regret when Eirlys and her father insisted that it was time to go. Even Percival ate without complaint when Annie served up some warm stew and freshly baked bread and they all declared it was their best day ever. Annie wondered whether they would be able to resist the temptation of running away from school if the snow was still there on Monday, and decided to ask Eirlys to walk them there and make sure they went in!

On the following Saturday, with the snow "still hanging around for more", as her mother insisted, Johnny called, and Eirlys apologised for not being ready to go out with him as planned. "The boys are due back from the fields any minute and Mam has had to go out. Sorry Johnny, but I have to be here to dry them off and get them a hot meal."

"Something smells good," Johnny sniffed appreciatively.

"They're up in Sally Gough's field next to where Mr Gregory's donkeys spend the winter. Spending the morning sledging down the sloping grass on a sled Dad made them," Eirlys explained. "Not much snow left, but they insisted on trying to find a place. Why don't you stay and eat with us? I'm cooking one of their favourites, sausages and mash."

"Thanks, I will. Is your dad eating with us?"

"How do I know? If Mam is in, Dadda is out and vice versa. I don't know what's wrong, but they've had a serious quarrel about something."

"They'll soon forget it. This isn't the first time, is it?"

"Not by a long way." She smiled ruefully. "Always arguing about something or other, and Mam usually wins. Even if she's in the wrong it's Dadda who does the apologising. Daft isn't it?"

"Anything for peace. I know a few blokes like that." He looked at her quizzically. "Will I have to say sorry when it's you who burns my dinner?" He nodded towards the grill, where the sausages were beginning to spit angrily.

She took them away from the heat and on to a rack to drain the fat into a basin. "Can't waste good dripping. Not now fats are rationed."

Johnny helped set the table then the boys came in, soaking wet, freezing cold and starving, and excited by a letter from their mother telling them that a few weeks ago, "their" River Thames had frozen over. He waited contentedly while Eirlys took the boys upstairs to rub them dry and dress them in clean, warm clothes.

Stanley and Harold cleared their plates fast, but as usual, Percival pulled a face and chewed the same mouthful for a long time, reluctantly, with his lips apart.

"These sausages is boverin' me," he whined in a low voice. Before the words were out, two forks were winging through the air and the sausages were whipped off his plate.

"You could at least ask!" Eirlys scolded, glaring at the two elder boys happily chewing their extra treat. Then she saw Johnny trying in vain to hide his laughter and they relaxed and enjoyed the joke. Pudding was chocolate cake heated and served with custard, and this Percival ate with relish.

"I'm concerned about Percival's poor diet," Eirlys said as she washed the dishes.

"'These sausages is boverin' me'." Johnny mocked Percival's complaint, laughing. "I don't see why you worry. He eats what he wants and he's the best judge of what's good for him. You worry too much," he said, standing close, nuzzling her neck affectionately, his arms around her trim waist. "If you're like this with strangers, what will you be like with your own?"

The prospect made her blush. "I can't imagine letting my child go away from me to live with strangers. I'd want to be with him every minute. As he grows up, and wants to go out on his own, I'll delay the day for as long as possible, then I'll march up and down until he comes back to me." She smiled. "That's how I feel now but I expect mothers gradually learn to let them go. We have to or we'd be a nation of madwomen."

"You'll be a wonderful mother," he assured her.

"Talking about mothers, I saw Hannah on my way home from work. She was dressing a small snowman for Josie and Marie. I watched as Josie and Marie threw snowballs at it, laughing, even throwing one at their mother.They were so excited. I think she's wonderful the way she copes without any help. Don't you think so?"

"I do. Those little girls are so content and well behaved, she must be doing a remarkable job. We were right to invite them to share our Christmas, weren't we?"

"Perhaps we can invite them to tea when the weather is better and they can play in the garden with the boys."

"Or sooner, so the boys can introduce them to Snap, Old Maid and dominoes."

"All right then, what about tomorrow?"

Having given up on the walk they had planned, Johnny left by mid-afternoon. It was Saturday and he had promised to help his father in the chip shop that evening to give him an evening off.

"He's still very shocked and I know he isn't sleeping very much," he explained. "I hear him wandering downstairs at odd times, and I sometimes find him sitting looking through photograph albums as though trying to find a clue to her unhappiness. It was the way she died that makes it worse," he went on. "Dad can't accept that Mam chose to leave us. We hoped the verdict would be accidental death, but the note, and the deliberate way she went to a place where she was unlikely to be seen, all suggested suicide."

"Was she always ill? I mean, when you were small, did she play games and have fun?"

"It was Dad who played games and provided our fun. I asked him if he knew before he married her that she suffered with her nerves, and he said her family kept it from him. That was wrong, I think."

"I wish I could help, but your father is a solitary man, isn't he? He'll deal with it in his own way and in his own time."

When Johnny left Eirlys, he didn't go straight home. There were a couple of hours yet before he needed to get ready for the chip shop. Unplanned, his feet led him to Hannah's door.

With the brief discussion about his mother still in his mind, when Hannah invited him inside, leaving the door open and letting in the cold wind, he continued his thoughts with her.

"Why can someone hate life so much they want to die?" he asked. They were in the kitchen leaving the girls in the living room where they were too far away to hear him.

"I know that kind of despair," Hannah told him sadly. "I wanted to die when I could see no way out of my situation. But with your mother it couldn't have been anything like that," she added hastily. "She seemed to me to have everything she could possibly want."

"I should have seen her desperation and been able to help her."

"You have to accept that she was sick, Johnny, seriously sick, and no one could help her get well. There are many kinds of terminal illnesses, remember. She suffered from one that is less easy to accept."

Her words soothed him as no others had. He felt the strain of the past weeks leaving him. Her suffering had not made her bitter but more sympathetic; she had a greater understanding because of it.

"Your marriage was deeply unhappy. Can I ask you whether he was violent before you married, and whether you were warned?"

"He had beaten up a young boy once, when he was sixteen. His parents and he convinced me it had been an experience he would never repeat. When you're in love, Johnny, you hear what you want to hear, believe what it's comfortable to believe."

"Dad and Mam didn't have a real marriage. Eirlys's parents are rowing all the time. You suffered real distress. I wonder if there is such a thing as a happy marriage."

"Don't become cynical. Some couples argue but still love each other. Don't mistake that for an unhappy marriage. Like terminal illnesses, there are many different kinds of marriage, except most kinds of marriage are good." She went in to see that the girls were warm enough then returned to the kitchen where, for the moment, with her mother out shopping, they were able to talk in private.

"I married at twenty-two, to escape from my parents' criticism and disapproval, and went from one set of problems into another. They disliked me for being alive when my brother was dead. He died of pneumonia you see. I had the flu first, just after the last war, when I was eight. I recovered, I passed it to him and he died, so his death was my fault and there was never a day when they didn't remind me of that."

"That's so cruel," Johnny gasped.

"Yes, I found it hard to bear. So when Laurie came along and offered freedom, I took it. We had two rooms over a china shop in Barry, and I thought I was in heaven. I worked in a shop not far from where we lived and he worked on the docks. The first few months were good ones. Then he was injured. He suffered a broken leg, crushed ribs and head injuries as he was unloading a cargo of pig-iron, and he changed from a loving husband into a foul-tempered bully.

"He accused me of neglecting him if I was late back from the shop. Then I discovered that he was using our money for drink. We couldn't pay the bills and were thrown out of the flat. I found us a room and he went on blaming me for everything. He hit me if the meal wasn't to his liking, or for some other imagined slight." Her lovely eyes clouded. "I lost the baby I was carrying, and he and my parents blamed me for not taking proper care of it. My parents told me it was God's punishment. As if a caring God would kill an innocent baby to punish me! I was never that important, was I? No God of Love for them. Their God was just an excuse for disapproval and punishments."

"So you left him," Johnny coaxed as she paused.

"So I left him. My parents disapproved of my leaving him and wouldn't help. I stayed with a friend, Iolo James, but my mother told Laurie where I was and he came and—" She couldn't go on.

Johnny guessed she was thinking about rape and he hugged her until her sobs subsided. "Don't tell me any more, love. It's upsetting you too much."

"If you can bear it, Johnny, I want to tell you the whole story. I can't talk about it to anyone else."

Johnny continued to hold her as she went on, "One day he attacked my friend Iolo thinking it was me and the police caught up with him.

Iolo and her husband took me to a doctor then to a solicitor, and they supported me through the divorce. Then, unfortunately, they moved away to look for work. It was Eirlys and her parents who were my only friends at that time. Using their quasi-religion against them they persuaded my parents it was their Christian duty to give us a home. My parents reluctantly agreed to my sharing their house. I'm here under sufferance, but I stay so Josie and Marie can have some stability in their lives."

"I think your parents should be immensely proud of you," Johnny said, pressing her against him as her sobs began again. For a long time they didn't move. The kiss when it came seemed the most natural thing in the world, and when they walked back into the living room to sit with the girls, who were playing with a doll's house Hannah had made from shoeboxes, they sat close together, hand in hand, silently digesting what had just happened between them.

Annie didn't think she would have coped with Morgan's revelation without Stanley, Harold and little Percival. Although she had been unwilling to accept them at first, she dreaded every letter they received from their mother, expecting that, like the rest of the evacuees, she wanted her boys to go home. So far the feared bombing of London had not happened, with the Germans fighting on land, pushing their way through France, and using the might of the Luftwaffe to destroy shipping.

Teresa's letters were full of cheerful little anecdotes about the building of air raid shelters and the boring lectures given to householders about the way to deal with incendiary bombs. She wrote about the queues and the meanness of the grocers when they doled out the ration of butter; no pleading would persuade them to allow the knife to slip back beyond the weekly allowance of four ounces, she reported. Annie sent her a cake, made with butter, for which she had exchanged some sugar of which she had plenty.

She wrote assurances that the boys were missing her but were well and happy, reminding Teresa of the importance of their staying in St David's Well where they were safe. With the estrangement between her and Morgan continuing into the forseeable future, she needed the boys as much – if not more – than they needed her.

Johnny couldn't get Hannah out of his mind. They had parted that afternoon without anything being discussed. Memories of the kiss had shone in Hannah's eyes as they said their goodbyes, and he knew she could recognise the desire lingering in his. He had to talk to someone, but who?

He was in love with Hannah. He had to admit it and face the consequences. She refused to marry him but how could he marry Eirlys feeling this way about another woman? Could he persuade Hannah to change her mind? Every strand of common sense told him he was being stupid, giving up someone like Eirlys for a woman who was older, divorced and with two little girls. He was very fond of Eirlys and she was a perfect choice for a wife – clever, ambitious and quite lovely – so what was wrong with him? Perhaps he should wait until the army took him away from St David's Well and marry neither.

The thought of going to war loomed and momentarily obliterated his confusion. He could walk away. He had to forget Hannah and marry Eirlys. Once they were married the dreams of another life would fade. Wouldn't they?

He went to the chip shop and worked there until eleven o'clock, staying behind to drain the fat, clean out the cooking range and wash the last utensil. His actions and responses had been automatic and he remembered hardly a thing about the hours he had spent cooking and serving the food.

He walked home past the houses of Granny Moll Piper and his Uncle Huw and Auntie Marged. No light was visible in either house, but on impulse he knocked on the window of Granny Moll's and waited to see if she answered.

The door opened and Moll's sharp voice asked who was there.

"It's Johnny, Granny Moll. I know it's late, but can I come in?"

Juggling with the blackout curtain, Moll led him into the living room, where a low fire still burned, grey ash at the front with only a faint glow of red at the back. "The fire's gone next door," Moll said, with a smile, adding a couple of logs to rouse it.

"I wanted to talk to someone and I thought you might still be awake," Johnny began. "Not the call-up, is it?" Moll asked at once. "I don't know how they expect us to run the business if they take all our able-bodied men."

"No, nothing yet, although I don't think they'll hang about much longer. Millions gone and it still isn't enough. No, it's about how I feel about Eirlys; that's what's worrying me."

"Don't tell me you've changed your mind about marrying her? I was depending on Eirlys joining the family to help us next summer! People will still want to come to St David's Well Bay for some fun, Hitler or no Hitler. We'll need her on the sands or in Piper's Café."

"I don't know how I feel about her any more."

"What went wrong?" Moll asked, pushing the kettle over on to the fire and stirring the coals with a poker.

"I have strong feelings for someone else."

"Who is she? Someone who'd fit in with the family business?"

"Granny Moll! It's my life I'm thinking about, not Piper's cafés and stalls!"

"We have to be practical." Moll grinned. She got up and began to mix cocoa, sugar and milk in the bottom of two cups, then added water from the gently simmering kettle. "Drink this and tell me all about it."

When Johnny mentioned Hannah she frowned. "She's too old and she's got a ready-made family. That's not what your father would want for you, Johnny."

They talked over the situation until two a.m., by which time Johnny was far more confused than when he came. Moll's advice was for him to arrange to marry Eirlys as soon as possible. He was assured that once he was married and settled down in a home of his own with a loving wife, all thoughts of other women would magically vanish from his mind.

Walking home through the dark, silent streets, Johnny wondered wryly whether Moll's solution was the best one for him or for herself and Piper's Café. She might be right about that early wedding, though. Several of his friends had married sooner than intended, wanting to be sure there was someone waiting for them when the war ended and they came home. They told him that it would make them strong to have someone to survive for and now he was beginning to understand what they meant.

When Johnny discussed Moll's idea of an early wedding, he put it to Eirlys as his own, explaining that his application to defer call-up on account of the family business might not be successful.

"I want to know you'll be here, waiting for me while I'm away.

Helping on the sands, keeping everything safe until I come home. Lovely word that, 'home', it's what you'll be making for us while I'm away."

There were the usual misgivings in Eirlys's heart, so she didn't answer him immediately. She loved Johnny, she longed to be his wife, but she didn't want to give up on her dreams and become a housewife until she had created a life of her own. So far the idea of how that would be achieved had not materialised.

"I love my job," she told him, trying to explain how she felt. "Now, with fewer men available, I'm being given more and more responsibility and I love it. The stalls in the summer would be fun but it wouldn't be enough for me, specially if you go away. I want a career or a business of my own, not sharing your family's."

"And is that the only reason you're refusing me?"

"I'm not refusing you. I love you, Johnny and I want to be your wife more than anything in the world. I want us to have a home of our own. I could build it ready for when you come home, but I don't want to give up my job and ambitions and work for Piper's."

"You don't have to. Although," he added with a grin, "I'll be surprised if Granny Moll doesn't persuade you to spend some spare time helping out, mind."

"I'd like that very much."

"So if we can find somewhere to live, a place where we can build a home, you'll say yes?"

She loved him. Why was she hesitating? Unromantically she knew too that at twenty-two she might not have another chance to do all the things women wanted to do, marry and have children, create a home. If she let Johnny go because of some vague idea of a business of her own she would be a fool. There would never be anyone else she could love as much as she loved Johnny. There was also the pull of belonging to the Castles' large and lively family. Apart from Taff's wife Evelyn, they had all been very welcoming.

"All right, Johnny, let's get married soon."

A little later, when they had celebrated their decision with a kiss, Johnny laughed and said, "I'm so happy, Eirlys." For a while, he meant it.

"Who knows," Eirlys laughed, "it might even bring Mam and Dadda together."

* * *

Predictably, Bleddyn and Taff were pleased but Evelyn was not.

They met as they were each calling separately on Bleddyn's house in Brook Lane. Evelyn proudly placed a cake on the kitchen table and told Bleddyn she had made it for him. Rather self-consciously Eirlys put her offering beside it. Annie had made him an apple tart with apple rings dried the previous summer. They eyed each other, the gifts a challenge.

Bleddyn smiled at them and said, "I'm beginning to see the advantage of having a couple of daughters-in-law."

"Rushing it, aren't you," Evelyn hissed when Bleddyn left the two girls alone, "getting married before you're even engaged?"

"It's Johnny who didn't want to wait," Eirlys explained. "Why don't you ask him?"

The wedding was fixed for the end of March, Saturday the thirtieth, and they both hoped that the army didn't claim Johnny beforehand.

At once Annie started talking to Morgan.

"You can forget that suit you wanted to buy, and your shoes will have to do for a while longer. I'm not having those Castles showing us up. You can hire a suit and I'll get a good dress and we'll show them how it should be done. Right?"

They had hardly exchanged a word since Annie had learned of his "carrying on" with Irene Castle, and Morgan had only been allowed to stay on condition that he slept in the boxroom with the suitcases and the artificial Christmas tree, the discarded picture frames and boxes of children's books and abandoned toys. She reminded him, when he complained, that a two-foot-six camp bed was better than he deserved.

Now that they had something to discuss, barriers fell, although the conversation was extremely one-sided. After Annie had reeled off lists of things to be done, she would glare at Morgan, who had been more or less silent throughout, and demand that he took a greater interest in his daughter's big day.

"I don't think our Eirlys is really sure about this," Morgan said, doubtfully.

"Nonsense. Of course she wants to marry Johnny Castle. They've been discussing it for weeks. It's only this war that's making them change their minds about waiting till next year."

"Will there be a party?" Stanley wanted to know.

"A boring one for grown-ups, I expect," moaned Harold.
"Food?"
"Plenty of it," Annie promised. "A really splendid meal."
"I just want the pudding," Percival told them firmly, "or I ain't going."

On the subject of where they would live, Johnny suggested asking his father if they could live there with Eirlys running the house for them.

"I'll be keeping my job," she told him, "but I can easily manage both."

When they put the idea to Bleddyn he rudely refused.

"I've run the house most of my married life," he said. "I don't see the need to change that. You two can find a couple of rooms somewhere, can't you, without me having to disrupt my life?"

Eirlys began looking at the "To Let" columns of the local paper and asking all her friends to make enquiries. "We'll find something soon," she said to Johnny, "and your father is right, we need to start off with a place of our own." She was hurt by the abrupt refusal but hid her feelings from him, supporting Bleddyn in his decision. She did not want to start married life by upsetting Johnny's father.

Two days later, Bleddyn called on her. When Morgan saw the big man walking up the front path, an aggressive expression on his face, his heart began to race and he was filled with the desire to run. His injured ankle throbbed in sympathy with the rest of him and he felt the strength leak out of him. He wanted to hide but knew his legs wouldn't support him. Bleddyn had found out about him and Irene! Why else would he call? He never called.

"Annie? Eirlys?" he called. "We've got a visitor." He waited for his wife or daughter to open the door. Like a coward he remained in his chair and succumbed to panic.

Bleddyn took off his hat and sat with it resting on his knee when Annie showed him into the living room. Morgan stuck out his injured leg as a shield to prevent attack, but Bleddyn smiled and shook his hand.

"Good news about your Eirlys and my Johnny, eh?" he said shaking the nervous Morgan's hand. "It's Eirlys I came to see. In, is she?"

Eirlys entered the room and he said at once, "I'm sorry, Eirlys. I was very rude to you when you suggested moving in with me. It was a generous thought and I shouldn't have been so unkind."

"It's all right, Mr Castle. It was Johnny thinking you needed looking after. I knew you were perfectly capable of running your life without any assistance from us," Eirlys replied.

She tried to smile but her lips were stiff with tension. From his demeanour it was clear he had something more to say, and she waited, dreading to hear his opinion that they were wrong to plan the wedding so soon. It had to be that. Why else would he have called? Like her father she thought, he never calls.

Bleddyn took a piece of paper out of his pocket and slowly unfolded it. Morgan, guilt making him imagine the worst, peered over to try and read it, envisaging a newly discovered letter from Irene, telling of his guilt. The man was tormenting him, playing him like a cat with a mouse, hoping he would relax before he dealt the first blow. Then he realised it looked like an address.

For a moment he felt relieved, then he remembered. The caravan! Bleddyn had found out about their meeting at the caravan! He sank deeper into his chair, wishing he could disappear.

"What's the matter with you?" Annie asked coldly.

"Bellyache. Too many pickled onions last night!"

"This shop is closing down," Bleddyn explained, handing the paper to Eirlys. "It was a wool shop and there are boxes and boxes of wool to be sold. Skeins of every colour so far as I could see. I thought, with your rug-making, you might take a look, and if you can use it, I'll help you to buy it if you wish. Some of it is in a right old muddle; looks as though a cat's had fun with it, so it's bound to be cheap."

Morgan was shaking when Bleddyn and Eirlys left to investigate the possibilities and Annie told him that if he was getting a cold he could sleep downstairs as she wasn't going to risk catching it. He wondered if anyone except Eirlys knew he and Annie weren't sharing a bed. It would only need a slight suspicion and something like that could start Bleddyn thinking.

Two and two weren't difficult to add up, he thought anxiously. He was still in danger of something being said. Someone could easily have seen them together and it would only take a word to Bleddyn for him to guess the rest. He shuddered.

"I've made a decision," he said to Annie firmly, although afraid to look her in the eyes. "I'm not sleeping on that damned camp bed any more. If you don't let me come back to a proper bed so I can have a good night's sleep, I'm going to find lodgings. And," he went on, as courage grew out of desperation, "and I won't go to our daughter's wedding either. It'll be a farce with me pretending to be your husband, and, well, I'm not doing it. So?" he asked, daring to look at her.

For a moment he thought his gamble had failed then she nodded and said, "All right, but—"

"No buts," he interrupted. To his relief she turned away, nodded and said nothing more.

He went upstairs and folded the camp bed and threw it at the bottom of the garden. The sooner it rotted the better.

Eirlys was smiling. Keeping her job and her interests wouldn't be a problem after all. With the strong-minded Moll as head of the family she had been so afraid it would be impossible to marry Johnny on her own, not unreasonable, terms. But Bleddyn was helping her with the rug-making so he must understand about her unwillingness to give up everything for the Pipers.

Marriage to Johnny; belonging to that large, affectionate family and keeping what she wanted from the old life to take to the new – everything was perfect. Nothing could happen to spoil it.

Nine

When Eirlys saw the amount of wool waiting for a buyer, she was daunted at first, but as she examined the variety of the stock, some very old and uselessly tangled, some perfect, she admired the colours and the varying thicknesses and began to imagine the swirls and concentric circles and diamonds within diamonds that she could create with them, and her interest grew.

"I don't think I can afford all this," she whispered to Bleddyn, who had come with her to introduce her to the owner, Mrs Hibbert.

"I could help if you think you can use it," Bleddyn offered. "I don't want you to take it if you aren't sure, mind. The amount could be frightening. Although you could sell most of it easily enough, I would think."

She stared around her at the dark and rather gloomy shop. The shelves were tumbling with piles of knitting patterns and needles were strewn about carelessly in their assorted sizes and colours. The wools were no longer set out in an orderly arrangement, but mixed up, higgledy-piggledy, revealing the lack of interest on the part of the owner.

"I know it's a mess," Mrs Hibbert smiled. "I've just lost interest and I want someone else to take it all off my hands." She shrugged and added, "I thought of having a closing-down sale, but the stock is in need of sorting and I can't be bothered."

The shop was far from full and the stocks hadn't been replenished for a long time. There were large quantities of some colours, small amounts of most. Customers would want enough of one colour and shade number to knit a jumper or something similar, and Eirlys surmised that there were few colours with sufficient amounts in the same shade. The yarns that remained in larger quantities were rather dull. Perfect for background for her rugs, but not exciting enough to tempt someone to tackle the work involved in knitting a complicated pattern.

An idea for using the smaller amounts and oddments began to grow and Eirlys searched through the piles of knitting patterns that littered the shelves and slithered to the floor.

After stepping outside and discussing it with Bleddyn, who seemed very willing to help, she made an offer, which Mrs Hibbert accepted with relief.

"I can change this back into a room where I can sit and watch people walking past," the old lady said happily. "Hate living at the back, I do. Nothing to look at and no one to talk to once the shop closes. I might rent the back of the house. It's too big for me to look after."

"That's a good idea," Bleddyn told her. "Better than being on your own in a big old place like this."

They made their excuses and left, after arranging for the goods to be collected on the following Sunday morning.

"Now," Eirlys laughed, "now, all I have to do is find somewhere to keep it all!" The van belonging to Piper's Café was filled twice with boxes of wool, which Eirlys would have to sort out at a later date. The priority was to empty the shop so Mrs Hibbert could arrange for it to revert to its previous use as a living room, or "best parlour" as she had called it.

The wool was taken to Brook Lane after further discussions, and housed temporarily in the stable in Bleddyn's yard. It couldn't stay there long as mice would quickly ruin it. Once there Eirlys and Johnny began sorting through it. The immediate fears over the large quantity had fled and for Eirlys, this was what she had been looking for: the beginning of a business of her own, a way of being independent. She wondered why she felt the need, now she and Johnny were planning their wedding. For most of her friends, marriage was an end of something, for her it was a continuation.

It was still very cold but on several evenings, sometimes with Beth's help and sometimes with Johnny and even Bleddyn, the wool was separated into colours and type and in quantities suitable for the various items Eirlys had in mind. Running through her fertile mind were ideas for soft toys, childrens' garments and simple novelties beside the rugs with which she had begun.

She became so absorbed in her plans she neglected the arrangements for her wedding. It was Annie who dealt with the immediate preparations which consisted mainly of making a great many lists.

One lunchtime, when Eirlys would have preferred to stay in the warmth of the office, she had to do some shopping in her lunch hour and had promised to go home. The weather was harsh and the town looked grey and gloomy from the effect of the lowered clouds. Even the slates on the roofs of houses looked a different colour, Eirlys thought, a dullness she associated with the approach of snow. The air was still and painfully cold and the streets were empty, the threat of more snow keeping most people indoors. Eirlys was curled up and tense with the effort of keeping warm as she ran from the bakery to the greengrocer where Johnny's cousin Beth worked.

She felt cold but Beth looked seriously chilled. "Can't you get an hour off and come home with me for a warm meal?" Eirlys coaxed. "I have lots to tell you, and Mam will be there with something hot ready for us."

A pleading look at her boss and Beth was given permission to take one hour. She pulled on a fur-trimmed coat and covered her black, neatly bobbed hair with a woollen scarf and the two girls ran through the streets to Eirlys's home where the fire burned brightly and Annie was warming up some potato and leek soup.

Annie finished work at one p.m. and Morgan was on a morning shift, but she had managed to get home to have food hot and the fire lit for when her daughter arrived.

"I'm looking for people to work for me," Eirlys explained to her mother and Beth. "I have design ideas for rugs which I will pay people to make for me, then once a month on my Saturday off I'll take a market stall and sell them."

"How many rugs d'you think you'll sell?" Annie asked pessimistically. "It's not like a packet of sweets. You'll be wasting your time."

"I'll have a shop one day," Eirlys said firmly.

"Selling only rugs? How often do people buy a rug?"

"If they only buy one every five years, I'll want them to buy it from me."

"Looking a long way ahead that is, Eirlys. In a small place like St David's Well you won't get rich on a few rugs. Best you marry Johnny and forget it."

"The wool from Mrs Hibbert's shop has started me thinking," Eirlys said, ignoring her mother's discouragement. "Most people knit and I could get people to knit toys from the small oddments of wool I've bought. I would make them up – that's where the skill lies, stuffing them and sewing them professionally – and I'll pay the knitters for their work." She looked at Annie, hoping for a show of interest or even an offer of help, but Annie shook her head.

"Toys? That's even dafter than selling rugs!"

"I'll ask a few people I know who might be interested," Beth offered, as they walked back to work, restored by Annie's soup and chunks of fresh bread. She listened for a while longer as Eirlys explained her plans more fully, then asked, "What does Johnny think of all this? Won't you be expected to work on the beach in the summer? I'd hoped you'd be working with me in Piper's Café, or with Johnny and Taff and my brothers Ronnie and Eynon on the sands below."

"Your Granny Moll has already decided where and what I'll be doing, but she'll be disappointed. I don't intend to give up my job for a summer session on the beach followed by a winter looking for anything that I can find . . . Oh, Beth, I don't mean to belittle what you do. In fact, when Johnny and I first started going out together, it was my dream, to work with the Piper family."

"Castle family," Beth corrected. "We're all Castles except Granny Moll and Auntie Audrey who hasn't married."

"Sorry. The truth is, I'd have wanted nothing more than to work with Johnny and the rest of you. But things have changed and I'm no longer so willing."

"What changed it? You still love Johnny, don't you?"

"I love Johnny, of course I do. I think my attitude changed when I was given more responsibility at work. I might have stayed an unimportant clerk, not believing I was capable of more, if it weren't for the war and men being called up. Now I have a big, big dream of owning my own business, and the trouble with having a really wonderful dream is that it throws all your other dreams into turmoil."

"I never wanted anything other than working on the beach and becoming Mrs Freddy Clements. Oh Eirlys, can't you do both? You'd have a perfect winter occupation and that's something most of us don't have."

"I've thought of it, but every time I think of doing something else, the big, big dream comes back and gives me a nudge and I know I can't do anything else but make a seriously concentrated attempt to succeed."

"Poor Johnny," Beth laughed.

"Why poor Johnny?"

"He's got a successful businesswoman on his hands and you know how men hate to be bested."

"He won't be bested," Eirlys said seriously. "He'll have as much from me as he needs, more probably, as I'll be happy doing something I enjoy."

"Good luck, Eirlys. I think Johnny's a lucky man."

Walking back through streets, taking care on the icy pavements, Eirlys was engulfed by feelings of guilt. Was Johnny lucky? She no longer felt able to offer him the commitment she had previously felt. The excitement of planning a future, of owning a business in which she was her own boss, had filled her mind to the exclusion of everything else. Plans for a wedding to take place in just over two months seemed trivial by comparison. She should be boring people by talking about nothing else, planning every last detail, dreaming romantic dreams. Nevertheless, rugs were what she dreamed about, and every spare moment she could find was used to build a stock of hand-made rugs.

Some would be thick and practical for kitchen use, made from strips of strong material given by various friends and sometimes found in second-hand shops. Others were less robust and delicately coloured, intended for a bedroom or a nursery.

She worked late into the night and sometimes woke bleary-eyed and had to force herself to get up and cook breakfast for Stanley and Harold and try to coax Percival to swallow a few mouthfuls of porridge. She even sat and cut strips of material ready for the evening as they ate their breakfast.

The disappearance of the camp bed gave Eirlys hope that the latest, and by far the fiercest row between her mother and father was fading away, although they were still not speaking to each other. Her parents sometimes sat and cut material for her during the evenings, and she tried to tease them out of their ill humour by laughing at them working together, looking in opposite directions and pretending not to know the other was there. On one occasion, Annie's response was to pick up a pile of material and throw it at Morgan.

Her father was working regularly, first having a lift to the factory on the back of a friend's motorbike and later, under his own steam, walking to the bus stop and being dropped at the factory gates by kindly bus drivers. The plaster was off and apart from a walking stick – to give him confidence rather than support – he was recovering satisfactorily from his accident.

He was gradually relaxing from the fear of Bleddyn learning about his "carrying on" with Irene, and growing more and more convinced that neither Bleddyn nor Eirlys would ever find out. Surely if they had been seen, if something had been noticed, it would have come to light before this?

The postman's visit was always one highlight of the boys' day as they waited for letters from Teresa. Her notes were short but filled with loving messages for each of her sons, and the pile under Stanley's pillow was taken out regularly and re-read when they went to bed.

Eirlys received letters from Ken describing his progress in becoming involved in the forces' entertainments plans. His letters were full of affection, and he always asked about her interests. "Have you learnt to drive yet?" he asked in one letter. "How many rugs have you sold?" in another. It was enjoyable to write back and tell him of her progress and her ideas for the future. Ken was a loving friend and she valued him greatly as such, but she always made sure she saved his letters for Johnny to read so they wouldn't give rise to misunderstanding. Sometimes Johnny even added a note of his own when she wrote to Ken, reassuring her he understood.

Johnny was a little worried, though. He sensed that something was worrying Eirlys and hoped it was not belated regret at letting Ken leave without her. His own recurring doubts made him aware that she too might be less than certain about their marrying. One evening when they were sorting through one of the boxes bought from Mrs Hibbert, he sat untangling a skein of soft blue baby wool and asked, "Are you going to tell me what's wrong, love?"

"Wrong? There's nothing wrong. I'm frowning because I'm concentrating, that's all."

"You haven't changed your mind about marrying me so soon?"

"I love you, Johnny Castle, and I want to be your wife. In fact, I think I might have found us a couple of rooms."

"Really? That's marvellous. Where?"

"Mrs Hibbert told your father and me that she's changing the shop back into a room where she can sit and look out at the street. She said she has always hated living at the back with nothing to look at except the garden. She has two other rooms downstairs and she said she might be renting them. Shall we go and take a look?"

They examined the two rooms and, seeing them overfilled with Mrs Hibbert's treasured possessions, Eirlys had to force herself to show interest. The rooms were shabby and would need a lot of work before they could move in. It would involve a lot of time and, for her at that moment, time was precious. Finding a place to live was beginning to become an upheaval and the thought of it had the opposite effect than it would have had a few months previously. Why couldn't they simply move in with her parents and wait until something really suitable turned up?

Right now, all she wanted was to find people to work for her and get her business under way. Home-hunting was an unwelcome chore. She was ashamed of her reaction and knew she was cheating on Johnny by not explaining how she felt.

Every day she was told of young men going away to join the army or the navy or the air force, and every week there were reports of injuries, imprisonment and deaths. She understood the urgency felt by Johnny and thousands of others, to marry and get their lives in order, but it was an urgency she didn't feel able to share.

Johnny too continued to have doubts but they were hidden in a flurry of enthusiasm for his marriage to Eirlys. He had to face a life without Hannah, and he constantly reminded himself how fortunate he would be to have a wife like Eirlys: talented, intelligent, very lovely, and someone who would build up a business of her own.

On that subject Granny Moll didn't agree with him and she asked him to try again to persuade Eirlys to help in the summer season on the sands. She promised help with the rug-making during the winter months as compensation. He had called to collect clean white overalls for the chip shop that evening and as Moll handed him the carefully ironed clothes, she asked him to talk to Eirlys.

"Don't count on it," he warned, then speaking proudly he added, "She wants to start a business of her own, Granny Moll. Isn't she marvellous having such a grand ambition? She'll succeed too for sure."

"She'll soon forget all that," Moll said confidently. "When she's a part of the Piper family, she'll be happy working with us all."

Johnny shook his head. "I want to help her get the business under way. I don't want to pressure her about Piper's in any way. Then, when she's ready I think she'll come and work with us at the beach, just part time, mind, when she can fit it in. She's told me several times how much she would love to work on the sands in the summer."

"She told me that too. Don't fret, boy, this rug-making is only a phase. Lots of girls worry a bit about committing themselves to a man and a marriage. An intelligent girl like your Eirlys, she's bound to feel trepidation at having to look at your face every morning!" she joked.

Johnny laughed at her teasing, told Moll how much he loved Eirlys and how lucky he was, but he was still unconvinced. How could he love Eirlys and still think about Hannah?

Johnny and Eirlys took the three boys to the pictures that evening and after walking them home and leaving Annie to put them to bed, Eirlys took out some of the diagrams she had drawn. Even with the straight lines that resulted when the "hairpin" method was used, variety could be added with pattern and colours.

"I thought I would use the same pattern and make it in several colours now I have plenty of wool in hand," she said, writing on the pattern the colours she planned.

"Good idea, although most people would chose something dark and practical," Johnny said. "Not that I want a room that's dull and sensible, mind. When are you going to make one for our fireside?"

She picked up a few skeins held together with an elastic band. "That's what I wanted to talk to you about. Do you like these?"

She handed them to him with a canvas on which a design was printed. A design of tree branches, leaves and cherries. The colours were bold, and he nodded agreement.

"Great," he said approvingly.

"Will you help me wind the skeins?" she asked. He held the wool on his hands with arms outstretched and she unwound the skeins and rolled it into a ball. As they worked they talked.

"Have you thought about next summer?" he asked. "I probably won't be here and neither will Taff. My cousin Ronnie will be called up too if our attempt at deferment fails and Granny Moll will be desperate for some help."

"Johnny, I don't want to give up my job," she said, putting down the finished ball of wool and taking up another skein. "I thought you understood. I earn a fair wage and it's right through the year, not just in the summer. We'll need a nice nest-egg for when you come out of the army. With the rug-making and perhaps expanding into other handcrafted items, I'll be building a secure base for us."

"You used to say how much you'd love to work on the sands."

"I did. I still would. It's just that now, with this rug-making idea, I'm distracted from it. I find the idea of having a business of my own, even though it's a lowly one compared with Piper's, great fun. I have to give it a try, Johnny. If it doesn't succeed I won't be as unhappy as I would if I don't try."

"I understand," he smiled, offering his hands for another skein of wool. "I'll help all I can; I promised Granny Moll I'd ask, that's all. Dad has agreed for you to use the spare bedroom as a store room indefinitely. Keep the wool and materials there and also the finished rugs, until you're ready to sell them."

"Thanks, Johnny," she said, hugging him. "It's our future, you know. I want to keep my job at the council offices and if I can start selling rugs too, well, we'll have a good start when you come home. I'll save every penny I can. I know how important the family business is to you and I'm grateful for your understanding, really I am."

They discussed the advantages of a market stall and other ways of displaying the rugs. Johnny suggested using one of the showcases in the seaside rock and sweet shop on the promenade which was run by Granny Moll's unmarried daughter, Auntie Audrey. "It's closed now of course, but later you could use it to show one or two samples, with your name and address on a card."

"Your Granny Moll Piper would never agree to that, specially when I tell her I can't help in the summer."

"Leave Granny Moll to me. She's very fond of me, and very susceptible to flattery! I've called her my gran since I learnt to talk. I can persuade her, I know I can."

When Johnny discussed the idea with his father, Bleddyn offered to go with him to talk to Granny Moll Piper. At first, Moll was doubtful.

"How can you put floor coverings and sweets in the same shop? It doesn't make sense," she complained. But when Bleddyn spoke to her alone and reminded her how worrying it was that Johnny was attracted to Hannah, and how much better it would be for Piper's if he married Eirlys, Moll agreed.

"In fact, there's no reason why she can't put one or two in the window now, while the place is closed," she offered. "People walk on the beach and along the prom even at this time of year," she added and glanced at Bleddyn for his smile of approval. "There are a few sticks of seaside rock in the window we'll have to dispose of, but I think Stanley, Harold and Percival Love might help us with those!"

Johnny met Eirlys from work the following lunchtime. He hadn't slept and yet his mind was clearer than it had been for a long time. He knew he had to commit himself to Eirlys. There were plenty of unhappy marriages because one or the other didn't do just that. Granny Moll was right, once he was married, he would forget he ever felt any doubts.

"I spoke to Granny Moll and she says using the shop to display your work is all right with her," he told her.

"Really?"

"In fact, she suggested putting one or two in the empty window now, as there are often people strolling along the prom when the weather is mild."

They hugged and walked home, buying chips on the way, talking excitedly about their plans. "Because," Johnny told her, "they are our plans, not just yours."

In the days following, they both felt as though they had reached a turning point in their relationship. Johnny faced up to the knowledge that his future did not include Hannah, while Eirlys began to believe that she could marry Johnny and still follow her dream.

Eirlys didn't think she could be happier. She still worked on the rugs in odd moments, completing the cherry design for her and Johnny's future home. Johnny came when he could to help her sort out colours and even added a few geometric designs to her book of patterns.

She loved the Readicut designs but still made many using the method with which she began, the strips of material and the giant "hairpin". These were popular and quick to make.

Bleddyn painted an old chest of drawers for her use, built shelves to store her wool and even sat patiently untangling some of the worse skeins, amid much teasing from his elder son Taff when he and Evelyn called.

Evelyn seemed to accept the forthcoming wedding with a distinct lack of enthusiasm, and when Taff and Johnny asked her to help with the redecoration of the two rooms in Mrs Hibbert's house, she refused.

"If you're getting married in March, Eirlys will have to forget her stupid mats and start making the rooms into a home, won't she? It isn't my place to do her work for her."

Puzzled by her attitude, Johnny and Taff failed to get her to explain.

"I suppose she simply doesn't like Eirlys. We none of us like everybody, do we?" Bleddyn said, unworried by the mild disturbance. "They'll settle down when they know each other better."

Eirlys's fears that the decoration of the rooms would use up too much of her time were unfounded. It was Johnny who worked there every moment he could find and his brother, Taff, who helped him. Bleddyn too did a lot of the initial cleaning and it was only a few weeks before the place was smart and looking inviting. They were given a few pieces of furniture to begin with, which they would discard when they could afford new. Bleddyn painted delicate floral designs on some of the dull pieces, much to Johnny's and Eirlys's surprise and delight.

Eirlys took Stanley, Harold and Percival to Mrs Hibbert's one day to show them the place where she intended to live with Johnny. The two rooms were freshly papered and the paintwork gleamed. The floor was covered in linoleum and she explained where the items of furniture they had managed to collect would be placed. There was a kitchen which she would share with Mrs Hibbert, and beyond, a short passage and an outside porch leading to a lavatory. There was no bathroom, but, she explained to the three boys, "Johnny and I will manage well enough in the kitchen with the door locked and we'll go home to bathe once or twice a week."

"We never had no bathroom," Harold told her disparagingly. "Our mum says a bath is a wicked waste o' space."

After showing them the bedroom, stripped of its wallpaper, ready to be transformed, she was conscious of how small the place was and wondered where she would find the space to work. Harold disagreed.

"Two great big rooms all for yourselves? Blimey, we've never had that much room, have we, Stanley?"

"Of course you have," Eirlys said disbelievingly. "You could hardly fit three boys like you, *and* your mother, into less space than this!" Annie had described the tiny room in which the Love family had lived but Eirlys had decided it had been an exaggeration. She thought the boys were exaggerating too.

"One room, we had. Although our mum called it a flat to show off a bit. Stick in a couple of beds and a cupboard and stuff, and there ain't much room to move, is there, our Stanley?"

"Surely there was a kitchen?" she teased. "And what about a bedroom?"

"A kitchen? What for?" Harold asked. "We ate out of the chip shop most nights, except when mum was broke and we just had bread."

"I like chips from our chip shop," Percival said, his whine suggesting serious deprivation.

The boys had never told her much about their home in London, and if she thought about it at all – even though her mother had told her of its lack of comfort and conveniences – Eirlys had imagined they had lived in a block of flats with better facilities than many families in St David's Well. No one could live in a room as small as Annie had described. She was convinced her mother had belittled their situation to increase her affection for the boys who had landed on their doorstep a few months ago.

She wondered what would happen to them when they eventually went back to Teresa. Unless things had changed, they would return to the small room her mother had visited when she took the boys to visit Teresa. It was hardly a flat, Annie had told her, just a large bedroom divided into two sections to provide a bedroom and a living room, with a sink and cooker which didn't work in one corner. There hardly enough room for one, and it was certainly not large enough to accomodate the boys plus all the possessions they had accumulated since they had come to live at St David's Well. Perhaps she hadn't overstated their situation after all.

They were the only evacuees left now. The others had trickled slowly back, having been collected by loving, caring families unable to bear being separated any longer, especially since there had been no bombing in London so far.

In her newly strengthened happiness with Johnny, and the reminder of the poverty from which they had sprung, she felt even more benevolent towards the three boys and after looking at the rooms being prepared for her and Johnny she took them to buy an ice-cream.

She let them choose and they bought a knickerbocker glory but after a few mouthfuls, Percival lowered his head and solemnly declared that, "This ice-cream is boverin' me."

"Eat it up," she told him. "If the war doesn't end soon, there might not be many more."

"Good," he grumbled, chewing painfully slowly on a piece of fruit and making them laugh.

Teresa had lost her flat. After failing to pay the rent and causing a disturbance one night when she brought a few rowdy friends back, she had been told to leave. At first she wasn't worried. There were several people who would let her sleep on their couch for a night or two. She managed to keep herself looking smart and picked up men easily enough. Offering money to her friends, insisting they took it, made it harder for them to tell her to go. But when she had spent a few days with everyone willing to help, and seeing the rest turn away, she began to wonder what would happen to her.

Her friend Maureen lived near with her ten-year-old daughter. Her husband was in the forces and for a while she was glad of Teresa's company. Meanwhile, Teresa looked for a flat she could afford, but without success. Then she saw an opportunity to steal the wallet of a man she was drinking with. She helped herself to twenty-four pounds.

She felt sick with excitement as she left him and hurried out of the pub, where she was well known. Foolishly, she hadn't been able to resist taking it out and counting it before she left, and several of the man's friends had seen her. She ran through back alleyways back to Maureen's flat.

When the man returned from the toilet, it was to a chorus of jeers as he announced he had lost twenty-odd pounds. He was soon given the facts and the laughter at his gullibility made his unreliable temper explode.

He ran from the pub and, after listening for a few seconds, heard her tip-tapping footsteps in her high heels and followed her. He caught up with her as she reached Maureen's door and shouted, threatening her with the police. Afraid of getting her friend into trouble by bringing the police to her door, she ran away, kicking off her shoes to run fast and silently, hoping he would be led away from Maureen.

Unable to return, she stayed in a cheap boarding house. Although she went to Maureen's several times in the days that followed her stupid mistake, there was always a man watching the place. She had made an error of judgement, presuming the man would be too embarrassed to complain, unaware of his friends' teasing and the man's hot temper. She shivered as she realised she had robbed a man who wouldn't give up.

If he was not there, waiting for her to return to Maureen's, another man would be standing in the same place. She had to move right away.

But where would she live? Twenty-four pounds was a lot of money but it wouldn't last for ever.

Maureen worked in the pub on the corner and she managed to see her and explain.

"I'm broke and with no place to live I can't see how I'll avoid ending up sleeping under the arches," she sobbed.

"Use Stanley, Harold and Percival," Maureen advised. "Go to the council and tell them you're separated from your sons because you have nowhere to live. They're bound to help you to get a place if there's children involved."

"Bring my clothes to the pub for me to collect, will you?" Teresa pleaded. "I can't afford new."

Maureen tried, but when she walked to work with a loaded suitcase it was taken from her by the man watching her flat and thrown into the canal.

The council were sympathetic when Teresa told them about her husband leaving, especially as she forgot to mention that he had been gone more than five years, soon after telling him she was expecting again. Then they told her they had to see the boys.

"They're on holiday in Wales," she explained. "I didn't have any money to feed them and they had no decent clothes. My husband took everything we had." A few tears here, then she went on, "I have a friend in a small seaside town called St David's Well. She offered to have them for a while, but they'll be back next week and I've got nowhere for them to sleep."

They were adamant. There would be no help unless she could produce the boys.

"This war is bringing a lot of people in for help, and we have to check that we're helping those in real need and not cheats," the women explained sympathetically.

With the money left in her purse, Teresa bought herself some clothes to replace those lost to her in Maureen's flat, and went to catch the train for St David's Well. At the station she shrieked and told the crowd that someone had stolen her purse, and several kind people offered to buy her food. She filled her pockets for later and went happily on her way.

Eirlys and Johnny were like two people who had recently discovered love. They couldn't bear to be apart. Their kisses were no longer gentle affairs, but passionate and filled with promise of wonderful times to come. Johnny was Eirlys's last thought each night and her first every morning.

If Johnny thought of Hannah at all, it was with the sadness of something beautiful that has passed into memory. He saw her sometimes and took chocolate or sweets for the girls on occasions. Sometimes he went alone, but he didn't go inside. At other times Eirlys was with him, and they stayed while he played with Josie and Marie and she and Hannah talked wedding plans, much of it in muffled, giggling whispers, as Hannah was making Eirlys's wedding dress and Johnny mustn't learn a single detail of it.

If it caused Hannah pain, she determinedly didn't show it.

Bleddyn was still supportive of Eirlys's business plans, thankful that his fears of a romance between Johnny and Hannah had come to nothing. He sold several rugs for her and took orders for more. He also took an interest in her other ideas, for making toys and dolls' clothes and children's clothes with the smaller amounts of the wool they had bought. He encouraged her to think seriously about a shop sometime in the future.

The boys had been promised new clothes for the wedding and Stanley in particular was excited at the prospect.

"Will I be a best man?" Percival wanted to know.

"The best there is," Eirlys laughed. "I couldn't imagine getting married without you three standing near me. I'll need your support, won't I? You are very important to me, all of you."

As she spoke the words she realised how much she meant them. The boys had become such an important part of their lives. With Mam and Dadda still not speaking except when necessary, their presence was especially valuable. The house would have been silent and sad without them. The home revolved around them and their various activities. It was impossible to imagine the house without their filling it with noise and muddle and laughter.

Annie and Morgan took them to the department store and besides buying them each a suit and shirt and shoes, they were given good quality warm coats. Spring was on the way but the weather would be cold for a few months yet, Annie reminded them.

She wanted them to look smart for her daughter's wedding, even if they weren't really her family.

* * *

It was cold and dark and Annie had put up the blackout curtains and lighted the lamps early. Morgan had carried in extra coal and a few logs and the place looked particularly cheerful when Eirlys came home from work. Johnny was working at the chip shop that evening, and she had planned a lazy few hours writing out wedding invitations and checking wedding lists to make sure nothing was being forgotten.

Annie had made a large fish pie, something that Percival occasionally ate with slightly more enthusiasm that other meals as it required little if any chewing. They were finishing off the food, talking about their various activities throughout the day, when there was a knock at the door – a loud, impatient knock.

"'Ere, come on, let me in before I'm frozen to the doorstep," Teresa complained, and the three boys jumped from the table and ran to greet her, loud in their delight.

She dragged a large suitcase inside, pointed to a collection of assorted bags borrowed from friends and packed with her possessions, and ran to the fire to warm herself, leaving Morgan to carry the luggage and Annie to find her some food.

"I couldn't stay in London any longer," she said by way of explanation.

"Missed us, did yer?" Harold asked.

"More than that, I couldn't go another day without seeing you," she said hugging them all.

After the initial surprise, Annie and Morgan set about finding her a place to stay, insisting that she stayed a day or so, as the boys needed to see her for more than the weekend she had mentioned.

"Sure, are yer? I can easy stay in a boarding 'ouse or something," she said airily as she handed Morgan the last of the bags she carried and settled herself in front of the fire.

She settled in, taking over the small boxroom recently used by Morgan, dumping most of the contents into other rooms to give herself more space. The camp bed was rescued from the bottom of the garden, brought in and put close to the fire to be aired, but this Teresa refused.

"That ain't big enough, for me," she complained. "No, let my boys share. Three to a bed they sleep at 'ome, cosy that is, then you can move the other single in for me."

At once they all set to and did what she asked. No one questioned her: the boys were happy to see their mother and that was enough for Annie, Morgan and Eirlys.

She unpacked her things and spread herself widely. She brought clothes out from her suitcases and hung dresses and skirts around the picture rails and jumpers over the banisters. Shoes and boots were spread along the walls, both upstairs and down, until Morgan offered her several of their cases to use as extra drawers.

"Wonderful. Just what I need," she said, pulling out underwear and dropping it carelessly into the new storage.

"Taken over the damned house she has," Morgan grumbled to Annie and their togetherness against the behaviour of the uninvited guest slowly began to repair their damaged relationship.

Eirlys heard them talking long into the night and was relieved to hear muffled laughter coming through the walls. Smiling, she covered her head with her pillow and settled to dream about being Mrs Johnny Castle.

There was no offer of any money to pay for her keep from Teresa and Annie's hints to that effect were disregarded.

"Another loaf of bread needed?" Annie sighed, when Teresa had been with them four days. "It's certainly more expensive having seven instead of six, isn't it, Morgan?"

"We can't afford any more housekeeping," he said supporting her. "By the time we've paid the bills there isn't enough left for extra." Then, "How long are you staying, Teresa?"

"Oh, I won't go just yet. I can't face saying goodbye to my darlin' boys just yet," Teresa said airily, helping herself to another slice of bread and some cheese.

"No butter on that slice, mind," Annie warned. "That butter has to last us till ration day, and that's Friday."

Making a *moue*, pleading with her eyes, Teresa took a small amount of butter and spread it on a corner of the slice, bit it and threw the rest aside.

A week after she had arrived, Annie and Morgan looked out of the window watching for her to come home from school with the boys. They were already half an hour later than usual. Teresa had gone to meet them, carrying the new winter coats Annie had bought them for Eirlys's wedding. Annie had argued, insisting they didn't need them as they were wearing jumpers and their macs, but Teresa had insisted.

"I like to see Stanley, Harold and my Percival looking smart," she said as though the coats were her gift to them.

When another half an hour had passed and they still hadn't arrived, Morgan suggested she might have taken them to the pictures.

"Typical of her not to bother to tell us," he said.

When Eirlys came in from work, it was six o'clock and Annie was torn between anger at Teresa's thoughtlessness and concern in case something had gone wrong.

"If one of them were hurt, one of the others would have come to tell us," Eirlys reasoned. But she went to see the schoolteacher who lived near and asked if they had been met.

"Yes, their mother met them; waiting outside she was, dressed up and carrying a couple of coats, if I remember."

"Thank you. Sorry I bothered you, but we were worried. They've probably gone to the pictures and forgot to tell us."

"Pictures? That's not likely. They went off in a taxi, and there were several suitcases with them. And more luggage waiting for them at the station I was told. Off for a little holiday with their mother, are they? She didn't say how long they'd be away."

Eirlys left the woman still talking and ran to find Johnny. As the station was on the way to Brook Lane, she ran there first and made enquiries.

"Yes," the ticket office clerk told her. "A young woman did buy tickets for her three boys. Singles they were and she had a return. Such a lot of luggage she had too, and not even a sixpenny tip for the porter."

Eirlys looked stricken with grief when she met Johnny and told him what had happened. Johnny hugged her and said, "They'll write and if things get bad up there, they'll be back."

When they returned to Annie and Morgan, her father told her he had looked into the rooms and discovered that all the boys' best clothes and toys were gone. Further enquires revealed that even the bikes had been sent on as advance luggage.

"So it's true," Eirlys said. "Teresa has taken the boys back to London."

Morgan nodded. "And it doesn't look as if they're coming back."

Ten

With the boys gone and her life lacking the need to keep busy in order to get everything done, Annie was lost. She read and reread the postcards they received, which were written by Stanley and signed by all three boys. They asked about their friends and the donkeys and whether there had been any more snow. Annie wrote back and asked about their new school and whether they had been to the pictures or anywhere else of interest, but her questions were ignored and she had the feeling they did nothing besides exist in the small flat their mother rented. She was even doubtful that they attended school.

She and Morgan went several times to stand and look into the room the boys had shared, as though half expecting them to appear and laugh and tell them it was all a huge joke.

Because of the gap in their lives, they tried to involve themselves in their daughter's wedding plans. Morgan went to see if anything needed doing at the rooms in Mrs Hibbert's house but Johnny and his father and Taff had dealt with the redecoration and everything was in place. He came home after each attempt to help feeling useless.

For Annie it was worse. Since Eirlys was born she had dreamed of the wonderful wedding she would arrange for her. Now, at a time when she needed to have something to fill her days, even that had been taken from her. The organisation of Eirlys and Johnny Castle's wedding had been taken completely out of Annie's hands. Once the wedding guest lists had been shown to Moll she had taken over, giving instructions to Annie and Morgan on their specific tasks and organising everything herself.

Aware of her parents' disappointment, Eirlys began to have qualms about belonging to a family in which Moll was matriarch, and in which everyone so willingly accepted it.

"There's room for thirty guests in the café and if the weather is fine it will be perfect for photographs," Moll announced one evening, having invited Annie and Morgan and Eirlys to discuss what had so far been planned. Evelyn and Taff were there too as well as Marged, Huw and their youngest daughter Beth, who was to be chief bridesmaid. Johnny was helping his father at Piper's fish-and-chip shop.

Eirlys told Beth, "I want to have flowers inside the church and around the porch, as well as on the tables for the reception. But I want you, as bridesmaid, and myself to carry a prayer book and a single rose. I've seen some in silver and white. What do you think?"

"I'd like that," Beth said, her dark eyes shining. "So stylish."

"It will hardly be the event of the year," Evelyn hissed. She made several snide remarks throughout Moll's announcements, most of which she was careful not to let anyone else but Eirlys hear.

Moll was tapping her pencil on her notebook impatiently and said sharply, "Can we get on with this? I have a lot to arrange. I take it that Piper's Café for the reception is all right?"

"How do you feel about using Piper's Café, Mam?" Eirlys asked Annie, hoping she would disagree. She had no real objection to using Piper's Café, in fact it would be a rather charming and unusual choice, high above the sands with wonderful views across the bay, but she felt the need to stop Moll on something, otherwise the wedding would have nothing at all to do with her or Johnny.

"I thought we'd have it in the room above the Oaktree café," Annie said. "They specialise in weddings." She was talked out of that in a few firmly spoken words.

"This is the Piper family and we always have our receptions at Piper's Café." There was no opportunity to argue. Moll had spoken, Annie thought, with irritation rising.

"Eirlys and I will be making the wedding cake," she said, but that idea was quashed too.

"No need, I've already ordered it, Mrs Price. Three tiers and all in white."

"I hope you haven't seen the dress," Eirlys said a little petulantly. "I want that to be a surprise for everyone."

She was shocked to be told even that had been checked by Moll. "I went to see the material to make sure it's the best," Moll said, unaware of the irritation she was causing.

Annie began to wriggle in her seat. Morgan put a hand on her shoulder and told her to stay calm.

"What about the honeymoon, a week in a caravan, is it?" Evelyn smiled, glancing first at Eirlys then at Morgan. Eirlys was startled at her father's reaction. He jumped up and insisted that enough had been settled for one evening and prepared to leave.

The three Prices left the house in Sidney Street and as soon as the door was closed behind them they began to verbalise their frustration.

"It's my wedding. Mine and Johnny's, and it's nothing to do with Granny Moll," Eirlys said, her voice low with simmering anger. "I feel like leaving her to carry on with the arrangements, then running away with Johnny and getting married in a register office!"

"What if we all went to London, so Stanley, Harold and Percival could share it?" Morgan said, and Eirlys spared a moment to remember how much her father was missing the boys.

"What did that Evelyn mean about you having a honeymoon in a caravan?" Annie asked.

"Nothing more than cattiness," Morgan said at once. "I don't know what's got into that girl. You'd think she was jealous of our Eirlys, or something."

"She doesn't consider me a suitable wife for Johnny," Eirlys told them, "but she won't explain why."

"Ask her," Annie said.

"Don't bother," Morgan shrugged.

A few days later, Eirlys and Evelyn came face to face in Woolworths. Eirlys was choosing some ribbons with which to bind a small rug she had made for a baby's room.

"Trimmings for your honeymoon nightie?" Evelyn asked.

Eirlys turned, smiling, prepared to enjoy some mild teasing, but Evelyn's face was stony.

"Why do you dislike me so much?" she asked.

"As if you didn't know!"

"That's the point, I don't know. Tell me, so we can sort it out, please."

"Pretending such innocence," Evelyn sneered.

"Tell me."

"Ask your father," was the swift reply.

Unsettled by the encounter, Eirlys went to see Hannah to see how her wedding dress was progressing.

Hannah was setting in gathers on the frilled layers down each side of the crinoline-style skirt. Bags made of muslin were fixed inside to rest on each hip which, on the day, would be filled with tissue to hold out the sides. Embroidered honeysuckle and Tudor roses trailed down the bodice and the centre panel of the skirt.

As she inserted each neat stitch, Hannah dreamed of wearing it, walking up the aisle to stand beside Johnny. In her head she could hear the organ playing, then the silence before the spoken words of the marriage service, and aloud she said, "I do."

When Eirlys knocked at the door she didn't answer. She went on sewing, a tear in every stitch.

Stanley, Harold and Percival were sitting reading old comics and watching the rain through the spotted window of the ground floor flat. Not really a flat, just a room divided into two sections by a pair of curtains.

"Wish we was with Auntie Annie," Percival said quietly.

"What, leave our Ma again?" Stanley said brightly. "You wouldn't want to go away again, not really?"

"I wanted to see Ma, but now I want to see Auntie Annie and Uncle Morgan," Percival said reasonably.

"We haven't even got our bikes," Harold added glumly.

Teresa had sold the three bicycles as soon as they had arrived on the carrier. She dealt with the sale swiftly and didn't think the boys had even seen them, but Stanley had. He guessed what had happened to them but patted Harold on his head and said, "They ain't come yet. That carrier takes 'is time, eh? Tomorrow; perhaps they'll come tomorrow."

Their new coats had disappeared too and several of their games and toys. Teresa had explained the absence of the toys by telling them there was no room, and they had gone to poor little children "who never had a thing to play with". In the sparsely filled room, with nothing but out-of-date comics to look at, that wasn't easy to explain to his brothers, so Stanley didn't try.

Teresa also tore up some of the letters Annie and Morgan wrote. She checked first to make sure there was no postal order inside then threw them into the rubbish bin. When she did find money she kept most of it but bought a few sweets and gave them to the boys as a gift, from herself. Best they didn't grieve too much for Annie and Morgan. She didn't think they would see them again.

They tried to talk to her about their lives with Annie and Morgan and the friends they made but she never had time to listen. She had heard a little about the grand Christmas concert and the fun they'd had in the snow but didn't question them and quickly changed the subject, reminding them how happy she was to have them back where she could look after them properly.

Partly her refusal to listen was fear that they might want to go back, partly it was because she wasn't really interested. What did she care about St David's Well? She loved them and did what she thought was best for them, but she didn't want them to leave again. At least, not till she had the council flat. Then she would manage without them while she built them a proper home.

She went out most evenings, leaving the boys to amuse themselves and put themselves to bed when they were tired. Coming back home about a week after they had returned, the man whose wallet she had stolen was waiting for her. She panicked and ran away, hoping to put him off the scent. She didn't want her boys harmed or frightened.

It was four in the morning before she felt safe to return. Stanley greeted her at the door.

"Thank heaven's you're back, Ma. Our Harold's got toothache and can't sleep."

Teresa cuddled him after giving him an aspirin and told him it was Annie and Morgan's fault for giving them too many sweets.

"Thank goodness I got you back home when I did, Stanley, or you could have suffered real bad 'ealth," she said.

"Yeah; lucky us, eh," Stanley said as he crawled into the damp bed beside his brothers.

"I'm lucky to have three wonderful sons like you, Stanley. Don't I know it."

When they woke the next morning, she began packing their meagre belongings into bag and said cheerfully, "Come on, stir your stumps, we're movin'!"

To fill in some of the empty hours, and escape from the lonely house, Annie went along to the ARP meetings and helped by making tea and supplying a few cakes. She soon became involved in learning some basic first aid, and attended lectures on dealing with incendiary bombs and other devastations which they secretly thought would never happen.

Morgan too became more involved and learned to recognise British and enemy planes by their silhouettes, as well as how to tackle more immediate problems – everything from using a stirrup pump to rescuing people from burning houses. It was so far from everyday life which, apart from the shortages of food, was going on much the same as always, that it was treated like a game.

Since the death of Irene, Morgan hadn't missed a single shift at the factory and he hadn't been late either. Annie began to hope that their problems were behind them.

"Saving to go and see the boys," he told everyone who teased him about his new-found reliability. "Annie and I want to go up and make sure they're all right."

"The wedding too," Annie reminded him. "We want to do our best for Eirlys – if that Granny Molly Piper will let us," she added with a frown.

"Eirlys and Johnny are happy, and they've found a home a long way from Sidney Street," Morgan said. "They'll be all right. Sure to be."

Annie and Morgan were upset to have a flood of letters from the three boys. Most of them arrived without a postage stamp and they had to pay before receiving them. These had probably been written without Teresa knowing, Annie guessed. There were no complaints, no criticism of their mother, but they were clearly not happy and they were not attending school regularly, their mother waking too late to send them most mornings.

From the postcards they learned that Teresa had a single room in which they all lived. Stanley wrote cheerfully and said nothing about his being unhappy although it was apparent between the lines.

He told them how they missed the walks in the countryside and hoped to see the beach in the summer. Harold wanted to see Mr Gregory and the donkeys. In a P.S. Stanley told them Percival promised he would eat his "taters" if he could come back. These words had been rubbed out but were still readable, and they brought Annie to tears.

"They aren't happy, that much is clear," Morgan said, walking up and down the living room agitatedly.

"You'd be more worried if you'd seen the flat Teresa lived in before," Annie told him.

They were still separated by his betrayal with Irene Castle. Althought outwardly relaxed, there were some days when Annie felt the hurt as much as she had in the moment she had been told. Then she would refuse to talk to him or even look at him, unwilling for him to see her pain. Even on the worst days, when they rarely exchanged more than the occasional word, where the boys were concerned they were in complete accord.

"Now she hasn't even got that miserable place," she went on. "Sharing they are, cramped four to a bed into a small room so the council will take pity on them and get them a decent flat."

"They should come back here," Morgan said, not for the first time.

"I know that, and you saying it won't make it happen!" Annie snapped. "I think I should go up there and talk to them, see if I can persuade Teresa it would be better for them."

"Careful, or you'll have her staying here as well, paying no rent and using us as child-minders so she can go out on the tiles!"

"She's stopped all that," Annie said. "She must have. She can't leave the boys alone at night, specially not now, with the blackout making it easier for thieves to break in. I can't bear the thought of them being alone at night." They looked at each other for reassurance. "She wouldn't, would she?"

Morgan thought it was quite likely she would but didn't say so and add to Annie's distress.

"And there's the risk of an air raid, and bombs dropping," she went on. "Just because it hasn't happened yet doesn't mean the danger has gone."

"Another reason for her to let them come home – I mean back here," he quickly amended.

"I think they were beginning to think of this place as home," Annie said softly. "That's probably why Teresa took them away from us."

"I suppose we can't blame her for that. They are her boys after all and she loves them."

"They'd be better off with us, though, wouldn't they?"

"No, Annie, don't torment yourself. With their mother they are and that's got to be the best."

Teresa was walking back home after seeing a man she had met the previous evening. The late evening was quiet, just a few cars passing by with their minimal lights, and even fewer pedestrians about. The public houses had closed an hour before and she had spent a while with the man in an empty house she sometimes used.

The figure darted out from the darkness of the passageway at the side of the building like a shadow. Without warning, he grabbed her from behind.

"All right, bitch, I want the money you owe me."

"But I—"

A hand covered her mouth, stifling her protest, then she was pushed and slapped hard across the cheek, turned around and slapped again until she didn't know where she was. The man pulled her handbag from her arm. "If there isn't twenty-five quid in here, you'd better leave it for me tomorrow at the pub. If I don't get it, you're dead, you *and* your kids, Teresa Love." He twisted her and tripped her until she lost balance and fell to the ground. He kicked her several times, then ran off.

She lay there for several seconds, confused and dizzy from the blows and the suddenness of the attack. Then she rose to her feet and hurried to the front door of the house in which she and the boys rented a room of a flat. She felt that vulnerable coldness between her shoulder blades. The darkness closed in around her, isolating her, and the shadows were filled with invisible threats.

Her leg hurt and her head was spinning but she ran as fast as she could, seeking the shelter and safety of the flat. So he had found her again, and was still insisting on getting his money, more than she had stolen in fact; interest, to pay for his humiliation, she guessed. Where could she find that amount? The twenty-four pounds she had stolen from him was long gone.

A lot of the men she was involved with were unable to cope with being bested by anyone, particularly a woman. Little men pretending to be big. Not many were as vicious as this one. Why had she chosen to steal a wallet from him? She had never done that before, she had always played fair with her clients.

Weakness overcame her when she had climbed the first two steps and she longed to collapse, to sit and recover, but he could be still there in the darkness, watching her, ready to come after her again. She clung to the rail at the side of the steps for support and dragged herself to the top, concentrating on staying upright, when all she wanted was to sit down and recover.

She was trembling when she reached the door and had difficulty finding the keyhole. This meant she would have to move again. It wouldn't be easy with the three boys to consider but she had to get away. She fell inside, closed the door behind her and stood for a long time to allow her heart to calm and her breathing to drop to a normal rate.

As she stood there she wondered whether she could leave the boys and go somewhere on her own until the man's anger had died down. Touching her stomach, she was comforted by the tiny bulge of notes she had hidden inside her knickers after her last client had left her in the empty house and she had cleaned herself up. Thank goodness her attacker hadn't known about them.

Her handbag contained less than a pound. Now she would be able to buy those new shoes she had set her heart on, and treat the boys to good meals for a few days. There was no point in trying to pay the man. He didn't want her money, he wanted revenge. He would be watching her, and waiting for the opportunity to hit her again.

Her face hurt and her leg ached where she had fallen awkwardly, and she knew there would be big bruises on her where the toe of his shoe had landed. Bruising was something she didn't like, they could give clients the wrong idea. "And I bet my last pair of stockings are laddered," she muttered to herself, worrying about the trivial to take her thoughts from the serious. It was past eleven thirty, and the flat, which she was sharing with a friend, was in darkness when she moved away from the door and adjusted the blackout curtain. She decided she would have to break her own firm rules; she wouldn't undress or have a thorough wash, in case she disturbed the rest of the household. She had promised her friend she would be home before ten.

Then she heard sobbing. It was quiet – muffled, she guessed, by the blankets across his mouth – but unmistakable.

"Percival?" she whispered, climbing painfully over Harold and Stanley to reach her youngest, squashed against the wall in the single bed.

"I want to go back to Annie an' Morgan," he blubbered.

"Soon, darlin', soon. I promise," Teresa whispered. She wondered how it could be arranged. Perhaps she *could* send the boys back now the housing officer had seen them. It would give her a real chance to save up for something decent if she didn't have the boys to worry about. This time she could really succeed, get them a decent home with proper beds and everything.

She had to get away from this flat, that much was certain. She couldn't risk the man hurting the boys or her friend who had helped her out by lending her a room. If she went far enough perhaps the man wouldn't find her again. If she was lucky with a few quality clients she might even pay him off! Leave his money at the pub he used. That idea was a novelty, being rich enough to pay him back. She might even deduct the money he'd taken from her handbag!

She would let the council housing officer know she'd had to move again, and if it was somewhere worse it wouldn't matter, just for a while, until she got that smart flat. Yes, everything would be settled if she could hand the boys back to Annie and Morgan for a while.

The idea was very tempting and she hugged the little boy and repeated her promise. "I'll write to Mr and Mrs Price tomorrow and ask if we can go back for a little holiday, shall I?"

"I'd rather 'ave a big 'oliday," Percival said sleepily.

"I love you, Percival," Teresa whispered.

Life was hectic for Eirlys, with customers arriving frequently to order one of her custom-made rugs. Some of the requests came as a result of the display Bleddyn and Johnny had set up in the sweet and rock shop on the promenade. Johnny's father was being very supportive of her enterprise.

The machine-made rugs didn't take very long, with her parents helping to cut the strips of material from coats and skirts, and in some cases heavy curtains. The hand-made designs took a lot longer and Annie began to help her make these as well as help with the preparation. So far they had been small hearth rugs and smaller ones for children. She knew she had to find a way of embarking on more adventurous sizes and even different shapes. She had to add variety to what she was offering if she were to expand.

She had spasms of guilt when she realised that she was more excited about her burgeoning business than the arrangements for her wedding. She reminded herself that most of it had been taken out of her hands by Granny Moll Piper, and found comfort in that. Yet she knew her lack of enthusiasm was really something far more serious: by her lack of involvement she was letting Johnny down.

On impulse one Saturday she arranged to go shopping with Johnny's cousin Beth.

"We'll look for some special underwear and night-clothes," Eirlys whispered, and they began to giggle like children at the implications.

They caught the train into Cardiff and began looking around the shops, eventually choosing the garments for Eirlys's honeymoon. Clutching their exciting purchases they wandered towards the market stalls, attracted by the buzz of activity now the day was ending and the stall-holders were anxious to sell the last of the perishables. Saturday afternoon was the time for bargains.

They didn't buy meat or fish. With nowhere to store it, their "bargains" would have ended in the dustbin. The fruit and vegetables looked fresh, though, the prices too good to miss, and by the time they reached the railway station they were staggering under the weight of it.

Eirlys and Beth noticed a thin, shabbily dressed man getting on their train but neither commented. The number of sick and exhausted soldiers returning from France made the young man a not uncommon sight. They looked away, embarrassed as he passed them. They felt sympathy but were unable to open a conversation with a stranger.

It was as they alighted at the platform that they saw him again and this time he approached them. It wasn't until he was close that they recognised him.

"Peter?" Beth said. "Peter Gregory? What on earth have you been doing with yourself? Your dad'll have a fit when he sees the state of you."

"Living rough you might say," Peter replied in his polite tone. "I dare say Dad will accept the challenge to fatten me up like one of his Christmas turkeys before I depart once more for – who knows what." He took some of the carrier bags with which they were struggling and they left the platform. To their delight, Mr Gregory was there with the pony and trap and they all piled in.

The conversation was general, Peter asking about their families and congratulating Eirlys on her imminent wedding.

"And you, Bethan?" he asked. "Are you and Freddy Clements still getting engaged on your birthday?"

"Fancy you remembering that!" Beth laughed.

Eirlys looked at Peter's expression as he gazed at Beth and thought it wasn't surprising at all.

* * *

Peter called for Beth the following day and invited her and Freddy to visit his father.

"There's a chicken cooking in honour of my return and we'd love you to share it."

"Thanks, Peter; I'm sure Freddy will be as pleased as I am."

"What about Eirlys, could she come too? I feel the need for a party. Father's chicken will be the equivalent of the fatted calf. Your cousin Johnny wouldn't refuse a meal I'm sure."

So it was arranged, and six people sat down in the living room of Mr Gregory's cottage that evening and enjoyed a delicious meal cooked in the oven next to the fire.

Peter asked a lot of questions, obviously anxious to hear the local gossip, but Eirlys noticed he rarely answered a question about his own life. Mr Gregory had told them he was unable to discuss his business and they accepted it.

Eirlys also noticed that Peter looked at Beth quite often and there was more than friendship on his mind. She suspected that the "party" was an excuse for him to see her. She wondered if Beth was aware of his interest but, seeing the way she clung to Freddy, she thought not. Interesting though. Attractions weren't always conveniently mutual.

Between working at the hardware store and helping his father at the chip shop, Johnny was kept busy, but he went to Mrs Hibbert's house when he had any spare time. He had finished decorating their future home, with the help of his father and Taff. The furniture was more or less in place, much of it given by family and friends.

Everyone was involved and it was only Evelyn who still treated Eirlys like the enemy. One day, several of her comments melded together and began to puzzle Eirlys rather than irritate her as in the past.

Evelyn's comment about the caravan for her honeymoon had been more than cattiness. She had been looking at her father when she had said it, as though the reference to a caravan meant something to him, and he had left so suddenly after that too. Angry? Upset? Embarrassed? She wasn't sure he had shown any of those emotions now, after so much time had passed. At the time she remembered thinking it was her father's concern for her that had made him leave so suddenly, getting her away from the frustration of Granny Moll's organising and from Evelyn's obvious dislike. Now she wondered if there was something more. She remembered the day she thought she had seen her father walking near where the caravan was parked not far from the old stone barn. Could there be a connection?

The thought drifted into her mind but didn't solidify into something on which she could act. It was curious, that was all. She did nothing about it, because she couldn't think of any way of solving the mystery. She didn't have sufficient facts. The main one was that Evelyn disliked her, and she seemed to dislike her father too.

While Peter Gregory was home he managed to see quite a lot of Beth Castle – sometimes with her soon-to-be fiancé, Freddy Clements, who worked in a gent's outfitters in the town, and sometimes on her own.

Wednesday was early closing and the afternoon was when Beth was free from the icy-cold shop selling vegetables. Peter was there when she pulled down the shutters and swept up the debris from the pavement.

"Are you and Freddy doing anything this afternoon?" he asked in his polite way.

"Not really, Peter. Freddy is going into town and I planned to do nothing except get warm," she told him with a demonstrative shiver.

"Come with me and groom the donkeys," he said. "Hardly an exciting invitation but they're very warm and, apart from Charlie, very friendly."

Mr Gregory greeted them and made them a pot of tea then left them to attend to other things. They went to the field in which the stables were situated and talked, using the excuse of grooming the donkeys for being there.

Peter made her laugh, telling her of the people he met and some of the things he had done. She was surprisingly happy. Then, when they were walking back home in the fading light, he stopped to help her over a stile and as her feet touched the ground he held her and kissed her.

"Peter!" she gasped, utterly surprised.

"Sorry, Bethan, but I've been wanting to do that all day."

"But we've never been more than friends," she said, still puzzled.

"Can't a friend kiss a friend?"

"I suppose not, it's just that Freddy and I—"

"Put it down to my long absence and the situation in which I've been working," he smiled. "I promise not to do it again. That is, unless you want me to."

Beth was unsure how to deal with this, but Peter returned to his previous manner and she was soon laughing, and answering him as easily as before. Nevertheless, a part of her felt a guilty wriggle of excitement.

Hannah walked into the house after taking her two children to school and nursery one morning, and a shout from her mother made her heart race. What misdemeanour was she accused of now?

"Your father's had an accident," her mother said. "He's in bed and can't be moved. You'll have to miss work this evening and tomorrow morning and help me look after him."

When the facts were explained, and Hannah learned that her father had fallen while riding a bicycle and was badly bruised, she carefully explained that it wasn't really serious enough for her to miss work.

"I'll help when I can, but I can't not go to work and I can't not finish the skirt I've promised Mrs Beynon for next Saturday," she explained. She spoke politely and quietly but the tirade she hoped to avoid came at once. Words like "selfish" and "ungrateful" and plenty more were thrown at her and when Johnny passed in the firm's van an hour later, she was standing in the shadows near the park gates crying.

He parked the van and ran to see what had happened. Hannah's mother saw them on her way back from the chemist.

"Are you all right? Are the girls all right?" Johnny asked, taking her in his arms.

"Don't, Johnny; I'm in enough trouble as it is," she sighed, trying to control her sobs.

She explained what had happened and he led her to the van and insisted she got in. He drove to a place where they could have coffee and cakes, and found them a corner seat where they could talk. Tight-lipped, Mrs Wilcox watched them go.

"We'll have to see if we can't get you a better place to live, Hannah, love. I know you should be grateful to your parents, but they're very misguided in the way they expect you to behave." He was careful not to criticise them, afraid she might turn away from him when he wanted only to help her.

"I can't go away. Where would I go? Living in rooms with strangers could be much worse. At least I know what to expect from Mam and Dad – nothing!" she said bitterly.

He coaxed her to sip the coffee and gradually she calmed down. "I'm going to be strong over this," she told him, forcing a smile that wrenched at his heart. "If I miss work, it's Josie and Marie who will suffer and they are more important than my parents."

When she walked back into the house, her mother said, "There are to be no more men in this house."

Hannah didn't understand quite what she meant until a man called to collect a blouse and skirt she had been altering for his wife, and Hannah was not allowed to give them to him.

When Johnny finished his deliveries and went back to the hardware shop, he was told someone had reported him for using the firm's van to give a lift to a young woman, and he was sacked.

Eirlys was very busy. At work there were so many extra arrangements to be made. Men had left without giving anyone a chance to train others to take their place. Eirlys and her assistants dealt with everything, including the deliveries of air raid shelters to those who requested them, arrangements for people unable to erect their shelters without help, and special protection for the elderly and infirm. There were pages and pages of information to distribute to grocers and butchers on dealing with ration-book registration, and dozens of complaints from irate customers who suspected the retailers of being unfair. The variety of her various activities seemed endless, and she loved it.

Permission had to be acquired from owners to enter buildings so that fire-watchers could stand guard, and their equipment had to be distributed. There were payments to be given, and in most cases later cancelled, for housing the evacuees. She and her staff worked many extra hours to deal with the increasing preparations of the country now at war.

When she reached home each evening, Johnny was usually there. He had been kept busy dealing with extra work too, packing and delivering goods which were already slower to restock, as people with sufficient money gathered as much as they could to prepare for the shortages that would surely come.

When he told her he had been sacked for giving Hannah a lift and buying her coffee because she was upset, she showed concern for Hannah. After she had heard the whole story she smiled and said, "Their loss, Johnny. I'm sure it won't take you long to find another job."

When they spent time with Johnny's Uncle Huw and Auntie Marged, Granny Moll, who lived a few doors away, usually appeared and Eirlys dreaded the detailed discussion of her wedding. It was becoming less hers and Johnny's as the days passed. She was relieved when the discussion changed from their wedding to the repainting of Piper's Café ready for the opening in May.

With the six-month summer season taking all the family's time, repairs and redecoration had to be done during the winter months. Much of the painting was done in the weeks running up to opening, but this year they were going to start on the café earlier so it would be looking its best for the wedding at the end of March.

Eirlys sat and thought about what awaited her at the office next day, or the rugs she was working on, and let the conversation drift over her. She knew she should be more involved, more excited, but the truth was, she couldn't rouse enough interest to make a single suggestion. "Partly because Moll always has the last word – and frequently the first as well," she told Annie and Morgan later.

"You are sure about this marriage, are you?" Morgan asked.

Eirlys stared at her father as though the question had never entered her mind. "Sure about it?"

"If you aren't absolutely certain you have to say, love."

"Of course I'm sure."

"You aren't thinking about Ken Ward?"

"Ken and I finished a long time ago."

"And it's really over and done with?" Morgan insisted.

"Over and done with," she echoed. "I'm fond of Ken but I love Johnny like never before."

The conversation disturbed her. It roused in her questions she had pushed aside, tried to ignore. Bringing them out and facing them when she lay in bed that night, she knew she had lied. She wasn't sure about becoming Mrs Johnny Castle. She loved Johnny, wanted nothing more than to be his wife, but she was more and more afraid that she wouldn't be able to cope with his family. The large family, the closeness she had wanted so much, was threatening to destroy her love for him.

She had a brief and foolish impulse to pack a suitcase and go away. It was ironic that less than a year ago she had said goodbye to Ken Ward because she had refused to do just that.

As she drifted into a restless sleep, she heard in her mind the sound of Ken, singing silly songs to the children at the last concert he had given before going back to London and applying to entertain the troops. She saw again the smiling faces of his young audience as they joined in lustily with the choruses. She was smiling with them as she slept.

The following morning there was a letter from Ken, the usual friendly note telling her of the various interviews and auditions and rehearsals that were gradually taking him towards entertaining the troops.

She was, as always, cheered by his letter and she settled to reply. As she wrote, her cheerfulness faded and she began to tell him about their worries for Stanley, Harold and Percival Love in the sad little room in London.

She usually heard within a week or so but this letter had a prompt reply. Ken offered to go and visit the Love family to find out how they all were.

With the work on the cafés and stalls looming, and the busy summer season not far off, Bleddyn was busy repapering his house. He felt the need to start a fresh phase of his life now Irene had gone. Starting in the bedroom they had shared, he chose a cheerful pattern and was given one of Eirlys's rugs to complete the transformation.

The living room was next and, unable to stop, he went on to do the hall and stairs, helped by Johnny who, as he frequently did, complained about his lack of height. Only Bleddyn in the Castle family was above average height and it was he who was called on to deal with any job that needed extra reach.

Between them he and Johnny completed the task very quickly. Johnny didn't think the work was needed but understood his father's need for changes.

"Just in time for the wedding," Johnny smiled. "Thanks, Dad."

Although the wedding was not taking place in Brook Lane, Johnny knew a lot of friends would be calling. He also hoped the redecoration was really a sign that his father was recovering from the shock of his mother's death.

One Sunday afternoon, when the sun shone weakly but with a promise of warmth to come, Johnny and Eirlys went over to the beach. There were other couples enjoying the pleasant hint of approaching spring, walking beside the waves, stopping occasionally to collect a shell or a particularly beautiful piece of rock. They recognised some friends but didn't join them, going instead to Piper's Café high above the sand.

They had been asked to measure the shelves so Marged could buy shelf paper to cover them. Johnny used the tape measure and Eirlys jotted down his instructions on a note pad.

They worked busily for a while, then Johnny took a bar of chocolate from his pocket and they sat to enjoy it. Eirlys said very little. He sensed her confusion, and apologised for Granny Moll.

"Sorry about Granny Moll's enthusiasm. She's always been in charge of us all and we just accept it. She's Uncle Huw's mother-in-law, besides being his boss, and he can expect her to make the decisions, but as for Dad, I don't know why he suffers it. He's worked for her since he was about twelve, and he's never known any other way, I suppose."

"She isn't even your gran," Eirlys protested, glad to be able to talk to him honestly about how she felt. "She certainly isn't mine! So why does she insist on arranging our wedding? I feel as though it's nothing to do with you and me, it's a Piper family affair. It's more an initiation ceremony, accepting me into the clan, than you and I starting a life together." She laughed to disguise her frustration and he hugged her, kissed away her frowns.

"Dad called her Granny Moll long before Taff and I were born. She needs to believe we are all one family. And you will be a part of it too. Aren't you happy about that?"

"I love you, Johnny. I want to belong to you – and perhaps one day I might even help on the beach," she added doubtfully.

"You don't have to work on the sands. Mam never did."

"Poor lady. If your father hadn't been so understanding, she would always have felt like an outsider."

"Perhaps that was why she was so unhappy. Taff and I loved the life so much, we should have understood that she didn't and tried harder to help her." He imagined her body lying in the cold, still water of that dock. "God, Eirlys, she must have been so unhappy to do what she did."

"Don't blame yourself or anyone else for her sad and lonely death. She wasn't deprived of happiness. I don't think she looked for it, she didn't think there was any."

"I sometimes think she must have been looking for something better than us. Where did she go on her long walks? Perhaps during her wanderings she found someone else, someone who understood and who made her feel better."

"You don't really think there was someone else?" Eirlys looked suitably horrified.

"I found a note once and it made me wonder. I've never told a soul so keep it to yourself, love. It was on the floor of her bedroom, as though it had fallen out of her drawer with some handkerchieves. It was addressed to 'My Love' and signed 'Your adoring slave'. I threw it away before Dad saw it and I didn't think much about it. But since her death, I have wondered."

"Johnny!" she laughed. "You're crazy if you think that was to your mother from a secret lover! That's definitely schoolgirl stuff! She probably picked it up intending to show you and make you laugh. She would never have looked at another man! Don't even think it."

"Her wedding ring was never found, or her watch. If we find them, we might learn more of what really happened that day. And a pair of wellingtons she used on her walks went missing too."

"She was probably carrying them home, put them down somewhere and forgot to pick them up. They probably ended up on a scarecrow in a farmer's field, or in somone's dustbin. You're letting your imagination go wild, Johnny. 'Adoring slave'! Who would talk like that, for heaven's sake! Don't think badly of her. She's your mam and now she's gone. Think only nice thoughts."

They spent an affectionate hour together in the privacy of Piper's Café, sitting at one of the tables looking down at the beach, the sun spreading its warmth around them. They sat close together, kissing, hugging and promising each other that they would talk over any problems and deal with them before they grew large enough to threaten their happiness. That night she tried to remember their conversation. Something was niggling at her memory and she couldn't bring it to mind.

Eirlys felt more positive about her wedding after those hours spent in Piper's Café. She was still very busy both at work and making her rugs, experimenting with wall hangings too after seeing some in a quality home-maker's magazine. When she and Johnny were together they talked easily and about everything. Eirlys knew she would be utterly content as Johnny's wife. She even helped out one evening in Piper's fish-and-chip shop when Bleddyn had a night off.

Unfortunately, that was the evening Taff and Evelyn came in.

"I don't think I want chips tonight," Evelyn said to Taff. Quietly, she added to Eirlys, "Not from your hands I don't."

"What is the matter with you?" Eirlys demanded loudly. "What have I ever done to you for you to treat me as though I'm not fit to look at you?"

Taff and Johnny looked at Evelyn, both waiting for her apology or at least an explanation, but Evelyn simply turned around and left the shop. Johnny went to run after her, but Eirlys stopped him. There was a long queue of customers waiting and enjoying the fun. Johnny smiled at the next customer and asked cheerfully, "What can I get you, Mrs Thomas, the usual cod and chips, is it? And the names and odds offered on the contestants in tonight's fight?" Everyone laughed and the moment was eased.

When the shop was closed, the cleaning done and Johnny was walking her home, Eirlys explained briefly some of the earlier incidents between herself and Evelyn and asked if he knew what had upset his sister-in-law.

He laughed and said, "Whatever it is, it can't be anything for us to worry about. She seems to have a problem accepting that I'm getting married. Perhaps being the only daughter-in-law, being fussed over by Dad, is a role she enjoys. Maybe she hates the thought of having to share his attentions with you, Dad having two of you to spoil and enjoy? He's fond of you, get on well you do, anyone can see that. She might feel put out. I don't know; let's forget it and enjoy the walk home."

It was a shared problem now, she thought with relief, and it drew them closer. The wedding day was something Eirlys began to think about more and more and with greater excitement. For Johnny too, confidence in their forthcoming marriage was stronger. He felt he would be able to visit Hannah and the girls without fear of being tempted by her.

He knocked on her front door one evening, straight from his new job at a greengrocer not far from the one at which Beth worked. A moon was showing through thin cloud and casting a magical beauty over the town.

He had no reason to call, but decided to ask whether the girls would like to go with himself and Eirlys to the last week of the pantomime. He was smiling, certain Eirlys would agree.

The door opened and Hannah stood there, her expression invisible in the poor light. There was no mistaking the voice, though. She had been crying.

"Hannah? What is it? Can I come in?"

"Sorry, Johnny. My mother insists that if I get any men callers I will have to take the children and find somewhere else to live."

"But that's ridiculous."

"I have to agree with her. I have no choice," she said. "I even had to refuse to hand over a child's dress yesterday when the husband of my customer called to collect it."

"Are there any restrictions on coming out for a walk? Josie and Marie aren't in bed yet, are they?"

"No, they haven't had their supper yet. I keep them up a bit later than I should because the evenings are so lonely."

"Get their coats then and we'll walk through the town and peer into shop windows. I used to love that when I was small, didn't you?" He produced an Aero, which he gave to the children. "Who cares if it spoils their supper? It doesn't hurt once in a while," he excused to Hannah, who thanked him then nodded to tell the girls it was all right to eat it.

The moon rose clear of the clouds and lit their way and they walked along the main road, where most of the shops were, stopping whenever something attracted the attention of the little girls. There was a toy shop, and Josie and Marie pressed their noses to the glass, covered the sides of their faces with gloved hands and tried to look at the wonders on offer for those with money. Bicycles and scooters, forts and castles, dolls' prams, houses and everything needed to enjoy them. They discussed what they would buy if they were given a choice and Johnny stood inside the porch with Hannah close to him.

Nothing was said, but their eyes told it all. What he felt for Eirlys was forgotten whenever he was close to Hannah.

In their black woollen stockings and sturdy boots they were well wrapped up, but the girls soon began to shiver and stamp their feet as an icy east wind stole the warmth from them.

"We should be getting back," Hannah said.

"Another five minutes?" he asked huskily.

"Johnny, please don't do this to me." She took her daughters' hands and began to walk away from him, not hurriedly, but slowly, waiting for him to join them after a few paces, talking to Marie and Josie, asking if they had room for supper after the chocolate, which biscuits they wanted with their night-time cocoa. Calm, easy questions, denying the tumult in her heart.

With the girls between them they wandered back, swinging arms and running at times to keep warm. At the gate, Johnny asked whether she would allow Eirlys and himself to take them all to the pantomime. He spoke quietly, afraid of disappointing the girls if their mother said no. He was holding his breath as he waited for her reply.

"No thank you, Johnny. It isn't fair. You and Eirlys have to do things together. I'll take them myself, they won't miss it, I promise."

"Hannah," he pleaded softly, but she told the girls to thank him and slipped inside, lost to him, it seemed, for ever.

He went to see Eirlys later and the confusion of his feelings led him to be extra loving with her.

Any doubts she had felt were long gone. She was marrying Johnny Castle and they were going to be blissfully happy.

She would cope with the strong-minded Granny Moll, and deal with Evelyn's disapproval with Johnny's support and help. They had a home of their own, and the promise of a summer helping out on the beach, but only if and when she wanted to. There was nothing but contentment ahead. Full of emotional well-being, she went in and hugged her parents as she hadn't done since she was a child.

Eleven

Eirlys's euphoria lasted until a week later.

During that week, she and Johnny spent evenings at Mrs Hibbert's, putting the finishing touches to their future home. Eirlys had made curtains and one of her rugs with its design of cherries lay beside the double bed that was already made up with crisp new linen and two Witney blankets.

A chest of drawers and a cupboard in a corner stood empty, waiting for the wedding gifts to come. Many more had been promised than originally expected. Moll had spread the word that one of the Pipers was getting married. She ignored the fact that Johnny was not a Piper but a Castle. As far as she was concerned, Johnny worked on the sands and was therefore family – her family. She had spent some considerable time reminding people of their connection with the Pipers, and contacted the people from whom they bought their supplies during the summer season. By these and other means, she had extended the circle of their acquaintances, making the list of promised presents very impressive.

It was one of those spectacular mornings that sometimes occur during early spring which deceive people into believing that summer is just around the corner. Eirlys was awake early and she knew she would not be able to stay in bed. She went down and found that, early as she was, someone had been up before her. She felt the teapot and found it was warm. Throwing away the dregs she made a fresh pot and considered taking one up to her parents, then decided against it. Sunday morning was not the time to be roused before you need be.

She drank two cups of tea and ate a few biscuits then, putting on a thick coat and warm scarf and gloves, went for a walk. She had no destination in mind, but when she saw the bright sun giving a rosy glow to the hedges and the graceful birch tree at the end of the road, which looked more perfect than a Christmas tree, she decided to go through the fields. With luck she might see a fox or another wild creature searching for food. There would be catkins or sticky-buds to pick and take home. Her mother loved to see them opening their fresh green leaves.

She walked fast at first to warm herself, swinging her arms, a feeling of well-being lighting her face with a smile. As she reached the lane she slowed her footsteps to gaze in admiration at the trees bordering the road, not quite bursting into leaf but with the blackthorn already decorating the lanes with its white blossom. In the grasses at her feet daisies and dandelions bloomed and celandines showed their golden faces rising from the clumps of heart-shaped leaves. Nature was wearing her ostentatious best as though sharing her joy. She wished she had remembered to bring a camera. The Brownie box camera wouldn't do it justice, but it would have been a memory of today, when she was so very happy.

The field in which the old barn stood was the usual muddy morass. A few weeks ago it had been surfaced with hard ridges, with frozen water shining dully in the dips between them. She stepped carefully across and stood near the entrance for a while, wondering which field the cows were now using. Using the ridges as stepping stones, she made her way across the field until she was in sight of the caravan. Someone was using it. Smoke rose straight up from its chimney in the clear air, and the door stood open.

Curious to know who could live in such a lonely place during the winter, she went to see if there was anyone home. She saw that the door was propped open with a pair of wellingtons. They were very like her father's. She called and stepped closer, then as she had heard nothing she went right up to the door and looked in. A woman's wellingtons were just inside. The thought flashed through her mind that Irene's wellingtons were missing, and her ring and watch had never been found. Perhaps she used this place; Eirlys remembered seeing her nearby once.

Daring to look further inside she saw a man sitting with a coat around him, looking as though he was fast asleep. She hesitated; she could hardly wake him up just to say "good morning". Slowly she tried to back away. Then he opened his eyes and turned to face her.

"Eirlys? What are you doing here?" her father asked.

"Dadda?" she asked with a confused frown. "Can I ask the same question?"

She went inside and saw to her horror that he had been crying. His eyes were bloodshot and tears wet his cheeks. Then she saw that the coat in which he had wrapped himself was not his coat. It was Irene Castle's. She recognised it easily with its brown fur collar.

A letter was near him and as he tried half-heartedly to pick it up, it fluttered to the floor. She stepped forward and was about to give it back but something stayed her hand and she read it.

"Darling M, I will be waiting for you tomorrow at two. Don't be late, I am desperate to see you." It was signed "I".

"Irene?" she gasped. "Were you and Irene Castle seeing each other?" When there was no reply she pleaded, "Dadda. Please tell me it isn't true?"

"It's true. You wouldn't understand." He pulled the coat tighter around him. "Bleddyn gave me her coat, this coat, and told me to cut it up for you to make rugs. I couldn't do that."

"Tell me I'm wrong," she said. "Please, Dadda, tell me I'm wrong."

"You wouldn't understand," he repeated, still not moving or even facing her, curled up hugging himself in Irene's coat.

"Understand? What is there to understand? You were carrying on with another woman and Mam didn't know!" She was trembling with shock and knew that if she didn't allow anger full rein she would howl. Her parents involved in something as sordid as this? It only happened in films, didn't it? Not in real life. She began to shout and scream at him and, as the full realisation came, that she could never marry Johnny after such shame, she began to hit him.

He held her arms and talked soothingly to her, then as anger abated and hopelessness and despair overwhelmed her, he cuddled her as he had when she was a child.

"If we tell no one, there's no harm been done." He deliberately misled her into believing that Annie did not know. If both kept their secret independently, then it would avoid further outbreaks of Annie's recriminations. The arguments, the recriminations, the anger, they would never go away. He didn't think he could cope with any more of it. "Why upset your mother now, when it's all over?" he reasoned.

"How can I marry Johnny after this?" she wailed.

"Not marry Johnny Castle? Why not? He doesn't know, so how can it affect your marriage? So long as we don't tell anyone nothing will change."

"Mam should be told. She has the right to know."

"Why, so you can feel better? Punish me? It won't do anything for your mother except destroy her happiness, and where's the sense in that, eh?" he insisted, continuing with the lie.

"I have to tell someone."

"No, Eirlys, you don't. If Irene hadn't died you might have been justified in telling everyone about us, but now she's gone, and talking about it would only bring more misery. To her family as well as ours," he reminded her.

She didn't wait to walk home with her father, she ran across the slippery, uneven ground and stumbled, still sobbing, into the lane. Several times she skidded on the treacherous surface but she hurried on, unaware. How could they keep it a secret? In a small town like St David's Well someone was certain to have seen them together and although weeks had passed since Irene Castle's death and funeral, that did not mean they were safe from an ill-timed comment that would start the rumours spreading.

Then a thought stopped her hasty retreat and she saw Evelyn's dislike of her very clearly. Evelyn knew. Somehow she had found out and that was the reason for her unpleasantness, her unwillingness to accept her as a suitable wife for Johnny. She knew!

The snide remark about a caravan honeymoon had been directed at her father, not her. The "ask your father" and the conviction that she, Eirlys, knew what had been happening between her father and Johnny's mother. It all fitted together now.

She didn't want to go home, but she had to. She would prepare the vegetables for dinner, and chat to her mother as though nothing had happened. Somehow she had to conceal from her the fact that her life was destroyed. Then, when she had recovered sufficiently, she would have to talk to Johnny, tell him their wedding was cancelled. She would have to tell him, but without explaining why. Only Evelyn would understand, and she would smile in satisfaction and say nothing.

The saddest part of all this was that there was no one in the world with whom she could discuss it, talk to about her feelings, ease away the pain by sharing the whole sordid story. The secret was hers and hers it had to remain.

Somehow she survived the day, using a headache as an excuse to stay in her room for much of the afternoon, and using the same excuse for not eating the meals. All the facts chased round and round in her head until she thought it would burst. She had decisions to make and they had to be made quickly.

When Johnny called, she longed to run downstairs and fall into his arms, tell him everything and beg him to make it all better. She couldn't. She loved him too much for him ever to be told. She persuaded her mother to tell him she was unwell and in bed. How could she see him now? Once she had her tears under control, then she would see him. Then she'd be strong enough to tell him she no longer wanted to marry him.

Darkness fell, ending that most awful of days. Annie came up and fixed the blackout and lit her lamp and still she didn't leave her room. How could she go downstairs and stay in the same room as her father, knowing what she did?

On Monday morning she surprised her boss by offering her resignation.

"If there's a chance of transferring to a similar job elsewhere, I would like to be considered," she told him, "but I have to get away from St David's Well."

Mr Gifford and Mr Johnston questioned her briefly but quickly accepted that it was something she did not want to talk about, for the moment at least. Mr Gifford guessed it was love trouble and thought it wise to do nothing for a while, in case the rift was mended and she changed her mind about leaving.

"Will you please say nothing to the others," she asked as she faced him across his large wooden desk, her fingers twisting, showing her anguish.

"I'll say nothing until you are sure you mean it," he promised kindly. "Problems have a way of sorting themselves out given enough time. If you change your mind and want to stay, then nothing would please me more. You've been an asset to the office from the day you arrived, Miss Price. Hard-working and willing to tackle any task you are given. Whatever you decide, I wish you nothing but the best."

His gentle understanding made tears threaten. She managed to say, "Thank you," before hurrying from his office.

She had to tell Johnny and her honesty wouldn't allow her to write him a note – that would be cowardly – although how she would face him, tell him she wouldn't marry him and at the same time refuse to give an explanation, was something she couldn't imagine. Then there was the other problem of how to tell her parents. She had to move away from St David's Well and start again somewhere far away, yet she didn't have any idea of where to go or how to set about finding accommodation or work. She was daunted by her naïvety, her ignorance. She had lived at home with her parents making all the decisions, happy to play a minor role in her own life, and now, at nearly twenty-three, she was trying to move out of that security and cope alone. How could she, without help? Then she thought of Ken Ward.

As Eirlys was dropping a letter addressed to Ken Ward into the post box, the postman was delivering a letter to her from Ken. With the letter from Ken, two letters from the boys were delivered.

Ken had tried to find Teresa and her sons but had failed. No one knew them at the address Eirlys had given him. He promised to try again when he had an opportunity.

The neat, careful writing of Stanley and the ill-formed impatient scribble from Harold were worrying. Annie showed them to Morgan at lunchtime, before he went off to work the two-till-ten shift at the factory. The two letters had been correctly addressed but had borne no postage stamps and Annie had willingly paid the excess amount. "That means Teresa didn't know they were writing," Morgan said unnecessarily. "They didn't want her to be upset at their asking if they can come back."

Stanley was worried about missing school and Harold grieved for his beautiful bike and asked if Morgan could find him another one, adding that he'd paint it himself if Morgan would show him how. The message from Percival was his wish to ride one of Mr Gregory's donkeys on the sands.

"They sound so unhappy," Annie said. "I wish Teresa hadn't taken them away from us. Who knows how long it will be before the bombs start dropping? How can she risk their young lives like this?"

"Most of the other evacuees have gone back too," Morgan reminded her. "I don't suppose you'd want to send your children away to live with strangers, no matter how strong the argument in favour of it, would you?"

"I could write and suggest they come down for a holiday, couldn't I?"

He laughed and said, "Knowing Teresa, I expect we'll have to send them the fare!" He looked at Annie, her face saddened by the words written by the unhappy boys. "Not that we'd mind that," he added soberly.

"Percival says he'll eat his taters, if you let him come back," Stanley had written. This time no attempt had been made to obliterate the sad message.

Harold had promised never to get in another fight, even with the boys at school.

"I think we should buy the train tickets and see if we can arrange for them to travel in care of the guard, if they still do that."

"I could go up," Annie mused.

"Could you cope with the disappointment if Teresa refused to let them come back?"

"We could both go. She might be less inclined to refuse if we turn up on her doorstep."

"No, I think it's best you go on your own. I'll stay here with Eirlys, we can't leave *her* on her own, can we?" he reasoned, unaware of the irony of his protectiveness for his daughter, who was making plans to move right away from their care and protection.

Teresa had a new boyfriend and a new job. She had met Ronald when she had moved once more in the hope of shaking off the determined man she had robbed. She wasn't doing right by her boys, she had to do better. Stanley was clever and needed regular school, and the others – well, sitting on their own all the time without even a wireless for company . . . Remorsefully she admitted to herself they were better off in St David's Well with Annie and Morgan.

She was smart and attractive enough and now that she had made up her mind, she went job-hunting with great determination. She loved her boys and she had to succeed for them as well as herself.

Another visit to the council and the story that her reason for moving had been rats, and she was put on the priority list for accommodation. If things worked out as she hoped, Ronald would move in with her and they'd be a proper family. He would help her manage her money. It had always been a problem. Once she had money in her pocket she was tempted by all sorts of things and was soon broke once again. If only she could save enough to pay the man who was dogging her footsteps.

Ronald wasn't fond of children, he'd told her that, but in her new mood of optimism she felt certain he would succumb to their fascination. Lovely boys they were, anyone would be proud of them.

With this decent job selling clothes on a market stall she'd be home in the evenings to talk to them and play games like they used to, except for when she went out for a drink with Ronald of course. He knew about her past.

"And that's just what it is," he told her. "It's past and gone for ever." By the end of summer they'd be settled. But first, she thought, handling the last few pounds in her pocket, first she needed some new clothes. Her own wouldn't do at all.

Beth was surprised to see Peter Gregory when she opened the shop one morning.

"I've come to apologise," he said.

"No need," she smiled. "What's a kiss between friends?"

"I've had a long, lonely and dangerous time recently and seeing you, so fresh and clean and familiar, I couldn't help it."

"It is dangerous work you do, isn't it, Peter?"

"Things will be easier from now on. I'll be able to get home occasionally and keep in touch. I don't suppose I could ask you a favour, could I, Beth?"

"If I can help . . . ?" She looked at him expectantly.

"I'd love it if you could write to me. Not regularly, but now and then, just to keep me in touch with things here. So I feel a part of it."

"Of course I will. I'd like that. I've never had a pen-pal before." There was some relief in Beth's reply. After that unexpected kiss, she had wondered what he was going to ask her.

"Thank you. Your pen-pal will be ever grateful. Dad will have my address – I won't know it myself until I get back. He could drop it off at your house, if you think your Freddy won't mind?"

She watched him walk down the road, tall, straight and purposeful. A warm feeling crept over her and she chided herself, reminding herself that Freddy was her love and always had been. Peter's interest was flattering, though, she admitted happily.

Days passed and Eirlys still hadn't found the right moment to tell Johnny or her parents. How many lives had Dadda wrecked by his stupid behaviour? It began with the death of Irene, depriving Johnny and Taff of their mother and Bleddyn of his wife. Her marriage was no longer possible, so both she and Johnny faced a different future to the one they had so happily planned. And Annie: how would she cope if she ever found out, Eirlys wondered, still unaware that her mother knew and was slowly forgiving her father for his weakness. Ken wrote to Eirlys quite often so his letter in reply to hers on Tuesday morning caused no speculation. Neither did the fact that she waited until she was in her room before she opened it. The letter was brief. She had told him only that her father and Johnny's mother had been carrying on and it meant she couldn't marry Johnny Castle. Ken made no comment on this, but stated succinctly that his parents had a spare bedroom which they were willing for her to use until she could get herself something more convenient. He included details of the journey and a diagram of where his parents lived. He also asked her to tell him the time of her arrival and added that, if she would like him to, he would meet her at Paddington. No criticism of her father, no comment on whether her decision was right or wrong, just an offer to help. It was exactly what she needed at that time.

She was working out her two weeks' notice. This wasn't essential – seven days would have been acceptable as she was paid weekly – but she had promised Mr Gifford she would stay until he had found a replacement, which he quickly did.

Three girls came for an interview and one was chosen. Still having said nothing to Johnny or her parents, she worked out the day on which she could leave. Unfortunately she would travel to London on Saturday March thirtieth, the day that was to have been her wedding day. Now, all she had to do was tell Johnny and her parents.

She didn't know how to begin. Johnny and she met one evening intending to go to the pictures, but she persuaded him to walk instead.

"There's something I have to tell you," she told him, her heart racing, painful in her chest.

Johnny smiled at her, her face a pale oval in the darkness. "You sound serious; can't you get the right hat to go with your going-away outfit?" he joked. "That reminds me, I have had a letter confirming our booking at the Sea Crest hotel in Porthcawl."

"Cancel it," she said, her voice little more than a whisper.

"What? For a moment there I thought you said cancel it."

"Cancel the booking, Johnny, I won't be going on our honeymoon.

You and I won't be getting married. I'm going away, leaving St David's Well."

"Is this some kind of joke?"

"No joke. Something has happened and it means I can't marry you, ever."

"What is it? There's nothing we can't work out together. Tell me, Eirlys! Let me put things right."

"No chance of that. I'll go to the church tomorrow and I'll send back the gifts and tell the rest of the guests. You can tell your father, and Granny Moll and the rest of your family."

"Tell them what?" he demanded. "You haven't told me anything!"

"I can't marry you. That's all you need to know."

"You don't love me enough, is that it? Pre-wedding nerves, that's all this is. You should have seen our Taff on the days before he and Evelyn—"

"I do love you, Johnny," she interrupted. "I love you more than enough. But something has happened to stop us marrying. It isn't nerves. It isn't anything that can be put right. I can't explain but you must accept that you and I can never marry."

He tried to put an arm around her, comfort her and reassure her, believing that he had been correct in his diagnosis of pre-wedding jitters. She pushed him away and her voice was ragged as she told him to go home and spread the news. "Your Evelyn will be pleased," she sobbed. "She never thought one of the Price family was good enough for you Castles."

"Not good enough? What are you saying? Please, Eirlys, let me—"

His voice carried on the still night air, there was the sound of her hurried footsteps fading, then he was alone, confused and devastatingly hurt. He stood there for what seemed an age, wondering what to do. Should he go after her and persuade her to tell him what was wrong? Or would it be better to go home and wait until the next day, then try to talk to her? It had to be something he could put right. Damn it all, the wedding was only days away!

He needed to talk to someone, but who? If it was sorted out in the next couple of days, he would probably regret telling anyone. His father would worry and Taff wouldn't understand even though he had experienced something similar himself. He was shaking with the shock of it all and he felt as stiff as if he had walked all day. His legs ached and his arms felt as though they had just dropped a heavy load. He was aware of pain around his shoulders and in sudden defeat he dropped onto the kerb at the corner of the street and with his head lowered so his chin was on his chest, he sat, his mind empty of coherent thought.

It was late evening and the girls should have been in bed, but the sky was clear and the stars were out in force. When Josie and Marie insisted they weren't tired enough to sleep, Hannah wrapped them up warmly and took them for a walk around the outskirts of the park, where, if they were lucky, they might hear the chirping, restless sounds of the birds settling for the night. It was something that always fascinated the girls and they stood, arms around each other, in the shadows, as the robin signalled the end of the day and the blackbird gave its mellow settling-down sounds.

"Time to go, the robin is saying," Hannah whispered.

"Can we wait for the owl?" Josie begged and, as they stood there for the promised, "two more minutes", Hannah became aware of the figure sitting not far from where they stood.

"Are you all right?" she asked hesitatingly, not recognising Johnny in the darkness.

"Hannah?" he said in disbelief. "What are you three doing here?" He was overwhelmed with the relief of not being alone, and jumped up and hugged all three in turn. "I have some sweets in my pocket for two good little girls," he said and made a big pretence of searching in every pocket until they were laughing. Then he handed them the bag of coconut mushrooms he had intended to give to Eirlys.

He walked back with them and at the door he hesitated. "Can I come in?" he asked.

"Johnny, you know how my mother feels about men coming to the house."

"All right, I understand."

Hannah had opened the door and the girls had slipped inside, carefully replacing the curtain behind them. "There's something wrong?" she asked softly.

He was aware of her standing so close that he could smell the clean, fresh night air on her cheeks and he longed to reach out and hold her close to him. He tried to bring his thoughts back to

Eirlys and could not. "Something wrong? The truth is, Hannah, I don't know."

He hurried away from her. The confusion in his heart had culminated in an almost overwhelming desire to kiss her. He had never been so mixed-up or unhappy in his whole life. He wandered along the empty streets, stopping sometimes to listen to the wireless programmes coming from a house, and, imagining the family groups sitting enjoying them, he felt that his world was in shatters. A surge of almost violent jealousy filled him at the sound of the contented murmur of voices and the occasional laughter. There was no point going home until he had exhausted himself enough to make sleep at least a possibility.

It was three in the morning before he headed for Brook Lane. No sounds from any of the houses now, everyone was tucked up in bed, trouble-free and with nothing to disturb their sleep. The wardens were still on their beat and offered a polite, "Goodnight, sir," as he passed the shop doorway where they hid to enjoy a cigarette. A policeman cycled past, stopping from time to time to check on shop doors to make sure they were firmly locked.

He stood for a while outside the house where Eirlys lived. He looked up at her window, shrouded in darkness, and wondered if she was sleeping soundly, at peace with her decision, or, like him, confused about whether or not they were making a mistake, or rectifying an earlier one.

Rumours were already beginning to reach Bleddyn, not about Johnny and Eirlys but about his wife. A woman further up Brook Lane, who seemed to spend a lot of her time standing outside wielding a sweeping-brush and watching what went on, had made several references to Irene's friend, and when he questioned her she smiled and said in a childish voice, "It's not for me to say, Mr Castle. Never speak ill of the dead, isn't that what we say?"

"I don't want you spreading gossip about my wife!" he said sharply. "My sons are upset as it is, losing their mother in that dreadful accident. Please don't make it worse for us all."

"Only saying what others are saying, that's all," she said, sweeping fiercely at a recalcitrant weed on her path. He tried to ignore the woman. Bored she was, always looking for excuses to gossip.

It was when he mentioned her remarks to Taff that he began to wonder.

Eirlys told the vicar that the wedding was cancelled and he spent most of her lunch break advising her not to be hasty. She smiled, listened with apparent interest, then repeated her instruction to cancel all the arrangements, promising that she would be in touch to compensate for any inconvenience.

She felt that her mind was floating through a different world. The pavement beneath her feet was there, but the street was no longer the familiar street, the town wasn't the same town, the people passing were strangers unable to see her.

She should have passed the fish-and-chip shop as she left the church and walked back to the office, but she darted down a back lane and avoided it, in case Bleddyn ran out and begged her to change her mind. Johnny would have told his father by now. She mustn't talk to anyone else before she told her parents. They had to be told soon, before they heard the news from someone else.

She tried to think of a convincing story to explain her behaviour to her mother, but failed. Her father didn't need telling, she thought bitterly. He, and only he, knew exactly why she was behaving in this way.

When she had helped her mother to put their evening meal on the table, she tried to build up to her announcement slowly but in the end she simply blurted it out.

"Johnny and I have cancelled the wedding. I can't marry him and I've told him so. The wedding is permanently off. We won't change our minds." As her mother stared at her in disbelief, she went on, "The church arrangements are cancelled, Johnny will tell Granny Moll Piper that the catering won't be needed, and tomorrow I'll start returning all the presents. Will you help me, Mam?" She was amazed at how matter-of-fact she sounded. She might as well have been telling them she'd changed her mind about which film she would see.

Demands for explanations were met with a stony silence. Morgan kept out of it, refusing to comment, fully aware of what had changed their daughter's mind.

The following day was Saturday and it was then that Johnny began to spread the news. He told his father, who pleaded with him to go and see Eirlys and put right whatever had gone wrong. Stubbornness, or something else, pride perhaps, made Johnny say angrily, "It's over, Dad. Eirlys has made that quite clear. There's nothing more I can say. And I wouldn't change it now if I could!"

He called to see his brother, Taff, and Evelyn. Evelyn's stilted, "I'm sorry," reminded Johnny about Eirlys's words and the long-standing disagreement beetween them.

"What did you say to her, Evelyn? This has to be down to you!"

At this Taff became roused in protection of Evelyn. Taff was rarely angry but he turned on Johnny and told him to go.

"How can you blame this on Evelyn? It's Eirlys's decision not to marry you and there's no point in looking for anyone else to blame. It's you she's turning down, nothing we could say would make that decision for her."

When the door slammed behind his distressed brother, Taff turned to Evelyn and demanded an explanation of her dislike of Eirlys. Sitting beside her, she gently told him the truth about his mother and Eirlys's father.

"I hated her because I thought she knew all along," she said sadly when the full story was explained.

Taff wanted to go at once to talk to his father but Evelyn stopped him.

"I don't think he knows and it's best he never finds out. Why add to his unhappiness?"

"It might ease his guilt," Taff said sadly. "He blames himself for not looking after her better."

Anger was Johnny's weapon throughout the day as he went to tell the family what had happened. He told Granny Moll to abandon her plans for the wedding breakfast and found himself going over the same ground as with his father and his brother Taff – "Talk to her, make her change her mind. Put right whatever's wrong." Each time he told someone, they gave the same responses and by midday he could have recited them in chorus with ease.

Several people called to see Eirlys, hoping for an explanation. Even Granny Moll Piper knocked on the door and demanded to know what she should do with the cake she had chosen and paid for. Eirlys refused to come down and speak to her, telling her mother, "She can throw it in the sea for the fish!"

Over the weekend, everyone who needed to be told had been notified. Then Eirlys told her parents her next item of news.

"I'm going away," she said. "I'm going to live in London. My boss has given me a good reference and has given me an introduction to a place looking for someone with my skills."

"What is the matter with you?" Annie demanded tearfully. "First the wedding and now this! Where will you go? Where will you stay? For heaven's sake, Eirlys, what has happened?"

"I'll be staying with Ken Ward and his family until I get a place of my own."

"But why? You've got a home here," Annie wailed.

Her father said little, except to plead with her not to go. He was sitting, his head drooped, a melancholy expression on his face, knowing he was responsible and could do nothing about it.

"It's Ken, isn't it?" Annie suddenly said. "He's the cause of this. Writing letters, unsettling you. He should have left you alone."

"It's nothing to do with Ken," she said.

Bleddyn threw down the cloth with which he was wiping up the last of the spilt paint.

"Damn it all," he said aloud, "this wedding cancellaton is because of Irene! Eirlys must be worried about her illness, afraid it's something Johnny and their children could inherit. Her suicide in the docks must have terrified her – and understandably, too."

He sat for a while working out how he could help, surrounded by paint pots and brushes and all the paraphernalia of decorating. He had been through the house with Johnny and Taff's help and every room looked different from when Irene was alive. He had needed the cleansing and a fresh start; could Eirlys be in need of the same?

He went firstly to see Mrs Hibbert and paid a month's rent on the rooms Johnny and Eirlys were to have made their home. That gave them time to reconsider.

When Johnny came in, he told him what he had done, but Johnny shook his head.

"Thanks, Dad, that was a kind thought and a good idea, but she's going away; she's got a job in London and for a while at least she'll be staying with Ken Ward's family."

"Is he the trouble?" Bleddyn asked.

"No, he's just a friend."

"Then has she told you why?"

"She won't say, just that we can't ever marry."

"I wondered, well, is she worried about the way your mam died? It's an awful thing to live with."

"How could it be to do with Mam? It's me. She doesn't want to spend the rest of her life with me, that's the only reason. It has to be. Anything else could have been sorted."

On what would have been her wedding day, Eirlys was at the station, coldly calm, alone, and waiting for a train to take her to London instead of catching a later train to take her and Johnny on their honeymoon, being cheered on their way by family and friends. It was so unfair. She steeled herself not to cry although inside she felt the aching, barely controlled agony of tears that needed to be shed.

In a corner where the rack to hold bicycles stood, a lone figure watched her board the train. He had to see for himself that she really was leaving. It still seemed impossible for their plans to come to such a sudden and unexplained end.

As the train moved away and disappeared, Johnny stared at the empty rails for a long time. This really was the end. There was no chance of her changing her mind.

Annie was devastated by her daughter's departure. The house echoed, the empty rooms mocked her as she wandered around as though the building might have an explanation. First Stanley, Harold and Percival, now Eirlys leaving; not to marry and live a few minutes' walk away, but to disappear into a place they didn't know.

Morgan's thoughts were equally morbid and he knew the only way he could help Annie was to coax her to go to London to see the place where Eirlys was living and to visit the boys. The Ward family had been friends; it wouldn't be unreasonable in the circumstances to ask them to find accommodation for Annie near them, so she could see for herself the place where Eirlys was living. It would help Annie if she were able to picture her daughter in her new surroundings.

Johnny on the other hand, was deliberately and excessively cheerful over the following days. He exaggerated his indifference to combat Taff's sympathy. He did lose his temper once and accuse Evelyn again of being the cause, although he failed to extract from her an explanation. Apart from that brief moment, he whistled and sang as he went about his greengrocery deliveries, making people smile, winking at young girls and old ladies as though life was particularly good.

Besides his unhappiness, Johnny felt embarrassed, a bit foolish. He'd been jilted and he didn't even know why.

The postman's visits were still eagerly awaited by Annie and Morgan, but with greater anxiety now that Eirlys had gone away. She wrote several times during that first week, telling them how interesting the area was and describing some of the places she had visited with Ken's sister Julia.

Like Johnny, she was over-bright, over-cheerful, laughing at everything and nothing, attempting to convince others as well as herself that she was content.

Annie wrote back and asked whether there was time for her to try and find Teresa and the boys. She knew London was big, but it must be possible to get around it on buses and the terrifying Underground trains, she thought.

The need to see that Stanley, Harold and Percival were all right was made doubly urgent after another letter came telling Annie they had moved yet again and were sharing a bed in what had once been a cellar. Stanley also told them that their mother had a new boyfriend called Ronald but that he didn't like Percival very much. Annie knew she had to go as soon as possible. Her greatest fear was that they might move once too often and she would lose touch with them altogether.

"I expect it's a basement flat, you know how Stanley can make a drama out of everything," Morgan said, trying to comfort her.

"I have to go to London, Morgan. I want to see that Eirlys is all right and although she's living in a different area from the boys, I could see them all if I stayed a night or two."

Morgan didn't try to persuade her against going, he encouraged her. He needed a rest from her abuse as well as wanting to know that Eirlys was settled safely. Guilt was a heavy cloak he was unable to remove. Annie had guessed the real reason for her daughter cancelling her wedding and her accusations against Morgan were destroying him. They rarely exchanged a civil word and he had taken to walking around at night rather than stay in the house and listen to her repeated accusations. He had long ago given up retaliation. He allowed her to rain the insults down on him without apparently hearing them. He wondered how much longer he could bear it.

He went to the station with her and kissed her awkwardly for appearances' sake. Then he went back home and for the first time in weeks he slept.

The train was full of uniformed young men. Normally Annie would have enjoyed talking to them, but today she had no interest in anyone. Her thoughts were ahead of her, wondering if Eirlys was happy, or ready to come back to St David's Well and face the gossip, and whether she would be able to persuade Teresa to allow the boys to come back to St David's Well until she had found them somewhere decent to live. If there was time, she might suggest going to the housing department with Teresa and finding out exactly what was happening.

Teresa had moved again, as the boys had told Annie and Morgan. It was far from comfortable. Any furniture and linen and china she'd had in the past had been lost during her frequent moves. Her attempts at hiding from the man who stalked her demanding his money had been futile anyway. He had found her easily, followed her when she left the public house one night and hit her so she had bruises on her body, making it difficult to work and earn the money to pay him back.

She still worked on the market stall but didn't earn enough for her needs. If only she could pay him back, although she suspected that by this time, the money was not the strongest reason for his persistence. He had been made to look a fool and he told her he wanted to see her come into the place where he and his friends were gathered and hand over the money and make an abject apology. Only then would he leave her alone.

The so-called romance with Ronald had lasted less than a week. He had left without a word but two days later, while she was out and Percival was home alone nursing a head cold, an officer from the housing department came and, finding the place unfit for habitation and the boy on his own, called the welfare authorities.

Two officials were waiting for Teresa when she arrived home at seven, having called in at the pub for a drink on the way. She wasn't a heavy drinker but had hoped to make a date for later on.

The three boys looked frightened, having been warned that they might have to go into a children's home until their mother could get decent accommodation.

"We could go and stay with Auntie Annie," Percival said hopefully.

The so-called "flat" was a single room below pavement level, small, dark and damp, and sparsely furnished. After coming in from work and feeding the boys, Teresa habitually left them there while she went out and hung around the pubs looking for likely customers.

Much of what she earned went on herself. Her clothes were smart and quite new. She had to look good, dress expensively, have her hair properly washed and set and, use make-up skilfully unless she wanted to end up with the dregs of humanity. When she met the welfare people, she was aware of the difference in her appearance and theirs and tried to make excuses.

She had to get money, enough to set them up. Her lovely boys deserved more than she'd given them. They'd be better off in a home.

When the boys were asleep she went out to find the man who she called her shadow. He was in the usual pub at his usual table with his cronies around him. She pleaded with him to leave her alone so she could get the boys a decent place to live. "I stole from you," she said. "None of this is their fault."

He hit her as she was laughed out of the place and said, "The money, here, tomorrow, or you're dead." He had no intention of doing more than frighten her, but she believed him. Perhaps she should go to the police? But who would believe her? No one.

The boys had not made the address very clear and after reaching the general area. Annie spent several hours searching for them. She was extremely tired. Having found a place to stay and deposited her small suitcase in her room, she hadn't stopped to eat, but had gone straight out to find the boys. Tomorrow she would go and see her daughter, but this evening was for Stanley, Harold and little Percival. She had a few pounds in the back of her purse hoping she would use it to take them back to St David's Well with her. First she had to find them!

The traffic was very different from back home, she thought, as two cars skidded around the corner and almost touched one another as they passed. So impatient, and, on the dark streets, very stupid too.

She was nearing the address where she thought she would locate the flat when she saw, running along the opposite pavement, a figure she thought she recognised. That funny, tippy-toed run in such ridiculously high heels couldn't be anyone else but Teresa hurrying home after her day in the market.

"Teresa!" she called, relief slowing her weary feet. "It's me, Annie. I've come to see the boys!"

Teresa appeared not to hear her and, still with that silly girlish run, hurried towards the corner. Exasperated, afraid she would lose her and perhaps not be able to find the boys, Annie ran after her, calling her name.

The car that slowly cruised out of a side road was barely visible. But here in London, with more traffic and the hooded traffic signals, the light was slightly brighter than at home. The car's shaded head lights snapped off and the car increased its speed. In the faint glow from other vehicles nearby, she saw quite clearly that the car was heading straight for Teresa. "Teresa!" Annie screamed. "Look out!"

The driver swerved away from Teresa at the very last moment, as he had intended, but couldn't avoid hitting, then running over Annie, who was heading for Teresa in blind panic.

Teresa gave a wail of horror and ran to where Annie's body lay in the dark road. The driver's shocked face was briefly visible as he stared back at what he had done, then he drove off, still without showing his lights. Only Teresa knew who he was.

Cars stopped, people arrived, instructions were shouted, and Teresa lay down beside the still form, unaware of them all, murmuring, "It was meant for me, Annie, it was meant for me." She lay beside her, hugging her, until an ambulance man came and took her away.

She was oblivious of what was said. Questions went unanswered, her brain dulled by the tragedy. Annie dead. And because of her. Stealing that twenty-four pounds had ruined everything and had now caused the death of a friend. How was she going to live with that?

Twelve

Teresa stared down at the peaceful face of Annie as the ambulance men lifted her body on to a stretcher. She knew she was dead. She remained still, her arms wrapped about herself, and silently wept.

In her head she relived the moment: the shouts, the revving engine, the squealing brakes as the car slewed momentarily out of control, then the thump, the awful thump. Unaware of the people approaching, slowly at first, then in a flurry of activity, she hadn't responded to the voices at first, but had sat there on the cold ground nursing Annie, talking to her, telling her it was going to be all right. Then the wailing approach of the ambulance broke into her consciousness. Someone lifted her gently away from Annie's still form and her hands covered her face as the sound of voices invaded her ears. Where had all these people come from? What had they to do with Annie?

Remorse hit her then. What had she done? By that stupid action, stealing the wallet of a man who wouldn't accept his humiliation, she had been chased and attacked and it had ended in not injury to her, but the death of Annie Price. How could she live with this? How could she tell the boys?

The sequence of the events went round and round in her mind, as though next time, the ending would be different.

The next hour was filled with confusion – seeing Annie's body taken away and then questions and more questions, until she told the police that her children were at home, unattended.

"We'll come back with you, and once we know they are safe, we can continue with the interview," she was told.

"Interview?" The word had connotations of guilt. Could they know what had happened, and understand that she was responsible?

"You say she was your friend, a good friend. You must want to help us in every way you can to catch the driver of that car."

"I don't remember anything. It's all a blur, all squealing brakes and the shouting and—"

She sobbed and the policemen accompanied her home and waited, silent and unmoving, until she had recovered. They then continued with their questions.

They were very persuasive and she eventually told them about the wallet, the threats and her convictions for prostitution.

"Just tell us who the man is and we'll do the rest," they told her.

"I'll be made to appear in court. I can't let the boys go through all that."

"Tell us his name, Teri," one of them said, making it clear he knew the name she used when working, and for her prosecutions. "Give us his name, description and the make of car and the number if you know it. There'll be enough evidence on the car to convict him," he coaxed.

Reluctantly, but with the image of Annie lying in the middle of the road to persuade her, she gave them a description, told them where he usually drank and everything else she could remember, to give them a picture of him.

When she fell into bed she was exhausted, but she didn't sleep. The images were too vivid. She lay there in the cramped bed, trying to hug all three boys at once, the need to feel she was protecting them paramount.

As dawn broke on the dark wet morning, she lay for a while longer listening to the rain dripping through the rotten window pane on to the old bedspread placed to catch it, dull and persistent. What should she do? Where should she go? Then the idea flooded her mind like a shaft of warm sunlight on a winter's day; comforting and filling her with a sensation of well-being. St David's Well. She would go and stay in Annie's home, with Morgan Price.

At once she felt more cheerful. With the first move planned she didn't worry about what would happen after that. Knowing her first action was sufficient for the moment.

She woke the boys and said excitedly, "Get dressed, we're going to see Morgan and all your friends in St David's Well. Just wait till summer. We'll see the beach in all its glory, just like Eirlys told you, remember? There'll be roundabouts and donkey rides and sticks of rock and ice-creams and picnics on the sand and more people having fun than you've ever seen!"

* * *

The news came to Eirlys via the police. There was a loud knock on the door of Ken's parents' house, a brief, whispered conversation, then they came and stood beside her while the constable told her that Annie was dead. She stared at the constable and he had to repeat it as she seemed not to have heard him.

Her first thought, after the inital shock had receded, was that she wanted to see Johnny. She needed him there to help her over this. Instead there was Ken and his family and she was so thankful that she had not decided to stay with strangers in some anonymous bed-sitter as she had originally planned.

"I'll go home with you," Ken said, putting an arm around her. "You aren't in a fit state to travel on your own."

Recovering fast, Eirlys shook her head. Tempting as it was, she knew that at a time like this she could easily give Ken the wrong impression. She loved him dearly, but had no thoughts of a future for them together and she couldn't allow herself to mislead him.

She asked him to let her new boss know what had happened, and then, carrying only a small suitcase, she went by bus to Paddington and commenced the long, sad journey home. She was unaware that on the same train Stanley, Harold and Percival were playing snakes and ladders with Teresa, in between marking their progress on a list of stations in a railway guide given to them by an elderly passenger.

Unaware of the tragedy that had taken place, Johnny stood outside Hannah's front door early that morning and knocked. He knocked loudly and stood prepared to push a foot in the door to prevent Hannah from closing it when she recognised him.

It was still dark and rain was falling, cold rain that threatened to turn to snow. As he waited, the first flakes settled on his shoulder, to vanish immediately into the soft navy cloth of his overcoat.

It was late in the season for snow. He remembered Granny Moll calling it "daffy" snow, sudden to cover the ground but staying only a short time. He was unaware of the cold, thinking only of what he would say to Hannah as soon as she opened the door to him.

The door shifted after he had heard the swishing sound of the blackout curtain being pulled across. Then she was there and at once he stepped forward into the hall.

"Johnny, you mustn't come in."

"I have something to say to you and it won't wait," he said, firmly guiding her back into her cramped living room.

"Who is it, Hannah?" a voice called from the back.

Stifling Hannah's reply, Johnny pressed a hand gently over her mouth and called back, "It's me, Johnny Castle, and I have business to discuss with your daughter. Private business, right?" There was anger in his voice but when they went inside the room where the gas light gave its friendly glow there was no anger in his eyes, only love.

"I don't want you to think this is desperation, or love on the rebound, or anything else except this. Hannah, I love you. I want us to be a familiar sight, walking around, doing everything together, as a family. You, me and Josie and Marie, never apart, so everyone knows we love each other."

"Johnny, what about Eirlys and—"

"No one else counts. There's just you and me and the girls. I love them as much as I love you."

"I can't do this, Johnny."

"Why? Don't you love me?"

"There's the age difference for one thing," she protested weakly.

"It hasn't made the smallest difference to how I feel for you so why worry about it?"

"Your father wouldn't be happy about us."

"He isn't marrying you. I am."

"How can you want to take us on, when you could find someone young and without all my encumbrances?"

"What encumbrances?"

So far he hadn't touched her and the air around them was fraught with barely controlled emotion. He lifted her chin with a finger and made her look at him.

"Tell me you don't love me and never will, and I'll go away," he said softly. "But before you decide, let me show you how much I love *you*."

For a long moment he stood there, looking at her, staring at her, pleading silently for her to give the answer he so desperately wanted. When he did open his arms and hold her, she couldn't explain the tears except to say that they were tears of happiness like she had never believed in before.

The news of Annie's death spread swiftly around the town and people visiting her home with sympathy for Morgan had him almost constantly in tears. He felt hollow but couldn't eat, he was exhausted but couldn't sleep. He just sat and watched the clock going around, drank gallons of tea, and waited for Eirlys to come home.

Mixed with his grief were regrets at how he had made Annie's last weeks so unhappy. Why had he been so stupid and started that affair with Irene Castle? If only Annie hadn't found out, he wailed inwardly. Irene hadn't been a serious threat to his marriage; in spite of his words of love and his promises, she would never have been important enough to persuade him to leave his wife. If only he had ended it sooner, Annie would have died without the distress of knowing.

He heard the latch on the gate click and jumped out of his chair. Through the front window he saw his daughter and for a brief moment wondered how she would behave towards him. Would this dreadful situation ease her return, make them forget the agony of their parting? The words with which he would greet her were on his lips, practised through the long night and day, but he didn't say them. Voices accompanied Eirlys's progress and he stared in disbelief when first Percival, then Harold and then Stanley and Teresa came into sight.

He didn't get to hug Eirlys, or say the words he had planned; instead he was leapt upon by the boys, their faces showing their grief. Yet their relief at being back in St David's Well was soon apparent by the way they wandered around the house reacquainting themselves with it. He was grateful that the moment was eased by their affectionate greetings. Teresa followed her small sons and hugged him as enthusiastically as her sons had done.

Eirlys had decided to ignore her father. How else could she deal with all this? She couldn't pretend to have forgiven him. The death of her mother couldn't wipe out his shameful behaviour towards her. Having someone to blame eased her pain, and added to his.

She had been shocked at his appearance when she walked in, and was glad of the chance to recover while the boys fell on him with such delight. He was pale and his face seemed to have lost its roundness, his eyes were large and deeper in their sockets. It was obvious he hadn't slept since being told of Annie's death last night, and sympathy swelled but receded quickly, as she thought of her mother and remembered how deceived she had been by Morgan.

Leaving Teresa and her sons talking to him, she went into the kitchen and began to prepare a meal for them all. Crosse and Blackwell tinned soups were always a favourite with the boys. With some bread, and with cakes and fruit to follow, it would have to do until she could do some shopping in the morning.

She began to work out where they would all sleep. She unkindly decided that the quickest and simplest arrangement was for her father to give up his room and allow Teresa to use his bed. When she suggested it his look of horror changed her mind for her and she was ashamed. How insensitive she was becoming.

She knew she should talk to him, let him share his grief with her, but she wasn't ready for that, although she knew the moment would come. With complete lack of logic she blamed Morgan for everything, and the pain inside her made her unaware of how unsympathetic she was being, thinking of herself and her own aching misery and not sharing with her father the tragedy of his terrible loss.

Teresa made herself at home, spreading her things around the various rooms, demanding various changes in the way the furniture was arranged and accepting Eirlys and Morgan running around after her as her right. While Eirlys and Stanley washed the dishes, Teresa announced that she was taking Morgan for a drink.

"Do 'im good, poor man, it'll make sure he sleeps."

Eirlys wanted to say something but she was too amazed at the woman's suggestion and too offended by her father's swift agreement. She ran upstairs. Teresa's clothes were everywhere, and she pushed them unceremoniously into a corner.

Stanley followed her and said, half apologetically, "'Ard work, ain't she, our ma. She loves clothes and she's pretty, ain't she?"

"Yes, Stanley, she's a very pretty lady, but she'll have to learn that there isn't room for her to spread all her things about. We're seven – I mean six," she corrected sadly, "and there isn't the room."

Hannah had persuaded Johnny not to make their love for each other public. They decided that they would wait a few months, and only gradually let it be known that they intended to marry. Johnny had willingly agreed with Hannah's wish, as he did not want people to whisper that he had turned to Hannah in his disappointment over Eirlys.

"It will soon be time for the new season to begin," he told her on the day that Eirlys returned to St David's Well. "I'll be caught up in the last-minute painting and repairing and all the usual stuff that the new season brings, so we won't be able to meet regularly. Then when the season begins you won't see much of me, except when you bring Josie and Marie to the beach, which I hope will be often. The family will soon get used to seeing us together and will soon love you as much as I do."

They had met on the morning Eirlys and the four Loves had arrived, and were taking Josie and Marie to Mr Gregory's small-holding, to see the donkeys. Mr Gregory took them to the barn, which he boastingly called the tack room, and explained about the repainting that would be done on the collars bearing the animals' names before the summer season began.

While Josie and Marie were happily entertained, Hannah asked, "What has happened about the rooms in Mrs Hibbert's house, Johnny?"

"Eirlys told her we won't be using them after all, and no, I don't have any regrets," he smiled. "I don't think Mrs Hibbert has any either; she's had the place cleaned up and decorated for nothing, and Dad paid her four weeks' rent, so she's happy."

He talked about the beach for a while, telling her she must ignore Granny Moll's inevitable pestering and decide for herself whether or not she wanted to help out now and again. "The trouble with Granny Moll Piper is that she loves the sands and can't understand those who don't."

"You love it though, there isn't any persuading needed to get you there, is there?"

"I've worked the beach for so long I can't imagine any other life. When Taff and I were at school, all our holidays were spent on the beach – helping Dad at first, then, as we grew older, we took on one of the regular jobs. In fact I think I learnt arithmetic and lots of other things besides, from the need to give change and to count the takings, and helping Uncle Huw and Auntie Marged with the orders and the like." He laughed, then his face took on a serious expression. "I don't know how much longer I'll be able to enjoy it, though. I'm afraid I might have to accept an enormous change before very long. The call-up of men is increasing to men a lot older than me. Most of my friends have already gone. One has been killed.

I have doubts about any chance of deferment, just because we work at Piper's."

"Let's not think about it and be happy while we can, Johnny. I can't bear to think of you going into danger."

Ignoring her reminder of what call-up actually meant, he said cheerfully, "The swingboats and helter-skelter and the stalls and Piper's Café stay open for as long as there's daylight, and I'll be there until everything is locked away for the night. You won't see much of me, but when we do have time to be together, I'll make sure every minute is treated as something precious."

It was as they were walking back across the fields that they learned of the death of Annie Price.

When Hannah recognised the figure of Eirlys walking towards them, she felt a sort of panic that threatened to close her throat so that she couldn't breathe. If Johnny saw her, would he regret telling her goodbye? Would Eirlys reclaim her place in his heart?

Johnny saw her at almost the same time and sensing Hannah's uneasiness, lifted Marie up into his arms and reached out for Josie's hand. Eirlys's first glimpse would see them as a complete group, a family. No words would be needed to explain.

"Hi, Eirlys," he called as they drew nearer. "Couldn't you stay away from us then? London not as exciting as you hoped?" he teased lightly. Then seeing her expression, he asked, "What is it? Is something wrong?"

"It's Mam. She was killed. Hit by a car in London when she went to see Stanley, Harold and Percival."

At once Hannah ran to her and held her. "Oh Eirlys, what a terrible thing to happen. You and your father must be distraught."

Johnny hugged her too, still holding Marie, who insisted she couldn't walk a single step more.

They walked back together, Eirlys explaining that she wasn't going anywhere, just out to get a breath of air and to escape the stream of visitors calling to offer help and sympathy. Johnny set a complaining Marie on her feet and took Hannah's hand in his.

"Your father?" Hannah asked. "Is he coping? Thank goodness you were able to get home so quickly. He must have been so in need of you."

Eirlys couldn't explain her inability to comfort her father, and she didn't reply.

Hannah went on, "My parents have never been very kind to me, they often told me they wish I had been the one to die instead of my brother. But in spite of that, I'd do everything I could if they were in trouble. It's a time for families, isn't it?"

Only then did it occur to Eirlys that Hannah and Johnny were holding hands, and she saw then that the group was more than a few friends out for a walk, but four people joined together in love.

It hurt. Seeing him with Hannah, knowing that he had found with her friend what she had thrown away, she was afraid to stay with them and drink in their happiness. She loved Johnny and her father had ruined her hope of a future with him.

"I have to go," she told them, but instead of running home she went across the fields and stood, looking at the caravan where her father and Johnny's mother had frequently met.

She felt about in the most likely places for a key and found it tucked behind one of the wheels. Going inside she was aware of the cold dankness of the place. Everything was dreary except for the moss which grew at the base of the windows, bright green and alien in that drab place. The windows were wet from winter's melted frost. The ice would have been beautiful, delicately ornamental, with leaves and exotic flowers formed by the tightening of the frozen water into many and varied shapes. If it was beautiful once, all that had gone, and what was left were smells, invasive mildew and cloth already beginning to rot.

She felt an aching and overwhelming sadness as she imagined her father seeking secret and forbidden pleasures in such a place. Mould was creeping across the cushions and there was a smell of decay and neglect. It was a sordid picture, she told herself, but her emotions twisted away from her resentment and anger and hurt and she began to think of her father as a lonely man, weak and foolish but not wicked. Locking the door and putting the key back in its hiding place, she went home. It was time for her to forgive.

They talked long into the night and both felt happier for accepting that they were still important to each other.

"I still want to keep my job in London, Dadda," Eirlys explained. "But I'll come home often and make sure you are all right."

"I'll manage fine," he assured her. "I'm not helpless and there are bound to be those willing to offer a hand. That's the best of living in a small town like St David's Well. There are plenty of friends when you need them. As long as you and I are still friends, that's all that matters to me, love."

The funeral took place in a cemetery which had a light covering of "daffy" snow, making the stark and gloomy place beautiful, if only for a while. Eirlys didn't attend; it was men only at the graveside. She stayed at the house, and, with Teresa doing her best to help, and several neighbours and friends doing what they could, she prepared the food for those who would return with her father.

Most of Johnny's family attended the service and many of them came back to the house. Johnny was there with his father Bleddyn, his brother Taff and Evelyn, but without Hannah, who had no one to look after the children.

In a brief moment between attending to the food and drinks, Johnny came into the kitchen and asked her how she was and what her plans were. It was strange to talk to him as though they were no more than friends. She coped by pretending he was someone she hardly knew, not the man she loved and had planned to marry. Then he spoilt it all by telling her how much he loved Hannah and how it was all for the best, even though he still didn't understand why she had suddenly left him.

"I can't explain, Johnny. Something happened that made it impossible for us to marry. Please don't ask me to tell you what it was."

Then Evelyn came in and, seeing their serious faces, presumed that Eirlys was telling Johnny about his mother and her father.

"So now you know, Johnny. Sordid, mind, hearing this about your own mother, but better that you know."

"Don't, Evelyn!" Eirlys pleaded.

But Evelyn went on, believing she was helping. Her voice was full of sympathy; there was no malice in her expression. She believed that telling Johnny was the best way of dealing with it, and that was what she thought was happening now. "I think Eirlys is very brave and honest to have told you. It couldn't have been easy. But secrets fester and it's always better to deal with things rather than try to hide them, isn't it?" She looked at Eirlys with an affectionate smile. "I'm so glad you faced it, Eirlys. I'm so sorry about the way I've behaved towards you."

In the stunned silence that followed, Eirlys felt tears falling down her cheeks.

"Please, Evelyn, don't say any more," she whispered. "Take no notice, Johnny, Evelyn's mistaken, that's all, it's a mistake." In vain she had tried to stop Evelyn, but by the time the other girl had realised her mistake, she had said too much for Johnny to be able to walk away.

He insisted on hearing the full story and was angry with Morgan and his mother, but, surprisingly, most of all with Eirlys.

"How could you not tell me?" he demanded

"What would have been the point? I thought the fewer people who knew the less chance of your father finding out."

"That was my reasoning too," Evelyn said. "That was why I hoped you and Eirlys would stop seeing each other. I'm very fond of your dad, Johnny, and I hoped that if you and Eirlys were no longer together, the secret would be safe and he would never know."

"Eirlys should have told me. There shouldn't be any secrets between two people who love each other."

"But you didn't love me, did you, Johnny?" Eirlys asked quietly before walking away.

Evelyn followed her and begged her to listen to her apology.

"Eirlys, I really thought you knew about your father and Johnny's mother. I was so upset for his father, who's such a kind, gentle man, so undeserving of such treachery. I was convinced you must know, you'd been to the caravan, you'd seen Irene wandering about, obviously waiting to meet your father. I hated you for it. I'm sorry. I'm really sorry."

Eirlys looked at her, and, seeing the tear-streaked face, believed her.

"I don't know whether you believe me, Evelyn, but I think I would have acted in the same way," she said as they hugged. "I'm fond of Bleddyn too. But," she added sadly, "I don't think you and I will ever be sisters-in-law as we once hoped. Johnny didn't deny it when I said he didn't love me, did he?"

Johnny hadn't been able to formulate an honest reply. He left the house and walked alone across the fields to think about what he had been told. It all came back: the death of his mother, the doctor explaining her earlier insistence that she was expecting a child and his telling her she was mistaken.

It was almost dark before he returned to the outskirts of the town and he stopped for a while and stared at the looming shadow of the caravan, where, he had been told, his mother had met Morgan Price and made love.

Like Eirlys he searched for a key, convinced that it would have been left somewhere close by. With the aid of a torch which he, like most people, habitually carried, he found it behind the same wheel. He went inside and, like Eirlys, was distressed at the sordid mess that was revealed by the thin beam of the torch.

There was a paraffin stove and, nearby, some matches in a tin which had previously held Oxo cubes. He tried to strike a match, intending to throw it among the bedclothes on the built-in couch, but, damp, they broke apart and he threw them down in disgust.

He was aching with pent-up fury that wouldn't be released. He couldn't bear the thought of people seeing this place and laughing. He tried to push the van off its support but failed at that too. He was sweating with his attempts to destroy the hated thing and all he could do was tie back the door and release the catches on the windows and let the elements do their worst. At the end of the summer there would be nothing left but a mouldering wreck. He'd come back and burn it. Then, as he prepared to leave, he shone the light around the place one last time, and it fell on his mother's coat. It destroyed him as no words had.

It all became real. Until then he had been trying to convince himself it was idle and mistaken gossip. He thought of the number of times she had been seen without a coat, and remembered the time when he had insisted that Eirlys had been wrong when she told him his mother was in the fields dressed only in a thin dress. She had been here, probably walking to meet Morgan Price.

As he walked away, the wind was already gusting in and moving the shabby curtains. The sooner it was a ruin the better. It was a memorial to his mother he didn't need.

He went back to Eirlys's house and when she opened the door, demanded, "You should have told me! I had a right to know why you were walking away from me, didn't I?"

"I hoped you would never find out."

"You didn't mind that everyone knew except Dad and me? That everyone was talking about us and probably laughing?"

"No one knows except Evelyn and she found out long before I did. Like me, she thought there was no value in telling you."

"We would have married if you hadn't discovered their secret, wouldn't we?" he said.

"Yes, and it would have been a mistake. I want more than St David's Well can offer me, and you – you love Hannah, don't you?"

He couldn't deny it.

"I wish you luck, Johnny," she said softly. "And I'm really sorry you had to find out about your mam."

His voice became calm to match hers. "Mam couldn't help it, but she always let us down." He frowned as he thought about his childhood. "When Taff and I were children she never did all the things mothers usually do. That's why Granny Moll and Auntie Marged were always so important to Taff and me."

"She loved you, Johnny. She wanted you and Taff to find the happiness that was denied her."

"Perhaps she did. Perhaps this disaster made us see things more clearly. You *and* me. She probably prevented us making a great mistake."

"That's a good way of looking at it, Johnny." She kissed him affectionately. "Being the sort of people we are, we'd have stayed together, but you and I would both have had regrets."

"How are you going to find room for all that wool?" he asked with a wry smile. "It looks as though Dad won't get his spare room back for a while."

"As soon as I can find a place I can afford, I'll send for it," she promised. "I haven't forgotten my dream."

"And Ken?"

"Ken is a kind and loving friend and he knows he'll never be anything more." As she spoke the words she had a vision of Ken waiting for her when she returned to London and the thought was far from displeasing.

When Johnny left, she sat and considered her life so far. It was filled with regrets. She had let Ken down and now her love for Johnny hadn't stood the test either. Perhaps she wasn't intended for love and marriage and motherhood, she thought sadly. She was a businesswoman with high ambition. But, she wondered, would that always be enough?

Eirlys didn't intend to stay with her father very long. Unless she left soon she would become caught up in running the home, making arrangements to see friends, and end up staying for ever.

She went to look for him the following day to tell him when she planned to leave. She found him on the allotment that had once been his, talking to the new owner. After telling him her plans, they walked back together with very little left to say.

She stayed to share a midday meal of lumpy mashed potatoes and crisply overdone sausages, prepared, with good intent, by Teresa.

"Not much of a cook, is she?" she whispered conspiratorially, when she found him later, clearing out the shed.

"She tried very hard and I was determined to eat it," he smiled. "Thank goodness for indigestion tablets, eh?"

"When is she going back? I thought I'd leave tomorrow, if that's all right."

"Fine, love. I'll miss you, mind. But I don't want you worrying or thinking of coming back. I'll be fine. You will write often and tell me what you're doing, won't you?"

"And Teresa and the boys?"

"I told them they can stay another day or so. I think Teresa was as affected by your mam's death as any of us, being there an' all. Seeing it happen. The boys are hoping to see something of the beach before they go back to London."

"Be careful you aren't too welcoming, Dadda, or you'll find it hard to tell them to go."

She was delighted when he explained the reason for clearing out the shed. "It's to store your wools and materials, so you can get back to your rug-making as soon as you have a place of your own," he told her.

All anger faded as she hugged him. "Thanks, Dadda. That's exactly what I needed, some help to rebuild my dream."

With the train time chosen for the following afternoon, she spent the hours before she left for the station walking around the town, seeing the familiar and loved places, saying her goodbyes.

She knew where Johnny and Taff and the others would be. With the days getting longer and the sun getting stronger, the thoughts of summer were not far from anyone's thoughts. They would be at the beach, getting everything checked in preparation for the opening of the 1940 summer season. The helter-skelter would be painted and all the safety checks carried out, and the swingboats made ready for their place on the sand. She wondered how she would live through a summer without having the sea so close. She knew she would miss it.

The bus took her to the sands, where several of the cafés were having a face-lift ready for the opening in May. There were quite a few people around, taking advantage of the sunshine. Leaning on the sturdy sea wall, she watched as children ran about and played. Their voices were shrill, and echoed amid the calls of the gulls gliding on the light breeze hoping for a tidbit or two. No summer dresses yet, but the hats and scarves added splashes of cheerful colour; a hint of the wonderful days to come.

As she strolled to the end of the promenade to where a cliff rose up to the path above, she looked at Piper's Café and saw a hand waving. Waving back she walked across the sand to the bottom of the metal steps and climbed up.

Moll opened the door and said, "Come in, girl, and we'll have a nice cup of tea and a Welsh cake. Let's sit in the window and enjoy this bit of sun."

She was disappointed not to find Johnny and Taff and Bleddyn there, but stayed a while, talking to Moll about her plans and listening to Moll telling of her new ideas for the approaching season. Moll said nothing about her cancelled wedding. It had all been said. She hugged the old lady affectionately, then caught the bus back home.

There wasn't time for more than a snack, so she prepared a few sandwiches to eat on the train, collected her suitcase and set off for the station. She hoped to get away without any further goodbyes but as soon as she was on the platform, Johnny came.

There were some rather formal requests to write, keep in touch and look after herself; all the usual clichés that fill the uncomfortable last moments before the train puffs into view. Both were thankful when the sound of the steam engine reached their ears. Johnny stepped back after kissing her affectionately, and Eirlys began patting pockets and looking in her handbag to make sure she had everything to hand. Then she gasped. "My wallet! I've left it home and it has my identity card and my ration book and heaven alone knows what else. Oh, Johnny, I'll have to go back. I'll have to catch a later train!"

They left the suitcase in the porter's room and hurried away, Johnny leaving her at her gate with a final goodbye.

She went in through the back door, careful not to make a sound. The last thing she wanted was another round of goodbyes! The house was silent and she was thankful for that. She wondered vaguely whether her father had taken Teresa and the boys to see the donkeys again, a walk of which they never tired.

She looked around her at the familiar room as she picked up her wallet and stored it safely in her handbag. More untidy than when her mother was there, she thought with a wry smile. Annie had been so fussy. She was sorry to say goodbye to her home, and felt guilty at walking away from her father, leaving him to cope alone.

Should she have stayed a while longer, helped him to get used to being alone? Promising herself she would visit often and make sure he was looking after himself properly, she turned to go. Poor Dadda, he'd find it hard to face the empty days, even though he had put on a brave expression and encouraged her to leave. Again guilt overwhelmed her and her footsteps faltered as she went towards the door.

Then she heard a voice upstairs, a soft chuckle. Teresa, she wondered? Still not making a sound and this time without really understanding why, she went up the stairs on tiptoe.

The door of her room was open and as she peered around the door she gave a wail of anguish. Teresa and her father were naked on the bed.

Slamming the door, and still issuing the wailing, distressed sounds that echoed around her head as though they came from someone else, she ran down the stairs and out of the house.

She ran until her legs threatened to give way and her lungs explode, then she paused and sat on the wall of a garden and stared back the way she had come as though expecting her father to loom into view.

Walking more slowly, she went on and after collecting her case, stood on the platform for the train promised in fifteen minutes. This time the platform was full. Soldiers, airmen and sailors mingled with the civilians who had come to see them off. She remembered the stiffness of her parting from Johnny and wondered if it was the same with most of them. Everything said, couples sharing nothing more than the occasional nervous smile, not willing to go until the last minute, but feeling enormous relief when the signal dropped and the train curved slowly towards them.

Then she heard shouting and pushing their way through the crowd came Stanley, Harold and Percival.

"Eirlys! Eirlys!" Stanley shouted. "Mum says we can stay in St

David's Well! Ain't that somethin'? On Monday Uncle Morgan's taking us back to school!"

Uncle Morgan. How different the honorary title sounded since she had witnessed the scene in the bedroom. Before, it had been so innocent, but Annie's death had changed that too. Morgan's resentment about Teresa's casual acceptance of their help had vanished. An uncle to the boys; one of a long line of them, the most recent being Ronald who didn't like Percival.

Strange how helpless some men are when faced with an attractive woman, she mused, her expression hidden as she hugged the three evacuees who had become locals. Specially when they find themselves alone. Solitude would not have been easy for Morgan Price. Why should she expect him to accept it? He couldn't hurt Annie any more.

Johnny had been weak too. He loved Hannah yet, afraid to face the doubts and criticism, he would have married her, Eirlys. She wondered if she would find a man who was strong, or whether a strong-minded man would bring less happiness than men like her father. An equal partnership sounded wonderful, but was it that easy to find?

She didn't have time to ponder the question; the train was hissing to a stop, and she had to find a seat. Amid the shouting of last goodbyes, and the scramble for seats, she heard her name called and, looking at the fence alongside the platform, saw Johnny and Hannah and the children. She blew kisses and smiled to show them she was happy for them, hoping her tears wouldn't show. Then a couple came and stood beside them; Teresa and her father, solemn-faced and ill at ease. A feeling of love for her father flowed over her. He was her Dadda and she couldn't pretend not to love him. Not even for the sake of her mother's memory.

Who was she to criticise? How could she accuse her father of callous indifference to her mother's death? She had made it clear that she wouldn't change her plans and stay home and look after him, hadn't she? She wasn't in the position to act as judge and jury, or to understand her father's need to be flattered and loved.

She forced a smile and waved a hand to them before stepping into the carriage.

A shrill whistle sounded, the guard waved his flag and slowly the giant pulled its load out of the station, and her journey towards a new life began.

Ironic, she thought, as the boys waved her off. It's only a few months ago that they were arriving and what a lot has happened since then.

If Teresa and Dadda stayed together it would at least be a happy ending for the boys. Annie would have been pleased about that.

Ken was waiting when the train puffed importantly into Paddington. He had waited while three trains arrived and departed, knowing she would eventually turn up and would be glad of a familiar face.

Paddington was crowded and among the uniforms she saw couples dressed smartly, some with confetti on their shoulders and in their hat-brims. Everyone was in such a hurry to marry. This damned war was to blame; everyone wanting to grab what they could just in case . . . The sentence was never completed, it was too frightening to contemplate.

She was in no hurry and walked along the platform allowing others to pass her. When she reached the barrier and held her ticket for the inspector, she saw him. He was smiling widely and obviously glad she was back. Ken, reliable, unjudgemental, and very dear.

He had a car parked close by and when they were on their way he asked casually,

"Did you see Johnny?"

"Yes. He and Hannah will marry, I think."

"And are you all right about that?"

"Yes, I am. But it doesn't say much for me as a person, does it? I left you, then Johnny. My love is very short-lived."

"Or stronger than you realise," he said enigmatically as he helped her out and kissed her lightly before following her into his family's home. "Maybe your dream of marrying Johnny, and being a part of the Castles on the sand," he joked lightly, "were short-lived because you were wrong to leave me."

One day, when her jangled thoughts settled, she might take his suggestion seriously; just for now, she wanted nothing more than to find a niche for herself and find out who she really was.

"Wait till summer," she smiled.

Swingboats on the Sand

One

At Piper's Café close to the sandy beach in the small town of St David's Well, the Piper family were all busily engaged in preparation for the new season. It was 1940 and the effects of the war were beginning to be felt, but for the people who worked on the sands at St David's Well, it was soon to be business as usual. Beth Castle and her sister Lilly were helping their mother Marged to clean the café after opening its doors and windows for the first time in months. Beth Castle's brothers, Eynon and Ronnie, and her cousins, Taff and Johnny Castle, were putting the finishing touches to the paintwork of the helter-skelter and the swingboats, ready to erect them on the sand.

The small beach was still dressed for winter, with the shops and stalls boarded up and with no more than a few people enjoying the golden sands. But soon the place would be transformed, as the day-trippers and the holiday-makers arrived in ever-increasing numbers.

Through the café doorway Beth could look down on to the beach where Ronnie, Eynon and her father Huw stood in deep conversation, punctuated occasionally by her father pointing up at the roof of the café. She climbed up on to a café chair and leaned out of the window to wave, but they were too intent on their work to see her. She saw her brothers leave, shrugging on jackets and heading for the bus stop.

Beth was excited. Her dark brown eyes shone and a smile was ever constant on her generous mouth. Her black hair looked like a polished cap; always neat, it was cut in a short bob with a fringe that just touched her eyebrows. Her mother often told her she looked like the beautiful film star Anna May Wong. She was just under five feet tall, a half-inch that she regretted; four feet eleven and a half sounded so childlike. But being a bouncy, happy person, rarely critical of anyone, a friend to every person she met, the lack of height added to her air of innocence and was an enhancement rather than a disadvantage.

She loved the summer season with its lively crowds intent on having fun. The days were hectic and she knew from previous years that she would sink into bed each night exhausted, but happy. Only a few more days and the place would be open for business. War or no war, St David's Well Bay would attract the crowds.

Looking across the sand to where the waves were lit by the early sun, she watched as her Uncle Bleddyn set out his pitch ready for the boat trips he would run on the following day. He launched his twenty-seven-foot, clinker-built boat, registered to take twelve passengers, with his son, Johnny beside him and put-putted gently around the area of bay they were allowed to use. Further out there were barricades and mines, and soldiers ready to shoot to kill, a grim reminder of what was happening in France.

Beth's brother Ronnie, who at nineteen was just a year older than herself, greeted the start of the summer season with as much happy anticipation as herself. For Eynon who was a surly seventeen, and her sister Lilly who was twenty-six, the prospect was gloomy.

"All the hours we have to work and for a wage most of my friends would laugh at," Lilly grumbled as she lifted the cover off a display cabinet behind the counter in the café and began to pile up the assorted bars of Cadbury's and Fry's chocolate.

"But it's such fun," her sister replied. "What other job could we do that would give us such fun?"

"I can't see the fun. Only months of hard slog. A waste of the summer. Everyone on holiday except us. We'd be better off working for someone else. Family loyalty is all very well, but I want to earn real money. Don't you?"

"This year will be a good one for me." Beth's eyes shone. "A time to remember. There's my engagement party on my eighteenth birthday for a start. Only three weeks away."

"Marrying that Freddy Clements isn't something to celebrate," Lilly warned. "I'm telling you now that if you marry him you'll regret it. Too fond of himself, that one."

"Come on, you're only jealous. Twenty-six you are, Lilly, and no sign of a fiancé for you yet, is there?"

"That's all you know. I don't share my private life with the whole town like you do."

"Still seeing this secret lover-boy then? Hard to believe in someone you keep so well hidden, mind."

"Shut up about a secret lover or you'll get a thump. Right?"

Their mother Marged walked in then, staggering under the weight of a long shelf, recently painted a cheerful blue, on which the glasses for the popular ice-cream sundaes would stand.

"Give me a hand, Lilly, you're a bit taller than our Beth."

"Oh Mam, I'm just finishing this."

With a barely audible sigh, Beth put down the glass shelf she had been polishing and went to help her mother.

Beth's soon-to-be fiancé, Freddy Clements, worked as "third sales" in a gents' outfitters in the town. As this was Wednesday, a day on which the shop closed at lunchtime, he went home to change out of the formal suit he wore for business, having promised to go and see Beth. He wore another suit, one reduced to second best since it was no longer smart enough for work. As he straightened his tie and admired himself in his wardrobe mirror, he wondered whether he dare raid the savings account he and Beth had started a year ago and buy another suit and a few shirts. If rumours of clothes rationing became fact, then he would need a good stock. He didn't think Beth, who wore white overalls over any old thing, would understand this.

Freddy himself was not tall, measuring only an inch and a half more than Beth. He jokingly told her that he would never marry her if she grew that extra inch and a half as she'd shame him. He was as fair as Beth was dark; he used to try and flatten his hair, which was a bit longer than most and deeply waved, with Brylcreem, but now allowed it to move freely around his ears. His boss was constantly complaining about it but Freddy knew that girls liked it and he prefered to please girls than his boss any day.

Aware of his lack of height, he walked with his shoulders well back and his neck stretched to hold his head high. Giving himself one last look in the mirror and seeing that his collar wasn't sitting flat, he called to his mother.

"Mam, can you give this shirt one more go? The collar isn't up to your usual standard, and I know you'd hate me to go out looking sloppy."

Twenty minutes later, declaring himself satisfied, he set off for the bus stop. He was a bit late, but he knew Beth would be waiting. Confidence widened his smile.

Beth left her cleaning and went to the bus stop to wait for him. She leaned on the sea wall and studied the groups of people dotted around the sand. Several families were painting their stalls, small wooden shacks in which they would offer for sale everything needed for a day on the beach. She waved to the people she knew, rivals but still friends.

Her cousins Taff and Johnny were helping to paint the swingboats and the helter-skelter in bright red and yellow stripes. Now, before the summer season began, the magic was yet to come. All there was to be seen were rather shabby wooden structures being disguised by cheerful paint, touched here and there with gold. Bright colours and glitter were essential elements of the seaside.

Many stretches of the coast, both isolated areas and a number of once popular beaches, were now inaccessible to the public, having been surrounded with barbed wire and concrete blocks to prevent invasion forces landing. In the more isolated places they had been heavily mined and flags and notices gave stark warnings of the dangers to those who thought of trespassing. It had been decided to leave St David's Well Bay relatively open, however, apart from defences further out to sea, to offer families a chance to forget the worries of the war for a week, or a day or even a few hours. Holidays at home were encouraged and every town, not only those on the coast, were providing entertainments to persuade people against travelling. "Is Your Journey Really Necessary?" asked the posters.

She saw the bus making its way around the funfair and turned to watch its approach. It was two o'clock and this was the third bus she had seen arrive. Freddy was sure to be on it, smiling, warming her with his obvious delight at seeing her. She walked towards the bus stop but the only passengers to alight were her two brothers, Ronnie and Eynon, struggling with a piece of glass and assorted packages. They explained they had been sent home for some tools, glass and putty to fix a loose window.

"Tell Mam I'll wait for one more bus," she told them, turning once more to look at the busy people on the sands.

Piper's Café had been started by Joseph and Harriet Piper, her

Granny Moll's grandparents. Joseph and Harriet had actually been Moll's husband's grandparents, but she always referred to them as her own. It was tucked into the curve of the cliffs on the eastern side of the bay and could be reached from the path along the headland or, when the tide allowed, by climbing metal steps leading up from the sand.

Some distance below the level of high tide, in front of the café steps, some council workmen were scrubbing the pool built from rocks that was filled regularly by the incoming tide. As the tide ebbed, it would slowly empty to await the next high tide, leaving small crustaceans, which colonised the cracks and hollows throughout the winter. These were now being evicted for the summer by men wearing waders and carrying brushes and spades, who were filling buckets with the winter residents, intent on making it more comfortable for the bare-footed children who would soon fill the place.

With hope slowly fading, Beth glanced towards the bus stop where a few people were waiting to return to the town. He wasn't coming, she thought sadly. Sitting once again on the strong sea wall she watched the activities below as the traders made the last-minute adjustments to their stalls and rides. A few people wandered around, idly watching others at work, intrigued perhaps at the sight of the flat boards and sections of corrugated iron that, by tomorrow, would be bright, cheerful, overloaded stalls.

She saw a bus in the distance, travelling up to turn and come down to the stop where she stood. This was her last chance. If Freddy wasn't on board she would have to get back to the café and finish the job she had started. Her sister Lilly was right – Freddy *wasn't* reliable – but they understood each other. After growing up only a street apart and spending most of their time together, they understood each other's failings better than most. She knew that love wasn't perfection. There were cracks in the best relationships; you only had to think about Mam and Dad to know that. Always arguing they were.

When the next bus spilled out its passengers, Freddy Clements was the first to alight and he hurried towards her, a smile to match hers on his handsome face.

"You look nice," she said shyly. "Not dressed for work, though. Painting it is today, mind."

"Not for me," he said, pulling a face, persuading her to laugh with him. "Wearing a good suit is my way of avoiding the jobs I hate."

"What are you planning to do, then?" she asked. "I thought you promised to help?"

"Windows?" he offered. "I don't mind cleaning windows."

They walked hand in hand along the promenade, their height practically the same, her dark head close to his fair one. They did not look like a couple; Beth was dressed in a skirt and blouse, both damp and stained from her work, while Freddy was dressed immaculately in his navy suit and white shirt. Beth was suddenly self-conscious, aware of the difference in their appearance, unable to excuse herself on the strength of eight hours' work in the café that day.

On the promenade they passed the shop also owned by the Castle family, although still bearing the Piper name after Moll's grandfather who had begun it. Like the rest of the shops and small cafés it was freshly painted. Beth was surprised to see that it had been decorated with stripes of pink and pale green and that on the window was written "Piper's Peppermint Rock".

"That's smart," Beth said, "but I'm surprised Granny Moll agreed. Adamant she was that it should be blue like the café. It looks much better, don't you think, Freddy?"

"Much better. More suitable than blue. Blue isn't a colour for eating, is it?" he agreed. "What can you eat that's blue? No, pink and peppermint green is much better." He looked in through the window. The shop was empty and the stands holding postcards were just inside the door.

"I wonder if someone has persuaded your gran to sell saucy postcards as well?" he grinned. Then his face sobered and he asked, "Why don't you forget the café and run this little seaside rock shop? Tidy little job that'll be, with no overalls and no messy cleaning to do. You could dress smart working here, couldn't you?"

Beth blushed then, even more aware of her untidy appearance. She knew Freddy hated her looking like a skivvy, despite the fact that cleaning was a part of her work.

"Cleaning is as important to the entertainments business as smiling and waving flags and selling sticks of rock, Freddy," she retorted. "And besides, Auntie Audrey's in charge of it."

"Auntie Audrey spends more time at the café, getting someone to take over for her here. It's obvious she prefers it there, so why don't you ask her if you can run the shop?"

"Because I like the café and being on the beach. Piper's is a family affair, remember, and we all have to do whatever's needed."

"Your dad and his brother don't think so, do they? Granny Moll never listens to them. In fact I'm amazed she let them have their way over the colour of the rock shop."

"She does listen! But we have to do what's best for the business, and sometimes Granny Moll has to disagree with Dad and Uncle Bleddyn."

"Sometimes?" Freddy said with a laugh. "Uncle Bleddyn and your dad have been trying to make some changes for a long time, but Granny Moll never listens to them, family or not."

She led him in silence to where her father and her brothers were preparing to climb a tall ladder to fix the loose window.

"Afternoon, Mr Castle," Freddy said and in reply was asked to help fix the window. "I've got a good suit on," he began to protest, looking at Beth for support.

"For God's sake someone, get him an overall," Huw ordered, and after borrowing an overall from Eynon, removing his jacket and placing it carefully over a chair, Freddy resignedly climbed the ladder after Huw to help him deal with the task.

They worked for most of the afternoon making sure everything looked its best, the men outside putting the finishing touches to the paintwork, cheerful reds, blues and yellows chosen to attract the customers. Beth and her mother Marged were both very tired as they put the finishing touches to the inside, decorating the fresh clean shelves with doilies and checked shelf-paper before filling them with glasses, cups, saucers and plates. Teapots and jugs were piled conveniently close to the small trays they would need, everything in readiness for the following day.

Their last task was to place a few artificial ice-cream sundaes in the window and hang pictures on the wall. A formal portrait of Granny Moll's grandparents looked down on the customers as they queued at the till, and there were old photographs of the beach in past years which showed the changes in dress to amuse the customers as they waited to be served.

Beth's grandmother, Molly Piper, no longer worked every

day in the café. When she had reached seventy, she had decided that it was time to relinquish her role and allow her daughter Marged and son-in-law Huw to run things their way. Although now, at seventy-four, she still liked to think her opinion was respected, as she told everyone who asked her about retirement. The truth was that she couldn't relinquish her position as head of the family to Huw and his brother and, for them, this refusal to "let go" was frustrating.

She arrived as Huw was locking the door and they were gathering up their tools and cleaning materials to go home for a well-earned meal.

"Hang about, hang about," she called as she hurried along the path towards them. "Let me get my breath."

"What d'you want, our Mam?" Marged asked, trying not to sigh. "Finished we have and off home for something to eat. I thought you were going home from the wholesaler on the bus with Audrey?"

"I came down to look at things after I'd been to the wholesaler and just as well I did. Have you seen what your Huw and that brother of his have done to the shop?"

Huw and Marged exchanged a look that told of their expectation of argument.

"I have, Granny Moll, and Freddy and I think it looks wonderful." Beth looked at Freddy for his agreement but he was half smiling, looking from one to the other, expecting fireworks.

"Stripes! And in green and pink! This will delay the opening, mind. We can't open it looking like that. You'll have to get it changed. I won't have it looking like a – a—"

"A seaside shop selling seaside rock?" Huw said threateningly.

Bleddyn arrived having made the boat safe and heard Moll's comments. He spoke in support of his brother. "All the others along there are painted either brown or dark green. It stands out and shows clearly what it sells, Moll."

"It won't open until you've changed it back to how it was!"

"Can we discuss this at home? I'm sinking for a cup of tea," Freddy said, winking at Beth. "This could go on all night and I'd rather be sitting down, eh?"

They started to move away again but Moll stopped them. "Hang about! I want to check that everything looks right for the first day," the elderly lady insisted, taking out her key and reopening the café door.

While no one was looking, Beth and Freddy held hands. Huw exchanged a glance of irritation with Marged, Bleddyn stood head down waiting for a decision to be made and the two boys groaned and asked if they could walk on home. Beth's sister Lilly drooped her shoulders and complained loudly that she had done enough. She was going to the pictures and didn't want to miss the beginning.

"You can all wait," Moll insisted. "This business was started by my grandparents and they had high standards. I don't want those standards slipping." She looked around her, an expression on her face suggesting disapproval, then she nodded. "It'll do," she said, touching a shelf, straightening a display. "Now, are you sure everything is ordered for the morning, Huw?"

Patiently, Huw and Marged went through the list of bread, cakes, milk and the rest until Moll announced she was satisfied. Thankfully, they all turned and walked towards the van, which bore the Piper name, with Moll mentioned as proprietor below.

"An' it's time that was changed, too," Huw muttered, before being shushed by Marged.

The ladders and benches and heavier tools were already on board and the rest was thrown casually on top of them. Huw drove with his mother-in-law next to him, and as the rest squeezed themselves among the tools they set off home.

"And don't think I've forgotten about what you did to the shop. Tomorrow you'll have to repaint it in the blue, like always. Right?"

"Fine, if you don't mind closing the café as well as the shop. If Bleddyn and I have painting to do we can't deal with the café."

"Or the boat trips," Bleddyn added quietly.

"I suppose it will have to stay for the moment – unless," she added, glowering at them, "the council sends someone to close us down!"

Two hours later, fully recovered from the hard work and fortified by a good meal of fish and chips from their Uncle Bleddyn's shop, Eynon and Ronnie were out with friends, Beth and Freddy were sitting hand in hand listening to the wireless, Huw was snoring, and Lilly had slipped away to see Phil Martin.

* * *

Phil was waiting as arranged at the corner of Garth Row and Angel Villas, a place where few were likely to see him. Both roads had few houses, just a few privately-built detached properties with high walls and gardens filled with shrubberies and tall trees.

"Oh, Phil." Lilly sighed as they hugged each other passionately. "I'm so glad you could get away. I've had the most awful day and you're the only one to make me forget it."

"You're opening Piper's Café and the stalls tomorrow, then?" he said. "It'll be more difficult for us to meet now the season's starting, what with your long hours and my wife wanting to go out and about. I hate the summer."

"I hate it because we can't see each other as easily, but I'd dread the season anyway. Why should I have to work in the family business when they won't give me a say in the way it's run? Mam and Dad and Granny Moll have all made it clear that I'll never be in charge. Only my brothers are good enough to run it. No matter that I'm the eldest and I've worked there since I grew tall enough to see over the counter. No, unless they can promise me one of the businesses to run as I want it run, then I'm going to tell them I'm finished."

"Best to hang on a bit longer, Lilly love. I don't think your Eynon is too keen to take it on and Ronnie, well, he's due for call-up soon and if he's in the forces fighting Hitler, then they'll need you proper, won't they? No, best you hang on."

"I hate it."

"What about the rock shop on the promenade? There's a tidy little back room there that would be handy on a quiet afternoon, eh?"

"I don't think Auntie Audrey will part with that job. Oh, have you seen what our Dad and Uncle Bleddyn did to it? Granny Moll asked them to touch up the dark blue paint and guess what they did? Painted it in stripes." They laughed as she described the various faces when her grandmother arrived at the café to complain, then grew serious once more.

"If I leave, show them I can be independent, then I could come back when they need me and make my own conditions."

"That's a clever thought. Bright girl you are, no mistake, Lilly Castle. But come here and forget it for an hour. I daren't stay longer; my wife will be back from her sister's by nine o'clock and we shouldn't waste valuable time on all this. Oh Lilly, if only things were different. You and I would make a wonderful team, we could do anything. If only—" His words were silenced by her kiss.

As the big clock on the church chimed the half-hour he walked her back to the corner of Sidney Street where she lived. Arms around each other, pressed as tightly together as possible yet still able to walk, they strolled through the dark lanes behind the houses, stopping for just one more kiss, a few murmured endearments and regrets, seeking privacy until the last moment, when they would step out into King Edward Street where they would part.

"I think I could persuade our Mam to let me find a job in a shop where the hours aren't so long and the work easier, but it's Granny Moll. She won't hear of it."

Stopping for a final kiss before going their separate ways, they were half hidden, having pressed themselves deep into an overgrown privet hedge. When they heard footsteps approaching they turned away, hiding their faces in the thick foliage and waited for the person to pass. To their consternation, the footsteps faltered and a female voice said, "Evening, Lilly."

Lilly froze and didn't reply, but once the footsteps began to fade she pulled away from Phil and looked along the quiet unmade road to see who had spoken. There was no one in sight. Whoever it was had disappeared into one of the houses on King Edward Street.

"Damn it all, Lilly," Phil muttered, "I hope whoever it was didn't recognise me. If my wife hears about us we're finished."

Lilly said nothing. She knew that forcing their relationship out into the open was her only chance of ever becoming more than a secret love, the one hope of a satisfactory end to all this. She wondered who had spoken, hope rising in a flood of excitement.

Beth was at home going over the endless lists that were an essential part of arranging an engagement party. The list of guests was growing by the minute and Marged glanced at it and shuddered. Beth was the first of her daughters to become engaged and she was determined to have a real good do but, with rationing already limiting her plans for a generous meal, she was doubtful of the wisdom of inviting so many.

"What about making it a late evening do instead of starting at teatime? That way we'd cut out the children and invite only the adults. We'd be able to give a better meal if we cut the numbers," she suggested. She and Beth discussed this idea for a few minutes but when Beth turned to ask Freddy how he felt, he looked bored.

"Let's leave it for now, Mam, is it?" Beth said, hiding her disappointment. "We've all had a busy day and we're tired."

"Great," Freddy said, jumping up enthusiastically. "Let's go to the pictures."

"Sorry, but I feel too tired, love. I want an early night."

"That's okay," he quickly agreed. "I'll get off home. An early night isn't a bad idea." He gave her a chaste kiss and left. But he didn't go home. He went to the Chain and Locker for a pint, then to catch the last showing at the pictures. Boring, that was what Beth had become. She talked about nothing but the engagement party or Piper's damned Café. When would she have time for him?

The picture house wasn't full. Most people came for the earlier performances and he chose a seat a few rows from the back and threw his coat across the seat next to his.

A few moments later someone lifted up his coat and put it on the arm and sat beside him. He took no notice as he was involved in the film, trying to work out the plot, which was difficult as it had been well under way when he had arrived. He didn't try to see who it was until a voice said, "Want a toffee, Freddy Clements? Or a marshmallow or a hard-boiled?"

Shirley Downs worked in a shop near the gentlemen's outfitters, selling newspapers and magazines and sweets. Freddy often stopped for a chat when he called for his paper. Shirley was taller than him by several inches and to compensate she usually leaned on the counter, or kicked off her high heels.

Sitting down, they were much of a height, but she slid down in her seat and lolled against the arm as she spoke. She held out a large paper bag and he smiled in the darkness and riffled around in it until she closed her hand and locked his among the sweets.

"Ooh, 'elp! Let go of me, Shirley Downs," he said in mock alarm. "Grip like a set of pliers you've got!"

Amid demands to "hush" she allowed him to choose a sweet and they laughed as they settled down to watch the film. They whispered as they each tried to work out the story and an irate patron warned that he would speak to the manager and have them thrown out if they didn't stop talking. So they moved places and sat in the back row.

Shirley usually wore her long hair fastened in a tight "sausage" around her head, rolled around a ribbon and held in place with clips, but tonight she had allowed it to fall about her shoulders and Freddy enjoyed the sensation of its fluttering touches as they leaned towards each other to whisper observations about the plot. He realised with some surprise that he didn't remember ever touching Beth's hair. He wondered whether the effect of caressing the short, orderly bob would be the same as running his fingers through the tempting tresses so close to him.

They watched the end of the main film and sat through the "B" offering, plus the news and all the shorts. Then they watched the main one again, hardly taking in what they saw.

At eleven o'clock, Freddy said, "I can't let you go home alone at this time of night. Where d'you live, Shirley?"

"Above the shop. Mam and I work there and live in the flat above. It's handy, but I've no excuse for being late for work, mind, and I start at five thirty. So get me home quick, so I can get some sleep."

"Fancy you living above the newsagent. All this time and I never knew."

"There's a lot you don't know about me, Freddy Clements."

"I might spend a bit of time finding out," he said, flirting with his eyes, receiving a promising response.

Crossing the park on his way home, Freddy sat on a bench for a long time, thinking a little about Beth and a lot about Shirley. As the day of his and Beth's engagement drew close, he had become less and less excited. Surely there should be more than lists and more lists?

The romance that had slowly grown out of friendship had vanished almost as soon as he had proposed. He remembered their most recent discussion on the subject, when he had failed to convince Beth of his plan.

"I know we've agreed that we'll live with your Granny Moll and your Auntie Audrey," he had said, "but it isn't too late to change our minds. Why can't we do what we originally planned and get rooms of our own?"

"We'll be fine with Granny Moll. She has such a big house it seems a waste of money to spend on rent while she has rooms empty. Oh Freddy, we'll be so happy with her to look after us. And we'll be only a few doors away from Mam and Dad."

He shuddered. Why couldn't Marged and Huw set them up in a flat? It wasn't difficult to rent a place and furnishing wouldn't cost much if they bought second hand.

"I want us to start out on our own," he had said, trying to provoke an argument.

"We can't afford it, Freddy."

"Yes we can, if your mam and dad would help and if we buy second hand. My mam and dad have a lot of spare stuff they want to give us. I want us to be free to do what we want, lock our door and go out when we choose to, come in with the milk if we like, without having to tell Granny Moll where we're going and what time we'll be back."

As he remembered, his frustration grew. He walked on until he was at his gate. It was almost midnight and his parents were in bed, trusting him to go in quietly and lock the door. It would be a return to childhood to be "looked after" by Granny Moll Piper.

Was becoming a part of the Piper family and the seaside café, shop and stalls what he really wanted? Or had he thought of it as an easy way to earn his keep? Was he ready to settle down? He wasn't yet eighteen and he and Beth had been together since their first day at school.

His thoughts returned to Shirley Downs and the way they had laughed together. He had felt more alive after talking to her for a few hours than he had felt for months.

Guilt touched him then, but he shrugged it off. Was he wrong to want a bit of fun before settling down with Beth and becoming a part of the Piper family's business? Security and money had been and still were the attraction, he admitted, as he leaned on his front gate and stared at the sky, but the thought of being married to the earnest and kindly Beth was losing its appeal.

Beth and Lilly didn't have a peaceful night but it wasn't thoughts of Freddy that kept Beth from sleep, it was the argument between her mam and dad, a shouting match that quickly woke Lilly and Eynon too. Huw and Marged had been late going to bed and by the time they had done so their low murmuring had grown into an enormous row.

Lilly covered her head with a pillow and, after wriggling about and complaining, fell back to sleep, but Beth was upset. Mam and Dad frequently argued and with the beginning of the season making everyone tired and edgy, their rowing was becoming worse by the day.

The morning of the opening of the summer season broke fair and Marged and Huw were up before six and on the sands by half-past. Everywhere was frantic activity as owners opened up the serving areas of their stalls and displayed their wares. Balloons and windmills on sticks were fixed all around the brightly painted stalls. Flags caught the morning breeze and waved a welcome to the crowds who were expected to come and buy.

In the café high above the sands, Marged and Huw were setting out the food, turning on the chip-fryer and filling the boiler for making tea. Occasionally they looked out to see their sons setting up.

Even from a distance, Marged could see the lack of enthusiasm in their younger son, Eynon. He stood looking towards the edge of the waves where their Uncle Bleddyn, their father's brother, was fixing the painted sign that advertised boat trips. Ignoring Ronnie's need for help, he stared while Ronnie climbed up on the helter-skelter to fill the spaces with the last of the flags, and only did something to help when chivvied by his brother.

Marged watched and wondered how long they would keep him working the beach. There was no doubt that his heart wasn't in it.

Huw looked over her shoulder and, guessing her thoughts, said succinctly, "Lazy sod."

Ronnie, who was nineteen, tried to encourage his younger brother.

"Do you want to finish off here, Eynon, or go and fetch the ice-cream with Dad?"

"I don't want to do either. I want to join the army and get away from this boring beach for ever!"

"Come on, you know the call-up isn't to take you on a picnic. I'm two years older than you and I'll have to go before long and believe me, I'd rather stay here than face guns and tanks and bombs and God knows what all, over in France."

"At least it won't be boring." Eynon kicked at the sand which had settled around the base of the round wooden stall, making it appear to have been there for ever.

"You're right there. You damned fool, haven't you seen Eddie Powell who's lost a leg? Or heard of the fathers who won't be coming back? Stop pretending and be thankful that you're here and safe!"

"Until they start bombing us!"

"Oh, go and fetch the ice-cream!" Ronnie snapped.

"No I won't! I'm going to find my mates."

"You'd better serve these kids first," Ronnie warned him.

"Any pop, mister?" the first customer requested.

"Waiting for it to come."

"Do you sell Snowfruits?"

"No, that's Wall's. We make our own."

"Is that the biggest balloon you've got?"

"Yes, and you can't have it, so clear off before I thump you."

Every request received a short and irritable response until Ronnie lost his temper with his brother. "Eynon, for heaven's sake, boy, these people are here to have fun, not to be shouted at by a misery-guts like you!"

"I hate this stupid stall. I'm off!" He reached for his jacket and slung it over his shoulder.

"Too late to slope off, boy, here's our Dad."

"Ronnie, d'you think you could help in the fish-and-chip shop this dinnertime? Your Uncle Bleddyn needs to get the boat ready; there are quite a few passengers waiting and he can't be in two places at once."

"Why can't I do that?" Eynon moaned.

"Because he asked for Ronnie. You'll stay here and serve on the stall, right?"

"Not much point without ice-cream or pop."

"They're on the way. Your cousin Johnny is bringing it all. He's been on the job since five o'clock this morning."

"More fool him," Eynon muttered.

"What about the shop?" Ronnie queried. "Did Granny Moll mean it when she said she wouldn't open it till the paint was changed?"

"Auntie Audrey is opening it later."

"I could open it now," Eynon said hopefully. Anywhere away from Mam and Dad and Granny Moll's eagle eyes. There would be a chance of a bit of flirting, and he might arrange a date for himself for later with a bit of luck.

"Gran's determined that Dad changes it back to blue, mind," Ronnie told him.

"Pity. Our Dad ought to get his own way sometimes. I wouldn't allow a woman to boss me around, would you? Oh," Eynon added cheekily, "I forgot. You already have Olive, haven't you!" He darted away to avoid the cuff aimed at his ear.

The café was busy that first day. Although it was not warm enough for bathing, several families had settled for the afternoon and the sand was dotted with deckchairs and brightly coloured towels. Buckets and spades were in action as the tide approached and children, mothers and a few grandfathers made channels inviting the water to flow in and fill the moats around castles. Using the iron steps, mothers climbed up to the café and ordered teas. Beth and Marged were kept busy serving meals and filling trays with cups and saucers and teapots and milk jugs for people to take down on to the sands, while Granny Moll and her youngest daughter Audrey made sandwiches, cut and filled scones and baked Welsh cakes on the heavy metal bakestone.

Beth's Uncle Bleddyn was not like her father even though they were brothers. Huw was small and slim, whereas Bleddyn was taller and heavier with a beard that disappeared during the winter and grew again in the spring to give passengers the romantic impression that he was a seasoned sailor – which he was not. He looked powerful and strong however, which he was. At forty-six, Bleddyn Castle, with his dark hair scattered with grey and skin toughened by summers spent in the open air, was still a handsome man. His recently widowed status had added to his appeal to the ladies of St David's Well.

The beach was far from crowded, but his boat set off several times. The passengers were few, but he didn't like disappointing them and took the sturdy flag-bedecked boat out as far as restrictions allowed, pointing out the various landmarks and the beauty of the headlands proudly, as though they were of his own making.

At five o'clock the stall-holders began to close. They would extend the hours of opening as the season progressed, but the summer visitors were yet to come in their thousands and they were content with the little they had done.

At the end of the day Bleddyn moored the boat and locked

it securely before going to open the fish-and-chip shop and the small café behind. After accepting the last of the trays returned from families who had picnicked on the sands, Beth and her Auntie Audrey began packing up the remainder of the food. Everything not sold would be discarded and fresh food bought for the following day. It was a matter of pride that they never sold food that was stale. The chip-fryer and pans would be emptied, the fat cooled and the utensils thoroughly scoured. Beth smiled as she saw Granny Moll's suspicious eyes on her.

"Don't think you can get away with a quick wipe around, my girl," the old lady admonished her. "Good shiny pans are what I want to see before I go home."

"I'll do the greasy old fryer and all that," Auntie Audrey told her. "You get ready to meet that young man of yours. I'm in no hurry tonight."

Gratefully, Beth accepted her aunt's help and hurried home. Freddy was coming over and they were going to write out the invitations to their engagement party.

"Do we have to do it tonight?" Freddy asked, as he watched her start to prepare the table for the family supper. "I don't feel like doing anything tonight. And," he added solicitously, "I bet you're tired, it being your first day on the sands and you up so early. Let's forget it for tonight and you have an early night, is it?"

As he spoke, his words, so low and sympathetic, had the effect of reminding her of the long day she had worked. She was aware of tiredness which a moment ago she would have denied. Her legs ached and she felt a stiffness across her shoulders.

"Perhaps that is a good idea," she agreed. "The party isn't for another fortnight, we can do them another time."

"Tell you what, why don't I take them to work and do some in my dinner hour?" he offered and, taking the list, the pile of envelopes and the writing pad, he kissed her and left.

Out of sight of the house where Beth lived with her parents and her sister and brothers he broke into a run. If he hurried, he might be in time to catch Shirley Downs before she and her mother closed the shop.

Before the start of the season Audrey had found an assistant for the shop, Alice Potter. The young girl was willing to help out when necessary and seemed amenable to irregular hours. After a few instructions, Audrey felt able to leave the girl in charge, calling once or twice during the day to see that everything was running smoothly. Meanwhile Eynon worked the swingboats and Taff and Johnny managed the helter-skelter and the stall selling ice-creams and items for the beach.

The stalls set up on the sand were very busy, with newcomers wanting buckets and spades and flags and windmills and water-wings. Dippers – the local name for bathing costumes – had to be measured for size, and beach balls blown up with a sense of fun. As visitors arrived they set themselves to enjoy the day, and everything – even the exhausting effort of filling a beach ball or changing into dippers covered by an inadequate towel – was accompanied with laughter.

Bleddyn's boys swopped occasionally to share the work evenly, as the stall was more hectic than the helter-skelter. It was truly a family affair with everyone capable of doing any job, although each of them had their favourites – except Eynon, who constantly told the others that he hated it all!

Business increased over the first weekend and the Castle family were forced to work non-stop from dawn to dusk making food and attending to the queues waiting for the helter-skelter and the ever popular swingboats. Even Eynon forgot to be miserable as groups of young girls began to flirt in the hope of a longer ride. He didn't mind helping on the swingboats. All he had to do was time the rides and take the money.

Marged sighed with relief to see her youngest smiling and enjoying his work – until Ronnie left the ice-cream stall and insisted it was time for a change. He wanted his turn at the swingboat ride. Eynon refused to change and an argument quickly ensued. When it was finally sorted, Marged sighed.

"When will our Eynon grow up?" she asked Huw.

"Will he ever?"

"I hope it isn't the army that does it. The time for our Ronnie to sign up is getting close and unless Hitler gives up quick our Eynon will soon follow."

In spite of the sun and the laughing crowds, the day grew suddenly grey.

Lilly was determined to show her parents and grandmother how efficient she was and she spoke briskly to the customers in the café as they hesitated about what they wanted. Twice

Beth had to push her sister aside and deal with customers herself because Lilly had made them so flustered.

"Talk to her, Mam," Beth pleaded. "She's making the customers feel they're a nuisance."

When the café was quiet, Marged took Lilly to one side.

"Even when the café is full and they're queueing down the steps and as far as the swimming pool, you give them all the time they need to decide what to order. Right? It's their holiday and we're here to make sure they enjoy it."

Turning away from her mother, Lilly poked a tongue out at Beth, who said softly, "Oh, very grown up and responsible, aren't we?"

At the end of the first weekend Granny Moll gave two shillings to Beth.

"What's this for, Gran?"

"Hush an' don't tell your sister. It's for your savings. Put it away quick."

"Gran, you're very generous. You've given us so many ten-shilling notes already. I'm sure you can't really spare it."

"Between now and when you get married, I'll help when I can. I know you're doing without things to put a bit by. Just a few shillings now and then. I want you to have a nice little nest-egg when you start off on your own."

"Thanks, Gran." Beth kissed her and they hugged.

That evening as she and Freddy were walking home from the pictures, where he had had to sit through the film he had already seen twice, she handed him the two-shilling piece. "Another gift from Granny Moll," she said. "She helps us a lot, doesn't she? How much have we got now, about forty pounds or more? We'll be able to buy our own house at this rate, specially if we live with her and Auntie Audrey for a while. Just think of it, Freddy, a house of our own, just you and me."

Freddy kissed her to avoid the need to reply. The savings had been reduced recently. With the rumour of clothes rationing, he had ordered a suit and a pair of trousers and a sports jacket. It wasn't really extravagant. He wouldn't have to buy any others for a while and he had to look smart in his position.

"When are we going to choose the ring?" she asked, as they hugged in the shadows of the fruit-and-veg warehouse. "You've been saving for that separately, haven't you?"

"It's difficult, me working in a shop and having the same half-day as the jeweller."

"What about me getting a few hours off and meeting you one dinnertime? I'm sure Mam and Dad won't mind, seeing as it's for such an important reason."

Evasion failed to work and Freddy arranged to meet her the following Tuesday.

Beth chose a double-twist diamond ring that cost seven pounds. She walked to the door as Freddy dealt with the transaction, her eyes shining. It was really happening. She was really going to marry Freddy Clements.

When they got outside she asked to look at it again.

"Sorry, but I've left it in the shop," he said, hurrying her down the street towards the café where they were going to eat. "The salesman wasn't satisfied with the fit, he wants to take it in just a half-size to make sure you don't lose it."

The engagement of Bethan Castle and Frederick Clements was displayed on a banner in the café a week later. The party was to be held there on Saturday after the trippers had gone home and the café closed.

Moll Piper and her two daughters were already setting out the food when Beth took the final few trays from the families leaving the beach and dealt with the last of the dishes. Lilly had gone early, insisting she had to have her hair set. Eynon was chatting up a couple of girls as he locked the swingboats and fastened the gate of the helter-skelter.

Beth had realised she would have no time to go home and had brought her new dress so she could change in the toilet when the work was finally done. She combed her dark hair and brushed it until it shone, then pulled the taffeta dress over her shoulders. It was coppery brown and had a full skirt. The wide belt showed her trim figure off perfectly.

Freddy forced a smile when he saw her and asked quietly why she had chosen such a dull colour for their celebration. She felt uneasy for the rest of the evening, especially as there was no sign of the ring.

Most of the guests were family. There were fewer than she had expected and the café was far from full. She missed a few faces she had expected to see but didn't have time to dwell on their absence as she greeted the newest arrivals.

Her father's brother Bleddyn and his sons burst in and filled the room with their size and their loud voices but they soon subsided into silence as though the smallness of the crowd inhibited them. Taff, whose real name was Arthur Brian, was twenty-six and large like his father. He was about to enlist. He and his wife, Evelyn, sat looking away from each other and almost back to back, and argued all evening. Johnny, who was twenty-two, had come with his girlfriend Hannah. She was thirty, divorced and had two children, and felt ill at ease meeting the family *en masse* for the first time.

As her brother Eynon came and slumped in a chair, fist under chin, obviously not wanting to be there, Beth's heart dropped like a stone. This was not a good start to the evening.

There were few of Freddy's family present when the time came to cut the rich fruit cake that Marged had robbed the café's store cupboard to make. His parents sat apart from the rest and made little effort to join in the chatter, the teasing or even, Beth thought sadly, the congratulations.

Once the cake was cut and distributed, Beth and Freddy opened the many gifts that had arrived for them. Tea-towels and towels, china and cutlery piled up. There were egg-cups and spoons, a tin kettle and a brown teapot and several ornaments. The largest gift was from her parents, a hearth tidy to place near the fire. It was in the shape of a cloaked figure with hooks around it on which hung a small shovel, a brush, poker and tongs.

Beth thanked them all and rubbed her wedding finger disconsolately. Somehow the excitement hadn't happened. "Where's the ring?" she whispered anxiously to Freddy.

Freddy led her into the kitchen. "Sorry I am, Beth, love, but the jeweller let me down proper. Not ready till next week he said. Shortages are already causing problems, he told me."

"He had to make it smaller, that's all. He didn't need to add anything, so how could shortages—"

Once again Freddy stopped her tearful protest with a kiss. Fumbling in his pocket he produced a tiny brass curtain ring. "We have to make our special day somehow, love, so will you wear this for a week until I get the ring and we can do it all proper? I'll go down on one knee an' all, mind."

He was rewarded with a smile and he placed the tawdry object on her slim hand and kissed it, and then her lips, slowly, and with a groan of passion that made her forget her disappointment.

They made a huge joke of the substitute ring and only Huw and Marged looked less than amused.

"There's another gift here," Beth's Auntie Audrey called, handing them a small box. It contained a china clock painted with roses and forget-me-nots and was quite the nicest present of all. It was from Bernard Gregory, the man who kept the donkeys that gave rides to children, and Beth suddenly realised that, although he had been on her list, he hadn't appeared.

"I wonder why he didn't come?" Beth frowned. Then, as she thought of those who had turned up, she realised how few of the people on her list had actually been there. Counting on her fingers, she began to list the people from the beach, people she had known all her life, who had not shown up. "None from the cafés and none from the other stalls. I hope I haven't offended them. Not even Sarah the fortune teller, and she never misses a party. And the two from the wholesaler didn't come. Neither did Alice, the new girl from the rock and sweet shop, or Granny Moll's friend Greta."

The list went on. Freddy felt a twinge of guilt. He had only written invitations to half the names on his list before getting fed up with the whole thing and throwing the list away. He covered up his concern at Beth's dismay, however, laughing to try to ease her disappointment that people whom she thought of as friends hadn't bothered to come and wish them luck. Who needed them?

That night when Beth was undressing, hanging up the lovely dress that had been ruined for her by Freddy's remark, she looked down at the brass curtain ring and a tear dropped into her small hand. When she went into the bathroom to clean her teeth and wash her face, the ring slipped from her finger and disappeared down the drain.

Two

Belgium and Holland surrendered to the German army at the end of May and a week later the British Army became caught between the sea and the determined attackers. The call went out for the owners of boats of thirty feet and over to go to their rescue. Bleddyn had already registered his boat, but as it was only twenty-seven feet he wasn't needed, although like many others he would have attempted to join in had he been near enough to respond to the call in time. What was being asked of them seemed an impossible task, but determination was a strong weapon.

In horror the audiences in cinemas all over the country watched the newsreels that showed the bravery of the rescuers as they lifted thousands of men from the beaches of Dunkirk under the persistent fire of Hitler's army. Fear filled the hearts of everyone and it was to the beaches they went: some to feel closer to their loved ones, others to help their family relax and forget, even momentarily, the dramatic events taking place across the water that could be changing history.

"Laughter always was good medicine," Moll told her family, "and it's our duty to provide it. The war effort isn't just making bombs and bullets, remember."

Huw was sent to repaint the rock and sweet shop and with ill grace he set off with the cans of dark blue paint to restore it to its previous dullness. He was just about to start rubbing down when Moll appeared.

"I need you to go to the wholesaler, Huw," she said.

"Can't. Sorry. Got this painting to do."

Moll looked undeniably shifty, Huw told Bleddyn later, as she said, "Perhaps we could leave it. Several people have remarked on its cheerfulness."

Huw dropped the sandpaper he was using and stared at her, enjoying her humiliation at having to back down.

"You mean I was right for once, Ma?" he grinned.

"No, you weren't!" she snapped. "Doing it without discussing it with the rest of us! This is a family business, Huw, and don't forget it!"

"As if I could," he retorted. "But it's the Castle family, no longer Piper's."

"Piper's it will always be."

"Face it, Ma, Bleddyn and I run it and we have for years. Bleddyn and me, Marged and our children. All Castles, not a Piper among us except you."

Muttering insults not intended for his ears, she scuttled off. Huw loaded the painting equipment back into his van and drove to Sidney Street, smiling. She'd give in eventually, she'd have to; she knew the business depended on Bleddyn and himself to survive, especially now with so many of the young men being called up to fight Hitler.

Presuming Huw was repainting the rock shop, Marged asked Ronnie to go to the wholesaler for more supplies. "You'll have to go on the bike, mind, your father's got the van."

"No thanks!" Ronnie replied. "I'll walk to the rock shop and borrow the van."

He walked up on to the promenade and along past the assorted shops and cafés but when he reached the rock shop, it was open for business with Auntie Audrey smiling behind the counter. There was no sign of his father's van.

After hearing Audrey's brief explanation Ronnie set off to walk to Sidney Street, where he joined his father in a sandwich and a cup of tea before setting off. He went first to Goose Lane where Mr Gregory kept chickens and ducks as well as his donkeys.

The house looked empty and Ronnie was writing a note asking Mr Gregory to deliver four dozen eggs the following day when a tall figure dressed in a heavy sweater and corduroy trousers came around the corner.

"Peter Gregory?" Ronnie said hesitatingly. "It is you, isn't it?"

"Ronnie Castle. How delightful to see you," Peter said, his voice lacking the local accent, the words formal and very polite. He held out a rather grubby hand. "Not called up yet, I see? Or are you on leave?"

"Not yet, but I'm expecting it any time. I can't wait to get stuck in. Still working on the beach until they want me, with Mam and Dad and the rest of them." He wondered why he was apologising, and lying about wanting to go. There was nothing he wanted more than another deferment. But seeing Peter Gregory, who had volunteered as soon as the word "conscription" was mooted, made him feel ashamed of being a civilian, especially after the tragedy of Dunkirk. "All set to go I am, but they know what's best, they'll send for me when they want me, eh?"

He paid for the eggs and placed them in the van.

"How are the family?" Peter asked. "Is your sister Beth still working the beach too?"

"We're all there, Uncle Bleddyn and my cousins Taff and Johnny, and Beth and Lilly and our Eynon and me. And Granny Moll of course, still thinks she's in charge she does."

"Perhaps I'll call and see you all. I sometimes walk down to help Father bring the donkeys back to their field."

Driving off Ronnie chuckled. Posh voice; "Father" instead of "Dad": what a boring bloke he'd turned out to be. Different from when they used to go out looking for apple orchards and helping themselves to the fruit, scrumping they called it. Now he'd probably call it "depriving the owners of their property by illegal means", he chuckled.

The weather turned nasty and the days at the beach consisted of bedraggled families coming into Piper's Café for shelter more than food. The place smelled of damp clothing as people who had booked into a bed and breakfast filled the hours before they could return to their accommodation, change their clothes and make themselves comfortable.

Marged and Huw felt sorry for them and initially allowed them to stay longer than the amount of money spent would justify. Many more arrived as the season moved towards the main holiday period, however, and they realised they couldn't fill the place with unprofitable bodies and exclude those who might spend money and eat the food they had prepared. Some of the stalls on the sand closed and Mr Gregory walked his patient donkeys home earlier than usual.

The cafés stayed open but few did more than cover their expenses, throwing left-over food away each evening. Mr

Gregory might have taken the discarded food for his pigs but it was too far to travel for a few cakes and sandwiches. Buses and trains continued to bring people but fewer and fewer left the town and braved the dampened splendour of the seaside. The weekdays were very quiet and Beth and Lilly were given time off to enjoy as they wished, though at the weekend the whole family turned out, the stalls were opened and even a few flags were set to wave and help create the illusion of enjoyment.

One evening as Beth, draped in her father's mac, had put the left-over food in the bins at the side of the café, she saw a young girl, who looked about eight, search through the rubbish and take several packages before running off, scuttling through the wet grass away from the headland and down towards the fields beyond.

It wasn't the first time Beth had seen the girl and she felt a growing concern. A child hungry enough to steal food from a bin? She made up her mind that in future she would make sure the best of the left-over food was wrapped carefully and left on the top. She mentioned the incident to her mother and Marged agreed to do the same.

There was more waste than usual during those two wet weeks and towards the end of each day they gave any customers they had more generous portions than usual rather than throwing the food away. Each evening, however, a couple of cleanly wrapped packages were placed at the top of the bin, and Beth waited until she saw the small child run out and take them. All the stale food that went into the bin was well wrapped in newspaper so she didn't feel too worried about the child eating any other food she might take.

On the days when she wasn't needed, Beth had been spending a few hours working on a rug she was making for the house she and Freddy would one day own. Taking an idea from a friend who had begun to build a business making rugs, but using the method of weaving scraps of material into sacking, she used old coats and skirts she was given and a backing made from a potato sack. With so many oddments of material, she worked with only the slightest attempt at a pattern. Most of the colours were either navy or brown. Drab, Freddy would call it, she thought with a stab of pain, remembering his unkind remarks about her engagement party dress.

At that moment she heard the wailing call of the rag-and-bone man, who wandered the streets of St David's Well with his horse and flat cart, begging for rags which he would later sell. On impulse she gathered the bags of material, all dark, practical colours, took the partly made rug with the hook she used to pull the scraps through, and gave them all to the surprised old man. She refused his offer of a mechanical singing bird or a goldfish and as she closed the door she saw he was examining her gift with interest. His wife might like to finish that; it would be better than putting it with the rest and getting a few pence. Pleased with the result of his day, he ambled slowly home.

"I brought this old skirt from Auntie Audrey," her mother said as she came through the door, shaking the rain from her umbrella. "Dark brown it is, just what you need for the border."

"I've thrown the rug away. I didn't want to finish it," Beth said, taking the baskets from her mother and beginning to sort out the tea-towels and tablecloths for the wash. "Dull, it was; boring."

"You can hardly want pale colours to put on the floor, love." Marged frowned. "What's the matter, fach?"

"The truth is, Mam, I don't feel engaged. I can't see that Freddy and I will ever get married if I don't even have a ring to show we're engaged."

"Two weeks and he still hasn't collected it from the jeweller?"

"Why don't you go in tomorrow and see what the trouble is?" Huw suggested, following Marged into the house. "Lord knows we aren't busy, what with this rain an' all, so get yourself down there first thing and sort him out, is it?"

Freddy didn't call that evening so Beth wasn't able to discuss it with him. She imagined going to the jeweller and then calling into the gents' outfitters and surprising him by wearing it. Or perhaps she would just give him the box so he could choose a romantic moment and place it on her finger. She was dreamily imagining it all as she walked to the jeweller's shop next morning.

The shop was being opened as she reached the door and she tentatively asked the rather haughty-looking young man if her ring was ready. The man was formally dressed in a three-piece suit, his hair slicked back severely, his mouth pursed in disapproval. Pimples in abundance failed to reduce the self-confidence that his position clearly gave him. He paused after she posed her question as though deciding whether or not she was a suitable person to enter, then he stood back for her to walk in.

She had never been inside a jeweller's shop before going with Freddy to choose the ring, and there was something intimidating about entering the sparkling shop where so many expensive items were on display, items she would never be able to afford. She waited, feeling like an interloper who was about to be thrown out.

There was much discussion going on behind the half-closed door and then the assistant came out and shook his head off-handedly. "I'm very sorry, Miss Castle, but we have nothing reserved or under repair in your name."

She began to leave, embarrassment colouring her cheeks, wondering how she could have made a mistake. Then the assistant was brushed rudely aside and the proprietor came forward, a kindly expression on his face.

"I'm very sorry, Miss Castle, but there is nothing reserved for you. Could you have perhaps made a mistake about the shop? There are other jewellers, and . . ." He smiled kindly.

Feeling marginally better she smiled and began to leave. Had she come into the wrong jewellery shop? Then she turned back. "Of course! It would be under the name of my fiancé, Mr Frederick Clements." She smiled.

"I'm sorry, Miss Castle, but Mr Clements didn't buy that ring after all. I understood you had changed your mind."

"Oh, no. Er, there must be some mistake."

The man felt sorry for her and said kindly, "If the mistake is ours, I apologise sincerely, Miss Castle. We will do everything we can to put things right."

She almost ran from the sympathetic voice, the knowing eyes, fumbling her way out, unable to see for humiliating tears.

Lilly's way of spending her spare time as the rain continued and the beach was quiet was to lie on her bed and read. Phil Martin worked in the back room of a wireless shop, on the outskirts of the town, repairing wireless sets and gramophones. The fact that he was married meant she couldn't go and see him, even as a customer. She had already done so twice and another visit in the guise of a customer was out of the question. With other members of staff there, she would soon be noticed; remarks would fly and Phil's wife would get suspicious. That would mean disaster. Or would it? Again she felt that impish desire to confront the woman, make her face the fact that Phil no longer loved her. Then she would have to let Phil go. It was an intoxicating prospect.

Why had she been unlucky in love? She comforted herself with the thought that her sister Beth wasn't any better off marrying Freddy Clements. Liked himself too much, that one. She threw down the book and stared at the ceiling. If only she had met Phil a couple of years earlier, she would be the one celebrating an engagement. She didn't think Phil would spend the money for the ring by putting clothes on his back, which was what Mam and Dad suspected Freddy Clements of doing. No, Phil Martin would buy her a beautiful ring and then the wedding ring to snuggle up beside it and they'd be so happy. If only he hadn't married so soon.

At four o'clock Auntie Audrey was due to call to pick up the freshly laundered gingham tablecloths for the next day. Regardless of how quiet the café was, the white tablecloths were washed daily and the gingham ones underneath were changed twice a week. Over-fussy Mam was. Lilly wouldn't waste time on unnecessary washing if she were in charge.

She heard the knock at the door and, picking up a duster and a tin of polish to make herself look busy, she went down to let her aunt in.

"Was that Phil Martin or whatever he calls himself that you were kissing in King Edward Street the other night?" Audrey demanded. "Want your head read you do, my girl."

"Phil who?" Lilly blustered.

"You know who I mean. What are you thinking of, carrying on with a bloke like that? Notorious he is, that one!"

"I didn't – we aren't—" Seeing the glare of confidence in her aunt's beady eyes, Lilly lowered her head, giving up trying to bluff her way out of the accusation. "You won't tell Mam, will you?"

"Best we forget it and you keep away from him. D'you hear? Or I'll have a little chat with your mam and your dad. Right?"

The fear that churned in Lilly gradually turned to excitement. Notorious! She was the reason for him being called notorious.

There's romantic! An illicit affair! That was what she had just been reading about. It was so thrilling, and it was her story too. A deep and forbidden love. She couldn't wait to see Phil and tell him again how much she loved him. She smiled at her aunt and tried to look contrite.

Audrey saw the gleam of excitement in Lilly's eyes and sighed. Her nieces didn't seem to be any luckier in love than she was.

Audrey Piper and Wilf Thomas had been courting for more than twenty years. Audrey lived with her mother and, she explained to anyone who asked, by the time she and Wilf began thinking about marriage she had felt unable to leave her. Wilf lived with his aged mother too and he didn't see how he could leave home and live with Audrey and Moll. The situation could have been resolved in the early days of their courtship, but there seemed to be plenty of time and now, with Wilf's mother in a wheelchair and Moll so dependent on Audrey, they were trapped.

Audrey had told the story so often she almost believed it herself – except at night, alone in her white counterpaned bed, when she imagined how it could have been.

Every New Year's Eve, she and Wilf opened a bottle of port and drank to the coming year, convinced that somehow their trap would be sprung and they would be free to marry. There was always a tinge of guilt in their eyes as they looked at each other and clinked glasses. The only solution to their dilemma was for both Wilf's mother and Granny Moll to die.

Bleddyn Castle had worked with his brother Huw since they were children, first running messages and helping out with a few chores for Moll and her husband Joseph, earning a few pennies, then, when they left school, coming to work for the Pipers full time, doing odd jobs in the winter and spending wonderful summers on the sands.

He had married Irene and they had had two sons. Taff and Johnny had taken to the beach and their life seemed set to continue into the foreseeable future, but Irene had died and for a while everything had changed. Nothing had seemed worth doing. But after a short time of mourning and regrets and guilt, Bleddyn revived his interest and his summer began as so many others had done, working happily among the holiday crowds.

Now Johnny and Taff seemed content to follow in the family tradition, with only Taff's wife Evelyn breaking out and refusing to take a share of the responsibility during the summer. At twenty-five, two years younger than Taff, Evelyn was basically very shy and hated the beach trade. The crowds embarrassed her and she was unhappy serving on the stall or in the café, fumbling with the change and getting flustered when orders came thick and fast. So the family had accepted her decision and she now worked as a supervisor and inspector in a factory that had once made enamel saucepans, washing-up bowls, food canisters and other kitchen equipment, but had changed to making items for the war machine. In this role she was efficient and well liked. On the beach, dealing with the public at play, she had felt like a stupid child.

Bleddyn's other son Johnny also loved the beach and dreaded the end of the season. He wasn't married but was seeing a divorced woman called Hannah. He didn't bring her home to meet the family very often as he sensed that it was an ordeal for her. At thirty, she was eight years older than him and although he wasn't concerned about the age difference or the fact that she had two daughters, Hannah was inhibited by it all. Occasionally she would bring the girls to the beach when she knew Johnny was working on the swingboats and he would give rides to the girls and spend a little time with them. But mostly they went for walks in the park or travelled into the next town to go to the cinema there. The outings always included the four of them, as Hannah's parents refused to help her, accusing her of bringing shame to the family by leaving her husband and having no sympathy for her difficulties.

Hannah and the girls, Josie who was four and Marie who was three, lived in two rooms in her mother's house but were not allowed to have any visitors. To earn money to keep herself and the children she worked as a cleaner, getting to offices very early in the mornings, when her mother grudgingly agreed to listen for the children waking, or during the evenings once they were asleep. She was an accomplished needlewoman, and she supplemented this small income with dressmaking. She loved Johnny dearly, but the children, the divorce and the age difference made her afraid. She left all the running to him and prayed he wouldn't grow tired of her hesitancy, mistaking it for lack of love.

Marged and Huw's son, Ronnie, loved the beach and looked forward to the opening of the holiday season with great joy. But his happiness was tempered by the discontent on his wife's face. Like Taff's wife Evelyn, Olive hated the summer. As the weeks passed, leaving winter behind, she had begun her campaign. Reasons why Ronnie should not join his family for the summer poured out in a steady stream. As the days grew longer, her frustration grew stronger.

"I have to give up my job and help out, and it just isn't fair," she complained one Wednesday morning as Ronnie gathered his white jacket and hat ready to work on the ice-cream stall.

"The money's regular and if we have a good season we all get a bonus; what's wrong with that? Your job will be waiting for you when the beach closes." Ronnie spoke calmly but he was tired of the constant battle. He had worked on the beach with his family since he was six, standing on a pop-bottle box to see over the counter as soon as he was capable of serving. He had been doing the job when he and Olive met, and she had joined in with enthusiasm then, so he couldn't understand why she now wanted him to change.

"I want your family to keep Piper's fish-and-chip restaurant open all year. You know it would pay for itself."

"Uncle Bleddyn runs the chip shop and he closes the café part for the summer. It's the way it's always been done, love, you know that."

"Because it's always been done doesn't make it right!"

"Look, I've got to go." He kissed her lightly then went to the door. "Don't forget you're taking over from Eynon at three so he can go to the pool. He's taking swimming lessons for some life-saving badge, him and Freddy, remember?"

"Just an excuse to get out of his shift if you ask me," she muttered.

"Who d'you mean, our Eynon or Freddy Clements?"

"Both! Your Eynon hates the beach as much as I do."

"Rubbish. Born to Piper's Café and the stalls he was." But Ronnie looked doubtful as he got on his bicycle to leave their rooms in Curtis Road and head for the beach.

Olive put down the hearth brush and ignored the mess of ashes from last night's fire. Granny Moll would be at home today; it might be worth trying once more to talk to her.

The day was dry but the sun was reluctant to show itself so

she put a short jacket over her cotton dress, slipped her feet out of slippers and into sandals and went to get the bus.

Moll answered the door and smiled a welcome. "Come in and stay for a bite to eat, Olive, we don't often get the chance to chat now summer's here. You aren't on till three, are you?" she continued as she led the way down the passage to the kitchen at the back of the house. She bustled about making sandwiches, grating cheese and mixing it with salad cream and chopped onion and adding a leaf or two of lettuce. "The thinnings," she said, to explain the smallness of the lettuce leaves. "Auntie Audrey and I thinned the row of lettuce plants and it's a pity to waste them."

"Granny Moll, don't you think it would be a good idea for me to keep the chip-shop café open? I'm not much use on the beach, am I? I don't like it and I find it hard to be polite some days. If I had one assistant I could run the café and it would bring in more than having me helping out on the beach, now wouldn't it?"

"Bleddyn has to close the café part so he can do the season with the boat trips, you know that."

"He could still do the boat trips, Granny Moll. All it would mean is that the man he employs to fry the fish would have to work a bit harder. I'd see to that." Olive smiled. "That café is popular with people coming out of the pictures and there'll be extra people in the summer months, won't there? The town is full of trippers and they all look for somewhere to eat that's good and reasonably priced and quickly served."

"We've always closed the café part for the summer, Olive love. It's tradition."

Moll's arguments were becoming weaker, Olive noted. "Things are changing, Granny Moll, and we have to change with them. A lot of the cafés are staying open till nine o'clock for the busiest weeks. I heard them discussing it last week."

"They can't do that!"

"They can, Granny Moll. There's a war on!"

When Olive left to walk to the beach at two thirty, Moll had agreed to think about it and discuss it with Bleddyn. Her last words were, "Fair play, Olive, I can see the sense in it."

Beth was waiting for five o'clock, when her brother Eynon and Freddy were due back from their swimming lesson. She had to find out what Freddy had to say about the non-existent engagement ring.

She was serving three young girls with chips and bread and butter – a scrape of margarine, in fact, but butter sounded better – when Freddy arrived.

"I passed with distinction," he told her as he walked in, fresh faced, his eyes glowing. "Fastest, calmest and with the highest marks in first aid; what do you think of that, then?" he boasted happily.

"How many marks did you lose for dishonesty, Freddy?" she asked quietly. Then she turned to her brother and congratulated him, having been told that he too had passed the exam. "Well done, Eynon. You'll be even more useful on the beach now, with a life-saving qualification."

"Wait a minute, Beth, you don't think I cheated on the exam?" Freddy demanded.

"No, just on me."

His thoughts fled to Shirley Downs, but there had been nothing to that. A chat in the pictures, that was all. "Who's been talking?" He added quickly, "And what about? I haven't cheated on anything." He stared at her, willing her not to have found out about the missing money in their savings account.

"I went to the jeweller today," she said, taking the one shilling and sixpence for the servings of chips.

"Oh, there's been a bit of a mix-up. I should have told you. I've been meaning to, mind."

Taking off her apron, she went into the small kitchen and turned to him. "Well? I'm waiting."

"Truth is, Beth, I didn't have enough money. I didn't expect you to choose one that cost seven pounds, see, and I only had four pounds ten shillings."

"Only four pounds – but you've been saving for the ring for months and months."

"I am sorry, love. I didn't know how to tell you, did I? Shall we go in next week and choose another one?"

"No, Freddy. I've already chosen the ring I want. It's up to you whether or not you buy it for me."

They were interrupted by Eynon. "Beth, I didn't do the life-saving to help on the beach. I've been offered a job in the pool. Every afternoon. Not much money, mind, but I want to take it. Anything to get away from Granny Moll and our Mam."

"Ask Mam," Beth said irritably. Pushing Freddy unnecessarily out of the way, she went back into the café.

The following day Freddy took his dinner hour early. The jeweller's assistant was at lunch and the proprietor was not very understanding. He remembered the embarrassment the pretty, dark-haired girl, Miss Castle, had suffered. After a stilted discussion, it was agreed that Freddy could pay for the ring by instalments.

"That will be two pounds ten shillings deposit, Mr Clements, and, er, five shillings a week?"

Freddy agreed, wondering how he would manage to survive while it was being paid off. It also crossed his mind that the money could have paid for a weekend away with the easy-going Shirley Downs. He tried to push the thought away but as he handed over the two pound notes and the ten shillings in half-crowns, he begrudged every penny, paying as it did for a closer tie with Beth, whom he was no longer sure he wanted to marry.

Unaware of Freddy's feelings, Beth too felt a certain unease as he kissed her and slipped the pretty, sparkling ring on her finger that evening. He said all the usual loving words and promised everything she wanted to hear. But something was missing and she couldn't explain, even to herself, what it was. Whatever the reason, the future as Mrs Fredrick Clements did not seem as rosy as it once had. The ring looked odd set on her finger, even cheap and garish, whereas in the shop and in her dreams it had glowed beautifully as a symbol of all she had ever wanted.

The young girl searching for food became a regular visitor to the café refuse bin, and although the food was well wrapped and left on the bin for only a short period, Beth wished she could help further. Granny Moll was so fussy about wrapping everything there wasn't much risk of contamination, but it was a sad way for such a young girl to have to live.

She wondered where she did actually live. It couldn't be in any kind of home or food would be provided. She must be living outside society, probably in a derelict house or a barn. All right now, with the summer ahead of them, but what did she do in winter? Where did she find food then? And where did she find clothes?

She said nothing to her parents, but she still had a few coats given to her for her famous rug. She took them to the café and left them draped across the bin after putting the food where the girl could find it.

Hiding in the kitchen, now spotlessly clean and ready for the following day, she looked through the window and saw the girl come, pick up one of the coats and examine it.

It was tempting to shout, to tell her it was all right and she could take them all if she wished, but Beth knew that if she did the girl would run away and might not come back. The food must be keeping the girl alive and she couldn't risk her losing it.

As Beth watched, the girl tucked the coat under her arm and, taking the two packages of food, ran down from the headland and disappeared once again into the fields.

Olive was closing down the ice-cream stall on the sands. She scraped the last of the ice-cream from the tin, and piled it dangerously high on to a double cornet for a small boy. "Lucky you are, that's the last of it and we're just closing down."

Half of the boy's face disappeared as he tucked into the soft, runny confection.

"Ta, missis," he said as he came up for air.

Olive was smiling as Moll and Marged walked towards her but the smile soon faded.

"Have you asked Uncle Bleddyn about the fish-and-chip café?" she asked, crossing two sticky fingers out of sight below the counter.

"Sorry, Olive dear, but Bleddyn won't change his mind about the café," Moll lied. In fact she hadn't mentioned the suggestion. Bleddyn might have agreed and she couldn't have that. The family dictating to her? That was something she couldn't allow! "He thinks we'll be spreading ourselves too thin if we keep it open," she told the disappointed girl.

"That's nonsense. We manage really well, plenty of people to help."

"We'd only need a bout of flu or summer colds to hit us and we'd be going round like headless chickens trying to keep it all going. No, love, he's right, best we keep it closed and concentrate on the beach in the summer, like we always do.

The Pipers have been here for a long time, we don't want to risk losing our place, do we?"

"If the family can't manage, there's a pool of casual workers looking for summer jobs," Olive pointed out.

"We like to keep it in the family, you know that," Moll replied. "Good idea, mind, shows you're thinking of the business now you're a part of the Piper family."

"I'm a Castle, Granny Moll. I married Ronnie Castle."

"But the business is called Piper's and always will be, you know that. And we keep it in the family, so the café has to close. You understand, don't you, dear?"

Olive didn't look convinced – in fact, Moll thought, she looked rebellious. "Now come on," she said in an effort to change the subject to a less contentious one, "it's our Ronnie's birthday next week; what shall we get for him? New shirt? That's always handy, specially if the clothes rationing happens like they're warning us."

Olive didn't reply. She gathered the tools for serving ice-cream and dropped them into one of the empty ice-cream tins ready to be cleaned. The serving counter flap was wiped and closed for the night and Moll helped lock everything away before she followed her granddaughter-in-law over the sand and up on to the promenade to the café.

Aware of the girl's disappointment, Moll said, "Go on home, Olive, love. I'll see to the rest."

Thankfully, Olive turned and went to stand at the bus stop. She saw Ronnie closing up the helter-skelter and flirting with a group of giggling girls. She didn't wait for him; she was in no mood to talk to any of the family for a while, not even her husband.

Marged watched her go and wondered if Ronnie would be wise to forget his dream of working alongside his wife during the summers.

"I think we'll lose Olive soon, Mam," she said to Moll as they approached the café high above the beach.

"She ought to do what her husband wants, Marged. If she'd been brought up proper she'd know that, wouldn't she?"

"Olive isn't a Piper, she married a Castle. I think we're being unfair to expect her to feel the same as us."

"Nonsense, Marged. A woman has to do her duty and follow her husband's wishes."

Marged wondered how much longer people would talk that way. The war, less than a year old, had already reminded women that they had choices. Factories paid better wages than shops and seaside stalls and Olive knew it. Who could blame her? she reasoned silently, as she walked into the café with the empty tins and utensils.

When Ronnie had closed up the swingboats and helter-skelter, she took the keys from him and said, "Go home, Ronnie, and talk to your wife – or, more important, listen to her."

"What's the matter?" Ronnie stared at Marged in alarm.

"Nothing's the matter, boy, but she needs a bit of maldod, a bit of spoiling. Not happy working the beach? Wanting something different, perhaps?"

"Oh, that old story. She knows what I do and she's always known, so why is she being so awkward?"

"She prefers working in the chip-shop café and Granny Moll won't agree to it staying open. Fed up she is, bach, and needs a sympathetic ear, that's all."

Lilly, whose turn it was to stay and load up the van, had slipped out of the door while attention was distracted and it was Beth and a reluctant Freddy who were left to finish the day's work. Beth closed the doors of the café, having watched the departure of her sister with dismay.

"It's not fair," Beth began, as Granny Moll tried to hush her. "Our Lilly gets away with it every time."

"Never does as good a job as you and me, Beth. Slapdash our Lilly is, and there's her expecting to share the running of the business one day. What a hope, eh?"

Huw stood looking up at the window they had replaced a few weeks before. A crack had appeared and was slowly moving down from the corner, and he knew that it would soon be unsafe. "One good storm and it'll blow in," he said to Marged. "We must have cut the glass a fraction bigger than we should and it's giving under the strain."

"We'll ask our Ronnie to get a new piece and fix it, shall we?" Moll said as Ronnie prepared to leave.

"No, the boy needs more time to talk to that wife of his, not less. We'll get it done tomorrow."

* * *

"Ronnie, I don't want to discuss it any more," Olive said irritably as she set the table for their evening meal. "I don't want to work on the beach and you won't accept it. There's no point talking about it; you never listen! I asked Granny Moll if she'd consider keeping the chip-shop café open, but she said Uncle Bleddyn refused. I don't believe she even mentioned it to him. She's that strong, she always does things her way and I don't know how you and the others stand it."

"What was her reason?"

"The usual, we've always done it that way and there's no reason to change."

"Is that all?"

"Oh, she said we'd be overstretched."

"Perhaps she's right. We do need you helping on the sands during the busiest weeks at least."

"Well, you'll have to find a way to manage without me. I'm going to look for a job in another café or perhaps a shop."

"Olive, we can't do without you. The family has to pull together; you know Granny Moll is against employing strangers. Piper's is a family concern."

"What about Taff's wife? Evelyn doesn't work for the family. Everyone accepted that."

"She had a career before Taff married her and he didn't expect her to give it up."

"Evelyn works as a clerk in a factory! Hardly 'career', Ronnie!"

"It was different with Evelyn, she didn't want to belong. And we have enough people, so long as you help. Granny Moll doesn't want to employ strangers; you know how strongly she feels about that."

"What about the call-up? How will you Pipers manage when half of you are in the army? It'll be down to your mam and dad and Beth and me. She'll have to agree to strangers working for her then. Your Lilly isn't keen on work, is she? Why won't Granny Moll listen to reason? With food rationing already tight and threatening to get worse, people will depend on cafés to eke out their food. It's bound to be a better investment."

"You've thought about this seriously, haven't you?"

"Ronnie, love, if you have to go into the forces, I don't want to be stuck all day in a job I hate then come home to these empty rooms. Misery all day and loneliness all night, that isn't much of a life, now is it?"

"I'll have another talk with Granny Moll."

"I mean it, mind. Tomorrow I'm starting to look for a job. There's plenty of factory work now, and good pay too I'm told."

"Not a factory. If I have to go away, I'd feel happier knowing you're with Mam and Dad and the rest. You'd be safer somehow than working in some factory."

"Munitions are part of the war effort and I might not have a choice." She hugged him, pressing her cheek against his. "I couldn't bear it, Ronnie, and you might as well face it. I'm dreading you going away to face such danger, and the only way I can survive is by getting involved in something I enjoy."

"And you enjoy serving chips?" He grinned at the stupidity and was rewarded by Olive returning his smile.

"All right, I know it sounds ridiculous, but it's better than the Pipers and their 'everyone having jolly fun' beach days. Uncle Bleddyn's fish-and-chip café will do for now, until I find out what I really want to do."

Ronnie was concerned. Olive had never really taken to the family business, but he hadn't realised just how strongly she resented having to be a part of it.

When the café closed the following day, Beth hid just inside the door while her mother and Auntie Audrey cleaned the oven and washed the floor. She didn't have to wait long before the little girl came around the corner of the path and strolled nonchalantly towards the bins. Beth held her breath as if afraid the girl would hear her. She intended following the girl and finding out where she lived that made the theft of food so important.

Meanwhile Huw collected putty and knife, pliers and tacks and a small hammer, all of which he stuffed into the pockets of his dungarees. Whistling cheerfully he climbed up the ladder to replace the pane of glass he had removed earlier. To his relief the new piece of glass fitted perfectly and, after working around the frame to make the bed of putty which would hold it firm, he pressed the glass in place. He was feeling in his pocket for the tacks when a movement caught his eye and he turned to see his daughter creeping across the grass heading for the fields.

"Where the 'ell's she off to?" he muttered. Stretching his neck and leaning away from the ladder, he saw the small figure just ahead of her. She was following someone, but why? Not a thief; everything would be locked up by now, surely.

He stretched a bit further and to his alarm felt the ladder move sideways. "Ronnie, hang on to the the flamin' ladder, boy!"

He dared to look down and saw that Ronnie had abandoned his job of putting weight on the bottom of the ladder and was playing football with a group of children further down the beach on the wet sand. He swore loudly and with feeling as the ladder slid further and further to one side. He tried to make a jump for it as it increased speed after sliding past the corner, but his foot was stuck and he landed heavily with his hands still foolishly gripping the hammer.

Marged was emptying a bucket of soapy water at the sink and saw the figure of her husband, his mouth in a rictus of fear, slide past the window. Calling the others with a scream of panic, she ran out.

Beth was unaware of the accident as she hurried after the fleeing figure of the young girl. But the girl was perfectly aware of Beth. Knowing she was followed, she darted on through the back streets and lanes, past the overgrown path leading to the abandoned stable where she lived. Amused at the unexpected fun, she led Beth to a field further on. Hiding one precious package under her coat, she opened the other and fed the contents to the horses who stood hopefully at the hedge.

Surprised, but amused and heartened by the young girl's kindness, Beth turned and went back to the café.

The girl waited until she felt safe from being followed and made her way slowly back to the stable. Lying in a corner, covered by Beth's gift of a coat, was another girl, aged about fifteen but looking younger.

The older girl sat up slowly and greeted her sister.

"Myrtle, you're late. I was wondering where you'd got to. No trouble, was there?"

"No trouble, but I'm afraid we've got half rations today. The girl from the café followed me so I gave one package to the horses." They tucked in to the sandwiches and cakes Beth had packed and Myrtle told the story of the chase again, with many exaggerations, before they both settled under the assorted covers to sleep.

When Beth returned to the café, hoping the family were still there to give her a lift home, voices led her to the crowd around her father. Seeing him on the ground, surrounded by the rest of the family and several onlookers, she ran down to investigate.

"It's your dad; he's fallen and I think his ankle's gone and broke," Granny Moll wailed. "Fixing that window he was, mind, when he should have left it till he had some help."

"Our Ronnie was supposed to be holding the ladder and he went off to play football," Marged sobbed.

"And that wife of his will have to put an end to whatever plans she's making to work somewhere else!" Moll added firmly.

It was late before Huw was comfortable in hospital and the family had dispersed to their various homes. Beth was tearful, convinced that her father's curiosity about what she had been doing had been the cause. All this was her fault. And all because a shy little girl liked to feed the horses.

Olive was silent as she and Ronnie left the hospital. Sorry as she was for her poor father-in-law, this would be another reason for Ronnie to want her to stay at the beach and help the Pipers and Castles with the café and stalls. She knew she should support them, but the fear of living alone and working on the beach all hours while he was away was daunting. If she could earn more money, then as soon as the war ended they could get themselves a better place than the two rooms they rented in Curtis Road.

She said nothing further. Today was not the right time to bring up the subject, not while Huw was in hospital and they were having to face managing without him for a while. Thank goodness Ronnie's calling-up papers hadn't been delivered; that would really have made life difficult for them all.

Letting themselves into their rooms, Olive picked up the post and gave a cry of dismay. She was trembling as she handed the OHMS envelope to her husband.

"Your papers; they've come," she said in a tight voice. Then she burst into tears.

Three

With Huw out of action as far as helping on the sands was concerned, Eynon was taken off the swingboats and made to help in Piper's Café, a job which he hated. The beach gave opportunities for flirting and making dates for later. In the café, even if attractive girls did come in, with his parents watching he had no chance for any fun.

Few of the Castle boys were above average height. Huw, Ronnie and Eynon were five feet four inches tall and all were of slim build. Ronnie was like his father, rather serious. He had married young and had settled down with Olive in their rooms in Curtis Street with no regrets. He pretended to flirt with girls on the beach knowing that was a part of the entertainment, but he was content with Olive, living with the hope that one day they would have children to follow him and work on the sands.

Eynon, with his wide-apart guileless brown eyes, had an air of confidence and boldness that was appealing to all ages. On first sight he appeared younger than his almost seventeen years, and the gleam in his eyes when he saw girls he liked first surprised then intrigued them. He had perfected the skill of revealing to them that although he looked young, he was no longer a child.

So far he had got nothing more than kisses and some gentle fondling, but he had hopes of celebrating his seventeenth in the best possible way. With any luck, he would have the willing assistance of Alice Potter, Auntie Audrey's assistant in the rock and sweet shop.

Huw Castle's brother Bleddyn was the exception to the rest by being both heavily built and tall. At five feet eleven, weighing about fourteen stone, and with a rather pugnacious jaw, he sometimes gave the erroneous impression of being aggressive. The heavy jaw had reappeared in Taff, who, although tall and powerful like his father, was also amiable and rarely roused to anger. Like his cousin Ronnie, Taff had married a girl who disliked working on the sands. Stronger and more determined that Olive, Evelyn stubbornly refused to help in the business.

With his leg in plaster, Huw wished the two young women were more amenable. The family was stretched severely and the situation would be even worse once the boys were called into the forces. He spent his days propped up near the till in the café, taking money and joking with the customers. It was obvious that he couldn't help with much else and, to avoid frustration, he spent a lot of time thinking about ways of improving the place, although his suggestions were usually quashed by either his wife or his mother-in-law.

"What about doing lots of different meals? Chips all the time is boring."

"No room, no time and too wasteful."

"What about salads like the posh hotels along Old Village Road? Them hotels make a packet. Their owners go abroad for holidays every October."

"Not now they don't! And salads aren't popular with our beach families. The kids complain."

"What about—"

"What about you getting on putting the small change into bank bags and letting us be?" Marged grumbled irritably, before turning to smile at a harrassed young woman with a brood of young children hanging around her skirts, shouting for crisps and chocolate and cakes.

"Rissole and chips for six," the woman ordered. She looked at Huw nervously. "Er – no salad, the children won't eat it," she added.

Marged gave Huw a "told you so" look and went on serving. Huw went on thinking, this time about his daughter Beth.

He had serious doubts about young Freddy Clements. He'd noticed the boy was wearing new clothes again, and wondered where he was finding the money to pay for them when he was too short of the readies to pay for his fiancée's ring.

"Pity he works in a clothes shop, it's making him one of the best-dressed people around. Better if he changed his job and worked for a bank," he told Marged during a lull. "Then he might think about saving. Or an ironmonger, so he could start getting interested in tools, and think about things for their bottom drawer!"

"I've tried to warn Beth that he isn't doing all he could," Marged said. "But will she listen? No."

"She's like you there, then!"

Ignoring his remark, Marged said, "Too vain that boy is, for sure."

"At least they have some savings, so when they get married they'll have a good start. And if he joins Piper's we can keep an eye on him."

"You don't think he's using their savings to pay for all these clothes he keeps buying, do you?" Marged looked alarmed at the thought.

"Never. He wouldn't do that, Marged, love. That would almost be stealing, wouldn't it?" But he didn't look as convinced as he sounded and when Beth called in to fill a basket with food for a picnic she was planning, he brought up the subject of savings.

"Savings are building up nice, then?" It was a question rather than a statement. "Reached your first hundred yet, have you?"

"No, Dad. But," she said, frowning thoughtfully, "we can't be far off forty, mind."

"Check with Freddy and if you're close, perhaps your mam and I can top it up. You'll have enough to buy your own house. Wouldn't that be great?"

"Thanks, Dad." She smiled. "I'll ask Freddy this afternoon."

She was puzzled by the strange look in her father's eyes as he replied, "Yes, my lovely girl, you do just that."

It was a Wednesday, Freddy's half-day, and Marged had given Beth the afternoon off so that she and Freddy could go out. Beth had packed a picnic that included a bottle of Tizer, which was Freddy's favourite, and they walked to the pebbly beach with the beautiful park close by.

"I can't think why you choose to spend your day off at a beach when you work on the sands seven days a week," Freddy grumbled, changing the basket from one hand to the other with exaggerated discomfort. "Damn me, this basket's heavy. What you got in there, table and chairs?"

"I thought you'd like a picnic."

"I hoped we'd go into town, do a bit of shopping and see a film."

"That's as far as your imagination goes, the pictures," Beth said, a smile disguising the edge of irritation in her words. She wanted to talk, make plans, share their thoughts and dreams, but he preferred to blank her out with soundtrack music and other people's words.

"Better than sitting on an uncomfortable beach surrounded by yelling kids."

"All right, we'll eat our food then go back and see what's on. OK?"

"It doesn't matter. I promised Mam I'd start decorating the kitchen. I'd better not be late," he said.

Beth hid her disappointment. Some day off this was turning out to be.

They found a comfortable place, built a wall of stones to protect them from the breeze and stripped to their bathers – or dippers, as they called them.

"Teas for trippers, donkeys and dippers, Sunhats, hoopla and rides, Piper's kingdom, cloths of fresh gingham, Fortunes, windmills and tides," Beth said softly.

"Did you make that up?" Freddy asked with a smile.

"No. It used to be printed on the window of Piper's Café when Granny Moll's grandparents first opened it."

"Piper's Café is important to you, isn't it?"

"Very. It will be to you too when we're married and you're part of the Piper family."

"Yes," he said without enthusiasm. "Lovely it'll be."

"Us married with a home of our own, and working together," she said dreamily.

"God 'elp, I don't have to change my name to Piper, do I?"

"Mr and Mrs Freddy Clements we'll be," she said, kissing him.

It wasn't warm but they braved the waves and swam a little.

Beth knew she had to talk to him about their future and she waited until they were dry and warm and were stretched out on their towels.

"How much have we got saved now, Freddy?" she asked, staring up at the sky.

"Don't remember for certain sure. We're doing all right, though. By the time we marry in a couple of years, we'll have the deposit for a house. Won't that be great? Just you and me in our own little home?"

"Yes, it'll be wonderful, Freddy love. I can hardly wait." She raised herself up on her elbow and looked down at him. "But how much do we have now, this minute?"

He frowned as though trying to think, not meeting her gaze. "Tell you what, I'll check in the book when I get home and tell you tomorrow, is it?"

"Fifty pounds?" she persisted, exaggerating to make him answer.

"Never! Nothing near fifty pounds!"

"Granny Moll has been good, giving us two shillings a couple of times a month, beside them all starting us off with twenty pounds, the same as they did for our Ronnie. Then there were gifts of money as part of our engagement presents from Mam and Dad and Uncle Bleddyn, and Auntie Audrey gave us two pounds ten shillings. So generous they've been."

"The Pipers can afford it, mind," Freddy added ungraciously. "Plenty of money they've got."

"Gifts from your mam and dad too. They gave what they could. We must be heading for forty at least."

"You dream on," he laughed.

He was being evasive. Beth knew that where money was concerned, Freddy was never this casual. He probably knew right down to the last penny piece. "I'll walk home with you and we can check it together," she said, watching his face, sad to be doubting him.

"No, don't let's waste this precious time together. Come here and let me show you how much I love you."

Hidden from the few others on the almost deserted beach, they kissed and apparently forgot their discussion, giggling when an elderly couple approached and separating quickly in case they were seen.

It was only five o'clock when they reached Sidney Street, having walked arm in arm back through the lanes behind the terraced houses of the old part of the town.

"We ate our picnic so early I bet you can do with something more to eat. Stay for supper?" she suggested. "Ham, salad and potatoes, without the ham," she added, only half joking. With fresh meat rationed and only three ounces of cooked meat per week allowed, meatless meals were becoming the norm.

Freddy made his excuses. "Best I go. Mam's expecting me back."

"How could she be? You thought we were going to the pictures!"

"Sorry, love. To be honest, I just don't feel like listening to your mam and dad talking about their day. The beach isn't my favourite topic."

"But Freddy, I thought you were keen to join Piper's when we get married?"

"I am. But it's a long way off and there are other more important things happening. I like the pictures because of the newsreels. This war is something that won't go away, love. While we're standing here safe as safe, people in the big cities are preparing the underground shelters, knowing that soon they're in for uncomfortable and dangerous nights with bombs falling all around them. Day after day our soldiers, sailors and flyers are fighting, young boys facing terrible dangers like we could never imagine, and we shouldn't forget it just because we're safe down here and spending our days playing on the sands." He hugged her and added, "We can't make no plans until Hitler is beaten."

"You still want to marry me, Freddy?"

"I do, of course I do. But unless this war ends miraculously quick, I might have to think about being called up. It's frightening, Beth. I can't concentrate on much else, specially now I'm eighteen. A turning point my birthday was. I'm liable for call-up at any time now, and I can't forget it for a moment."

He succeeded in making her feel selfish and uncaring. "Of course you're worried, Freddy, love. I didn't think. I should have realised."

"There you are, there's more to life than Piper's Café. You've seen the injured arriving in the town, young men only months older that me. I could be one of them soon."

"But," Beth insisted, still feeling guilty but determined he shouldn't forget, "you will let me know how our savings are doing. We ought to transfer them into National Savings; that would help the war effort a little, wouldn't it?"

He lowered his head, hesitating. Beth held her breath, not knowing what he was about to say, but certain it would be something she did not want to hear.

"Look, Beth love, I might as well tell you. I've used some

of our savings. I've drawn out some to buy some clothes which, because of my position, and being promoted to second sales now another of the salesmen has been called up, I really need. I've got to look smart, Beth, it's essential for my job."

Beth's mind flashed back to the rather quizzical expression on her father's face when he mentioned their savings. In that moment she understood that he had guessed. Why was she so naïve?

"You shouldn't have! Not without telling me."

"I am telling you. I think you should spend a few pounds too, get yourself some decent clothes before we lose the chance. Then we'll start again and nothing will make me part with a penny. We'll get that house and have a big wedding, a honeymoon, everything you want. And," he added quickly to appease her, "I took out enough to buy you a brooch. That one with daffodils you admired when we were looking at engagement rings. I couldn't bear to see you without it. You work so hard and get so few treats, I had to buy it for you. Beth, love, I want to buy everything for you. I want you to be the most cherished wife in St David's Well. I want you to look at the brooch when I'm away and know how much I love you." He held her tight, kissing her with more passion than ever before. "I've got it at home and I intended to give it to you on the day I left. There, now you know the truth."

She found herself apologising for his cheating and spending the money they had saved, most of which had come from her family. She went inside, delirious with happiness. She could hardly remember the daffodil brooch. But he must have seen her looking at it and had seen the way she had admired it, and had bought it for her. She put aside the niggling dismay at the loss of their savings. Freddy loved her and that was the most important thing.

She went to her room and sat for a long time imagining the loving letters he would write and how close they would remain even though he would be miles away from her. She had a chocolate box in which she kept pressed flowers. Emptying it, she put it in a drawer, ready for Freddy's letters.

After leaving Beth, Freddy went to a call box and telephoned his boss to ask if he could be an hour or so late the following morning, as he needed to go to the bank and to the jeweller.

He didn't feel like going home. It was not quite six and he

ran to the newsagent just in time to catch Shirley closing the shop door.

"Come to the pictures?" he invited, and stood around the corner in a doorway until she came. He felt a bit mean paying for Shirley when he should have been with Beth, but then, he comforted himself, Beth wasn't very keen on the cinema.

It was eleven o'clock when they came out, having shared a bag of hard-boiled and a brief cuddle in the back row.

"I'll walk you back," he said as they set off towards the newsagent.

"Thanks," Shirley said. "But why don't you come in? Mam will be up and she'll make us a sandwich and a cup of cocoa."

"I don't think so," Freddy hesitated. "Up early I am, and—"

"Not as early as me! Mam and I do the morning papers, remember." She smiled at him and said shyly, "Don't think I'm trying to steal you from your girlfriend. I know you're engaged to Beth Castle and so does our Mam."

"OK, why not? Go down a treat a cup of cocoa will."

Shirley's mother, a small, thin woman dressed in the overalls she wore in the shop, greeted them with little enthusiasm. After a nod, she went into the kitchen and began to fill the kettle and stir the cocoa and sugar and milk in the cups. "Nothing fancy, mind," she warned as she reappeared with a plateful of sandwiches. "Meat paste or bloater."

"Thank you, Mrs Downs. Very kind." Feeling a little uneasy, Freddy was glad when Shirley leaned across him and turned on the wireless. Dance band music issued forth and Shirley stood up and persuaded Freddy to dance.

Mrs Downs looked on and smiled. "My Shirley never could keep still when there's music to dance to," she chuckled.

"Beth doesn't dance," Freddy said. "So I'm not very good. I like it, mind. I just don't get no practice."

"Soon put that right," Shirley replied. "So long as you've got rhythm."

Freddy was surprised at how enjoyable it was to hold Shirley in his arms. She pressed close to him and, being slightly taller, leaned towards him until her head touched his. Her cheek was warm against his own, the illicit contact far more exciting than he would have imagined, and he didn't want the music to stop. He continued to hold her when the Sid Philips number came to an end; and the look in her eyes disturbed and excited him.

When they sat to enjoy their supper, Mrs Downs said, "Engaged to that Castle girl, aren't you?"

"Yes; we're getting married in a couple of years, if the war doesn't stop us."

"You don't sound very sure," Shirley said, looking at him quizzically, her head tilted to one side. "How can the war stop you?"

"Old enough for call-up, I am."

"So? If you want to marry Beth, then you will."

"Best you don't!" Mrs Downs said, unexpectedly fiercely. "Dishonest, deceitful family they are. Not a decent one among the lot of 'em."

"What d'you mean?" Freddy asked.

"No, Mam," Shirley pleaded. "Don't start on all that. Not tonight."

"All what? If there's something I should know, then you have to tell me," Freddy said.

"Stole that business of theirs from my grandfather, that's what."

"Your grandfather? A hell of a long time ago, then."

"The Pipers, Joseph and Harriet Piper, Moll's grandparents they were, put in a complaint about the state of the place, got a bunch of thugs to knock it about a bit, and bought it off him cheap. They built that place you see today by deceit and dishonesty, that's what."

"And when is all this supposed to have happened, Mrs Downs?"

"Don't matter when. It happened, and that's all you need to know before you tie yourself to that family."

It was only then that Freddy realised that Shirley's mother had been drinking. Soon afterwards he excused himself and left. That was a lot of ol' rot she was talking. As if the Pipers would do anything like that. Decent they were, and well known for their generosity.

As he let himself into his parents' house he made a decision. If Shirley's mother drank, then she might not always guard her tongue. Tomorrow he would tell Beth about going to the pictures and meeting Shirley there, and walking her home. She'd understand, probably admire him for his thoughtfulness. Best to cover the situation before it jumped up and knocked him between the eyes. Best too if he didn't see Shirley again, innocent or not. He closed his eyes and danced with Shirley blissfully, bewitched, into his dreams.

The following evening, he told Beth an edited version of his meeting with Shirley and her mother.

"I was miserable, Beth. I knew I'd let you down, so I went to the pictures."

"Oh, Freddy, I'm sorry. I should have gone with you."

"You wouldn't have enjoyed it, it wasn't much of a film. Gangster stories aren't your favourite, are they? Anyway, Shirley Downs was near by and as she had a big huge bag of sweets, I sat next to her and shared them," he grinned. "I walked her back to the shop after. It was late, see, after eleven. I didn't think she should walk back on her own."

"That was kind of you, Freddy."

"Well, I'd like to think someone would do it for you when I'm not here to look after you, love." He handed her the velvet-lined jeweller's box. She seemed oblivious to what he was saying as he placed the dainty, sparkling brooch in her hand. "I had to buy you a ring, it's convention, isn't it? But this was something different. I bought this not because it was expected of me, but because I wanted to." He lowered his voice, adding, "Because I love you."

She choked on tears of joy and, speechless, she hugged him. Then as she calmed down she told him he was marvellous, thoughtful, romantic and that she was the luckiest girl in St David's Well.

He felt euphoric at her reaction, his body fired with love, and this lasted until he left to walk home. As he walked past the newsagent and looked up at the blacked-out window above, he remembered the dance he had shared with Shirley Downs and despondency fell over him like a threatening shadow, an augury of a future without joy.

Beth proudly showed the brooch to her sister, but Lilly was far from impressed. She had just got home from a very unsatisfactory meeting with Phil Martin, and she was miserably aware that for her life was far from perfect. Then her stupid sister had come in boasting about some boring present from that cheat Freddy Clements, and she was supposed to be pleased? Fat chance. "It was probably your money he was spending anyway!" she snapped.

"The trouble with you, Lilly Castle, is that you're jealous! No one ever buys you presents!" Beth retorted and soon they were arguing as only sisters can.

Eynon came in after a while and said, "Stop it you two! I could hear you halfway up the street. It's bad enough our Mam and our Dad rowing all the time without you two joining in. Honestly, I'll be glad when I can sign on and join the army. It can't be much worse than living here!"

Slamming the door he ran upstairs and flopped on the bed. Through the wall, he could hear the subdued mutterings of his parents. They were not as loud as his sisters, but the tone told quite clearly that they were arguing.

Coming home from a date with Alice Potter he had felt great. Then, as soon as he stepped inside the front door, his mood had changed. He thought of leaving home with greater anticipation. If it weren't for the war he would be facing living here until he married, years ahead. At least the army was an escape available to him. Even if it meant danger it would be an improvement, he thought, as the voices downstairs rose to a crescendo, in counterpoint with the increasing volume from the next room.

A note pushed through Olive's door that evening asked her to call in to see Granny Moll on the way to the beach next morning. Curious, and preparing to stand her ground if there had been any complaints, she called and stepped into the large, three-storey house in Sidney Street a few doors up from the smaller one owned by Marged and Huw.

After the usual offer of a cup of tea from the blackened metal pot on the hearth, Granny Moll said, "We've been thinking about what you said about keeping the fish-and-chip café open. Do you think you could manage it without calling for help and expecting some of us to leave the beach and rescue you if you got into difficulties?" She handed Olive a cup of tea that was as thick as paint and waited for the girl's first polite sip.

"You really mean it? I can run the café instead of working on the beach?"

"You'll have a month's trial. Fair play, you should know all about it, working there all winter like you do, but we'll need to be sure. It will be different from working under Bleddyn. You'd have to organise the staff and deal with orders; it's a lot of responsibility."

"I won't have any problems. Just give me a girl to serve tables and some help with the dishes and you won't need to do anything more."

"What's wrong with your tea? I can spare another spoonful of sugar if it isn't sweet enough."

"Sorry, Granny Moll, but I find it a bit strong."

"Not expecting, are you?" The old lady looked hopeful.

"No, it's just too strong for me."

"I've been trying an experiment. Instead of emptying the pot, I put a small sprinkling of tea leaves on top, just to see if it saves on the tea. Now it's going to be rationed we have to try and save a bit."

"I think I'd rather drink hot water," Olive said, making a face.

"Shall we start next Monday then?" Moll suggested and Olive thankfully discarded the tea and nodded agreement.

"I know Ronnie wants to tell you himself, but he had his calling-up papers a couple of days ago."

"What? I thought he'd applied for deferment on account of the business?"

"Turned him down it seems."

They discussed their fears for a while, both trying not to remember the steady stream of injured young men returning to the town and the increasingly long list of the missing and killed.

"The best way of helping Ronnie is to appear matter of fact about it. We'll talk about it when he comes home, plan for the future as though it's only around the corner," Moll said, holding Olive's trembling hands.

They comforted each other and with their fears talked out honestly and fully, they agreed to try not to think about the dangers Ronnie would undoubtedly face. They agreed to take it for granted that he would return, soon and unharmed, to take his place once more within the Piper family.

"There is one thing, Olive, love," Moll said sadly. "This news changes things. I think our plans to reopen the café will have to wait or at least be reconsidered. We'll need you to replace Ronnie on the stalls."

Thinking of Ronnie leaving her, at that moment Olive was too distressed to care. Telling Granny Moll the news, saying it aloud, had been almost as shocking as when she saw that dreaded envelope with OHMS on the corner.

For the next couple of weeks Ronnie concentrated on "training" his wife to run the two stalls for which he was mainly responsible, which sold everything needed for the beach, including ices and pop, plus the swingboats and helter-skelter.

Disappointment over the refusal to run the café was given greater emphasis, a cover for her real distress at Ronnie having to leave her. She tried to hide the true cause of her unhappiness, instead being as difficult as she knew how when Ronnie and the others tried to encourage her to take an interest in the beach. How could she admit that her real reason for hating the business was that she was shy? Even a light-hearted joke from a customer made her colour up and want to run. She was being forced into something for which she was totally unsuitable.

"Eynon will give a hand when you're busy, and when you aren't he'll deal with the helter-skelter," Ronnie told her one afternoon, when the cloudy weather had brought disappointingly few people in search of fun. "There's no set job for any of us. We all muck in where we're most needed."

"I know that, Ronnie. I'm not stupid!"

"You'll be fine, love," he said, hugging her. "It's only till I come back and then you can give it up. Keep it all going for me, will you?"

"It seems fine on a day like today when most of the trippers have stayed in the cafés and shops. But when there's a queue and I'm running out of ice-cream, or short of change, what d'you expect me to do then?"

"Taff's job is to keep an eye on us all and help where needed, you know that." He was beginning to become concerned by Olive's obvious reluctance to learn. Then he sighed. "Look, love, I know you're disappointed not to be running the café, but—"

"Restaurant! It would have been a restaurant." She turned away so he couldn't see tears. How could she tell him that she was crying for him?

A group of young girls walked up, chiffon scarves in their hair, sand on their feet where they had been walking along the edge of the tide, blue with cold in their bathing suits but determined to have fun. Olive watched as he turned to present them with his special smile.

"You need something more than dippers on today, girls," he said. "I'm not complaining, mind." He served them generously with top-heavy cornets and when he turned to speak to Olive she was on her way up the metal steps to Piper's Café.

He couldn't understand her attitude. Knowing he was going away any day, he had expected these last hours to be special, but instead of being more loving, she was more prickly and bad-tempered.

He was appeased a little when she returned ten minutes later with a tray of tea and sandwiches for them both.

"Sorry I've been awkward, Ronnie," she said, staring down into her teacup. "I'm finding it hard to accept that you're going away and I won't know what you're doing or even where you are. Since we married we haven't been apart for more than a few hours."

"I'll write, love. I'll write as often as I can, although from what I understand there won't be much time in the first weeks; they really put us through a grilling. I promise I'll write but don't be upset if you don't hear for a while. The training is important, see. Our lives depend on knowing what to do in any situation. But I'll be all right, I just know it. You have to believe that. It'll help me to cope, knowing you're here with the family. I'm the lucky one. I will know what you're doing and where you'll be."

"I'll keep the stalls going as well as I can. I know you'll need a job to come back to and no other job will do." She smiled and, forgetting their tea, they kissed, much to the amusement of the girls who had returned for another ice.

"Make the most of it, ladies," Ronnie said as he served them. "There isn't much more where that came from, thanks to Adolf, rot his socks."

Beth watched each evening as the young girl casually walked up to the bins outside Piper's Café and took the parcels of food. She saw her run off over the path, across the headland and through the fields. One day she failed to arrive and Beth wondered if she were ill, or had just got tired of feeding the horses. The following evening she was there early and hovered around until the food was placed in the bin. Beth stopped her cleaning and watched as the girl went only as far as the grass and, with her back to the café, opened the packet and began to eat.

So the food *was* for herself! Beth was glad she hadn't altered her habit of putting out only the best food for her, and had not decided that the horse might not be very fussy. She tried to follow, but the girl easily evaded her and she walked disconsolately back to the café. The following night she tried again, then, realising that the girl was well aware of her intentions, decided it was best to do nothing for a while and hope the girl would regain her confidence and allow her the chance to get close.

Beth had told her parents nothing about Freddy using their savings. She proudly showed them her beautiful daffodil brooch and boasted about how well their savings were growing. If Marged, Huw and Moll had their doubts, they said nothing to her. There was plenty of time before they would be married and everything could change before a wedding took place.

There were evenings when she and Freddy didn't meet and on those, Beth worked at making tablecloths and embroidering cushion covers for her future home. She had three large boxes in her bedroom, boxes in which the local shop received its five-weekly orders of cigarettes and tobacco. Strong and roomy, they were gradually filling up with the necessities for beginning to build a home.

Occasionally Freddy would contribute something. His mother found a pair of pillow cases she had never used, a saucepan that she no longer needed. In spite of the fun of watching the collection grow, Beth sometimes felt a melancholy surround her as she took out the items and listed them, writing down items they still needed and planning how they would be used.

On the day Ronnie left, a travel warrant and a small suitcase his only possessions, she stood with the rest of the family outside the family home and wondered how long it would be before Freddy went off in the same way.

"I wish I was going with him, don't you, Freddy?" her youngest brother Eynon said.

"Shut up, you damned fool!" Lilly said. "No one in their right mind would want to go and fight in a war!" She was tearful. Phil had told her the previous day that he too was waiting to be called up.

"Yes, use your sense," Marged scolded him. "Can't you see how upset we all are? Especially Olive, seeing him go like this."

As the others tried to hush him for Olive's sake, Freddy agreed with Eynon.

"I can't say I'll be sorry to go, Eynon. This waiting around is terrible when we want to go and help fight."

Surprised, Beth turned to him and asked, "You really want to go and fight in a war?"

"I don't want to leave you, Beth, love, you know that, but I can understand the excitement Eynon's feeling."

"You're the only one, then."

"Wearing a uniform and carrying a gun and hand grenades; I'll show 'em," Eynon said. "I can't wait till I'm old enough."

"The way it's going over there, you'll have your chance," Huw said gruffly, as Bleddyn put the clutch in and began to move off with Ronnie and Olive inside the van. "Me an' all, perhaps, even though I'm past fifty." He dragged himself inside with the aid of crutches, the reason why he hadn't driven his son to the station.

As the van moved off, taking Ronnie and Olive to the railway station, and the rest of them stood in the road waving until they disappeared around the corner, Moll said sadly, "Your brother's boys will be going next, Huw. I don't know how we'll manage without Taff and Johnny."

"We'll all have to work that much harder, that's all," Huw said, his voice choked with fear at the thought of the danger Ronnie would soon be facing. "We'll work hard to keep everything going till they come home."

"You don't really want to go away, do you, Freddy?" Beth asked as they made their way back into the house.

"Of course not, love. Specially now I've been made second sales," he joked.

When he went into the shop the following morning, wearing his newest suit and a crisp white shirt, he was told his services were no longer required.

"What? I've just spent a hell of a lot of money on new clothes, and for why? So I can look my best for you, that's for why! You can't tell me you're sacking me. With men being called up you'll need me to keep the business running." He was red in the face, disbelief in his blue eyes. This couldn't be happening. What would Beth say? How could he tell her he'd just spent another ten pounds on three pairs of shoes, a dozen pairs of socks and a new trilby hat?

"One of the men who was called up has come back, with part of his hand missing. We have to find him a place. It's only fair and proper when he's been fighting for us all," the manager said. He handed Freddy his cards and pay packet and thanking him formally for his work for the company, opened the door for Freddy to leave.

Lilly's reaction to her brother joining up was to burst into tears every time he was mentioned. She wrote to him twice in the first week.

"I don't know what's got into our Lilly," Marged said one day as she prepared toffee apples for the sweet and rock shop. "Her and our Ronnie have always quarrelled and now it's as though he was her greatest friend."

"Had a row with this mysterious boyfriend probably. Who is he, d'you know?" Huw asked.

"No, and I don't intend to question her. She'll tell us when she's ready."

"You're her mother, she should talk to you," he complained. "You should know what's going on."

"I can't interfere. God 'elp, Huw, she's twenty-six."

"And without the sense she was born with!" Huw heaved his heavy leg off a stool and walked to the door. Making sure it was closed, he asked Marged, "Has our Beth said anything about Freddy's savings? I bet you anything you like he's spent them."

"She's said nothing to me."

"Then we should make her talk to us, warn her about him. Take everything that's going, he will."

"We can't say anything. Mam says she has to learn for herself."

"Oh, Mam says, does she?" There was incipient argument in the words. "That's typical of you, Marged! Bury your head, pretend nothing's happening! God alone knows who our Lilly's carrying on with, and there's our Beth being cheated on by young Freddy. You know he's been seen in the pictures with that Shirley Downs, don't you? Or are you pretending that isn't happening too? Mam says this, Mam says that! You're their mother and it's up to you to look after them!"

Tightening her lips, Marged said, "There isn't much of the Luxona ice-cream powder left. Shall we use it, or save some for a celebration at the end of the war?"

"What are you asking me for? When do you ever listen to

my opinion? Ask Mam; she's in charge of this house as well as her own!" Thumping down heavily on his plaster-encased leg he stormed out and went to join some friends for a drink.

Beth tried a new tactic in her determination to discover where the young girl who stole the food was living. Instead of waiting in the café kitchen, she finished early with her mother's willing permission and hid in the field through which the girl regularly ran. She waited until the girl was running well ahead and had stopped glancing behind her, obviously free from worries about being followed, then set off after her.

Beth was led through back lanes, pausing at each corner before catching up with her quarry. They were in the poorer part of St David's Well, where houses had fallen into neglect and many were abandoned and beginning to fall down. Beth would never normally have ventured into this part of town, where broken-down stables and warehouses made it an alien landscape, where danger lurked in the shadows and the fallen buildings leaned towards her, daring her to enter. Even though the evening was still light, her heart raced and her body was tense, prepared for flight. She felt a presence behind her and her skin tingled with fear of an imminent attack. She felt that vulnerability between her shoulder blades but was afraid to look around.

Wondering how best to make her retreat, she was startled by a loud noise. She froze and waited for long seconds, expecting discovery, before slowly easing herself around the corner of a building. She looked along a back lane where weeds and saplings were growing out of the broken concrete. A drainpipe had fallen and was still rolling a little. Beth wondered if the girl had knocked it as she passed.

Looking down the length of the narrow lane with its crooked buildings and air of menace, there was no sign of the girl, or of anyone else. The broken and distorted doors leading to once smart stables and warehouses were still and there was no sound other than the pipe that still moved slightly, its weight giving it momentum for longer than Beth had expected.

A shiver of fear twisted her shoulders as she turned and retraced her steps. There was no point in searching through the desolate buildings. Once away from the area she walked hurriedly, trying to tell herself it was common sense and not cowardice that had persuaded her to leave without investigating.

Ronnie wrote regularly both to his wife, Olive, and to his mother. Olive wrote back assuring him that she was happy and managing well on the stalls, but it was not the truth.

"Granny Moll," she said one day, "I'm sorry, but I can't carry on working the stalls. I hate it and although I promised Ronnie I'd help while he's away, I just can't."

"Give it time," Moll began, but Olive interrupted.

"If you don't let me work in the chip-shop café or the sweet and rock shop, there's plenty of call for factory hands. I might have to go soon anyway. At least that way we'll have some money when Ronnie comes home, enough to get out of our two miserable rooms in Curtis Road and into a place of our own."

"Take these toffee apples down to the shop, will you, dear? I promise I'll talk it over with Marged, see what we can sort out, is it?"

Audrey was serving a family with seaside rock to take back after their holiday and, placing the toffee apples and some slabs of coconut ice on the counter, Olive waited until Audrey had finished. Before she could ask Ronnie's aunt what she thought of her working there, Lilly came in.

"Mam says I've got to stay here while you go and get some lunch," she said sulkily.

"It's all right, I'll stay if you like," Olive offered.

"No, you go back and fetch me a few sandwiches and a pot of tea, Lilly, I'll eat here. Wilf is coming to share it with me."

Lilly wandered slowly along the promenade, looking over the sea wall, down to where the Punch and Judy man was about to begin his midday performance in front of a group of children who were sitting cross-legged on the sand. To her surprise she saw Phil walking towards her. She ran towards him but to her shock and dismay he pushed her aside as though he didn't know her and hurried on.

She stared after him in disbelief. Had he seen someone he knew, someone who might tell his wife he was talking to a woman? Tears welled up. This was no way to live, she thought sadly. She watched as he went past where the audience of the Punch and Judy theatre were sending up shouts and laughter, enjoying the fun. Every eye was turned to the puppet swinging the string of sausages and she approached him again.

"Phil, I—" He glanced at her, then stopped and began to turn away once again. She darted around until she was facing him. At that moment the beach photographer jumped out in front of them and snapped. Walking backwards beside Phil, he tried to persuade him to buy the photograph. So that was why he was so cautious. He was unwilling to have his photograph taken, although she had tried to persuade him on several occasions.

"Keep away," Phil hissed and Lilly stood back and watched as he strode towards the road.

Almost without thinking, Lilly ran to the photographer who had given up and was looking around for a better prospect.

"That last photograph you took. Can I have a print, please?" she asked.

The small triumph was short lived. As she turned to go back to Piper's Café, she began to feel angry. She tried to fuel the anger, telling herself she would finish it, that Phil was treating her badly and she deserved better, but the emotion flared only briefly and was done, stifled by the achingly empty thought of life without him. She tried to tell herself that any hopes of his eventually marrying her were nothing more than foolish dreams, but while there was a chance, however slim, she had to cling to it. She knew she was being a fool, but hope flowered through her humiliation and disappointment. At least she would have a photograph, around which she could spin fantasies. A picture of them together. That would be something to help her pretend that one day everything would be perfect.

Four

The town was awash with posters warning about careless talk, unnecessary travel and the need to save fuel and food and paper and almost everything else. Besides these posters there were others telling mothers to let their sons and daughters go to war. Men walked around with feelings of guilt if they were not in uniform and informed everyone who would listen that they were exempt either on health grounds or age, or because their work was of national importance; excusing themselves for being there and not on some distant battlefield.

The men who were called up to serve in the armed forces put on a brave expression and told their family that they couldn't wait to get stuck in. Any fears they had were hidden behind confident smiles and light-hearted words.

It was not only the men who were worried. Wives, girlfriends and sisters, besides being frightened for their men's safety, were concerned about their own ability to cope alone. For Olive, the suggestion that she give up the two rooms where she and Ronnie had lived since their wedding seemed the end of everything.

"It's our home, Ronnie," she said sadly when on his first leave he suggested she went back to live with her parents until he came home.

They stood together looking around the small, over-filled room with its basic furniture and the clutter of their own belongings with which they had tried to create a place that was clearly theirs and couldn't belong to anyone else.

"Perhaps Mam and Dad could find room for it all in the store room at the ice-cream factory?" he suggested.

"I want to stay, be here when you come back and we can pretend nothing's happened."

"Think about it, Olive, love. I'd be happier knowing you were with your mam and dad and not on your own. What if there's an air raid? We've already had a few. What if the town gets bombed? Please, love, think about it."

Later that day, while they were counting up the takings on the stall, Granny Moll came across the sand, pausing to speak to them. Huw was struggling to close up the helter-skelter with one of Bleddyn's sons. He limped across to speak to her but she waved him away.

"It's amazing how quickly this war is changing things," Ronnie said. "We won't be selling ice-cream, the sweets and crisps will be on allocation if not rationed. What are we going to give the trippers when we can't give them those things, Granny Moll?"

"We'll think of something," Moll smiled. "And in the mean time, Olive dear, what about you? Ronnie's right. You can't stay in those rooms on your own, can you?"

"Why not? I'm married. I can't run home to Mam when things get difficult, Granny Moll."

"That's what Ronnie wants you to do, isn't it? Happier he'd be, knowing you weren't on your own."

"I can't go back to live with Mam and Dad. Not after running my own home. I've got used to doing things my way."

"Then I've got a suggestion. What about coming to live with me and our Audrey? The house is too big for just Audrey and me. And," she went on quickly as she saw that Olive was about to refuse, "with all my spare rooms, I'll be having soldiers or evacuees billeted on me if you don't come and use a couple of them."

The suggestion was discussed all that day, Moll and Audrey deciding which rooms would be best for Olive, Olive asking Ronnie if he thought he would be able to accept not having a place of their own when he came on leave.

"I'll put up with that knowing you're not on your own," he replied, then he looked at her with a suspicious grin on his face. "There's something else stopping you, isn't there? You're thinking you'll be unable to refuse to work on the sands if you take two rooms with Granny Moll?" He hugged her and asked, "What if I make sure she knows you aren't willing?"

Moll promised she wouldn't try and persuade Olive. "Just give me a couple of weeks when I can call on you if I'm real desperate at weekends and when you're not working, and as soon as I can find some extra help I won't ask you again, right?"

To add further persuasion, she added, "And think of how much cheaper it will be, easier for you to save for a place of your own, better than two rooms, eh?"

So it was arranged and before Ronnie left, he saw their possessions packed away and his wife settled into two rooms in his grandmother's house.

At first Olive spent the evenings with Moll and, when she was in, with Audrey. But she gradually spent more time in her own room. She couldn't write to Ronnie in the loving way she wanted to with Granny Moll there. Moll's presence inhibited her from expressing her feelings.

Audrey was out several evenings each week. She had joined the Air Raid Precaution group who met in the school, learning ways of dealing with the air raids they were sure would come. She had also started organising weekly sales of unwanted items to raise money for servicemen's comforts. Using a wooden barrow she walked the streets knocking on doors collecting items for sale, and every Saturday afternoon she set up a stall on the pavement outside Woolworths to sell them all.

Olive thought that having to live without her husband's presence and suffering the occasional session on the beach stall was enough support of the war effort for her to give, and ignored Audrey's attempts at persuading her to help with these activities.

Huw, with an ankle almost healed, but still using a stick, had joined the Local Defence Volunteers which many had joined at its conception in May. They had been promised weapons and a uniform and a new title in the near future and in July, Churchill gave them the more impressive title of the Home Guard. Their ages varied from seventeen to over sixty – although most were in the upper age limits – and they quickly earned the nickname "Dad's Army".

Everyone seemed to be doing something to support their country on the home front when they couldn't help further afield.

Freddy quickly recovered from the shock of losing his job. Perhaps he would be lucky and find himself a position in a reserved occupation and evade call-up, he thought hopefully. He was not as keen to serve as he pretended and had nightmares of himself in battles surrounded by faces filled with hatred and hands threatening him with guns.

He went to the Labour Exchange straight away, hoping to find a position that would exclude him from call-up. There were plenty of reserved occupations, although he didn't think that experience working for a gents' outfitters qualified him for many.

"Certain farm workers are exempt," the man in the labour exchange told him. "But without experience I doubt that you'd qualify."

"Thank God for that!" Freddy replied fervently. He thought of all that mud – and worse – and large smelly animals and decided he'd rather take his chances against Hitler's army.

Prospective employers always began an interview by asking his age and, knowing he was ripe for call-up, were unwilling to take him on.

"Hardly worth our time training you, see," he was told. "You'll be off before you can be any use to us."

There were vacancies at one of the factories that had changed from constructing machinery to making munitions and aeroplane parts. When Freddy arrived for an interview he was offered work on the bench with a lot of women, for which he would wear greasy overalls, or an office job with less money but for which he could dress in a tidy suit. He chose the office job and was determined to become so indispensible he would evade conscription.

Moll called Beth aside one morning and handed her a pound note. "Here, love, put this with the rest. Best to save while you can."

"Granny Moll, it's too much. A whole pound! Freddy earns less that in a week!"

"Take it and start building on it."

"Thank you, Gran," Beth said, hugging her.

"There won't be much for him when he gets army pay."

"He isn't getting much now, Granny Moll."

"I thought the pay was good at the munitions?"

"Yes, but he's in the office and the pay is less than he was earning in the shop." She shrugged. "Not everyone will make money out of the war. Although I'm sure there's some who will, mind."

"Didn't fancy dirtying his hands? Don't be shamed by that," she added as Beth was about to protest. "Freddy is who he is.

Don't be one of those girls who marry someone they want to change." She opened her purse. "Here, love, put this with the rest." She handed Beth another ten-shilling note. Ignoring her granddaughter's protest, she pushed it into her pocket. "Piper's is a good business and you should benefit from all the work you do. I want you to have a real good start. Put it in a savings book in your name. Keep it as a surprise for Freddy when this lot is over and you can plan your wedding, is it?"

When Beth met Freddy later that evening she had the money in her handbag to give to him. Granny Moll had advised her to put it into a savings account of her own, and add to it regularly every week, but Beth felt she had to show Freddy she still trusted him after his confession about taking money from their joint savings. It had given her so much pride, knowing they had a bank account with a real bank and not a post office book like most of her friends. Surely he wouldn't take from it again?

"Here you are, Freddy, this is to start our savings for our own house." She handed it to him and felt only the briefest of doubts as he took it and put it in his inside pocket.

"Marvellous she is, your Granny Moll. I wish I could contribute more, but my wages are worse than before. Fancy me being given the push. Just when I was promoted to second sales too. I've been there since I left school at fourteen, and that's the way they treated me. I wouldn't mind if I'd been called up, but just to be told to go – insulting it is, Beth. Damned insulting."

"Think of the chaos there'll be when the war's over. All the men coming back and wanting to return to their jobs and the replacements told they're no longer needed."

"Doesn't bear thinking about. I hope I can stay where I am for the duration. Small pay is better than none, eh?"

"You don't think you'll be called up, then? Thank goodness for that."

"Couldn't bear to leave you, Bethan." He kissed her firm little mouth and thought of the soft generous lips of Shirley Downs and the sensations she created with a kiss. He held Beth close to hide the disappointment in his blue eyes.

Lilly still met Phil whenever he could get away from his family. During the summer months, with the evening too light for concealment, they had been desperate for a safe place to meet. On one occasion they shared a shed with a couple of sheep, on another they jumped over a farm gate for an hour's privacy, burrowing deep into haystacks when the weather was kind. Back lanes, shop doorways and certain places in the woods all had their uses, but with the end of summer in sight they needed to find a sheltered place to meet. Then Lilly had an idea.

"Piper's Café closes about eight," she said excitedly. "I've got keys, so why don't we meet there?"

The beach was never as busy in the evenings, although some of the cafés stayed open and the fairground was still packed with those looking for thrills. As the evening wore on the lights from the rides grew brighter, until the time for blackout came and they were all snuffed out. The voices became more shrill for a while as young people held out before setting off back home, but fewer and fewer stayed to stroll along the beach. The bay gradually became shrouded in darkness and was abandoned. Seagulls strutted along the edge of the sea looking for food left by the trippers. A few older children searched for empty pop bottles which they could return and claim a few pennies for. An elderly man stacked the last of the deckchairs under the promenade where he was supposed to lock them up for the night, though he never actually bothered to find the chains and padlocks.

Wardens were strutting about warning people not to show a light. A man struck a match to light his pipe and the warden ran after him shouting angrily, "Oi, put that light out! Don't you know there's a war on and you can be fined for striking an unguarded match?"

Lilly watched with amusement. She wondered whether the warden really thought a match flame could be seen by a German pilot as he flew over or whether he was just being officious. Although, she remembered, there had been a fine for that offence in the paper recently. What a farce. They'd never be bombed; the Germans wouldn't waste effort on a small town like St David's Well.

She watched as the pipe-smoking man walked slowly up the slope leading to the promenade and headed for a pint of beer to celebrate the end of his long day. She was sitting at the bottom of the rocks in the shadows at the end of the promenade, the smell of the warm wet sand redolent of a thousand summer days. When she felt it was safe to do so, she crossed the sand, climbed the metal steps up to the café on the cliff path and unlocked the door. She went through the seated area and as she opened the main door, Phil slipped inside and took her in his arms.

The chairs were hard and too small for comfort, entwined as they were, so they sat on the floor in the corner near the door, where passers-by wouldn't see them. They held each other close, spoke in whispers and thought they were in heaven.

"What did you tell your wife so you could get away?" Lilly asked when they were sitting smoking a cigarette, the glow lighting their faces at intervals and lighting up their expressions of love.

"I'm walking the dog," he grinned.

"Where is it then?"

"Left it with a mate."

That evening visit was the first of many. They left no evidence of having been there, even disposing of the rubbish that was sometimes pushed through the letter box by passers-by too lazy to find a rubbish bin. No one guessed the café had nightly visitors.

As weeks went by, Lilly persuaded Phil to reveal more about his unhappy marriage.

"She's out all the time, see," Phil explained when Lilly asked why he worked such long hours. "Never home to get my tea. I usually go in to find something keeping warm on top of a saucepan of hot water."

"That's terrible." Lilly longed to help him, spoil him, look after him as a wife should.

"I might as well stay at work and earn a bit extra," he went on. "Putting it away in secret I am; she's a bit extravagant and always short of cash. I need to have a bit put by to dig her out when she gets into debt."

"You deserve better treatment," Lilly said, knowing she was the one to provide it. If only he would face the fact that his marriage was a terrible disaster, a mistake to be rectified.

"I hope to be running Piper's one day," she said, hoping he would understand what she was offering him. "Our Beth and my brothers and cousins will stay in the business of course, but it needs a strong person in charge. I'm like my Granny Moll, and I'm the one to do it after her time. Plenty of money then. If I marry, my husband won't have to work such long hours."

"And your husband will have something to hurry home to," he whispered. "Lucky he'll be, no mistake."

Lilly was better tempered now she and Phil were meeting regularly and had reached a new level of understanding. They seemed able to talk about anything now the barriers were down and he had told her about his unhappy marriage. She began to believe that he would one day leave his wife and, far into the future, would marry her.

She worked a little harder on the beach and didn't complain about the various jobs she disliked. She was anxious to show her father and mother how much she deserved to be given more responsibility, building up to the time when they would retire and leave the business in her hands. Me and Phil running Piper's, she dreamed. Handyman he was, good at fixing things; he'd be an asset to Piper's with its almost continuous maintenance problems. Yes, life looked good. If only she could persuade him to leave his uncaring wife.

Beth continued to pursue the little girl who came each evening to take the food. The girl was now well aware of being followed and easily evaded Beth's attempt to follow. Beth tried leaving Piper's early and waiting near the lane to which she had been led, the place where she suspected her quarry lived, but although she waited long after the girl should have returned, she didn't appear.

With the familiarity of several visits, the run-down places had lost some of their terror but it still wasn't a place where she liked to dawdle. The semi-derelict buildings seemed to hold unseen dangers, their interiors dark and threatening. She saw a door move occasionally as though someone was watching, hidden behind its rotten wood. A cat paused to look at her as it slunk along the gutter about its business and a rat sat for a while, watching her with beady, intelligent eyes, but there was no sign or sound to suggest human habitation.

She tried putting a note with the food, but saw it flutter to the ground and dance away on the breeze. It seemed she needed some assistance if she were to find out more and be able to help the child further. She decided to ask her family.

Lilly told her she was stupid, and Eynon said he hadn't the time. Both were involved in their love lives and when they weren't meeting their loved ones they were dreaming about meeting them. Eynon had met a girl who was holidaying in the town, and he was determined to pursue her during the few days left. She lived about sixty miles away so the romance was unlikely to continue after the holiday, but at seventeen he found that an advantage rather than a problem. Beth pleaded with them both to no avail.

Ronnie came home on embarkation leave and Beth asked him to help. When the situation had been explained, he agreed. On the following evening he went to the field near the café and settled down in a spot from where he could see the café bins. Olive was with him, lying down in the tall ripe summer grass. They were inseparable during those precious days and Beth had to accept the help of both of them or neither.

They saw the girl take the food, which Beth now left on top of the bin, the packages having increased in size and the contents more varied. Olive spoke aloud to Ronnie, who replied as though angry and stayed where he was. Olive walked off in the same direction taken by the girl, making sure she had the girl's attention. A lover's tiff would reassure her as to their presence there. She wouldn't see them as a threat.

Ronnie waited until they were both out of sight then darted through the lanes to the area Beth had described. Beth waited at the far side of the field but was careful not to show herself.

As the girl reached the lane behind the run-down houses, she paused and looked around her. Feeling safe from curious eyes she ran softly up the worn concrete with its immature forest of weeds and saplings. She gave another brief look around before she darted in through a stable door and closed it softly behind her.

Half an hour later, the three conspirators met and discussed their next move.

On the following day, Beth did not put out the usual bundle. She watched as the girl came and searched through the bin, which Beth had filled with unwrapped fish leftovers to discourage her. She was crying when she ran off and Beth's eyes filled with guilt at the way she had made the girl suffer disappointment.

An hour later she took a generous packet of food, which included fresh fruit and some chocolate, and made her way to the stable. Ronnie and Olive met her and together they went in. Darkness and silence greeted them and they stood for a long time while their eyes grew accustomed to the poor light. Then they made out a mound in one corner and on investigation discovered a child who looked about twelve lying, obviously ill, under a heap of old coats.

"Who are you?" the girl asked, her voice low and wheezing as though with a heavy cold.

"Friends," Ronnie said. "Come to help you we have."

"Please, go away."

"You have to see a doctor."

"No need for a doctor, my sister is looking after me."

"So is *my* sister, though you don't know it," Ronnie replied.

"It's you who puts out the food?" The girl turned her head slowly to look at Beth, who nodded. "Thank you." She lowered her head as though the weight of it was too much for her slender neck.

"We can't leave you here like this," Olive said, compassion softening her voice.

"We manage fine," the breathless voice insisted.

"We could take you to the hospital," Ronnie offered. "When you're well again maybe you will manage fine, but you have to be fit to live rough like this."

"And what about school?" Beth asked. "Doesn't someone at school try to help you both?"

"None of your business!" a voice shouted and they turned to see the small figure of the younger sister silhouetted against the open door. "Go away and leave us alone. We don't want no interfering busybodies!"

"Either you accept our help or two of us will stay here and the other will go and fetch the police," Ronnie said firmly. "The choice is yours and you have one minute to decide." He deliberately panicked the girl, knowing that if they went away, allowing them time to consider, the girls would have moved on before they could return, even though the older one looked too sick to be moved.

"No police, please, and no hospitals," the elder girl pleaded between coughing.

"They'll send us back, see," her sister added. "We can't go back; we're trying to find our brother." She crouched down beside her sister in a protective way.

"Back where?" Ronnie asked, bending down to talk to them. "Do you have a mother somewhere? We'll help you find your brother if we can," he offered encouragingly. "Or take you back to your mother."

"Dead, she is, and our dad. We were put in a home, see, and our brother was sent somewhere else, and we can't find him. He'd look after us if we could find him."

"Take them to Granny Moll," Olive suggested. "She'll know what to do."

With Ronnie half carrying the sick sister and the other fussing around her like a distraught mother hen with a solitary chick, they made their way through the lanes towards Sidney Street.

Before they were halfway there, Ronnie had to lift the girl and carry her. She smelled unpleasantly of perspiration and the dampness of the bedding in which she was wrapped. She felt very light and he wondered how long they had been surviving on what the younger sister could steal. They were both so thin and gaunt, he didn't think they had had sufficient food for a long time.

Olive opened the door and called to Granny Moll. She was convinced that Moll would get the two girls into hospital and back into the care of the council as soon as they explained, but Moll had different ideas.

"Food and some cough medicine, that's all they need," she said when she had heard the impassioned pleading of the two girls not to send them back to the home. "We'll see if a bit of maldod will put them right, then we can think again."

Somewhat doubtfully, Ronnie, Olive and Beth agreed.

Moll rang the police later and rather evasively explained the situation.

"They aren't criminals – and they aren't running away from conscription," she joked. "Two children in need of a home, they are. I'll keep an eye on them and you say nothing to your superiors or the authorities till I tell you, right?"

"If they're runaways, I need to—"

"You didn't find them, you don't know where they are, so how can you tell anyone?"

"But it's my duty to—"

"Forty-eight hours, that's all I'm asking."

"I have to see them and find out where they're from. You can't just casually take on someone else's children."

Moll could hear a lot of noise in the background, people talking, shouting, arguing, laughing. She guessed the man was in the middle of something important. Depending on it, she added more weight to her argument. "I'll take responsibility for them, and you've got plenty of other things to see to with this war an' all. So give me a couple of days, right?"

"All right," the constable agreed reluctantly, knowing he was wrong but too harassed by the local residents classed as aliens to argue. The front desk was crowded with Italians and Germans who had lived in the town for many years, many of them sailors who had liked the town and found work and stayed. These foreign residents now had to report weekly to be checked, or risk being imprisoned. After being kept waiting, they were becoming restless and noisy and he gave up. "Keep them for tonight and I'll be over first thing tomorrow. And make sure you're there," he warned as a pretence that he was in control.

"Oi! Where d'you think you're going?" Moll demanded of Beth and Olive as they went towards the kitchen door. "Staying here you are, the three of you. I'm not doing this on my own."

"We were going to make some tea and get them some hot food," Olive explained.

"Washing comes first," Moll said firmly. "A wash and a clean bed is what these two want most. Then we'll see about cawl and a cwlff. Right?" "Cawl and a cwlff" was a bowl of home-made soup and a thick slice off the loaf. Once the two girls were settled between Moll's clean white sheets, Olive and Ronnie were allowed to relax and eat their own share of the food, and Beth was allowed to go home.

Moll smiled. The house had felt empty for years. Once Marged had left, she and Audrey had rattled around in the three-storey building. Now, with Olive and Ronnie staying there and these two children desperate for a home, the place was filling up nicely.

The sergeant came the following morning and after numerous phone calls it was agreed that the children would stay with her until something else could be arranged. Myrtle and Maude burst into tears at the policeman's words.

"We don't want to go back."

"We have to find our brother," Maude wailed.

"Don't worry, trust Granny Moll," the old woman promised. "You won't go anywhere you don't want to go. The sergeant is too busy with important things to worry about a couple of tiddlers like you."

* * *

Before July ended, Bleddyn's two sons received their call-up papers. Marged and Huw wondered how they were going to cope with the severe shortage of staff. Marged asked Freddy to help by giving up his job at the factory and joining them, but he refused. He didn't explain that he hoped to avoid being sent into the army; instead, he told them that the factory desperately needed his organising skills and war work was more important that holidays on the beach.

"That's where you're wrong, boy," Huw replied. "Wars aren't only fought on the battlefields, it's on the home front too that wars are won or lost! Morale is important and we have to do everything we can to keep it high."

"Selling ice-creams and making money from rides?" Freddy was sarcastic, almost believing his story about the importance of his position. "Bullets and bombs we need, not ice-cream."

In spite of several enquiries, Moll could find no information about the family of Maude and Myrtle. The girls insisted that they had a brother whom they had never met, but the matron of the Children's Home – where they had been taken after several attempts at finding them a foster home had ended in failure – knew nothing about any relations apart from an aunt, who had since died.

Moll called a family conference and everyone attended, including Freddy. It was held at Moll's house as it was the largest, and they all squeezed into the parlour, even Bleddyn, Johnny – who arrived with Hannah and her two daughters – and Taff with his wife Evelyn. The idea was to decide on the best way of dealing with the shortage of help now the army was taking the young men. Moll also hoped they might come up with some ideas for extending the search for the girls' family. They had been surprised to learn that Maude, who was recovering well from her illness, was fifteen, and Myrtle, whom they had guessed was eight, was in fact twelve.

With regard to the beach, Freddy offered to help when he could, but reminded them with importance that with the factory working around the clock with different shifts, he might not be reliable. Bleddyn decided to cut out the boat trips. "I can't go very far out and they'll soon be stopping me altogether I expect," he said gloomily. "So I'll deal with the chip shop full time." Huw and Marged insisted they were unable to do more than run Piper's Café, and they needed Beth's assistance to do it properly.

"Can I help?" Maude asked. "I can take the money for the swingboats or the helter-skelter. Love that we would, me and Myrtle could do that easy."

"Threepenny ride, how much change from half a crown?" Huw asked and neither girl could work it out. "All right, try this. You're given a shilling, how much change for a threepenny ride from that?"

Maude felt her fingers as she counted and came up with the answer eventually but Myrtle looked as blank as before.

"You have been to school?" Marged asked them.

"Not much," Maude admitted. "We didn't go much after Mam and Dad died, then we went for a while when we lived with Auntie Hazel and again when we were with Auntie Rita and—"

"When did you last go to school?" Moll asked Myrtle, who shrugged and looked at her sister for an answer.

"You're too old for school, Maude, we'll have to get you some help from somewhere else, but you, Myrtle, you'll go back to school as soon as the new term starts, right?"

Myrtle looked frightened and hugged her sister. "I can't. They laughed at me before, for not knowing how to read," she said. "I can't go back."

"I'll help you," Beth said, feeling a sense of responsibility for the two girls she had rescued from dire poverty. "We all will."

Huw emptied his pockets and began at once to teach the girls the names of the various coins.

"It seems like we're stuck with you two until we find that brother of yours," Moll said, smiling at the two thin, pale children. "Best we do what we can for you while you're here."

The two girls settled in happily with Granny Moll and Auntie Audrey. With decent food and proper care their skin glowed with health and their hair shone. But their insecurity was still clearly shown by the way they clung to each other in sleep. Moll and her daughter Audrey always looked in on them before they went to their beds and they were touched by the sight of the two little girls tightly clasped in each other's arms, using only a fraction of the big feather bed. Sometimes one of them would cry out in her sleep and the other would whisper soothingly to reassure her that everything was all right and they were safe.

Enquiries went on to try and discover any relations or friends who could give them some information about their early years, but so far nothing had been learnt. Moll repeatedly discussed the situation with her family and others and most were of the opinion that they would never find any relations as they did not want to be found.

"Best we don't tell Maude and Myrtle how hopeless it is, mind," Moll warned. "We don't want them to give up hope, or run off again. Not now, when they're beginning to settle down and build a life for themselves with us."

Audrey, and on occasion Wilf, spent time with the girls helping them to master reading skills and basic adding and subtraction. Myrtle, who at first had understood nothing about reading, was a quick learner and one day Moll was amused to see that the younger sister was helping the older one with a task set her by Audrey.

Hannah came to see the girls sometimes, bringing her two small children, Josie aged four who was already at school, and Marie who was three. Using the books bought for her own girls, Hannah patiently encouraged the four girls to play "schools", thereby adding to the development of them all.

"Great with the kids, isn't she, Granny Moll?" Johnny whispered when they were watching Hannah playing a counting game with the children. "Endlessly patient and so gentle when she has to correct them."

Moll looked at Bleddyn's son fondly. "Besotted you are, young Johnny."

"You do like her, don't you, Granny Moll?"

"How could anyone not like Hannah?" Moll replied. "She's beautiful inside and out." Johnny smiled at her until she spoilt it by adding, "Too old for you to think of marrying, mind."

"I loved her long before I knew her age," Johnny said. Moll recognised a quiet determination in his young face and said nothing more.

Johnny left her and went to join the game of I Spy, which Hannah had changed into a more beneficial game by telling them the object they chose had to be written down. Moll watched them and her eyes softened. Hannah was beautiful and she had helped generously in the teaching of Maude and Myrtle. Bleddyn would be fortunate to have her as a daughter-in-law.

The girls were excellent pupils, she thought, as she watched them laboriously writing on the paper she had supplied, Hannah helping her own two and ready to assist the others when necessary.

Everyone needs an incentive to persuade them to work at a new skill, and for both Maude and Myrtle the urgency was to acquire sufficient ability to be allowed to help on the beach. Moll's motives weren't entirely selfless. With the boys all likely to go to help the fight against Germany, she knew that two other members of the family, even though temporary, would be a valuable asset.

The first week of August was the busiest of the beach season and the family asked friends, neighbours and even a small band of children to help out. Little boys standing on pop crates, wearing outsized shirts back to front in place of overalls, stretched over the small counter to reach for the pennies, which they counted carefully into the biscuit tin which served as a till. Arms waved like frantic jellyfish as everyone tried to be served at once. Ice-cream melted and ran down chubby arms to be licked off when no one was looking, leaving faces sticky as well as rosy in the warm sun, and causing havoc when wasps were attracted by the delicious confection.

The beach filled up until there was hardly any sand to be seen when the tide was high. Screams filled the air as children splashed in the sea and performed wobbly walks both around the edge and inside the beach pool. The uneven surface hurt their feet, adding to the excuses to shout and scream.

More and more day-trippers came: mums, dads, aunties, grandmothers and grandads, arriving by train, bus, bicycle or on foot. They were mostly loaded with heavy baskets and bags filled with whatever they considered necessary for a good day out.

Besides the increasing number of visitors, more vendors came in the hope of a successful day, and Beth noticed that the men who came were generally older than usual, fathers and uncles and brothers with things to sell, services to offer, taking the place of those gone to serve their country, trying to keep the business alive for when their loved ones returned.

Cyril the Snap, the street photographer, abandoned his occasional pitch in the centre of a large city and came for his annual "holiday", smiling hopefully at young girls, flattering them and persuading them that, "Not to take your photographs, beautiful girls that you are, Duw, it would be a crime."

They accepted his words willingly, laughing, half believing him, and he thanked them, told them they were adorable, blew kisses and went to look for more prospective customers.

Mystical, Magical, All-Seeing, All-Knowing Sarah, the Gypsy Princess, advertised her psychic powers on her booth on the promenade. An exotic addition to the rest, her tent was decorated in bold colours and bedecked with gold and silver, attracting some and frightening others. She would sometimes appear, draped in layer after layer of dark-coloured skirts and shawls edged with sparkling designs, and smiled to herself when some hurried past, afraid of those dark, intelligent eyes, which sometimes looked at them boldly and sometimes softened into a wink.

Candy floss failed to appear, obviously a victim of sugar rationing, but Moll dug into her store cupboard and continued to offer coconut ice, Turkish delight and toffee apples made from the last of her stock, selling it in the rock shop run by Audrey, as well as on the stalls where ice-creams were still the favourite.

Bernard Gregory was kept busy with his team of donkeys and the small cart, decorated with flags and pulled by his pony, which gave rides to children. Bernard had retired from the sands several years previously and left the happy business to his son, Peter, but with Peter previously studying for better things and now serving in the forces, Bernard had returned to enjoy his summer with the children.

During a particularly busy day, Beth stood at the top of the café steps, after having been down to the sands to make sure there was no crockery left abandoned, and looked at the scene below. Colour and noise was everywhere: children yelling, mothers shouting louder to attract their attention, and, in many cases, surprisingly, being heard. Every colour imaginable was shown in the summer dresses and dippers and towels, and tablecloths too, as families set out picnic meals. The only dull spots were the men, most of whom sat wearing their suits, sporting a handkerchief on their heads, the only concession to summer being the few inches they exposed of their ankles by rolling up their navy serge trousers. Some had removed their jackets which were folded neatly beside them, but most still wore shirts and ties; loosened, but still respectably in place.

Beth thought of Freddy working in that stuffy factory and felt sorry for him missing these wonderful days.

Freddy had worked a morning shift, finishing at two p.m. and at five o'clock he called to see Shirley.

"Decision day today," he told her when she had finished serving a customer and was free. "Today I'll know whether or not my application for deferment will be approved."

"Good luck," Shirley said, but she sounded far from interested.

"Is everything all right?" Freddy asked, slightly offended. "I thought you'd want to know."

"I might be signing up myself," she said.

"You, signing up? Leaving your mam to cope on her own? You can't do that."

"The shop has been sold and the new owner will let us stay in the flat but we're losing our jobs."

"Sorry I am, Shirley. There's me worrying about my own problems and you're facing this." He was still unappeased, thinking she should have been more concerned for him, but he bravely ignored his own worries and suggested, "Tell you what, I know that Piper's are looking for staff, for the last weeks of summer at least. Shall I put in a word for you and your mam?"

"Lovely – I don't think! With Mam convinced that the Pipers stole the business and it should rightly be hers, she'd love working for them, wouldn't she?"

"Sorry, I didn't think."

"I wouldn't say no to working on the beach," Shirley's mother surprised them by saying. "And I'd be good at it. It's in my blood after all – not that they'd think so, the thieving lot!"

"No, no, no!" Huw was adamant. "I don't want that woman working for us."

"We're desperate, Huw. I don't think we can refuse," Marged said.

"She's trouble. She might think I've forgotten, but I remember the way she called us everything she could lay her tongue to and that's plenty, telling everyone your grandparents stole the business from her grandparents."

"Load of ol' rubbish that was," Moll said, agreeing with Huw for once. "We don't want her sort here, cause trouble she would for sure."

Marged argued and finally threatened to go on strike. "I can't do all the cooking and serve tables with only our Beth to help. Lilly is worse than useless, half the time she doesn't turn up and when she does she's only in the way. I have to have help until the end of summer and this Mrs Downs is all we've found."

"You're right, Marged," Moll conceded eventually. "It's only for the last few weeks, so what harm can she do?"

"Damn it all, Marged, when am I going to have some say in what happens at Piper's?" cried Huw. "Never listen to me, none of you. I make suggestions and you throw them out without discussion, you employ the staff without consulting me, but on this I'm determined. Mrs Downs will be trouble and I don't want her here, right?"

"What about starting her daughter Shirley as well?" Freddy suggested, a flutter of amusement in his throat.

"No, no, no!" Huw shouted angrily, but the idea was discussed as though he hadn't spoken.

"Let's see how Mrs Downs gets on first," Moll said.

"We're not taking on either of them. I forbid it." Huw's voice was losing its power, knowing he was making no impression on the others.

"We'll have a vote," Marged said, realising that she was on safe ground. Huw was outvoted and Mrs Downs arrived the following morning to start work at Piper's Café.

Some of the boats were still managing to give short rides when the tide was high and the barricades built to deter invaders far out to sea. Bleddyn had put his boat in storage for the duration, however, sadly covering her with tarpaulin after giving her an extra coat of paint to protect her.

It was sad to see the small craft hugging the shore and giving a pretence of danger to a few passengers, while others looked on and patiently waited their turn. Bleddyn preferred not to look.

On the morning of Mrs Downs's first day, she collected the rubbish that had been pushed through the letter box during the night and sniffed disapprovingly.

"Don't you clean up before you go home?"

"Yes we do," Marged retorted. "Everything here is shining

spotless and all the left-over food is thrown away. You know how fussy we are about quality and cleanliness. This cigarette packet is what some idle creature has pushed through after we've closed. Don't think you can tell me anything about cleanliness, Mrs Downs."

It was not an auspicious start. With another busy day, there was little time for point-scoring though, and Marged had to admit that Mrs Downs – Hetty, as she chose to be called – worked as hard as any of the others, needing little instruction, seeming to understand what was needed, and to learn quickly where everything was kept. When she mentioned this to Huw he only grunted.

Freddy turned up at five o'clock and offered to help clear the tables and stack dishes for washing. He had been to the swimming baths in his occasional role of lifeguard, which meant a free swim after he had kept watch for a few hours. His towel and dippers were in his bag, which he put on a chair near the door. He thought he might get a swim in the sea later, although he was never very keen, preferring the more orderly pool with its changing rooms and lockers and no waves to worry about. The waves were rough that day, and increasing in size as the tide grew towards its highest point. Perhaps he wouldn't bother. He wouldn't admit it but he never felt easy about sea bathing, in spite of his training as a lifeguard. He preferred to have a safety rail handy and near enough to grab.

He kissed Beth when Marged wasn't looking, then stood beside Shirley's mother and settled to the routine work of cleaning up. The day had been a very busy one, with a continuous queue of people wanting food, partly to save on their rations by eating out. The sea was too rough for most people to enjoy bathing and the sand was being blown about by a frivolous wind, making picnics less pleasant, so instead many trippers had found their way into the café to eat in comfort.

Beth felt a slight twinge of jealousy when Mrs Downs's daughter Shirley arrived to meet her mother. She saw Freddy invite her to join them in the kitchen and shortly afterwards laughter swelled out interspersed by whispered conversation. She went in once to find them doubled over with mirth and asked what the joke was.

"Too complicated to explain," Mrs Downs said, and this increased the laughter as Beth walked away.

It was fast approaching closing time but still the people came and still Marged and Huw and Beth served meals.

"More plates, please," Beth called, popping her head into the kitchen. Shirley and Freddy were wiping plates and stacking them, laughing at something Shirley's mother was saying, and she felt again that surge of jealousy, a sensation of being left out, pushed aside by the girl and her mother. Perhaps her father had been right, and they shouldn't have invited Mrs Downs to help, she thought, although honesty made her admit to herself that the woman worked hard and didn't need constant reminders of what was expected of her.

Bleddyn called unexpectedly to borrow some cooking fat, since he was running low at the fish-and-chip shop, and as he left, carrying the white slab in its greaseproof wrapping, a roar was heard coming from below them. Beth and her parents ran to the window and, looking down, saw that there had been an accident. A crowd was gathered and more people were running towards the edge of the tide. Some were pointing to where one of the small pleasure boats had overturned.

"Freddy!" Beth called. "There's been an accident! Quick, you'll have to help!"

Freddy ran to see what had happened and his heart began to thud painfully. The sea had turned quite rough and he couldn't face diving in and swimming out to where people struggled in the water far beyond the surf, where breakers rose and fell in giant peaks and valleys. The sea was rising and falling like some great boiling cauldron. How could he swim out through that? He was afraid of the sea. Panic set in and his mind whirred. How could he get out of helping without disgracing himself in the eyes of Beth and her whole family?

He glanced at Shirley and knew at once that she understood. She could offer no help, though, and he grabbed his towel, hid in a corner and struggled into his wet bathers. He appeared to rush but many precious seconds passed before he stepped out and began to go down the metal steps to the beach.

"Two children and two women there are," Beth shouted to him as she ran beside him, "besides the boatman."

"I think I'd do better to run to the first-aid hut and ask them to phone for help," he said, slowing down and standing near the edge of the tide. "I can't go out there and bring five people back! What can I do?"

"Do what you can, just get out there," Beth pleaded, thinking of the people in such danger only yards from where they stood. "Someone has already gone for help. We can't stand here and watch them drown!"

He dived in and began to swim but was making little progress, faking cramp, when Bleddyn, who had just realised what had happened, stormed down the beach and dived in. He swam strongly and was soon overtaking Freddy.

The children were crying, the women close to collapse. After talking to them briefly and making sure they had something to hold, he supported each child with a hand under their heads, coaxing them, encouraging them when he realised they could actually swim a little but had been terrified out of trying by their distance from the shore and by the danger represented by the barricades and the mines frighteningly close.

He hadn't wanted to leave one behind while he helped the other. He had thought the women and the boatman would be able to cope but it would have taken only one extra strong wave to have sent the child way beyond the beach and out of reach. Their being able to float enabled him to bring them both in together, kicking strongly with his legs until he could touch the bottom, then wading out, carrying them one under each arm, laughing, persuading them it had been an adventure, something to relate to their friends.

The owner of the boat had persuaded the two distressed women to hold on to the upturned boat, assuring them that the children were safe, and he waited with them while Bleddyn swam to safety with his precious charges and handed them over before swimming back to help the man bring the two women ashore. Like Bleddyn, he had been afraid to leave one of them for fear of them relaxing their tenuous hold and being swept out beyond help.

Bleddyn looked with utter disgust at Freddy when he walked past the younger man. He was carrying one of the women and was followed by the boat owner carrying the other.

Freddy turned to Beth and mouthed silently, "What's up with him? I was on my way, wasn't I?"

"Were you, Freddy? Or were you waiting for someone else to do what you're supposed to be trained to do?"

"Beth, be fair. I did try but I got cramp and—" But Beth was running up the beach beside her uncle, hoping the reason for her tears would be presumed to be relief and not shame.

Five

Beth looked at the ring on her third finger and thought it had lost its sparkle. How could Freddy have been so useless when five people were in danger? She had hardly spoken to him since the accident. Thank goodness nobody had been hurt. He could have been responsible for someone's death, she kept reminding herself. Trained in life saving and too cowardly to swim out when he was needed.

It was early morning and she had been awake since five thirty, the brightness of the day making it impossible to chase sleep any longer. Hearing sounds from above her, she went into the kitchen and filled the kettle. Mam was usually first to rise and would be glad of a cup of tea.

"How long have you been up?" Marged asked as she came into the kitchen in her ancient woollen dressing gown. "Couldn't you sleep?"

"I keep thinking of that boat overturning and Freddy pretending he had cramp. Mam, what would have happened if one of those people had drowned? I couldn't ever have forgiven him."

"You won't be a very suppportive wife then, will you?" Marged said sharply. "The minute he makes a mistake or loses his nerve, you'll stop loving him, is it? Fine start to an engagement that is. I love your father and that means I forgive him whatever he does and support him when he's done something foolish. And he'd do the same for me. I only have to reach out a hand and I know he'll be there. That's what love is, not being so sure of your own perfection. It's knowing you'll give, and have, understanding and forgiveness."

"Mam!"

"All right, I don't like the boy very much and I'd hoped you'd choose to marry someone else, to be honest. But you chose him and you should honour your decision."

As they cleared up after breakfast and prepared to leave for the beach, Beth said, "Can I come over later? There's something I want to do."

Marged only nodded.

The factory worked shifts, but recently Freddy had worked days only, starting at nine and finishing at six o'clock. Instead of the usual stream of people rushing in to clock on before they were late and would miss a quarter of an hour's pay, that morning at ten minutes to nine there were only seven people strolling through the entrance. Beth saw Freddy immediately, and ran up to him before he could disappear through the heavy reinforced metal gates with their barbed wire mounting.

"Freddy? I'm sorry I've been so upset with you."

"I'm sorry too. I should have been braver. But I was so scared. I didn't know what to do; my brain seized up. I couldn't think how to deal with it, how I could possibly rescue five people when I got out there. I had no idea what to do. Ashamed I am, and I don't blame you for hating me."

"I don't hate you, you know that. My shame is that I reacted like I did."

Freddy pulled her round to face him and took her hands in his. People were calling him from the gate but he ignored them. "I'm no film-star hero, am I?" he said sadly.

"None of us are. I don't know how I'd react when faced with sudden danger."

A security man came towards them looking angry.

"For God's sake, come in if you're coming, boy! Lost your shift work because you were always late for shift and now you can't even be on time at nine o'clock!"

"What does he mean, Freddy? You moved to a more important job, didn't you?"

"I missed the six a.m. start a few times, that's all, and the foreman's got it in for me, Beth." He gave her a quick kiss and hurried inside the factory.

Beth wandered back through the town, heading for the small railway station. She would need to catch a train since she'd missed her ride to work. Mam had been right about her lack of loyalty, but she was more unsettled than ever after her attempt to make amends. Freddy had told her he'd been promoted to a more important job, but that wasn't true. He'd lost his position because he was often late. Just how important had his job been, she wondered? Just how well did she know Freddy? They had been together since they were four years old, but she was beginning to think he was a stranger.

The reason the boat had overturned was that the boatman had gone too close to the defences and it had become caught on a metal spike. Held in place, the next wave partly filled it. That it had overturned rather than sank was pure good fortune.

A few days after the incident, the army came and blew up the boat; a frightening reminder that they were at war.

Under Moll's tuition, helped by other members of the family, Maude and Myrtle quickly improved their ability to handle money. To encourage them, Marged allowed them to work on the stalls taking money and giving change under supervision. The knowledge that they were useful was like magic medicine and as their abilities developed so their health improved. A nurse attached to the welfare department of the council visited them at intervals and declared herself satisfied that they were being cared for adequately.

"I think a family environment is what most of these abandoned children need, Mrs Piper," Nurse Francis told Moll one morning. "Pity is that there aren't enough families for them all." She sighed gently. "With any spare spaces being used by evacuees, there are fewer than usual."

"And things will be far worse in the big cities, Miss Francis, with bombing taking away so many houses, and families separated by evacuation as well as everything else. How will it ever get sorted once we've seen an end to it? Lucky we are, to live in a small unimportant place like St David's Well."

"Indeed," Miss Francis agreed. "Now, have you learned anything to suggest there might be some truth in this story about them having a brother?"

"They insist that they have a sister-in-law, which presumably means they have a brother somewhere, but nothing we've discovered gives any clue to where this sister-in-law might be, or even if she exists. Could they have invented her?"

"It's possible. Children who have no one of their own have been known to dream about discovering a long-lost aunt or invent a story that their mother isn't really dead and one day will come back to find them. Sometimes they come to believe it."

"Poor dabs," Moll said sadly. "Never mind, they've got us Pipers now and we'll look after them like they're our own."

"In the circumstances Maude and Myrtle are lucky girls."

Beth's younger brother, Eynon, resented the beach. As far back as he could remember he had been made to help on the stalls or doing menial jobs in Piper's Café. As a child he had enjoyed it – he'd made his friends envious when he described his days on the sands – but now he wanted something different, something that didn't take so much of his time. He had discovered the joy of girls.

Today he had sloped off when his cousin Taff had come to repair a wooden support, and he had no intention of going back. Let them find someone else. The day was warm, summer was coming to its end, the girls were out in force and he was free.

He wandered aimlessly through the busy little town, where shops had filled their windows with patriotic displays supporting the soldiers and sailors and airmen. A pretty, dark-haired girl was standing looking at a tobacconist's window and he strolled casually up and offered her a cigarette from his gold-coloured case, "borrowed" from his father's drawer.

"No thanks, I don't smoke. I think it's a filthy, smelly thing to do," she said, tilting her pert little nose.

"Neither do I," Eynon said, hiding the cigarette he had taken out. "I just keep some on me and offer them to any soldiers I see. Got it hard they have, not much money an' that."

"You are kind," she purred and as he stretched up to his full height and smiled modestly, she added brightly, "Here's my boyfriend, perhaps he'd like one."

With a forced smile, Eynon opened his cigarette case and invited the soldier to help himself. "Greedy bugger needn't have taken two," he muttered as he walked away.

From then on, every likely girl he saw was either with her parents or had a member of the armed forces on her arm. When he met Freddy coming out of the factory at six o'clock, they agreed immediately about the boredom of working for the Pipers.

"Granny Moll thinks that as I'm family I'm bound to love working the beach, but I hate it," Eynon moaned.

"I think it's madness you wasting your talents serving kids with buckets and spades or helping them on and off the swingboats," Freddy said. "Your Beth wants me to work for the Pipers when I come back from the services, but I don't think I'll settle for that, not when I've travelled the world."

"Travel the world?" Eynon said, his mouth open in awe. "Is that what you do in the army? I thought you'd go no further than France, stay a while blasting away at the enemy until you got wounded, them come back home."

"Of course I'll travel. They can send you anywhere they like – and you can bet it won't be anywhere near St David's Well Bay! It's the RAF for me, Eynon. Smart uniform and plenty of girls." Freddy suddenly realised he probably shouldn't be talking to Beth's brother about other women. Never mind; Eynon was a kindred spirit. He'd understand.

Eynon looked starry-eyed. "Just think, Freddy, you might be a pilot! Imagine that, skimming over the towns in France and Germany." He smiled dreamily at the thought of himself wearing his wings proudly on his sleeve and having girls pleading for his attention.

"I'm thinking of enlisting," Freddy told him. "Not waiting for my papers, but signing on for a few years, official like. Then I'll be able to choose which service I join. That's got to be better than waiting to be called up. They can put you where they like then. So I'm told, mind."

"I'm not eighteen till next year, Freddy. I wish I was old enough to go with you."

"They'll take you as a regular, won't they? You're old enough for that. Grab a fine lad like you without hesitation they will. You sign on for five years and you'll come out smarter than you'd be after five years working on the sands. What can you possibly learn on the sands?"

Freddy didn't tell the gullible young boy he had recently learned that his application for deferment had been turned down and that he was expecting his papers any day. "Come on, Eynon, let's see what they tell us at the recruitment office, is it?"

"Is there a place for Royal Navy volunteers, Freddy? I fancy that uniform more than the RAF, don't you?"

"No, I fancy that forage cap. Racy that looks, mind."

During the busy weeks when factories and employments of all kinds normally closed to allow their workforce to take a week's holiday, most continued working. But the beach was still packed and the café had a continuous queue from the moment it opened until the family thankfully closed the door and fell exhausted into the kitchen chairs.

People who didn't usually take a holiday away from home were making the most of the short time before their sons or husbands went into the forces and the atmosphere was lively, with a kind of forced gaiety.

Maude and Myrtle were learning fast and were already very useful members of the Piper team. Lilly had found a new way of avoiding the tasks she hated, insisting she was teaching the youngsters the basics of working on the sands. She also realised that with the place so busy, Marged and Huw didn't have time to check on what she was doing and she became adept at looking busy whenever they approached.

Beth was aware of her sister's idleness but after complaining several times and having nothing done about it, she ignored Lilly and got on with her work. She knew that Lilly wasn't the only one of the family who wasn't doing their fair share, although for the past week her younger brother had seemed much more cheerful.

Eynon stood near the swingboats and was smiling and helpful to the steady stream of customers. Marged and Huw were relieved at his change of attitude. That he was especially charming to the young girls just made them smile. He was growing up. Huw and Marged were just thankful for the effort he was making at this particularly busy time.

Freddy came every evening in time to help, and even Lilly seemed willing to join in with the cleaning at the café when it came to the end of the day, so they could get off a little bit quicker. The family were unaware that she would soon be back there. Marged sighed contentedly as she told Moll that the family were pulling together and everyone seemed to be content despite the long, tiring days.

Audrey's assistant at the rock shop, Alice Potter, worked for several hours each day, though she couldn't work regular shifts as she was needed to look after her father. Colin Potter was an ex-boxer who had been injured in a fight. He couldn't stand without support as he kept losing his balance and he was also deaf.

Alice found looking after him a thankless occupation. No praise was given, however well she managed. They lived in a building that had once been a shop. The room at the front, with its once grand entrance, was empty. The windows were streaked with dirt, and the whole place had a neglected air. Many rooms were unused, since they could afford to furnish and heat only a few.

Eynon saw Alice serving novelty rock when he was on his way to collect more crisps from the store room in Moll's house and he went in to talk to her. That evening, when the rock and sweet shop closed and Audrey came to deal with the money, he was there to walk her home.

Alice was small and very thin, and dark haired like most of the Castle family. Audrey remarked that they could be mistaken for brother and sister. Eynon laughed and winked at Alice. He wasn't feeling at all brotherly.

Alice and her father lived in a dingy lane and the back entrance to their home was blocked with abandoned shelving from the shop. Immediately behind it was another similar terrace. The place was dark and gloomy and from what Eynon could see when he glanced inside, the long passage leading through to the back door, past the hollow space of the shop area, was bare of lino. The walls were in serious need of fresh wallpaper.

On impulse, when he was on his way home, he went to the shops, which were just closing, bought a bunch of chrysanthemums, and returned to Alice's house. When she opened the door her smile was rewarding, and he was about to invite her to go with him to the pictures when another figure appeared.

Leaning on the wall, Colin Potter came down the passageway in a series of jerking paces, angled oddly and using the walls for support. He demanded to know what Eynon wanted.

"Just to thank your daughter for helping my aunt out today, sir," Eynon said politely and after a sly wink for Alice, he went home.

* * *

War or no war, Marged still insisted on throwing away what hadn't been used, and starting each morning with clean shelves and fresh food. A man called Richards arranged to collect the discarded foodstuffs and he came every evening and emptied the separate bins containing food, which he took back to his farm and boiled up for his ever-hungry pigs.

Maude and Myrtle often stood for long periods, staring up into the faces of passers-by.

"I'm sure I'd know our brother if I saw him," Maude would say repeatedly. "He must look like us."

"And Dad used to talk about St David's Well Bay, didn't he?" Myrtle said, never tiring of the stories her sister told about what she remembered of their parents.

"Yes, he did, and that's why we came here, because this is where we'll find our sister-in-law and our brother."

The business during those last few weeks of that first season of wartime increased instead of slowly fading. Even with the whole family working all the hours of daylight, Marged and Huw had difficulty coping. Alice was invited to work as often as possible, releasing Audrey to assist in Piper's Café. Lilly was given clearly defined tasks to do, much to Beth's satisfaction. Freddy helped out as and when he could, spending a lot of his spare time on the sands working the helter-skelter and the swingboats with her brother Eynon, with whom he had developed a kinship not previously apparent. Beth also suspected that the pair of them sloped off early some evenings to go to the pictures. Still they needed extra hands, and small children known to Marged and Huw, who were on holiday from school, were occasionally employed to help serve.

The youngsters tried to outdo other stall-holders, shouting to attract customers and having a wonderful time, with the added bonus of getting some pocket money at the end of each day. Tin buckets and spades, flags and balloons were in constant demand. There had been no sign so far of the shortages they had been warned to expect, so stocks were not conserved. There seemed no need when there was an apparently endless supply. The war would surely be over before they need worry about supplies for the next season, eight whole months away.

The summer was one of the busiest and happiest they could

remember. The youngest assistants hoped the men wouldn't come home too soon and spoil their fun. As the family's confidence in them grew and the stalls were at their busiest, they were each wrapped around several times with a white aprons and, wearing saucy hats pinned to size, they were soon selling ice-cream. They tried not to be seen licking their hands or the scoops too often, because Moll had threatened them with a cut in their pocket money if they were caught.

Youngsters ran with the donkeys too. Old Bernard Gregory walked sedately with the older patrons but when children wanted a more daring ride, one of the band of enthusiastic helpers would run behind the patient donkeys, urging them into a gallop. All the beach people were sunburnt and happiness shone in every eye. It was with surprise, therefore, that the family greeted Freddy's words one Saturday night when they were making their way homewards.

"I won't be able to help you after next week."

"Why not?" Beth demanded. "Don't tell me you're fed up with the beach already?"

Making the most out of the situation, lying with ease, Freddy said sadly, "I was devastated at my cowardice when that boat overturned, and, well, I had to prove to myself that I'm not a coward, so I ignored the fact that I'm in a reserve occupation, getting the bombs and bullets out to our boys. Sorry, Beth, but I've enlisted. It's the army uniform for me instead of a white jacket." Dramatically, he opened his arms to Beth to be hugged, and they clung together, oblivious of Huw and Marged's stare.

"Joined up voluntary, like?" Huw said, amazed.

"When you didn't have to go?" Marged asked with a frown.

"Oh Freddy, I wish you hadn't," Beth said. "Why didn't you discuss it with me? I am your fiancée."

"I knew you'd try and talk me out of it, and this is something I have to do," he said emotionally.

Moll just stared at him enigmatically. This wasn't what she had heard from others who worked at the factory. She said nothing. Perhaps her information was wrong.

"There is something I'd like to suggest," Freddy went on. "I know how desperate you are for help, so I asked Shirley Downs if she'd be willing to give up the job she found at the café in town and come here to help you. She's experienced now, waiting table at that café."

"No! We've got her mother against my wishes. That's bad enough," Huw complained. "Why should we give them work when they call us names? Just let me see her mother drunk, just once, and she goes, right? So we don't want no Shirley Downs, right?"

"Wrong," Marged said. "We're too desperate to argue. Bleddyn's boys are off in two weeks' time and we'll take who we can."

Huw appealed to Moll, but she agreed with her daughter. "It's only through these next few weeks, the busiest times will be over by then. Not worth making a fuss about, Huw."

Huw walked a little way past the van and stared out across the slowly emptying promenade. He wondered how Marged could accept help from Hetty Downs after all the accusations she had made about Marged's great-grandparents cheating her family. The woman must be exaggerating about the dishonesty of Moll's parents. There was certain to be a grain of truth in the story, there usually was, but that would be all.

He ignored the struggles of the women as they put all the tablecloths and other washing into the van and fitted themselves around it. He didn't try to help, and he drove home in silence. Why did no one ever listen to his opinion? He was the man of the family, its head, yet it was as though he were invisible. He wasn't a Piper, he seethed, he was a Castle, and one day he'd remind them of that fact.

The Castle family had a party the night before Bleddyn's two sons left for the forces. As Freddy was due to go soon afterwards, he was included in the capacity of departing friend as well as part of the family and Beth's fiancé.

Moll's house was the largest so it was there they all gathered, each wondering how to set the tone for the evening. Although it was an excuse for a family get-together, the occasion had sombre undertones as they were saying farewell to those they loved as they left to face untold dangers.

Music was the way they set the mood, Huw playing piano and Bleddyn on mandolin. They started with comic, music-hall songs, laughter a release from the inhibitions of not being sure of what role they should play. The conversation was stilted for a while, but as the flagons emptied and the singing began, the mood swiftly passed through the usual stages of laughter, nonsense and into the sentimental or downright maudlin as they sang the melodies of years ago.

Bleddyn spoke very rarely to Hannah. He didn't like the closeness she and Johnny were showing. The glances they shared were very revealing. She was too old and too worldly, with a divorce behind her. The fact of her parents being unwilling to support her told of some other event to discredit her and he didn't want his son to become embroiled in anything sordid.

Hannah sensed his disapproval and was saddened by it, but she didn't push Johnny away when he took advantage of a quiet moment and kissed her. Then he sang a love song, smiling towards the corner where she sat with a sleepy Josie and Marie. Taff looked shyly at his wife Evelyn and slid his hand into hers. Beth glanced at Freddy, but he was looking across the room towards Eynon as though they shared a secret.

It was when this late stage had been reached that Moll suddenly realised that Lilly had failed to appear. Before she could remark on the fact, Lilly came in, apologising none too sincerely for being late.

Moll looked at her, assessing her granddaughter's mood. Lilly's eyes were shining, her hair dishevelled, her face aglow with intoxication that had nothing to do with alcohol. Moll knew the signs of love-making; she had seen it on her own face many years before and on the face of her daughter. Her granddaughter had been with a man, not a casual friend either, someone to whom she was strongly attracted and she showed the headiness of having that love returned.

In Piper's Café, where Phil and Lilly had spent a blissful two hours, a cigarette burned slowly in a corner near the door. It glowed with one last burst of energy before guttering out.

Bleddyn was at a loss. He no longer ran boat trips, and the fish-and-chip shop was easily managed with the competent staff he had. Time hung heavily, and with his sons gone he had little heart for the beach. He kept looking up, expecting one of them to come and relieve him. He knew he should spend more time talking to Taff's Evelyn and Johnny's Hannah, comforting them, discussing their plans, offering help where needed, but when he met them he had nothing to say.

Subliminally he blamed them for his sons' leaving, as if by looking after them better they could somehow have prevented it. They came to see him as often as they could and sometimes stayed at the beach all day, wanting to help, to lose themselves in work. He should have been grateful, but distress and fear obliterated all compassion for them.

One morning, after heavy rain during the night, they even managed to remove the stiff and awkward covers from the swingboats and the helter-skelter by themselves. Although he didn't want to help, he was offended by their unwillingness to ask for it.

He took over the ice-cream making, using the last of their stock of powder, and spent time in the pop factory dealing with the jobs no one else wanted to do, clearing out corners, painting areas that were looking shabby, seaching for tasks he could do alone. He relieved his brother Huw of the ordering and checking the deliveries of foodstuffs, but all without any joy. It was as though he had presumed the deaths of his sons, knew they would never survive and was already in mourning.

As Marged and Beth were setting the tables with the freshly laundered gingham cloths one morning, Marged complained that the floor hadn't been washed properly the evening before.

"Look at this, there's dirty ol' ash down in this corner. Whose job was it to mop the floor?" she demanded angrily.

"Lilly's, I think," Beth said as she straightened the cutlery.

"She never does anything proper and still thinks she could take over from me," Moll added, outraged at the negligence. She collected brush and dustpan and dealt with the ash and cigarette ends. "Imagine if our first customers came and saw that," she tutted.

"I did the floor last night and I didn't miss that corner," Mrs Downs said, having overheard. "However it got there, it wasn't there when I washed the floor." Her eyes were bright as she prepared to defend herself.

Seeing her mother about to argue, Beth said curiously, "Mam, the same thing happened a few days ago. I'd done the floors the day before, and I didn't skimp on the cleaning either. I think someone pushes rubbish through for a joke or because they're too lazy."

"That's likely," Mrs Downs agreed.

Marged disagreed. "I don't think so. It isn't in the right spot to have fallen through the letter box."

With customers already banging on the door, they didn't discuss it further, but they were all puzzled about the overnight appearance of the cigarette ash. Could someone be using the place after they left? It seemed impossible. The place was firmly locked each evening and nothing had changed when they arrived in the morning, except the occasional appearance of cigarette ash. Moll sighed and put it down to tiredness. It was not surprising that after a long busy day they were less than fussy over the final cleaning job.

Aware that they were in danger of being found out, Lilly and Phil still used the café, but were more careful not to leave behind any evidence of their nocturnal visits.

Because he had been employed to work in the parks during most of the summer, it was for two weeks only that the Punch and Judy man joined the other entertainers on the sands. Twice every morning and three times every afternoon, a crowd of children and adults would gather, sitting cross-legged on the sand to watch the performance. Boos for the villain, cheers for the hero, sympathy with the victims were all interspersed with laughter. Nothing changed from year to year and it was the repetition, the knowing what came next, that gave the performance its special delight.

Audrey Castle did very little on the beach these days. Leaving Alice Potter in charge more and more often, she cleaned and ran her mother's home, leaving Moll free to help where she was needed. Besides looking after her own mother's place, Audrey also spent a lot of time helping Wilf's mother run hers.

Geraldine Thomas was a semi-invalid, rising late, going to bed early and taking a rest each afternoon. Wilf worked as a storeman in a wholesale fruiterers and besides working at the early morning market, he was training as an auxiliary fireman with special emphasis on how to deal with incendiary bombs in case of air raids.

Audrey went up to King Edward Street after she had

dealt with breakfast for her mother, Maude, Myrtle, Olive and herself, and prepared a late breakfast for Mrs Thomas. When the rush of early customers had slowed, Wilf cycled home to join her. Audrey went shopping then, shopping for her own meals as well as food for Wilf and his mother. Wilf went with her and this was the longest time during their busy days that they spent together. This was the extent of their "courting". Sometimes they went into a café and enjoyed a cup of tea, although instead of personal conversation, Audrey usual whispered criticisms on the way the place was run, comparing it unfavourably with Piper's.

She did a little housework, although most was dealt with by Mrs Thomas and Wilf, and usually stayed to get their midday meal on the table before going back home in time to cook the evening meal for her family.

"One day, my dear. One day," Wilf always whispered as they parted.

"Yes, dear, one day," she would whisper back. The remark and response were automatic, having lost their excitement over the years they had been repeated. She had almost stopped dreaming about being married to Wilf and having a home of their own. Being needed, flattered and complimented, she was content.

Despite local enquiries, the Castle family had failed to learn anything about the girls they had taken under their wing. Maude was fully recovered and Myrtle was preparing, somewhat nervously, to return to school.

Both girls were able to read simple stories, although understanding arithmetic had come easier. Huw had been right: having a reason to learn – their desire to help more fully on the beach stalls – had given them the incentive they needed to understand the mathematics of money.

Eynon was talking to the donkey man, Bernard Gregory, one day and the old man thought he remembered the family. "Maude and Myrtle are easily remembered," he told Eynon. "They sound like a music-hall act. If you call round the house one evening, I'll let you see the snapshot album, old snaps taken years ago. I've got a feeling that Maude and Myrtle are in some of them. If I'm right, then the family used to work the beach, but I can't remember what they did."

Eynon told Beth and they arranged to go to see the man together.

Bernard Gregory lived in an area just outside the town, where he had a couple of fields for his donkeys and hen houses as well as a pond for ducks. Beth and her brother Eynon walked down there one Sunday evening and found the old man carrying a bucket of warm mash to feed the chickens.

They walked around the smallholding with him, admiring the ducks as they were locked up for the night and the hens and the thirty cockerels – which, he informed them, were being fattened up for Christmas. Beth shuddered. Even though she ate chicken with as much relish as the rest of her family did, she didn't like looking at the beautiful creatures and being aware of their purpose.

They went inside the cosy, over-furnished living room and Mr Gregory handed them three battered photograph albums. He pointed out the children, then very young, whom he thought were the sisters and invited Beth and Eynon to take the albums home in the hope that they might trigger some memories. But as to who Maude and Myrtle were, he insisted he could not remember.

Beth came away convinced he knew more, that his memories of the children were clearer than he admitted.

"Perhaps it's not his story to tell," Beth said thoughtfully.

"Or it might involve a juicy bit of scandal," Eynon said.

"You don't think Granny Moll or Mam and Dad are pretending not to know, do you?"

"Why not? You can't imagine they're connected to St David's Well, without someone recognising them, can you?"

Eynon had persuaded Alice to go to the pictures with him several times and had managed a few brief kisses. One rainy evening when they had run from the picture house and were very wet, she invited him in to dry his hair.

"What about your Dad?" he asked

"Fast asleep by this time, don't worry," she whispered as she opened the front door.

They walked on tiptoe along the dark passage and went into the kitchen beyond. As Alice filled the kettle and set it to boil, upstairs her father stirred. He could barely hear a sound, but some sixth sense told him there was someone in the house. Not bothering to find anything for his feet and not possessing a dressing gown, he moved quietly down the stairs, walking with his body slanted, his shoulders leaning against the grimy walls.

Eynon turned off the gas under the kettle and said, "Why don't we go upstairs, Alice?" She took his hand and they had actually begun to climb the stairs when they saw Mr Potter on his way down. "Who's there with you, Alice?" he shouted and Eynon tried to leave.

The door was stiff and the man was moving very fast. Eynon abandoned the door and ran down the passage. There might be a high wall, but the approach of Alice's father promised him wings!

The uneven footsteps scurrying along the bare floor behind him were frightening. The man ran leaning against the wall to stay upright but it didn't slow him down and he reached out and gripped Eynon's shoulder painfully tight.

"I only came in for a moment," Eynon said. "I wanted the lav, see."

"The lav's out the back, not upstairs like the posh Piper family."

"I'm a Castle," Eynon said weakly. For someone supposed to be deaf, this one was quick to understand what was being said, Eynon thought. He hadn't seen Alice repeat the words slowly so her father could lip-read. Confused by the pain, he struggled to escape the man's firm grasp.

"It's all right, Dad." Alice tried to pull her father's fingers free. She could see that Eynon was in pain.

Mr Potter gave Eynon a powerful push before letting him go and he slithered along the passage, fell but immediately recovered and made for the door. Alice opened the door and whispered, "See you tomorrow," before he was out in the night and running down the road. His shoulders hurt, but before he reached the corner he was laughing.

Marged and Moll looked through the albums sent by Mr Gregory but saw no one they recognised. Marged showed several of the snaps to Huw but he was clearly not interested – although she did see him looking through the tattered pages once, when he thought she wasn't looking.

"See anyone you know?" she asked and he shook his head and threw the book down.

The girls browsed through the pages time after time, refusing to give up hope of finding someone they knew, but eventually the albums were put aside, another dead end.

Eynon considered himself one of Freddy's closest friends since their talk regarding conscription. When he spoke of him he referred to him as "my butty", the local name for a close friend. So when he was walking along the main road with his sister late one evening, after a second visit to Mr Gregory to return the albums, and saw Freddy coming out of the picture house with another girl, he quickly led Beth away so she wouldn't see them. He was bubbling with barely controlled laughter, which eventually exploded as they turned a corner and left the main road behind, along with any possibility of the couple being seen by his puzzled sister.

"Eynon? What's struck you as so funny?" Beth asked with a frown. "You're always laughing these days." The frown faded and she began to smile, amused by his helpless laughter. They were soon sharing the merriment even though Beth still didn't know the reason.

"That Bernard Gregory, he's got them long teeth and miserable eyes," Eynon spluttered between bouts of laughter. "He's beginning to look like one of his donkeys."

At any other time Beth would have been angry with her young brother for being so unkind, but with laughter already irresistibly out of control, she giggled louder. They went home in a cheerful mood but with no news for the two girls searching for their brother.

"He found a few more photos of them but couldn't remember a thing," Beth giggled.

"We'd have done better to ask his donkeys," Eynon gasped, his eyes full of tears.

Irritated with their stupid behaviour, Marged told them to "be'ave", and got on with her knitting.

"Eh up, boy," Eynon said when he and Freddy met the following day. "You owe me a favour."

"What's that, then?"

"Saw you and some girl coming out of the pictures and I made sure our Beth didn't see you, that's what! I dragged her round that corner so quick she must have thought Hitler was coming!"

"Oh, that was only Shirley Downs. Her mam works for your mam and dad. I met her inside and we walked out chatting, that's all. Tell Beth if you like, but she won't be very bothered," Freddy said. He hoped Eynon wouldn't tell, however. He and Beth were supposed to be careful with their money and visits to the pictures were forbidden as unnecessary extravagances. He felt a surge of resentment. He enjoyed the pictures, Beth didn't, so it was easy for her to give up going, pretending she was depriving herself of a treat!

Shirley was different. She loved the glamour of the beautiful women and the grand houses and the suggestions of wealth portrayed. She loved dancing too and twice they had slipped into the local dance hall, pretended surprise at meeting and danced happily for several hours. Beth and he never went dancing and she worked rather anonymously in the beach café, hidden away in the kitchen most of the time, so it was unlikely she would be told. He was recognised, of course, having worked in the town's main gentlemen's outfitters until recently, but Shirley Downs was such a good dancer and such lively company, he thought it worth the risk.

With news of the war shown on the Gaumont British News every day, many went just to see a pictorial version of the latest events. The next day Beth decided she would like to go, since the newsreel was said to contain pictures of the new Home Guard. Huw and Uncle Bleddyn had joined and she had a fanciful idea that they might be shown. Once again, Freddy had to pay to see a programme he had already seen right through. It was as they were coming out that someone remarked on his enthusiasm for the film.

"So good you've seen it twice?" one of his friends called. Quickly, Freddy hustled Beth out on to the street, but the young man followed. "Oh, aye, a different girl too. You old devil, Freddy Clements!"

"Get lost! You've mixed me up with someone else."

Beth stared back at the young man as Freddy hurried her along pavements which were wet after several days of rain.

"Ignore him, Beth. Stirring up trouble is his idea of fun. Start a war he could with his so-called 'only joking'!"

He was irritable when Beth tried to question him and when

they got back to Sidney Street, Beth didn't invite him in. She was frowning as she went into the living room, where her brother Eynon was the only occupant.

"He's always bumping into that Shirley Downs," she said half to herself.

"He told you then, did he?" Eynon said. He was studying the evening paper, quite unconcerned, and didn't see the shock that crossed his sister's face. "I told him I wouldn't split as you'd be sure to get the wrong idea. Met her inside he did, nothing suspicious about that, is there?"

"Nothing," she said, the words forced out of tight lips. "Except that we're trying to save and he'd promised not to go without me." Memories of their laughter the previous evening returned and she glared at her brother, who was trying to read the newspaper, with suspicion in her dark eyes. "You saw them, didn't you?"

"Yes, I did, and he was upset, afraid I'd tell you, so he must have decided to tell you himself." He tutted and looked superior. "Fancy getting married to a bloke and not trusting him. Asking for trouble that is, sis. He's all right, our Freddy. Real butties we are."

Freddy walked around the town, restless and unable to face going home, getting to bed and trying to sleep. Having signed on for the armed forces was no longer an adventure, a bit of fun. It was frightening. Now he was on the edge of losing his job again, and being made to do something about which he had no choice until he was called up, all because the foreman had it in for him and complained about his timekeeping. He felt cut off from everything that had once seemed normal. He was detached from Beth too: his happiest moments had been spent with Shirley during the past weeks and instead of feeling guilty about that, he felt trapped.

He no longer felt safe and secure. A door was opening and he was going to step through with no idea what was on the other side. When he tried to analyse how he felt, he had a premonition of death. There was no one he could talk to. Perhaps his thoughts were usual at such a time and everyone went through a period of morbid imagination? He needed someone to tell him this was so, and that he would feel different once he met others and found companionship and confidence from the numbers involved. He wouldn't be alone, he kept telling himself, and alone was how he felt at the moment.

The following morning he went to the bank and withdrew the remainer of his and Beth's savings. What was the point of leaving it there if he was going to die?

Mrs Downs again found a small amount of tobacco ash in the corner of the café one morning and she told Moll. "This time it couldn't have been pushed through the letter box. It's too far away and so neatly placed there had to be an intruder, or someone wasn't doing their job!"

"It has to be inefficient cleaning," Moll insisted. "The place is securely locked."

When Huw told her he had cleaned the floors the previous evening, she still argued that it was the only explanation. A few days later the same thing happened and this time it was Mrs Downs who had dealt with the mop and bucket.

"I'll do it myself tonight," Moll said. "Then I'll believe it's something other than sloppy cleaning. Right?" She and Huw both suspected that the culprit was Mrs Downs, the only non-family member in the café team. The woman did her job but resentment was there. The occasional snide remark showed it. Huw believed the mystery of the litter on the floor was nothing more than Mrs Downs trying to agravate Moll and Marged, and recommended they forgot it. As usual, they ignored him.

When they left, the floor gleaming with the thorough treatment Moll had given it, Mrs Downs dropped a few matches, throwing them unnoticed behind the door as Marged and Huw locked up. That'll show her, she thought. Accusing me of not washing the floor properly! Well, Moll Piper left herself open for that one! She enjoyed telling Shirley when she got home.

Shirley still worked for the small café in the town, having refused to consider working for the Pipers. But she hoped that the following year she might be offered a full-time summer job now an approach had been made. Freddy would put in a good word for her, she thought with a smile. The beach was a more exciting place to work than a café patronised by the boring and the elderly who came to sit and gossip. She would pick up a nice tan and put on pretty dresses instead of the black dress and white apron she was presently forced to wear.

She met Freddy on the day he finally got his cards from the factory. He had overslept again and when he walked in, to the jeers and cheers of his workmates, his wages were made up and he was told to leave.

Shirley had been sent to the wholesaler to try and buy some tomatoes for the café where she worked, and was carrying the box out of the entrance when Freddy approached.

"Freddy! What a bit of luck. Can you help me to carry this box? It's cutting into my side something chronic."

He walked with her back to the café, then stayed and was rewarded with a cup of tea and a cake.

"What's up?" Shirely asked as she pretended to take his money. "Why aren't you in work? Your papers haven't come already, have they?"

"I was sacked for bad timekeeping. You'd think they needed people desperate enough to overlook a few minutes, wouldn't you? Where's this war effort we're being told about? A few minutes late and I'm sacked."

"I bet it wasn't the first time." Shirley grinned. "Late nights and early mornings don't go well together, do they? Dancing – pictures . . ." she teased.

"Fancy going to the dance tonight? There's a live band on."

"And I bet there's not one of them under fifty," she laughed. "Yes, I'll come, Freddy. We won't have many more, will we?"

"Don't say that!"

"I only meant for a while, you daft thing. You'll be home for leaves with stories to make me laugh sooner than you think. And this nuisance of a war won't go on for ever. We'll celebrate every leave, shall we? You and me? And we'll really celebrate when the war ends and you come home for good."

She could see he was still unhappy so she added, "In fact, let's really celebrate tonight, shall we? Just for the practice?"

Promise was in her dark brown eyes and neither of them heard when her employer twice called for her to serve some newcomers who were becoming impatient.

Mrs Downs went in first when they got to the café next

morning. She opened the door wide and held it for the others to enter. Moll saw the matches on the floor and looked accusingly at Mrs Downs, who stared at her enigmatically.

"Did you just drop these?" she asked, pointing at the pink-tipped matchsticks.

"How could I? I've just opened the door for you. What are you looking at me like that for? You did the floor. Going to show us all how it should be done, weren't you?"

"You left them there," Moll said. "You dropped them last night as we were leaving."

"Ridiculous!" Mrs Downs replied angrily.

"Look at them. The ends have softened and spread. They were put on a wet floor, wet like when we all went through the door last night."

"You can't accuse me, we all left at the same time."

"But you were expecting me to find them," Moll insisted. "It was written on your face." Taking money from the float she handed Mrs Downs her wages. "I'm not telling you to go because of a few matches, whatever you choose to tell your friends. I can't work with people I don't trust."

"I'll work the day. I'll stay in the kitchen and do the dishes, you'll be hard put to manage on your own." Mrs Downs was beginning to regret her stupid action.

Marged saw this, and also saw the queue already forming. She forestalled Moll's refusal. "She's right, Mam. We're going to be busy today and we'll be glad of your help today, Mrs Downs. Thank you."

How stupid of Moll to sack someone over a bit of nonsense that should have been treated as a joke! Staff were more and more difficult to find, with women being offered good wages in factories and taking jobs previously undertaken by men. They needed to build goodwill, to have people they could call on when the new season began. It seemed a long way off, but it was essential to look forward and plan ahead.

Mrs Downs was smiling when she left. She was leaving sooner than she had hoped, but the scene was set for a revenge for which she had waited a very long time.

Six

"What about painting the helter-skelter and the swingboats red, white and blue?" Huw suggested one morning as they were leaving for the beach.

"That's ridiculous, Huw," was Marged's instant response. "They've always been yellow and red."

"That's no reason not to change them. All the businesses in town are doing something to make people proud of being British, so why shouldn't we?"

"We'll keep them the same, Huw. Mam wouldn't hear of making them so gaudy."

"Gaudy? It's patriotic!"

"Why d'you always want to be different, Huw?" Marged asked in exasperation. "Whatever will you think of next?"

"There was something else," he said, eyeing her to assess his chances.

Marged put down the bag she was filling with the laundry and stared at him, lips tight, a look of irritation on her face. "Look, it's Piper's and we'll keep everything the way it was first planned. Right?" She bustled around gathering everything they needed to take with them. But curiosity got the better of her and she asked, "What was it then, this other fancy idea you had?"

"The Home Guard need somewhere to sit and have a cup of tea during their shift, and the fire-watchers and the wardens pass there often. I thought Bleddyn and I could take it in turns to provide teas and perhaps a cake or sandwich during the evenings. What d'you think?"

"I think we're going to be late, and you and Bleddyn have enough to do helping to keep my business running. Piper's is as much as you can manage without idling your time chatting to the Home Guard and their buddies."

"*Your* business?" He said the words slowly. "Your business

is run by me and my brother, and we're Castles, not Pipers. It hasn't been Pipers running things since you married me. Bleddyn and I do most of the work, you run the café. Without us you wouldn't last a month. Yet I can't offer an opinion. The time will come, Marged *Castle*, when Bleddyn and I will have had enough. Right?"

Halfway down the stairs, Beth and Lilly listened in horror. They hated hearing their parents argue. Lately the arguments were increasing and they were always about Piper's.

"Dad's right, mind," Beth said. "Gran and Auntie Audrey are the only Pipers left. The name should be changed. Dad is head of the family. It should be called Castle's."

"You think the man should be in charge whatever the situation?" Lilly sneered. "I don't think so. If our Ronnie and Eynon gave up the beach and I married, there's no chance *my* husband would ever be in charge!"

"I don't think that's right."

"You ought to be thinking the same," Lilly went on. "Imagine if you took over. Your Freddy would never keep his hands out of the till for a start. And as for work, well, it isn't his favourite pastime, is it? No, with Freddy in charge you'd fade to nothing in weeks. Your Freddy hasn't the head for business, he'll never succeed."

Beth continued to defend Freddy but her heart wasn't in it. She had the strongest of feelings that Lilly was right.

In a small town like St David's Well nothing could remain a secret for very long. Several people asked Beth whether she and Freddy had broken off their engagement and more than one commiserated before asking for confirmation, having seen Freddy once or twice with Shirley Downs.

She soon became adept at lying, insisting that she knew and understood about Freddy's addiction to the films and that he occasionally met Shirley, also a film fan, inside.

She told him quite casually what she had been told, and he said apologetically, "Sorry, Beth, but I really enjoy the pictures and, knowing that you aren't so keen, well, I sometimes go on my own."

"That's all right, Freddy, I'm not going to be the jealous girlfriend, just because I'm wearing your ring." She smiled and added, "Just as well you enjoy the pictures. When you're away from home it will be a way of filling in the lonely hours, won't it?"

Freddy hugged her but in his mind he saw crowds of girls filling his hours, drawn to him by his uniform, begging to be taken out to have fun. Not girls like Beth who was his safe, comfortable future, but girls like Shirley Downs offering excitement during his short-lived freedom.

When Moll came to the house to ask for a lift to the café a couple of days after Mrs Downs had left, Beth said, "Granny Moll, all the shops in town are dressing their windows in red, white and blue to show their support for the forces. Couldn't we do the same? Patriotism helps the war effort, doesn't it?"

"Nonsense, girl. Paint to support the war effort ready for next season? The war will be over and done with long before that!"

"You'd better ask her to come back," Huw said when he, Marged and Moll discussed the departure of Mrs Downs.

"Get her back? I thought you didn't want her to work for us in the first place," Moll said irritably. "Worse than a woman for changing your mind you are, Huw Castle!"

"She's a nasty bit of work and you know the way she gossips," he said, "but if we're desperate for help until the end of September, she might be the simplest choice."

It was eight thirty and they were on their way to the café. Beth had said she would catch the bus and join them later. As Marged put the key in the lock and opened the door an unpleasant smell met them.

"What the 'ell—" Huw went into the kitchen, sniffing and pulling faces. "Smells like something's crawled in and died!"

The three of them searched the whole place but found nothing. The smell was strongest in the kitchen and with nothing but fresh air beneath the concrete floor of the café and a solid wooden floor beneath the kitchen area, there didn't seem to be anywhere else to search. Opening the windows and doors as wide as they'd go, they started preparing for the day.

The smell increased as the hours passed. The sun was shining cheerfully and it was one of the hottest days so far that year. Disinfectant was poured everywhere but the smell returned to greet them next morning.

Lilly and Phil were still using the café for their secret

meetings but even passion was defeated by the foulness of the air. They dared to leave the door open, hoping no one would walk up the metal steps and come in to request tea and sandwiches. Giggling at the unexpected problem, stretching the joke and laughter to the utmost, they didn't stay long, choosing instead to go separately through the roads and lanes to the park where bushes and trees gave some privacy.

They felt complacent about Phil's deferment from call-up. As the only member of staff able to run both the shop and repair-workshop, he was certain he was safe as, without him, the business would have to close down.

During the last days before Freddy had to report to camp for training, he and Beth saw each other often, but there was a coolness between them that neither mentioned and which Freddy couldn't understand. He thought the explanation about his love of the cinema had satisfied Beth's initial dismay at the rumours about himself and Shirley, and there didn't seem to be anything else amiss.

He came to the beach late in the afternoons, helped the family to clear up and tried, with the rest, to solve the mystery of the dreadful stink. He often went back to Marged's for a late supper but always left early, explaining thoughtfully that he knew Beth rose early and needed her sleep.

Once out of sight of the house in Sidney Street, he hurried to the flat above the newspaper shop and called to see Shirley. Besides the pictures – the town offered a generous choice with three cinemas which all changed their programme halfway through the week – there was also dancing.

Freddy still planned to marry Beth; it was the best way of ensuring a good future. The Pipers and Castles owned entertainments, stalls, cafés and ice-cream and pop factories and their business was sound. He would always have to work, but not too much. He believed that Beth offered him an easy life married to a family who were never likely to be short of the readies. He had to hang on to Beth. He thought he loved her in his own way, but he wanted some fun first.

There was an air of exhilaration about Eynon during those last days on the sands, a hint of a secret about to be told. Blowing up balloons to decorate the stalls to attract the dwindling crowds, he popped one behind Beth, laughing at her alarm. He marked Marged's best mirror with a candle so it looked as though it was cracked, and couldn't contain his laughter when she stared at it in horror before telling her it was a trick. He livened them up with his cheerful presence both on the beach and at home, and nothing was too much trouble. He had never been so helpful or willing. Huw and Marged smiled and put it down to his newly awakening interest in girls. When he asked for a day off Marged didn't hesitate.

"You've worked so hard you deserve it," she smiled, handing him a ten-shilling note. "Take this and give yourself a good time."

Without explanation and also without denying the many hints about a girl that issued from Huw's lips during breakfast, he left early. Long before the post arrived.

It was when they got home from the long day at the beach that Marged picked up the letter from the doormat.

"Funny," she frowned. "It looks like our Eynon's writing."

"Some joke I'll bet. He's full of nonsense at the moment – in fact, I'm beginning to wonder whether that stink at the café that's beginning to smell fishy isn't down to him. Some stink bomb from the joke shop or something."

The letter with Eynon's handwriting on it was puzzling and Marged stared at it for a while before opening it. She frowned, then glanced at the clock, automatically thinking as a caring mother. "Funny, he didn't say what time he'd be back," she said vaguely. "He'll have to have something cold." She opened the envelope, unfolded the sheet of paper, and screamed.

Huw ran to her and snatched it from her trembling hands. "What does he mean, he's joined the army?" he demanded as though Marged had the answers. "He isn't old enough for call-up till next year!"

"He's volunteered. He's old enough to volunteer," Marged wailed.

Phone calls and visits to the police, the army recruitment office and every other organisation they could think of to demand his return were met with the solid stone walls of officialdom. Eynon was old enough and he was on his way to the camp where initial training would take place. They weren't even told which one. All they could do was wait until he made contact.

"There *is* a war on," the sergeant in the recruitment office reminded them with unnecessary sarcasm.

"So we're short of another pair of hands," was one of Huw's comments the morning following a sleepless night.

"Is that all you can think about?" Marged said unfairly. "Eynon, our youngest, has gone to war!"

"Tomorrow we open the café as usual, and we help others to forget their war for an hour or two. We need someone extra to help on the stalls." He spoke firmly, determined that Marged wouldn't collapse into despair.

"I'll call and ask Mrs Downs to come back, I suppose," she said quietly. "I'll have to grovel a bit, but compared with our Eynon running away, a bit of grovelling isn't important." She looked at the face of her husband, seeing the lines of distress there, she was reminded that for him too this was a difficult situation to deal with; she wasn't alone. "He's only a boy," she said and they hugged, seeking comfort from each other.

A second letter arrived a few days later, a letter full of apologies and cheerful with news of Eynon's first few days as a soldier. He told them he was already making new friends and wondered whether he could bring a couple of the lads home on his first leave, as several had never seen the sea.

"He has the right attitude, our Eynon," Huw said emotionally. "He'll do well, for sure."

"There are a couple of camp beds in the loft." Marged was already planning Eynon's first leave. "And we'll keep that tin of salmon. It's his favourite with a bit of salad."

Eynon was bitterly regretting his decision to join up. Why had he listened to Freddy? The glorified portrayal of adventure and brave acts had stirred his imagination and thrilled his young mind, but the reality was very different from his dreams.

The exercise had been something he had looked forward to with excitement. He considered himself a fit young man, running everywhere and rarely catching a bus. He was sure he'd show the rest how things should be done. He hadn't been prepared for the long hours of marching with heavy kit and little prospect of a rest. Nor had the constant punishments entered into his thoughts. He was there because he had chosen to be, so why punish him for mistakes he couldn't avoid?

His attempts at humour were considered childlike and when

he heard the others talking about their lives before they had joined up he realised how sheltered his own life had been. He was smaller than most and that too had been pounced upon as a likely subject for teasing.

Then there was Kipper, so called because of his constant smoking and the fact that he was so dark skinned and thin. He was a sadistic bully and as soon as he saw Eynon, he knew he had found his victim. For a while others took Eynon's side but they quickly realised that if they wanted a reasonably peaceful existence they would have to turn the proverbial blind eye. Kipper tolerated no one else's opinion. After just ten days, Eynon was on his own.

It wasn't the unseen punches and kicks, or the constant "jokes" of making his kit filthy just before inspection, or even the nail that had been driven up inside his boots before a five-mile run. It was the loneliness. He missed his family more than he had imagined. He had no one to talk to and he didn't dare write home complaining.

People walking to the station in a steady stream to see husbands, sons and loved ones off was an almost daily sight. When Beth walked with Freddy one late August morning, her emotions were mixed. In tune with others on the same duty as herself, she looked suitably sad, but inside there was an air of relief. Ashamed of the sensation, she was nevertheless filled with the excitement of being on the verge of something new.

She had been dreading this day, and like many others wondered how she would cope. To her surprise she now knew she would cope very well. She couldn't admit that to Freddy of course and although they said very little, she promised him she would write regularly and would miss him something awful.

Assurances were given that he would miss her too, but to the newly awakened Beth the words had the discordant ring of insincerity. She wondered whether, like herself, he welcomed the break from their very close and long relationship. The saying "absence makes the heart grow fonder" seemed to her at that moment to be wishful thinking.

Their final kiss was less than heartwarming; with others watching and shedding a few tears, she felt uneasy, aware that her falseness matched Freddy's as she clung to him briefly, anxious to be gone.

* * *

Mrs Downs returned to help in Piper's Café and the smell lingered in the air for a while but soon faded. She had removed the kipper she had nailed to the back of a drawer and had thrown it into the tide. Huw watched and frowned but said nothing.

"All the place needed was a good scrub," she said with a superior tilt to her head.

Bleddyn lived for letters from his sons. He didn't hear from either of them often, but heard a little news from the letters Taff wrote to Evelyn.

Hannah didn't make many attempts to keep in touch with Bleddyn. Knowing how much he disapproved of his younger son's choice, she didn't know how to be supportive now Johnny was away. She wanted to call, but Bleddyn had made his feelings quite clear on the evening of the farewell party and she was too unsure of her welcome.

She visited Huw and Marged, taking the children and staying for a cup of tea. At these times she was able to impart small items of news, which she hoped would be passed on to Johnny's father. She still continued to help Maude and Myrtle with their reading and Moll was always pleased to see her. The news went in the other direction too. She was able to write to Johnny and tell him of the daily happenings and keep him in touch with the Piper businesses while he was away.

The news of embarkation leave was something Bleddyn was dreading. The night the news had reached him, via a brief letter and a visit from Taff's wife, Evelyn, he was unable to relax. He went for a walk along the edge of the tide, the gentle shushing of the waves soothing his taut nerves. Sitting on the wall, a man's overcoat draped around her, was Olive.

"Can't sleep either?" he asked, sitting beside her and staring out to sea.

"I know it doesn't really make sense, but I feel this is the closest I can get to Ronnie," she said. "He's over there somewhere, beyond that land and over another great stretch of water, but this is the closest I can get."

"I can't explain why I came," Bleddyn said. "I just couldn't sleep and this seemed a good place to come and think back on how good life was until this damned war opened its hungry jaws and took our boys."

"I wish I'd appreciated the happy times more," Olive sighed. "I fought Ronnie, told him I hated working on the beach. I tried so hard to persuade him to leave and get a better job. Now, seeing how people need the nonsense, the laughter and the escape we offer here . . . well, I know its value and wish I'd known it before. Ronnie and I would have been happier. I wish I'd helped more and complained less."

"I've been told that both my sons will be coming home on embarkation leave, and you know what that means."

"It means you have to hide your fears and be cheerful and let them be happy." She smiled. "We'll all be accomplished actors by the time this lot is over, won't we?"

"You're right, and they'll go back smiling. Thank you, love, you're a good kid and Ronnie is a lucky devil to be married to you."

"I'll make sure he knows it when he comes on leave." She smiled again. "How are Evelyn and Hannah coping? They must be frightened too. I know; I've been through it, remember."

"Evelyn is putting on a brave face – for my sake, I think – but I don't know about Hannah. She – well, she can't be a serious girlfriend for our Johnny, can she? She so much older and with two children an' all."

"From what I've seen of them it's very serious. Johnny loves her very much, and her children. You should go and see them; it's what Johnny would want, you keeping an eye on them for him."

"I don't think she'd want to see me, I've never been very friendly."

"Then it's time you were." She smiled to ease the criticism and said, "Come on, what about a bag of chips before we go for the bus?"

"Chips? When I run a chip shop most of the year?"

"Why not? You can pretend you're checking on the competition!"

The beach was as full as it could possibly be. Whereas in low season families came and found a circle of sand to call their own, now the tide was high during the afternoon and there were so many trippers flooding into the bay that there wasn't the space to offer any prospect of temporary ownership. Buckets and spades, sun hats and windmills as well as the rest of the paraphernalia of the day out became mingled with the group next along, and cardigans disappeared under sand as people walked past trying to find a place to sit and spread themselves out. The smell of wet sand filled everyone's nostrils and the children glowed with the sun and happiness that only a holiday beach can provide. And still they came. Marged and Beth were serving meals without a moment's rest from the time they opened the café doors.

The wind got up during the afternoons, and Beth ran up and down the steps gathering trays and returning deposits, afraid to leave the trays of china for the users to return, knowing from past experience that some would be lost under the spraying sand or be broken under careless feet. The number of spoons they lost each season was countless, even though the deposit slip clearly marked every item.

Shirley was back working in the paper shop. As with so many other businesses, the men had disappeared and women were in demand. She went back with fewer hours and a ten-shilling increase in wages.

She had worked in the shop for as long as she could remember, standing beside her father and mother, going with her dad to the wholesaler to collect the odd magazine and to pay the weekly account. Helping to carry newspapers out on to the bogie cart her father had made for the paper boys to use on their deliveries was something she had done as soon as she was strong enough, and when she was eight she had been given a round of her own, with money at the end of each week.

She had been only six when her father had left to live somewhere else, and twelve years old when he disappeared from her life completely. She remembered the confusion of her thoughts when she was told he would never come back. For a long time she had looked at people in the street hoping it had been a mistake and he would suddenly appear.

Now she looked at the old bogie cart and wondered whether she could tow it behind her as she had done years ago. Experimentally she pulled it around the small yard behind the shop. If the paper boy let them down again, she might try. Pulling it up Grantly Rise and Channel View Avenue might be less of a struggle than having that heavy bag on her shoulders, she thought with a wry smile.

Shirley was puzzled by her mother's attitude towards the Pipers. She had been told the story about her mother's grandparents losing the business because of Moll Piper's grandparents, but there were stories about lost wealth in every family, apocryphal, the stuff of legends. She had always thought the story about the Pipers was the same. Her mother had hinted about something else, something equally wicked, but Shirley had put that down to a desire to keep the story alive, to continue the hatred, nothing more.

Why was her mother working for the Pipers, whom she insisted she hated? And why, after being dismissed for causing mischief, had she been willing to return?

The Castle family believed that they had lost all their young men and there were no more surprises in store, but Lilly was still to become the final victim of the urgent demands from the government for more soldiers. The shop where Phil worked in apparent safety had been handed over to a fifty-six-year-old man, releasing Phil for call-up. He went just three weeks after being told that the decision on his deferment had been revised.

Lilly was devastated and, because of the situation, couldn't even seek sympathy from friends and family. From being the one member of the Castle team to work hard at avoiding work, she needed to pack as much into her day as possible. She needed to fill the hours and also tire herself for sleep. After only a few days the plan began to work, and she found the untypical enthusiasm exhausted her so much that bed was welcome. In fact she fought against tiredness sometimes during the afternoons.

She interfered with everyone's tasks, disrupting the routines that had been set out at the begining of the season and were working well. She often seemed to be on the verge of tears but Beth, instead of being irritated by her, was patient and understanding. Beth hadn't been told the reason for Lilly's unhappiness but as her sister hadn't been out during the evening for weeks, she guessed that her secret boyfriend had either left her or had been called up.

Lilly was desperate to fill the hours, and even found some

extra cleaning to keep herself from grieving. As the secret lover of a married man, she couldn't expect to have news of him, as any letters would go to his wife. Until he was given leave and could slip away for an hour, she wouldn't know where he was or how he was feeling. He had already told her he wouldn't be able to write.

"Everything I write will be read before it's posted," he had explained, "and I can't risk anyone finding out about us. Not yet, not until I decide the time is right for my wife to accept that our marriage is over. I have to choose my time, love, for your sake. You can see that, can't you?"

Since he had never been so specific before about his intentions to leave his wife, Lilly was deliriously happy. Of course he couldn't write while he was away, she understood that, but as soon as his wife could cope with it she would be told. For herself and Phil, it would mean their love would be out in the open for everyone to see how happy they were. Once the war was over, life would be bliss.

Eynon sat in the lorry that was taking them into mid-Wales for an exercise and listened to the chatter all around him, news and opinions and confidences which he was not allowed to share. His leg ached badly from last night's violent kicking after he had inadvertently touched Kipper's bed. He wondered how he was going to climb mountains and march over rough ground for endless hours and cope with the pain.

The lorry lurched to a stop and they began to jump down.

"Wait there, Titch," Kipper growled as Eynon stood and allowed the others to get down. "Wait there till I say you can jump."

"Why don't you give up this tormenting and leave me alone," Eynon sighed. The response was a punch that sent him reeling, staggering against the sides of the vehicle and making the dark night even blacker.

He was aware of voices, of soft laughter, and then the lorry crunched into gear and began to move. He had to get out. There would be no excuses allowed if he lost contact with the others. He scrambled over the tailgate and, although the lorry had picked up speed, he dropped off. There was a sharp bend at that moment and the driver, with a view hampered by the low lights, didn't see it until he had almost passed it. The resulting swerve as Eynon fell caused him to knock his head on the corner of the lorry, and he fell and rolled until his fall was stopped by a boulder placed to mark the edge of the road.

He wasn't sure how long he had lain there. It was only very slowly that his memory returned. It was still dark. Perhaps it had been no more than a few minutes. He stood, groggily wondering which direction to take, and tried to walk, staggering along holding his head in his hands. He had to find the others. He listened but there was a ringing in his ears that made it impossible to hear anything else. Perhaps he was deaf like Alice Potter's father and would only be able to walk by leaning against a wall? Holding back the need to sob, he made his way back in the direction he thought he had been travelling.

Huw was nervous when Mrs Downs was in the café. He avoided talking to her and when he had any instruction he asked his wife to convey it.

"Come on, our Dad," Beth teased, "she isn't exactly a dangerous woman, is she? Poor dab, she lost her husband in a road accident more than ten years ago and lives in a poky little flat above a newsagent; what can she possibly do to harm you?"

Huw didn't tell her, but he lived with the fear that one day Hetty Downs would tell his family the truth. He watched the woman, convinced that she was planning some disaster in which he would be the central player.

Marged was pleased with the way the woman worked, often staying late when the day had been particularly busy and never complaining about sharing the tedium of washing endless dishes and cleaning the same things day after day until they all felt like robots.

September dragged lazily on and the people who had booked into hotels and boarding houses diminished to the families and couples not tied to school holidays. Fewer children being around changed the mood, but the buses and trains still brought day-trippers. Now the busiest days were at the weekend, when coaches would growl their way into the car parks and trains puffed their fussy way into the railway station, unloading streams of excited hordes set on having a day to remember. By this time, many of the beach traders were weary and longing for a break in the daily round, but none of their tiredness showed in their faces. They all treated the newcomers as they had treated the first to arrive, months before, determinedly making sure their holiday or their day out sent them home with only good memories.

Bleddyn's two sons came home for their embarkation leave and they chose to spend it working on the beach with the rest of the family, insisting that they too needed the memories to see them through whatever lay ahead. Taff's wife, Evelyn, came with him when she could, but working in a factory meant shift work and sleeping at odd times of the day. Hannah was less willing to spend time with the Castles, still afraid of being made to feel unwelcome at this emotional time. But one afternoon, she brought her two girls down and stood with Johnny as he served ice-cream and sold buckets and spades, flags, balloons and windmills and the rest. The day was warm for so late in the season and Josie and Marie stripped their clothes off with her help, giggling behind the stall, and got into their bathers.

"You can't go in the sea, mind," Hannah warned the disappointed girls. "I didn't bring my bathers with me and you can't go in on your own." There were wails of disappointment but she was adamant.

During a lull, Bleddyn left the swingboats to come over and talk to them. He heard of their dismay and said, "I've got my dippers on under these white trousers, I can go in and look after them if you like, Hannah?"

Hannah was about to refuse, belligerent in preparation for the rebuffs she had expected, but seeing the rather anxious expression in his face, she changed her mind, smiled, thanked him and told the girls they could paddle after all.

Taking an inflatable beach ball with them they walked to the water's edge, the girls glancing back occasionally for their mother's encouraging wave. Then they forgot about her as Bleddyn played games and they were soon shrieking with laughter with the rest.

Bleddyn was happier than he had been for a long time during the hour that followed. He lifted the children one after the other and, wading out, allowed them to kick in the waves. He pretended to struggle to blow up the beach ball until the nonsense brought them to their knees laughing at his uselessness.

"Mam can do it easy," they said scornfully when he allowed the air to escape once more. He blew up the ball with their shouted encouragement and threw it for them, fell when he missed it, and generally acted the clown.

Hannah and Johnny were laughing too when the three of them walked back up to the stall.

"Two delightful youngsters you've got there, Hannah," Bleddyn said. "I hope you'll bring them to see me some time."

"Thank you," Hannah said hesitantly. "They'd like that."

"They've just invited themselves to tea in Piper's Café," Bleddyn went on. "And I'm told that it's to be beans on toast with tomato sauce like their Uncle Johnny makes it," he teased, looking at his son.

The nights were drawing in more quickly as summer came to its end but the gloomy evening seemed less so that day as Bleddyn walked home, still smiling at the happiness of his time with Marie and Josie and the glimmer of understanding with their mother and his younger son.

When Johnny was helping at the beach a few days later, Bleddyn decided he would call on Hannah and the girls.

"No, I won't come in," he said when he presented himself at the neat little house near the centre of town. "I just came to tell you that I'm there if you need anything, and if you and Marie and Josie would like to come and spend a little time near the beach, well, I'd like to see you, that's all." He turned and walked away. Hannah had been slow to reply and he didn't want to cause embarrassment to her or himself if she did not want to give him any of her time.

He was closing the gate to the small front garden when she called, "Mr Castle, thank you. That's very kind and, if you like, you can come to tea on Sunday and the girls will make you a cake."

Bleddyn turned and nodded. "Thanks, Hannah. I'll come – when, about four?"

She smiled agreement and he went home proud of his good sense in contacting the little family whom his son loved so much. He had gained three friends where he might have lost a son. He must remember to thank young Olive.

Hannah took a deep breath. Now she had to tell her parents.

* * *

Marged and Huw were concerned about Eynon. His letters were short and there was no mention of his having leave. Marged continued to write and one morning she was startled to answer a loud knock at the door to see two military policemen standing there.

She listened in disbelief as they told her that Eynon was absent without leave.

"He must be hurt. He wouldn't do that without a reason," she said. "What have you done to him? Tell me the truth, where is he? What's happened?"

Coldly, indifferent to her distress, they told her that if he got in touch she must inform the police immediately, and if she did not, she would be committing an offence. Questions tumbled out of her mouth but they walked away as though she hadn't spoken.

In utter panic she ran out of the door, remembering after several seconds that Huw was at the beach and not there to comfort her. When she found him, Huw stared in disbelief. "He must be injured, lost somewhere, he wouldn't run away. Not our Eynon." He tried to picture the happy boy who had left and could only visualise him dead. He said nothing of his fear to Marged.

"He'll get in touch as soon as he's able," he said reassuringly. "It has to be a mistake." But within himself there was a paralysing fear for his son's safety.

Ronnie was in France and his letters were short and heavily blue-pencilled. Olive tried with a magnifying glass to read beneath the heavy pencil in the hope of gleaning more of his thoughts. She wrote to him regularly and hoped that somehow he would receive her letters. But for the past few weeks she hadn't heard from him. She still kept on writing but terror filled her heart and she had to calm herself for fear the worries would reveal themselves in her letters to him.

She said nothing about her fears to his parents, or to Granny Moll. She lied about hearing from him and assured them that everything was all right. She didn't want Marged or Moll worrying him about not hearing from him. She tried not to imagine him in the thick of the fighting. There were plenty of other reasons why he could have been unable to write. She tried to think of some, but her mind was a blank. Best she kept her fears to herself, she realised; she didn't want him upset by the others writing and complaining and telling him how worried they were. However well meant, anxiety from home was something he could do without.

With the season coming to an end, the café was less busy and Marged told Mrs Downs that after the end of the week she wouldn't be needed any longer.

"Haven't you got anything in one of the other businesses?" Hetty asked, glancing at Huw. "There's the fish-and-chip shop and café, couldn't I work there, at least part time?"

Huw turned away after giving Marged a warning stare, and Marged said with regret that there was just enough work for the family. "We usually have to look for winter work ourselves, but with the boys away, we can probably manage without having to," she explained, untruthfully. "There aren't any places to fill, sorry."

The following morning, there was evidence that once more someone was using the café after it closed. A toffee paper was found and a small amount of cigarette ash. Lilly was involved in the discovery, but this time she knew that she and Phil were not the culprits. Phil was a member of His Majesty's forces and couldn't even write to her, she reminded herself sadly.

The mystery was still unsolved by the time October came and they had to close the café for the winter. After a week's rest, the family was kept busy cleaning everything and making sure the building was secure enough to cope with the winter weather.

Phil came home on leave and Lilly expertly escaped from the final cleaning, taking the spare tablecloths and tea-towels home and forgetting to go back.

When she and Phil met it was already dark. They let themselves into the café, which was redolent with the smell of strong carbolic soap, and settled into "their" corner. They laughed about the mystery of the cigarette ash and Phil dropped some more to cause puzzled frowns when Granny Moll and Marged came on one of their weekly checks throughout the winter to ensure there were no leaks or other damage.

Their need for each other was greater because of the weeks they had been apart. They were reluctant to go, knowing it would be several weeks before they could meet again.

"It's past eleven o'clock," Lilly whispered, shining a small torch on to her watch. "What did you tell your wife?"

"I told her it was a friend's stag party. I wish it was mine, the night before our wedding," he said as desire for her grew once more.

Passion spent, they lay together and Lilly asked, "Isn't there a way that I can write to you? I need to tell you things and not being able to write is cruel."

"What things? You can tell me things now, can't you?"

"Special things. I want to write them down as I think of them, so you know what I'm thinking, what's happening to me. And I want to hear the same from you."

She did have something to say but avoided saying it. She knew that a letter, which he could reread and mull over before deciding on a reply, was the best way of telling him.

"I'm cold," she complained as a shiver ran through her. He wrapped his arms around her once again as they promised themselves just half an hour longer.

Marged and Huw were relaxing, having finished the seemingly endless chores. Huw had changed out of his work trousers and wore grey ones with a V-necked Fair Isle pullover and an open-necked checked shirt underneath it. He puffed slowly on a pipe, his face brown with sunburn which ended at his collar line, his hair slicked back with Brylcreem.

Marged's hair was tightly enclosed in dinkie curlers and she wore a skirt and blouse with fluffy slippers on her feet as she concentrated on finishing the khaki sock she was knitting. She and her daughters and many other enthusiastic people were helping the war effort by knitting socks and scarves for the forces. Clothes factories had been modified and instead of making civilian clothes had been set up for the manufacture of khaki battledress, kit bags, camouflage net, parachute silk, tents, and all the other necessities of war. But there was a shortage of woollen items and women were encouraged to make scarves and socks which were collected at special centres and sent to where they were most needed.

"It's late, Huw, our Lilly should have been in ages ago." Marged looked up from her casting off. "Did she say she'd be late?"

"Probably meeting her secret boyfriend," Beth said. "If he

exists. She's invented him if you ask me, as an excuse to get out of work."

The door opened at that moment and Lilly came in, greeted them mournfully and went to the cupboard to take out writing paper. Huw stood up and went to throw the bolt on the front door. "Thank goodness you're in, Lilly," he said. "Now we can go to bed."

Lilly grunted and, with her arm shielding what she was writing, began to scribble on the paper.

"Where's your boyfriend, then?" Beth wanted to know. "Too ashamed to bring him home, are you?"

To everyone's surprise, Lilly burst into tears.

"Whatever is it?" Marged asked, trying to comfort her daughter.

Lilly couldn't explain that Phil was at that moment on his way home to prepare to return to duty after a forty-eight hour leave. Between sobs she explained that she was thinking of Ronnie, Taff and Johnny.

"I was trying to write to our Ronnie but I don't know what to say," she wailed, tearing up the paper and throwing it into the embers, poking it until it flared and blackened.

At that moment there was a loud knock at the door. Puzzled, Huw went to open it, with Marged close behind him. "Bleddyn? What is it?"

"Fire. The café's on fire, you'd better come quick."

By good fortune, a courting couple had passed when the fire near the door of the café was slowly gathering momentum, and they quickly alerted the fire brigade. Their response was fast. Lights had to be extinguished as fast as possible, fires in particular, in case they were intended to be a signal to the Luftwaffe. When Marged, Huw, Bleddyn, Beth and Lilly, who looked decidedly sick, tumbled out of the van, the flames were all but out, but the dining area was a smoking ruin.

The café was made mostly of wood, and they had expected to see nothing left but a pile of smouldering ashes, but from the outside the walls looked undamaged. Inside, however, they saw that the floor, in places, was burnt right through. The sight of the sand and a couple of abandoned deckchairs below, visible with the aid of brief flashes of the firemen's torches, gave them a sick, dizzy sensation akin to vertigo. This was a view they hadn't seen before.

It was difficult to assess the damage to the rest of the place but on inspection with the weak, shaded torches, it appeared that the walls were mostly firm, just blackened, the once neat paint now blistered.

Lilly felt sickness overwhelm her. She and Phil must be responsible for this. They had smoked, left their cigarette ends; they must have forgotten to make sure they were completely out. She tried to think clearly about whether Phil had slipped the evidence of their clandestine visit into a cigarette packet to be thrown away later, as he usually did, but everything was a blur. Her memory jerked from one thing to another and wouldn't settle down. All she could think of was seeing their cigarettes balanced on the edge of a matchbox.

No one else could have started it; there hadn't been time. How could she tell her parents and Granny Moll that she was the cause of this terrible disaster? Just lately it had been one problem after another. In a few hours Phil would be far away and she wouldn't see him for months. She needed to talk to him. He'd help her decide what to do about all this.

A taxi drew up as they were locking up as best they could and preparing to leave. Moll stepped out and stared at the still smoking mess that had been Piper's Café.

"Oh, my God, look at it! Oh, my God, what happened? How will we sort it? Oh, Marged, what will we do? Who did this?"

Lilly was shaking but she went to her grandmother and hugged her, tears for herself being mistaken for tears for Moll. "Granny Moll, the season's finished. We'll have it sorted long before next year. It isn't as bad as it looks." She held Moll more tightly and said, "I'm so sorry."

"You're sorry? You aren't to blame. But whoever did this will be sorry all right," Moll sobbed. "Piper's, gone. I can't believe it."

"It isn't gone," Lilly soothed. "Dad and Uncle Bleddyn will have it looking better than before in plenty of time for next year's opening."

Marged looked at her elder daughter in surprise. She hadn't expected Lilly to be the one offering sympathy to her grandmother. It would have been more in character for Lilly to cheer to see Piper's go up in smoke. Perhaps she had misjudged the girl.

There was nothing more they could do. They all went back to Sidney Street, Beth and Lilly walking with Uncle Bleddyn, Moll in the van with Marged and Huw. Beth told Bleddyn about the mysterious cigarette ash that had been found several times and the suspicion that someone had been using the place after they had locked up and gone home.

Lilly said nothing. She was still trying to decide what to do. By the time she reached home, she had made up her mind that, having allowed so much time to pass without confessing, the wisest move was to do nothing and say nothing. The moment to confess had passed. Besides, there were other things on her mind – predominantly, Phil Martin.

As the van driven by Huw turned the corner into Sidney Street, Moll lurched against him and at first he thought she had fallen asleep. "Get her off me, Marged, I can't drive with her leaning over me. Poor old girl, she's exhausted. I'd better get her straight home."

Marged tried but couldn't rouse her mother. Standing at their front door was Audrey, with Maude and Myrtle dressed in night-clothes with blankets over their shoulders. Huw stopped and leaned over to open the passenger door, calling for Audrey to, "Come and help your mam, fallen asleep she has. Would you believe it?"

Moll wasn't asleep. The shock of the last few hours had brought on a sudden heart attack which had ended her life. Audrey was now the only Piper left.

Seven

The fire at Piper's Café and the death of Moll Piper caused quite a stir in the town of St David's Well. Moll had been a familiar figure and had been well liked. Her death so quickly after the fire seemed to make it a greater tragedy and people speculating about how the fire had begun suggested reasons that varied from spite for the family's success to enemy action!

A pale Marged seemed suddenly older, supporting her sister Audrey, both of them busy making preparations for the funeral in three days' time. Beth and her father looked stunned. Lilly sat and cried. Maude and Myrtle looked scared.

"We'll have to leave, there's no doubt about it," Maude whispered to her young sister. "Now Granny Moll has gone, the others won't want us hanging around."

"Where will we go?" Myrtle asked as they sat, shivering, in the yard behind Moll's house.

"Don't know, but we'll find somewhere warm for the winter."

"Perhaps they'll let us stay till the spring and we can work on the sands again."

"Maude? Myrtle? Are you out there?" Audrey called and they grabbed each other's hand for comfort and went inside.

"We have to go to the shops, you'll need some dark clothes for the day of the funeral," Audrey told them. "Get your best shoes on and we'll go straight away."

The dresses and cardigans she chose for them were too large and in a style unsuitable for their youth. The clothes made them look smaller and thinner but they didn't care. "It'll be extra layers to wear when we leave," Maude whispered. "Perhaps we'll be able to steal a couple of blankets too. I don't think Granny Moll would mind if we took the spare ones in the old trunk, do you?"

"Why did she have to go an' die?" Myrtle sobbed.

Cards of sympathy arrived for the family, cold, stark white ones with an edging of black. Myrtle was frightened by seeing them standing along the mantelpiece.

"Perhaps we should buy one?" Maude suggested.

"Perhaps." Myrtle didn't look convinced. The sight of them made her shiver.

Marged didn't like the clothes Audrey had bought for the girls. "They're miles too big. They make them look like orphans."

"That's what they are!"

"Just because they're orphans they don't have to look like them!"

"They'll only be worn once, it wasn't worth spending more," Audrey defended her decision.

"Then why did you buy them to fit them in two years' time?"

There wasn't time to go back and change them so they had to suffice. The days went quickly and everyone had jobs to do to ensure the smooth running of the funeral and the gathering afterwards at the house.

They had heard nothing more about Eynon, though there had been several further visits from the military police. Nevertheless, Marged wrote to Eynon at the only address she knew to tell him about the death of his grandmother. "Surely he'll be found and given leave to attend," she said to Huw. Huw nodded agreement, but knew the letter, like all the others, would receive no reply. Wherever Eynon was, he was in a situation in which he couldn't make contact.

Staggering along the unmade road for a few yards, Eynon had known he couldn't hope to catch up with his group. He looked around him, moving his head slowly to avoid the pain such movement produced. There was no light to be seen. Everywhere was blackness and he felt the openness of wild countryside surrounding him. He had to sleep. Taking his groundsheet from his pack took ages but eventually he lay down and, wrapping it around him, slept.

When he woke the day was far from new. He guessed that evening was approaching and he had practically slept the clock around. A wound on his head had bled profusely and was stuck to his great-coat. He stood and looked around. He could hear the trickle of water and made his way to where he could wash the wound. Examining it carefully he felt the damage. It was large and gaping and needed attention, but attention it wouldn't get. He was not going back to accept punishment for Kipper's cruelty. However long this war lasted, he wasn't going back.

The funeral of Moll Piper was a small one. With so many men away fighting the war, and no women allowed at the cemetery for the brief service, the huddle of men surrounding the grave was fewer than a dozen.

Huw and Bleddyn stood together and wished their sons were safe at home and able to stand with them. Neighbours and those who worked the beach were represented although, like the Castles, their numbers were reduced by the call-up.

Bleddyn knew that his sons, Taff and Johnny, would be there had they not been overseas, and Huw thought of Ronnie, from whom they hadn't heard for several weeks. Bleddyn had seen Johnny's girlfriend, Hannah, at the house with the rest of the women, and he had managed to have a word with Marged and Beth to ask them to make her welcome.

Bernard Gregory was there with his son, Peter, who was on leave. Few greetings were exchanged but the young man seemed aloof, as though the death of an old friend was unimportant and he was there under sufferance. At twenty-seven, Peter had already seen so much death he was unaffected by the loss of the old lady, but he comforted his father and made all the right noises to the family. He felt no strong emotion and had no need to hide his tears behind a handkerchief as his father did. He tried to pretend, but could not.

He had been in the army since before war broke out, spending time in France and Holland and Germany and witnessing at first hand atrocities which had not yet come to light. Now he was in the intelligence service, still dropping into enemy-held territory, forming resistance groups, extending his knowledge and, recently, sending others into danger. It was impossible to witness so much without becoming immune to the display of sadness at the death of Granny Molly Piper. He was there solely to support his father, although he had known and liked Moll.

As with many others, the beach had been his playground as a child. He had helped his father as soon as he grew old enough, running with the donkeys, helping to look after them during the winter as well as the summer. Calling into the café or begging sweets from one of the stalls, he had grown up as part of the wider family of beach traders, knowing them all, calling them aunties and uncles, safe under their watchful eyes. Yet seeing the sad faces around the open grave, something in him had hardened. Moll had been nearly seventy-five and she'd had a good life compared with the eighteen-year-old he had seen die two days previously. He felt a surge of impatience and wanted to be gone.

"You'll come back to the house, Peter?" Huw asked. Although he had been about to shake his head, a glance at his father's face told him he would be needed there.

"Just for half an hour," he said, leading them towards the pony and cart waiting at the cemetery gate. "I've no wish to listen to eulogies about a woman who, by dying, has become a saint!"

Bernard was aware of some of his son's experiences and understood his attitude.

"I've known Moll since I was a snotty-nosed kid," Bernard said to his son as the sturdy Welsh cob trotted towards Sidney Street. "Your mam and I did our courting under that café, freezing cold in the winter, or huddled among the rows and rows of deckchairs in the summer. When you were born Moll and her Joseph came to the house and brought us some hand-knitted clothes and a blanket for your cot as though we were both part of her own family. Miss her something awful I will."

"No one likes to lose a friend." Peter was thinking about his young, innocent friend who had died a couple of days before.

"Besides the loss of a friend," his father went on, as the pony walked lazily through the streets, "besides knowing I'll never see old Moll again, it's a warning to get my own life in order. I'm on the front line now, in a row facing the last trumpet."

"Come on, Dad!" Peter turned and smiled with strong affection at his solemn-faced father. "You've got a long way to go yet, and besides, we're supposed to cheer the relatives today, not remind them of their mortality."

"There won't be one around my age who won't be thinking the same," Bernard defended.

When they arrived at the house of Moll and Audrey Piper,

there was a knot of neighbours outside, arms folded, leaning towards each other with words of praise for Moll, sympathy for the family and whispered criticism of the hats. Pushing past them, his tall figure in the smart uniform very impressive, his blue eyes carrying an air of authority, Peter went to find Beth.

The front room, rarely used, which Moll had called the parlour, was full of people, all in dark clothes, moving sluggishly like a tide caught against the sea wall, a seething homogenous mass of humanity. Heads were bowed and voices were slow and low. The curtains across the windows added to the gloom and Peter thought they looked as though they had been drenched in black treacle.

He thought the crowded room smelled of decay, filled as it was with the strong odour of stale clothes, dampness and mothballs. Dull clothes suitable for funerals were kept in the backs of wardrobes; suits and bowler hats for the men and, for the women, ill-fitting black dresses smelling slightly of damp and hats with the greenish tinge of mildew. These had all been brought out, brushed, and worn as a mark of respect for the dead. Tomorrow they would return to their dark places to await the next solemn occasion.

Peter found Beth, her mother and her Auntie Audrey in the kitchen where the air was cleaner, attending to the wants of their guests. Olive had broken down and was talking to Uncle Bleddyn, who was trying to reassure her about Ronnie's lack of letters.

"Never you mind, Olive, love. Ronnie is a thoughtful boy and he'll get a letter to you as fast as he can, but there are bound to be times when it's difficult. He won't be able to trot down to the corner and pop it in the pillar box as easy as you can, will he?"

Peter waved at Beth who looked up in surprise.

"Peter? How kind of you to come." She offered a hand, which he took, pulling her forward and kissing her.

"Beth! How grown up you look. It seems everyone has changed in the time I've been away." His voice was carefully modulated, the accent no longer familiar.

When they had exchanged a few pleasantries, Marged handed Peter two plates of food. "Take these for you and your father in case he can't get to the table, will you, Peter? There's a love."

When Peter had obediently struggled out of the kitchen in search of his father, Auntie Audrey mimicked his voice. "'Beth, how you've grown.' Fancy talk for a boy who ran with the donkeys, eh?"

"None of your, 'Hi yer, how've you bin?'," Marged agreed. "Always fancied himself, that one."

Beth blushed a little, afraid Peter might have heard and been embarrassed. When the food was more or less dealt with, she went to find him. With Freddy so poor at writing letters, she needed to understand something about life in the forces. Through Peter Gregory, she might learn something about the way Freddy lived, even though he was in a different service.

"To say that Freddy is not very good at writing letters is an understatement," she laughingly told Peter. "Three the first week, one the next – and that was to ask for money! And it's now two weeks since I've heard from him. I hear from my brother Ronnie more often than Freddy," she sighed. "Although we haven't heard from him for a while."

"I don't write to Dad as often as I should," Peter confessed. "Walking into the barracks is stepping into a separate world, an alien place where none of the normal rules apply. We cope better by forgetting how things were and concentrating on how they are. I'm part of that different world, Beth, so I can understand how he feels; being taken away from everything familiar, dealing with the day-to-day activities that often make very little sense, pretending the people I share my life with are my friends. It's better to cut yourself off from the real world and accept the artificial one. That way you might survive. So don't be hurt when he doesn't write. He's coping with something he was never prepared for, a way of life he would never have chosen."

He pointed to the corner near the fireplace, now visible as the crowd was thinning. "Who are those girls?"

"Maude and Myrtle, the two girls I found living on the streets and stealing food to survive." She explained about the food left out for them outside Piper's Café, and the devious way she had tracked them down. "Maude was ill and poor little Myrtle was trying to keep them both safe. Granny Moll took them in and, as they refused to go back to the children's home and Granny Moll agreed to be responsible for them, they've stayed with us ever since."

"What's going to happen to them now your grandmother has

gone? From the anxious look on their faces, that seems to be their question too." Maude and Myrtle sat huddled together, two pale, thin children dressed in the over-large and sombre clothes, silently watching the people come and go. "Dresses chosen for suitability rather than flattery, by the look of them," Peter whispered.

Beth walked over to the silent girls and Peter followed.

"Has Auntie Audrey spoken to you yet?" Beth asked. "About what's going to happen?"

"No, but we know she'll be telling us to go," Maude said stiffly. "Stands to reason. Now Auntie Audrey and that Wilf Thomas can get married, they won't want us hanging around, getting in the way, for sure."

"Nonsense! There's no question of you going anywhere. Auntie Audrey needs you for company in that big old house."

"And we'll be staying for ever?" Myrtle said in delight. "Always?"

"For as long as you want to stay," Beth smiled. "But remember your promise to Granny Moll, Myrtle. You're going to work real hard at school."

Myrtle nodded and hid her face. She was not getting on very well, but if it was the only way they could stay and be a part of the Castle family, then she'd have to face it. Young as she was, she knew Maude couldn't cope with another winter on the streets. The only other choice was for her to go back into that home – and without her sister, who was considered old enough to look after herself.

Peter was looking amused. "You don't like school?"

"They tease me because I don't know anything," Myrtle muttered.

"They both missed a lot of school," Beth explained.

"But I can read a bit now," Myrtle told him, "and I can give change for half a crown an' all, mind."

"You'll be fine." Peter delved into his pocket and brought out a shilling. "Here, take this and buy yourself some sweets."

Beth smiled her thanks for his kindness. "Your father thought he could help us find their family. They must have someone, somewhere." She explained about the old snapshots and Peter turned back to the girls.

"What do you remember about your mam and dad?" he asked.

Myrtle shrugged. "I only know what Maude tells me," she said.

They turned to look at Maude. "I remember they laughed a lot," she said. "Mam used to tease Dad and say he had sticky-outy ears. He pretended to be cross and they chased each other around the room and laughed."

Peter shrugged. "That isn't much to go on," he said, "but you never know. Someone might remember those sticky-outy ears. Lucky you haven't got them too," he teased.

Maude lifted her long hair and said, "But I have, look." She revealed small ears that indeed did not lie flat against her head.

Beth smoothed her hair down and said softly, "Beautiful ears you've got and not at all sticky-outy, I promise."

Peter solemnly agreed.

Lilly had been in the kitchen when the food was being prepared, but after that she had disappeared. Marged asked where she was once or twice, but with all the activity in the house, trying to deal with food and talk to the people who had come to pay their respects, she didn't have time to dwell on her daughter's absence. Lilly had always been adept at avoiding work, she thought to herself grimly. Now, with Granny Moll gone, she would be needed to do her share, but she knew her daughter well enough to know that the extra effort would not be forthcoming voluntarily. If Lilly were to help, it would mean arguments and ultimatums, and Marged knew that life would be easier if they allowed Lilly to go her own way. But that wouldn't be fair on Beth, who had always done more than she was asked.

Marged and Huw had been surprised at the grief Lilly had shown. The depth of feeling had been unexpected. Marged could see by her daughter's eyes that the girl hadn't been sleeping. And her restlessness was apparent by the tangle of sheets and blankets each morning when she went to make the bed. Lilly looked ill and her appetite was no longer enormous; in fact she picked, pulled faces and pushed her plate away barely touched most mealtimes. She had been more fond of her grandmother than Marged had realised.

Lilly was in the park, staring around her but seeing nothing. The October day was drawing to a close, the autumn mist with a hint of bonfire smoke on its breath settling over the trees and bringing a chill to her shoulders. She hadn't bothered to bring a coat. She was responsible for Granny Moll's death and she couldn't talk about it to anyone.

With no one close enough to help her, except her parents to whom she could never confess, she was weighed down with guilt and unable to ease her mind by having someone tell her it was an accident and no one was to blame. She wouldn't believe them if they did, but it would have been soothing to be told. If only Phil were here. He would comfort her, help her to deal with it. An hour with Phil and she would be able to sleep.

A vision of the burnt-out café came to her then. She saw in her mind's eye the corner where she and Phil had sat to tell each other how much they were loved. Because of her carrying on with a married man, meeting him in secret, Granny Moll was dead and the café was a smoking, distorted ruin.

Remorse, shame and the need to tell someone was overwhelming. The café wasn't the only thing to be ruined. If Phil were here, they wouldn't have their secret hideaway any more. It was as though, with the burning of the café, she and Phil and all they had said and done had been destroyed too.

She had been writing long, loving letters to Phil but not posting them. She planned to read them to him when he came home on leave. He had warned her that letters could easily allow their secret to escape. "If people find out before we're ready," he had said, "it will be more difficult for us. And it will delay the time when we can be together all legal, and safe from difficulties. We have to keep our secret until the moment is right for me to ask my wife for a divorce. She mustn't know about you or she'll never agree." She knew he was protecting her, making sure she wasn't shamed by being named in the divorce. She hugged herself. Dear Phil. He was so thoughtful. But now there were things to discuss, urgent things. Surely he wouldn't expect her not to tell him about the fire they had caused? She had to write to him. There was no one else.

She walked down the road, past Granny Moll's house where a few mourners remained with Audrey, who wanted them gone. Her parents looked at her but didn't demand an explanation of her absence. The room was not in its usual state of orderliness. Cups and saucers and plates were piled on the table ready to be returned to the café when it was once again habitable, the burn marks on some of the boxes a stark reminder of her guilt.

Taking out the writing pad, she began again to write to Phil, telling him all her fears and worries: the fire, the death of Granny Moll and all the other things that were on her mind.

Beth had written to Freddy and they walked together to the pillar box and dropped their letters in, both with the fervent hope of a swift reply.

Freddy was on leave but he wasn't sharing it with Beth and he knew nothing about the fire or the death of Granny Moll. Listening to the exploits of others in his group, he wanted some true stories to tell to add to the many untrue ones he had boastfully recited. So he had gone home with a mate and they had gone on the town dressed in uniform and tried their luck at the local dance.

When the last evening of their leave arrived and they were about to give up hope of a flirtation, Freddy caught the train and went to St David's Well to call on Shirley. The dark evenings and the black-out meant there was little chance of them being seen.

She didn't mention the tragedy that had hit the Castles, thinking that there was no point in spoiling the one evening they'd have together, so when Freddy saw the headline in the local paper he didn't at first realise it referred to Beth's family. When he did, he was in a state of shock. He needed to go and see Beth, make sure she was all right, although the article said nothing about anyone being injured. But how could he go? He wasn't supposed to be there. He went back to camp filled with shame at the way he had cheated on her, hiding away and meeting another girl when he should have been with her.

Once the funeral was over, Huw and Marged started making arrangements to repair and redecorate the café.

"Now Moll is gone, and Audrey is the only member of the Piper family left, I think it would be a good time to change the name," Huw said, as they looked at the blackened interior and began to assess the work that needed to be done.

"Of course we won't change the name!" Marged said in surprise. "Piper's it is and always will be."

"But there aren't any Pipers working for the firm. We're

all Castles! You and I are Castles. Bleddyn and his sons are Castles. I think it's about time we faced the fact that it's run by Castles. We should make the name match the business. You ashamed of the name you married into or something?"

"Of course I'm not ashamed. I'm always known as Mrs Castle, aren't I? What else would I be called?"

"Then give the café the name of the family who run it."

"No. I'm sorry, Huw, but I can't do that. My great-grandparents started the business and Piper's it will remain."

"Then let the Pipers sort out this little lot!" He left her in the doorway of the damaged café and walked off. At the van he hesitated. He couldn't very well leave her to catch a bus home; she'd be furious with him for days. But he couldn't help her with the plans for reopening either. Castle's it should be and would be before he set foot inside it again. He didn't have a say in anything, yet he and Bleddyn carried most of the responsibility. He wasn't going to put up with it any longer.

"If you want Bleddyn and me to get this place sorted in time for next season, you'll have to change a few things," he called to her.

"You were *glad* when my mother died," she accused as she walked back to the van. "You think that with her out of the way you'll get anything you want. Well, you're wrong!"

"Rubbish, woman. I liked the old girl, but it's time to rethink."

"What a time to choose, when I'm grieving."

"Whatever time I chose it would be wrong," he muttered. "You never allow me any say. I didn't want you to employ that Hetty Downs, for a start. Went ahead and did it, though, didn't you? And who's to know that it wasn't her who set fire to the place because of some imagined cheating on the part of your great-grandparents about fifty years ago?"

"You don't think she burnt the place for spite, do you?"

"I'm only saying you should have listened to me and not allowed her anywhere near the place. She knew where to go to sort out that disgusting stink that time, didn't she? A bit of rotten fish she found, and she knew exactly where to go to find it. She thinks I didn't see her, but I did. And she blamed our Eynon! I don't trust the woman, she's cracked when it comes to your family, but, as usual, you wouldn't listen to me."

"Perhaps we ought to talk to the police—"

"How can we without evidence?"

Huw drove home in silence, Marged tight lipped and offended, he himself determined not to give in. This was his only chance of succeeding with his plans for the business.

Huw went to see his brother that evening and found him writing letters. "God 'elp, Bleddyn, writing letters is all anyone seems to do these days. Writing letters or knitting socks for soldiers. There's our Beth writing to that Freddy and facing disappointment whenever the postman comes without a reply. There's Marged writing to everyone she's ever known to tell them about Moll, and praying every night for news of our Eynon, and our Lilly is writing to some bloke in secret. A mysterious boyfriend who, like that Freddy Clements, brings nothing but disappointment."

"Let's talk about opening the stalls next spring, shall we?" Bleddyn said, putting the letter aside. "There's plenty to sort out. More restrictions, and ice-cream making is banned. Although I think we might risk a fine or two to give the kids a treat now and then, what d'you say?"

"I told Marged I'm not going to help," Huw told him. "I want to change the name to Castle's. There are more Castles than there'll ever be Pipers. I don't think Audrey will produce an illegitimate son in Moll's memory, do you?" he joked.

"I don't think now is the time," Bleddyn said quietly. "Marged was close to her mother and they've worked together for so long it must be difficult for her to cope with Moll's death, losing her so sudden an' all."

"I still think she should listen to me sometimes," Huw argued.

"I think she will now. After all, there is no one else."

"Thanks. Last-hope Huw, that's me!"

"Come on, let's go and see what we can salvage. Thank goodness we'd reached the end of the season. Just think how much worse it would have been if this had happened in May."

Peter Gregory called on the Castles to see Beth. He brought the snaps from his father's collection and together they showed them again to the girls, this time with a powerful magnifying glass. Maude, being the oldest, thought she might recognise others in the group photograph but she didn't.

"Can you see your father there?" Peter coaxed.

Maude shook her head. "I look too old. I think this was when we were with Auntie Flossie."

Myrtle stared at the pictures as though begging them to reveal a secret, but it was a waste of time and Peter put them back in his pocket disappointed. As he was leaving, he told Beth, "My father doesn't have a clear memory of the girls, but I suspect there was some scandal attached to them. It's frustrating to have a glimpse of their past and nothing more."

"Thank you for trying to help, Peter. Somewhere someone must have that snippet of information that will set us on the right track. There's nothing more your father can tell us?"

"I'll talk to him again; you never know, something I say might trigger his memory of that time." He left a card when he went, propped on the mantelpiece with the others, still in its envelope.

Marged opened it and said in surprise, "It's from an old friend of your gran's, she must have just heard."

"Isn't it too late?" Maude asked.

"Never too late for a kind word, fach," Marged smiled.

That afternoon, Maude and Myrtle went to the newsagent above which Mrs Downs lived and chose a sympathy card. "I told you we should have sent one," Maude admonished her sister.

Mrs Downs was in the shop and she saw the two girls giggling as they read some of the words they considered too fancy. Then they looked at postcards and laughed at one which showed a cartoon of a young boy with very large ears.

"Sticky-outy ears just like our Dad had!" Maude said.

Mrs Downs came over and looked at them as though she hadn't seen them before. "What's your name?" she demanded.

"Maude Carpenter, and this is my sister Myrtle."

"How old are you?" They gave her their birthdays and she asked, "Your father, what did you mean about big ears?"

"Our Mam used to tease him and they'd laugh," Maude said, holding her sister's hand and edging out of the shop away from this angry-looking woman.

"Get out of here! D'you hear me? Get out and don't come back!"

"Mam?" Shirley asked, coming out of the back room. "What is it?"

"These girls, they were giving me cheek."

Maude and Myrtle fled.

Forgetting his ultimatum, over the next few days Huw helped Bleddyn sort out the demolished stalls. Some cafés were still open and they managed to serve a few of the diminishing number of visitors, most now without children, who still found their way by bus and car and train to enjoy the quiet of an autumn break.

The weekend still produced trippers, coaches bringing families on day trips, leaving earlier than in the summer but enjoying themselves just the same. There was lethargy among the few still trading and a false gaiety about the beach, fewer people making more noise to fill the void.

The rock and sweet shop still opened with Alice serving, thankful to get away from her difficult father for a few hours each day. The number of customers dwindled but Audrey kept the shop open for them, glad of the few extra pounds they brought.

Bernard Gregory spent some hours on the wilder beaches with his pony and flat cart gathering driftwood, which he would saw and chop to sell around the houses now fires had become a necessity once more. The rumours about coal being rationed made him more diligent in his searches and he went further afield than usual, the amiable pony taking him to the less frequented beaches to increase his stock.

While the Castle family gradually recovered from the loss of Moll, and continued to grieve over the disappearance of Eynon, Beth and Lilly each waited for a letter. A postcard came from Freddy addressed to the whole family and containing no words of love. It showed a view of another seaside town, in the west country, and he told them how pretty it was and how much more lively than St David's Well Bay.

Beth read it and reread it, trying to find some comfort hidden in the casual words. Surely he should have received her letter telling him about Granny Moll by now? But then, if he was away from camp on some exercise, he might still not know.

Audrey Piper and Wilf Thomas spent some time clearing out

Moll's bedroom. In privacy they put their arms around each other, looked at the huge white-counterpaned bed and dreamed of sharing it as Mr and Mrs Wilfred Thomas.

"I have bouts of guilt about Mam's death," Audrey told him. "All these years we've delayed getting wed, looking after your mother and mine, hoping for a miracle that would make it possible for us to marry, and knowing that the death of one of them was the only hope."

"Now it's too late," Wilf said sadly. "You're free but my mam is too frail to face it."

"There's plenty of room for her here," Audrey suggested. "I have to stay because Maude and Myrtle need a home, and Olive is here of course. But there are spare rooms. We could live on the top floor. Three nice rooms there are up there and we could make them into a beautiful home for the two of us, and I could still run the house. What d'you say?"

"It's too early, love. There's some who'll say we've benefited by poor old Moll's death and that would be hard to live with."

"In a month or so? What about the spring?"

"Well, we could think about it, but d'you think Mam could cope with the upheaval at her time of life?"

"Probably not," Audrey sighed, content to continue as they had done for so many years, unable to relish the idea of upheaval herself but unwilling to admit it. Pretence was kinder for them both, she thought philosophically.

They put aside some of Moll's jewellery for Beth, and for Ronnie's wife Olive. Some of the best pieces went to Lilly – who cried as loudly as she had when Moll had passed away.

Beth was surprised at the regret Lilly had displayed. Her sister hadn't been particularly fond of Granny Moll when she was alive, had often moaned when told to do something to help her, yet since her death Lilly seemed to be continually weeping.

With the approach of winter, and with the café in the hands of builders, the Castle family were taking on work for the winter months. Lilly went back to the café at the back of the fish-and-chip shop run by Bleddyn, but after two weeks she admitted that she no longer wanted to work there for six months of the year.

"I need something out in the open," she explained. "The smell of that fish makes me feel quite ill."

"You've done it every winter for years," Beth protested. "Why suddenly is the job beneath you?"

"If you must know I've never liked working there, coming home with the stink of fish and fat in my hair! I did it because I had to. It's a family business and I'm family!"

"When it suits you!" Beth retorted.

"Stop it, you two," Marged sighed. "If Lilly doesn't want to work in the café, we'll find someone who does. What about you, Beth, fancy giving it a try?"

"All right, I'll try," Beth said, relieved that she didn't have to take a job in one of the cold, open-fronted greengrocers like she had the winter before.

"Jump in my coffin so quick, would you?" Lilly snapped. "I haven't decided no for definite yet!"

Before Beth could retaliate and start a serious quarrel, Marged raised a hand and told them to hush.

"What would Granny Moll think of you two arguing all the time like a couple of kids?" she demanded and Lilly, predictably, collapsed once more into tears.

Lilly made little effort to find work. She made no comment when Beth started in the job that she had always considered her own at Uncle Bleddyn's café. She rose late and went to bed early, and, in between, did as little as she could get away with. Marged threatened her with a visit to the doctor, thinking that the mourning and grieving had gone on too long for a healthy young woman, and were now simply an excuse to be idle.

Letters were eagerly awaited by most families, and friends and neighbours shared what little news they had with others. Beth received a short note from Freddy, full of what he had done and making it seem that life was one long, laugh-filled pub crawl. He taught her a new word, "skiving", which was an essential skill for survival, he told her. He then asked whether she could send him some money as he was finding it difficult to manage. She threw it down in disgust. Why hadn't he responded to the news about the fire and Granny Moll? Her letter must have reached him by now!

The following day she received a second letter, this one full of remorse at his previous one. He told her the letter had been mislaid and he'd just read it. He explained that he wrote all that nonsense as a way to fill the pages, because life was really very dull and he missed her and longed to be home once again. He was sympathetic, concerned and as loving as she could wish. Saying nothing to her parents, she went to the post office, took out ten shillings and popped it into her next letter.

Thoughts of money made her decide to check on their savings. Freddy had taken it out of the bank and had told her it was safe in National Savings. A word with his mother, a hint that she intended to surprise Freddy by adding to it, and the book was in her hands. It contained only three shillings. Once again he had spent all they had saved. It was no more than she had suspected.

Marged picked up a letter from the doormat one morning and puzzled over the writing. It wasn't a hand she recognised. Fear clutched her heart. It was Eynon. Someone was writing to tell her he was dead! Audrey was there and Marged handed it to her; she was unable to open it and her hands shook as she waited for her sister to tell her what it contained.

"It's from someone calling himself Ross, but I think it's Eynon."

Marged snatched it back and read, "Dear Auntie Marged, Just to let you know I'm all right and will get in touch soon."

"You'll have to take it to the police, Marged. The boy has to be found for his own safety."

"They can put me in prison first! If he comes here I'll do everything to make sure he doesn't go back."

The long-awaited letter from Ronnie arrived and Olive was told that he was injured and would be coming home. She ran to tell Marged and Huw.

"What happened?" they demanded in unison. Handing them the letter, she said breathlessly, "An injury to his knee, apparently, but he's alive and he's coming home!"

One morning, as her father and Uncle Bleddyn were setting off to begin to grease the joints of the dismantled stalls and put them away for the winter, Beth received two letters. One was the usual brief note from Freddy with a PS thanking her for the money. The other envelope was addressed in handwriting she didn't recognise.

She sat down in surprise when she unsealed it. It was from Peter Gregory. Very different from Freddy's hastily scrawled note, it was full of amusing observations about people he remembered from when they were children. He asked about the two girls, Maude and Myrtle, and remembered to ask about Freddy, Eynon and Ronnie too, something Freddy never did. His PS was to hope she was well and had found interesting work for the winter.

Feeling a bit guilty at the comparisons she was making, she handed it to her mother and father then said, "I might go and see Mr Gregory. I expect he'd like to read it too. Can't have too many letters at a time like this."

"I wonder why he wrote to you?" Marged said, hope of a separation from Freddy Clements adding a sparkle to her eyes.

"I think they like to keep in touch with home. Writing is a way of making contact." Beth's tone was casual, but she was already mentally composing her reply.

The stalls were taken apart and cleaned before being stored in their winter premises, a barn on a farm a few miles out of town. They would be repainted in the spring, and Huw was determined they would be a patriotic red, white and blue.

Bernard Gregory's donkeys had been taken to their winter home, where they had two large fields and comfortable stables. As Beth was working in Bleddyn's fish-and-chip shop, she was free during the afternoons. She took the letter and cycled to the house in Goose Lane where Bernard Gregory lived.

She found him in a large shed at the back of the premises, cleaning the saddles ready for waxing. The donkeys all had names and holidaying children grew to know each one. Dolly, Bertha, Pat, Hazel, Charlie, Bertie, Clifford: the names were brightly painted on the headbands. Without their name plates Beth was never sure which was which, but Bernard knew the names and characters of every one.

"Dolly is as gentle as you could wish, but Hazel, she has to be treated with caution. Anyone too heavy and she won't move, and she has been known to tip a persistent rider off! Charlie has to be leader, or he kicks . . ." He laughed affectionately as he remembered.

Beth handed him the letter and his eyes filled with tears as he read it. "Thanks for bringing it down, lovely girl. Peter writes as often as he can, but it's difficult at times. This is a bonus."

"Will it be all right if I write back?" she asked.

"Good heavens, why not? Love to hear from home, they do."

"I only thought that he might not want to bother writing to me again. It's more important that you get letters, after all, but if I write and tell him I don't expect a reply—"

"If you have the time to tell him about what's happening here, it would help him. Just casual chat about home, that's all they want, everyday things. A reminder about the sanity of home."

Talking to Peter's father she picked up on several things to tell him in her letter and as she cycled home she felt excited at the prospect of another letter in response. Writing to Freddy wasn't much fun, she had to admit, and his replies were hardly worth the cost of the stamps – which she had paid for anyway, stamps she sent him to encourage him to write.

In defiance of his wishes, Lilly had written several times to Phil but every day the postman passed without bringing her a reply, until one day she lost her temper and wrote a fiercely angry letter, threatening to go and see his wife if she didn't get a response in two weeks. At last, in November, the long-awaited letter arrived.

With trembling hands she opened it, and burst into tears.

"What's the matter with the girl?" Huw demanded irritably. "Waiting for the postman with more interest than that snappy terrier on the corner and when he finally brings her a letter what does she do? She cries! God 'elp, Marged, the girl is beyond me."

Lilly looked up and in a low voice said, "Mam, Dad, I'm expecting and the father is married and won't leave his wife. He refuses to help in any way, says it can't be his."

Eight

Marged stared at Huw and they both stared at Lilly as though waiting for her to explain her words, tell them she had been joking, that they hadn't heard properly, anything other than face the situation with which she had presented them.

"It's true," she said harshly. "I'm expecting and there's no one to help me. There'll be no hasty marriage to try and make this respectable, Mam. I'm on my own."

"Just tell us who the father is and I'll see if you're on your own," Huw growled.

She looked at him contemptuously. "Don't you listen? There is no father. This baby will just have me. No one else, understand, Dad? No need for you to flex your muscles and start playing the outraged Victorian parent. This baby has no father. Right?"

Too shocked to complain at her rudeness, Huw looked at his wife for support.

"We have to do something, Lilly," Marged said. "There's more than you involved here, whatever you say."

Lilly shook her head, screwing up Phil's letter and throwing it into the flames of the fire so nothing could be gleaned from it. Cajoling, threatening, pleading, nothing did any good. On the matter of the baby's father, Lilly would not budge.

As though she was not there, Marged and Huw discussed the possibility of sending Lilly away, having the baby adopted. Lilly refused to consider it.

"I'm having this baby, Mam, and if you don't want me, then I'll find somewhere else to live." She had no idea how she could possibly cope on her own, but was determined not to give in to threats.

Marged looked at Huw and said softly, "How are we going to tell Audrey?"

Beth was the next to be told and it was Lilly who told her when they were alone and she could put her case to her sister for having the child, without her parents adding their opinions.

"I'm convinced that when – my boyfriend – sees the beautiful baby he'll love her and want us both," Lilly told Beth, looking at her for reassurance.

"Have you written to him since he told you he wouldn't help?" Beth asked, avoiding a reply. "Perhaps when he's had time to think, he'll at least help financially."

"Yes, I wrote back, not angry, not pleading and helpless either, mind. I just stated the facts, and reminded him that the baby is his, and he'll regret it if he abandons her."

As the sisters sat and talked, all previous antagonism faded. Beth felt a strong need to defend her sister and take care of her through the difficult weeks ahead.

"If it's a daughter, he'll definitely want her then. Fathers are notoriously soft when it comes to daughters," Lilly went on. "Remember how we used to run to our Dad when Mam told us off?" They both smiled at the memories of Huw's spoiling.

"I'll stay with you when you tell Auntie Audrey, shall I?" Beth offered. "You're not alone, Lilly, we're all here and the baby won't lack love." She hugged her sister and was surprised to feel a painful tinge of envy.

Audrey told her much the same as Beth. She didn't mention the baby's father, but she could guess who it was. She would help in any way she could and heaven help anyone she heard gossiping about Lilly. "Put them to rights straight off I will," she promised.

Wilf nodded tacit agreement, but his eyes and his tightly clenched mouth told a different story. Disapproval was clear and as soon as they were on their own, he told Audrey so.

"Why is everything being made so easy for her?" he asked.

"Times change, Wilf. You wouldn't have our Lilly treated like a criminal, would you?"

"No, but it's so unfair."

"I know, dear, but when is life ever fair?"

"It certainly wasn't for us, was it?" he said, taking her hand and holding it tight.

Uncle Bleddyn was philosophical about it. "I don't think

you'll be the only young woman in this situation, fach," he said hugging her. "Men away from home month after month, women tempted by men who are available, stands to reason, we'll soon have a whole flock of 'em."

"No more knitting for soldiers," Marged said. "I'll be knitting for my grandchild, won't I?"

Huw remained determined to find out who the man was, and make him pay.

A visit to the doctor confirmed Lilly's fears and she was told the baby would be born early in May. Quickly working it out in her head, she realised that their visits to the café after closing had made hers and Phil's love-making too easy. The dark, cosy privacy had relaxed them, made them forget the danger of their growing desire. If they had stuck to the park and back lanes she might have been saved this distress, but somehow, even with Phil's refusal to become involved, she wasn't sorry.

It was unlikely she would marry. She loved Phil and because of his determination to remain married, he had made love to her, told her how much he cared, then let her down in the worst possible way. She would never feel the same way about anyone else, so this baby would be all she had to fill her life. While her mother and father continued to discuss ways of finding out who the father was, she gently dreamed of girls' names and boys' names and wondered if she might be the first in the family to produce twins.

"So I have to plan for May," Lilly said one day as she and her mother were washing up after supper. "I'll have the winter to get everything ready, won't I?" She sighed happily. "A spring baby will be lovely."

"Typical!" Huw grumbled. "Right at the start of the season. It couldn't be worse."

Beth silently thought that Lilly being unable to work wouldn't change much; she never had been too keen to do her share. "Don't worry, Dad," she said. "With Freddy away, I'll have plenty of spare time."

"And besides," Huw went on, glaring at his daughter, "what's lovely about having a baby and everyone knowing you haven't been churched? No engagement ring or even a visible boyfriend. People'll think you're a tart, that's what they'll think, mind. Carrying on like a tart. What's lovely about that, eh?"

"That's enough, Huw," Marged warned, and Huw stomped off to look at the garden to cool his anger.

Apart from Beth, it was Hannah who helped Lilly the most. Bleddyn had told her about the pregnancy when she visited him with her two girls to share one of Johnny's letters with him.

"D'you think I could call on Lilly?" she asked, and Bleddyn walked up to Sidney Street with her and Marged invited them in. While Bleddyn and his brother went out to look at the garden, a euphemism for talking in private, Lilly and her mother went to make tea. Leaving Josie and Marie listening to the wireless, Hannah followed them into the kitchen.

"Johnny's dad has told me about the baby," she said hesitantly to Lilly. "I wondered whether you'd like to borrow my pram? It's in Mam's loft and it's been well polished and covered against dust, so it should look smart enough."

"Thanks, that's kind of you, Hannah." Lilly was delighted with this positive response to her news. "I'd be glad to borrow it. There's so much to get, isn't there, and me without a husband." She lowered her eyes, expecting sympathy, but Hannah's reaction surprised her.

"You're on your own, but at least you know it. Some mothers think they're safe and secure in a marriage and find they are not. That's worse. Forget looking for sympathy, face the facts and get on with it, that's my advice."

Shock and the beginnings of anger showed in Lilly's face but then she relaxed and smiled. "Thanks again, I think I needed that."

"Sorry if I was rude," Hannah apologised.

"No, not rude, just reminding me that I've got myself into this mess and I have to – as you put it – face facts."

"Married, was he?" Hannah asked, thinking of her own ex-husband's games.

"I don't want to talk about him," Lilly said quietly.

"If ever you do, then come and see me. I've had plenty of disasters in my life and it's taught me, among other things, to be discreet. And I love Johnny and would never do anything to hurt his family."

They arranged to meet at the weekend, when Hannah would help her make lists of what she would need. "I might even find a few baby nightgowns and a cardigan or two. I don't think I'll be needing them any more," Hannah told her.

* * *

When Ronnie was released from hospital, Olive went to the station to meet his train. She stood on the platform, watching the few passengers wandering about, some carrying shopping bags and others with briefcases and a newspaper. It was all so different from the day Ronnie had left. The platform had been crowded then, groups surrounding young men as they left to join their training camp, travel warrant ready to show the inspector, small suitcases with all they were allowed to take held tightly in one hand, the other in most cases around a mother or a sister, a wife or a lover.

It had been quiet then as now, in spite of the crowd; the departing ones having nothing left to say, wanting to be gone, to get the painful parting over with. Those staying behind had given up repeating the same clichés about taking care, avoiding damp socks and eating well, and there were no more promises from both sides to write regularly. It had all been said. Now, waiting for the train to bring Ronnie back, Olive couldn't help feeling relief and gladness that her husband was coming home safe and relatively sound.

As the train puffed importantly into the station and squealed to a stop, she looked up and down the train as doors opened and people stepped out. Not so many. At three in the afternoon few people travelled. He came out backwards, awkward on his crutches, an elderly woman helping him, much to his embarrassment. Olive ran to him, thanked the lady and hugged Ronnie, almost falling against the train as she did so.

She was glad to hide her shock and distress from him by burying her face against his shoulder. He looked thin and so very, very pale. No sign of the suntan that darkened his face in the summer months. He looked as though he hadn't seen the sun in years. His hair was unbelievably short and a bandage was visible under his hat. She felt his bony body and wondered how she could hide her alarm.

After a moment, composing herself, she eased away from him, a smile fixed on her face, and stared into his eyes. Although they were more deeply set in his wasted face it was Ronnie she saw there and she knew it was up to her to make the rest of him strong again.

The lady who helped him was standing there, obviously with something to say.

"I hope you'll be going back when your wounds have healed, young man," she said warningly. "Hitler won't be beaten if we shirk our duty."

"Of course," Ronnie said, then, in a whisper, he added, "Not it I can help it!" making Olive laugh.

Linking arms, Ronnie using two sticks, they made their way to the exit where a taxi was found to take them back to their two rooms in Moll's house in Sidney Street. After greeting Auntie Audrey and assuring her he was really quite well, Ronnie went upstairs. Refusing Olive's assistance, he sat on the bottom step and went up backwards.

"Perhaps you'd better have a bed downstairs," Audrey said. "I can get it ready in no time."

Ronnie refused. "Thanks, Auntie Audrey, but I have a goal in mind. I'm going to get up and down stairs without sticks before the end of the month. I can't give up that easy."

The war news was becoming serious and very frightening with stories of air raids and threats that the bombing campaign would get far worse as Hitler tried to destroy cities and lower morale to the point where Britain would surrender. But for Olive that day, looking across the fireside at her husband, the war belonged to other people. Sympathy was there for the families who had lost their homes through the fierce bombing, and the hundreds who had lost their loved ones, but it was lessened by her relief that for Ronnie, the war was as good as over.

Beth had an occasional note from Freddy and on almost every occasion there was an accompanying letter from Peter. She always gave Peter's letter to her parents to read as there was nothing more than casual friendship displayed. He wrote amusing descriptions of the people he met, and his observations were real enough for Beth to see them clearly. He wrote of his own mistakes and foolishness, and Beth began to look for his letters with more enthusiasm than for Freddy's.

Freddy usually filled the short page with complaints, wanting sympathy for his boredom, and often asking for money to help him afford the pictures when a rare pass enabled him to go into the town near which he was based. She wondered whether he had a girl to take. Freddy had never minded going alone, but he preferred someone beside him to share the laughter and the fear and all the other illusory emotions the film world offered him.

Beth hadn't mentioned the disappearance of their savings. He was a man who had to have money to spend, she knew that. The temptation of knowing money was available was too much for him when there was something he needed or just wanted. In future, any saving would have to be done in her name. She already had twenty-two pounds put aside but she said nothing about it to Freddy.

She knew that both Johnny and Taff both sent money home for Hannah and Evelyn to save for them. It wasn't much, just a gesture to remind them they were together and planning for the future. She didn't think Freddy would send money to his mother and he certainly wouldn't think of adding to their savings. No, Freddy liked money to spend. He had no thought of looking further than today. Looking into the future and planning a home was for her to deal with. Like Lilly with her baby, she was on her own. But she bought a five-shilling postal order and put it in with her reply.

She had continued to take Peter's letters to his father. Bernard Gregory was always very pleased to see her and sometimes she stayed a while and helped him feed the chickens, stack the firewood he sold or fill barrels with seaweed gathered from the beach, which he sold further inland as manure for allotments and gardens. He was always busy, making a few shillings in one of many ways, occasionally using the donkeys to bring seaweed and wood along the narrow paths from the beach, but whenever possible taking the larger cart and the pony. He delivered for a few shops too, when they lost their drivers to the army, and transported furniture when required. Anything that would bring in a few shillings, providing for himself and the animals by his efforts.

A procession was arranged by the local churches and the donkeys were employed to take part, although this was voluntary. It was to raise money for the Red Cross. Beth went along to help with the costumes, enjoying the unexpected activity when winter and the black-out brought its gloom.

One mid-November evening Marged gave her a cake to take to the old man. She was hoping that Peter would be a greater attraction that Freddy, she admitted to her sister Audrey as they watched Beth set off for Goose Lane.

"Selfish and greedy, that's what Freddy Clements is, and I'd be delighted if she gave him the push and married Peter Gregory instead."

"We all make our own choices," Audrey said. "Beth would find someone else if she thought Freddy's selfishness was going to be a problem. Some women like a man to have faults, it makes them feel needed. People say that Mam was selfish, stopping Wilf and me from marrying," Audrey went on. "And that's true, she was." Her eyes went misty as she thought back to those difficult times. The memories were still painful. "She did it because it suited her. No other reason. Wilf and I wanted to marry but once the problems we had were sorted, there was never any great urgency after a while. I began to think she had been right, but she wasn't, she was just selfish."

"Beth wouldn't marry him if she wasn't sure he'd change. It isn't down to us to tell her how to live her life."

"Freddy is cheating on her and he used money that was for their future. Yet she still plans to marry him." Audrey stared at her sister with a quizzical tilt of her head.

"What are you saying? Beth wants to look after Freddy and feels the need to accept him faults and all?"

"Some women like that, enjoy being a bit of a martyr. Although with Freddy it might be different. Perhaps Freddy doesn't want to get married but hangs on to Beth in case he doesn't get a better offer, and he wants to make sure there's someone to look after him."

"Audrey! That doesn't say much for our Beth!"

"It says even less for Freddy," Audrey retorted.

When Beth arrived at the cottage on Goose Lane there was no sign of Mr Gregory. The door was never locked and she went inside, intending to leave the cake, the letter and a note for him. She was stepping into the kitchen when she heard voices. Calling to let Mr Gregory know she was there, she stepped out into the back garden, still bright with fuchsia bushes, dahlias and a few late roses, and saw Mr Gregory walking up from the beach with Peter. A sudden shyness overwhelmed her and she darted back into the kitchen, hoping to avoid being seen.

"Beth?" Peter called. "Is that you?"

"I only brought a cake for your father," she said shyly. "Mam sent it. Not much fat in it, rationing, see, but I hope you'll enjoy it," she prattled on, backing away as though in a hurry.

"How kind," Peter said, running forward and taking both of her hands in his. "I hope you aren't dashing back home? You must stay and taste it with us. Dad?" he called back to where Mr Gregory was putting the harness away in the shed, which he rather grandly called the tack room. "The kettle is as good as on, don't delay."

He busied himself in the kitchen, putting china and cutlery on a tray, which he carried to the table. Beth felt the need to help, but having had no female to run the house in the past ten years, she could see that setting tables and the tasks usually dealt with by the woman of the house came easily to him.

She usually cycled to call on Mr Gregory but today she had chosen to walk, so Peter offered her a lift home.

"No need," she said, longing to accept. The prospect of another half an hour in Peter's company was alarmingly tempting, but she had to refuse. "I can easily walk," she assured him. "You need to spend as much time as possible with your father. He looks forward so much to your visits."

"He values your visits too," he said. "Thank you so much for being kind to him. I really appreciate it. I'm very fond of the old boy, you know."

She hesitated so long about how to reply that she ended up saying nothing and felt silly for being so unaccomplished a conversationalist. She imagined that Peter's girlfriends would always know exactly what to say.

He handed her her coat and as she put it on she felt a wave of disappointment flood over her. Why hadn't she said yes, she would like him to walk home with her? Why hadn't she acted the helpless woman and told him she was nervous out alone in case there were parachutes falling out of enemy planes and . . . She knew she couldn't act the helpless woman and she'd make a mess of it if she tried.

Turning to call goodnight to Mr Gregory, she saw that Peter was putting on his overcoat. A repeat protest almost reached her lips, but not quite.

The night was clear, the moon a Chinese lantern floating in a velvet sky, large and bright as though lit from within. The lights from the town were blocked by the black-out curtaining and wardens stalked the streets warning people to "put that light out!" if a glimmer were allowed to escape. Peter took her hand and tucked it under his arm companionably.

"I'd hate to lose you," he teased. As they walked, they talked about their plans for the future. Peter wanted to move to Cardiff and run an agency finding work for people, covering all occupations.

"I have some qualifications in running a business," he explained. "Accountancy and other aspects of the day-to-day running of a business of my own. And I have a theory that once this war is over, nothing will be the same and, among other things, employment will change dramatically. Women are beginning to realise that they needn't stay at home all day every day to run a home. Until they have children and when the children are grown, or even when the children are at school, they can spare a few hours a day to earn some extra money. I want to expand on that."

"I can't imagine working anywhere else but the beach," Beth told him. "Mam and Dad have always worked there with Granny Moll. Even when we were small we went over to the sands with them. I can't imagine doing anything different. I work in town in the winter, of course, but there's always the beach to come back to."

"I think you're very fortunate to have a dream and be able to live it. So few of us manage that." He squeezed her arm against him and smiled down at her, and in the intimacy of the darkness his nearness was as exciting as a kiss.

"I should be doing more to help, but Dad says what I do on the sands is part of the war effort, helping people to relax and have fun and pretend for a while. So my conscience isn't too troubled."

She asked him about his occupation in the forces but he told her it was secret work and it would be tantamount to treason if he revealed the details of what he was doing.

It wasn't until they were almost there that Beth realised she had been talking about herself and not her and Freddy. She thought perhaps she was guilty of a different kind of treason for enjoying Peter's company so much. Again an explanation almost reached her lips, but not quite.

"Come again tomorrow," Peter suggested. "We can go and see the donkeys in their winter quarters."

"Love to," she said at once, willingly pushing thoughts of Freddy Clements from her mind.

* * *

Investigations into the cause of the fire had ended with the conclusion that the fire had begun near the door, but there was no evidence about how it had started. Anything combustible that might have been either thrown behind the door or pushed through the letter box had been swallowed in the flames.

Whatever the cause, Marged and Huw decided that there would be no letter box on the new door. It had never been needed and people had been known to push rubbish through. Perhaps a cigarette end had been included with an empty packet or matchbox, they suggested to the investigators.

Both really believed that the fire was a deliberate act, perpetrated by a resentful Mrs Downs, and Huw constantly reminded Marged of his suspicions about the woman and of how his warnings about her had been ignored.

Beth returned to Goose Lane the following day, the last day of Peter's leave. She should have cycled, but the thought of Peter walking her home again made her decide to walk.

They sat and talked for a while, Mr Gregory smiling, puffing on his old pipe, contented it seemed to see the young couple enjoying each other's company. He knew Peter had plans for when the war ended, plans that would take him far away from St David's Well, but he hoped that, with a local girl stealing his heart, he might change his mind and stay closer to home.

He didn't go with them when they went to see the donkeys. "I'll be going up later with the food," he said. In the summer the donkeys managed with grass and an occasional treat, but as winter approached their feed increased and they were given mash each evening before being locked into their stables.

Peter didn't walk Beth home that evening. Instead he used the pony and flat cart and they clip-clopped slowly around the lanes, in no hurry to reach their destination. As the streets with their darkened windows were reached, he stopped the pony, turned to Beth, and kissed her.

"There, complain if you must, but I've been wanting to do that for so long."

"Why should I complain?" She leaned towards him and they kissed again.

"Please write often," he whispered, his breath feather light on her cheek. "I look forward to your letters more than you can imagine."

"Kiss me again," she replied, "in case I forget how it feels."

"I'll never forget our first kiss. Never," he said drawing her close to him.

"I'll remember every moment," she whispered, before being silenced once again by his lips.

Lilly was still up when Beth went in and a glance told her that Beth had done more than walk down to Goose Lane. "Peter home, was he?" she asked.

"Peter was there, yes, but he's going back tomorrow."

"He didn't make you forget you're engaged to Freddy Clements, did he?"

"Of course not," Beth said, too quickly.

"Oh, like that, is it? Absence makes the heart grow fonder? Don't make me laugh! Plenty of men will come home to disappointment after this war."

"Oh, Lilly, he's so nice. We talked so easily and about everything. I don't remember enjoying myself so much in ages. I like him so much I feel" – the word came back to her – "like a traitor, forgetting all about Freddy while I was with Peter."

"How d'you think *I* feel? I encouraged – him – and I feel traitorous when I think about his wife. It wasn't just a nice chat and a casual kiss." She patted her slightly extended belly. "This isn't a pimple, is it!"

Work on restoring the café on the cliffs above the beach began in earnest once the insurance company were satisfied that no further investigation was required. Bleddyn and Huw had to do much of the work themselves as so many builders had left to serve in the forces. Finances were another consideration. They were worried that they might no longer be able to depend on a good summer season to boost their income. They had to conserve as much of their savings as possible in case the worst happened and the beach had to close.

The framework of the building was metal and the wooden floor was made of thick timbers, which in most areas were scorched rather than seriously damaged. So apart from cleaning, sanding and replacing the windows and some of the furniture, decoration was the biggest task.

Huw and Bleddyn left the choice of colour to Marged, but when she chose what he considered a rather dull yellow and a dark blue, he ignored her and bought white.

"Now and then I have to remind her who's boss," he joked to his brother, but he made sure Bleddyn wasn't there when Marged saw their effort for the first time.

Expecting a row, he was relieved when she agreed with his choice. "Practical having all one colour, and cleaner looking too," she said. "We'll stick to blue for the curtains and tablecloths, shall we?"

Huw frowned. Why was she asking his opinion – was she building up to ask a favour? Something he wouldn't like?

Huw found work for the winter in a factory, and was alarmed when given a reminder that when the new season began he might not be able to leave. War work was increasingly important and more and more people were having to accept work in stores or factories. There were dozens of items needed to keep the army supplied: uniforms, kit bags, metal tools, cooking equipment, cutlery and survival gear, besides the many and varied weapons.

Beth, Audrey, Marged and Lilly went on knitting, sometimes for the soldiers and sometimes for the baby. Olive helped when she wasn't attending to Ronnie, who walked with difficulty, was easily exhausted and still needed constant attention. Living with Audrey and Maude and Myrtle meant she had help and someone with whom to discuss the future.

"Ronnie won't ever be strong on that leg," Audrey said one morning when the five of them were finishing breakfast. "I don't think he'll be able to manage a long day on the beach with Huw and Bleddyn and the others."

"What will he do? He loved the beach," Olive said, looking sadly at Ronnie who sat half smiling, amused at being talked over as though he were a helpless and not very bright child.

"I've thought of that and I've decided what we'll do, if you agree, Olive," he said, and the others stared at him in surprise. "I want us, you and me, Olive, to take a market stall."

"A market stall?"

"Selling vegetables, fruit when we can get it, and perhaps fish."

"Fish?"

"Stop behaving like a parrot and listen," he teased. "The stall at the back of the market, near the door into Frog Street, has had to close as the man who ran it has joined up, so I suggest we reopen it. I'm sure the previous owner would help us with suppliers and all that. I could sit down for a lot of the time. It would be perfect. What d'you think?"

Olive's first instinct was to say no, but she remembered how happily Ronnie dealt with the crowds on the beach. He liked people, he enjoyed working with them. A market stall would suit him perfectly. For herself she had doubts, but she smiled at him, her eyes shining, and said, "Ronnie, love, I think it's a wonderful idea."

During November and December people began to hoard what they could, and save from their rations to prepare for Christmas. Besides trying to work up excitement for the celebration, every household seemed to live for the postman's visits, longing for news while avoiding thinking about the visits of the telegram boys who brought the worst news of all. Every day, Marged looked out and watched as the postman approached, praying for a letter to tell her Eynon was coming home. He hadn't been home once since joining up and now she didn't even know whether he was alive or dead. She was convinced that he must have refused the offer of leave initially, afraid for some reason to face them all. Now the only news of him was the negative kind, when army representatives called to ask if he had made contact.

The last time she had shouted at them, "I had him for seventeen years without a problem. You had him five minutes and you lost him!" Stony faced as always, the men left with a repeat of the warning about informing the authorities the moment she heard from him.

She took out the pathetically few letters and cards he had sent. In the first ones he had told them he was enjoying his training. Then one told her he wouldn't be coming home on his leave because a friend from Yorkshire had invited him there. Marged relived the disappointment of those words. She remembered how she had forced a smile and said to Huw, "Grown up he is and able to choose his friends. He'll be home next time for sure."

She now knew there had been other reasons for not coming home. Had he been in trouble? What trouble could there be that he couldn't tell her about? He must have been desperate if he'd run away. Was he regretting signing up for five years? Had he been wishing he could come home but was afraid of breaking down when he saw all the familiar places and faces?

She still wrote to him almost daily; cheerful letters, full of reminders about the summers to come when he could decide for himself whether or not he would work on the sands.

"We'll be so used to managing without you, me and your dad and Uncle Bleddyn, Beth and Lilly, and Ronnie too when he's well enough, that we won't have to press-gang you into service," she joked.

She had told him about Lilly and teased him about being an uncle. The bulk of her letters were about the family and the people he knew, giving details about them, about where they had been and what they had been doing, telling him that the beach was still attracting visitors this late, and about the stalwarts who swam in the cold months of the year "like Bleddyn used to do".

"It's as though he's in prison with no hope of getting out ever again," Marged said to Huw after her most recent letter to him had been returned. "So homesick he must be."

"At least the occasional card tells us he's alive, and that's all he can tell us until he decides to give himself up. Once he decides to face it, he'll settle down to army life. He must have had a bad start. I don't think it's easy for some. Got to be a part of it, see, be thought of as a character, one of the lads. He won't be down for long, not our Eynon."

Eynon was washing the gash on his head and wondering if it would ever heal properly. The bruises from the kicking and beatings from Kipper had faded to yellow and they would be gone soon.

For the past week he had been sleeping in a barn about five miles outside Aberystwyth. He had been found on the third night huddled in the hayloft with chickens and dogs below, dogs who were friendly and shared his supper of chips, bought in the town with money he had stolen and eaten in the solitude of the barn cold and greasy but sufficient to ease the pangs of hunger. He could have eaten them hot, straight from the shop, but there was a need to pretend he was going home, and the dogs were there waiting for him, a substitute family.

It was when they were sharing the last of the chips that a man appeared in the doorway. Eynon didn't see him at first, but the dogs wagged their tails and looked towards the door and he knew he had been discovered. He felt a flash of relief that it was over and he could return to something like normal, then the instinct to run.

"I'm not doing any harm, mister," he said softly.

"Runaway, are you?"

"I just couldn't resist the chance when it came. Ashamed I am, but I couldn't take it."

The man came in and Eynon was alarmed to see a shotgun over the man's arm. He foolishly grabbed one of the dogs and held it close to him. He hadn't suffered all this to be shot in a farmer's barn, had he?

The man broke the gun and laid it down. "Thought you might be a Jerry parachutist," he explained.

To Eynon's relief he was offered a bath and some food before going on his way. The wound on his head was dressed and the farmer told him it wouldn't heal until it was stitched into place; the lip of it would constantly pull away and start the bleeding until the flap was secured properly. Eynon thanked him but knew he wouldn't try to see a doctor; not yet. Not until he was ready.

While he was washing the filth of weeks from his skin he listened anxiously, half expecting the police to arrive, but he was allowed to sleep peacefully until the following morning then sent on his way with his pockets filled with food.

The coming of autumn heralded the start of a more intense bombing campaign on London and other major cities. The Luftwaffe seemed in control of people's lives, forcing thousands of Londoners to pack their most valued possessions and hurry underground night after night in the hope of evading the bombs. It was a campaign with which Hitler hoped to destroy the capital's commercial centre.

A new menace increased the danger to shipping and warnings of even greater shortages of food were announced. The war was being fought a long way from St David's Well but it was involving every man, woman and child in the fight.

Freddy had written to tell Beth he was coming home for three days, and like Olive when she had gone to meet Ronnie after his injury, Beth waited at the railway station and compared the calm of his return with the chaos of his departure.

The train was full with office workers and shop assistants coming home at the end of their day, and she stood near the ticket-office wall looking anxiously around, afraid they would miss each other in the crush.

Freddy stepped out on to the platform right in front of her, and he turned to help a trim little WAAF girl, who clearly didn't need it, putting his arms around her and lifting her down from the step. Beth looked away, wanting to hide so she could pretend not to have seen the incident. Glancing back she saw they were kissing.

She backed towards the fence, urgently needing to run away, but there wasn't time. Freddy waved and blew another kiss as the girl hurried away through the barrier, where the ticket collector stood checking everyone who went through.

The platform had almost cleared before Freddy saw her. He looked fit and confident and, after a brief hug, immediately asked her if she had any money to spare. "For a taxi, see, I haven't any change," he explained as she stared at him in surprise.

"Freddy," she laughed dryly, "at least wait until you've said hello before you ask for money!"

She handed him a few shillings and they climbed into the back of the Austin, where he immediately put his arms around her and kissed her – a surprisingly passionate kiss, and from the way he looked at her, she knew he wanted more. This was a very different Freddy from the one revealed in his scrappy letters. He missed her, wanted her, and actions were more his way of telling her than writing letters, she thought as the taxi wound its way through the streets of the town.

"Who was the girl?" she asked.

"The WAAF girl? Oh, no one; she'd hurt her arm and I helped her, that's all."

Beth wondered how many other girls he had been kind to in such an affectionate way.

There was no one in the house and he coaxed her upstairs under the pretext of wanting to look at the view.

"Freddy, when were you interested in a view from a window?" she laughed as he pulled her up the lino-covered stairs behind him.

"Who said anything about looking out of a window?" he said, pushing her jacket off her shoulders and kissing her neck, his lips moving lower until they reached the swelling of her breast. "I love you, Beth, and I've been dreaming of this moment."

Alarmed, tempted, afraid of discovery, imprisoned by desire and frightened by what was happening to her, she tried to push him away. His hands were everywhere and eventually fear blocked out desire and she hit him hard, on the side of his face.

Shocked, he stared at her and in a bewildered, little-boy voice said, "Beth, the way you kissed me in the taxi, I thought you wanted me as badly as I want you. Come on; I have to have something to keep me going while I'm away. I might not come back, Beth; you know that, don't you? Hundreds are dying and I could easily be one of them. This is embarkation leave. This could be our last chance."

The dreaded word "embarkation" almost persuaded her, but not quite. It was a vision of Peter that kept appearing in her head that prevented her from succumbing to desire and blackmail, so that she did refuse and allowed her anger to show.

"Stop it! What have you been up to, Freddy Clements? What makes you think you can come back here and treat me like some common tart?"

"I love you, Beth. I'm going a long way from home and I want memories to take with me. What's wicked about that, eh?"

"Three days? I thought embarkation leave was longer?" she said as he sat and stared at her.

"It's all I've got, then I'll be sent abroad and I won't get any home leave then. Please, Beth." He stood and walked towards her, his arms spread wide, but she slipped past him and ran down the stairs.

Whenever they were alone he tried to persuade her to make love, and it was becoming increasingly difficult to refuse. But refuse she would. She didn't want to be in the same position as Lilly. Freddy might tell her how much he loved her, but she had a thinly veiled conviction that his love wasn't strong enough to cope with her having his child. However passionately he loved her, she didn't think Freddy was ready for marriage and responsibility. That brought a shadow of sadness to the three days he was home.

Freddy didn't spend the whole time with Beth. She thought her refusal was the reason for his disappearances but he explained that, faced with a long absence, he wanted to say cheerio to his friends. In fact the only friend he saw was Shirley Downs, and although his leave was actually seven days, he had kept the other four days free. He didn't want to spend it all here, where, besides being uncooperative, Beth restricted his activities. He had grown away from all that. He had quickly discovered that not all girls were like Beth. With the girls who were attracted to the uniform, there wasn't much persuasion needed before moral stands were abandoned.

On the last of his three days he and Beth walked over to St David's Well Bay to the now empty sands. There was no sign now of what had been a holiday beach. The stalls had long gone, and only a few people strolled, perhaps remembering the frenzied activity of the past summer, when the clean golden sands, the varied stalls and amusements had attracted hundreds of families to come and have fun.

Seeing the café with its boarded-up windows shocked him.

"I'd forgotten about the fire," he said. "Did you find out who started it?"

"Not really. But Mam and Dad are convinced that Mrs Downs was responsible," she said.

"What d'you mean, responsible? Was she careless about things? Like leaving the gas burning?"

"No, worse than that. They think she burnt it down deliberately. She hates my parents and accused Granny Moll of stealing her grandfather's business or something. I don't remember the facts, although it's a regularly told story."

"That's a lot of rubbish!" Freddy said angrily. "Mrs Downs wouldn't do anything like that! They shouldn't say such things."

"Mrs Downs accused Granny Moll's grandparents of cheating, of stealing the business from her family."

"Who told you that? Granny Moll, I'll bet! Her grandparents bought it from Mrs Downs's grandparents. How can Mrs Downs resent that? It's all in Granny Moll's head. She made it up!"

"Freddy, it's true, you know it is!" Beth was alarmed at his anger and his refusal to support her.

"Damn it all, Mrs Downs worked for them, didn't she? If they really believed she hated them enough to burn the place, would they have employed her? Just using her as a scapegoat they are, and you're as bad for repeating it. What's Shirley or her mam ever done to you, eh?"

His anger frightened her and she backed away from the furious expression on his face. He ran off then and after a moment's hesitation she hurried after him. A bus came around the corner and was moving off as he reached the bus stop. She slowed down in disbelief as he jumped on it and left her standing there.

She was furious about the way he had treated her, accusing her of lying about Mrs Downs, walking off and leaving her to walk home alone like an abandoned puppy. She walked fast, releasing her anger, but slowed as outrage left her. By the time she had reached home she had calmed down and was able to put his unexpected outburst down to his stress at the end of his leave, and having to go back and face the dangers of the front line. But she did wonder why he was quite so vehement in his protection of Shirley's mother, a woman he barely knew. Unless, as many hinted, Shirley Downs really was more than a girl he occasionally bumped into at the pictures.

Nine

Ronnie and Olive's market stall idea was under way by the end of November, but it was a bad time to begin. Seasonal fruits were finished, apart from a few scruffy apples, the import of bananas and oranges had all but finished permanently, and there were few vegetables to be found.

Leeks and cabbages and carrots and swedes were the mainstay, with potatoes being the most important item they offered. The government was beginning to suggest more ways of using the vegetables that were available, to make them more interesting, but sales were poor and Ronnie and Olive were afraid the stall would only support itself until the spring. Profit was an unlikely outcome.

Olive continued to work at the factory, but helped out on the stall when she could and, to her surprise, began to enjoy it. The bustling market with its hordes of busy shoppers looking for bargains or a commodity in short supply gave her an excitement she had never found on the beach. There were no frantic crowds fooling about and looking for excuses to laugh and shout, just people quietly searching for ways to feed their families. The place hummed with activity whereas the beach had shrieked.

They were situated close to the back entrance to the market hall and close by there were shoe stalls selling bargain-priced footwear and handbags and purses. Another vendor offered remnants of floor covering, mostly linoleum and cheaper imitation, and rugs of various sizes. On occasion there would be a few pieces of carpet at very low prices and, as though by bush telegraph, the news went out and a queue would quickly form.

"If only we were in the other entrance, catching the customers as they come in," Ronnie sighed as a couple of chattering women walked past with their baskets packed high. "I hope we didn't make a mistake."

Olive looked around them.

"No, Ronnie love, I don't believe we did."

"You like working here, don't you?" Ronnie asked her later as she took the money for a few tired-looking tomatoes they had bought from Mr Gregory.

"Yes, I do. I didn't think I would. I imagined the market would be the same as the stalls on the sand, but it isn't. The customers here are more inclined to stop and chat for one thing. When we're busy on the beach I seem to do nothing more than look at their hands, take the money and return the change. I often stop and realise that I haven't looked at a face for ages. And" – she looked at Ronnie, touching his arm, hoping he wouldn't be offended – "I think part of the reason I'm so happy is that it's ours, yours and mine, and we don't have to do what others tell us."

Ronnie had to sit on a high stool for much of the day, but his cheerfulness and ready wit attracted customers and they were soon recognising the same people returning once or twice each week. Their names were unknown and they began to give them nicknames, which they would whisper to each other. One elderly lady always wore a startlingly bright green hat; another carried a basket made from raffia-covered milk-bottle tops sewn together, in which a tiny Pekinese puppy travelled. These women received polite names, but others did not. Adenoids, Woodbine Winnie, Big Nose and Slipper Feet were some of the names they would whisper. Others were named for the words they always used, like "What you got then?" and "Too dear" and, one of their favourites, known to every stall-holder selling food in the hall, "Any throw-outs I can use to make a soup?" These and many others became regulars. Then there were the wounded men who came past on crutches or with a sleeve folded and pinned, and the sad-faced women who looked as though everything it was possible for them to bear had already weighted down their shoulders. There were those with children being carried or walking holding their mothers' skirts for fear of being lost. To these Ronnie and Olive were generous, even though their profits were almost nil.

The war raged on, the bombing killing hundreds and making thousands homeless, far from the boundaries of St David's Well, but touching them all the same.

One lady, whom they had seen passing on several occasions, a fair-haired woman of about twenty, surprised them one day by bringing them a cup of tea each from the café at the entrance where she worked.

"There's cold you look," she said handing them the cups and saucers over the piled-up vegetables. "Have these on me and if you want the same tomorrow I'll bring them over and you can pay at the end of the week. Eleven a.m. and three in the afternoon all right, is it?"

Olive and Ronnie thanked her and the cups of tea and a brief chat were a welcome break in their morning and afternoon. The woman, who was unmarried, was called Janet Copp, and she managed the small market café. She told them some of her story over the first few days.

"I haven't got no family. But," she said thoughtfully, "I suppose I might have cousins somewhere. Mam never said much about them, mind. They moved away years ago. But neighbours hinted at some dark secret. Perhaps Mam did something shameful and was cut off from the rest of the family. Exciting, eh? Just think, they might be rich enough to save me from the boring ol' café. There's lovely that would be."

Olive and Ronnie told her about Lilly expecting a child without naming the father, who was married to someone else.

"Mam and Dad wouldn't dream of refusing help, or cutting her off from the family like that," Ronnie said. "Our Lilly's a part of the family and nothing would be allowed to separate us."

"Ronnie's mother is so kind, even to strangers. She even took in a couple of children who were living rough. They hadn't been abandoned, though. Their parents are dead and they had run away from a children's orphange," Olive explained.

"Thank goodness I was too old to go through that. I'd have hated being cared for with dozens of others in a place like that." She grinned at Ronnie as she collected their empty cups. "Their name isn't Copp, is it?"

"Sorry, but life isn't that tidy I'm afraid," Ronnie smiled. "Carpenter they are and, like you, they'd love to find their family. Not much hope though. They do talk about a sister-in-law and a brother, but we've never been able to find them."

"Pity," Janet sniffed. "I'd like a couple of sisters."

Bleddyn's daughter-in-law, Evelyn, didn't call on him very often. With the work she did involving odd hours, and Bleddyn's house a long way off her regular route, she rarely found herself in that part of town. In his letters, Taff often asked whether she had seen his father but she evaded replying.

Like many others, she was beginning to find the restrictions of wartime life tedious. With Taff away she wouldn't go dancing like many of her friends did; she didn't want even a whisper of trouble to reach him. So there was only the pictures where she went sometimes with Maude and Myrtle and on rare occasions with Audrey and Wilf too. The girls with whom she worked came in most mornings full of the fun they'd had the night before and, although not envious, she felt dull being unable to join in. Listening to the wireless, doing the week's ironing, racing home to catch the shop, it was hardly riveting. There were the letters from Taff of course, but unlike some of the others she didn't want to read out his words to have them mulled over and laughed at.

When one of the girls was celebrating her birthday and asked her to join them, she agreed, and wondered afterwards where her common sense had been at the time. Before the planned night out, she went on one of her rare visits to Bleddyn and found Hannah and her two girls there. Shame, jealousy and embarrassment made her abrupt with her greeting and Hannah stood at once to leave.

"Well, Mr Castle, I'll leave you to talk to Evelyn, shall I? We'll all be down to see you on Sunday, unless you'd like to have tea with us?"

Evelyn stood with a look of impatience on her face as Hannah dressed the children against the cold, discussed final arrangements for Sunday and left.

"Why did you do that? Is there anything wrong?" Bleddyn asked when they were alone.

"Do what?"

"Rush Hannah away like that. What is it you have to tell me that she can't hear?" His voice was slow and soft, but Evelyn sensed the anger.

"Sorry, Dad, but I was disappointed to find her here. She works a few hours in the mornings and evenings, she has plenty of time to visit you. I have to come when I can and I hoped you'd be alone."

"She's very kind and calls often, sometimes bringing me a letter she's had from Johnny."

"Dad, I'm going out tomorrow night, with the girls from the

factory. One of them is eighteen and she's going to join up, so it's a celebration and a farewell."

"Good, you shouldn't be stuck in night after night. Taff wouldn't want that."

"It's only a drink. I wanted to tell you, so you know it's nothing more."

"I hope you enjoy yourself," Bleddyn assured her, forcing a smile. When she left, the smile changed to a frown as he stared at the closing door. He hoped this was not the beginning of trouble. Women who went out without a man, especially in a group, might be tempted to stray out of boredom. Perhaps he ought to visit her more often, make sure everything was still all right.

Maude and Myrtle were intrigued by the story of Janet Copp who, like themselves, had no family. They made Olive and Ronnie repeat it several times, like the children they still were. Although the story had nothing in it to offer them hope, it cheered them to know there were others in a similar state to themselves.

Coming out of the pictures a few days later, standing still to accustom their eyes to the darkness, they heard a voice call, "Hey, Mrs Carpenter, over here!"

The two girls reacted as though in shock. They stared, trying to pierce the darkness and by force of will trying to see the woman who was referred to by their name. Gripping each other's gloved hands, they pushed through the crowd to where they had heard the voice. Fortunately the woman called again, "Mrs Carpenter, yoo hoo!" The two women were all but concealed in the blackness, but they made out the figure of a young woman pushing herself through the closely gathered bodies, making for the person who had called and who was now waving her hands in encouragement.

"She might be our sister-in-law," Myrtle breathed.

Maude dragged Myrtle behind her and followed as the two women set off along the street.

The two women, one of whom was wearing a fur coat, went through the doorway of a public house, the sounds from within bursting forth as people chattered, shouted and laughed. Tinny notes from a piano were heard, and a few were singing a sad song tunelessly. The girls grinned. The discordant, harsh sounds swelled up then stopped abruptly as the doors swung behind them.

The black-out arrangement involved two doors positioned at either end of an angled, covered passageway. Still holding hands, the sisters crept in through the first door and pushed the second open to look into the bar room. They looked around and eventually recognised the two women they had followed. They were at the bar trying to get served by a barman who was determined to serve all the men first. He didn't approve of unaccompanied women in his pub.

"Shall we wait?" Maude suggested, and in the darkness she felt her sister nod her head.

Still looking through the slit, Myrtle gasped and told Maude to look in the corner close to the fire. Around a table about eight women and two soldiers were sitting, and one of the women was Evelyn.

The group were giggling and rosy faced and they saw that one of the soldiers had his arm around Evelyn's shoulder. They couldn't hear what was being said as she tried to move away, but guessed that the others were encouraging Evelyn to have some fun.

The two girls stepped backwards and out into the dark night. They didn't want to see any more, but eventually couldn't resist one more peep. Evelyn was now looking angry and they saw her take a glass of beer belonging to one of the soldiers and pour it over the head of the one who was annoying her. Helpless with laughter, the girls ran out once more into the night.

It was tempting to run home and tell Auntie Audrey what they had seen, but the need to talk to someone bearing their name was too strong. Hiding in the shadows, stifling giggles, they didn't have to wait long. The two women, easily recognised by their voices and the fur coat, came out and they followed.

Having to keep back and occasionally hide, they lost their quarry after a few short cuts through lanes, but found them again waiting at a bus stop. It was almost half-past ten by now and they both knew they should really be going home.

"If we can find out where she lives, we can go back another day," Maude said when Myrtle became worried. "We won't talk to her tonight."

At home Audrey was knitting, stopping every few rows to stand on the front doorstep and listen for sounds of them coming. They had never been this late before. She wished her mother was there. She wouldn't dither, she'd do something.

She gave herself another fifteen minutes before going to tell Marged and Huw that they hadn't returned.

The girls followed the two women on to the bus and asked for the terminus. When the women alighted near a row of small terraced houses outside the town, still apparently oblivious of the girls trotting along behind them, they followed.

The inadequately lit bus lumbered off and before Maude could reach for her sister's hand, they were grabbed roughly. Amid their screams of fright, the women demanded, "What are you doing following us? If my husband has asked you to see what I'm up to, you can tell him—"

Swearing their innocence, the girls cried and promised that they hadn't been sent by anyone.

"We're looking for our brother, and we heard someone call you Mrs Carpenter and we thought—" Maude's voice faded as the woman began to laugh.

"Carpenter? My name isn't Carpenter, it's Callender."

The girls waited for a long time but no bus appeared to take them home, so with only a vague idea of where they were, they set off to walk home. Myrtle was dragging her feet and complaining and Maude tried to carry her so that both girls were exhausted when they eventually turned into Sidney Street.

Something was wrong. There were voices shouting, asking questions, making suggestions, someone was crying and, most remarkable of all, lights were escaping from doorways and streaking across the street. Slowing to a hesitant crawl, they soon realised that every house was open, the neighbours were out in force, some in groups talking, others with torches stabbing the ground in front of them. Everywhere men and women were hurrying around. In a doorway they saw two wardens, who seemed oblivious of the black-out regulation being flouted. Cups of tea were being handed out and men with torches were approaching from a different direction from those setting off.

"God 'elp, Myrtle, they're all looking for us. Auntie Audrey'll kill us!"

It was one a.m. before their story was told and everyone was settled, and Audrey had relieved her fears by telling them off. The last thing they heard before going to sleep was the warden shouting for someone to "put that light out", adding, "You needn't think you can make an 'abit of this, mind!"

* * *

Peter continued to write regularly to Beth, but it was two weeks before Beth heard from Freddy. Then it was a picture postcard and the frank told her it was posted in Blackpool. She wondered what he was doing there. It was a long way from his barracks. The note was the usual scrawl, casual, friendly, with no mention of missing her or with any reference to their brief time together. He didn't refer to his imminent departure either and she began to wonder whether his words were prevarications when he wrote later, this time from his usual address, and told her that another leave might be possible very soon.

Was it loyalty that kept her pretending he was the man she loved? Or was the war a pause in in her life, a time that was not real, a time to hold back and not think too deeply about what was happening to closeness, love and trust? When the world returned to normal, she would remember how much she loved Freddy, wouldn't she? She wouldn't think about Peter every moment. Everything would be fine.

Once the soldiers began training for their posting overseas, they weren't allowed out of camp: she had learned that much by talking to friends. There was the danger of spies learning of their possible movements and passing on information to the enemy. She thought of asking Peter if he knew what might be happening but decided not. Talking about Freddy would be an intrusion, an unwanted, jarring note in their happy hours together.

She and Peter never did anything that Freddy would consider very exciting when Peter managed a few days' leave. When he was free on one of Beth's days off, they walked in the gradually fading colours of autumn, talking, stopping sometimes for refreshment at an inn or café, or taking a picnic and finding a sheltered corner of a local beach. Between times they wrote long, chatty letters, broadening their knowledge of each other, growing closer, but without the complications of love. They kissed on meeting and when they parted, but rarely did more than hold hands otherwise. Beth knew it was because of the engagement ring she wore and foolishly began to feel irritation with Freddy: resentment, too, for being there, clearly visible on her finger, while he was unlabelled and free to do what he wanted.

She remembered with surprisingly little pain the kiss he had given the WAAF girl on the train, and the way he had leapt to the defence of Shirley's mother, Mrs Downs. He was not being faithful, something deep inside her told her that.

She talked to Lilly about her doubts and Lilly advised her to tell him goodbye.

"I can't, Lilly. Not when he's on the point of going overseas. I'd feel so guilty, him not having anyone to write to him. They all need someone at home who cares for them. It gives them hope, being able to plan for when the war's over."

"And you've just told me you suspect there's someone else he's seeing!" Lilly said in exasperation. "Why pretend you're the only one who'll write to him? Are you the only one to help him spend his leave? I doubt it, and so do you if you're honest. Why don't you face facts, Beth? Freddy's seeking pastures new in more ways than one and only bothering to write when he wants money. Peter is here, asking nothing of you, writing to you, and spending every moment he can with you. How much more do you need before you stop kidding yourself that Freddy loves you?"

Using her pregnancy as an excuse, Lilly rarely worked. She appeared to be busy helping Marged in the house, but in fact did very little. Every afternoon she insisted she needed a rest, and most evenings she either went to the pictures or visited friends. One of her friends was Hannah, for a while at least.

Hannah worked longer hours now Josie was back at school and Marie was at nursery school, but she welcomed Lilly whenever she called, even though she was usually very busy. At first they talked happily about the birth of Lilly's baby and discussed ideas for making and knitting the little garments she would need, but Hannah began to lose patience when she realised that although they talked, nothing was ever achieved by Lilly, only by others doing things for her. Time, she thought, for some serious discussion.

"When are you going to stop feeling sorry for yourself and get organised?" Hannah asked when Lilly had sat in her room all afternoon drinking tea and talking about the unfairness of life, that she had chosen to fall in love with a married man.

"I'm not sorry for myself, I don't go screaming to his wife do I? I'm sorting myself out without causing trouble like some would in my situation," Lilly protested.

"Sorting yourself out does not mean leaning heavily on your

mother. Sorting yourself out is getting up and doing what you can to prepare for this baby! How are you going to support it? Have you thought of a job? You should be using these months to train or at least decide what you'll do."

"I can work on the beach in the summer like always," Lilly defended.

"That isn't a job. You take the wage, but from what I understand, you don't do much to earn it."

"Why are you being so unkind? I thought you were my friend," Lilly said tearfully.

"I am, and I hope you value my friendship enough to listen to what I'm saying. I do like you, I would like you to be my friend, my real friend, but you aren't even a friend to yourself, living like you do."

"I dream of having a decent job sometimes," Lilly said. "But working on the beach year after year with Mam and Dad has made me think of work as boredom. How would you like it, doing the same thing day after day?"

"I clean up after other people, the same old chores, day after day after day," Hannah said softly. "Boredom? You don't know what boredom is until you've cleaned floors and walls and lavatories, with the only variety being the different sorts of litter or the colour of the soap."

"Lavatories? Ugh! How can you do it, Hannah?"

"Because of my girls. I do whatever is necessary to keep them fed, clothed and happy." Hannah spoke softly and stared at Lilly, allowing the words to sink in. "They are my responsibility, my joy, my life and I'll do anything for them."

"Having parents who can afford to keep me makes all that noble stuff unnecessary," Lilly replied.

"Until you develop some pride."

"Fat lot of pride in cleaning lavatories!" she retorted as she flounced off.

With Hannah's words ringing in her head, Lilly went for a long walk, through the park, passing places where she and Phil had stopped to kiss, remembering how wonderful it had been. Overwhelming self-pity enveloped her. She hadn't needed Hannah's words to tell her how lazy she was. All her other friends had work, many of them in munitions factories or other work that contributed to the war effort. Even Auntie Audrey went around collecting money for National Savings and was a volunteer fire-watcher, besides running the big house where Granny Moll had lived all her married life.

The baby wasn't due until May. She could work through the winter, and suddenly she knew she wanted to. She had to put aside her easy acceptance of idleness, using the excuse that she was different, that it was her basic character. The question was, with the fish-and-chip shop shop still making her feel queasy, what could she do?

It was the beach, the place she said she hated, that gave her employment. Two of the cafés remained open during the winter. They had small rooms which offered teas and snacks during the summer, but in the winter they made a reasonable living by opening the top room, which was enormous, for dances, tea dances and, on occasion, celebration dinners for various firms. Lilly went there and offered her services as waitress and occasional kitchen hand.

The wages were small, but there was the promise of tips, which appealed. She would be so charming that the tips would give her baby all he or she needed. But she would have to avoid mention of that or she wouldn't get the job in the first place!

Hannah loved Johnny Castle but she still had no illusions about him marrying her. Although he had declared his love for her and had told her he wanted them to marry, he had also said he wanted to delay the announcement in case people thought he was marrying her on the rebound from his broken engagement to Eirlys Price.

Eirlys had been in London for almost a year and he still hadn't made the announcement. With two children and him being so much younger, she had to settle for friendship. Johnny was a good friend. From the morning they had met outside the greengrocer when her paper carrier bag had collapsed and sent all her vegetables rolling down the street and he had stopped to help her, they had been friends.

He had walked home with her to the house where she lived with her parents, using two rooms and with restricted use of the kitchen. He didn't need any explanation of their attitude. Their disapproval showed on their faces and in the way they spoke to her and the little girls, their granddaughters. They were embarrassed and angry at having a daughter who was divorced and bringing up children without the father's presence or help.

"Shamed they are," she had told Johnny one day, when she had been forbidden to allow the girls to play in the garden. Johnny had asked her to explain.

"I had a husband who refused to work," she began. "He spent most of his time in the snooker hall, or in friends' houses playing cards. At other times, when he could find the money, he was in the pubs, or at dances, and . . ." She hesitated before he nodded for her to tell him more. "There were other women, and he didn't even try to hide them from me." She avoided telling him the full story of how he had hit her in drunken rages, and how her parents refused to support her.

"When I sued for divorce, he forced himself on me one day and, well, the result was Josie. Another time, when he was really angry with me for the statement I'd made, he did it again and I had Marie. Born out of fear and anger they were, yet they're the sweetest, gentlest of girls."

"Poor love," Johnny had said. "But I don't understand why your parents aren't more helpful. Surely they love their granddaughters?"

"They reckon they were born out of wedlock, as, officially, we were separated. So that makes me a loose woman. They don't believe rape is possible between husband and wife, even in those circumstances."

Hannah thought of that terrible confession as she opened one of Johnny's letters. In it, he asked whether the garden was still out of bounds. Holding the letter, she went through to the kitchen and asked her mother if the girls could play outside for a while before supper.

Tight-lipped, her mother shook her head. "I don't want you flaunting your shame for all the neighbours to see."

She wrote a cheerful letter to Johnny, ignoring his question and giving him details of a trip the three of them had made to see his father, followed by a fish-and-chip supper for herself and the girls, served by Beth. "Your father is so kind to me; I can't tell you how much it means to be able to talk and laugh, without feeling ashamed of showing happiness," she wrote. Then she tore that piece off. She didn't want to sound even slightly dejected. She wanted to visualise him reading the letter and smiling. Instead she wrote about something amusing that Josie had told her and ended on a happy note, before signing it "your loving friend, Hannah".

To make extra money, she did sewing for various people. She had worked as an alteration hand in one of the larger gown shops before her marriage, but with the two girls she couldn't return to the shop and they weren't willing for her to do the work on their very expensive gowns at home, in case of accidents.

She had promised to finish a dress for one of Josie's friends and it had taken much longer than she had expected. Already late with some other work she had promised for the following week, she was sitting near the window, concentrating on the smocking that would decorate the front of the pretty yellow party dress for the six-year-old, when there was a knock at the door.

Johnny was home on leave and after seeing his father and changing his clothes, he had come straight away to see Hannah. The door was answered by her mother, who left him waiting on the doorstep while she told Hannah he was there.

"Johnny! I didn't know you were coming home!" She smiled and hugged him as her mother quickly pushed the door shut so no one could see them.

"Can you get out for an hour?" he asked. "You don't have to meet the girls until half-past three, do you?"

"I have some sewing to finish by tomorrow, but, yes, of course I can spare an hour!" She collected a coat and looked at the dress with its half-finished smocking. She would have to work half the night to finish it anyway.

They walked hand in hand through the small park, where, wrapped up against the autumn chill, children played and mothers stood in groups.

"Dad said you go down and show him my letters," he said. "Best I just write the one and you can share it." He grinned to show he was teasing.

"Oh, no. Don't stop writing to me, please! I look forward to your letters so much, and besides, your father likes to have a second news report to know you're safe and well."

"He likes you calling to see him too."

"Does he? I hope so."

"Thanks, Hannah. He's very much alone these days, with Taff and me in the army and the beach no longer filling his time. He has the fish-and-chip shop, but the clientele isn't the same. At the beach everyone is out for a good time, there's laughter and nonsense as they forget the tragedy of the war and have fun. The people who queue for their supper talk about nothing else but the latest war news and who is dead or injured. He finds it very depressing."

"Thank goodness he has Evelyn. Taff's wife calls often, doesn't she?"

"She used to, but this winter the war seems to have changed everything. She works in a factory and goes out with the girls a couple of times a week, and just calls on Dad when she happens to be passing."

After that brief walk before rushing back to meet the girls, Hannah felt more secure in her relationship with Johnny. Nothing important had been said, but his fondness for her was more apparent, and when they parted, his kiss was more than the usual affectionate salute of friends, containing the promise of something more.

She felt more secure, but as she allowed her imagination to roam, also more afraid. She didn't know how she would cope with a relationship with Johnny, or anyone else, once they reached the stage of making love. Her experience of love-making had been so unhappy. But she pushed the thought aside, her emotions like a switchback ride.

How could she imagine Johnny loving her? She was older by eight years and she had nothing to offer. Johnny was living far away from home, in an artificial situation with men from every strata of life teaching him things he would never have learned if life had remained normal. He needed her, but only while he was living away from home, afraid and lonely, where contact from the real world was desperately needed. Any day he could meet someone younger and without the trappings of children, an ex-husband and difficult parents, someone young and trouble free with whom he could live happily ever after.

The thought wouldn't go away as she sat into the early hours finishing the smocking. Ever afterwards, smocking on a yellow dress reminded her of that solemn night when she faced the fact that Johnny was unlikely to ever be more than a loving friend.

She finished the dress and took the small payment, wondering why people refused to pay a reasonable portion of the money charged by a shop when the same work was done in the back room of a terraced house. War changed many things, but not attitudes like that, she thought wryly.

Lilly started work at the café at nine thirty the following

Monday. She was half an hour late but this was excused, she thought, by the fact she was unused to finding a moment to wash with the rest of the family already in their routine. She smilingly told her boss that once the family had accepted that she was a working girl too, things would improve.

After telling her three times to hurry and constantly having to remind her to go at once when someone entered and sat at a table, she was told, not very politely, that she would not be needed the following day.

She smiled without rancour and told the boss it was for the best. She wasn't used to having to rush. She then told her parents that someone else had applied and been given the job and they had forgotten to tell her she wasn't needed. Then she happily settled to read the magazines she had bought and asked Beth to make her a cup of tea. Her burst of heroic industry had fizzled out like the proverbial damp squib.

Freddy managed to get a weekend pass but he didn't write to tell Beth. Instead he telephoned the paper shop and told Shirley.

"I can't meet you in St David's Well, mind," he said conspiratorially. "You'll have to meet me somewhere out of town."

Boldly, Shirley suggested the Grantham, a rather run-down hotel that had once been as grand as its name implied.

"It's a hell of a long way out," he said.

"We could stay overnight," she said as the pips went. She stood by the phone, ignoring the customers that were patiently waiting to be served and, as she expected, the phone rang again and a breathless Freddy said, "Did you mean it?"

"Of course. I'll book for us, shall I? Friday till Sunday?"

"Well, yes, but—"

He didn't have the chance to say more, as Shirley interrupted him with, "Meet you there then." She smilingly replaced the receiver and went to serve her customers.

Serve Beth right, she thought as she looked up the number of the Grantham to arrange the booking. If she doesn't know how to keep someone like Freddy Clements happy, she can move over for someone who does!

Myrtle was slowly making progress in school and, to her surprise, became a bit of a celebrity, once her story about living off her wits and sleeping in an abandoned stable rippled through the classrooms. She began to use her experiences during the writing lesson, impressing her classmates by asking the teacher how to spell "orphan", "abandoned" and "deprived", all words she had overheard Granny Moll and Auntie Audrey whisper when they were talking about her and Maude. Her writing was still large and untidy, but she began to practice after school and Audrey took great pleasure in helping her.

"Why are you so determined to write well?" Audrey asked one day. "You never practice your sums like you used to, and they're equally important."

"I want to put a letter in the paper when I'm old enough, asking if anyone knows where our brother and sister-in-law are," Myrtle explained.

Audrey hugged her and told her that if she thought it would do any good she would do that for her at once.

"Then will you, please? They could be living near and not know how to find us."

A letter to the editor of the local paper resulted in a photograph of both girls appearing in the paper with an article explaining how they had come to live in Sidney Street with the Pipers.

"Damn me," Huw grumbled. "When will I be allowed to use my own name? We're the Castles. And I'd like people to know it, right?"

The argument about the name of Piper's Café wouldn't go away. Marged insisted that the tradition was important, and it was such a well-known name that it would cause confusion to change it, but Huw argued that no one called Piper worked the stalls and cafés any more. "Castle's, it should be," he insisted with increasing frustration over his wife's stubbornness.

"Castle's Café," Marged sneered. "It sounds like something from Comic Cuts!"

"Then call it just Castle's."

"On a beach? It's so daft it'll seem like a joke!"

The café was almost back to normal now. The building work was completed and a new fridge and a larger cooker had been installed. This had caused another argument, but one which Huw had won.

"There'll be more and more visitors now travel is restricted, what with petrol getting scarce and the trains being needed for the transport of soldiers and the rest," he prophesied. "There's this meeting in town of all the people involved with holidays, not just us café owners but landladies and that newly formed entertainment committee. Rumour has it that the government is already talking about big campaigns to persuade people to spend their holidays at home. We've got to be prepared for the opening next May. Really prepared. It's no good waiting till then and finding we need a bigger cooker." So Marged had agreed.

"I miss your Granny Moll," Marged told Beth when they went to see the newly restored café. "She always had the last word and it made everything easier. However seriously your father and I disagreed, we both had to accept her final word. Now we seem to disagree on everything and there's no one to help us settle it."

"The new sign isn't up yet," Beth remarked, looking up at the front.

"That's something else we can't agree on," Marged said. "It's always been Piper's and your father wants to change it to Castle's."

Looking down at the deserted sands below, Beth grinned and said, "Castles in the air, eh?"

"Daft name, Castle's."

"You're Mrs Castle, I'm Bethan Castle, you aren't ashamed of it are you?"

"Of course not! What an idea."

"Dad probably thinks you are."

"Don't be silly," Marged said dismissively, but Beth continued to look at her.

"There's only Auntie Audrey and if she eventually marries Wilf . . . Why don't you do it as a surprise, Mam? I think Dad's right, Castle's it should be."

"No!"

That evening the subject of the new name came up again and to Beth and Audrey's alarm the argument was louder and more unpleasant than ever before.

"You've already ordered it?" Huw said angrily. "You've no right, Marged. This is a family business. It belongs to Bleddyn as well as the rest of us. We all contribute and we all have a say. We're supposed to talk about things, not watch you go out and do what you want."

"Forget it, Huw, the sign's going up and that's the end of it."

"Don't do it," Huw warned. "Or I won't wait for Mrs Downs to burn it down again, I'll damned well burn it down myself!"

"It's Piper's. That's final."

"Then you work it without me. You never listen to me, do you? If you hadn't employed that Downs woman against my wishes this wouldn't have happened and we wouldn't be arguing like this. Damn it all, I might just do it, too," he said, staring at her and striking his thumb against the wheel of his lighter. "Down to you the fire was, and I'll never let you forget it."

Lilly, who was struggling to knit a pair of tiny socks, burst into tears.

"What now?" Huw said, exasperated.

"Don't argue about burning the place down," Lilly sobbed.

"Joking he was, girl. As if one of us Pipers would burn down our own place," Marged soothed, at which point Lilly cried even louder.

"It was me," she wailed. "I went to the café and – the man I was with – left a cigarette burning, I know he did and that was how it was burnt down and it's all my fault."

Beth and Marged stared at her in disbelief. Only Huw spoke.

"Thank God you didn't own up before the insurance paid out!"

Lilly took a lot of calming as she went on to tell them she felt responsible for Granny Moll's heart attack and death.

"I'm not thrilled to be told that you and this man, whoever he is, crept into the café and—" Huw couldn't finish the sentence. "But I still think that Mrs Downs had something to do with it. There was something about her face, the smirk she wore like a badge."

"It started in the corner behind the door where we used to sit," wailed Lilly.

"Just near the letter box," he pointed out.

"Yes."

"Where people were in the habit of pushing rubbish through."

"Yes," she said again.

"Then that's most likely what happened," Marged said, guessing Huw's intention of exonerating their distressed daughter.

In Beth's next letter to Freddy she told him that Lilly thought she might have been responsible for the fire and that they were all sorry that they had accused Mrs Downs. She also told Peter's father when she went to Goose Lane.

"Don't tell anyone else," Mr Gregory warned. "You could get

your father into real trouble if the insurance people think there's been intent to defraud."

"It isn't certain," Beth told him. "She only told us that she and this mystery man used to go into the café after hours and sometimes smoke a cigarette. Dad still believes it was Mrs Downs, because of her grudge against the Castles."

"Best if you think so too. Saves complications."

They walked over to see the donkeys in Sally Gough's field and Beth helped give them their bran and potatoes. She watched while Mr Gregory examined each one, talking to them as though they were friends.

"I saw Mrs Downs's daughter last week – Shirley, isn't it?" Mr Gregory said as they walked back to Goose Lane.

"She works in the paper shop," Beth explained, "and they live above the shop."

"She was a long way from home then! I was delivering a new farm gate in one of the villages and she was coming out of the Grantham. I thought I saw Freddy with her, but I must have been mistaken; so many men are in uniform it's easy to make a mistake."

"What would Freddy be doing at the Grantham?" Beth laughed. "If he had some leave he'd come home."

"Of course he would, home as fast as he could with a pretty girl like you waiting for him." He spoke brightly but he wore a frown. It had been Freddy. He had been too close for him to have made a mistake. And he could guess why he and Shirley Downs had been there. No mistake about that either.

Beth sensed Mr Gregory's unease and that evening she wrote to Freddy asking why he hadn't come home when he had had leave. She also asked what he had been doing in the Grantham in the village of Gorsebank. She didn't mention Shirley Downs. She waited with something bordering on detached amusement for his reply, vaguely wondering why his behaviour was no longer capable of hurting her.

Freddy received her letter and thought carefully about how to handle it. He eventually decided on a devious plan. Basically, he would write as though he had not yet received her letter.

"Dear Beth," he began.

> I was sent out for some extra training last weekend and we were staying in digs with some of the locals in the village

called Gorsebank. You'll never guess who I bumped into? Mrs Downs's daughter Shirley! We had a drink in some pub there, a bit scruffy it was, mind, but the beer was welcome.

He signed it just "Freddy" and Beth put it on the table for the family to see. Lilly picked it up and said, "D'you still think you're the only one to write to him? They must have arranged it somehow!"

Beth didn't reply, but she knew Lilly was right. Freddy was a cheat and an accomplished liar, but she still felt unable to tell him goodbye. It was the war, the knowledge that tomorrow you might be dead, that was why he was cheating on her. Once the war was over, everything would be fine.

She kept telling herself this and at times almost believed it. But as she tried to envisage a future with Freddy she knew she was lying to herself. She was not so feeble that she could pretend to feel the same about him. When he was home and safe, she knew they were unlikely to stay together. Too much had happened to them both. The idea of telling Freddy goodbye no longer gave her pain, just sadness, and guilt at the way she felt about Peter Gregory.

She settled down to write to him. She would keep writing, keep up the pretence. She would post it when she went to start her lunchtime shift at the fish-and-chip shop. Still called Piper's, the name was still a contentious issue between her parents. It was unlikely that she would change her own name from Castle to Clements. Her eyes blurred with tears as she thought defiantly that she didn't like the name anyway. Bethan Castle was good enough for her. And Mrs Freddy Clements was not.

Ten

Winter slowly drifted in, dusk settling in over the town a little sooner each day, filling the corners with shadows, making silhouettes of the once vibrant trees. Spiky remnants of flowers gave gardens a neglected look, a devastation that had taken only weeks to achieve yet had the appearance of age-old abandonment.

Children no longer pleaded to be taken to the beach, and street games came into their own. Hopscotch numbers were drawn on pavements, skipping ropes were unearthed and long lengths were held across the road in deep loops for children to jump in and out, counting and chanting well-known rhymes. Home-made whips sent coloured tops spinning, hoops made from wheel rims were bowled along with small sticks, and bogie carts were already doing the rounds, their owners begging rubbish for the bonfire that, this year, would not be allowed, though the children hoped to sneak away into the fields, defy the ban and outrun the wardens.

Fire-watchers and wardens were on patrol each evening and Audrey went around the streets selling National Savings and collecting for a Christmas savings scheme she and Marged had always organised for the neighbours. She was out very late one evening, and she was alarmed when she realised that it was past nine o'clock and she hadn't given Myrtle and Maude their supper.

At fifteen, Maude was quite capable of finding food for herself and Myrtle, but she never did. With food rationed, she was well aware of how carefully the day-to-day use of commodities like butter and sugar and meats were apportioned. Audrey organised the food strictly, and only she knew what they could use each day. Over-generous help-yourself was not possible; it could make the time spent waiting for Friday, which was ration day, seem very long.

She dashed into the house apologising for making them wait, but when she pushed open the door to the living room, where there was always a fire burning, the room was empty. Filled with remorse now, she ran up to their bedroom, ashamed that they had put themselves to bed hungry. The beds were neatly made and empty.

"Oh no," she murmured, "surely they haven't gone off again to look for that brother!"

A search of the house, a hasty visit to Marged and Huw, even a foolish run around the street calling their names produced no response. She was convinced that this time they had run away.

Ronnie and Olive told her not to worry.

"Why should they leave a comfortable home, Auntie Audrey? It isn't as though they have anywhere else to go. They'll be back soon." They went back to their card game unconcerned.

"Of course they haven't run away! They haven't taken anything with them, for a start," Huw said, to calm everyone down. "I bet they heard something that they thought would lead them to this fictional brother and sister-in-law, and they took off, too impatient to wait for you."

"More likely they've gone to look for you, Audrey," Marged offered.

"I was out so late," Audrey wailed. "Where will they be?"

"They were talking to Olive and our Ronnie earlier when we went up to borrow a candle for the outside lav," Huw offered. "Perhaps they'll know something."

"I've already asked and they said not to worry."

"Go and ask them again," Marged suggested.

Back to the house, and a knock on the door of Olive and Ronnie's room resulted in the information that the girls had been interested in Olive's talk about Janet Copp, the lady who worked in the market café, and had learnt that, like them, she was without a family. "I bet they've gone to see her."

"Poor little kids," Marged sighed. "Desperate they are for this sister-in-law."

They were standing at the gate of Audrey's front garden when they heard the sound of singing, punctuated by footsteps. Hope brought them all out on to the pavement in time to see Janet Copp arm in arm with Myrtle and Maude dancing and singing, "Show me the way to go home".

"I hope you weren't worried," Janet called cheerfully, "only we had a bit of a chat. They told me about their name and we compared what we knew of our families, but found no connection. Then we walked over to your Bleddyn's chip shop. Hungry they were."

When the girls were in bed, Janet explained.

"They thought that as I had no family and had narrowly escaped being sent to a home, I might be their sister-in-law, or know something of her and their brother," she said sadly. "Desperate they are and me unable to help."

"Thanks for talking to them. I think they both know it's hopeless but a dream is hard to discard," Audrey said. "They don't even know his name, this brother they want to find. I don't know whether he really exists."

"They seem convinced about having a sister-in-law, mind. But even the name they were given could be wrong. Things get muddled so easily. A spelling mistake perhaps, then someone else thinking to correct it and filling in a different name altogether. I'm called Cope sometimes and have to point it out."

The fortune teller, who had a stall on the beach until the end of summer, continued to trade. Sarah lived in two rooms on Sunnyside Road, and her living-cum-consulting room was bedecked with scarves and shawls and sparkling mirrors, and stars and moons and many other mysterious symbols. Low-wattage light bulbs draped with thin veils of cloth added to the mood and people who came quickly absorbed the atmosphere and were ready to believe anything.

Sarah was standing on her front doorstep one evening when Maude and Myrtle passed on their way home from the pictures. A glimpse of the interior made Myrtle want to hurry past, but Maude held her back.

"Can you help us find our sister-in-law and our brother?" she asked, her heart racing with her own temerity.

"Come with money and your friend, Audrey Piper, and I'll seek knowledge from within the crystal ball," the woman said, before Myrtle grabbed her sister's arm and pulled her away.

"You'll never guess what Maude did," Myrtle said as they burst through the door and greeted Audrey. "She went up to that gypsy woman and asked her to find our sister-in-law."

"Oh? What did she say?" Audrey asked, smiling at Wilf who was chuckling at their story.

"She said we have to go with you and take some money, and she'd insult the crystal. What d'you think she means? Will she help us?" Myrtle asked in a hushed voice. "Will she find them, d'you think? If we pay her?"

"It's *consult* the crystal," Maude said scathingly, "and of course she will. You only have to look at her to know she's clever about such things."

"Then why didn't we ask her before?" Myrtle demanded.

"Don't get your hopes up, girls," Wilf said. "She might have the gift of seeing, I'm sure some have, but there are also those who are cheats and just take your money, talk a lot and tell you nothing."

"But we'll try?" Maude asked hopefully.

"We'll see what Auntie Marged has to say."

Maude's shoulders drooped. "She'll tell us no," she said sadly.

Surprisingly, Marged, again defying Huw's common sense, agreed.

"Where's your sense, woman?" Huw protested. "Gullible they are – like you and your Audrey – and they'll believe everything the woman says and expect miraculous results. We don't want them upset for nothing. Best they forget they ever had a sister-in-law. We don't even know if that's true, do we?"

"It won't do any harm. We have to show the poor dears we're willing to help."

"Daft nonsense. I should have said yes, shouldn't I? You'd have been sure to say no then, contrary woman that you are," Huw muttered.

Freddy came home on a "forty-eight" and Beth dreaded his arrival. She didn't know what to say to him. Should she mention Shirley Downs again? Or just pretend she hadn't given her a thought since Freddy was last home?

It was Freddy who broached the subject.

"Would you mind if Shirley came to the pictures with us tonight?" he asked.

"The pictures? Why are we going to the pictures? You've only got a few hours before going back to barracks. I thought we'd go somewhere where we can talk." She didn't see the pained expression on Freddy's face at the prospect of "talk". "And why should Shirley Downs want to tag along? She has friends of her own, surely?"

"You don't like Shirley, do you? And your father hates her mam. Have you ever wondered why?" Freddy asked.

"I suppose it was the story about Granny Moll's grandfather buying Piper's from Shirley's great-grandfather. The place being a mess and Piper's working the business up from nothing."

"That isn't what I've been told. The Downs were cheated."

"Granny Moll said the place was run down and filthy, and her grandfather bought it from Mrs Downs's grandfather and built it up. Mrs Downs and her daughter are talking rubbish. Piper's Café's success is due to my family's hard work, not robbery."

"And there's nothing else?"

"I haven't heard anything more, but I think my father upset her again somehow. No one will talk about it. Mam gets all tight-lipped if I ask, so I've given up being curious about it all. They dislike each other, that's plain to see. And, at first, Mam and Dad believed Mrs Downs set fire to the café as some sort of revenge. That's all I know."

"There is something else, but Shirley doesn't know the story either."

"Talk about us often, do you? Is that why you go out with her?" she asked. "So you can solve the mystery and get hold of some sordid gossip about the Pipers and the Castles?"

"I don't 'go out' with her!" he protested. "We've met by accident once or twice, that's all."

She tried, but couldn't believe him. "I don't think I want to go to the pictures tonight," she said, "but you can go if you like. It's rare for me to have a Saturday off; Uncle Bleddyn only agreed because you were coming home. I'd rather spend it somewhere else. A walk perhaps?"

She was horrified when he accepted her invitation for him to go without her.

"You wouldn't mind?" he asked cheerfully. "Only I promised Shirley that we'd go. Come on, love, come with us. You'll enjoy it. We can have some chips after, and—" He grinned as he realised what he'd said. "No, not chips; you see enough of them, don't you?"

"Quite enough."

"All right, then," he retorted. "and remember I get enough

of walking, usually wearing heavy boots and weighed down with kit."

They went to the pictures.

"Why don't you tell him goodbye?" Lilly asked when a despondent Beth came in. "He doesn't even try to hide the fact that he's more interested in Shirley, does he? Give him more than you do, does she?" she asked coarsely.

"Freddy is sorry for her; she doesn't have much of a life, living in that flat with her mother, working all hours selling papers, up at the crack of every dawn and delivering them too when the boys don't turn up."

"Aw! Pity for her too," Lilly mocked. "What about the long hours we work over the beach week after week in the summer?"

Beth declined to argue about just how much of that work involved Lilly.

"I bet she sees more of his money than you do too," Lilly went on. "In fact, I bet you paid for the pictures and for the sweets he bought her."

"Don't be daft," Beth protested.

Lilly grinned. "I've seen you putting postal orders into the letters you write."

Eynon was still on the run. Since leaving the farmer's house near Aberystwyth, he had continued to sleep rough, staying away from habitation except at night, when he would go searching for food.

The closest he'd been to home was when a lorry driver offered him a lift one evening. He had approached as close as he dared to Sidney Street and had stood for long hours, just watching the comings and goings of his family.

He saw Mam and Dad, arguing as usual, go in with some shopping. He watched as Audrey and Maude and Myrtle set off to collect National Savings, smiled at the warden's "put that light out" and marvelled at the ordinariness of it all.

Later he dared to walk through the streets, half hoping, half dreading being seen by someone he knew. He knew he was reaching the stage when to be caught would be a relief. He couldn't walk into a police station and give himself up, but knew he would be relieved to be caught and taken back.

The only person he met that he knew was Mrs Downs. She stared at him and said clearly, "Well, if it isn't Eynon Castle."

Panic overwhelmed him and he said quickly, "No, I'm not, I'm Frankie Davies." He tried to walk away but she caught hold of his overcoat and pulled him towards her. It was then that he realised that she was drunk.

"Frankie Davies I am and I've never heard of this Evan, or whatever you called him."

Confused, the woman released her hold and wandered away. Lowering his head, Eynon went through the lanes intent on putting as much distance as he could between himself and St David's Well. It had answered one question for him. He might be a bit low, but he was not ready yet to give himself up!

He had regretted joining up before he was made to, and now he regretted even more the foolish impulse that had led to his absence without leave. "AWOL", it sounded daring and a bit of fun, but he knew the punishment he would receive if he were caught would be far from funny.

Turning off the quiet road as the sillhouette of buildings appeared in the distance, he walked along the hedgerow and found the bedraggled remnants of a haystack. This would have to do for a resting place until the early hours, when he would be able to wander around and find something to eat undetected. He was lucky, there was a piece of tattered tarpaulin which had kept a section of the rotting hay relatively dry. Luxury indeed, he thought sadly, as he curled up and settled to sleep.

His head throbbed alarmingly, the wound still refusing to heal properly due to the knocks it received when he went in and out of his various shelters. He'd get it seen to one day, when he was ready to face up to the punishment that awaited him.

Maude and Myrtle looked eagerly at the local paper, read the letter they had submitted and waited hopefully for a response. None came. A week later, Audrey took them to see Sarah.

The late autumn day was bright, with a watery sun creating shadows reminiscent of summer. Walking into the overheated and dark room was unnerving.

The old woman looked into their palms for a long time, glancing up, dark intelligent eyes twinkling, smiling at them as if highly amused at their nervousness. She told them only good things about their future. "Love and laughter, comfort and ease," was her summing up. "A very good reading, the best I've seen all this week. Go, children, and be happy." Then she removed the black velvet cover from her crystal ball and stared into its depths for a long time.

"You will find the answer to your question in the grave," she said briefly as she held out her hand and stood, dismissing them. Audrey placed the coins on the outstretched hand and, thanking Sarah, led the girls out again into the bright sun.

"Did she mean we won't know till we're dead?" a frightened Myrtle asked.

"I thought she'd be able to tell us," Maude said sadly. "Uncle Huw said she'd talk a lot and say nothing; I know what he meant now!"

"Why didn't she tell us?" Myrtle asked Beth when they returned home and told her about their expedition.

"Perhaps she did," Beth said. "I think she meant that you'll have to search in the cemetery, you know, look at the names on the graves."

Accepting that the cemetery was where they would find the graves of their parents they pleaded with Audrey to take them. She adamantly refused.

"No! I will never set foot in the place, now or ever! So don't you dare ask me again."

The girls were surprised at her implacability. She rarely refused to help. But on this she remained firm. They put it down to the fact that as she was quite old, she had a fear of the place where she would certainly end up.

Huw promised to take them, but when Marged heard of their plan she persuaded him not to go. Eventually it was Beth who set off one Sunday afternoon for the cemetery with two subdued and anxious girls, without telling either Marged or Audrey where they were heading.

A horse and cart approached as they walked hand in hand, arms swinging, along the road towards the cemetery gates, and Beth was delighted to see Peter and his father riding on the pony and cart, waving to them enthusiastically. The cart was filled with bales of hay which they were taking up to the donkeys' winter home.

"Climb up if you can and we'll give you a lift," Mr Gregory called. And with some apprehension regarding their Sunday best dress and coat and shoes, Beth sat between Peter and his father on the board seat and the girls laughingly found places for themselves between the hay bales.

"Which first, cemetery or donkeys?" Peter asked, when told of their destination.

"Donkeys," Myrtle said at once. She was afraid of the gloomy place visible over the wall from their high perch, and besides, if yet another disappointment was in store for them, she wanted to delay it.

A chill wind blew as they left the houses and rode out to the field where the donkeys lived. They were in a huddle, heads together, backsides to the wind. "Like a group of gossiping women," Peter said, making the girls laugh.

While Bernard Gregory attended to the daily feed of hot bran and potatoes, Myrtle and Maude admired the donkeys and Beth and Peter talked.

"Heard from Freddy lately?" Peter asked.

"Just the usual scribbled note, nothing of interest," she replied.

"How much longer are you going to put up with him making a fool of you, Beth?" he asked softly.

"He's so far away from home, how do I know how he's coping with it all? How can I judge when I've no idea what's happening to him? We aren't all natural letter writers like you are, Peter."

"You say that as though I should be ashamed of my ability to write when life is difficult."

"Peter, I love your letters. I read them again and again, they're full of interest, amusement and – and—"

"Affection?" he offered.

"And affection," she agreed with a smile. "Please don't stop writing."

"But it's Freddy from whom you want to hear, isn't it?"

"Freddy isn't the most thoughtful of men, I know that, but we've been together all our life and I can't abandon him at a time when he's unable to defend himself against my decision, can I?"

"Does he correspond with anyone else?" He meant Shirley Downs but it would have been indelicate to name her.

Beth smiled to herself. "Correspond" indeed. She would have said "write".

"Why are you smiling?" he asked.

"I like the way you say things," she replied.

"And does he? Keep in touch with anyone else?"

"His mother and father of course, and I think he might write to Shirley Downs. He feels sorry for her. Her mother is deeply unhappy, mixed up, disappointed with life, and she sometimes drinks heavily. It's difficult for Shirley to cope with it."

"Freddy can be thoughtful at times, then," Peter said pointedly. "Look, I know I haven't the right to say anything, to interfere in your private life, but don't let him make a fool of you, Beth. You're worth more than that."

Before she could reply, the girls shouted with laughter and, turning, they saw that Mr Gregory's arm had been knocked by an enthusiastic animal and the food he was carrying had spilled on the grass.

"Damn and blast it, Dorothy, when will you learn to wait for it?" Mr Gregory said as the donkeys pushed him aside and began to eat.

Beth and Peter said very little as the now empty cart wended its way slowly back to the ornate gates of the cemetery. Mr Gregory tied the pony to a convenient post and they all went in, without any set plan, to read the inscriptions on the gravestones.

"Wait a minute," Peter said, waving them back to where he stood. "Let's do this military style. You two look on the left, and Dad, you look on the right. Beth and I will take the next path."

Beth had brought a notebook and with Peter searching one side of the path, she bent to examine every inscription, looking for some name that might tie in with the little they knew about the girls.

The name given to the home had been Carpenter and this was the name they hoped to find. They found several, but none were the right time or the right age to have been Myrtle and Maude's parents. Nevertheless Beth wrote the details meticulously into her notebook in case something fitted into the information they already had, limited as it was. Any entry might be the clue that would lead them, eventually, to the answer they sought.

Mr Gregory called urgently to Beth and his son, signalling them not to alert the girls.

"This is strange, Beth; is this one of yours?"

A small tombstone, barely visible amid ivy, brambles and nettles in a neglected corner, had been partially cleared by Mr Gregory's rough hand. A small bunch of roses, faded and brittle, falling into fragments, lay across it, and at one side another bouquet, brown and even older than the roses, was half pressed into the earth. Mr Gregory rubbed his hand across the lettering to reveal the legend:

BOBBIE PIPER
BORN SEPTEMBER 1910
DIED NOVEMBER 1910
GREATLY MISSED BY HIS MOTHER

"Could it have been a brother?" Beth wondered as she wrote the information down with a trembling hand. "A baby born to my mother before she married my father?" She felt a sense of guilt, as though she had been caught prying into someone else's business.

"Your mother?" Mr Gregory said, staring at her strangely. "Why not your Auntie Audrey? She's a Piper too, isn't she?"

"But she couldn't have—"

"Couldn't have what, loved someone when she was a young woman?" Mr Gregory said.

"I don't know." Beth shook her dark head in confusion. "I can't imagine her in that situation, I suppose."

Mr Gregory smiled sadly. "Why are the young incapable of seeing the older generation as anything but ancient? Why do they never accept that we were once young and capable of love?"

A shout of excitement came from a short distance away, in a section that, though newer, was almost as neglected.

"Beth, come quick. I think we've found something," Maude was calling.

The three left the mysterious and uncommunicative grave and went to where the girls were dancing up and down and pointing to an ivy-covered gravestone.

Peter and Beth knelt down, scraped away more of the moss and pulled at the persistent ivy, and Peter read:

IN MEMORY OF MARTHA MAUDE COPP
MOTHER OF MAUDE AND MYRTLE COPP
DIED 1931

"If that's us, then our name isn't Carpenter, it's Copp. Janet Copp must be a relation," Maude said.

"No, I don't think so. Don't get your hopes up," Beth told them. "This can't be your mother. It's just a coincidence."

"But it says 1931, that's when Mam and Dad died," Maude argued.

"Then why isn't your father buried here too?" Peter asked softly.

Frantic now to prove the connection, Maude and Myrtle sobbed as they read the stones nearby. The others helped but without much enthusiasm.

"I know this was our mam," Maude said, "I can't explain the name, but I'm sure it's our mam." She hugged her sister and they stared, white faced, at the neglected grave.

"Why did Mam tell everyone we were called Carpenter, then?" Myrtle wanted to know.

"I don't understand why," Maude said tearfully, "but it's her, I'm sure of that."

"Perhaps she was ashamed of us," Myrtle said, also on the edge of tears. "Mam hated us and pretended we weren't her daughters, that's why."

Ashen faced, the two girls were led from the gloomy grounds and helped back on to the cart.

Peter told them silly stories in an attempt to cheer them and Beth started singing one of their favourite songs, "When Father Papered the Parlour". Mr Gregory joined in, but the girls remained silent and tense, each wrapped in their own thoughts, trying to come to terms with what they had learnt.

"I really don't think that grave was anything to do with you," Peter said, "but perhaps you could write to the paper again, this time in the name of Copp?"

Beth agreed with forced enthusiasm, but the gloomy expression of the girls' faces didn't change.

When Olive and Ronnie were told the outcome of the search, they explained it all to Janet Copp when she brought tea to them on their stall at the market. When she heard the story, she promised to befriend the girls and help them to gradually accept that they were on their own.

"They'll soon realise how lucky they are to have found the Castles and been given a ready-made family. Just think of what might have happened to them if Beth hadn't been curious about young Myrtle. For one thing, Maude might not have survived the winter."

Hannah continued to visit Bleddyn and give him news of his son Johnny whenever she received a letter. Then she had a letter that made her hesitate. In it, Johnny asked her to marry him.

> I love you more than I can tell, and I want to be with you for always. Marry me, darling Hannah, and I'll ask nothing more of life. I love you and I adore Josie and Marie, and I know we can create a happy home for them to grow up in. On my next leave – heaven alone knows when that will be – we can make plans. I want us to get married as soon as we can arrange it. Don't let's wait, this is a precarious life and I don't want to waste another moment of it.

There were more endearments and pledges and promises and as a PS he had written, "I bet this is one letter you won't show my Dad!"

She was smiling as she handed it to Bleddyn, watching his face for his first reaction: a reaction on which her answer would depend.

"Darling girl, I'm delighted. I couldn't wish for a better daughter-in-law." He hugged her and handed back the letter. "Thanks for showing me. I don't think Johnny expected you to, mind! That PS wasn't a joke, it was a plea, so if you don't tell him, then I won't."

"Thank you. I was going to ask you not to say anything; I'd hate him to be embarrassed – although, why is it, d'you think, that love and affection and caring for someone other than ourselves causes embarrassment? More than some crimes cause, it seems to me."

"When will you tell the girls?" Bleddyn asked.

"As soon as I've posted my reply" – she patted her pocket – "and told the rest of your family. There's your Taff, and Evelyn. Perhaps I could write to Taff, if Evelyn doesn't mind? Then Beth and the others, quite an ordeal."

"I'll come with you to see Evelyn if you like. She'll be pleased, as we all will."

"Perhaps."

"Why are you so worried? Is it because you were married before?"

"That and the children, and the fact I'm eight years older than Johnny. It's a big difference."

"Rubbish! You and our Johnny are perfect together. Come on, let's go straight away. Evelyn'll be back from the factory about now."

Evelyn was abrupt in her congratulations. "Although," she pointed out rather coldly, "it isn't official yet, is it? You haven't replied and Johnny hasn't asked you face to face. It might have been a moment's loneliness that made him write that letter and afterwards regretted it. I'd wait before you tell everyone, in case it falls through."

"Evelyn!" Bleddyn said. "What an odd way of greeting the news. Of course Johnny meant it. He's already spoken to me about how he feels about Hannah and her girls." He glanced at Hannah and added, "It wasn't such a surprise as you thought, but I didn't want to spoil your telling me, unlike some!"

"Sorry. Well then, congratulations, Hannah." The words had softened but not the coldness of Evelyn's expression. "Will you marry soon?"

"Johnny is somewhere in Europe so far as we know so it's impossible to answer that. But it will be as soon as we can arrange it – if that's what Johnny really wants," Hannah couldn't help adding.

"Wouldn't it be wiser to wait until the war's over?" Evelyn persisted.

"I don't think either of us wants to wait that long. It could go on for another year or more."

Telling the rest of the Castle family was easier. Beth hugged her and Marged too. Huw shook her hand and asked when she was going to bring the children to see them again.

Lilly looked up from the magazine she was reading and asked, "Will you want the baby clothes back in case you and Johnny have another, then?"

"Of course not," Hannah said, her face reddening in embarrassment in case they thought she was expecting a child. "That isn't the reason Johnny wants to marry so soon. It's the war and the uncertainty of everything. If he manages to get home he'll certainly be sent abroad again, he could be away for a very long time the way things are going, and he wants to know we're there, building a home for when he comes back."

"Where will you live?" Beth wanted to know.

Hannah laughed breathlessly. "I haven't given it a thought. This is all so new. I'm so excited about his proposal. I won't be able to stay with Mam and Dad, that much is certain. When he gets his next leave we'll plan everything and hopefully book the wedding date."

When she walked back to collect the girls whom she had left playing with friends at a neighbour's house, she felt a sudden draining of confidence and began to feel that she had spoken too soon. When another letter appeared the following day, repeating his proposal and threatening to ask her every day until she said yes, she was relieved. That one was more loving than the last and it was one she didn't show to Bleddyn.

A meeting was called by the entertainments officer for the town. He asked that everyone connected with holiday-making attend. Beth went along with her parents and Uncle Bleddyn, anxious to know what was being planned for the following year, now that there were so many restrictions on everything they had previously taken for granted.

A gloomy audience awaited the speakers, expecting to be told that, like so many other places, St David's Well Bay would be sealed off from the public for fear of invasion. In fact the opposite was true.

"With fuel in short supply, and transport needed for our servicemen and their needs, the call is on for people to forget travelling to other towns for their holidays, and the slogan is 'Holidays at Home'," the chairman announced. "Every town in the country is asked to make plans for next year's season, and make sure no one wants to go anywhere else but the area in which they live. We have to do everything we can to persuade the local people that the best holiday they can have is right here. In St David's Well we are fortunate. We have the beach, numerous parks and many other attractions and we have to make sure everyone knows it. This means starting now, to plan for the summer."

The first business was to find a representative for each of the the various groups involved: landladies, hoteliers, café owners and of course the beach stall-holders, who voted for Huw to stand as their representative.

Once this was acomplished, and some shuffling had taken place to allow the various delegates to sit together, the chairman asked for suggestions. The other two speakers on the platform started it off by giving their ideas for entertainments that would involve the whole town.

A carnival with floats representing every organisation, a choir chosen from the schools to sing in the parks, brass bands, dancing, sandcastle competitions and a donkey derby were all proposed. The list went on until the noise in the hall was deafening. People forgot about addressing the chair and spoke to their neighbours, sharing ideas and forgetting the speakers completely.

Shouting for order, the chairman smiled, said he considered the meeting a rousing success and suggested they all stood to sing the national anthem before leaving to continue with the discussions in the newly formed individual groups.

While the meeting went on, Johnny was on a ship making his way home across the channel. The darkness hid the small ship from some dangers but others lurked below and he stood on deck wondering whether he would survive the perilous journey and see Hannah again, or whether one of the unseen U-boats would destroy the ship and the men whom it carried.

He knew that even if he did survive this journey, he wouldn't be home for more than a few days. He was being sent to Scotland for more training before being sent to Italy – or at least that was the whispered rumour surmised from the snippets of unreliable information they had received.

He arrived safely and after leaving his kit with his father and quickly eating a meal while catching up on the news, he went to see Hannah. The following day they arranged a marriage by special license.

With no time for the niceties, it would be a small affair, with only the family, including her still disapproving parents, and the girls, for whom she had promised to make very special dresses. Hannah's parents refused to discuss it. All they did was remind her that in the eyes of the church she was still a married woman and what she was doing was a sin.

Slowly Hannah rolled up her sleeve to reveal the scar left by one of her husband's drunken rages.

"Where were the eyes of the church then, Mam?" she asked.

"You're married. What you're doing is not right and you'll never be happy until you tell this Johnny Castle goodbye and return to your rightful husband. You can't build happiness on the destruction of someone else's."

Their remarks were hurtful but with so much to do to arrange the wedding in so short a time, she pushed her parents' attitude aside and concentrated on the list of things she had to do.

Inexplicably, the news of the wedding upset Marged. It was the thought of having a family celebration without Eynon being present. She looked at the calendar and counted the days since she had last seen her son. It seemed like a lifetime.

Marged and Bleddyn, like most others in the town, spent a lot of time writing letters. Marged told herself that this was something cheerful to report. Bleddyn wrote to Taff, told him about the wedding and enclosed the note Hannah had written. And Marged wrote to Eynon.

She wrote every week. But the letters always came back, having been read, and with a note reminding her that if he should turn up, then it was her duty to inform the authorities. She ignored the warning, stacked them away for Eynon to read when he came back, pretended he was replying and wrote again, telling him that everything was all right.

She did receive an occasional card, signed in strange handwriting as though from a cousin, Ross, or a friend called Reginald, and even on one occasion from a girl called Bessie. She tried writing with her left hand, to see whether that explained the unusual writing. There was no news, just a sentence telling her he was all right and not to worry. After showing them to Huw, she hid them upstairs in the back of the wardrobe. One day he would be home and able to tell her everything that had happened. For now she would write and tell him about Johnny's wedding, and pretend that he would soon be reading about it.

Johnny would be married in uniform and Hannah, defeated in her effort to treat the day as being in any way joyful by her mother's constant reminders of her wrongdoing, decided on a brown dress and coat with a handbag rather than flowers or a prayer book.

Beth quickly persuaded her to change her mind and, with Marged a willing supporter, the three of them went shopping and bought her a pale blue dress worn with a silk scarf. Hannah also borrowed one of Lilly's hats, which she decorated in the same trailing silk. She looked lovely and they all knew how thrilled Johnny would be when he met her at the register office. Flowers were ordered and Cyril the Snap promised to give them some photographs to treasure, which were paid for by Bleddyn.

"You're all so kind. You shouldn't be doing all this," Hannah protested as Bleddyn gave her money to buy a gift for each of the girls.

"You're a Castle now," Bleddyn told her fondly. "And you'll do us proud."

The day was dry and bright and they walked to and from the register office along the busy roads past the shops, where shoppers stopped to look and admire the little girls following their mother and their new stepfather. Some clapped and Bleddyn hid a tear, and Johnny looked as proud as proud, and after a few yards walking with her head down, Hannah looked at him and smiled, forgot her mother's bitter words and raised her head proudly, looking forward to a happy future as Mrs Johnny Castle.

There was no cake apart from a small sponge Marged and Audrey had swopped various rationed goods to make. A couple of ounces of tea for some sugar, a piece of bacon in exchange for some margarine. It somehow made everyone appreciate the spread more and several admitted that the wedding was happier than many they had attended in the past.

Lilly cried, of course, but no one was surprised. This was a moment she still dreamed about, and one that most knew would never happen, not with the child growing within her and no man willing to accept responsibility for it. Hannah left Johnny's side for a moment and sat with her.

"We're cousins now, Lilly. I hope you're as happy about that as I am. The girls are a part of your family and if you're willing, I'd like them to call you Auntie Lilly."

Bleddyn heard her and smiled. Hannah was an asset to the Castle family, he thought proudly. No mistake about that.

"Johnny," he said to his son. "You're a lucky devil and don't forget it."

"How could I?" Johnny smiled, putting an arm around his glowingly beautiful bride.

Eleven

"We aren't the only family of Pipers, for heaven's sake!" Marged said impatiently. Ever since Beth and the two girls had returned from the cemetery, the questions had come at her from all sides.

"At least come and see it, Mam," Beth pleaded. "It could be a distant cousin. Families never keep in touch after the cousins grow up, do they?"

"I haven't the time to go off wandering around the cemetery to look at the grave of a stranger!"

"You know something about it, don't you?" Huw accused. "Why else are you so angry?"

"I'm not angry," she protested. "I just don't want to give Myrtle and Maude any hope of finding their family. Too much time has passed and looking at gravestones isn't the occupation for young girls."

"We're talking about the child's grave, someone called Piper." Beth frowned. "Nothing to do with Copp."

"You know what I mean. We'll go exploring and they'll be searching for some family that might not even belong to Myrtle and Maude. Plenty of families could be using those names."

Beth knew her mother was deliberately misunderstanding her, trying to edge the discussion away from the Piper child and confusing her with talk about the Copp burial. Abandoning the attempt to get some information from her mother, she asked her father to go with her.

"Why bother?" he asked. "Your mother won't help us solve the mystery even if we do go. What'll be achieved, besides another argument with your mam?"

She decided to go alone. She still worked most lunchtimes and evenings at the chip shop, however, and with the days so brief and so dark, there wouldn't be much time to go and examine the grave during the afternoon. With the weather a mixture of gusty wind, short showers and dark clouds, the prospect of visiting the eerie place without company was not very cheering.

The heavy clouds that day prevented anything resembling daylight. From the almost indistinguishable dawn, the sky was hidden, the houses were wrapped in heavy mist and there was only a sort of twilight that was uneased by shop or street lighting.

The hedges bordering the pavements as she approached the cemetery were dripping with moisture and there were few people around. Her footsteps echoed back at her, and at times it sounded as though there was someone following her, as she forced herself to go on. She glanced around nervously, peering uselessly through the threatening gloom.

She almost turned back; the heavily ornamented iron gates and the rows of solemn graves were daunting in the semi-darkness. She walked briskly, purposefully, and headed straight for the area where the small grave lay, half hidden by the overgrown hedge.

To her surprise she saw fresh flowers there, bright in the surrounding gloom. She stopped and looked around, half expecting to see the person who had placed them there. But nothing stirred except the trees, moving in the wind, shedding the remnants of the recent shower.

Curious, she didn't approach the grave but instead ran back to the main path where she saw a figure in the distance, a figure she knew.

"Auntie Audrey," she called, running to join her. "What are you doing here?"

"Oh, I suppose it was the thought of that poor little grave you told us about, neglected, no one to remember, so I took some flowers."

"Why didn't you say? We could have come together," Beth said.

"You know what your mam's like. If she said we shouldn't bother it's best not to tell her."

Beth laughed. "Not scared of our Mam, are you?"

"Best to avoid arguments, don't you think?"

"Will you come back with me? I thought I'd look around the area in case there are other Pipers buried there. Families are buried together when possible."

"I'll come back with you, dear, but I don't think you'll find any other family near by."

"You've looked, have you?"

"Yes, I've looked."

They cleaned the stone and pulled some more of the stubborn ivy off the small plot, and Beth suggested they came again, this time armed with scissors and a sharp knife, so they could cut back some of the brambles and make the memorial more visible.

That evening, when Beth and her parents were finishing their meal, Audrey came with Myrtle and Maude, and Olive and Ronnie.

"We have news for you," Ronnie said, limping in and sitting beside his father. "Tell them, Olive, love."

"I – we – we're going to have a baby," Olive said shyly. "Some time in July."

"Bang slam in the middle of the busiest month!" Huw said, smiling to show he was teasing.

"That's what Ronnie said!" Olive laughed.

"Congratulations, to both of you," Marged said, hugging them.

"Yes, well done," Huw added.

Audrey said nothing, remembering the tiny grave and the tragedy of that birth.

"Such a happy occasion, a time to celebrate," Marged went on, unaware of her sister's distress.

"Yes," Audrey said quietly, "a happy time, isn't it, Marged, except when a baby is born out of wedlock. Then it's a different story, isn't it?"

"What d'you mean?" Huw asked. "These two have been married for ages, there's no problem there."

"That little grave the girls found—"

"Not now, Audrey," Marged interrupted quickly. "Talk about someone else's problems another time, not now when we're celebrating Olive and Ronnie's news."

She spoke sharply in a tone that would normally have silenced Audrey, but Huw said, "No, don't let's forget it. There's no harm in reminding ourselves that we're the lucky ones and others don't have such fortunate lives."

"Not *now*," Marged almost shouted, but Huw looked at Audrey with a determined frown.

"You know something about the grave of that child, don't you?"

"The grave is that of my son. Ten weeks and two days he lived. Wilf and I were to have married that year but Mam forbade it, insisting that Wilf, being a bank official, wouldn't help in the family business and I couldn't be spared."

Utter silence greeted her words. Beth went over and put her arms around her aunt. No one else moved. Huw stared at Marged and waited for her to speak. But it was Beth who broke the painful silence.

"Why didn't you tell us before, Auntie Audrey? You shouldn't have kept it to yourself. We all lost the baby, he was a cousin for me and Lilly and Ronnie and our Eynon."

"I couldn't tell you because I was constantly reminded of how I had disgraced the family name," Audrey said harshly. "The neighbours were told that I was looking after the baby because his mother had died. Wilf wasn't allowed to see him, not once. And it was not until after little Bobbie died that we were allowed to meet. Then it was only when we had a chaperone, usually Mam."

"You knew?" Huw asked Marged, who looked away, up into the corner of the room, refusing to comment.

"Yes, Marged knew," Audrey answered for her. "She supported Mam and Dad at the time and has since refused to discuss it. I needed to grieve. But they wouldn't even allow me to do that."

Beth stared at her aunt, seeing the coldness, the bitterness in her usually gentle face, the dry eyes that sparkled, not with tears, but with the pain of the memories.

"Damn me, Moll has a lot to answer for," Huw muttered. "Giving out that she was so kind and caring, yet she could do that to her own daughter."

"I can still remember the sigh of relief she uttered when poor little Bobbie died," Audrey whispered.

"Why didn't you and Wilf marry?" Beth asked softly.

"I was told I must never marry him because of what he'd done. Punishment was always Mam's first thought. And although we planned to run away and defy them, first Dad died, then Wilf's mother became ill, and slowly the years passed, and we drifted into middle age and the urgency was gone. Poor little Bobbie. When he caught pneumonia everyone was happy. Except Wilf and me."

Marged stood up, still unable to look at them. Red faced, she stared unseeingly through the doorway to the kitchen, longing to escape but unable to. She knew that if she ran from this now, she would never be able to face any of them again. Yet how could she turn and face the accusation in every eye?

"You should never have told them, Audrey. How could they understand?" she said finally, her voice harsh, defensive. "Mam did what she did because she thought it was for the best."

"Best for her but not for her daughter! Plenty of people marry just in time for the birth," Huw said.

"Not the Pipers."

"Damn it all, Marged, it's not a criminal act, it's an act of love!"

Maude and Myrtle hugged each other and stared, white faced, at Audrey.

"Do you have a photograph?" Olive asked, reaching out and touching Audrey's arm.

"Your Granny Moll burnt them all. At least, she thought she had." Taking a wallet out of her handbag, Audrey pulled out a faded, dog-eared snap showing her with the baby in her arms. It was passed around without comment. No one knew what to say. There were no words that would offer comfort.

Olive and Ronnie left soon after, with Audrey and the two girls. Beth hugged Olive and said enthusiastically, "There's thrilled I am to be an auntie. Auntie Beth, how does that sound?" The telling of their glad news had been marred by Audrey's revelations and Beth knew how disappointing that must have been. She smiled until they were at their door, then her face collapsed from the false smile as thoughts of Auntie Audrey's tragedy hit her once again.

She stood on the doorstep long after they had disappeared through their front door a few yards up the street. The revelations of the evening had distressed her, partly for the grief her gentle aunt had suffered, and also for the realisation that although she had loved Granny Moll, she had not really known her at all.

She went to bed without any further discussion, leaving her father and mother in a silence that was prickling with words waiting to be said, and for most of the night she was disturbed by arguments and shouting. The argument ended with her father slamming the front door and walking with swift, angry strides up the road.

With the approach of Christmas, women prowled the streets looking for anything that would help make the season a cheerful one. It threatened to be the oddest one in most people's memory, with shortages making it impossible to plan for the usual overeating and the generous welcomes in every home. The government had announced that the ration would include an extra four ounces of sugar and an extra two ounces of tea.

"How will that help us make a Christmas cake?" grumbled Marged. "It's fat we want and some good dried fruit and fresh oranges and lemons for the juice and peel."

"Carrots, that's what Lord Woolton recommends!" Beth laughed. "It'll be interesting to see what sort of a cake you make with carrots."

Huw said nothing. He rarely spoke these days and Beth knew that her parents were sleeping in separate bedrooms. She discussed it with Lilly, who had not been present when Audrey told her story, and Lilly said she thought it was their mother keeping the truth from him that had upset him. "When you've been married as long as they have I don't think you'd expect any surprises like that one," she said, adding with a laugh, "I bet Granny Moll would have had something to say to Auntie Audrey for spilling it out like that, just when Olive and Ronnie announced their news of a baby due to be born all respectable, in wedlock!"

"It isn't funny. Poor Aunt Audrey."

"Poor Olive too, having that reception when she told the family their news."

"It was us finding the grave."

"You aren't sorry, are you? At least Auntie Audrey can share her sadness. It is sad. Losing a baby must be the very worst. No replacing it, is there?" She frowned and added thoughtfully, "And when you think of how many parents are having to face that terrible loss every day, it's hard to imagine how they must feel. Just when their children have grown up and they think they're safe from childhood illnesses and accidents, this war comes to threaten them."

Beth was surprised at her sister's compassion. Expecting a child had made her a nicer person.

She had written to Peter telling him the outcome of their sad discovery and he had written back, promising to go with her and her aunt and clean up the site when he was next home, "which won't be until after Christmas," he added.

When she had a letter a few days later telling her that Freddy would be unable to get home for Christmas, it was less of a disappointment. He still wrote occasionally, and she had developed the habit of sending him ten shillings every two weeks, for which he thanked her.

She saw Peter's father often. He called sometimes to see whether they needed fresh vegetables and when he had a few rows of young leeks which he wanted to clear so he could plant broad beans, he offered them to Olive and Ronnie for their market stall. This had led to them buying and selling on other things, including rabbits, which were a popular addition to the meat supply.

Towards Christmas he began taking orders for chickens, which so far were not included in the weekly meat allowance.

"Got a couple of geese too, mind," he said when he called into the bustling, noisy market. He wrote their order in his scruffy notebook, which he kept tucked inside the lining of his hat.

"Never cooked a goose," Olive said. Mr Gregory enjoyed a few moments telling them the best way of putting it in the oven, hanging it above a drip tray to remove much of the grease.

"And keep the goose grease, mind," Janet Copp said as she arrived with their morning tea. "Good for rubbing on chests when you've got a cold, mind."

"Thanks, Janet," Olive laughed. "But I think I'd rather have a cold!"

Between dealing with the occasional customer, they watched as the Christmas decorations went up. There was such a happy atmosphere they were unaware of the time passing. It was a surprise when the inspector came out of his cubby-hole of an office to remind them it was time to close.

"Tomorrow we'd better do something to add to the rest," Ronnie said as they set off for home. "I bet Auntie Audrey will have some trimmings tucked away. She's sure to find a few streamers and baubles we can borrow."

As the next day was Sunday the market was closed. On Monday, Ronnie tried to deal with the complicated task of fixing the trimmings, but he didn't get very far. Besides the impossibility of bending his injured knee, his fear of climbing too high in case of falling and damaging it further thwarted him. Exasperated by his uselessness he sat on his stool and resigned himself to waiting for Olive to help.

"Stuck for a bit of help, is it?" the woman on the other fruit and veg stall called. Ronnie shrugged expressively and she gave her husband a nudge. "Go on, Arthur, give the poor lad a bit of a hand."

Arthur came across smiling cheerfully and, with his wife shouting instructions and Ronnie helping where he could, the stall was soon as brightly decorated as the rest, right down to the sprays of holly, which Arthur sold on his stall, and the strategically placed bough of mistletoe.

Ronnie was as pleased with the Christmas display as he remembered feeling as a child. Every year about this time he had come downstairs one morning with Beth and Lilly and Eynon to find the tree sparkling and the room filled with streamers that dipped down from the centre light to the corners and along the walls to the door. Magic. The stall was almost as good; he couldn't wait for Olive to see it.

Olive declared it "wonderful", and went straight away to thank the couple for their help. Arthur and Sally told her it was a pleasure.

When the market closed and everyone had finished packing their stalls away for the night, Olive called to Janet and told her about the discovery of the grave of Ronnie's baby cousin and the distress it had caused in the family. Inevitably the conversation then returned to the discovery of that other grave, Myrtle and Maude's mother, a few weeks previously. "Copp she was called, like you. Strange, isn't it?"

"I don't think it's any relation of mine, though," Janet said. "Pity, mind; I'd have liked a couple of long-lost sisters. But so far as I know I don't have any other relations. Certainly not round here. From Birmingham my family were, not South Wales. But, tell you what, I'll wrap up a parcel for each of them girls for you to put under the tree, and tell them that having the same name is sure to make us friends. How will that be?"

Lilly's pregnancy progressed easily. She did less and less around the house, insisting that she needed fresh air every day and had to avoid any heavy work. As "heavy work" included practically every type of housework, she found very little to tax her energy.

She daydreamed a lot, imagining seeing Phil on the day he was demobbed and presenting him with the beautiful child and him falling in love with them both and leave his wife and – There the dream ended every time, bringing her down to earth with a jolt.

She had never discovered exactly where he lived or she would have paraded up and down from time to time hoping to catch him on one of his leaves and persuade him to at least help her. When she had asked about his home he had been evasive and the only clues she had were that he came from the direction of the beach when he walked up to meet her. She had also seen him on one occasion walking along one of the roads not far from the promenade, with a slim, fair young woman carrying shopping. Lilly presumed she was his wife.

She had walked along that road once or twice but hadn't seen Phil or the woman he had been with that day. So she enjoyed a dramatic few moments every day wondering if he was safe or injured, or perhaps a prisoner of war in some dreadful camp. If only she had news of him. Perhaps his wife didn't write very often. He might be glad of more letters from home. If only there was some way of finding out what was happening to him.

She found out in the harshest way possible. Each week the local paper listed the reported deaths and there was his photograph and his name, Philip Martin Denver. Not Philip Martin, the name he had given her, but there was no doubt about the picture. It was Phil, and while she had been daydreaming about a joyous reunion and being happy ever after, he had been killed.

Surprisingly she didn't burst into noisy tears. She was stunned by the news; her head hurt as though from a blow and was filled with a kind of pressure that blocked out all sensation and all thought. As the shock slowly receded she was calm and controlled. There was absolutely nothing that she could do. Nothing at all. She couldn't tell anyone and she couldn't be seen to grieve.

She knew that even at a moment like this she couldn't tell anyone. Selfish as she often was, she couldn't distress his wife more by letting her know that her husband had been unfaithful. She grieved silently, seeing before her a future empty of love. In the privacy of her room she hugged herself, seeking comfort from her unborn child who was unequivocally without a father, even an absent one.

Marged and Huw noticed how quiet she was, how less inclined to argue, but they decided there was no serious problem.

"Nothing to be alarmed about," Marged said, and Huw agreed.

"Our Lilly's always been moody."

The shops lacked their usual displays. They all had black-out material over their windows, so instead of the usual glitter of Christmas cheer, with grocers and butchers and toy shops, making a walk through the main shopping streets an exciting event for the town's children, everything became dark as soon as the day ended. No coloured lights enticed window-shopping children with bright eyes, marvelling at the magic, to wander and hope and dream.

Once darkness fell, most people stayed home and listened to the wireless, where news came of waves of German aircraft filling the skies night after night, many of them to be destroyed, but others coming in their place, relentlessly continuing to bomb the larger cities, leaving them wondering how anything could survive. Pity for the victims was mixed with relief that that St David's Well had nothing of strategic importance to the enemy.

Eynon gravitated towards St David's Well as Christmas drew closer. He didn't know what to do to extricate himself from the mess he had made. One evening, he walked along the promenade where the silent shops gave no sign of the bright days of summer. Some were boarded up against the winter gales, others still showed posters advertising the ice-creams that were no longer allowed to be sold. Leaves and piles of sand filled the once neat doorways and everywhere was a travesty of the golden days of the past summer.

At the rock and sweet shop he stopped and thought of Alice. Where was she now – still looking after her sick and foul-tempered father? He smiled sadly as he remembered his plans to save her from that, dreams in which he would flirt a little and perhaps become seriously involved. Then he had been ready for fun and adventure, now he would settle for having a friend.

Footsteps approached, running, accompanied by soft laughter. They slowed to a walk, then were running again. There was a shout of anger, then more running.

He stepped into the doorway of the rock and sweet shop and hoped the shadows would hide him. His eyes were used to the dark, living as he had far from towns and people for the past months, so as the girl and the dog who was causing the trouble passed the doorway, he recognised her.

"Alice!" The word was out before he thought of the risk he was taking. Appearing like that so soon after she had filled his thoughts, he was unable to help himself.

"Eynon? But I thought – I thought you were missing," she said, grasping the dog's collar in an effort to hold him still.

"I shouldn't have spoken," Eynon said. "Please, Alice, please forget you've seen me."

"Is it true then? You did run away?" she gasped.

"I ran away from a situation that I thought couldn't get worse, and I was wrong. Now I don't know what to do."

"Everyone thinks you're missing, or a prisoner of war."

"That's what I am, but I'm in a prison without walls."

"Dad'll be asleep; will you come back and have a bath and some food? I can cook you something."

"I can't do that. If you're seen to be helping me, you'd be in serious trouble."

She stepped into the doorway beside him. "I'll risk it. Come on, I'll tell them I was trying to persuade you to give yourself up." Then she saw the unsightly scar on his head and asked, "What's that? It looks painful."

"I did it when I fell from the lorry on manoeuvres, the day I ran away. I was knocked out for a few minutes. That was weeks ago and it just won't heal. It's a bit sore at times because I keep knocking it."

"You needed a few stitches, that's why it won't heal."

"I know, but it's too late now," he shrugged.

With Alice's father asleep upstairs, Eynon went into the kitchen and filled the galvanised bath with warm water and soaked luxuriously for a while. Beside him, half shielded by a curtain, Alice prepared eggs on toast, planning to tell her father that she had dropped them while cleaning the cupboard.

Daringly, she led him upstairs after he had eaten and showed him the spare room. There was a gas lamp on the wall and the curtains were open.

"Don't light that, whatever you do," Alice whispered.

He opened the window and stared out. The sky was clear and a moon shone over the town. Roofs were touched with its silver light and the street below, sharply etched, looked unreal.

Homesickness overwhelmed him and Alice held him as he took deep breaths to contain his grief. Then he slipped under the sweet-smelling sheets and was asleep within minutes. Alice watched for a while, thinking about how young he looked, in spite of a roughly chopped beard, and of how unfair life could be.

The next morning she called him early and he left with pockets filled with bread and her ration of cheese, promising he'd be back as soon as he had sorted everything out.

"Write to me," were her last words before he slipped out of the back gate and hurried away in the early dawn.

Two weeks after the death of Phil had been reported, Lilly was idly looking through her "treasure box", a chocolate box with a sentimental picture of kittens on the front, in which she kept her private memorabilia. She found the only photograph she had of Phil, taken when the beach photographer had snapped them unaware. If he'd thought about it at all, he would have presumed the negative had been destroyed without a copy being made, but he would have been wrong. She had kept it hidden in her treasure box, to take out occasionally and relive some precious moments. She had hoped that one day, when they were together and their love was no longer a secret, she would show him and they would laugh at her mild deception.

Now she wondered whether she should give it to Phil's wife. She needn't tell her the truth, just that she knew Phil from the repair shop. She could say that the photographer had taken the snap when they had met by accident, and that she had kept it as it was a flattering one of herself. It was a plausible story and to add to its authenticity, she would wear a wedding ring to reassure the poor widow that she was no threat. Granny Moll's ring was in the house and would fit well enough.

Most people managed to decorate their rooms with either home-made streamers or ones saved from previous Christmases, but for Beth, any attempt at adding the usual trimmings came to nothing. Every time she painstakingly put something up, her father frustrated her by pulling it down.

"What is it, Dad?" she asked when the artificial tree she had found in a cupboard had been thrown into the ashbin. "You might be angry about something, but for the rest of us, it's Christmas and we want to enjoy it."

"No cheek from you!" he snapped and she sat down, the crêpe-paper streamers she had made resting on her lap.

"Dad, why are you so angry? It's been ever since Auntie Audrey told us about the baby. Why has that upset you?"

"I can't talk to you about something like that, girl!"

"Why not? Our Ronnie's wife is expecting and I do have an idea of how that happens, Dad!"

"None of your impertinence, right?"

"Cheek, impertinence, there's a terrible daughter I am," she teased, hoping to coax a smile.

"All right, it isn't about the baby, it's about your Granny Moll. She ruled this family, insisting on having the last say in everything."

"Piper's was her business, and her father's before her. I suppose she thought she had the right."

"It was me and your Uncle Bleddyn who ran it, and we ran it in spite of her interference not because of her help. Lazy sod her old man Joseph Piper was. Never did a stroke of work unless he was forced. Bleddyn and I came into the firm when we were still at school, working dawn till dark. We worked full time, and I mean full time, when we were only fourteen and slaved like fools all these years with neither praise nor credit. And all the time Granny Moll was telling everyone how her grandfather Joseph brought the business round after he took over from Mrs Downs's grandparents."

Beth only half believed what her father was saying. Anger

and disappointment can easily distort the truth in the most honest people.

"But why are you suddenly angry about this now?" she asked.

"Because of what she did to your Auntie Audrey. She was a bully, her righteousness was a hammer which she wielded on us all, me, Bleddyn, your mother, poor inoffensive Audrey, and even you, Lilly, Ronnie and our Eynon, insisting that you worked on the beach even though you might have wanted something different."

"I didn't, though," she protested.

"How do you know? Ever since you were born, you and Lilly and Ronnie and little Eynon weren't given the choice. You were told by devoted Granny Moll that your future was Piper's. Damn it all, it's a couple of cafés and stalls, not a flamin' dynasty!"

He went out soon after and later Beth learned that he had gone to the fish-and-chip café, after collecting the sign he had ordered some days before – which had been changed to "Castle's".

Huw was still sufficiently angry to relish the moment when Marged first saw it, and he smiled in anticipation. He was determined it would stay if he had to sit up on the roof all night and guard it!

Lilly made up her mind. With the item in the newspaper giving her sufficient clues, she would find Phil's wife and give her the photograph. It was the last thing she could do for him. He had let her down when he learned about the baby she was carrying, but she still loved him and knew that he had loved her, at least a little. Not enough to behave honourably, but she could hardly blame him for that. Every family had its secrets, she knew that, particularly now, since the truth had come out about Auntie Audrey's lost child. It had made her feel less alone, knowing poor Auntie Audrey had been through something similar although with a far less happy outcome.

She searched through her mother's small collection of jewellery and slipped her Granny Moll's ring on her wedding finger. Tomorrow she would go to Queen Street and knock doors until she found her.

The road was a long, stone-built terrace, one of three

closely arranged rows climbing, one behind the other, up a steep hill from one of the town's busy shopping areas. She went to the first house and asked for the family of Denver and was directed to the house at the far end. She knocked and waited apprehensively for the woman who was Phil's wife to answer.

Suddenly she was afraid, and wanted to run away. How could she face the woman she had cheated on in the most degrading way? What had happened to Auntie Audrey could have happened to her: Mam and Dad could have forbidden her to keep the child. Then she might have been forced to tell the truth about its father. How could she stand here so blatantly and face the woman and pretend she was on an errand of kindness and friendship?

Her heart was racing and she had begun to move away when the door was opened and a rosy-faced woman of about fifty stood there. Her arms covered in flour, her apron folded up and held to save spilling more flour on to the shining doorstep, she stood there smiling. The appetising smell of apples cooking issued forth around her.

"I hope you're not selling nothing, love. Broke I am," she said at once.

"I heard about the death of Phil, I knew him from taking things to be repaired in his shop. I have a photograph, taken when we met by accident over the beach last summer. Cyril the Snap took it, thinking we knew each other, and I was curious to see how I looked so I bought it." She held out the rather tatty snap. "I thought his wife might like it, see, and as it's no real use to me as I didn't know him, I thought I'd bring it for her."

"For who, love?"

"Like I said, for his wife."

"Phil wasn't married, never had been. Plenty of women, mind, never no shortage of women with my Phil, but never no wife."

The street seemed to spin, the houses dancing as though in some crazy dream. Lilly reached out to grab the door frame for support and instead found herself held in the woman's arms and being guided inside the house. The once delicious smell from the apples began to make her nauseous. She thought she might be sick. She also thought that the sharp scent of apples cooking would always bring back memories of that moment.

"Is it Phil's child you're carrying?" Mrs Denver asked in a matter-of-fact tone as she helped her visitor to drink some hot, sweet tea. "Told the tale of being married regular he did, so's not to be expected to marry them."

"Them?" Lilly asked, her voice slurred, her mouth dry.

"Two children he's got and I never see a hair of either of them. I know they're both boys, but I don't even know their names. Sad it is, not even being able to send them a card on their birthdays or a present at Christmas."

She saw the ring on Lilly's finger then and hurriedly apologised. "Oh, you're married. Sorry, I thought – oh dear, I've really said the wrong things. Just a friend, are you, genuine friend and nothing more?"

Lilly took off the ring and placed it on the plush-covered table. "It was my gran's," she explained. "I thought Phil's wife would believe the story of us hardly knowing each other if I pretended to be a married woman. I didn't want to distress her with the truth."

"Such a kind girl you are. Here, let me get you another cup of tea – and a piece of my tart wouldn't go amiss, I'll be bound. Sugar for shock don't they say? And I put half my extra Christmas ration in that tart!"

Lilly was trembling and Mrs Denver sat and talked to her, coaxing her to drink the tea. She urged her to eat the oversweet tart on to which she had sprinkled even more sugar.

As Lilly calmed down they talked, Lilly explaining that she had kept Phil's identity a secret in respect for his non-existent wife. Phil's mother told her of her disappointment over her son's behaviour.

"Now he's gone and I've no real family left," Mrs Denver said sadly. "Only a sister who lives in London who I never see, and two grandchildren I'll never be allowed to meet." She looked at the distraught girl sitting huddled close to the fire trying in vain to warm away the chill within her, and said, "Will you come and see me? When the baby's born, I mean? I know I can't be a real grandmother, you and Phil not being wed and all, but I could be a sort of friend, couldn't I?"

Looking up into the round, motherly face, Lilly smiled

shakily and said, "I'd like that. I've a feeling I'll need a few friends once the secret is out."

"When is she due?" Mrs Denver asked, her deep blue eyes shining with happiness. "I'll be able to start counting the weeks."

"Some time in May, early in the month I think."

"Perfect."

"Mam and Dad don't think so," Lilly grumbled, then, having explained about Piper's Café and the stalls, she added, "I'll be expected to work on the beach or the chip shop as soon as I'm out of bed!"

"Then stay there for an extra week or so!" Mrs Denver said with a laugh. "Men don't like to ask questions when it's to do with women's problems, do they?"

"To be honest, I've worked that out myself." Lilly gave a tentative smile. "I haven't done much work since I knew this little one was on the way."

"Good on you. Take advantage of it. We don't get many opportunities in life!"

Like two conspirators they talked about the beach and how it would not be good for the baby, at least for the first two years.

"I'll have to find some way of earning money, though," Lilly said. "I don't want to lean on Mam and Dad for ever."

"Plenty of work about with this war on," Mrs Denver said confidently. "Factory work pays well and you can easily find someone to look after the little girl."

"You said 'she' and now 'little girl'; are you so sure?" Lilly asked curiously.

"Never been wrong yet. The others were boys," she added sadly.

Lilly walked to the bus stop with her new friend and felt happier about the forthcoming birth than at any time since it had been confirmed.

Huw was disappointed by Marged's reaction to the new sign above the chip shop and café. Although he hung around as often as he could, she saw it for the first time when he was not there. She went to speak to Bleddyn about something and walked in without noticing it. As she was on the way out, Beth called, "Hello, Mam. What d'you think of the new sign, then?"

It took a split second for Marged to realise what had happened and, having her back to Beth and Bleddyn as she pushed her way through the queue of customers, she was able to hide her initial fury. She walked on through the shop and out on to the pavement, then looked up at the brand new sign and nodded casually at them.

"Very nice," was all she said before walking on.

"She took that well," was Beth's comment.

"I wouldn't fancy being in your Dad's shoes, all the same," Bleddyn laughed as he shook salt and vinegar on to a bag of chips.

Marged didn't go straight home. She went to the sign-writing business, which was now run by the once retired father and uncle of the owner, who was now painting camouflage on army lorries, guns and tanks.

"There's been a terrible mistake, Mr Morton. The sign was ordered and paid for by Mr Castle, but the sign should have read 'Piper's'."

She spoke briskly and with an edge of irritation at their incompetence, so that they hovered over their order book and both agreed that they could see how easily the mistake could have been made.

"I'll be generous, considering the mistake was yours," she told them, and offered to pay a small sum for the correct sign – the old one repainted, for quickness – to be erected on the following Sunday.

"Sunday? We don't usually work on a Sunday, Mrs Castle."

"No? But then, I don't suppose you usually make a mistake and paint the wrong name on a sign for a long-established business, do you?"

They agreed to fix the old sign, repainted, on Sunday morning.

Lilly went to see Mrs Denver a week after her first visit and once again the lady was baking.

Lilly wondered where she found the ingredients and Mrs Denver smiled as though reading her thoughts.

"I do a bit of cooking for the café down the road," she explained. "Get an allowance they do and I'm good at ekeing out the stuff and making more for them to sell. Tell the truth, Lilly, love, I use smaller tins too and a slice of cake is a slice of cake, eh? Nobody bothers to measure it, do they?"

It was obvious from her home that Mrs Denver was far from wealthy, but one day she insisted on going shopping to buy what they could for the baby.

After an initial refusal, Lilly agreed. She could see that Mrs Denver wanted to be a part of the baby's life and with her only son dead, there was no other family for her to cherish, so she agreed.

As she explained to Beth a few weeks later, "I can always find ways of repaying her, give her things she needs and won't be able to buy."

Beth went to see Freddy's parents one morning and when she went into the living room she was instantly aware of an atmosphere. Then she saw a forage cap on the arm of the sofa.

"Is that Freddy's? Is he here?" she asked, excitement mixed with confusion. "He didn't tell me he was coming on leave."

"Well, I—"

Mrs Clements seemed unable to decide what to say and suspicion coloured Beth's face as she began to walk towards the door. "He told you not to tell me, didn't he?" Then there was the sound of feet running down the stairs and Freddy burst in.

"Beth, love. How did you know I was home? It was meant to be a surprise!"

She wasn't sure she believed him, but it was easier to pretend so she joined in the joke, telling Mrs Clements she wasn't a very convincing liar and telling Freddy he was a dreadful tease.

"Back to camp tomorrow, mind. This was so short it was hardly worth the fare, except that I had to see you," he told her when his mother had left the room.

"What d'you want to do, then?" she asked, expecting him to say, "the pictures", as usual.

"I want to walk in the dark and kiss you and tell you how much I love you," he said.

"I did have something arranged for this afternoon but it's easily cancelled. And I'll go and see Uncle Bleddyn; I'm sure he'll find someone else to take my place lunchtime and tonight," Beth responded, pleasantly surprised.

"No, love, it's impossible. That's what I *want* to do, but it isn't what I have to do. Special leave this is. I have to go and see the wife of a chap who was killed a week ago. I promised him that if he – you know – if he didn't come back, I would go and see his wife and children. Take the letter he left with me."

"Oh Freddy, not even an hour?"

"Hell of a war, this, isn't it, love? I want to be with my girl but I can't even spend an afternoon telling her how much I miss her."

"You were going to call, though?" she asked doubtfully.

"On the way back to the station, yes. Just time to tell you how much I love you and miss you." They kissed and hugged each other but it was clear that Freddy wanted her to go and disconsolately she walked back to Sidney Street and changed out of her best clothes for the two hours serving fish and chips and the ever more mysterious rissoles.

When she finished clearing up after the lunchtime session, she didn't go home. Instead she walked to Goose Lane. She supposed she might as well keep the arrangement she had made. The disappointment with Freddy was something she was becoming used to.

Peter had an unexpected pre-Christmas leave. He wasn't able to tell her why, but she gathered that there was a meeting he'd had to attend. She knew from a few things he had let slip that he was involved with codes and cyphers and she wondered whether he was involved with men working behind enemy lines. She wondered, but didn't ask. Peter was easy to talk to and open about everything else, but his work was a strictly forbidden subject.

He and Beth had planned to spend an hour or two cleaning up the small grave. She walked up and he was waiting for her at the gates, with a few tools in a bag beside him. Audrey and a slightly embarrassed Wilf met them there and, armed with their selection of assorted tools, they began to clean the stone and make the inscription easy to read.

It was cold, frosty and damp, and as soon as they broke through the soil they were surrounded by an unpleasant earthy smell which seemed to permeate their clothes. They were soon scratched and bleeding from the determination of the brambles to defy their efforts to remove them, and Peter and Wilf, who was now fully involved, tried to persuade the two women to leave it to them.

They organised a rota with each man taking it in turns digging out a root and passing it to the other to be cut and packed for removal. When the pathetically small grave was cleared, a rose bush planted and seeds of forget-me-nots scattered, Beth and Peter walked away leaving Audrey and Wilf to remember and grieve.

"It was so cruel for Auntie Audrey to have to grieve alone, and for Wilf never to have been allowed to see their child."

"It was considered to be such a disgrace, wasn't it?"

"I suppose Granny Moll thought she was doing the best thing."

"I would never have allowed anything like that to happen to you, Beth. I would have fought and fought for you, whatever the family thought."

"Would you, Peter?"

"I care for you, Beth, you know that, and I'd never let anything bad happen to you." He put an arm around her and pulled her against him. She relaxed against the strength of him, knowing she only had to raise her head to share the kiss that was waiting for her. The moment was fraught with longing, and slowly Beth moved closer. A flash of Freddy's face drifted across her mind and was discarded together with his lies and cheating. This was now, and Peter was showing her a different future. Why should she hesitate?

Then over Peter's shoulder she saw Audrey and Wilf, and the sight of them, familiar, a part of the real world, the world in which she had promised Freddy she'd be his wife, brought her down to earth. Moving reluctantly away from Peter, her hand grasping his as if through the door of a prison, her inside and him unattainable on the outside, she called to the other couple, "Peter's father has invited us back for a cup of tea. All right?"

They all went back to the house on Goose Lane and took the smell of the dank graveside with them. Mr Gregory offered tea and as darkness brought an end to the day, Peter took them all back to Sidney Street on the cart. He looked at Beth longingly as she stepped down and she felt aching regret as, with tears welling, she turned away.

Twelve

Shirley's mother was beginning to wish she had not encouraged her daughter to befriend Freddy Clements. All she had hoped for was to separate the boy from Beth to spite the Castles and give them some grief. Now it seemed that her daughter Shirley was more involved that she had intended. Freddy was a nice enough boy, she mused, and while he had worked for the gents' outfitters, a likely prospect as a husband. But now he was in the army as a regular, and that meant absences and opportunities to seek the company of other women. Nice he might be, but trustworthy he was not, she decided. She knew from bitterly learnt lessons that most men were weak when faced with temptation or the demands of a strongly sexual woman. She didn't want Shirley to have the same disappointments as herself. Freddy Clements was vain, and the type of man who'd be as easily flattered as her husband Paul had been.

"Don't you think you could do better than Freddy?" she asked her daughter one morning as she was getting her coat on ready to go to work. "You won't see much of him, even after this war is over, him being a regular."

"Five years he's signed for, not life. He'll be out when he's twenty-three, Mam. He could go back to the shop – or perhaps he'll learn a trade while he's in the army and come out qualified to do something better."

"You've talked about it, then? You and him, after the war?"

"Talked about it, yes, but not him and me. He's engaged to Beth Castle, isn't he? I just provide a bit of company now and then."

"As long as that's all you're providing!"

"I don't think he and Beth are all that well suited, mind," Shirley replied, ignoring her mother's remark. "A bit boring she is. Doesn't like dancing and Freddy loves it. She won't go into a café because she would rather eat at home."

"Not surprising she won't eat in cafés, she works in them most of the year!"

"She doesn't like the pictures, she only goes to please him – and I bet she makes sure he knows it, too!"

"And you're better suited, you and Freddy?"

"I think so. He just got trapped with Beth Castle. They started off at infant school and it's nothing more than habit that kept them together all this time."

"Be warned that if he's unfaithful to Beth, he could be the same with you. I know what it's like living with a man who doesn't remain faithful. Laughing at me he was, your father."

"Just friends we are, Mam, that's all."

"Them Castles are no better than they should be," Hetty Downs sniffed, wrapping a thick scarf around her head. "Lilly expecting and not saying – perhaps not even knowing – who the father is!"

"Lilly's all right. It's Beth I don't like. At least Lilly's ready for a bit of fun."

"And she's got a souvenir of some man's 'fun', hasn't she? Don't make the same mistake, Shirley. A man doesn't respect women who're easy."

Shirley smiled to herself. What made people think sex was a chore for women and only fun for a man? She knew better than that!

Hetty dragged on her short, fur-lined boots and picked up her handbag and umbrella. "Got to go. It's mornings like this when I wish I still worked in the shop below. At least you haven't got to face the icy cold weather and walk to that icy cold factory."

"You've forgotten quick! The shop door open all the time, and only a small electric fire for a few hours? Frozen stiff I am, long before you get to your factory!"

They both thought about Freddy during the morning, Shirley wondering how soon she could suggest to him that he broke off his engagement to Beth, and Hetty wondering how she could break them apart. Neither was concerned about Beth. If they considered her at all, it was with the casual attitude that she deserved to be abandoned by Freddy because she did nothing to try and keep him.

* * *

In Audrey's house the post arrived and was casually put on a small table to be inspected later. When Ronnie came down he saw that one of the letters was headed OHMS and he opened it to learn that he was to attend a medical examination to see whether he was fit to return to active service.

Olive ran down and read the letter and, trying to stop him worrying, said cheerfully, "Don't worry, love. You'd be a liability to anyone except me!"

"It'll be routine, won't it? They can't send me back, not like this." Unconvinced, he added, "I'll go this morning to see if Mr Gregory has any ideas where we can get a few Christmas trees to sell on the stall, shall I?"

In Sidney Street, at both Audrey's house and Huw and Marged's further down the road, the day had begun slowly. Long after Shirley and her mother had started work, Marged was cooking breakfast for Lilly, Beth and herself while they all tried to persuade Beth to leave Freddy.

"Face up to the facts," Marged said, slapping a plate of toast and one of Mr Gregory's hard-boiled duck eggs in front of her. "You know he's been coming home on leave and not telling you. You suspect he's seeing more of Shirley Downs than he's telling you. There's certainly a lot he isn't telling you! What more do you need to be convinced?"

"I'd know what he's up to if he was my fiancé," Lilly said. "You wouldn't catch me playing second fiddle."

"You what?" Beth laughed. "What's that lump then, if it isn't second fiddle?"

"Enough," Huw said. "Lilly's only trying to make you see sense, like the rest of us."

"Let her try and sort herself out," Beth retorted. "Why doesn't she go and see the man and tell him he has to help?"

"Because he's dead, that's why." In the silence that followed, Lilly told them that the man had been killed in combat. Then she decided to tell them the rest. "I had a photograph of him and I put on Granny Moll's wedding ring so she wouldn't be upset, and went to give it to his wife."

"You met her?" Beth sat down and stared at her sister. "That was brave – or stupid; I don't know which."

"Stupid as it happens. He wasn't married after all, he'd only told me that so I couldn't expect him to marry me. It was his mother I saw." Lilly glared at her sister and went on, "So you're right, I don't have the sense I was born with, and shouldn't be trying to tell you what you should do about that waster of yours. At least Freddy isn't very good at covering up."

No one knew what to say. Beth hugged Lilly and Marged stared at Huw, urging him to say something, anything, to make Lilly feel better.

"Glad we are that you won't have to marry him," Huw said gruffly. "I don't want to lose either of my girls just yet and I certainly won't want to lose this baby of yours. He's a next-generation Castle, and we'll love him, won't we, Marged?"

"Mrs Denver thinks it might be a girl," Lilly said, attempting to laugh.

"Then she'll have to keep her name when she marries, eh?"

"Denver?" Marged frowned. "Not Phil Denver, him who calls himself Phil Martin?" She stared at her daughter in disbelief. "But everyone knows about him telling that old story! It's been a joke for years!"

Lilly lifted her head, her face pale and taut with dismay. "Everyone knew, did they? Then why didn't someone tell me?"

Ronnie still limped badly and the doctor told him that he would not improve much further when he was called back for another medical to see if he was fit enough to return to his unit. He and Olive waited nervously for the decision. He knew it was unlikely that he would have to go back – even with a desk job he would be a liability if his unit was sent to the front line – but with more and more men, and women, being called to register every week, nothing was certain.

When the letter came, he and Olive looked at it together.

"No return to active service," they read aloud.

"That's such a relief," Olive said. Then she looked at her husband's serious face as he read further. "Ronnie? What is it?"

"I have to work in a munitions factory, reporting in two weeks' time, unless there are extenuating circumstances for which a waiver might be granted."

They wrote straight away, pointing out that without his help, as his wife and partner in business was expecting their first child, the market stall, their only source of income, would have to be closed. The reply came almost by return post; their request was denied.

Another form was filled in explaining their need to keep the business intact, this time with a word from Ronnie's own doctor to add weight to the plea.

With the war changing everything and many families in mourning, the town had an air of false gaiety as December speeded up, heading for the celebration. Cakes concocted with the most unlikely ingredients were made and were the cause of much laughter. Flagons of beer were carried back home to be stored until Christmas Day with a bottle of port or sherry, which for most was as much as they could afford.

The shops quickly emptied of anything that could be considered seasonal, queues forming when anything in short supply was rumoured to be available. Chickens and rabbits were snapped up by those who had the money to buy them and the bacon ration was saved for several weeks so a small joint could give the illusion of extravagance.

Marged couldn't think of Christmas with her usual enthusiasm. How could she when she didn't know where Eynon was? A couple of cards arrived purporting to come from Auntie Ethel and a Mrs William, a sentence to let them know he was well and hoping to see them soon. Although the writing was a scrawl, Marged knew the cards had been sent by Eynon. William was his second name. But she was unable to discuss them with anyone except Huw, and there was also the fear that something had happened since they were written and now, this moment, he could be far from well, all alone and in serious trouble.

The military police still called on occasion, starting by warning her of the seriousness of keeping his whereabouts from them, but as she didn't know where he was, and the postcards wouldn't have helped anyway, she said nothing. Now, with this everlasting disagreement between her and Huw, she grieved for him in lonely silence.

Beth didn't relish the thought of the holiday. With her parents hardly speaking to each other, Audrey and Wilf grieving anew for the child lost so many years before, and Lilly insisting on being spoilt, it was only the thought that it was Maude and Myrtle's first Christmas as a part of the family that made her do what she could to add some festivities to the house on Sidney Street.

Mr Gregory had promised them a chicken so it was with some surprise that she saw one arrive, in a box, well and truly alive.

"He wouldn't send it for us to kill!" Beth said, reaching for her coat, intending to go to Goose Lane.

Huw came in just as she was leaving and said, "Oh, it's arrived then."

"And I'm just off to tell him he can come and take it back!" she said.

"What's the matter with it? I won it fair and square, I did."

"Won it?"

"In a raffle at the pub. With the one we've ordered from old Gregory we'll have enough to invite the whole family around."

Thankfully, Beth removed her coat and sat down. "What will you do with it, Dad? You can't kill it."

"Who can't? Of course I'll kill it. What d'you expect me to do, buy it a present for under the tree?"

Beth reached for her coat again. She had kept well away from Mr Gregory's while the slaughtering was going on, but she had to stop this situation at once. He would give the poor thing a home. What was her father thinking of?

"I'm going to see Mr Gregory. And," she told her father, "I'm not going to let you kill that poor little creature, whatever you say. Even if I never have a Christmas dinner ever again!"

Huw watched his daughter leave then picked up the beautiful speckled hen. He went into the yard and with feet wide apart took hold of the hen's body in one hand and its head in the other. Then a scream rent the air and he dropped it. The hen ran off and hid behind the shed. Maude and Myrtle stood at the door with such an expression of horror on their faces Huw felt like a man caught about to commit a murder.

"Murderer," Myrtle choked, confirming his thought.

"How can you, Uncle Huw?" Maude said, sobbing loudly.

The chicken came out from behind the shed pecking the ground, aimlessly searching for edible morsels, apparently unharmed and unfazed by her narrow escape.

"What d'you want me to do with it?" Huw asked irritably. "Keep her as a pet?"

"Oh, Uncle Huw, thanks," Maude said.

"This is the best Christmas present we've ever had," Myrtle echoed.

Leaving the girls to decide on a name, Huw chuckled as he went back inside. Thank goodness they had ordered one from Mr Gregory. At least they wouldn't recognise that as anything more than a few slices of meat. Then he crossed his fingers. He didn't want them refusing to eat the meat they had spent so much money on, or spoiling his own appetite by making him feel guilty! He sighed, a mixture of irritation and amusement. "I suppose I'd better build the thing a coop," he shouted after the girls.

Later he sat listening to the wireless and wondering how he could prevent Christmas being spoilt for the rest of the family by Marged's attitude. They tried to keep it from the family, but they hardly spoke to each other and continued to sleep in separate rooms.

Beth, Lilly and Ronnie knew that their parents were having difficulties and Lilly was worried. It is frightening to realise that your parents, on whom you rely for security and comfort and advice, aren't getting on. In a rare fit of willingness, Lilly was helping Beth wash up after supper when she voiced her worries.

"What will become of us if they decide to leave each other?" she whispered to Beth. "Our Dad's gone to meet friends and colleagues from the beach this evening, and Mam refused to go with him."

Peeping through the door, they looked at Marged sitting in her usual chair at the side of the fireplace, knitting furiously and saying nothing, anger apparent in her expression and in the speed of the flashing needles.

"It was a meeting about next season, and the restrictions on catering and all that. Important enough for her to want to be there, don't you think? Running the stalls and the cafés is her life. It must be serious if she's refused to go."

"Mam? Why didn't you go with Dad?" Beth asked. "The new season is going to be difficult with the new regulations and all. You have to know what's happening."

"I don't need to go to listen to a lot of gossiping old men trying to tell me what to do. I know how to deal with the beach trade. I'm a Piper and I've done it all my life."

"At least Dad and Uncle Bleddyn have gone."

"And they needn't think they can come back here and tell me what I must do," Marged warned.

"It's their business too, Mam," Lilly dared to say. "God 'elp, they've been involved since they were about eight!"

"None of your cheek! And I get enough of that talk from your father. It's Piper's, and your father won't change that."

"But we're Castles. Dad and Uncle Bleddyn run it now Granny Moll is dead."

"And we've run it since we were children!" Huw had walked in and stood, glaring at their mother.

The two girls backed away into the kitchen and continued to discuss the rift in whispers. They finished clearing up and got into bed while below them the row still rumbled on.

"What will we do?" Lilly said. "I can't bear it, Beth. If only Granny Moll was here none of this would be happening. Talk some sense into them she would."

"I think it's Granny Moll that's the trouble," Beth told her. "Ever since Dad found out about Auntie Audrey and the punishment she suffered – Granny Moll not allowing her to marry, treating her and Uncle Wilf like criminals – Dad's been angry. Mam obviously supported Granny Moll, didn't she? The worst bit of all for Dad was being married to our Mam all these years and not being told. Since then they haven't spent an hour in each other's company without rowing, have they?"

"I still don't understand why."

"Neither do I. It must be something to do with Granny Moll being so hard. I think Dad and Uncle Bleddyn want some recognition of the work they've done to keep the business running. The story of Auntie Audrey just made him realise how much she needed her own way in everything."

Lilly shrugged. "It still doesn't make sense."

The bedroom door opened and their father stood there.

"Sorry I am that you've heard all this. But your Mam and I don't seem able to sort this out. I'm going to stay with Uncle Bleddyn for a while, until she accepts that we're a partnership, all equal. Me and your mam and Uncle Bleddyn. All of us Castles."

They stared at the closing door, their hearts racing with fear. What would happen to them now? Predictably, Lilly began to cry.

They heard the front door close and their father's footsteps fading as he walked up the street to where he parked the van. They heard the van drive away and a few minutes later, in the silence of the night, they heard the water drawn to fill the kettle and the fire being poked to boil it.

"Come on, Lilly. I think we're entitled to hear Mam's side of things, don't you?" Together, they went down the stairs to face her.

Huw went into his brother's house and Bleddyn saw at once that something serious had happened. Evelyn was there and Hannah was ironing in the kitchen.

"How are those girls of yours?" Huw asked Hannah after greeting the others. "Looking forward to Father Christmas's visit? I'm hoping for a new razor; I think Marged trimmed the oilcloth with mine," he joked.

Evelyn went out into the kitchen and closed the door, guessing that the brothers needed to talk in private.

"Can I stay a couple of nights?"

"Stay here? Why?" Bleddyn asked.

"Marged and I've had a row and until she sees sense I'm not going back," Huw replied. "I can't get her to see that this business wouldn't be here at all if it wasn't for you and me. Moll did all the shouting, but we did all the work. Wicked she was, treating us like idiots and poor Audrey like a criminal. I can't really explain why, but it was the last straw for me, her treating her own daughter so badly and Audrey still doing penance all these years after."

"You won't get anywhere by staying away, not talking to Marged. Go home and insist on her listening to what you have to say. That's my advice."

"She never listens. As soon as I start talking, her ears close and you can see her about to explode with the need to say her piece. No matter what I said, the answer would be no."

"Shall I try?"

"If you want to, but I don't think it'll do any good. Moll trained her well. Thinks she's the top of the heap because she's a Piper. Being married to me all these years hasn't altered that!"

"You've seen the chip shop then?"

"She never changed the sign back!"

"She did. Got Will Morton to take down the new one and put the old one back."

"Well, tomorrow it's coming down again. No sign at all it'll be, just an empty board, until she agrees to it being called Castle's. Right?"

"Right. Er – I think. What will we do if she refuses right up to the new season?"

"Then there won't be a season, will there? If it's Piper's she wants, then she and Audrey can run it and see how well they do. Now, have you got a bed I could use? I'm worn out with all this wrangling, and that's a fact."

They talked a while longer. Evelyn and Hannah and the two sleepy girls said goodnight and left, with Bleddyn and Huw walking them home to where they all now lived, as the night was so dark. When they returned, Bleddyn settled Huw into a single bed in his own room, as it had been simplest for both of them to use the room in which there was a heater, and lay there wondering what would become of them.

Huw also lay with his eyes open, sleep a vague hope. He thought about Lilly and her baby, about Beth and that pain in the arse Freddy, Marged and her stubborn righteousness – inherited from the other pain in the arse, Moll.

"Damn it all, Moll wasn't a Piper anyway until she married that useless Joseph! She was a Jones!" Huw said in exasperation.

"Shut up and go to sleep," growled Bleddyn.

"Made me suffer all these years because of—"

"Shut up!"

Beth and Lilly tried to persuade their mother to talk about what had happened between her and their father but Marged refused. She made tea, gave them a cup and sent them back to bed.

"It looks serious," Beth whispered, "our Dad walking out like that. What will happen, d'you think?"

"Mam won't let the café go, whatever happens she'll open that next year."

"She can't do it all on her own though."

"We'll have to help as much as we can."

"I can't!" Lilly said at once. "I'll have a baby to look after."

"So did our Mam when we were small, remember. She still managed to keep everything going, didn't she?"

"I'm not like Mam. I couldn't do it," Lilly admitted as she drained her cup. "But I can't see any other way of earning my keep and with our Dad gone, I suppose I'll be expected to, won't I?" On that sad note, she turned over and tried to sleep.

Christmas was the happiest time but it could also be the loneliest, Eynon thought as he trudged along an empty country road on Christmas Eve. He thought longingly about the Christmas dinners he'd enjoyed at home, and the games they had played after tea. Hot and tired and overfed he'd been, and so happy that laughter came without the need of an excuse.

In his pockets now he carried a couple of maggotty apples and a bar of chocolate stolen from a shop when he went to ask the time. Both had been saved for the day when the celebrations would be under way. He would pretend to be sharing Christmas day with his family. And Alice.

He was so deep in thought he wasn't aware of the rumbling sound that seemed to make the road on which he walked vibrate. It gradually entered into his consciousness and looking back he could see a great cloud of dust where the mud on the road had been disturbed by many wheels. There was a convoy, an army convoy coming his way.

Cutting across a field, he ran hurriedly to where a secondary road, little more than a track, emerged. He didn't bother to look either way as he clambered over the hedge and slid down on the other side. The armoured car was almost upon him and he tried to get back up and over the hedge, but because the bank was steep and very slippery after a succession of frosty nights he found himself sliding, unable to gain purchase with his worn shoes, and he was soon out of control, falling inexorably into the path of the vehicle.

The driver stopped the car but not soon enough. Eynon felt a blow and then waves of darkness, but he didn't quite lose consciousness. He was aware of footsteps crunching towards him. The pain in his head was severe and he felt the unmistakable sensation of blood running down his face.

He came to fully with a voice asking his name and whether he was all right. Then a hand was slapping him gently on his cheek, and he looked up into the rugged features of a man wearing a forage cap. An army uniform appeared below the face and his brain cleared in seconds. He opened his eyes wide and recited his name and army number clearly and confidently.

"Where are you from, son?" the man asked.

At this Eynon frowned and looked frightened. "I don't know, sergeant. I can't remember." Then acting for all he was worth, he sat up and began to behave in an agitated manner. "I should be back there with – the lorry. It's gone." He repeated the same words several times in a variety of ways, acted confused and recited his name and number again, and was eventually taken back to camp.

There he underwent severe questioning and he told most of the truth, just adding that since the fall from the lorry he had been confused about where he should be and how he could get back there. He hid his excitement. Soon he would be able to receive letters and find out how his brother Ronnie was, and Johnny and Taff.

On Christmas Eve, two military policemen knocked loudly on the door of Marged's house and told her that Eynon had been found and was in hospital. "Private Eynon William Castle is accused of absconding," they told her in their cold indifferent manner. "If it is proved, he will be sent to a military prison before being returned to his unit for further punishment."

Laughing between tears, Marged's only thought was that he was safe, and that their news was the best Christmas gift she had ever had. Then she sent Beth down to tell Huw. This must surely bring him home.

Christmas Eve brought news for Ronnie too. Their second appeal had been successful. He would be allowed to continue working at the market stall. He and Olive hugged each other and, like Marged, thought this was the best news they could receive now they knew Eynon was safe.

Ronnie handed the letter to Olive and said, "Don't forget to read the last bit." He was warned that should his situation be changed, then he had to let them know.

"That's all right; we don't plan a return to the beach next summer, do we?" Olive spoke the words lightly but she held her breath for Ronnie's reply.

"No, love. I think we'll stay on the stall. There are plenty of Castles and hangers-on to run the rest of it, eh?"

Olive thought she couldn't be happier. She had found her niche and was sharing it with Ronnie.

Christmas morning was the strangest one Beth could remember.

Their father was still sleeping at Bleddyn's and presumably he would eat Christmas dinner there too. Mam was busy in the kitchen, throwing pots and pans about, the noise and the muttering revealing the extent of her frustration. After unpacking the presents that had been displayed under the tree, except the four awaiting Huw's return, and those for Audrey and Maude and Myrtle who were coming later with Ronnie and Olive, Beth suggested a walk.

"If you aren't going too far, I might come with you," Lilly said.

"Call for the girls, they might like to get out for an hour," Marged suggested.

"Why don't you come too, Mam?"

"Christmas morning? Don't be ridiculous, there's far too much to do!"

"The chicken is cooking, the pudding's simmering nicely, it's too soon for the vegetables and we'll only be half an hour."

Marged finally agreed in the hope that Huw would call and find them all out. Dressed in their warmest coats and wearing the new scarves and hats and gloves Marged had given them, the five of them set off through the town, intending to go to the park and feed the ducks, something Myrtle particularly enjoyed.

At the park gates they came face to face with Mrs Downs and her daughter Shirley, who had been on a similar errand, Shirley celebrating one of only two mornings in the year when there were no morning papers to deal with.

Beth was embarrassed, having to speak politely to the girl she suspected of seeing Freddy. Wishing Shirley and her mother a Happy Christmas stuck in her throat.

"Pity your Freddy couldn't get home for Christmas, eh?" Shirley said. "Send you a card, did he? I had a big-huge one a week ago."

"Kind of him," Beth said stiffly.

Although they had all spoken to Mrs Downs, she had said nothing. She was staring at Maude and Myrtle.

The shy girls backed away from her nervously, remembering the woman's anger when she had chased them out of the shop. She took a step towards them.

"So you're Maude and Myrtle," she said, and her eyes were filled with pain. "Not much like your father, are you?"

From Maude came a deep intake of breath. "You know him?"

"Knew him more like! He's dead. And it's all because of your husband, Mrs High and Mighty Castle! He was responsible, your Huw. For that and all the rest!"

It was only then that they realised that the unhappy woman had been drinking.

"Come on, Mam." Shirley put an arm around her mother and tried to lead her away.

"Please, tell us who he was," Maude begged. "We want to find our sister-in-law. We might have a brother, see."

"What are you talking about? You haven't got a brother, you stupid girl." Pulling away from Shirley, Mrs Downs lurched towards Marged and said, "Killed in an accident he was, when your husband got him drunk and left him and that woman of his to find their way home."

"What is this to do with Maude and Myrtle?" Marged asked, looking at Shirley for the answer. Shirley said nothing, concentrating on getting her mother to move away.

Mrs Downs shrugged herself away from her daughter's grip and said belligerently, "He was their father, wasn't he? Your Huw introduced my husband to Martha Copp, and he left me for her. Even that wasn't enough. Oh no! No, he left them drunk, in a strange town and they were killed on the road. All down to your husband, Mrs High and Mighty Castle. Proud of him now, are you?"

Shirley apologised and succeeded in guiding her tearful mother away from them. "Always bad at Christmastime, she is. It was this time of year that Dad died, see."

The questions came in a torrent from the girls and Marged tried to answer evasively, unsure of how much of the woman's outpourings were fact and how much was fiction, a fantasy built over the years to pass the blame on to someone else, excusing her husband for his infidelity and abandonment and making it easier to bear.

When they got back to the house, Marged put the vegetables on, following the routine like an automaton, unaware of what she was doing. When she did remember it was Christmas dinner she was cooking she wondered, as she had no appetite and the others were silently lost in their own thoughts, who was going to bother to eat it.

* * *

In the flat above the paper shop Hetty Downs had calmed down a little. Shirley took the opportunity to learn a few facts before her mother sobered completely and refused to discuss it.

"Strange, wasn't it, Beth finding Maude and Myrtle and then discovering they were Dad's daughters?"

"Illegitimate they are. Nothing to do with us. At least your father had the decency not to give them his name."

"Decency? What's decency? Whatever you feel about Dad, they are his children and my half-sisters. I don't think I can ignore that, Mam."

"Just remember that I had to face the shame of living with a man who was unfaithful, who left me for another woman and gave her the children that I was denied. Oh yes, everyone will know and once this gets out – and it will – memories will be uncovered and I'll have to live it all over again."

"I'll be here, Mam. I'll help you deal with it."

Hetty seemed not to hear. "How can you think of marrying when you could be facing something like that?"

"D'you think she called them Carpenter so the secret would be safe?"

"How do I know how her mind worked?"

"If so, it might have been to protect you," Shirley said, but her mother didn't answer. Hate was a habit and she wasn't ready to give up on it yet.

The girls went several times to the grave of their mother over the Christmas period. Now they knew the truth, they also found the burial plot of Paul Downs, their father. Both of their parents had been killed in December. That seemed more poignant, as they had found him so close to the anniversary.

Maude and Myrtle went with Beth and knocked on the door of Hetty Downs. There were a multitude of questions the girls needed to ask, but Mrs Downs refused to open the door.

"Is Shirley really our half-sister?" Myrtle asked.

"Yes," Beth told her. "You had a half-sister, not a sister-in-law, so no brother I'm afraid. But when things have settled, I think you might be able to talk to Shirley and learn something about your father."

Audrey and Wilf were married quietly in January 1941. They

said nothing to Marged. When Wilf's mother passed away two weeks later, Wilf moved his belongings into the house that had been Moll's home. The move was accomplished quietly and without fuss, and Wilf's house was sold in the same way.

Since the revelation about their child had been aired, Wilf had spent more and more time with Audrey. They had arranged for a retired nurse to look after his mother, who by that time no longer knew whether he was there or not, or even who he was. So slowly did the change take place, it wasn't noticeable enough for Maude or Myrtle to mention it with any degree of importance when he moved in altogether.

Although tradition in the town disapproved of women attending an interment, there were so few mourners that Marged went to Wilf's mother's funeral and stood beside Huw and Bleddyn silently, as though they were all strangers. They both knew that they would have to discuss what was happening with regard to the stalls and the café before the new season, but neither of them felt able to make the first move. Huw was still angry and determined that the business should be renamed Castle's, Marged was equally determined that it remain Piper's, and Bleddyn thought it politic to stay out of it until the couple had at least reached the stage at which they were willing to discuss the situation without quarrelling. All they did at this stage was repeat recriminations with tedious regularity.

During the time following the funeral of Wilf's mother, Marged was aware of Audrey spending time helping Wilf to sort out Mrs Thomas's possessions but took little interest. Time was passing and she was becoming more and more worried about the approaching season.

"Uncle Wilf is here," Myrtle told Marged one afternoon when she called with some shopping.

"That's nice," Marged said casually. "Company for you and your sister as well as Audrey."

"Staying for supper, as well, mind," Myrtle insisted, but Marged only smiled. She was too wrapped up in worries about what would happen to her and Huw and Piper's for her to show any concern about her sister.

Eynon had recovered his health rapidly once he had been taken to the military hospital. The wound on his head which had taken so long to heal had needed a small operation and was now settling down to what he thought would be an interesting scar around which to weave stories to tease his friends and family.

He stuck to his story of being unaware of what had happened to him and where he had been during the months of his absence, and his word was finally accepted. One day he wrote home joyously to tell his family that leave had been granted and he would be home to see them very soon.

Marged immediately began to think about the food she would prepare for him, and insisted that his bedroom was freshly decorated. "It's like Christmas all over again," she said as she began to reply to his letter. She thought of all the letters she had written and which had been returned. He would be able to read them now and know just how much they had all missed him. Huw was as excited as she, but he still didn't return home.

It wasn't until Audrey invited Marged for supper one day in late January that Marged was finally faced with the fact of her sister's marriage. She walked into the house just a few doors from her own and was surprised to see balloons decorating the walls and a slab of fruit cake sprinkled with icing sugar on the table, amid sandwiches and pasties, garlands of evergreens and even a few coloured candles.

"What's this?" Marged asked. "I haven't forgotten a birthday, have I?" She began to smile but the movement froze on her face as Huw stood up from the couch and stared at her.

"A celebration, Marged. A celebration of a wedding that should have taken place years ago." He picked up a glass containing a small serving of port. "A toast, to Audrey and Wilf, Mr and Mrs Wilfred Thomas. Married a couple of weeks ago. Aren't you going to congratulate them?"

The room went out of focus as a shocked Marged took in what he was telling her.

"Married? You and Wilf are married? But when did this happen? Why wasn't I told?"

"We wanted it to be our day, no one else's," Audrey said quietly.

"We had to wait a very long time for it," Wilf added, "and we were determined to make it special."

Marged felt anger rising. She looked around the room for a sign of support but although all the family were there, including Bleddyn, Evelyn and Hannah with Josie and Marie, no one looked anything but delighted. Only Huw's face showed disapproval but that was for her, a silent warning for her not to spoil this moment.

To hide her face and give herself a chance to recover, she hugged her sister and wished her luck. Then the room was filled with noise and laughter as everyone relaxed now the possibility of argument was gone. The food was dispensed by Beth and Lilly, helped by the kindly Hannah.

Later, Marged was glad to immerse herself in clearing up and washing dishes, away from the rest, remembering the day she had told her sister's secret and persuaded her mother that she should work at the beach café and Audrey should be punished for the shame she had brought on them by being made to run Moll's house, away from the fun and prying eyes.

Marged had always behaved herself and didn't see why she should be the one stuck at home doing housework. Now there was a chance to put that right.

As they were about to leave, Audrey took out the wedding photographs. She had worn a dress made by Hannah from delicate lace and lawn which had been dyed a pale primrose colour and decorated with embroidery in pearls and gold thread. Marged stared at her sister's smiling face. She was too old to be a sparkling bride yet she did sparkle. And Wilf made a handsome enough bridegroom. Then, as she was about to remark on the charming picture they made, she looked at the rest of the group and gasped.

Beth was bridesmaid, Ronnie was best man. Huw was there too. She later discovered he had given the bride away. They all knew but had kept it from her. Her gentle sister had taken her revenge.

"Why? Why didn't you tell me?" she asked, her voice low with pain.

"You spoilt everything for them once; we were determined you wouldn't do it again," Huw said. "Ambition is all right, but not when it makes one person consider themselves more important than the rest."

"I didn't see why I should have to to run the house. I wanted to work on the beach," Marged explained. She realised how bad the words sounded as soon as they were spoken.

"So did I," Audrey said softly. "But only one of us could. One had to stay home."

"And you made sure it wasn't you," Huw said to Marged, bitterly.

Marged kissed her sister and Wilf, who had remained silent throughout. "I'll go now," she said, forcing a smile. "I'll come and see you tomorrow, shall I? We can talk about what we all want to do."

"I don't want to change anything," Audrey said. "Not now. It's too late. Wilf and I will live here and do what's necessary to help. I'll organise the rock and sweet shop. Alice will probably help me again. Glad to get away from that foul-tempered father of hers she is."

"I admire a strong woman," Huw told Marged in one of their rare quiet moments together, "and there's no doubt a strong woman was need to run Piper's. But there's never any need for greed and ruthlessness, and determination to get your own way whatever the cost."

"I'm not like that!" she said horrified. "Huw, you can't see me like that?"

"You were willingly led by Moll, weren't you? She pulled all the switches and made certain we understood who was boss, and she could always rely on you for support. But it can't go on. Not now. It's caused too much unhappiness."

Marged had to agree. "I was young, outraged morality was a wonderful feeling. At the time Mam was very convincing."

"That was her biggest and most dangerous fault. She was always convincing."

Beth was happy that her aunt had married at last, but she was less happy about her own marriage plans. Freddy was unreliable and he was hopeless with money. But true love had no boundaries and she supposed she had to accept him with all his faults, as she expected him to accept her. Occasionally she felt a stabbing fear when she thought about the future, imagining sitting at home wondering whether Freddy was being unfaithful. She was ashamed to realise that these thoughts were greater worries than concern for his safety.

There were stories in the newspapers of men being let down by women while they fought the enemy and she determined that, whatever her doubts, she would remain loyal and support Freddy until the fighting stopped. Then Peter came home on leave and her strength was sorely tested.

She went for a walk one Sunday morning in February when the sun was beginning to spread its warmth, with a promise of the better days to come. Before she reached Goose Lane she met Mr Gregory and his flock of donkeys heading for the cliffs. Bernard was walking beside a small cart being pulled by the donkey known as Gus and the cart was loaded with hay bales and the drum of food for the donkeys' evening feed.

Mr Gregory knew the story about Paul Downs and his affair with Martha Copp, and he filled in a few gaps. "Things aren't ever forgotten, Beth, my dear. The gossip dies down but the facts lie dormant, simmering beneath the surface, and ready to pop up and start all over again. Remember that it's the girls who are the victims in all this. The less they hear of the worst side of the story the better. They should know only that their father and mother loved them dearly."

"I agree," Beth said. "I've told them that already. And that their father loved their mother so much he gave up a great deal to be with her."

"Good girl," he said approvingly, puffing fiercely on his pipe. "I knew you'd say the right things." He smiled at her proudly and tilted his head as a salute. "Now why don't you come with me to Sally Gough's field, then we'll go back for a cup of tea."

Enjoying the slow, unhurried pace of the donkeys, Beth walked beside the cart with him, one of them on either side of Gus, through the lanes.

"Peter's due home tomorrow," Bernard told her. "Will you be able to get off for an hour or so? It being a Monday, you don't open the chip shop, do you?"

"I might," she told him. "Although Mam is already getting started on the café over the beach. With Dad not willing to help, and Uncle Bleddyn keeping away afraid of being involved, there's a lot to do before the May opening."

"Peter'll be disappointed not to see you," Mr Gregory said. "He loves your letters and looks forward to seeing you when he gets home. He reckons his leaves will be few and far between from now on. He can't tell me of course, but I think there's something serious in the offing."

"I'm not promising," she said, her heart racing as she tried to speak the words she didn't want to say. "It's Freddy, see. I'm not sure, but perhaps he'll be home and I won't be free."

"You and this Freddy, still engaged, are you?"

"Still engaged. This isn't the time to break off engagements, is it, with the men likely to go out to France or further afield, facing danger at any moment."

"You know he sees Shirley Downs and writes to her and you don't mind?" the old man asked curiously. "You modern women mystify me and that's a fact!"

"He feels sorry for her, that's all. She'll find herself a real boyfriend soon and then Freddy will forget her. Men and women can be friends without it developing into – you know – something deeper," she admonished.

"Oh, can they?" Mr Gregory didn't sound convinced. "The back row of the picture house wasn't for innocent friendships in my memory."

She didn't ask if he had seen Freddy with Shirley recently. She didn't want to know. Just get the war over, she told herself, and then they would sort their lives out. Now, she owed Freddy loyalty and support, whatever he felt about Shirley Downs.

They sat in the field that sloped down to the rocky edge of the sea for a while as the donkeys explored their temporary home. The sea was empty of boats. The restrictions on their movement meant that the all-important fishing went on within a rigid timetable or they risked being shot out of the water by patrols.

There was no sound apart from the waves dashing against the rocks. Whereas the regular movement of the sea would normally have relaxed her, Beth felt an increasing restlessness that was nothing to do with the sea and everything to do with Peter, who was coming home tomorrow.

"I can't be more than a friend to Peter," she said sadly. "Tomorrow I'll tell him so."

"Sure about that, are you?"

When they left the cliffs, having settled the donkeys in and seen to their feeding, she didn't go back to the friendly cottage in Goose Lane. Instead she went back home to write to Freddy and Peter and Johnny and Taff. It was her war effort and a very important weekly chore, she told herself. Nothing to do with the aching need to see Peter, and feel his arms around her, have her lips touch his, telling him how much he was loved. She wrote Peter's letter first, describing the peace and beauty of the cliffs and the contentment of his father. She mentioned in a casual way that she and Freddy would probably marry the moment he was demobbed. She read the lines that were filled with untruths in writing that was decidedly wobbly and told him nothing of how she really felt, and kissed the pages before putting them into the envelope, imagining him kissing them too.

Eynon came home for a forty-eight hour visit and the family celebrated with a party. No one outside the family was invited but that didn't stop them coming. From every house neighbours poured, most bringing something to add to the feast. Bottles left over from Christmas, food stored for that special occasion.

The scar was admired as though it had been earned in an honourable battle and even when he told people he'd done it falling from a lorry, no one believed him. There was a war on, they wanted a hero, and he was it!

He invited Alice but she didn't stay long, afraid of her father's wrath if she wasn't there when he looked for her. She promised to write, though, to his delight. He returned to camp to a different group of boys, stronger and with no fear of bullying, prepared to do what had to be done, older than his years and more sure of himself than ever before.

Shirley Downs called at Audrey and Wilf's house and was made welcome. She spent time with Maude and Myrtle, filling in gaps and talking about their father. She was surprisingly happy as she remembered incidents involving her father when she was young. Her stories were soaked up like a sponge by the girls as they built up a picture of Paul Downs, their father, who was buried not far from their mother.

During March, which came in like a lamb and therefore threatened to go out like a lion, Huw still lived at his brother's house. They did nothing towards preparing for the new season at the beach and if Bleddyn thought Huw and Marged were stupid, he kept it to himself.

Bleddyn continued to run the fish-and-chip café and he occasionally asked Beth how Marged was, but it never went further than the kind of brief, polite remark that warranted nothing more than a brief, polite reply. Both were determined not to become involved in taking sides. Mostly they talked about the latest letters from Johnny and Taff, and now Eynon too.

Beth kept away from Goose Lane while Peter's leave progressed. It would be a forty-eight, Mr Gregory had told her, so she felt safe to go there the following weekend. As she touched the gate she heard laughter and saw Peter coming around the corner arm in arm with a pretty girl of about her own age. She stopped and looked around as though preparing to run, but Peter had seen her, called to her and she was rooted to the spot.

"Beth, how wonderful. I thought you weren't going to visit us this week. Do come and meet Diana. Diana, this is Beth about whom you have heard so much."

Taking in the small neat figure, the pale baby-pink skin enhanced with rouge and lipstick, and the fair hair with its bow of ribbon tying back curls, Beth felt untidy and wished she had bothered to change out of the casual clothes she habitually wore when visiting Mr Gregory and his donkeys. She felt sick with jealousy, frighteningly, horrifyingly sick, afraid that if she didn't get away from this happy-looking couple she would almost certainly throw up on Mr Gregory's neat garden.

"I was on my way to the cliffs," she said. "Can I use your lavatory?"

Why had she said that? Why ask to use the lavatory before even responding to Peter's introduction to his friend? What a stupid remark! How embarrassing! Why couldn't she be self-assured like Diana obviously was? Then she thought, Why does it matter? I'm going to marry Freddy Clements. But even to her, that sounded more stupid than asking to use the lavatory.

She didn't stay. She went into the garden behind the house and walked down to the euphemistically named ty bach – little house – and stayed a moment, combing her hair and wishing it was fair and curly instead of straight and black. She examined her face in the speckly mirror and pretended the freckles were in fact marks on the glass, wishing she had bothered to smear a little lipstick on her lips.

When she came out, the girl was talking to Peter's father over near the chicken house and Peter was waiting for her in the kitchen.

"Peter," she said, wrapping her scarf tightly around her head. "I don't think I should write to you any more. Freddy doesn't like it and as I've asked him not to write to Shirley, who was only a friend, it seems only fair," she lied.

"What harm were we doing, getting to know each other better?"

"You know how painful jealousy can be," she said, glancing towards the pretty young girl.

"I understand jealousy," he said slowly. "I'm extremely jealous of the time you spend writing to Freddy. Are you sure you want to stop writing to me? I don't know how I'll bear it, Bethan."

"It's the best thing to do," she said, with the conviction that she was being more stupid than at any time during her life.

Her dismay gave her face an expression of stubbornness and Peter stared at her for long moments before saying, "Of course. I understand. You love Freddy and I have to accept that. I'll miss your letters enormously. They were the highlight of my week." He stepped towards her but she moved away, unable to trust herself. She was afraid to look at him; he would surely see in her face the tumult of her emotions.

"Goodbye," she said, stepping towards the door.

"If you should change your mind, Beth, I'd be so happy," he replied.

She hadn't realised just how strong an emotion jealousy could be. Beside the sick feeling that hadn't gone away, she felt as though her racing heart would explode with the agony of it. Peter and that fairy doll of a girl. Imagine her feeding the donkeys on a wet and windy hillside, Beth thought. She'd still manage to look beautiful.

There was a letter waiting for her when she reached home, and she recognised the writing as Freddy's. It was longer than usual and she took it to her room to sit in privacy and read it. It said he thought they should end their engagement, as he was seeing rather a lot of Shirley and thought he and she were better suited.

Beth was still staring at the words when there was a knock at the door. Shirley Downs stood there.

"I think we ought to talk about Freddy," Shirley said.

"Don't worry, Shirley. I've had a letter that makes everything clear. He's right, you'll make him happier than I ever would," Beth said, trying to keep her voice steady.

"I don't suppose you'll ever like me, but I hope we can be friends, if only for Maude and Myrtle's sake," Shirley went on. "They aren't guilty of any of what went on between my family and yours. Even Mam can see that, and I think she'll be able to get to know them once the pain of finding them has eased."

"Let's meet in a day or so and take the girls somewhere where we can talk," Beth suggested, forcing a smile.

There was nothing to be gained by being bitter. The end of her engagement to Freddy was completely painless. At least, it would have been if she hadn't been so determined to tell Peter goodbye, she thought sadly as Shirley left.

She had to get out of the house so she went to talk to the girls. When she got back her father was there. She went straight to the kitchen and shut herself in, afraid of interrupting what might be an attempt at reconciliation.

Marged and Huw at last began to talk to each other. With so much to do before the opening of the new season, common sense had prevailed. Marged's first act of surrender was to arrange for the new signs. The Pipers were all gone; even Audrey was now Mrs Wilf Thomas. The new name would show proudly above each of their businesses.

Lilly was given the task of dealing with the laundry and the daily ordering of fresh food, a side of the business previously dealt with by Moll. She agreed, but hoped that the baby would excuse her from most of it by being born so conveniently in May when the season started.

Beth had watched through a crack in the door with her fingers crossed that first day when her parents had begun to communicate, and heard her father say, "Most importantly, we'll listen to each other, won't we, Marged?" He was smiling but there was a threat in his glinting eyes and the stiffness of his lips. "All of us. We'll all have our say; the Castle family is a strong, unbeatable team."

A rota was arranged for washing woodwork and painting, especially the helter-skelter, which would proudly bear the colours red, white and blue. The new season was rapidly approaching, but although relieved that her parents were talking again, Beth was unable to involve herself in the excitement.

She had told Peter she didn't love him out of misplaced loyalty. Now it was up to her to try to put things right.

She met Mr Gregory, who told her that Peter was leaving on the nine o'clock train the following morning, and she decided to try and see him. If she could just write to him again, and continue to watch for the postman with such hope, that would be better than nothing. She stood at the station, trying to decide what she would say and how she would say it. She remembered Freddy's first departure and his first leave and wondered how this railway station meeting would end.

Peter came on his father's cart, his father driving, while Peter sat beside him writing something on a pad of paper.

"I just wanted to say goodbye properly, Peter," she told him when, with a great smile, he jumped off the cart and ran to where she was waiting. "I will still write, if you want me to, and if Diana doesn't mind. I wouldn't want to do anything to spoil things."

"Diana? She's a customer of Dad's, Beth! There's nothing there to spoil, and as for writing, I've just started a letter to you, begging you not to abandon me." He handed her the piece of paper on which he had written, "Darling Beth, please tell Freddy goodbye, and marry me."

With only a few moments before the train was due to leave, they hugged and kissed and promised to write every day. Peter said, "We'll marry as soon as the war is over and I've set up my employment agency."

"Not before? But what if things change?"

"If I die, you mean? You'd rather be my widow than my loving friend?"

"Oh Peter, I didn't mean that! Please, don't die. I meant that you'll be away from me and might meet someone else."

"I don't need anyone else. All I need is to imagine you on the beach, helping everyone suffering because of this terrible war to relax and have a good time."

Their parting was swift and painful, the kiss harsh and greedy and they were breathless as Peter turned and waved to his father who was waiting with the pony and cart to take Beth home.

"Peter and I—" she began to explain.

He interrupted with, "An' about time too."